For a complete list of books by Jean Plaidy
please see pages 678 and 679

Isabella and Ferdinand

In the first book of the trilogy Isabella of Castile is seen as a young girl in the care of her ambitious but unbalanced mother and at the court of her brother Henry IV whose wife's illicit love affairs result in confusion and scandal. These were momentous years in Spanish history and Isabella emerges, serene and courageous, determined to bring law and order to Castile and marry Ferdinand. In *Spain For the Sovereigns* Isabella and Ferdinand have to fight and win the war of succession. About the sovereigns move people notorious in history, such as Torquemada who is determined to establish the Inquisition in the land; Boabdil, the last Sultan of Granada; and Christopher Columbus, dreaming of a new world. The last of the trilogy, *Daughters of Spain*, concerns the daughters of Isabella and Ferdinand; young Isabella, the tragic widow; mad Juana; mild Maria; and Catalina, who left all she loved in Spain to become Katharine of Aragon, Queen of England.

Isabella and Ferdinand

JEAN PLAIDY

ROBERT HALE · LONDON

© *Jean Plaidy 1970*
This omnibus volume first published 1970

Reprinted 1971
Reprinted 1973
Reprinted 1981

ISBN 0 7091 1104 5

Robert Hale Limited
Clarkenwell House
Clerkenwell Green
London, EC1

Printed and bound in Great Britain by
Richard Clay (The Chaucer Press) Ltd.,
Bungay, Suffolk

CONTENTS

Castile for Isabella

© *Jean Plaidy 1960*

FLIGHT TO AREVALO

THE Alcazar was set high on a cliff from which could be seen the far-off peaks of the Guadarrama Sierras and the plain, watered by the Manzanares River. It was an impressive pile of stone which had grown up round what had once been a mighty fortress erected by the Moorish conquerors of Spain. Now it was one of the Palaces of the Kings of Castile.

At a window of this Palace, a four-year-old child stood looking towards the snow-topped peaks of the distant mountains, but the grandeur of the scenery was lost to her, for she was thinking of events inside the granite walls.

She was afraid, but this was not apparent. Her blue eyes were serene; although she was so young, she had already learned to hide her emotions, and fear above all must be kept hidden.

Something extraordinary was happening in the Palace, and it was something quite alarming. Isabella shivered.

There had been much coming and going in the royal apartments. She had seen the messengers hurrying through the *patios*, stopping to whisper with others in the great rooms and shake their heads as though they were prophesying dire disaster, or wearing that excited look which, she knew, meant that they were probably the bearers of bad news.

She dared not ask what was happening. Such a question might bring a reproof, which would be an affront to her dignity. She must constantly remember her dignity. Her mother had said so.

"Always remember this," Queen Isabella had told her daughter more than once. "If your stepbrother Henry should die without heirs, your little brother Alfonso would be King of Castile; and if Alfonso should die without heirs, you, Isabella, would be Queen of Castile. The throne would be yours by right, and woe betide any who tried to take it from you." Little Isabella remembered how her mother clenched her fists and shook them, how her whole body shook, and how she herself wanted to cry out, "Please, Highness, do not speak of these things," and yet dared not. She was afraid of every subject which excited her mother, because there was something terrifying in her mother's excitement. "Think of that, my child," she would proceed. "Indeed, you must never forget it. And when you are tempted to behave in any manner but the best, ask yourself: Is this worthy of one who could become Queen of Castile?"

Isabella always said on such occasions: "Yes, Highness, I will. I will." She would have promised anything to stop her mother shaking her fists, anything to drive the wild look out of her mother's eyes.

And for this reason she always did remember, for when she was tempted to lose her temper, or even to express herself too freely, she would have a vision of her mother, veering towards one of those terrifying moods of hysteria, and that was all that was needed to restrain her.

Her thick chestnut hair was never allowed to be disordered; her blue eyes were always serene; and she was learning to walk as though there was already a crown on her head. The attendants in the royal nursery said: "The Infanta Isabella is a good child, but she would be more natural if she would learn to be a little *human*."

Isabella could have explained, if it had not been beneath her dignity to do so: "It is not for me to learn to be human. I must learn to be a Queen, because that is what I may one day be."

Now, much as she longed to know the reason for the tension in the Palace, this hurrying to and fro, these expectant looks on the faces of courtiers and messengers, she did not ask; she merely listened.

Listening was rewarding. She had not *seen* the end of her father's friend, the great Alvaro de Luna, but she had *heard* that he had ridden through the streets, dressed as an ordinary criminal, and that people, who had once hated him so much that they had called for his death, had shed tears on seeing such a man brought low. She had heard how he had mounted the scaffold with a demeanour so calm and haughty that he might have been arriving at the Palace for an interview with Isabella's father, the King of Castile. She knew that the executioner had thrust his knife into that proud throat and cut off the haughty head; she knew that de Luna's body had been cut into pieces and set up for the people to shudder over, to remind themselves that this was the fate of one who, such a short time before, had been the King's dearest friend.

All this one could learn by listening.

The servants said: "It was the Queen's doing. The King . . . why, he would have taken de Luna back at the last moment. Yes . . . but he dared not offend the Queen."

Then Isabella had known that she was not the only one who was afraid of her mother's strange moods.

She loved her father. He was the kindest of men. He wanted her to learn her lessons so that she might, as he said, appreciate the only worthwhile things in life.

"Books are a man's best friends, my child," he told her. "I have learned this too late. I wish I had learned it earlier. I think you are going to be a wise woman, daughter; therefore when I pass on this knowledge to you I know that you will remember it."

Isabella, as was her custom, listened gravely. She wanted to please her father, because he seemed so weary. She felt that they shared a fear of which neither of them could ever speak.

Isabella would be good; she would do all that was expected of her, for fear of displeasing her mother. It seemed that her father, the King, would do the same; he would even send his dearest friend, de Luna, to the executioner's knife because his wife demanded it.

Isabella often felt that if her mother had been always as calm and gentle as she could be sometimes, they could have been very happy. She loved her family dearly. It was so pleasant, she thought, to have a baby brother like Alfonso, who was surely the best-tempered baby in the world, and a grown-up brother like Henry—even though he was only a stepbrother—who was always so charming to his little stepsister.

They ought to have been happy, and could so easily have been, apart from the ever-present fear.

"Isabella!" It was her mother's voice, a little harsh with that strident note which never failed to start the alarm signals within Isabella's brain.

Isabella turned without haste. She saw that her governess and attendants were discreetly leaving. The Queen of Castile had intimated that she wished to be alone with her daughter.

Slowly, and with the utmost dignity that a child of four could possibly display, Isabella came to the Queen and sank to the floor in a graceful curtsey. Etiquette at Court was rigid, even within the family circle.

"My dear daughter," murmured the Queen; and as Isabella rose she embraced her fervently. The child, crushed against the jewel-encrusted bodice, endured the discomfort, but she felt her fear increasing. This, she thought, is something really terrible.

The Queen at length released the little girl from that violent embrace and held her at arms' length. She studied her intently, and tears welled into her eyes. Tears were alarming, almost as alarming as the fits of laughter.

"So young," murmured the Queen, "my four-year-old Isabella, and Alfonso but an infant in the cradle."

"Highness, he is very intelligent. He must be the most intelligent baby in the whole of Castile."

"He'll need to be. My poor . . . poor children! What will become of us? Henry will seek some way to be rid of us."

Henry? wondered Isabella. Kind, jovial Henry, who always had sweatmeats to offer his little sister and would pick her up and give her a ride on his shoulder, telling her that she would be a pretty woman one day! Why should Henry want to be rid of them?

"I am going to tell you something," said the Queen. "We will be ready . . . when the time comes. You must not be surprised if I tell you that we are to leave at once. It will be soon. It cannot be long delayed."

Isabella waited, fearful of asking another of those questions which might win a rebuke. Experience told her that if she waited attentively she could often discover as much as, or even more than, if she asked questions.

"We may leave at a moment's notice . . . a moment's notice!" The Queen began to laugh, and the tears were still in her eyes. Isabella prayed silently to the saints that she would not laugh so much that she could not stop.

But no, this was not to be one of those terrifying scenes, for the Queen stopped laughing and put a finger to her lips. "Be prepared," she said. "We will outwit him." Then she put her face close to the little girl's. "He'll never get a child," she said. "Never . . . never!" She was close to that terrifying laughter again. "It is the life he has led. That is his reward. And well he deserved it. Never mind, our turn will come. My Alfonso shall mount the throne of Castile . . . and if by some chance he should not reach manhood, there is always my Isabella. Is there not, eh? Is there not?"

"Yes, Highness," murmured the little girl.

Her mother took the plump cheek between thumb and forefinger, and pinched it so hard that it was difficult to prevent the tears coming to those blue eyes. But the little girl knew it was intended as a gesture of affection.

"Be ready," said the Queen.

"Yes, Highness."

"Now I must be back with him. How can one know what plots are hatched when one's back is turned, eh? How can one?"

"How can one, Highness," repeated Isabella dutifully.

"But you will be ready, my Isabella."

"Yes, Highness, I will be ready."

There was another embrace, so fierce that it was an effort not to cry out in protest against it.

"It will not be long," said the Queen. "It cannot be long now. Be ready and do not forget."

Isabella nodded, but her mother went on with the often repeated phrase: "One day you may be Queen of Castile."

"I will remember, Highness."

The Queen seemed suddenly calm. She prepared to leave, and once more her little daughter gave her a sweeping curtsey.

Isabella was hoping that her mother would not go into that room where Alfonso lay in his cradle. Alfonso had cried in protest last time his mother had embraced him so fiercely. Poor Alfonso, he could not be expected to know that he must never protest, that he must not ask questions but merely listen; soon he would be old enough to hear that one day he could be King of Castile, but as yet he was only a baby.

When she was alone, young Isabella took the opportunity of slipping into the room where Alfonso lay in his cradle. He was clearly unaware of the tension in the Palace. He lay kicking joyously, and he crowed with pleasure as Isabella appeared.

"Alfonso, baby brother," murmured Isabella.

The baby laughed up at his sister and kicked more furiously.

"You do not know, do you, that one day you could be King of Castile?"

Surreptitiously, Isabella bent over the cradle and kissed her brother. She looked furtively about her. No one had noticed that little weakness, and she made excuses to herself for betraying her emotion. Alfonso was such a pretty baby and she loved him very much.

* * *

The Queen of Castile was on her knees beside her husband's bed.

"What hour is it?" he asked her, and as she dropped her hands from her face he went on: "But what matters the hour? My time has come. It is now for me to say my farewells."

"No!" she cried, and he could hear the rising hysteria in her voice. "The time has not yet come."

He spoke gently, pityingly. "Isabella, my Queen, we should not deceive ourselves. What good will it do? In a short time there will be another King of Castile, and your husband, John II, will begin to be a memory—a not very happy one for Castile, I fear."

She had begun to beat her clenched fist lightly on the bed. "You must not die yet. You must not. What of the children?"

"The children, yes," he murmured. "Do not excite yourself, Isabella. I shall arrange that good care is taken of them."

"Alfonso . . ." muttered the Queen, "a baby in his cradle. Isabella . . . just past her fourth birthday!"

"I have great hopes of our sturdy Isabella," said the King. "And there is Henry. He will be a good brother to them."

"As he has been a good son to his father?" demanded the Queen shrilly.

"This is no time for recriminations, my dear. It may well be that there were faults on both sides."

"You . . . you are soft with him . . . soft."

"I am a weak man and I am on my death-bed. You know that as well as I do."

"You were always soft with him . . . with everybody. Even when you were well, you allowed yourself to be governed."

The King lifted a weak hand for silence. Then he went on: "I believe the people are pleased. I believe they are saying 'Good riddance to John II. Welcome to Henry IV. He will be a better king than his father was.' Well, my dear, they may be right in that, for they would have to search far and wide for a worse."

John began to cough and the Queen's eyes widened in fear. She made an effort to control herself. "Rest," she cried. "For the love of the saints, rest."

She was afraid that he would die before she had made her plans. She distrusted her stepson Henry. He might seem to be good-natured, a less intellectual, a more voluptuous replica of his father, but he would allow himself to be ruled by favourites who would not easily tolerate rivals to the throne. They would impress upon him the fact that if he displeased his subjects they would rally round young Alfonso and Isabella. Therefore he would be watchful.

She trusted no one, and she was growing more and more determined that her own son should inherit the throne.

And what shall I do? the Queen asked herself; and her fist began to beat once more upon the bed. I, a weak woman, surrounded by my enemies!

Her wild gaze rested on the dying man in the bed.

He *must* not die until she was ready for him to do so; he must remain King of Castile until she was prepared to whisk her little son and daughter from Madrid.

They would go to a place where they could dwell in peace, where there was no danger of a morsel of poison's being slipped into their food or drink, where it would be impossible for an assassin to slip into their sleeping chamber and press a pillow over their baby mouths as they slept. They should go where they might bide their time until that moment—and the Queen was sure it would come—when Henry should be ousted from the throne and little Alfonso —or Isabella—triumphantly take it, King—or Queen—of Castile.

* * *

King John lay back on his pillows watching his wife.

Poor Isabella, he thought, what will become of her—she who was already tainted with the terrible scourge of her family? There was madness in the royal house of Portugal; at the moment it had not completely taken possession of Isabella, his Queen, but now and then there were signs that it had not passed her by.

He was by no means stupid, bad King though he had been, and he wondered now whether that tendency to insanity had been inherited by their children. There was no sign of it as yet. Isabella had inherited none of the hysteria of her mother; there could rarely have been a more serene child than his sedate little daughter. Little Alfonso? It was early to say as yet, but he seemed to be a normal, happy baby.

He prayed that the terrible disease of the mind had passed them by and that Isabella had not brought its taint into the royal house of Castile to the detriment of future generations.

He should never have married Isabella. Why had he? Because he was weak; because he had allowed himself to be led.

When Maria of Aragon, Henry's mother, had died, it had naturally been necessary for John to find a new wife, and he had believed it would be an admirable gesture to ally himself with the French. He had considered marriage with a daughter of the King of France; but his dear friend and adviser, Alvaro de Luna, had thought differently. He had seen advantages to Castile, he said—and to himself, which he did not mention—through an alliance with Portugal.

Poor misguided de Luna! Little did he realize what this marriage was going to mean to him.

The dying John allowed himself to smile as he thought of de Luna in the early days of their friendship. Alvaro had first come to Court as a page—handsome, attractive, he had been a dazzling personality, a skilled diplomat, a graceful courtier, under whose spell John had immediately fallen. He asked nothing more than to stay there, and, in return for the pleasure this man's company brought him, John had bestowed on him all the honours for which he craved. De Luna had been not only Grand Master of St. James but Constable of Castile.

Oh yes, thought John, I was a bad king, for I gave myself completely to pleasure. I had no aptitude for statecraft and, because I was not a stupid man, because I had some intellectual leanings, my behaviour was the more criminal. I have not the excuse of inability to rule; I failed through indolence.

But my father, Henry III, died too young. And there was I, a minor, King of Castile. There was a Regency to rule in my stead. And how well! So well that there was every excuse why I should give myself to pleasure and not concern myself with the government of my country.

But regrettably there had come the day when John was old

enough to be King in more than name. And there he had been, young, good-looking, accomplished in the arts, finding that there were so many more interesting things to do than govern a kingdom.

He had been frivolous; he had loved splendour; he had filled his Court with poets and dreamers. He was a dreamer himself. He had been touched perhaps by the Moorish influence of his surroundings. He had lived rather like a Caliph of some Arabic legend. He had sat, with his friends around him, reading poetry; he had staged colourful pageants; he had roamed about the brilliant gardens of his Madrid Alcazar with his tamed Nubian lion for companion.

The splendour of the Palace was notorious; so was the extravagance and frivolity of the King. And side by side with royal extravagance was the hardship and poverty of the people. Taxes had been imposed to provide revenue for favourites; there was misery and privation throughout the land. These were the inevitable results of his misrule and, if the country had been split by civil war and his own son Henry had taken sides against him, he blamed himself because here on his death-bed he saw more clearly where he had failed.

And always beside him had been his beloved Alvaro de Luna, who, having begun life humbly, could not resist the opportunity to flaunt his possessions, to show his power. He had made himself rich by accepting bribes, and wherever he went he was surrounded by lackeys and trappings of such magnificence that the King's retinue was put in the shade.

Some said that de Luna dabbled in witchcraft, and it was to this cult that he owed his power over the King. That was untrue, John told himself now. He had admired the brilliant, dashing courtier, this illegitimate son of a noble Aragonese family, because he was possessed of the strong character which John himself lacked.

John was the sort of man who seemed willingly to accept the domination of others. He had been as docile as usual when he agreed to his marriage with Isabella of Portugal.

If that marriage had brought him little peace, it had brought disaster to de Luna, for the bride was a woman of strong character in spite of her latent taint. Or was it that he himself was so weak and feared her outbursts of hysteria?

"Who," she had demanded, "is King of Castile, you or de Luna?"

He had reasoned with her; he had explained what good friends he and the Constable had always been.

"Of course he flatters you," she had retorted scornfully. "He coaxes you as he would a horse he was riding. But he holds the reins; he decides which way you shall go."

It was when she was pregnant with Isabella that the real wildness had begun to show itself. It was then that he began to suspect the taint might exist in her blood. Then he had been ready to do anything to calm her in order not have to face the terrifying fear that he might have introduced madness into the royal blood stream of Castile.

She had fretted and worked for the disgrace of de Luna, and now he felt bitterly ashamed of the part he had played; he tried to shut this out of his thoughts, but he could not do so. Some perversity in his dying self forced him to face the truth as he had never done before.

He remembered the last time he had seen de Luna; he remembered what friendship he had shown the man, so that poor Alvaro had reassured himself, had told himself that he cared nothing for the enmity of the Queen while the King was his friend.

But he did not save his friend; he loved him still, yet he had allowed him to go to his death.

That, he thought, is the kind of man I am. That action was characteristic of John of Castile. He entertained warm feelings for his friends, but he was too indolent, too much of a coward to save one whom he had loved more than any. He had been afraid of angry scenes, of being forced to face that which he dared not; and so the Queen, balanced very delicately between sanity and insanity, had achieved in a few months what his ministers had plotted for thirty years : the downfall of de Luna.

John felt tears in his eyes as he thought of de Luna's brave walk to the scaffold. He had heard how gallantly his friend had gone to death.

And up to the moment of de Luna's execution he, the King, who should have been the most powerful man in Castile, had promised himself that he would save his friend, had longed to quash the sentence of death and bring de Luna back to favour; but he had not done so, for he, who had once been dominated by the charm of de Luna, was now the thrall of the latent madness of his wife.

All I wanted was peace, thought the dying King. All? It was more difficult to find than anything else in turbulent Castile.

* * *

In his tapestried apartment of the Palace, Henry, heir to the throne, was waiting to hear the news of his father's death.

The people, he knew, were eager to acclaim him. When he rode through the streets they shouted his name; they were tired of the disastrous rule of John II and they longed to welcome a new King who could bring a new way of life to Castile.

As for Henry, he was very eager to feel the crown on his head, and he was determined to keep the popularity which was his. He had no doubt that he could do this, for he was fully aware of his charm. He was good-tempered, easy-going, and he had the art of flattering the people, which never failed to delight them. He could condescend to be one of them without apparent condescension; that was the secret of the people's love for him.

He was determined to dazzle his subjects. He would raise armies and achieve victories; he would go into battle against the Moors, who for centuries had remained in possession of a large part of Spain. The Moors were perennial enemies, and the proud Castilians could always be brought to a wild enthusiasm by talks of campaigns against them. He would give them pageants to delight their eyes, spectacles and entertainments to make them forget their miseries. His reign should be one of continual excitement and colour.

And what did Henry want? He wanted more and more pleasure —that meant new pleasures. They would not be easy to find, for he was a man of great erotic experience.

While he was waiting, his wife, Blanche, came to him. She too was expectant, for would she not be Queen of Castile when the news was brought to them? She would wish to receive the homage, to stand beside Henry and swear with him to serve the people of Castile with every means at her disposal.

He took her hand and kissed it. Always affectionate in public, even when they were alone he did not show his indifference; he was never actively unkind, for it was against his nature to be so. Now the look of affection he gave her disguised the distaste which she was beginning to rouse in him.

It was twelve years since Blanche of Aragon became his wife. At first he had been delighted to have a wife, but she was not his kind; she could not share his pleasures as his many mistresses could; and since the union had proved fruitless he had no further use for her.

He needed a child—never more than at this time—and he had recently been considering what action he might take to remedy matters.

He had been a voluptuary from boyhood, when there had always been pages, attendants, and teachers to encourage a very willing pupil; and the exploitation of the senses had appealed to him so much more than book-learning.

His father had been an intellectual man who had filled the Court with literary figures, but Henry had nothing in common with men such as Iñigo Lopez de Mendoza, Marquis of Santillana, the great literary figure, nor for the poet John de Mena.

What had such men done for his father? Henry asked himself. There had been anarchy in the Kingdom and unpopularity for the

King—civil war, with a large proportion of the King's subjects fighting against him. If he had pursued pleasure as indefatigably as his son he could not have been more unpopular.

Henry was determined to go his own way and now, looking at Blanche, he was making up his mind that since she could not please him she must go.

She said in her gentle way: "So, Henry, the King is dying."

"It is so."

"Then very soon . . ."

"Yes, I shall be King of Castile. The people can scarcely wait to call me King. If you look out of the window you will see that they are already gathering about the Palace."

"It is so sad," she said.

"Sad that I shall soon be King of Castile?"

"Sad, Henry, that you can only be so because of the death of your father."

"My dear wife, death must come to us all. We must take our bow at the end of the performance and move on, so that the next player may strut across the stage."

"I know it, and that is why I am sad."

He came to her and laid an arm about her shoulders. "My poor, sweet Blanche," he said, "you are too sensitive."

She caught his hand and kissed it. Temporarily, he deceived even her with his gentle manners. Later she might wonder what was going on in his mind as he caressed her. He was capable of telling her that she was the only woman he really loved at the very moment when he was planning to rid himself of her.

Twelve years of life with Henry had taught her a great deal about him. He was as shallow as he was charming, and she would be a fool to feel complacent merely because he implied that she still held a high place in his affections. She was aware of the life he led. He had had so many mistresses that he could not have been sure how many. He might, even at a moment when he was suggesting that he was a faithful husband, be considering the pursuit and seduction of another.

Lately she had grown fearful. She was meek and gentle by nature, but she was not a fool. She was terrified that he would divorce her because she had failed to bear a child, and that she would be forced to return to her father's Court of Aragon.

"Henry," she said on impulse, "when you are indeed King it will be very necessary that we have a son."

"Yes," he replied with a rueful smile.

"We have been so unfortunate. Perhaps . . ." She hesitated. She could not say: Perhaps if you spent less time with your mistresses we might be successful. She had begun to wonder whether it was possible for Henry to beget a child. Some said that this could be a result of a life of debauchery. She could only vaguely visualize what went on during those orgies in which her husband indulged. Was it possible that the life he had led had rendered him sterile?

She glanced at him; did she imagine this or had his gaze become a little furtive? Had he really begun to make plans to rid himself of her?

So she was afraid. She realized that she was often afraid. She dared not state frankly what was in her mind.

Instead she said: "There is trouble at my father's Court."

He nodded and made a little grimace. "It would seem that there must be trouble when a King has children by two wives. We have an example here at home."

"None could prevent your taking the crown, Henry."

"My stepmother will do her utmost, never fear. She is already making plans for her little Alfonso and Isabella. It is a dangerous thing when a King's wife dies and he takes another . . . that is, when there are children of both first and second unions."

"I think, Henry, that my stepmother is even more ambitious than yours."

"She could scarcely be that; but let us say that she has as high hopes for her little Ferdinand as mine has for Alfonso and Isabella."

"I have news from home that she dotes on the child, and that she has influenced my father to do the same. Already I hear that he loves the infant Ferdinand more than Carlos, myself and Eleanor combined."

"She is a strong woman and your father is her slave. But never fear, Carlos is of an age to guard that which is his—as I am."

Blanche shivered. "Henry, I am so glad I am not there . . . at my father's Court."

"Do you never feel homesick?"

"Castile became my home when we were married. I have no other home than this."

"My dear," he said lightly, "it makes me happy that you should feel thus."

But he was not looking at her. He was not a man who cared to inflict cruelty; indeed he would go to great lengths to avoid anything which was unpleasant. That was why he found it difficult to face her now.

She was trembling in spite of her endeavours to appear calm. What would happen to her if she were sent back to her father's Court, she wondered. She would be disgraced, humiliated—a repudiated wife. Carlos would be kind to her, for Carlos was the kindest of men. Eleanor would not be there, for her marriage with Gaston de Foix had taken her to France. Her father would not be her friend, for his affection was all for the brilliant and attractive Joan Henriquez who had given him young Ferdinand.

Carlos had inherited the Kingdom of Navarre from his mother; and, should Carlos die without heirs, Navarre would fall to Blanche herself as her mother, who had been the widow of Martin, King of Sicily, and daughter of Charles III of Navarre, had left Navarre to her children, excluding her husband from its possession.

She had, however, stated in her will that Carlos should, in governing the Kingdom, seek the good will and approbation of his father.

On his inheritance Carlos, since his father had not wished to give up the title of King of Navarre, had allowed him to keep it, but insisted that it was his own right to rule Navarre, which he did as its Governor.

So at this time Blanche was the heir of Carlos; and if he should die without issue, the right to govern Navarre would be hers, as also would be the crown.

She was foolish perhaps to let these fancies upset her; but she had a premonition that some terrible evil would befall her if she were ever forced to return to Aragon.

Here she felt safe. Henry was her unfaithful husband; she had failed to give him children, which was the whole purpose of marriages such as theirs; yet Henry was kind to her. Indolent, lecherous, shallow, he might be, but he would never use physical violence against her. And how could she know what would befall her if she returned to her father's Court?

Now he was smiling at her almost tenderly.

Surely, she thought, he could not smile at me like that unless he had some affection for me. Perhaps, like myself, he remembers the days when we were first married; that must be why he smiles at me so kindly.

But Henry, although he continued to smile, was scarcely aware of her. He was thinking of the new wife he would have when he had rid himself of poor, useless Blanche; she would naturally be young, this new wife, someone whom he could mould to his own sensual pleasure.

Once my father is dead, he told himself, I shall have my freedom.

He took Blanche's hand and led her to the window. They looked out and saw that he had been right when he had said the people were beginning to gather down there. They were waiting impatiently. They longed to hear that the old King was dead and that a new era had begun.

* * *

The King asked his physician, Cibdareal, to come closer to him.

"My friend," he whispered. "it cannot be much longer."

"Preserve your strength, Highness," begged the physician.

"Of what use? That I may live a few minutes more? Ah, Cibdareal, I should have lived a happier life, I should be a happier man now if I had been born the son of a mechanic, instead of the son of the King of Castile. Send for the Queen. Send for my son Henry."

They were brought to his bedside and he looked at them quizzically.

The Queen's eyes were wild. She does not regret the passing of her husband, thought the King; she regrets only the passing of power. "Holy Mother," he prayed, "keep her sane. Then she will be a good mother to our little ones. She will look after their rights. Let not the cares, which will now be hers, drive her the way her ancestors have gone . . . before her children are of age to care for themselves."

And Henry? Henry was looking at him with the utmost compassion, but Henry's fingers he knew were itching to seize the power which would shortly be his.

"Henry, my son," said John, "we have not always been the best of friends. I regret that."

"I too regret, Father."

"But let us not brood on an unhappy past. I think of the future. I leave two young children, Henry."

"Yes, Father."

"Never forget that they are your brother and sister."

"I will not forget."

"Look after them well. I have made provision for them, but they will need your protection."

"They shall have it, Father."

"You have given me your sacred promise and I can now go to my rest content. Respect my children's mother."

"I will."

The King said that he was tired, and his son and second wife moved away from the bed while the priests came forward.

Within half an hour the news was spreading through the Palace: "King John II is dead. Henry IV is now King of Castile."

* * *

The Queen was ready to leave the Palace.

Her women were clustered about her; one carried the baby in her arms; another grasped the hand of Isabella.

Muffled in her black cloak the little girl waited—listening, watching.

The Queen was in a mood of suppressed excitement, which caused Isabella great anxiety.

She listened to her mother's shrill voice. "Everything must appear to be normal. No one must guess that we are going away. I have my children to protect."

"Yes, Highness," was the answer.

But Isabella had heard the women talking: "Why should we go as though we are fugitives? Why should we run from the new King? Is she mad . . . already? King Henry knows that we are leaving. He makes no effort to detain us. It is of no consequence to him whether we stay here or go away. But we must go as though the armies of Castile are in pursuit of us."

"Hush . . . hush. . . . She will hear." And then, the whispers: "The little Isabella is all ears. Do not be deceived because she stands so quietly."

So he would not hurt us, thought Isabella. Of course dear Henry would never hurt us. But why does my mother think he would?

She was lifted in the arms of a groom and set upon a horse. The journey had begun.

So the Queen and her children left Madrid for the lonely castle of Arevalo.

Isabella remembered little of the journey; the movement of the horse and the warm arms of the groom lulled her to sleep, and when she awoke it was to find herself in her new home.

Early next day her mother came into that apartment in which Isabella had slept, and in her arms she carried the sleeping Alfonso, and with her were two of her trusted attendants.

The Queen set Alfonso on the bed beside his sister. Then she clenched her fists together in the well-remembered gesture and raised her arms above her head as though she were invoking the saints.

Isabella saw her lips move and realized that she was praying. It seemed wrong to be lying in bed while her mother prayed, and Isabella wondered what to do. She half rose, but one of the women shook her head vigorously to warn her to remain where she was.

Now the Queen was speaking so that Isabella could hear her.

"Here I shall care for them. Here I shall bring them up so that when the time comes they will be ready to meet their destiny. It will come. It will surely come. He will never beget a child. It is God's punishment for the evil life he has led."

Alfonso's little fingers had curled themselves about Isabella's. She wanted to cry because she was afraid; but she lay still, watching her mother, her blue eyes never betraying for a second that this lonely place which was now to be her home, and the rising hysteria in her mother, terrified her and filled her with a foreboding which she was too young to understand.

JOANNA OF PORTUGAL, QUEEN OF CASTILE

JOHN PACHECO, Marquis of Villena, was on his way to answer a summons from the King.

He was delighted with the turn of events. From the time he had come to Court—his family had sent him to serve with Alvaro de Luna and he had entered the household of that influential man as one of his pages—he had attracted the notice of the young Henry, heir to the throne, who was now King of Castile.

Henry had delighted in the friendship of Villena, and John, Henry's father, had honoured him for his service to the Prince. He had been clever and was in possession of great territories in the districts of Toledo, Valencia and Murcia. And now that his friend Henry was King he foresaw greater glories.

On his way to the council chamber he met his uncle, Alfonso Carillo, Archbishop of Toledo, and they greeted each other affectionately. They were both aware that together they made a formidable pair.

"Good day to you, Marquis," said the Archbishop. "I believe we are set for the same destination."

"Henry requested me to attend him at this hour," answered Villena. "There is a matter of the greatest importance which he desires to discuss before making his wishes publicly known."

The Archbishop nodded. "He wants to ask our advice, nephew, before taking a certain step."

"You know what it is?"

"I can guess. He has long been weary of her."

"It is time she returned to Aragon."

"I am sure," said the Archbishop, "that you, my wise nephew, would wish to see an alliance in a certain quarter."

"Portugal?"

"Exactly. The lady is a sister of Alfonso V, and I have heard nothing but praise of her personal charms. And let us not dismiss these assets as frivolous. We know our Henry. He will welcome a beautiful bride; and it is very necessary that he should welcome her with enthusiasm. That is the best way to ensure a fruitful union."

"There must be a *fruitful* union."

"I agree it is imperative for Castile . . . for Henry . . . and for us."

"You have no need to tell me. I know our enemies have their eyes on Arevalo."

"Have you heard news of events there?"

"There is very little to be learned," Villena replied. "The Dowager is there with her two children. They are living quietly, and my friends there inform me that the lady has been more serene of late. There have been no hysterical scenes at all. She believes herself to be safe, and is biding her time; and, while this is so, she devotes herself to the care of her children. Poor Isabella! Alfonso is too young as yet to suffer from such rigorous treatment. I hear it is prayers . . . prayers all the time. Prayers, I suppose, that the little lady may be good and worthy of any great destiny which may befall her."

"At least the Dowager can do little mischief there."

"But, uncle, we must be ever watchful. Henry is ours and we are his. He must please his people or there will be those ready to call for his abdication and the setting up of young Alfonso. There are many in this kingdom who would be pleased to see the crown on Alfonso's baby brow. A Regency! You know how seekers after power could wish for nothing better than that."

"I know. I know. And our first task is to rid the King of his present wife and provide him with a new one. When the heir is born a fatal blow will have been struck at the hopes of the Dowager of Arevalo. Then it will matter little what she teaches her Alfonso and Isabella."

"You have heard of course . . ." began Villena.

"The rumours . . . indeed yes. The King is said to be impotent, and it is due to him—not Blanche—that the marriage is unfruitful. That may be. But let us jump our hurdles when we reach them, eh? And now . . . here we are."

The page announced them, and Henry came forward to meet them, which was characteristic of Henry; and whilst this show of familiarity pleased both men they deplored it as unworthy of the ancient traditions of Castile.

"Marquis! Archbishop!" cried Henry as they bowed before him. "I am glad you are here." He waved his hand, signifying to his attendants that he wished to be entirely alone with his two ministers. "Now to business," he went on. "You know why I have asked you here."

The Marquis said: "Dearest Sire, we can guess. You wish to serve

Castile, and to do this you have to take steps which are disagreeable to you. We offer our respectful condolence and assistance."

"I am sorry for the Queen," said Henry, lifting his hands in a helpless gesture. "But what can I do for her? Archbishop, do you think it will be possible to obtain a divorce?"

"Anticipating your commands, Highness, I have given great consideration to this matter, and I am sure the Bishop of Segovia will support my plan."

"My uncle has solved our problem, Highness," said Villena, determined that, while the Archbishop received the King's grateful thanks, he himself should not be forgotten as chief conspirator.

"My dear Archbishop! My dear, dear Villena! I pray you tell me what you have arranged."

The Archbishop said : "A divorce could be granted *por impotencia respectiva.*"

"Could this be so?"

"The marriage has been unfruitful, Highness."

"But . . ."

"There need be no slur on the royal virility, Highness. We might say that some malign influence brought about this unhappy state of affairs."

"Malign influence?"

"It could be construed as witchcraft. We will not go too deeply into that, but we feel sure that all would agree, in the circumstances, that Your Highness should repudiate your present wife and take another."

"And Segovia is prepared to declare the marriage null and void!"

"He will do that," said the Archbishop. "I myself will confirm it."

Henry laughed. "There could surely not be a better reason." He repeated. "*Por impotencia respectiva. . . .*" And then : "Some malign influence."

"Let us not worry further on that point," said Villena. "I have here a picture of a delectable female."

Henry's eyes became glazed as he looked at the picture of a pretty young girl, which Villena handed him; his lips curved into a lascivious smile. "But . . . she is enchanting!"

"Enchanting and eligible, Highness, being none other than Joanna, Princess of Portugal, sister of Alfonso V, the reigning monarch."

"I can scarcely wait," said Henry, "for her arrival in Castile."

"Then, Sire, we have your permission to go ahead with these arrangements?"

"My dear friends, you have not only my permission; you have my most urgent command."

The Marquis and the Archbishop were smiling contentedly as they left the royal apartments.

* * *

The Queen begged an audience with the King. One of her women had brought the news to her that the Marquis and the Archbishop had been closeted with the King, and that their discussion must have been very secret, as the apartments had been cleared before it began.

Henry received her with warmth. The fact that he would soon be rid of her made him almost fond of her.

"Why, Blanche my dear," he said, "you look distressed."

"I have had strange dreams, Henry. They frightened me."

"My dear, it is folly to be afraid of dreams in daylight."

"They persist, Henry. It is almost as though I have a premonition of evil."

He led her to a chair and made her sit down, while he leaned over her and laid a gentle and caressing hand on her shoulder.

"You must banish these premonitions, Blanche. What harm could come to the Queen of Castile?"

"There is a feeling within me, Henry, that I may not long be the Queen of Castile."

"You think there is a plot afoot to murder me? Ah, my dear, you have been brooding about the Dowager of Arevalo. You imagine that her friends will dispatch me so that her little Alfonso shall have my crown. Have no fear. She could not harm me, if she would."

"I was not thinking of her, Henry."

"Then what is there to fear?"

"We have no children."

"We must endeavour to remedy that."

"Henry, you mean this?"

"You fret too much. You are over-anxious. Perhaps that is why you fail."

She wanted to say: "But am I the one who fails, Henry? Are you sure of that?" But she did not. That would anger him, and if he were angry he might blame her; and who could say what might grow out of such blame?

"We must have a child," she said desperately.

"Calm yourself, Blanche. All will be well with you. You have allowed your dreams to upset you."

"I dream of going back to Aragon. Why should I dream that, Henry? Is not Castile my home!"

"Castile is your home."

"I dream of being there . . . in the apartment I used to occupy. I dream that they are there . . . my family . . . my father, Eleanor, my stepmother holding little Ferdinand—and they approach my bed. I think they are going to do me some harm. Carlos is somewhere in the Palace and I cannot reach him."

"Dreams, my dear Blanche, what are dreams?"

"I am foolish to give them a thought, but I wish they did not come. The Marquis and the Archbishop were with you, Henry. I hope they had good news for you."

"Very good news, my dear."

She looked at him eagerly; but he would not meet her gaze; and because she knew him so well, that fact terrified her.

"You have a great opinion of those two," she said.

"They are astute—and my friends. I know that."

"I suppose you would put their suggestions to a Council . . . before you accept them."

"You should not worry your head with state affairs, my dear."

"So it was state affairs that they discussed with you."

"It was."

"Henry, I know I have been an unsatisfactory wife to you because of my inability to bear children, but I love you and I have been very happy in Castile."

Henry took her hands and drew her to her feet. He put his lips to her forehead and then, putting an arm about her shoulders, he led her to the door.

It was her dismissal.

It was kindly; it was courteous. He could not treat me thus, she assured herself, if he were planning to rid himself of me. But as she went back to her own apartments she felt very unsure.

When she had gone, Henry frowned. He thought: One of them will have to break the news to her. The Archbishop is the more suitable. Once she knows, I shall never see her again.

He was sorry for her, but he would not allow himself to be saddened.

She would return to her father's Court of Aragon. She had her family to comfort her.

He picked up the picture of Joanna of Portugal. So young! Innocent? He was not sure. At least there was a promise of sensuality in that laughing mouth.

"How long?" he murmured. "How long before Blanche goes back to Aragon, and Joanna is here in her place?"

* * *

The procession was ready to set out from Lisbon, but the Princess Joanna felt no pangs at leaving her home; she was eager to reach Castile, where she believed she was going to enjoy her new life.

Etiquette at the Court of Castile would be solemn, after the manner of the Castilians, but she had heard that her future husband entertained lavishly and that he lived in the midst of splendour. He was a man devoted to feminine society and, if he had many mistresses, Joanna assured herself that that was due to the fact that Blanche of Aragon was so dull and unattractive.

But she had no intention of putting too strong a curb upon him. She was not herself averse to a little amorous adventuring; and if Henry strayed now and then from the marriage bed she would not dream of reproaching him, for if she were lenient with him so must he be with her, and she foresaw an exciting life in Castile.

Here in Lisbon she was, in her opinion, too well guarded.

Therefore it was with few regrets that she prepared to leave. She could look from the windows of the castle of São Jorge on to the town and say goodbye quite happily. She had little love for the town, with its old cathedral, close to which it was said that St. Anthony was born. The saints of Lisbon meant little to her. What cared she if after his martyrdom Saint Vicente's body was brought to Lisbon along the Tagus in a boat which was guided by two black crows? What did she care if the spirit of St. Anthony was supposed to live on and help those who had lost something dear to them to recover it? These were merely legends to her.

So she turned away from the window and the view of olive and fig trees, of the Alcaçova where the Arab rulers had once lived, of the mossy tiles of the Alfama district and the glistening stream of the Tagus.

Gladly would she say farewell to all that had been home, for in the new land to which she was going she would be a Queen—Queen of Castile.

Soon they would depart, travelling eastwards to the border.

Her eyes were glistening as she took the mirror which was held to her by her maid of honour; she looked over her shoulder at the girl, whose eyes danced as merrily as her own.

"So, Alegre, you too are happy to go to Castile?"

"I am happy, my lady," answered the girl.

"You will have to behave with decorum there, you know."

Alegre smiled mischievously. She was a bold creature, and Joanna, who herself was bold and fond of gaiety, had chosen her for this reason. Her nickname, Alegre, had been given her some years before by one of the Spanish attendants: The gay one.

Alegre had had adventures; some she recounted; some she did not.

Joanna grimaced at the girl. "When I am Queen I must become very severe."

"You will never be that with me, my lady. How could you be severe with one who is as like yourself in her ways as that reflection is like your own face?"

"I may have to change my ways."

"They say the King, your husband, is very gay . . ."

"That is because he has never had a wife to satisfy him."

Alegre smiled secretly. "Let us hope that, when he has a wife who satisfies him, he will still be gay."

"I shall watch you, Alegre, and if you are wicked I shall send you home."

Alegre put her head on one side. "Well, there are some charming gentlemen at your brother's Court, my lady."

"Come," said Joanna. "It is time we left. They are waiting for us down there."

Alegre curtsied and stood aside for Joanna to pass through the apartment.

Then she followed her down to the courtyard, where the gaily-caparisoned horses and the loads of baggage were ready to begin the journey from Lisbon to Castile.

* * *

Before Joanna began the journey Blanche had set out for Aragon.

It seemed to her that the nightmare had become a reality, for in her dreams she had feared exactly this.

It was twelve years since she had left her home to be the bride of Henry; then she had been fearful, even as she was now. But she had left Aragon as the bride of the heir to Castile; her family had approved of the match, and she had seen no reason why her life should end in failure.

But how different it had been, making that journey as a bride, from returning as a repudiated wife, one who had failed to provide the necessary heir to a throne.

She thought now of that moment when she had been no longer able to hide the truth from herself, when the Archbishop had stood before her and announced that her marriage was annulled "*por impotencia respectiva*".

She had wanted to protest bitterly. She had wanted to cry out: "What use to throw me aside? It will be the same with any other woman. Henry cannot beget children."

They would not have listened to her, and she could have done her cause no good. What was the use of protesting? She could only listen dully and, when she was alone, throw herself upon her bed and stare at the ceiling, recalling the perfidy of Henry who, at the very time when he was planning to be rid of her, had implied that they would always be together.

She was to return to her family, who would have no use for her. Her father had changed since his second marriage; he was completely under the spell of her stepmother. All they cared for was the advancement of little Ferdinand.

And what would happen to her . . . she who would have no friend in the world but her brother Carlos? And what was happening to Carlos now? He was at odds with his father, and that was due to the jealousy of his stepmother.

What will become of me at my father's Court? she asked herself as she made the long and tedious journey to the home of her childhood; and it seemed to her then that the nightmares she had suffered had been no dreams; when she had been tortured by them she had been given a glimpse of the future.

* * *

Life in the Palace of Arevalo had been going smoothly.

We are happier here, thought young Isabella, than we were in Madrid. Everybody here seems serene and not afraid any more.

It was true. There had been none of those frightening interludes when the Queen lost control of her feelings. There was even laughter in the Palace.

Lessons were regular, of course, but Isabella was quite happy to receive lessons. She knew she had to learn if she were to be ready for her great destiny. Life ran to a set of rules. She rose early and retired early. There were many prayers during the day, and Isabella had heard some of the women complaining that to live at Arevalo was to live in a nunnery.

Isabella was contented with her nunnery. As long as they could live like this and her mother was quietly happy and not frightened, Isabella could be happy.

Alfonso was developing a personality of his own. He was no longer a gurgling, kicking baby. It was a great pleasure to watch him take his first steps, Isabella holding out her arms to catch him should he stumble. Sometimes they played these games with one of the women; sometimes with the Dowager Queen herself, who occasionally would pick up the little boy and hug him tightly. Then the ever alert Isabella would watch her mother for the tell-tale twitching of the mouth. But Alfonso would utter lusty protests at being held too tightly, and often an emotional scene was avoided in this way.

Isabella missed her father; she missed her brother Henry; but she could be happy like this if only she could keep her mother quiet and contented.

One day she said: "Let us stay like this . . . always. . . ."

But the Dowager Queen's lips had tightened and begun to twitch, so that Isabella realized her mistake.

"You have a great destiny," began the Dowager Queen. "Why, this baby here . . ."

That was when she picked up Alfonso and held him so tightly that he protested, and so, fortunately, his protests diverted the Queen from what she was about to say.

This was a lesson. It showed how easily one could stumble into pitfalls. Isabella was aghast on realizing that she, whose great desire was to avoid hysterical scenes, had almost, by a thoughtless remark, precipitated one of them.

She must never cease to be watchful and must not be deceived by the apparent peace of Arevalo.

There came a terrifying day when their mother visited the two children in the nursery.

Isabella knew at once that something unfortunate had occurred, and her heart began to hammer in an uncomfortable way. Alfonso was, of course, unaware that anything was wrong.

He threw himself at his mother and was picked up in her arms. The Queen stood holding him strained against her, and when Alfonso began to wriggle she did not release him.

"Highness . . ." he cried, and because he was proud to be able to say the word he repeated it. "Highness . . . Highness. . . ."

It seemed to Isabella that Alfonso was shouting. That was because everything was so quiet in the apartment.

"My son," said the Queen, "one day you will be King of Castile. There is no doubt of it."

"Highness . . . you hurt me . . ." whimpered Alfonso.

Isabella wanted to run to her mother and explain that she was holding Alfonso too tightly, and to remind her how much happier they were when they did not talk about the future King or Queen of Castile.

To Isabella it seemed that the Queen stood there a long time, staring into the future, but it could not have been more than a few seconds, or Alfonso's whimper would have become a loud protest.

Meanwhile the Queen said nothing; she stared before her, looking angry and determined, as Isabella remembered so well to have seen her in the past.

Then the little girl could bear it no longer; perhaps because it was so long since she had had to restrain herself, or because she was so very eager to preserve the peace of Arevalo.

She went to her mother and curtsied very low. Then she said: "Highness, I think Alfonso is hungry."

"Hungry, Highness," wailed Alfonso. "Highness hurts Alfonso."

The Queen continued to stare ahead, ignoring their appeal.

"He has married again," she resumed. "He thinks he will beget a child. But he never will. How could he? It is impossible. It is the just reward for the life he has led."

It was the old theme which Isabella had heard many times before; it was a reminder of the past; it warned her that the peace of Arevalo could be shattered in a moment.

"Alfonso hungry," wailed the boy.

"My son," the Queen repeated, "one day you shall be King of Castile. One day . . ."

"Don't want to be King," cried Alfonso. "Highness squeezing him."

"Highness," whispered Isabella earnestly, "shall we show you how far Alfonso can walk by himself?"

"Let them try!" cried the Queen. "They will see. Let them try! The whole of Castile will be laughing at them."

Then, to Isabella's relief, she set Alfonso on his feet. He looked at his arms and whimpered.

Isabella took his hand and whispered: "Walk, Alfonso. Show Highness."

Alfonso nodded gleefully.

But the Queen had begun to laugh.

Alfonso looked at his mother and crowed with pleasure. He did not understand that there were more kinds of laughter than one. Alfonso only knew about laughing for amusement or happiness, but Isabella knew this was the frightening laughter. After the long peace it had returned.

One of the women had heard and came into the apartment. She looked at the two children, standing there watching their mother. Then she retired and very soon a physician came into the room.

Now the Queen was laughing so much that she could not stop. The tears were running down her cheeks. Alfonso was laughing too; he turned to Isabella to make sure that she was joining in the fun.

"Highness," said the physician, "if you will come to your bedchamber I will give you a potion which will enable you to rest."

But the Queen went on laughing; her arms had begun to wave about wildly. Another physician had now joined them.

With him was a woman, and Isabella heard his quiet order. "Take the children away . . . immediately."

But before they went, Isabella saw her mother on the couch, and the two doctors holding her there, while they murmured soothing words about rest and potions.

There was no escape, thought Isabella, even at Arevalo. She was glad Alfonso was so young that, as soon as he no longer saw his mother, he forgot the scene they had just witnessed; she was glad that he was too young to understand what it might mean.

* * *

Henry was happy in those first weeks of his marriage. He had arranged ceremonies and pageants of such extravagance as had rarely been seen before in Castile. So far he had not displeased his subjects, and when he rode among them at the head of some glittering cavalcade, towering above most of his retinue, his crown on his red hair, they cheered him vociferously. He knew how to dispense smiles and greetings so that they fell on all, rich and poor alike.

"There is a King," said the people of Castile, "the like of whom we have not seen for many a year."

Some had witnessed the departure of Blanche and had pitied her. She looked so forlorn, poor lady.

But, it was agreed, the King had his duties to Castile. Queen Blanche was sterile, and however virtuous queens may be, virtue is no substitute for fertility.

"Poor Henry!" they sighed. "How sad he must be to have to divorce her. Yet he considers his duty to Castile before his own inclination."

As for Henry he had scarcely thought of Blanche since she had left. He had been delighted to dismiss her from his thoughts, and when he saw his new wife his spirits had soared.

He, who was a connoisseur of women, recognized something beyond her beauty . . . a deep sensuality which might match his own, or at least come near to it.

During those first weeks of marriage he scarcely left her. In public she delighted his subjects; in private she was equally satisfactory to him.

There could not have been a woman more unlike poor Blanche. How glad he was that he had had the courage to rid himself of her.

Behind the sparkling eyes of the new Queen there was a certain purpose, but that was not evident as yet. Joanna was content at first merely to play the wife who was eager to please her husband.

Attended by the maids of honour whom she had brought with her from Lisbon, she was always the centre of attraction. Full of energy, she planned balls and pageants of her own to compete with those which the King gave in her honour, so that it appeared that the wedding celebrations would go on for a very long time.

Always to the fore among those who surrounded the new Queen was Alegre. Her dancing, her spontaneous laughter, her joy in being alive, were already beginning to attract attention.

Joanna watched her with some amusement.

"Have you found a Castilian lover yet?" she asked.

"I think so, Highness."

"Pray tell me his name."

"It would scarcely be fair to him, Highness, for he does not yet know of the delights in store for him."

"Am I to presume that this man has not yet become your lover?"

"That is so," answered Alegre demurely.

"Then he must be a laggard, for if you have decided, why should he hold back?"

"Who shall say?" murmured Alegre. Then she laughed and went on: "It is a great pleasure to all of us who serve Your Highness to note how devoted the King is to you. I have heard that he has had hundreds of mistresses, yet when he is with you he is like a young man in love for the first time."

"My dear Alegre, I am not like you. I would not tolerate laggards in love."

Alegre put her head on one side and went on: "His Highness is so enamoured of you that he seems to have forgotten those two cronies of his, Villena and the Archbishop . . . almost."

"Those two!" said the Queen. "They are for ever at his elbow."

"Whispering advice," added Alegre. "I wonder if they have advised him how to treat *you*. It would not surprise me. I fancy the King does little without their approval. I believe he has become accustomed to listening to his two dear friends."

Joanna was silent, but she later remembered that conversation. She was faintly irritated by those two friends and advisers of the King. He thought too highly of them and she considered he was ridiculously subservient to them.

That night, when she and the King lay together in their bed, she mentioned them.

"I fancy those two are possessed of certain conceits."

"Let us not concern ourselves with them," the King answered.

"But, Henry, I would not see you humbled by any of your subjects."

"I . . . humbled by Villena and Carillo! My dear Joanna, that is not possible."

"They sometimes behave as though they are the masters. I consider that humiliating for you."

"Oh . . . you have been listening to their enemies."

"I have drawn my own conclusions."

He made a gesture which indicated that there were more interesting occupations than discussing his ministers. But Joanna was adamant. She believed those two were watching her too intently, that they expected her to listen to their advice, or even instructions, simply because they had played some part in bringing her to Castile. She was not going to tolerate that; and now, while Henry was so infatuated with her, was the time to force him to curb their power.

So she ignored his gestures and sat up in bed, clasping her knees, while she told him that it was absurd for a King to give too much power to one or two men in his kingdom.

Henry yawned. For the first time he was afraid she was going to be one of those tiresome, meddling women, and that would be disappointing, as in many ways she was proving to be satisfactory.

* * *

It was the next day when, making his way to his wife's apartment, he encountered Alegre.

They were alone in one of the ante-rooms and Alegre dropped a demure curtsey at his approach. She remained with her head bowed, but as he was about to pass on she lifted her eyes to his face, and there was a look in them which made him halt.

He said: "You are happy here in Castile?"

"So happy, Highness. But never so happy as at this moment when I have the undivided attention of the King."

"My dear," said Henry with that characteristic and easy familiarity, "it takes little to make you happy."

She took his hand and kissed it, and as she did so she again raised her eyes to his. They were full of provocative suggestion which it was impossible for a man of Henry's temperament to ignore.

"I have often noticed you in the Queen's company," he said, "and it has given me great pleasure to see you here with us."

She continued to smile at him.

"Please rise," he continued.

She did so, while he looked down at her neat, trim figure with the eyes of a connoisseur. He knew her type. She was hot-blooded and eager. That look was unmistakable. She was studying him in a manner which he might have considered insolent if she had not possessed such superb attractions.

He patted her cheek and his hand dropped to her neck.

Then suddenly he seized her and kissed her on the lips. He had not been mistaken. Her response was immediate, and that brief contact told him a good deal.

She was ready and eager to become his mistress; and she was not the sort of woman who would seek to dabble in state matters; there was only one thing of real importance in her life. That short embrace told him that.

He released her and went on his way.

Both of them knew that, although that was their first embrace, it would not be their last.

* * *

Under the carved ceiling in the light of a thousand candles the King was dancing, and his partner was the Queen's maid of honour.

Joanna watched them.

The woman would not dare! she told herself as she recalled a conversation concerning Alegre's lover, who had not then known the role which was waiting for him. The impudence! I could send her back to Lisbon tomorrow. Does she not know that?

But she was mistaken. Alegre was by nature lecherous, and so was Henry; they betrayed it as they danced, and when two such people danced together. . . . But that was the point. When two such people as Alegre and Henry were together there could be but one outcome.

She would speak to Henry tonight. She would speak to Alegre.

She was not aware that she was frowning, nor that a young man whom she had noticed on several occasions had come to take his stand close to her chair.

He was tall—almost as tall as Henry, whose height was exceptional. He was strikingly handsome with his blue-black hair, and eyes which were brilliantly dark; and yet his skin was fairer than red-headed Henry's. Joanna had considered him as one of the handsomest men at her husband's Court.

"Your Highness is troubled?" he asked. "I wondered if there was aught I could do to take the frown from your exquisite brow."

She smiled at him. "Troubled! Indeed I am not. I was thinking that this is one of the most pleasant balls I have attended since coming to Castile."

"Your Highness must forgive me. On every occasion when I have had the honour to be in your company I have been deeply conscious of your mood. When you smiled I was contented; when I fancy I see you frown I long to eliminate the cause of that frown. Is that impertinence, Highness?"

Joanna surveyed him. He spoke to her with the deference due to the Queen, but he did not attempt to disguise the admiration she aroused in him. Joanna hovered between disapproval and the desire to hear more from him. She forgave him. The manners of Henry's Court were set by the King; as a result they had grown somewhat uninhibited.

She glanced towards the dancers and saw Henry's hand was laid on Alegre's shoulder caressingly.

"She is an insolent woman . . . that!" said the young man angrily.

"Sir?" she reproved.

"I crave Your Highness's pardon. I allowed my feelings to get the better of me."

Joanna decided that she liked him and that she wanted to keep him beside her.

"I myself often allow my feelings to get the better of the dignity expected of a Queen," she said.

"In such circumstances . . ." he went on hotly. "But, what amazes me is—how is this possible?"

"You refer to the King's flirtation with my woman? I know him; I know her. I can assure you there is nothing to be amazed about."

"The King has always been devoted to the ladies."

"I had heard that before I came."

"It was once understandable. But with such a Queen. . . . Highness, you must excuse me."

"Your feelings have the upper hand again. They must be strong and violent indeed to be able to subdue your good manners."

"They are very strong, Highness." His dark eyes were warm with adoration. She forgave Henry; she even forgave Alegre, because if they had not been so overcome by desire for each other she would not at this moment be accepting the attentions of this very handsome young man.

He was, she congratulated herself, far more handsome than the King; he was younger too, and the marks of debauchery had not yet begun to show on *his* features. Joanna had always said that if she allowed the King to go his own way, she would go hers, and she could imagine herself going along a very pleasant way with this young man.

"I would know the name," she said, "of the young man of such powerful passions."

"It is Beltran de la Cueva, who places himself body and soul in the service of Your Highness."

"Thank you," she said. "I am tired of looking on at the dance." She stood up and put her hand in his; and while she danced with Beltran de la Cueva, Joanna forgot to watch the conduct of the King and her maid of honour.

* * *

The Queen was in her apartment, and her ladies were preparing her for bed.

She noticed that Alegre was not among them.

The sly jade! she thought. But at least she has the decency not to present herself before me tonight.

She asked one of the others where the girl was.

"Highness, she had a headache, and asked us, if you should notice her absence, to crave your pardon for not attending. She felt so giddy she could scarce keep on her feet."

"She is excused," said the Queen. "She should be warned though to take greater care on these occasions."

"I shall give her your warning, Highness."

"Tell her that if she becomes careless of her . . . health, it might be necessary to send her back to Lisbon. Perhaps her native air would be beneficial to her."

"That will alarm her, Highness. She is in love with Castile."

"I thought I had noticed it," said the Queen.

She was ready now for her bed. They would lead her to it and, when she was settled, leave her. Shortly afterwards the King, having been similarly prepared by his attendants, would come to her as he had every night since their marriage.

But before her ladies had left her, the King's messenger arrived.

His Highness was a little indisposed and would not be visiting the Queen that night. He sent her his devoted affection and his wishes that she would pass a good night.

"Pray tell His Highness," she said, "that I am deeply concerned that he should be indisposed. I shall come along and see that he has all he needs. Although I am his Queen, I am also his wife, and I believe it is a wife's duty to nurse her husband through any sickness."

The messenger said hastily that His Highness was only slightly indisposed, and had been given a sleeping draught by his physician. If this were to be efficacious he should not be disturbed until morning.

"How glad I am that I told you of my intentions," declared Joanna. "I should have been most unhappy if I had disturbed him."

The King's messenger was ushered out of the Queen's bedchamber, and her ladies, more silently than usual, completed the ceremony of putting her to bed and left her.

She lay for some time contemplating this new state of affairs.

She was very angry. It was so humiliating to be neglected for her maid of honour; and she was sure that this was what was happening.

What should she do about it? Confront Henry with her discovery? Make sure that it did not occur again?

But could she do this? She had begun to understand her husband. He was weak; he was indolent; he wanted to preserve the peace at all costs. At all costs? At almost all costs. He was as single-minded as a lion or any other wild animal when in pursuit of his lust. How far would he allow her to interfere when it was a matter of separating him from a new mistress?

She had heard the story of her predecessor. Up to the last poor Blanche had thought she was safe, but Henry had not scrupled to send her away. Blanche had had twelve years' experience of this man and she, Joanna, was a newcomer to Castile. Perhaps she would be unwise to unleash her anger. Perhaps she should wait and see how best she could revenge herself on her unfaithful husband and disloyal maid of honour.

She was, however, determined to discover whether they were together this night.

She rose from her bed, put on a wrap and went into that apartment next to her own where her women attendants slept.

"Highness!" Several of them had sat up in their beds, alarm in their voices.

She said: "Do not be alarmed. One of you, please bring me a goblet of wine. I am thirsty."

"Yes, Highness."

Someone had gone in search of the wine, and Joanna returned to her room. She had made her discovery; the bed which should have been occupied by Alegre was empty.

The wine was brought to her, and she gazed absently at the flickering candlelight playing on the tapestried walls, while she drank a little and began to plot some form of retaliation.

She was very angry to think that she, Joanna of Portugal, had been passed over for one of her servants.

"She shall be sent back to Lisbon," she muttered. "No matter what he says. I shall insist. Perhaps Villena and the Archbishop will be with me in this. After all, do they not wish that I shall soon be with child?"

And then she heard the soft notes of a lute playing beneath her window, and as she listened the lute-player broke into a love song which she had heard at the ball on this very night.

The words were those of a lover, sighing for his mistress, declaring that he would prefer death to repudiation by her.

She took the candle and went to the window.

Below was the young man who had spoken to her so passionately at the ball. For a few moments they gazed at each other in silence; then he began to sing again in a deep voice, vibrating and passionate.

The Queen went back to her bed.

What was happening in some apartment of this Palace between her husband and her maid of honour was now of small importance to her. Her thoughts were full of Beltran de la Cueva.

THE BETROTHAL OF ISABELLA

ISABELLA was aroused from her sleep. She sat up in bed telling herself that surely it was not morning yet, for it was too dark.

"Wake up, Isabella."

That was her mother's voice and it sent shivers of apprehension through her. And there was her mother, holding a candle in its sconce, her hair flowing about her shoulders, her eyes enormous in her pale wild face.

Isabella began to tremble. "Highness . . ." she began. "Is it morning?"

"No, no. You have been asleep only an hour or so. There is wonderful news—so wonderful that I could not find it in my heart not to wake you that you might hear of it."

"News . . . for me, Highness?"

"Why, what a sleepy child you are. You should be dancing for joy. This wonderful news has just arrived from Aragon. You are to have a husband, Isabella. It is a great match."

"A husband, Highness?"

"Come. Do not lie there. Get up. Where is your wrap?" The Dowager Queen laughed on a shrill note. "I was determined to bring you this news myself. I would let no one else break it to you. Here, child. Put this about you. There! Now come here. This is a solemn moment. Your hand has been asked in marriage."

"Who has asked it, Highness?"

"King John of Aragon asks it on behalf of his son Ferdinand."

"Ferdinand," repeated Isabella.

"Yes, Ferdinand. Of course he is not the King's elder son, but I have heard—and I know this to be the truth—that the King of Aragon loves the finger nails of Ferdinand more than the whole bodies of his three children by his first marriage."

"Highness, has he such different finger nails from other people then?"

"Oh, Isabella, Isabella, you are a baby still. Now Ferdinand is a little younger than you are . . . a year, all but a month. So he is only a little boy as yet, but he will be as delighted to form an alliance with Castile as you are with Aragon. And I, my child, am contented. You have no father now, and your enemies at Madrid will do their utmost to keep you from your rights. But the King of Aragon offers you his son. As soon as you are old enough the marriage shall take place. In the meantime you may consider yourself betrothed. Now, we must pray. We must thank God for this great good fortune and at the same time we will ask the saints to guard you well, to bring you to a great destiny. Come."

Together they knelt on the *prie-Dieu* in Isabella's apartment.

To the child it seemed fantastic to be up so late; the flickering candle-light seemed ghostly, her mother's voice sounded wild as she instructed rather than prayed God and his saints what they must do for Isabella. Her knees hurt; they were always a little sore from so much kneeling; and she felt as though she were not fully awake and that this was some sort of dream.

"Ferdinand," she murmured to herself, trying to visualize him; but she could only think of those finger nails so beloved of his father.

Ferdinand! They would meet each other; they would talk together; make plans; they would live together, as her mother and the King had lived together, in a palace or a castle, probably in Aragon.

She had never thought of living anywhere other than in Madrid or Arevalo; she had never thought of having other companions than her mother and Alfonso, and perhaps Henry if they ever returned to Madrid. But this would be different.

Ferdinand. She repeated the name again and again. It held a magic quality. He was to be her husband, and already he had the power to make her mother happy.

The Queen had risen from her knees.

"You will go back to your bed now," she said. "We have given thanks for this great blessing." She kissed her daughter's forehead, and her smile was quiet and contented.

Isabella offered silent thanks to Ferdinand for making her mother so happy.

But the Queen's mood changed with that suddenness which still startled Isabella. "Those who have thought you of little account will have to change their minds, now that the King of Aragon has selected you as the bride of his best-loved son."

And there in her voice was all the anger and hate she felt for her enemies.

"Everything will be well though now, Highness," soothed Isabella. "Ferdinand will arrange that."

The Queen smiled suddenly; she pushed the little girl towards the bed.

"There," she said, "go to bed and sleep peacefully."

Isabella took off her wrap and climbed into the bed. The Queen watched her and stooped over her to arrange the bed-clothes. Then she kissed Isabella and went out, taking the candle with her.

Ferdinand, thought Isabella. Dear Ferdinand of the precious finger nails, the mention of whose name could bring such happiness to her mother.

* * *

Joanna noticed that Alegre did not appear on those occasions when it was her duty to wait on the Queen. She sent one of her women to the absent maid of honour with a command to present herself at once. When Alegre arrived, Joanna made sure that no others should be present at their interview.

Alegre surveyed the Queen with very slightly disguised insolence.

"Since you have come to Castile," said Joanna, "you appear to take your duties very lightly."

"To what duties does your Highness refer?" The tone reflected the insolence of her manner.

"To what duties should I refer but those which brought you to Castile? I have not seen you in attendance for more than a week."

"Highness, I had received other commands."

"I am your mistress. It is from me only that you should take orders."

Alegre cast down her eyes and managed to look both brazen and demure at the same time.

"Well, what do you say?" persisted the Queen. "Are you going to behave in a fitting manner or will you force me to send you back to Lisbon?"

"Highness, I do not think it would be the wish of *all* at Court that I should return to Lisbon. I hear, from a reliable source, that my presence is very welcome here."

Joanna stood up abruptly; she went to Alegre and slapped her on both sides of her face. Startled, Alegre put her hands to her cheeks.

"You should behave in a manner fitting to a maid of honour," said Joanna angrily.

"I will endeavour to emulate Your Highness, who behaves in the manner of a Queen."

"You are insolent!" cried Joanna.

"Highness, is it insolent to accept the inevitable?"

"So it is inevitable that you should behave like a slut at my Court?"

"It is inevitable that I obey the commands of the King."

"So he commanded you? So you did not put yourself in the way of being commanded?"

"What could I do, Highness? I could not efface myself."

"You shall be sent back to Lisbon."

"I do not think so, Highness."

"I shall demand that you are sent back."

"It would be humiliating for Your Highness to demand that which would not be granted."

"You should not think that you know a great deal concerning Court matters merely because for a few nights you have shared the King's bed."

"One learns something," said Alegre lightly, "for even we do not make love all the time."

"You are dismissed."

"From your presence, Highness, or from the Court?"

"Go from my presence. I warn you, I shall have you sent back to Lisbon."

Alegre curtsied and left. Joanna was very angry; she cursed her own folly in bringing Alegre with her; she should have guessed the creature would make trouble of some sort; but how could she have foreseen that she would have the temerity to usurp her own place in the royal bed?

* * *

She was thoughtful while her maids were dressing her. She felt she could not trust herself to speak to them, lest she betray her feelings.

It would be so undignified to let anyone know how humiliated she felt, particularly as her common sense told her that if she did not want trouble with the King she would have to accept the situation.

Her seemingly indolent husband, while he remained indifferent to the affairs of the kingdom, would commit any folly to please his mistress of the moment. She would never forget the sad story of Blanche of Aragon, and she knew she would be foolish to let herself believe that, because he appeared to have an affection for herself, he would hesitate to send her back to Lisbon if she displeased him.

After all, she was no more successful than Blanche had been in achieving the desired state of pregnancy. She was alarmed too by the whispers she had heard. Was it really true that Henry was unable to beget children? If so, what would be the fate of Joanna of Portugal? Would it be similar to that of Blanche of Aragon?

She listened to the chatter of her women, which was clearly intended to soothe her.

"They say he was magnificent."

"I consider him to be the handsomest man at Court."

Joanna said lightly: "And who is this magnificent and handsome personage?"

"Beltran de la Cueva, Highness."

Joanna felt her spirits lifted, but studying her face in the mirror she saw with satisfaction that she gave no sign of this.

"What has he done?"

"Well, Highness, he defended a passage of arms in the presence of the King himself. He was victorious; and rarely, so we hear, has a man shown such valour. He declared that he would uphold the superior charms of his mistress against all others at this time or any time, and that he would challenge any who denied his words."

"And who is this incomparable woman? Did he say?"

"He did not. It is said that his honour forbade him to. The King was pleased. He said that Beltran de la Cueva's gallantry had so impressed him that he would build a monastery which should be dedicated to St. Jerome to celebrate the occasion."

"What a strange thing to do! To dedicate a monastery to St. Jerome because a courtier flaunts the charms of his mistress?"

"Your Highness should have seen this knight. He was as one dedicated. And the King was so impressed by his devotion to the unknown lady."

"And have you any notion who this unknown lady is?"

The women looked at each other.

"Well?" prompted Joanna.

"Highness, all know that this knight is devoted only to one who could not return his love, being so highly placed. There could only be one lady at Court to answer that description."

"You mean . . . the Queen of Castile?"

"Yourself, Highness. It is thought that the King was so pleased by this man's devotion to yourself that he made this gesture."

"I am grateful," said Joanna lightly, "both to Beltran de la Cueva and to the King."

Joanna felt that in some measure her dignity had been restored, and she was conscious of infinite gratitude towards Beltran de la Cueva.

* * *

Joanna had retired; she did not sleep. She knew that very soon the man who was clearly asking to become her lover would be standing below her window.

It would be so easy. She need only give one little sign.

Was it dangerous? It would be impossible to keep such an affair entirely secret.. It seemed that there were few actions of Kings and Queens which could be safe from the light of publicity. Yet he had made that magnificent gesture for her.

Moreover she had a notion that the King would not object to her taking a lover. Henry wanted to go his own promiscuous way, and she believed that what had irritated him in his first wife was her virtue. To a man such as Henry the virtue of one whom he was deceiving could be an irritation. What if the rumours were true and Henry was sterile? Would she be blamed as Blanche had been? Henry would be more likely to keep her as his wife if she remained charming and tolerant in spite of his scandalous way of life.

There was another point; she had always been aware of her own sexual needs. The second Queen of Henry of Castile was quite different from the first.

She felt reckless as she went slowly but deliberately towards the window.

The night was dark and warm, soft with the scent of flowers. He was standing there as she had known he would be, and the sight of him excited her. None could say she would demean herself by taking such a lover. He was surely not only the handsomest but the bravest man at Court.

She lifted a hand and beckoned.

She could almost feel the waves of exultation which flowed from him.

* * *

Beltran de la Cueva was well pleased with himself, but he was too clever not to understand that this new path on which he was embarking was full of dangers.

The Queen had attracted him strongly since the time he had first seen her, and it had been one of his ambitions to make her his mistress; but he knew that his advancement would have to come from the King. He was pondering now how he could continue in the King's good graces while at the same time he enjoyed his intimacy with the Queen.

It was an odd state of affairs, since he was hoping to enjoy the King's favour while he was the lover of the Queen. But Henry was a meek husband; he was a man who, while devoting himself to the lusts of the flesh, liked to see those about him acting in like manner. He was not one to cherish the virtuous; they irritated him, because he was a man with a conscience which he was trying to ignore, and the virtuous stirred that conscience.

The future was hopeful, thought Beltran de la Cueva. He really did not see why he should not profit doubly from this new relationship with the Queen.

It was impossible to keep it secret.

The Queen had invited him to her bedchamber, and it was inevitable that one of her women would discover that these nightly visits were taking place; and one woman would pass on the secret to another, and sooner or later it would become Court gossip.

He hid his anxiety from the Queen.

He told her in the quiet of her bedchamber: "If the King should discover what has taken place between us, I do not think my life would be worth very much."

Joanna held him to her in a gesture of mock terror. It gave an added charm to their love to pretend it was dangerous.

"Then you must not come here again," she whispered.

"Do you think the fear of sudden death would keep me away?"

"I know you are brave, my love, so brave that you do not consider the danger to yourself. But I think of it constantly. I forbid you to come here again."

"It is the only command you could give me which I would not obey."

Such conversations were stimulating to them both. He enjoyed seeing himself as the invincible lover; her self-esteem was reinstated. To be so loved by one who was reckoned to be the most attractive man at Court could make her quite indifferent to the love affair between her husband and maid of honour.

Moreover she had heard that Henry was now dividing his attentions between Alegre and another woman of the Court; and this was gratifying.

Henry must have heard of her own attachment to Beltran, and he showed not the slightest rancour; in fact he seemed a little pleased. Joanna was delighted with this turn of events. It showed that she had been right when she had decided that, if she allowed Henry to take his mistresses without a reproach from her, he would raise no objection if she occasionally amused herself with a lover.

A very satisfactory state of affairs, thought the Queen of Castile.

Beltran de la Cueva was also relieved. Henry had become more friendly than ever with him. A fascinating situation, he reassured himself, when he might expect advancement through the Queen and the King.

* * *

Meanwhile the little girl was growing up in the Palace at Arevalo.

When she looked back she thought pityingly of that Isabella who had lacked her Ferdinand, for Ferdinand had become as real to her as her brother, her mother or anyone within the Palace. Occasionally she heard scraps of news concerning him. He was very handsome; he was the delight of the Court of Aragon; the quarrel between his father and Ferdinand's half-brother was all on account of Ferdinand. It was a continual regret to the royal House of Aragon that Ferdinand had not been born before Carlos.

Often when she was in a dilemma she would say to herself: "What would Ferdinand do?"

She talked about him so much to Alfonso that her young brother said: "One would think he was really here with us. No one would believe that you had never seen Ferdinand."

Those words had their effect on Isabella. It was almost a shock to have it brought home to her that she had never seen Ferdinand. She believed too that she had departed from her usual decorum by talking of him so much. She must remedy that.

But if she did not talk to him, that did not stop her thinking of him. She could not imagine life without Ferdinand.

Because of him she determined to be a perfect wife, a perfect Queen, for she believed that one day Ferdinand would be King of Aragon in spite of his brother Carlos. She mastered the art of the needle and was determined not only to become an expert in fine needlework but to be a useful seamstress as well.

"When I am married to Ferdinand," she once told Alfonso, "I shall make all his shirts. I shall not allow him to wear one that is made by another hand."

She was interested in affairs of state.

She was no longer a child, and perhaps, when she was fifteen or sixteen, she would be married. Ferdinand was a year younger, which could cause some delay, for she would be the one to wait for him to reach a marriageable age.

"Never mind," she consoled herself, "I shall have a little longer to perfect myself."

Now and then she heard news of her half-brother's Court. Henry was a very bad King, she feared, and her mother had been right, no doubt, to insist that herself and her brother should go away and live like hermits. This was the best way to prepare herself for marriage with Ferdinand.

As she had even as a very small child, she listened and rarely interrupted when she heard the conversation of grown-up people; she tried to hide her interest, which was the surest way of making them forget she was present.

One day she heard a great deal of whispering.

"What a scandal!"

"Who ever heard of such behaviour by an Archbishop!"

"And the Archbishop of St. James at that!"

Eventually she discovered what this misdemeanour of an Archbishop had been. It appeared that he had been so struck by the charms of a young bride that he had attempted abduction and rape as she left the church after her marriage.

The comments on this scandal were so illuminating.

"What can one expect? It is merely a reflection of the manners of the Court. How can the King censure the Archbishop when he behaves equally scandalously? You have heard, of course, that his chief mistress is the Queen's own maid of honour. They say she keeps an establishment which is as splendid as that of the Queen, and that people such as the Archbishop of Seville seek her favour."

"It is not as though she is the King's only mistress. The latest scandal is that one of his ladies wished to become an abbess, if you please! And what does our loving King do? He dismisses the pious and high-born abbess of a convent in Toledo and sets up his paramour in her place. It is small wonder that there are scandals outside the Court when they so blatantly exist inside it."

Isabella began to learn from her mother and her teachers how the state of Castile was being governed; she was made aware of the terrible mistakes which were being made by her half-brother.

"My child," said her pastor, "take a lesson from the actions of the King, and, if ever it should be your fate to assist in the government of a kingdom, make sure that you do not fall into like pitfalls. Taxes are being imposed on the people. For what reason? That the King may sustain his favourites. The merchants, who are one of the means of providing a country with its riches, are being taxed so heavily that they are prevented from giving the country of their best. Worst of all, the coinage has been adulterated. You must try to understand the importance of this. Where we had five mints we now have one hundred and fifty; this means that the value of money has dropped to a sixth of its previous value. My child, try to understand the chaos this can bring about. Why, if matters do not mend, the whole country will be on the verge of insolvency."

"Tell me," said Isabella earnestly, "is my brother Henry to blame for this?"

"The rulers of a country are often to be blamed when it falls on evil times. It is their duty to efface themselves for the love of their country. The duty of Kings and Queens to their people should come before their pleasure. If ever it should be your destiny to rule . . ."

Isabella folded her hands together and said. "My country would be my first consideration." And she spoke as a novice might speak when contemplating the taking of her vows.

And always on such occasions she imagined herself ruling with Ferdinand; she began to realize that this prospective bridegroom, who was so real to her in spite of the fact that she had never seen him, was the dominating influence in her life.

Later came news that Henry had decided to lead a crusade against the Moors. There was nothing which could win the approval of the people so surely as an attempt to conquer the Moors. Spaniards smarted in the knowledge that for centuries the Arabs had remained in Spain, and that large provinces in the south were still under their domination. Since the days of Rodrigo Diaz of Bivar, the famous Castilian leader who had lived in the eleventh century and had been known as the Cid Campeador, Spaniards had looked for another great leader; and whenever one appeared who proposed to lead a campaign which was calculated to drive the Moors from the Iberian Peninsula the cry went up : "Here is the Cid reborn and come among us."

Thus, when Henry declared his intention of striking against the Moors, his popularity increased.

He needed money for his campaigns, and who should provide it but his long-suffering people? The riches of the countryside were seized that armies might be equipped for the King's campaign.

Henry, however, was a soldier who could make a brave show, marching through the streets at the head of his troops, but was not so successful on the battlefields.

Again and again his troops were routed; he returned from the wars, with his dazzling cavalcade making a brave show; but there were no conquests, and the Moors remained as strongly entrenched as ever.

He declared that he was chary of risking the lives of his soldiers, for in his opinion the life of one Christian was worth more than those of a thousand Mussulmans.

This was a sentiment which he hoped would find favour with the people; but they grumbled, particularly those in whose districts the fighting had taken place.

It would seem, said these people, that the King makes war on us, not on the Infidel.

And each day in the schoolroom at Arevalo Isabella would hear of the exploits of Henry, and must learn her lessons from them.

"Never go to war," she was told, "unless you have a well-founded hope of victory. Fine uniforms do not necessarily make good soldiers. Before you go to war make sure that your cause is just and that it is wholeheartedly yours." "Never," said their preceptor, instructing Isabella and Alfonso, "had a prospective ruler a better opportunity of profiting from the folly of a predecessor."

The children were told why, on every count, Henry was a bad King. They were not told of his voluptuous adventures, but these were hinted at, and mistresses and ministers were spoken of under one category as Favourites.

He was extravagant almost to the point of absurdity. His policy was to give bribes to his enemies in the hope of turning them into friends, and to his friends that they might remain friendly.

Mistaken policies, both of them, Isabella and Alfonso were warned. Friends should be kept by mutual loyalty, and enemies met by the mailed fist and not by placatory gold.

"Learn your lessons well, children. There may come a time when you will need them."

"And we *must* learn our lessons, Alfonso," said Isabella. "For it may well be that one day the people will have had enough of Henry; and if he has no son they will call upon you to take the throne of Castile. As for myself, one day I shall help Ferdinand to rule Aragon. We must certainly learn our lessons well."

So, gravely, they listened to what was told to them; and it seemed to them both that the years at Arevalo were the waiting years.

* * *

Isabella sat thoughtfully over her needlework.

At any moment, she thought, there may be change. At any moment the people may decide that they will have no more of Henry; then they will march to Arevalo and take away Alfonso to make him King.

She had heard that the debasing of the coinage had caused chaos among certain sections of the community; and the result was that robbery had increased.

Some of the noblest families in Castile, declaring themselves to be on the verge of bankruptcy, lost all sense of decency and took to robbery on the roads. Travelling was less safe than it had been for centuries; and castles, which had once been the homes of noble families, were now little less than robbers' dens. Some of these nobles even attempted to put right their reverses by selling Christian men and women, whom they seized during raids on villages, as slaves to the Moors.

Such conduct was quite deplorable, and it was clear that anarchy reigned in Castile.

Much reform was needed; but all the King seemed to care about was his fancy-dress parades and the pleasure of his Favourites.

Isabella prayed for the well-being of her country.

"Ah," she told herself, "how different we shall be—Ferdinand and I—when we rule together!"

One day her mother came to her in a mood of great excitement, and Isabella was reminded of the night when she had been called from her bed to give thanks because the King of Aragon had asked that she might be given in marriage to his son Ferdinand.

"Isabella daughter, here is wonderful news. The Prince of Viana is asking for your hand in marriage. This is a brilliant offer. Not only is Carlos heir to Aragon, but Navarre is his also. My dear Isabella, why do you stare at me so blankly? You should rejoice."

Isabella had grown pale; she lifted her head and held herself at her full height, for once losing her sense of decorum. "You have forgotten, Highness," she said. "I am already betrothed to Ferdinand."

The Dowager Queen laughed. "That . . . oh, we will forget it. Ferdinand of Aragon? A very good match, but he is only a younger brother. Carlos, the heir of Aragon, the ruler of Navarre, is asking for your hand. I do not see why the marriage should be long delayed."

On one of the few occasions in her young life Isabella lost control. She knelt and, seizing her mother's skirts, looked up at her imploringly. "But, Highness," she cried, "I have been *promised* to Ferdinand."

"The promise was not binding, my child. This is a more suitable match. You must allow your elders to know what is good for you."

"Highness, the King of Aragon will be angry. Does he not love the finger nails of Ferdinand better than the whole body of his elder son?"

That made the Dowager Queen smile. "Carlos has quarrelled with his father, but the people of Aragon love Carlos, and he is the one whom they will make their King. The territories of Navarre are also his. Why, there could not be a better match."

Isabella stood rigid and for the first time showed distinct signs of a stubborn nature.

"It is a point of honour that I marry Ferdinand."

Her mother laughed, not wildly nor excitedly, merely with faintly amused tolerance; but now Isabella was past caring about the state of her mother's emotions.

The Dowager Queen said once more: "Leave these matters to your elders, Isabella. Now you should go on your knees and give thanks to God and his saints for the great good fortune which is to be yours."

Wild protests rose to Isabella's lips, but the discipline of years prevailed, and she said nothing.

She allowed herself to be led to her *prie-Dieu* and, while her mother prayed for the speedy union of her daughter and the Prince of Viana, heir to the throne of Aragon, she could only murmur: "Ferdinand! Oh Ferdinand! It must be Ferdinand. Holy Mother of God, do not desert me now. Let anything happen to me or the Prince of Viana or the whole world, but give me Ferdinand."

SCANDAL AT THE COURT OF CASTILE

In the Palace at Saragossa Joan Henriquez, Queen of Aragon, was discussing the effrontery of Carlos with her husband, John.

"This," declared Joan, "is meant to insult you, to show you how little this son of yours cares for your authority. He knows it is a favourite project of ours that Ferdinand shall mate with Isabella. So what does he do but offer himself!"

"It shall not come to pass," said the King. "Do not distress yourself, my dear. Isabella is for Ferdinand, and we shall find some means of outwitting Carlos . . . as we have in the past."

He smiled fondly at his wife. She was much younger than he was, and from the date of their marriage he had become so enamoured of her that his great desire was to give her all she wished. She was, he was sure, unique. Handsome, bold, shrewd—where was there another woman in the world to compare with her? His first wife, Blanche of Navarre, had been the widow of Martin of Sicily when he had married her. She had been a good woman, possessed of a far from insignificant dowry, and he had been well pleased with the match. She had given him three children: Carlos, Blanche and Eleanor, and he had been delighted at the time; now, having married the incomparable Joan Henriquez and having had issue by her in the also incomparable Ferdinand, he could wish—because Joan wished this—that he had no other children, so that Ferdinand would be heir to everything he possessed.

It was small wonder, he assured himself, that he should dote on Ferdinand. What of his other children? He was in continual conflict with Carlos; Blanche had been repudiated by her husband, Henry of Castile, and was now living in retirement on her estates at Olit, where, so Joan insisted, she gave assistance to her brother Carlos in his disagreements with his father; and there was Eleanor, Comtesse de Foix, who had left home many years before when she married Gaston de Foix, and was a domineering woman of great ambitions.

As for Joan, she doted on Ferdinand with all the force of a strong nature, and was resentful of any favours which fell to the lot of the other children.

In the first days of their union she had been gentle and loving, but from that day—it was the 10th March in the year 1452, some eight years ago—when her Ferdinand had been born in the little town of Sos, she had changed. She had become as a tigress fighting for her cub; and John, being so devoted to her, had become involved in this battle for the rights of the adored son of his second wife against the family of his first.

It was a sad state af affairs in any family when there was discord between its members; in a royal family this could be disastrous.

John of Aragon, however, could only see through the eyes of the wife on whom he doted, and therefore to him his son Carlos was a scoundrel.

This was not the truth. Carlos was a man of great charm and integrity. He was good-natured, gentle, honourable, and in the eyes of many people a perfect Prince. He was intellectual and artistic; he loved music; he could paint and was a poet; he was something of a philosopher and historian, and would have preferred to live quietly and study; it was the great tragedy of his life that he found himself drawn, against his will, into a bloody conflict with his own father.

The trouble had begun when Joan had asked that she might share the government of Navarre with Carlos, who had inherited this territory on the death of his mother, the daughter of Charles III of Navarre.

Joan's intention was to oust Carlos from Navarre that she might preserve it for her darling Ferdinand, who was only a baby as yet but for whom her ambitions had begun to grow from the day of his birth. Joan's manner was arrogant, and her policy was to create disturbance, so that the people would become dissatisfied with the rule of Carlos.

Joan was considerably helped in her desire to cause trouble by two ancient Navarrese families who for centuries had maintained a feud—concerning the origin of which neither was absolutely sure—which gave them the excuse to make forays into each other's territory from time to time.

These families were the Beaumonts and the Agramonts. They saw, in the conflict between the Prince and his stepmother, an excuse to make trouble. The Beaumonts therefore allied themselves with Carlos, which meant that automatically the Agramonts gave their support to the Queen; as a result war had broken out and the Agramonts, being the stronger party, took Carlos prisoner.

Carlos was confined for some months, the prisoner of his father and stepmother; but eventually he escaped and sought refuge with his uncle, Alfonso V of Naples. Unfortunately for Carlos, shortly after his arrival there, Alfonso died and it was necessary for Carlos to attempt reconciliation with his father.

Joan was eager to keep the King's heir in disgrace, and Carlos lingered in Sicily, where he became very popular, but when news of his popularity was brought to the Court of Aragon, Joan was disturbed. She saw a possibility of the Sicilians setting up Carlos as their ruler; and of course Joan had long ago decided that Sicily, together with Navarre and Aragon, should become the domain of her darling little Ferdinand.

It was necessary, she said, to recall Carlos to Aragon. So Joan and the King met Carlos at Igualada, and the meeting appeared to be such an affectionate one that all those who witnessed it rejoiced, for Carlos was popular wherever he went, and it was the desire of the majority that the family quarrel should cease and Carlos be declared without any doubt his father's heir.

This was exactly what Joan intended to prevent, as in her opinion there was but one person who should be declared his father's heir; and the people must be brought to accept this. She prevailed upon her husband to summon the Cortes and, there before it, declare his unwillingness to name Carlos his successor.

Carlos, bewildered and unhappy, listened to his advisers, who assured him that his best plan, since his royal house of Aragon was against him, was to ally himself with that of Castile.

This could be done through marriage with the half-sister of Henry of Castile, little Isabella, who was now being carefully guarded at the Palace of Arevalo.

She was as yet a child, being some nine years old; and in addition she had been destined for Ferdinand. But the King of Castile and the child's mother would be far more likely to smile on a match with the elder son of John of Aragon than the younger. Moreover, nothing could be calculated to flout the authority of his stepmother so completely as to snatch the bride she had intended for Ferdinand.

This was the plot, reports of which had reached Joan Henriquez; and it was on this account that she raged against Carlos, to her husband, and determined to bring about his destruction.

"That poor child," she cried. "She is nine years old and Carlos is forty! It will be at least another three years before she is of an age to consummate the marriage. By that time he will be forty-three. Ferdinand is now eight years old. What a charming pair they would make! I hear she is a handsome girl; and Ferdinand . . . our dearest Ferdinand . . . surely, John, you must agree that there is not a more perfect child in Aragon, in Castile, in Spain, in the whole world!"

John smiled at her fondly. He loved her more deeply in those moments when her habitual calm deserted her and she showed the excessive nature of her love for Ferdinand. Then she became like another woman, no longer the Joan Henriquez who had such a firm grasp of state matters; then she was the predatory mother. Surely, thought John, there cannot be another child in Aragon who is loved as fiercely and deeply as our Ferdinand.

He laid his hand on her shoulder. "Dearest," he said, "we will find some means of preventing this calamity. Isabella shall be for Ferdinand."

"But, husband, what if Henry of Castile decides to accept Carlos' offer? What if he says Carlos is the rightful heir of Aragon?"

"It is for me to decide who shall succeed me," said John.

"There would be trouble if you should choose any other than the eldest son. Ferdinand is young yet, but when he grows up, what a warrior he will be!"

"Alas, my dear, he is not grown up yet; and if Carlos married and there were children of the marriage. . . ."

Joan's eyes flashed with purpose. "But Carlos is not yet married. It will be some years before he can marry, if he waits for Isabella. She could not possibly bear a child for another four years at least. A great deal can happen in four years."

The King looked into her face, and it seemed as though deep emotions within him were ignited by the passion he read in her eyes.

Ferdinand was the fruit of their union. For Ferdinand she was ready to give all that she possessed—her honour, her life itself.

There was exultation in her voice when she said: "I believe that I have been blessed with second sight, John. I believe a great destiny awaits our son. I believe that he will be the saviour of our country and that in years to come his name will be mentioned with that of the Cid Campeador. Husband, I believe that we should deserve eternal damnation if we did not do all within our power to lead him to his destiny."

John grasped his wife's hand. "I swear to you, my dearest wife," he said, "that nothing . . . *nothing* shall bar Ferdinand's way to greatness."

* * *

In her retreat at Olit, Blanche lived her quiet life.

She had two desires; one was that she might be allowed to pass her time in peace at this quiet refuge, the other that her brother Carlos might triumph over his stepmother and win his way back into their father's good graces.

Occasionally she heard news of Castile. Henry had had no more good fortune with his new wife than he had had with Blanche. There was still no sign of an heir for Castile, and it was seven years since he had married the Princess of Portugal. She knew that Castile was almost in a state of anarchy; that there were armed bands of robbers on the roads and that rape and violence of all sorts were accepted in a light-hearted fashion, which could only mean that the country was bordering on chaos. She had heard rumours of the King's scandalous way of life, and that his Queen was by no means a virtuous woman. Stories of her liaison with Beltran de la Cueva were circulated. Blanche feared that affairs in Castile were as chaotic and uncertain as they were in Aragon.

But Castile was no longer any great concern of hers. Henry had repudiated her, and she would ignore Henry.

Aragon was a different matter.

Who was there left in her life to love but her brother Carlos? Dear Carlos! He was too good, too gentle and kindly to understand the towering ambition, the jealousy and frustration of a woman such as Joan Henriquez. And there could be no doubt that their father was completely under the influence of Joan.

She longed to help Carlos, to advise him. Strange as it might seem, she felt she was in a position to do so; she believed that, from her lonely vantage point, she could see what was happening more clearly than her brother could, and she was sure that now was the time for him to be on his guard.

Every time a messenger approached her palace she was afraid that he might be bringing bad news of Carlos. She experienced that premonition of evil which she had known during that period when Henry was preparing to discard her.

When her father had gone to Lerida to hold the Cortes of Catalonia—soon after Carlos had asked for the hand of Isabella of Castile—he had asked Carlos to meet him there.

She had warned Carlos, and she knew his faithful adherents had done the same. "Do not go to Lerida, dear Carlos," she had implored. "This is a trap."

But Carlos had reasoned : "If I will not negotiate with my father, how can I ever hope for peace?"

And so he had gone to Lerida where his father had immediately ordered his arrest and incarceration, accused, falsely, of plotting against the King.

But the people of Catalonia adored their Prince and demanded to know why the King had imprisoned him; they murmured against the unnatural behaviour of a father towards his son, and they accused the Queen of vindictiveness and the scheming design to have the rightful heir disinherited in favour of her own son.

Deputations arrived from Barcelona, and as a result it was necessary for John to leave Catalonia for the safer territory of Aragon without delay, and in a manner which was far from dignified. And the result : rebellion in Catalonia.

Back in Saragossa, John had gathered together an army, but meanwhile the revolt had spread, and Henry of Castile, who now looked upon Carlos as his sister's prospective husband, invaded Navarre on the side of Carlos against the King of Aragon. Carlos up to this time had been held prisoner, but in view of the state of the country John saw that his only course was to release his son.

The people blamed Joan for what had happened and, in order to win back their love for his beloved wife, John declared that he had released Carlos because she had begged him to do so.

Carlos, the kindest of men, bore no grudge against his stepmother, and allowed her to accompany him through Catalonia on his way to Barcelona, where John had hoped his presence would restore order; and the fact that his stepmother accompanied him led the people to believe that Carlos had returned to the heart of the family.

Blanche shook her head over these events. Now was the time for Carlos to beware as never before.

What would Joan be thinking during that ride to Barcelona, when she saw the people coming out in their thousands to cheer their Prince and having only sullen looks for his stepmother?

But Carlos seemed unable to learn from previous experience. Perhaps he was weary of strife; perhaps he wished to leave the arena and return to his books and painting, perhaps he so hated strife that he deliberately deluded himself.

He refused to listen to warnings. He preferred to believe that his father and his stepmother were genuine in their assertions that they desired his friendship. But the Queen was warned that she would be unwise to enter Barcelona, where a special welcome was being prepared for Carlos.

And now the Catalans all stood behind their Prince. Blanche had heard of the great welcome they had given him when he entered Barcelona.

"It is Catalonia today," it was said; "tomorrow it will be Aragon. Carlos is the rightful heir to the throne and wherever he goes is loved. 'We will have Carlos,' the people cry. 'And the King of Aragon must either accept him as his heir or we will see that there is a new King of Aragon. King Carlos!' And King John? He has deeply offended the people of Catalonia. They will never allow him to enter their province unless he craves and obtains the permission of his people."

Triumph for Carlos, thought Blanche. Oh, but Carlos, my brother, this is your most dangerous moment!

And so she waited, with that fearful premonition of evil.

She was even at the window watching when the messenger arrived.

"Bring him to me immediately," she told her attendants. "I know he brings news of the Prince, my brother."

She was right; and she saw by the messenger's expression the nature of the news.

"Highness," said the messenger, "I crave your pardon. I am the bearer of bad news."

"Please tell me without delay."

"The Prince of Viana has fallen ill of a malignant fever. Some say he contracted this during his stay in prison."

She said: "You must tell me everything . . . quickly."

"The Prince is dead, Highness."

Blanche turned away and went silently to her apartment; she locked her door and lay on her bed, without speaking, without weeping.

Her grief as yet was too overwhelming, too deep for outward expression.

* * *

Later she asked herself what this would mean. Little Ferdinand was now the heir of Aragon. His rival had been satisfactorily removed. Removed? It was an unpleasant word. But Blanche believed it to be the correct one to use in this case.

It was a terrifying thought. If her suspicion were true, could her father have been cognizant of a plot to murder his own son? It seemed incredible. Yet he was the blind slave of his wife, and she had coaxed him to worship, with her, the beloved Ferdinand.

"My only true friend!" she murmured; and she thought of her brother, who, had he been allowed to reach the throne, would have been a good ruler of Aragon—just, kindly, generous, learned.

"Oh my dear brother!" she cried. And later she said: "And what will now become of me?"

She remembered, when the first shock of her loss had diminished, that Carlos' death left her the heiress of Navarre, and she knew that greedy hands would be waiting to snatch what was hers.

Her sister, Eleanor de Foix, would be eager to step into her shoes, and how could she do that except through the death of her elder sister? Carlos had been removed. Would the same fate fall upon her?

"Holy Mother of God," she prayed, "let me stay here, where at least I know peace. Here in this quiet spot, where I can watch over the poor people of Olit, who look to me for the little I am able to do for them, I can, if not find happiness, be at peace. Let me stay here. Preserve me from that battlefield of envy and ambition which has destroyed my brother."

Navarre was a dangerous possession. Joan Henriquez would want it for Ferdinand; Eleanor would want it for her son, Gaston, who had recently married a sister of Louis XI of France.

"If my mother had known how much anxiety this possession would bring to me, she would have made a different will," she told herself.

So Blanche continued to wait. Nor did she have to wait long.

There arrived a letter from her father, in which he told her he had great news for her. She had been too long without a husband. Her marriage to Henry of Castile had been proved null and void; therefore she was at liberty to marry if she wished.

And it was his desire that she should marry. Moreover, he had a brilliant prospect to lay before her. Her sister Eleanor enjoyed the favour of the King of France, and she believed that a match could be arranged between Blanche and the Duc de Berri, Louis' own brother.

"My dear daughter," wrote the King, "this is an opportunity of which we have not dared dream."

Blanche read and re-read the letter.

Why is it, she asked herself, that when life has treated one badly and seems scarcely worth living, one still fought to retain it?

She did not believe in this talk of marriage with the Duc de Berri. If Carlos had met his death by poison, why should not she, Blanche? And if she were dead, Eleanor would take Navarre. What a great gift that would be to her son; and since he was the husband of the French King's sister, Blanche did not believe that Louis would raise any objection if such a crime were committed in his territory.

"You must not go to France!" There were warning voices within her which told her that. Her servants, who loved her, also warned her against going. So, she thought, I am not the only one who suspected the manner in which Carlos died.

"Marriage is not for me," she wrote to her father. "I have no wish to go to France, even for this brilliant marriage. I intend to spend the rest of my days here in Olit, where I shall never cease to pray for the soul of my brother."

Perhaps the mention of her brother angered her father. How much, she wondered, was there on his conscience? He wrote in extreme irritation that she was foolish to dream of casting aside such a wonderful opportunity.

"Nevertheless," was her reply, "I shall stay at Olit."

But she was wrong.

Late one night there was a clattering of horses' hoofs in the courtyard, followed by a hammering on the door.

"Who goes there?" called the guards.

"Open up! Open up! We come in the name of King John of Aragon."

There was nothing to be done but let them in. Their leader, when he was taken to Blanche, bowed low with a deference which contained a hint of authority.

"I crave your pardon, Highness, but the King's orders are that you prepare to leave Olit at once."

"For what destination?" she asked.

"For Béarn, Madam, where your noble sister eagerly awaits you."

So Eleanor eagerly awaited her—yes, with a burning ambition for her son Gaston which equalled that of Joan Henriquez for the young Ferdinand!

"I have decided to stay in Olit," she told him.

"I am sorry to hear you say that," was the answer, "for the King's orders are, Highness, that, if you will not consent to go, you must go by force."

"So," she cried, "it has come to that!"

"These are the King's orders."

She said: "Allow me to go to my women that I may make my preparations."

"Holy Mother of God," she prayed, "why should there be this desire to cling to a life which is scarcely worth the living?"

But the desire was there.

She said to her most trusted women: "Prepare. We have to leave Olit. We must escape. It is imperative that we are not taken to Béarn."

But where could she go? she asked herself. To Castile? Henry would befriend her. He had repudiated her, but he had never been actively unkind. For all his faults she did not believe Henry would connive at murder. She would explain to him her suspicions of Carlos' end; she would implore him to save her from a like fate.

To Castile . . . and Henry. It was the answer.

If she could slip out of the Palace by some secret way . . . if a horse could be ready for her. . . .

She whispered instructions. "We must be swift. My father's men are already in the Palace. Have the horses ready. I will slip out, and my head groom and one of my ladies will accompany me. Quick . . . there is not a moment to lose."

As she was being dressed for the ride she could hear the sound of voices outside her door, and the tramp of her father's soldiers' feet in her Palace.

With madly beating heart she left the Palace by a secret door. The groom was waiting, and silently he helped her into the saddle. Her favourite woman attendant was with her.

"Come," she cried.

Lightly she touched her horse's flank, but before he could spring into action, his bridle was caught in a pair of strong hands.

"Our grateful thanks, Highness," said a triumphant voice at her side. "You have dressed with great speed. Now we will not delay. We will leave at once for the border."

And through the night they rode. It was dark, but not darker than the sense of foreboding in Blanche's heart as she rode towards Béarn.

* * *

A great event had burst upon the Court of Castile. That which most Castilians had begun to believe would never happen was about to come to pass.

The Queen was pregnant.

"It cannot be by the King," was the comment. "*That* is an impossibility."

"Then by whom?"

There was only one answer. Joanna's faithful lover was Beltran de la Cueva, who was also a friend of the King.

He was clever, this brilliant and handsome young man. He knew how to entertain the King, how to be his witty and adventurous companion while at the same time he was the Queen's devoted and passionate lover.

There were many to laugh at the audacity of this man, some to admire it; but there were also those whom it angered and who felt themselves neglected.

Two of these were the Marquis of Villena and his uncle, Alfonso Carillo, Archbishop of Toledo.

"This," said Villena to his uncle, "is a ridiculous state of affairs. If the Queen is pregnant it is certainly not with Henry's child. What shall we do? Allow an illegitimate child to be heir to the throne?"

"We must do everything to prevent it," said the Archbishop righteously.

They were both determined to bring about the fall of Beltran de la Cueva, who was gradually ousting them from the positions of authority over the King which they had held for so long.

It was not that Beltran alone was politically ambitious, but about him, as about all favourites, there gathered the hangers-on, the seekers after power; and these, naturally enough, were in opposition to Villena and the Archbishop and desired to snatch from them the power they had held.

"If this child is born and lives," said Villena to his uncle, "we shall know what to do."

"In the meantime," added the Archbishop, "we must make sure

everyone bears in mind that the child cannot possibly be the King's, and that without a doubt Beltran de la Cueva is its father."

* * *

Henry was delighted that at last, after eight years of marriage, the Queen had become pregnant.

He knew that there were rumours, not only of his sterility, but of his impotence. It was said that it was for this reason that unnatural and lascivious orgies had to be arranged for him. Therefore the fact of Joanna's pregnancy delighted him. It would, he hoped, quash the rumours.

Did he believe himself to have been the cause of it? He could delude himself. He had come to depend more and more on delusions.

So he gave balls and banquets in honour of the unborn child. He was seen in public more often with his Queen than hitherto. Of course Beltran de la Cueva was often their companion—dear friend of both King and Queen.

When Henry raised Beltran to the rank of Count of Ledesma, the Court raised cynical eyebrows.

"Are there now to be honours for obliging lovers who supply that which impotent husbands cannot?"

Henry cared not for the whispers, and pretended not to hear them.

As for Joanna she laughed at them, but she constantly referred to the child as hers and the King's, and in spite of the whispers there were some who believed her.

Now the Court was tense, waiting for the birth. A boy? A girl?

Would the child resemble its mother or its father?

"Let us hope," said cynical courtiers, "that it resembles somebody in some way which can be recognized. Mysteries that cannot be solved are so wearying."

* * *

Change came to Arevalo on that March day, such change as Isabella would never forget, because there came with it the end of childhood.

Isabella had been living in a state of exultation since she had heard of the death of Carlos. It seemed to her then that her prayers had been answered; she had prayed that there should be a miracle to save her for Ferdinand, and behold, the man who was to have taken his place had been removed from this world.

It was her mother who brought the news, as she always did bring news of the first magnitude.

There was the wildness in her eyes once more, but Isabella was less afraid than she had been as a child. One could grow accustomed to those outbursts, which almost amounted to frenzy. On more than one occasion she had seen the physicians, holding her mother down while she laughed and cried and waved her arms frantically.

Isabella accepted the fact that her mother could not always be relied upon to show a sane front to the world. She had heard it whispered that one day the Dowager Queen would have to retire into solitude, as other members of her family had before her.

This was a great sadness to the girl, but she accepted it with resignation.

It was the will of God, she told Alfonso; and both of them must accept that and never rail against it.

It would have been comforting if she had a calm gentle mother in whom she could have confided. She could have talked to her of her love for Ferdinand—but perhaps it would have been difficult to talk to anyone of a love one felt for a person whom one had never seen.

Yet, said Isabella, to herself, I know I am for Ferdinand and he is for me. That is why I would rather die than accept another husband.

But how could one explain this feeling within her which was based, not on sound good sense, but on some indescribable intuition? It was, therefore, better not to talk of it.

And in the peace of Arevalo, Isabella had gone on dreaming.

Then came this day, and Isabella had rarely seen her mother look more wild. There was the angry light in her eyes. So Isabella knew that something alarming had happened.

Isabella and her brother Alfonso had been summoned to their mother's presence and, before they had time to perform the necessary curtsies and bows, the Dowager Queen exclaimed: "Your brother's wife has given birth to a child."

Isabella had risen to her feet with astonishing speed. Her mother did not notice this breach of etiquette.

"A girl . . . fortunately . . . but a child. You know what this means?" The Queen glared at Alfonso.

"Why, yes, Highness," said the boy in his high-pitched voice, "it means that she will be heir to the throne and that I must step aside."

"We shall see," said the Queen. "We shall see who is going to step aside."

Isabella noticed that a fleck of foam had appeared at the side of her mouth. That was a bad sign.

"Highness," she began, "perhaps the child is not strong."

"I have heard nothing of that. A child there is . . . a girl brought into the world to . . . to rob us of our rights."

"But Highness," said Alfonso, who had not learned to keep quiet as Isabella had, "if she is my brother's child she is heir to the throne of Castile."

"I know. I know." The Dowager Queen's eyes flashed briefly on Isabella. "There is no law to prevent a woman's taking the crown. I know that. But there are rumours about this girl. You would not understand. But let us say this: Has she a right to the throne? Has she . . . ?"

"Holy Mother of God," prayed Isabella. "Calm her. Do not let the doctors have to hold her down this time."

"Highness," she said soothingly, "here we have lived very happily."

"You are not going to live here happily much longer, my daughter," spat out the Queen. "In fact, you are to prepare for a journey at once."

"We are going away?"

"Ah!" cried the Queen, her voice rising on a note of hysterical laughter. "He does not trust us here. He thinks that Arevalo will become a hot-bed of rebellion now. And he is right. They cannot foist a bastard on Castile . . . a bastard who has no right to the crown. I doubt not that there will be many who will want to take Alfonso and put a crown upon his head. . . ."

Alfonso looked alarmed.

"Highness," said Isabella quickly, "it would not be possible while the King my brother lives."

The Queen surveyed her children through narrowed eyes.

"Your brother commands," she said, "that I, taking you two children with me, return at once to Court."

Isabella's heart was leaping within her, and she was not sure whether it was with fear or pleasure.

She said quickly: "Highness, give us your leave to retire and we will begin preparations. We have been here so long that there will be much for us to do."

The Queen looked at her eleven-year-old daughter and nodded slowly.

"You may go," she said.

Isabella seized her brother's hand and, forcing him to bow, almost dragged him from the apartment.

As she did so she heard her mother's muttering; she heard the laughter break out.

This, thought Isabella, is really the end of my childhood. At Court I shall quickly become a woman.

How would she fare at that most scandalous Court—she who had been so carefully nurtured here at Arevalo? She was a little alarmed, remembering the rumours she had heard.

Yet she was conscious of an intense elation, for she believed that she must now grow up quickly; and growing up meant marriage . . . with Ferdinand.

LA BELTRANEJA

THE March sunshine shone through the windows of the Chapel in the Palace of Madrid on to the brilliant vestments of those taking part in the most colourful ceremony Isabella had ever witnessed. She was awed by the chanting voices, by the presence of glittering and important men and women.

She was not unconscious of the tension in the atmosphere, for she was wise enough to know that the smiling faces were like the masks she had seen worn at the fêtes and tournaments which had heralded this event.

The whole Court pretended to rejoice because of the birth of Isabella's little niece, but Isabella knew that those smiling masks hid the true feelings of many people present at this christening.

There stood her half-brother Henry, looking very tall indeed and somewhat untidy, with his reddish hair straggling out beneath his crown. Beside him stood his half-brother, nine-year-old Alfonso.

Alfonso was quite handsome, thought Isabella, in his robes of state. He appeared to be solemn too, as though he knew that many people would be looking his way on this occasion. It seemed to Isabella that Alfonso was one of the most important people present —more important than the baby herself perhaps—and Isabella knew why. She could never entirely escape from that high-pitched voice of her mother's, reminding them that, should the people decide they had had enough of Henry, they would turn to Alfonso.

Isabella herself had an important part to play in the christening.

With the baby's sponsors, of whom she was one, she stood beside the font. The others were the Frenchman, Armignac, and the brilliantly clad Juan Pacheco, Marquis of Villena, and his wife. It was the Marquis who held her attention. Through eavesdropping whenever possible, she had heard his name mentioned often and she knew a great deal about him.

Echoes of conversations came back to her. "He is the King's right hand." "He is the King's right eye." "Henry does not take a step without consulting the Marquis of Villena." "Ah, but have you heard that . . . lately there has been a little change?" "It cannot be . . ." "Oh, but they say it is so. Now that *is* a joke."

It was so interesting. Far more interesting here at Court, where she could actually see the people who had figured so largely in the rumours she had overheard at Arevalo.

The Marquis was smiling now, but Isabella felt that his mask was the most deceitful of them all. She sensed the power of the man and she wondered what he would look like when he was angry. He would be very formidable, she was sure.

Now the heavy, dark brows of Alfonso Carillo, the Archbishop of Toledo, were drawn together in a frown of concentration as he performed the christening ceremony and blessed the baby girl who had been carried to him under a canopy by Count Alba de Liste.

There was another whom Isabella could not fail to notice. This was a tall man, who might be said to be the handsomest man present; his clothes were more magnificent than those of any other; his jewels glittered with a brighter lustre—perhaps because there were so many of them. His hair was so black that it held a bluish tinge, his eyes were large and dark, but he had a fine fair skin which made him look very young.

He was particularly noticeable, standing close to Henry, for he was almost as tall as the King; and, thought Isabella, if one did not know who was the real King and was asked to pick him out from all those assembled, one would pick Beltran de la Cueva, who had recently been made Count of Ledesma.

The Count was another of those people who were attracting so much attention, and as he watched the baby under the canopy, many watched him.

Unaccustomed though she was to such ceremonies, Isabella gave no sign of the excitement which she was feeling; and, if it appeared that there was a certain watchfulness directed at those three—the King, the Queen and the new Count of Ledesma—Alfonso and Isabella also had their share of this attention.

The thought was in many minds on that day that, if the rumours which were beginning to be spread through the Court were true—and there seemed every reason why they should be—these two children were of the utmost significance. And the fact that the boy was so handsome, and clearly showed he was eager to do what was expected of him, was noted. And so, also, with the decorous behaviour of the young girl, as she stood with the other sponsors, rather tall for her eleven years, her abundant hair—with the reddish tinge inherited from her Plantagenet ancestors—making a charming frame for her placid face.

* * *

In a small ante-chamber adjoining the chapel, the Archbishop of Toledo, whilst divesting himself of his ceremonial robes, was in deep conversation with his nephew, the Marquis of Villena.

The Archbishop, a fiery man, who would have been more suited to a military than an ecclesiastical career, was almost shouting: "It is an impossible situation. I never imagined anything so fantastic, so farcical in all my life. That man . . . standing there looking on . . ."

Villena, the wily statesman, had more control over his feelings than his uncle had over his. He lifted a hand and signed towards the door.

"Why, nephew," said the Archbishop testily, "the whole Court talks of it, jeers at it, and the question is asked: 'How long will those who want to see justice done endure such a situation?' "

Villena sat on one of the tapestry-covered stools and sardonically contemplated the tips of his shoes. Then he said: "The Queen is a harlot; the child is a bastard; the King is a fool; and the people in the streets cannot long be kept in ignorance of all that. Perhaps there have been wanton Queens who have foisted bastards on foolish kings before this. What I find impossible to endure is the favour shown to this man. Count of Ledesma! It is too much."

"Henry listens to him on all occasions. Why, in the name of God and all His saints, does he behave with such stupidity?"

"Perhaps, Uncle, because he is grateful to their Beltran."

"Grateful to his wife's lover, to the father of the child who is to be foisted on the nation as his own!"

"Grateful indeed," said Villena. "I fancy our Henry did not care to see himself as one who cannot beget a child. Beltran is so obliging: he serves the King in every way . . . even to providing the Queen with his bastard to set upon the throne. We know Henry is incapable of begetting children. None of his mistresses has produced a child. After twelve years he was divorced from Blanche on the grounds that both were impotent. And he has been married to Joanna for eight years. It is surprising that Beltran and his mistress have taken so long."

"We must not allow this child to be foisted on the nation."

"We must go carefully, Uncle. There is time in plenty. If the King continues to shower honours on Beltran de la Cueva, he will turn more and more from us. Very well then, we will turn more and more from him."

"And lose our places at Court, lose all that we have worked for?"

Villena smiled. "Did you notice the children in chapel? What a pleasant pair!"

The Archbishop was alert. He said: "It would never do. You could never set up young Alfonso while Henry is alive."

"Why not . . . if the people are so disgusted with him and his bastard?"

"Civil war?"

"It might be arranged more simply. But, Uncle, as I said, there is no need to act immediately. Keep your eyes on those two . . . Alfonso and Isabella. They made a good impression on all who beheld them. Such pleasant manners. I declare our mad Dowager Queen has made an excellent job of their upbringing. They already have all the dignity of heirs to the throne. Depend upon it, their mother would raise no objection to our schemes. And what struck you most about them, Uncle? Was it the same as that which struck me? They were so docile, both of them, so . . . malleable."

"Nephew, this is dangerous talk."

"Dangerous indeed! That is why we will not be hasty. Rumour is a very good ally. I am going to send for your servant now to help you dress. Listen to what I say in his hearing."

Villena went to the door and, opening it, signed to a page.

In a few moments the Archbishop's servant entered. As he did so, Villena was saying in a whisper which could easily be heard by anyone in the room: "It is to be hoped the child resembles her father in some way. What amusement that is going to cause throughout the Court. La Beltraneja should be beautiful, for her true father, I believe, is far more handsome than our poor deluded King; and the Queen has beauty also."

"La Beltraneja," mused the Archbishop, and he was smiling as the servant took his robe.

Within a few days the baby was being referred to throughout the Palace and beyond as La Beltraneja.

* * *

In the apartments of the Dowager Queen her two children stood before her, as they had been summoned. Isabella wondered whether Alfonso was as deeply aware as she was of the glazed look in their mother's eyes, of the rising note in her voice.

The christening ceremony had greatly excited her.

"My children," she cried; then she embraced Alfonso and over his head surveyed Isabella. "You were there. You saw the looks directed at that . . . at that child . . . and at yourselves. I told you . . . did I not. I told you. I knew it was impossible. An heir to the throne of Castile! Let me tell you this: I have the heir of Castile here, in my arms. There is no other. There can be no other."

"Highness," said Isabella, "the ceremony has been exhausting for you . . . and to us. Could you not rest and talk to us of this matter later?"

Isabella trembled at her temerity, but her mother did not seem to hear her.

"Here!" she cried, raising her eyes to the ceiling as though she were addressing some celestial audience, "here is the heir to Castile."

Alfonso had released himself from the suffocating embrace. "Highness," he said, "there may be some who listen at our door."

"It matters little, my son. The same words are being spoken all over the Court. They are saying the child is the bastard daughter of Beltran de la Cueva. And who can doubt it? Tell me that . . . tell me that, if you can! But why should you? You will be ready to accept the power and the glory when it is bestowed on you. That is the day I long for. The day I see my own Alfonso King of Castile!"

"Alfonso," said Isabella, quietly, authoritatively, "go and call the Queen's women. Go quickly."

"It will not be long," went on the Dowager Queen, who had not noticed that Isabella had spoken, nor that her son had slipped from the room. "Soon the people will rise. Did you not sense it in the chapel? The feeling . . . the anger! It would not have surprised me if the bastard had been snatched from under her silken canopy. Nothing . . . nothing would have surprised me. . . ."

"Holy Mother," prayed Isabella, "let them come quickly. Let them take her to her apartment. Let them quieten her before I have to see her held down by the doctors and forcibly drugged to quieten her."

"It cannot go on," cried the Queen. "I shall live to see my Alfonso crowned. Henry will do nothing. He will be powerless. His folly in showering honours on the bastard's father will be his undoing. Did you not see the looks? Did you not hear the comments?" The Queen had clenched her fists and had begun beating her breast.

"Oh let them come quickly," prayed Isabella.

* * *

When her mother had been taken away she felt exhausted. Alfonso lingered and would have talked to her, but she was afraid to talk to Alfonso. There were so many imminent dangers, she felt certain, and in the great Palace one could never be sure who was hidden away in some secret place to listen to what was said.

It was highly dangerous, she knew very well, to discuss the displacement of kings while they still lived; and if it were true—which of course it was—that she and Alfonso had been brought to Court so that their brother might be sure that they should not be the centre of rebellion, it was certain that they were closely watched.

She put on a cloak and went out into the gardens. Those occasions when she could be alone were rare and, she knew, would become more so, for she must not expect to enjoy the same freedom here at Court as she had in the peace of Arevàlo.

Still, as yet, she was regarded as but a child and she hoped that she would continue to be so regarded for some time to come. She did not want to be embroiled in the rebellious schemes which tormented her mother's already overtaxed brain.

Isabella believed firmly in law and order. Henry was King because he was the eldest son of their father, and she thought it was wrong that any other should take his place while he lived.

She stared down at the stream of the Manzanares and then across the plain to the distant mountains; and as she did so she became aware of approaching footsteps and, turning, saw a girl coming towards her.

"You wish to speak with me?" called Isabella.

"My lady Princesa, if you would be so gracious as to listen."

This was a beautiful girl with strongly marked features; she was some four years older than Isabella and consequently seemed adult to the eleven-year-old Princess.

"But certainly," said Isabella.

The other knelt and kissed Isabella's hand, but Isabella said: "Please rise. Now tell me what it is you have to say to me."

"My lady, my name is Beatriz Fernandez de Bobadilla, and it is very bold of me to make myself known to you thus unceremoniously; but I saw you walking alone here and I thought that if my mistress could behave without convention, so might I."

"It is pleasant to escape from convention now and then," said Isabella.

"I have news, my lady, which fills me with great joy. Shortly I am to be presented to you as your maid of honour. Since I learned this was to be I have been eagerly awaiting a glimpse of you, and when I saw you at the ceremony in the chapel I knew that I longed to serve you. When I am formally presented I shall murmur the appointed words which will convey nothing . . . nothing of my true feelings. Princesa Isabella, I wanted you to know how I truly felt."

Isabella stifled the disapproval which these words aroused in her. She had been brought up to believe that the etiquette of the Court was all-important; but when the girl lifted her eyes she saw there were real tears in them, and Isabella was not proof against such a display of emotion.

She realized she was lonely. She had no companion to whom she could talk of those matters which interested her. Alfonso was the nearest to being such a companion, but he was too young and not of her own sex. She had never enjoyed real companionship with her mother, and the thought of having a maid of honour who could also be a friend was very appealing.

Moreover in spite of herself, she could not help admiring the boldness of Beatriz de Bobadilla.

She heard herself say: "You should have waited to be formally presented, but as long as no one sees us . . . as long as no one is aware of what we have done . . ."

This was not the way in which a Princess should behave, but Isabella was eager for this friendship which was being offered.

"I knew you would say that, Princesa," cried Beatriz. "That is why I dared."

She stood up and her eyes sparkled. "I could scarcely wait for a glimpse of you, my lady," she went on. "You are exactly as I imagined you. You will never have reason to regret that I was chosen to serve you. When we are married, I beg you let it make no difference. Let me continue to serve you."

"Married?" said Isabella.

"Why yes, married. I am promised to Andres de Cabrera, even as you are promised to Prince Ferdinand of Aragon."

Isabella flushed slightly at the mention of Ferdinand, but Beatriz hurried on: "I follow the adventures of Prince Ferdinand with great interest, simply because he is betrothed to you."

Isabella caught her breath and murmured: "Could we walk a little?"

"Yes, my lady. But we should be careful not to be seen. I should be scolded for daring to approach thus, if we were."

Isabella for once did not care if they were discovered, so urgently did she desire to talk of Ferdinand.

"What did you mean when you said you had followed the adventures of Prince Ferdinand?"

"That I had gleaned information about him on every possible occasion, Princesa. I gathered news of the troublous state of affairs in Aragon, and the dangers which beset Ferdinand."

"Dangers? What dangers?"

"There is civil war in Aragon, as you know, and that is a dangerous state of affairs. They say it is due to the Queen of Aragon, Ferdinand's mother, who would risk all she possesses in order to ensure the advancement of her son."

"She must love him dearly," said Isabella softly.

"Princesa, there is no one living who is more loved than young Ferdinand."

"It is because he is so worthy."

"And because he is the only son of the most ambitious woman living. It is a mercy that he has emerged alive from Gerona."

"What is this? I have not heard of it."

"But, Princesa, you know that the Catalans rose against Ferdinand's father on account of Carlos, Ferdinand's elder brother whom they loved so dearly. Carlos died suddenly, and there were rumours. It was said he was hastened to his death, and this had been arranged so that Ferdinand should inherit his father's dominions."

"Ferdinand would have no hand in murder!"

"Indeed no. How could he? He is only a boy. But his mother—and his father too, for she has prevailed upon him to become so—are overweeningly ambitious for him. When his mother took Ferdinand into Catalonia, to receive the oath of allegiance, the people rose in anger. They said that the ghost of Ferdinand's half-brother, Carlos, walked the streets of Barcelona crying out that he was the victim of murder and that the people should avenge him. They say that miracles have been performed at his grave, and that he was a saint."

"He asked for my hand in marriage," said Isabella with a shudder. "And shortly afterwards he died."

"Ferdinand is intended for you."

"Yes, Ferdinand and no other," said Isabella firmly.

"It was necessary for the Queen of Aragon and her son Ferdinand to fly from Barcelona to Gerona; and there, with Ferdinand, she took possession of the fortress. I have heard that the fierce Catalans almost captured that fortress, and only the Queen's courage and resource saved their lives."

"He was in such danger, and I did not know it," murmured Isabella. "Tell me . . . what is happening to him now?"

Beatriz shook her head. "That I cannot say, but I have heard that the war persists in the dominions of the King of Aragon and that King John and Queen Joan will continue to be blamed for the murder of Carlos."

"It is a terrible thing to have happened."

"It was the only way for Ferdinand to become his father's heir."

"He knew nothing of it," affirmed Isabella. "He can never be blamed."

And to herself she said: Nor could Alfonso be, if they insisted on putting him in Henry's place.

"I think," she said aloud, "that there are stormy days ahead for both Castile and Aragon—for Ferdinand and perhaps for me."

"A country divided against itself provides perpetual danger," said Beatriz solemnly; then her eyes sparkled. "But it will not be long before Ferdinand comes to claim you. You will be married. I shall be married. And, Princesa, you said that, when we were, we should still be . . . friends."

Isabella was astonished that she could be so touched by this offer of friendship.

She said in subdued tones: "I think it is time that I returned to my apartments."

Beatriz sank to her knees and Isabella swept past her. But not before Beatriz had lifted her face and Isabella had given her a swift, almost shy smile.

From that moment Isabella had a new friend.

* * *

The Queen's little daughter lay on her silken cushions under a canopy in the state apartments, and one by one the great nobles came forward to kiss her hand and swear allegiance to her as heiress of the throne of Castile.

Beltran de la Cueva looked down at her with satisfaction. His position was unique. So many suspected that he was the baby's father, and yet, instead of this suspicion arousing the wrath of the King, it had made Henry feel more kindly towards him.

He could see a glorious future before him; he could still remain the Queen's very good friend, the King's also. And the child—now generally known as La Beltraneja—was to inherit the throne.

He fancied he had behaved with great skill in a difficult situation.

As he stood smiling with satisfaction his eyes met those of the Archbishop of Toledo, and he was quickly conscious of the smouldering anger there.

Rant as much as you like, my little Archbishop! thought Beltran. Plot with your sly nephew whose nose has been considerably put out of joint during this last year. I care not for you . . . nor does the King nor the Queen, nor this baby here. There is nothing you can do to harm us.

But Beltran de la Cueva, gallant courtier though he was, so expert in the jousts, such an elegant dancer, lacked the sly cunning necessary to make of himself a statesman. He did not know that, even while they kissed the baby's hand and swore allegiance, the Archbishop and his nephew were planning to have her proclaimed illegitimate and oust her father from the throne.

* * *

The Marquis of Villena called on the King. Henry was with his favourite mistress. There had been many since Alegre, and if she had been mentioned in his hearing it was doubtful whether he would now have remembered her name.

Henry had grown more indolent with the years. He was pleased that the royal cradle was at last occupied, and did not want to raise the question as to how this could have come about. Suffice it that there was an heir to the throne.

There were entertainments to be planned—those orgies which were growing more and more wild in an endeavour by those, whose duty it was, to tempt his jaded palate.

What new schemes, Henry was wondering, had they thought of this time? What pleasures would they show him that could give him new sensations, or could help him to recapture the old?

Then the Marquis of Villena was announced and with him, to Henry's dismay, was that villainous uncle of his, the Archbishop. Reluctantly and with a show of irritation Henry dismissed his mistress.

"We crave leave to speak to you, Highness, on a very important matter," said Villena.

Henry yawned. Angry lights shot up in the Archbishop's eyes but Villena flashed a warning glance at him.

"I think, Highness," said the Marquis, "that this matter is one to which it would be well to give your close attention."

"Well, what is it?" Henry demanded ungraciously.

"Grave suspicions have been cast on the legitimacy of the little Princess."

Henry shrugged his shoulders. "There are always rumours."

"These are more than rumours, Highness."

"What do you mean by that?"

"We fear something will have to be done. The peace of the country is threatened."

"If people would stop meddling we should have peace."

"The people must be assured," said the Archbishop, "that the heiress to the throne is the legitimate heiress."

"The Princess is my daughter. Is not my daughter the legitimate heir to the throne?"

"Only if she *is* your daughter, Highness."

"You are not going to say that another child was smuggled into the Queen's bed?"

"Rather, Highness," said Villena with a snigger, "that another *lover* was smuggled therein."

"Gossip! Scandal!" muttered Henry. "A plague on them. Have done. Let us accept what is. There is an heiress to the throne. The people have been crying out for an heir; now they have one let them be satisfied."

"They'll not be satisfied with a bastard, Highness," said the fierce Archbishop.

"What is this talk?"

"Highness," said Villena, almost placatingly, "you should know that throughout the Court the Princess is known by the name of La Beltraneja—after the man who, the majority are beginning to declare, is her father, Beltran de la Cueva."

"But this is monstrous," said the King with a mildness which exasperated the Archbishop.

"Your Highness," went on Villena, "puts yourself in a difficult position by showering honours on the man who is believed to have cuckolded you."

Henry laughed. "You are angered because honours and titles have gone to him which you believe should have found their way to you two. That is the point, is it not?"

"Your Highness surely will admit that it is unseemly to honour the man who has deceived you and attempted to foist his bastard upon you?"

"Oh, have done. Have done. Let the matter be, and let us have peace."

"I am afraid, Highness, that is not possible. Certain of your ministers are demanding an enquiry into the birth of the child you are calling your daughter."

"And if I forbid it?"

"Highness, that would be most unwise."

"I am the King," said Henry, hoping his voice sounded strong yet fearing that it was very weak.

"Highness, it is because we wish you to remain King that we beg you to give this matter your closest attention," whispered Villena.

"Let them leave me in peace. The matter is done with. There is a Princess in the royal cradle. Leave it at that."

"It is impossible, Highness. There is also a Prince in the Palace now, your half-brother Alfonso. There are many who say that, should the new-born child be proved a bastard, he should be named as your successor."

"This is all very wearying," sighed Henry. "What can *I* do about it?"

Villena smiled at the Archbishop. "There was a time, Highness," he said gently, "when I heard that question more often on your lips. Then you knew, Highness, that you could rely upon me. Now you put your faith and trust in a pretty young gentleman who makes scandals with the Queen herself. Highness, since you have asked me, this is my advice: Cease to honour Beltran de la Cueva so blatantly. Let him see that you doubt the honourable nature of his conduct. And allow a commission of churchmen—which I and the Archbishop will nominate—to enquire into the legitimacy of the child."

Henry looked about hopelessly. The only way to rid himself of these tiresome men and to bring back his pretty mistress was to agree.

He waved his hand impatiently. "Do as you wish . . . do as you wish," he cried. "And leave me in peace."

Villena and the Archbishop retired well satisfied.

* * *

It had become clear to all astute observers of the Castilian scene that the Marquis of Villena would not lightly abandon his hold upon the King, and if the King and Queen persisted in their allegiance to Beltran de la Cueva, Villena would raise such a strong party against them that it might well lead to civil war.

There was one who watched this state of affairs with great satisfaction. This was the Marquis of Villena's brother, Don Pedro Giron, a very ambitious man who was a Grand Master of the Order of Calatrava.

The Knights of Calatrava belonged to an institution which had been established as long ago as the twelfth century.

The Order had sprung into being because of the need to defend Castile against Moorish conquerors. Calatrava stood on the frontiers of Andalusia, which was occupied by the Moors, and the town, which commanded the pass into Castile, became of paramount importance. The Knights Templar had attempted to hold it, but, unable to withstand the constant and ferocious attacks of the Mussulmans, had abandoned it.

The reigning King of Castile, Sancho, the Beloved, offered the town to any knights who would defend it from the Moors, and certain monks from a Navarrese convent immediately took possession. The situation captured the imagination of the people and many rallied to the defence of the town, so enabling it to be held against all attacks.

The monks then founded an order which consisted of knights, monks and soldiers; and this they named the Knights of Calatrava; it was recognized by Pope Alexander III as a religious Order in 1164, adopted the rules of St. Benedict and imposed strict discipline on its community.

The first and most important rule of the community was that of celibacy. Its members were to follow the rule of silence, and to live in great austerity. They ate meat only once a week; but they were not merely monks; they must remember that their Order had come into being through their prowess with the sword; and it was their custom to sleep with their swords beside them, ready to go into action against the Moors at any moment when they might be called upon to do so.

Don Pedro Giron, while enjoying the prestige his position in the Order brought to him, had no intention of carrying out its austere rules.

He was a man of tremendous political ambition and he did not see why, since his brother the Marquis was reckoned to be the most important man in Castile—or had been deemed so before the coming of the upstart Beltran de la Cueva—he should not bask in his brother's glory and use the influence of the Marquis to better his own position.

He was ready to obey his brother's wishes, to rouse the people to revolt if need be, to spread any rumour that his brother wished to be spread. Nor did he hesitate to follow his own life of pleasure, and he had a score of mistresses. Indeed the Grand Master of Calatrava was noted throughout Castile for his licentious habits. None dared criticize him; if he saw a flicker of disapproval on any face he would ask the offender if he knew his brother the Marquis of Villena. "We are great friends, my brother and I. We are jealous of the family honour. His enemies are mine and mine are his."

Consequently most people were too much in awe of the powerful Villena to continue the criticism of his somewhat disreputable brother. He was greatly amused by the scandal which the Queen of Castile had caused in the Court.

It pleased him to consider that Queens were as frail as other women, and as he was a vain man, he began to fancy himself as the lover of Joanna. She however was besottedly devoted to Beltran de la Cueva, and he himself was not an overwhelmingly handsome or attractive man.

Then one day he saw Isabella, the Dowager Queen of Castile, walking in the grounds, and he considered her.

She was still an attractive woman; he had heard rumours of her wildness and how it was sometimes necessary to lure her from her moods of hysteria by means of soothing powders and potions.

His brother the Marquis was turning more and more from King Henry and his Queen, which meant that he was turning towards the young Alfonso and Isabella. There was no doubt that the Dowager Queen, who was obviously ambitious for her children, would welcome the friendship of the Marquis of Villena.

And if she is a wise woman, mused Don Pedro, she will be eager to be on the best of terms with all our family.

So he watched her on more than one occasion, and it seemed to him that his latest mistress had little charm for him. She was a beautiful girl, but he had set his heart on sharing the bed of a Queen.

He swaggered about the Court, seeing himself as another Beltran de la Cueva.

At last he could contain his patience no longer; he found an opportunity of speaking alone to the Dowager Queen.

He had formally requested a private interview, and this was granted him.

As he dressed himself with the utmost care, as he demanded flattering compliments from his valets—who gave them slavishly, realizing that if they did not it would be the worse for them—it did not occur to him that he could fail in his plans regarding the Dowager Queen.

* * *

The Dowager Queen was with her daughter.

She had sent for Isabella, although she knew that Don Pedro Giron was on his way to visit her.

When Isabella saw her mother, she was quick to notice the suppressed excitement shining in her eyes. Yet, there was no hint of the madness. Something had made her happy, and Isabella had come to know that it was depression and frustration which brought on those attacks of madness.

"Come here, daughter," said the Dowager Queen. "I have sent for you because I wish you to be aware of what is going on about us."

"Yes, Highness," said Isabella demurely. She *was* aware, more than she had ever been. Her constant companion, Beatriz de Bobadilla, was proving to be very knowledgeable on Court matters, and life had become full of intrigue and interest since Beatriz had formally been presented to her as her maid of honour. Now Isabella knew of the scandal concerning Queen Joanna and the birth of the baby who, many were beginning to say, was not the true heiress of Castile.

"I do not think it can be long now before your brother is proclaimed the King's successor," said the Dowager Queen. "There are protests from all directions. The people are not going to accept Beltran de la Cueva's daughter as their future Queen. Now, my dear Isabella, I have called you to me because I am expecting an important visit very shortly. I did not send for Alfonso because he is too young, and this concerns him too deeply. You are going to be present during the interview, although you will not be seen. You will be hidden behind the hangings there. You must stand very still, that none may know that you are present."

Isabella caught her breath in fear. Was this a new version of that wildness? Her mother, actually arranging that she should eavesdrop!

"Very soon," went on the Dowager Queen, "the brother of the Marquis of Villena is to call upon me. He will come as his brother's messenger. I know the reason for his coming. It is to tell me that his brother's adherents are going to demand that Alfonso be acknowledged as Henry's heir. You will hear how calmly I accept his statements. It will be a lesson to you for the future, daughter; when you are Queen of Aragon you will have to receive ambassadors of all kinds. There may be some who bring startling news to you. You must never betray your emotions. Whatever the news . . . good or bad . . . you must accept it as a Queen, as you will see me do."

"Highness," began Isabella, "could I not remain in your presence? Must I hide myself?"

"My dear child, do you imagine that the Grand Master of Calatrava would disclose his mission in your presence! Now . . . obey me immediately. Come. This will hide you completely. Stay perfectly still, and listen to what he has to say. And particularly note my acceptance of the news."

Feeling that it was some mad game she was being forced to play, a game not in accord with her dignity, which had increased since her coming to Court, Isabella allowed herself to be placed behind the hangings.

After a few minutes Don Pedro was ushered into the apartments of the Dowager Queen.

"Highness," he said, kneeling, "it is gracious of you to receive me."

"It gives me pleasure," was the answer.

"I had a feeling within me, Highness, that I should cause you no offence by coming to you thus."

"On the contrary, Don Pedro. I am ready to listen to your proposition."

"Highness, have I your permission to sit?"

"Assuredly."

Isabella heard the scrape of chair-legs as they sat down.

"Highness."

"Well, Don Pedro?"

"I have long been aware of you. On those happy occasions when I have been at some ceremony which Your Highness attended I have been aware of no one else."

There was a strange silence in the room, not lost on the hidden Isabella.

"I trust that you, Highness, have not been completely unaware of me."

The Dowager Queen answered, and her voice showed she was bewildered: "One would not be unaware of the brother of such a personage as the Marquis of Villena."

"Ah, my brother. Highness, I would have you know that his interests are mine. We are as one . . . in our desire to see peace in this Kingdom."

Now the Queen felt and sounded happier. "I had guessed that, Don Pedro."

"Would it surprise you, Highness, if I told you that there have been occasions when my brother, the Marquis, has discussed his policies with me and listened to my advice?"

"It would not. You are Grand Master of a Holy Order. Naturally you should be able to advise your brother . . . spiritually."

"Highness, there is one thing I would work for . . . body and soul . . . that is the acceptance of your son the Infante Alfonso as heir to the throne of Castile. I would see the little bastard girl, now known as the heir, proclaimed for what she is. It need not be long before this happens . . . if . . ."

"If, Don Pedro?"

"I have made Your Highness aware of the influence I have with my brother, and you know full well the power he wields in this land. If you and I were friends, there is nothing I would not do . . . not only to have the boy proclaimed heir, but to . . . I must whisper this . . . Come, sweet lady, let me put my lips to your ear . . . to depose Henry in favour of your son Alfonso."

"Don Pedro!"

"I said, my dearest lady, *if* we were friends."

"I do not understand you. You speak in riddles."

"Oh, you are not so blind as you would have me believe. You are still a beautiful woman, dear lady. Come . . . come . . . I hear you lived most piously at that deadly place in Arevalo . . . but this is the Court. You are not old . . . nor am I. I think we could bring a great deal of pleasure to each other's lives."

"I think, Don Pedro," said the Dowager Queen, "that you must be suffering from a temporary madness."

"Not I, dear lady, not I. As for yourself you would be completely well if you lived a more natural life. Come, do not be so prudish. Follow the fashion. By the saints, I swear you will never regret the day you and I become lovers."

The Dowager Queen had leaped to her feet. Isabella heard the urgent scrape of her chair. She heard also the note of alarm in her mother's voice. Looking through the folds of brocade she saw a purple-faced man who seemed to her to symbolize all that was beastly in human nature. She saw her mother—no longer calm—afraid and shocked beyond her understanding.

Isabella knew that unless the man was dismissed her mother would begin to shout and wave her arms, and he would witness one of those wild scenes which she, Isabella, was so anxious should not be seen except by those whom she could trust.

Isabella forgot the instruction that she was to remain hidden. She stepped from her hiding-place into the room.

The purple-faced man with the evil expression stared at her as though she were a ghost. Indeed it must have seemed strange to him that she had apparently materialized from nowhere.

She drew herself to her full height and never before had she looked so much a Princess of Castile.

"Sir," she said coldly, "I ask you to leave . . . immediately."

Don Pedro stared at her incredulously.

"Is it necessary," went on the young Isabella, "for me to have you forcibly removed?"

Don Pedro hesitated. Then he bowed and left them.

Isabella turned to her mother, who was trembling so much that she could not speak.

She led her to a chair and stood beside her, her arms about her protectively.

She whispered gently: "Dearest Highness, he has gone now. He is evil . . . but has left us. We will never see him again. Do not tremble so. Let me take you to your bed. There you will lie down. He has gone now, that evil man."

The Dowager Queen stood up and allowed Isabella to take her arm.

From that moment Isabella felt that she was the one who must care for her mother, that she was the strong one who must protect her brother and her mother from this wicked Court, this whirlpool of intrigue which was threatening to drag them down to . . . what? She could not imagine.

All she knew was that she was capable of defending herself, of bridging the dangerous years through which she must pass before she was safe as the bride of Ferdinand.

* * *

The Dowager Queen sent for Isabella. She had recovered from the shock of Giron's proposals and was no longer stunned; she was very angry.

"I am sorry, my daughter," said the Queen, "that you should have overheard such a revolting outburst. That man shall be severely punished. He shall very soon regret the day he submitted me to such indignity. You are coming with me to the King, to bear witness of what you overheard."

Isabella was alarmed. She fully realized that the Grand Master of the Order of Calatrava had behaved disgracefully, but she had hoped that, once the man had been dismissed from her mother's presence, his conduct might be forgotten; for remembering it could only serve to over-excite her mother.

"We are going to Henry now," said the Dowager Queen. "I have told him that I must see him on a matter of great importance, and he has agreed to receive us." The Dowager Queen looked at her daughter, and tears came into her eyes. "My dear Isabella," she said, "I fear you are fast leaving childhood behind you. That is inevitable, since you must live at this Court. I could wish, my dear, that you and I and your brother could return to Arevalo. I think we should be so much happier there. Come."

Henry received them with a show of affection.

He complimented Isabella on her appearance. "Why," he said, "my little sister is no longer a child. She grows every day. We are a tall family, Isabella; and you are no exception."

He greeted his stepmother with equal warmth, although he was wondering what grievance had brought her—he felt sure it was a grievance.

"Henry," said the Dowager Queen, "I have a complaint to make . . . a complaint of a most serious nature."

The King put on an expression of concern, but Isabella, who was watching closely, saw that it thinly veiled one of exasperation.

"I have been insulted by Don Pedro Giron," said the Dowager Queen dramatically.

"That is very shocking," said Henry, "and I am grieved to hear it."

"The man came to my apartment and made outrageous proposals."

"What were these proposals?"

"They were of an immoral nature. Isabella will bear witness, for she heard all that was said."

"He made these proposals in Isabella's presence then?"

"Well . . . she was there."

"You mean he was not aware that she was there?"

"No . . . he was not. I know, Henry, that you will not allow such outrageous conduct to go unpunished."

Henry shifted his gaze from his stepmother's face. He said. "He did not . . . attack you?"

"He attacked my good name. He dared presume to make immoral suggestions to me. If Isabella had not come from her hiding-place in time . . . I think it is very possible that he might have laid hands on me."

"So Isabella was in hiding?" Henry looked sternly at his half-sister.

"I thank the saints that she was!" cried the Queen. "No woman's virtue is safe when there are such men at Court. My dear son, you will, I know, not suffer such conduct to go unpunished."

Henry said :"Dear Mother, you excite yourself unnecessarily. I have no doubt that you protected your virtue from this man. You are still a beautiful woman. I cannot entirely blame him—nor must you—for being aware of that. I am sure, if you consider this matter calmly, you will come to the conclusion that the best of men sometimes forget the honour due to rank when beauty beckons."

"This is carnal talk," cried the Queen. "I beg of you not to use it before my daughter."

"Then I marvel that you should bring her to me when making such a complaint."

"But I told you she was there."

"She had been concealed . . . by your wishes, or was it some sly prank of her own? Which was it, eh? You tell me, Isabella."

Isabella looked at her mother; she dared not lie to the King, yet at the same time she could not betray her mother.

Henry saw her embarrassment and was sorry for her. He laid a hand on her shoulder. "Do not fret, Isabella. Too much is being made of very little."

"Do you mean," screeched the Queen, "that you will ignore the insulting behaviour of this man towards a member of the royal family?"

"Dear Mother, you must be calm. I have heard how excited you become on occasions, and it has occurred to me that it might be advisable if you left Court for some place where events which excited you were less likely to occur. As for Don Pedro Giron, he is the brother of the Marquis of Villena, and therefore not a man who can be lightly reprimanded."

"You would allow yourself to be ruled by Villena!" cried the Queen. "Villena is important . . . more important than your father's wife! It matters not that she has been insulted. It is the brother of the great Villena who has done it, and he must not be reprimanded! I had thought Villena was of less importance nowadays. I thought there was a new sun beginning to rise, and that we must all fall down and worship it. I thought that since Beltran de la Cueva—that most obliging man—became the friend of the King . . . and the Queen . . . the Marquis of Villena was not the man he had once been."

Isabella half closed her eyes with horror. Previously the scenes had been threatening in the private apartments. What would happen if, in the presence of the King, her mother began to shout and laugh!

She longed to take her mother by the hand, to whisper urgently that they should beg permission to go; and only the rigorous training she had received prevented her from doing so.

Henry saw her distress and was as eager to put an end to this discussion as she was.

"I think," he said gently, "that it would be well if you considered returning to Arevalo."

His quiet tone had its effect on the Dowager Queen. She was silent for a few seconds, then she cried out: "Yes, it would be better if we returned to Arevalo. There I was safe from the lewdness of those whom Your Highness is pleased to honour."

"You may leave when you wish," said Henry. "I only ask that my little sister and brother remain at Court."

Those words completely subdued the Queen.

Isabella knew that they had touched her with a terrible fear. One of the worst terrors of her mother's wild imagination had always been that her children might be separated from her.

"You have leave to retire," said Henry.

The Queen curtsied; Isabella did the same; and they returned in silence to their apartment.

MURDER AT THE CASTLE OF ORTES

There were days when the château of Ortes in Béarn seemed like a prison to Blanche, and her apartments there took on the aspect of a condemned cell.

Within those ancient walls she felt as though assassins hid behind the hangings, that in dark corners they waited for her.

Sometimes, after she had dismissed her servants, she would lie in bed, tense . . . waiting.

Was that a creak of a floor-board? A soft footfall in her room?

Should she close her eyes and wait? How would it come? A pillow pressed over her mouth? A knife thrust into her breast?

Yet what is my life that I should cling to it? she asked herself. For what can I hope now?

Perhaps there was always hope. Perhaps she believed that her family would repent; that ambition, which had dominated it for so many years and had robbed its members of their finer feelings, would miraculously depart leaving room only for loving kindness.

Miracles there might be, but not such miracles as that.

Here she lived, the prisoner of her sister and her sister's husband. It was terrible to know that they planned to rid themselves of her, that they were prepared to kill her for the sake of acquiring Navarre. It was a rich province, and many had cast covetous eyes on that maize and wheat-growing, that wine-producing land. But what land was worth the disintegration of a family, and the sordid criminality of its members against each other?

It would have been better, she often thought, if her mother had never inherited Navarre from Charles III, her father.

Often she dreamed that Carlos came to her, that he warned her to flee from this grim castle. In the mornings she was never sure whether she had dreamed that she had seen him or whether he had actually been with her. It was said that his ghost walked the streets of Barcelona. Perhaps the ghosts of murdered men did walk the earth, warning those they loved who were in similar danger, perhaps seeking revenge on their murderers. But Carlos had never been one to seek revenge. He had been too gentle. If he had been less so, he could not have failed to lead the people successfully against his father and his stepmother, and would doubtless now be the heir of Aragon in place of little Ferdinand. But it was the gentle ones who were sacrificed.

Blanche shivered. Her character was not unlike that of Carlos, and it seemed to her that there were warnings all about her that her time must come, as had that of Carlos.

There were occasions when she felt that she wanted to make the journey into Aragon to reason with her father and her stepmother, or to go to her sister, Eleanor, and her husband, Gaston de Foix, and tell them what was in her mind.

To her father and stepmother she would say: "What has your terrible crime brought to you? You have made Ferdinand heir of Aragon in place of Carlos. But what has happened to Aragon? The people murmur continually against you. They do not forget Carlos. There is continual strife. And one day, when you come near to the end of your days, you will remember the man who died at your command, and you will be filled with such remorse that you would rather have died before you committed such a crime."

And to Eleanor and Gaston: "You want me removed so that Navarre can pass to you. You desire your son Gaston to be the ruler of Navarre. Oh Eleanor, take warning in time. Remember what happened to Carlos. Do not, for the sake of land, for the sake of wealth, for the sake of ambition—even though this is centred in your son—stain your souls with the murder of your sister."

One must not blame young Gaston. One must not blame young

Ferdinand. It was for their sakes that their parents were ready to commit crimes, but these boys were not parties to those crimes. Yet what kind of men would they be, they who must eventually know that murder had been committed for their sakes? Would they, as their parents had, make ambition the over-ruling feature of their lives?

"I am a lonely woman," she told herself, "a frightened woman."

Yes, she was frightened. She had lived with fear now for two years; each day on waking she wondered whether this would be her last, each night wondered whether she would see the morning.

When she had come into Béarn she had been frantic, looking about for means of escape.

There had seemed to be no one to help her . . . until she remembered Henry, the husband who had repudiated her. It was strange that she should have thought of him; and yet was it so strange? There was about him a gentleness which others lacked. He was a lecher; he had deceitfully led her to believe that he intended to keep her in Castile even while he was planning to rid himself of her; and yet it was to him she had turned in her extremity.

She had written to him then; she had reminded him that he was not only her former husband but her cousin. Did he ever remember their happiness when she had first come to Castile? Now they were parted and she was a lonely woman, forced to exile far from her home.

Now, recalling that letter, she wept a little. She had been happy during those first days of her marriage. She had not known Henry then; she had been too young, too inexperienced to believe that any man, so gentle, so determined to please her as her husband had seemed, could be so shallow and insincere, not really feeling the deep emotion to which he had falsely given expression.

How could she have guessed in those days that tragedy was waiting for her in the years ahead? How could she have visualized those barren years, the inevitable conclusion of which had been banishment to this gloomy castle where death lurked, waiting to spring upon her at an unguarded moment?

"For two years I have been here," she murmured. "Two years . . . waiting . . . sensing evil . . . knowing that I have been brought here to end my days."

In that last frantic letter to Henry she had renounced her claim to Navarre in favour of the husband who had repudiated her, for it had seemed to her then that if she removed the cause of envy she might be allowed to live.

Was that letter a plea to Henry? Was she telling him that she was handing him Navarre because she was in Béarn, a lonely frightened prisoner? Did she still believe that Henry was a noble knight who would come and rescue the lady in distress, even though he had ceased to love her?

"I was always a foolish woman," mused Blanche sadly.

Henry in Castile was living his gay and voluptuous life, there surrounded by his mistresses and his wife who shared his tastes, it seemed. How foolish to imagine that he would have a thought to spare for the dangers of a woman who had ceased to concern him once he was satisfactorily—from his point of view—divorced from her and had sent her away. There was no help from Henry. She might as well never have offered him Navarre. He was too indolent to take it.

So Navarre remained—her inheritance, the coveted land, on account of which death stalked the castle of Ortes, waiting until the moment was propitious to strike.

With the coming of night her fears increased.

Her women helped her to bed. They slept in her apartment, as she felt happier with them there.

They could not be unaware of the sense of fear which pervaded the place; she noticed how they would start at a footfall, leap to their feet when they heard voices or footsteps at the door.

* * *

A messenger arrived at Ortes with a letter from the Comtesse de Foix to her sister Blanche. It was an affectionate letter, containing news of a marriage the Comtesse was trying to arrange for her sister. Because of that unfortunate incident in Castile, Blanche must not imagine that her family would allow her to lead the life of a hermit.

I do not care if I live the life of a hermit, thought Blanche. All I care is that I live.

In one of the kitchens the messenger from the Comtesse de Foix was drinking a glass of wine.

The servant who had brought it to him lingered as he refreshed himself, and there came a moment when they were quite alone. Then the messenger ceased to smile pleasantly as he sipped his wine.

He frowned in annoyance and said to the servant: "Why is there this delay? If it continues you will have some explaining to do."

"Sir, it is not easy."

"I cannot comprehend the difficulties; nor can others."

"Sir, I have attempted . . . once or twice."

"Then you are a bungler. We do not suffer bunglers. Can you guess what your fate may well be? Put out your tongue. Good! I see it is pink, and that I believe is a sign of health. I'll swear it's plausible too. I'll swear it has played its part in luring the maidens to your bed, eh? Ah, I know. You have paid too much attention to them and neglected your duty. Let me tell you this: that tongue could be cut out, and you'd be a sorry fellow without it. And that, my friend, is but one of the misfortunes which could befall you."

"Sir, I need time."

"You have wasted time. I give you another chance. It must happen within twenty-four hours after I leave. I shall stay at the inn nearby, and if the news is not brought to me within twenty-four hours . . ."

"You . . . you shall not be disappointed, sir."

"That is well. Now fill my glass. And . . . remember."

* * *

The messenger had left and Blanche felt easier in her mind as she watched him ride away.

She always believed that her sister or her father would send their creatures to do their work.

She called to her women to bring her embroidery. They would work awhile, she said.

There was comfort in the stitching; she could believe she was back in the past—in her home in Aragon when her mother had been alive, before sinister schemes had rent their household—when she had been a member of a happy family; or in the early days of marriage in Castile.

And thus, during those hours which followed the departure of the messenger, her fears were less acute.

She took her dinner with her ladies, as was her custom, and it was shortly after the meal that she complained of pains and dizziness.

Her women helped her to bed and, as the pain grew more violent, Blanche understood.

So this was it. It was not a knife in the dark, nor murderous hands about her throat. Foolish again to have suspected that it would be, when this was the safe way . . . the way Carlos had gone. They would say: She died of a colic, of a fever. And those who doubted that she had died a natural death would either not bother to question the verdict or not dare to.

"Let it be quick," she prayed. "Oh Carlos . . . I am coming to you now."

* * *

A message was taken to the inn, and when it was handed to its recipient he read it calmly and gave no sign that he was surprised or shocked by its contents.

He said to his groom: "We shall return to the castle." And they left at once, riding full speed towards Ortes.

When he arrived there, he summoned the servants together and addressed them.

"I am speaking in the name of the Comte and Comtesse de Foix," he told them. "You are to go about your business as though nothing has happened. Your mistress will be quietly interred, but news of her death is not to go beyond these walls."

One of the women stepped forward. She said: "I would like to say, sir, that I fear my mistress is the victim of an evil assassin. She was well when she sat down to her meal. She suffered immediately afterwards. If you please, I think some investigation should be made."

The messenger lifted his heavy-lidded eyes to stare at the woman. There was something so cold, so menacing in his look, that she began to tremble.

"Who is this?" he demanded.

"Sir, she served Queen Blanche and was much beloved by her."

"It would account for her derangement perhaps." The cold implacable tone held a warning which was clear to everyone. "Poor lady," went on the messenger, "if she is the victim of hallucinations we must see that she has proper attention."

Then another of the women spoke. She said: "Sir, she is hysterical. She knows not what she says. She had a great affection for Queen Blanche."

"Nevertheless, she shall be cared for . . . unless she recovers her balance. Now do not forget the orders of the Comte and Comtesse. This distressing news is to be a secret until orders are given to the contrary. If any should disobey these orders it will be necessary to punish them. Take care of the late Queen's poor friend. Make the wishes of the Comte and Comtesse known to her."

It was as though a shudder ran through all those listening.

They understood. A murder had been committed in their midst. Their gentle mistress, who had harmed no one and done much good to so many, had been eliminated; and they were being warned that painful death would be their reward if they raised their voices against her murderers.

ALFONSO OF PORTUGAL—A SUITOR FOR ISABELLA

QUEEN JOANNA let her fingers play in the dark glistening hair of her lover. He bent over her couch and, as they kissed, she knew that his thoughts were not so much with her as with the brilliant materialization of his dreams of fortune.

"Dear Beltran," she asked, "you are contented?"

"I think, my love, that life goes well for us."

"What a long way you have come, my Beltran, since I looked from my window and beckoned you to my bedchamber. Well, one way to glory is through the bedchambers of Kings. Also through the Queen's, you have discovered."

He kissed her with passion. "To combine desire with ambition, love with power! How singularly fortunate I have been!"

"And I. You owe your good fortune to me, Beltran. I owe mine to my own good sense. So you see I may congratulate myself even more than you do yourself."

"We are fortunate . . . in each other."

"And in the King, my husband. Poor Henry! He grows more shaggy with the years. I often think he is like a dear old dog, growing a little obese, a little blind, a little deaf—figuratively, of course—but remaining so good-tempered, never growling even when he is neglected or insulted, and always ready to give a friendly bark, or wag his tail at the least attention."

"He realizes his good fortune in possessing such a Queen. You are incomparable."

She laughed. "Indeed I begin to think I am. Who else could have produced the heiress of Castile?"

"Our dearest little Joanna—how enchanting she is!"

"So enchanting that we must make sure no one snatches the crown from her head. They will try, my love. They grow insolent. Someone referred to her as La Beltraneja yesterday in my hearing."

"And you were angry?"

"I gave evidence of my righteous anger, but inwardly I was just a little pleased, a little proud."

"We must curb that pride and pleasure, dearest. We must plan for her sake."

"That is what I intend to do. I visualize the day when we shall see her mount the throne. I do not feel that Henry will live to a great age. He is too indulgent in those pleasures which, while giving him such amusement, rob him of his health and strength."

Beltran was thoughtful. "I often wonder," he mused, "what his inner thoughts are when he hears our darling's nickname."

"He does not hear. Did you not know that Henry has the most obliging ears in Castile? They are only rivalled by his eyes, which are equally eager to serve him. When he does not want to listen, he is deaf; when he does not wish to see, he is blind."

"If only we could contrive some magic to render the ears and eyes of those about him equally accommodating!"

Joanna gave a mock shudder. "I do not like the all-important Marquis. He has too many ideas swirling about in that haughty head of his."

Beltran nodded slowly. "I have seen his eyes resting with alarming speculation on the young Alfonso. Also on his sister."

"Oh, those children! And especially Isabella. I fear the years at Arevalo, under the queer and pious guardianship of mad Mamma, have done great harm to the child's character."

"One can almost hear her murmuring: 'I will be a saint among women.' "

"If that were all, Beltran, I would forgive her. I fancy the murmuring is: 'I will be a saint among . . . *Queens.*' "

"Alfonso is of course the main danger."

"Yes, but I would like to see those two removed from Court. The Dowager has gone. Oh, what a blessing not to have to see *her*! Long may she remain in Arevalo."

"I heard that she has lapsed into a deep melancholy and is resigned to leaving her son and daughter at Court."

"Let her stay there."

"You would like to banish Alfonso and Isabella to Arevalo with her."

"Farther away than that. I have a plan . . . for Isabella."

"My clever Queen . . ." murmured Beltran; and laughing, Joanna put her lips to his.

"Later," she said softly, "I will explain."

* * *

Beatriz de Bobadilla regarded her mistress with a certain dismay. Isabella was sitting, quietly stitching at her embroidery, as though she were unaware of all the dangers which surrounded her.

There was about Isabella, Beatriz decided, an almost unnatural calm. Isabella believed in her destiny. She was certain that one day Ferdinand of Aragon would come to claim her; and that Ferdinand would conform exactly with that idealized picture which Isabella had made of him.

What a lot she has to learn of life! thought Beatriz.

Beatriz felt as though she were an experienced woman compared with Isabella. It was more than those four years seniority which made her feel this. Isabella was an idealist; Beatriz was a practical woman.

Let us hope, thought Beatriz, that she will not be too greatly disappointed.

Isabella said: "I wish there were news of Ferdinand. I am growing old now. Surely our marriage cannot long be delayed?"

"You may be sure," Beatriz soothed, "that soon there will be plans for your marriage."

But, wondered Beatriz, bending over her work, will it be to Ferdinand?

"I hope all is well in Aragon," said Isabella.

"There is great trouble there since the rebellion in Catalonia."

"But Carlos is dead now. Why cannot the people settle down and be happy?"

"They cannot forget how Carlos died."

Isabella shivered. "Ferdinand had no hand in that."

"He is too young," agreed Beatriz. "And now Blanche is dead. Carlos . . . Blanche. . . . There is only Eleanor alive of King John's family by his first wife, and she will not stand in the way of Ferdinand's inheritance."

"He is his father's heir by right now," murmured Isabella.

"Yes, but . . ."

"But what?" demanded Isabella sharply.

"How will Ferdinand feel . . . how would anyone feel . . . knowing that it had been necessary for one's brother to die before one could inherit the throne?"

"Carlos died of a fever . . ." began Isabella. Then she stopped. "Did he, Beatriz? Did he?"

"It would have been a most convenient fever," said Beatriz.

"I wish I could see Ferdinand . . . talk to Ferdinand . . ." Isabella held her needle poised above her work. "Why should it not be that God has chosen Ferdinand to rule Aragon, and it is for this reason that his brother died?"

"How can we know?" said Beatriz. "I hope Ferdinand is not made unhappy by his brother's death."

"How *would* one feel if a brother were removed so that one inherited the throne? How should I feel if Alfonso were taken like that?" Isabella shivered. "Beatriz," she went on solemnly, "I should have no wish to inherit the throne of Castile unless it were mine by right. I would wish no harm to Alfonso of course, nor to Henry . . . in order that I might reach the throne."

"I know full well that you would not, for you are good. Yet what if the well-being of Castile depended on the removal of a bad king?"

"You mean . . . Henry?"

"We should not even speak of such things," said Beatriz. "What if we were overheard?"

Isabella said: "No, we must not speak of them. But tell me this first. You do not know of any plan to remove . . . Henry?"

"I think that Villena might make such plans."

"But why?"

"I think he and his uncle might wish to put Alfonso in Henry's place as ruler of Castile, that they might rule Alfonso."

"That would be highly dangerous."

"But perhaps I am wrong. This is idle gossip."

"I trust you *are* wrong, Beatriz. Now that my mother has gone back to Arevalo I often think how much more peaceful life has become. But perhaps I delude myself. My mother could not hide her desires, her excitement. Perhaps others desire and plan in secret. Perhaps there is as much danger in the silences of some as in the hysteria of my mother."

"Have you heard from her since she reached Arevalo?"

"Not from her but from one of her friends. She often forgets that we are not there with her. When she remembers she is very melancholy. I hear that she lapses into moods of depression, when she expresses her fears that neither Alfonso nor I will ever wear the crown of Castile. Oh, Beatriz, I often think how happy I might have been if we were not a royal family. If I were your sister, shall I say, and Alfonso your brother, how happy we might have been. But from the time I was able to speak I was continually told: 'You could be Queen of Castile.' It made none of us happy. It seems to me that there has always been a reaching out for something beyond us . . . for something that would be highly dangerous should we possess it. Oh, you should be happy, Beatriz. You do not know how happy."

"Life is a battle for all of us," murmured Beatriz. "And you shall be happy, Isabella. I hope I shall always be there to see and perhaps, in my small way, contribute to that happiness."

"When I marry Ferdinand and go to Aragon, you must accompany me there, Beatriz."

Beatriz smiled a little sadly. She did not believe that she would be allowed to follow Isabella to Aragon; she herself would have to marry; her husband would be Andres de Cabrera, an officer of the King's household, and her duty would be to stay with him, not to go with Isabella—if Isabella ever went to Aragon.

She smiled fondly at her mistress. For Isabella had no doubt. Isabella saw her future with Ferdinand as clearly as she saw the piece of needlework now in her hand.

Beatriz gazed out of the window and said : "There is your brother. He has returned from a ride."

Isabella dropped her work and went to the window. Alfonso looked up, saw them and waved.

Isabella beckoned, and Alfonso leaped from his horse, left it with a groom and came into the Palace.

"How he grows," said Beatriz. "One would not believe he is only eleven."

"He has changed a great deal since he came to Court. I think we both have. He has changed too since our mother went away."

They were both more light-hearted now, Beatriz thought. Poor Isabella, how she must have suffered through that mother of hers! It had made her serious beyond her years. Alfonso came into the room. He was flushed and looked very healthy from his ride.

"You called me," he said, embracing Isabella and turning to bow to Beatriz. "Did you want to talk to me?"

"I always want to talk to you," said Isabella. "But there is nothing in particular."

Alfonso looked relieved. "I was afraid something had gone amiss."

"You were expecting something?" she asked anxiously.

Alfonso looked at Beatriz.

"You must not mind Beatriz," said Isabella. "She and I discuss everything together. She is as our sister."

"Yes, I know," said Alfonso. "And you ask if I am expecting something. I would say I am always expecting something. There is always something either happening or threatening to happen here. Surely all Courts are not like this one, are they?"

"In what way?" asked Beatriz.

"I do not think there could be another King like Henry in the world. Nor a Queen like Joanna . . . and a situation such as that relating to the baby."

"Such situations may have occurred before," mused Isabella.

"There is going to be trouble. I know it," said Alfonso.

"Someone has been talking to you."

"It was the Archbishop."

"You mean the Archbishop of Toledo?"

"Yes," said Alfonso. "He has been very gracious to me of late . . . too gracious."

Beatriz and Isabella exchanged glances of apprehension.

"He shows me a respect which I have not received before," went on Alfonso. "I do not think the Archbishop is very pleased with our brother."

"It is not for an Archbishop to be displeased with a King," Isabella reminded him.

"Oh, but it could be for this Archbishop and this King," Alfonso corrected her.

Isabella said: "I have heard that Henry has agreed to a match between the little Princess and Villena's son. Thus he could make sure of keeping Villena his friend."

"The people would never agree to that," said Beatriz.

"And," put in Alfonso, "there is going to be an enquiry into the legitimacy of the little Princess. If it is found that she cannot be the King's daughter, then . . . they will proclaim me heir to the throne." He looked bewildered. "Oh, Isabella," he went on, "how I wish that we need not be bothered. How tiresome it is! It is as it was when our mother was with us. Do you remember—at the slightest provocation we would be told that we must take care, we must do this, we must not do that, because it was possible that we should one day inherit the crown? How tired I am of the crown! I wish I could ride and swim and do what other boys do. I wish I did not have to be regarded always as a person to be watched. I do not want the Archbishop to make a fuss of me, to tell me he is my very good friend and will always be at hand to protect me. I will choose my own friends, and they will not be Archbishops."

"There is someone at the door," said Beatriz.

She went towards it and opened it swiftly.

A man was standing there.

He said: "I have a message for the Infanta Isabella." And Beatriz stood aside for him to enter.

As he came towards her Isabella thought: How long has he been standing outside the door? What has he heard? What had they said?

Alfonso was right. There was no peace for them. Their actions were watched; everything they did was spied upon. It was one of the penalties for being a possible candidate for the throne.

"You would speak with me?" she asked.

"Yes, Infanta. I bring a message from your noble brother, the King. He wishes you to come with all speed to his presence."

Isabella inclined her head. "You may return to him," she said, "and tell him that I am coming immediately."

* * *

As Isabella entered her brother's apartments she knew that this was an important occasion.

Henry was seated, and beside him was the Queen. Standing behind the King's chair was Beltran de la Cueva, Count of Ledesma; and the Marquis of Villena, with his uncle the Archbishop of Toledo, was also present.

Isabella knelt before the King and kissed his hand.

"Why, Isabella," said Henry kindly, "it gives me pleasure to see you. Does she not grow apace!" He turned to Queen Joanna, who flashed on Isabella a smile of great friendliness which seemed very false to the young girl.

"She is going to be tall, as you are, my dear," said the Queen.

"How old are you, sister?" asked the King.

"Thirteen, Highness."

"A young woman, no less. Time to put away childish things, and think of . . . marriage, eh?"

They were all watching her, Isabella knew, and she was angry because she was aware of the faint flush which had risen to her cheeks. Did she show the joy which she was feeling?

At last she and Ferdinand were to be united. Perhaps in a few days they would be meeting. She was a little apprehensive. Would he be as pleased with her as, she was certain, she was going to be with him?

How one's thoughts ran on. They went beyond one's control.

"We keep your welfare very close to our hearts—the Queen, myself, my friends and ministers. And, sister, we have decided on a match for you, one which will delight you by its magnificence."

She bowed her head and waited, hoping that she would be able to curb her joy and not show unseemly delight in the fact that at last she was to be the bride of Ferdinand.

"The Queen's brother, King Alfonso V of Portugal, asks your hand in marriage. I and my advisers are delighted by this offer and we have decided that it can only bring happiness and advantage to all concerned."

Isabella did not believe that she heard correctly. She was conscious of a rush of blood to her ears; she could hear and feel the mighty pounding of her heart. For a few seconds she believed she would faint.

"Well, sister, I see that you are overcome by the magnificence of this offer. You are a personable young woman now, you know. And you deserve a good match. It is my great pleasure to provide it for you.

Isabella lifted her eyes and looked at the King. He was smiling, but not at her. He knew of her obsession with the idea of the Aragonese marriage. He remembered hearing how upset she was when she heard that a match had been arranged for her with the Prince of Viana. It was for this reason that he had told her in a formal manner of the proposed marriage with Portugal.

As for the Queen, she was smiling brightly. The match was entirely to her liking. She wanted to see Isabella safely out of Castile, for while she remained there she was a menace to Joanna's daughter. She would of course have preferred to remove young Alfonso, but that would have presented too many difficulties at the moment. However, the brother would now be weakened by the loss of his sister's support.

One of them will be out of the way, mused Joanna.

Isabella spoke slowly but clearly, and no one in that chamber remained unimpressed by the calm manner in which she addressed them.

"I thank Your Highness for making such efforts on my behalf, but it seems that a certain fact has been overlooked. I am already betrothed, and I and others consider that betrothal binding."

"Betrothed!" cried Henry. "My dear sister, you take a childish view of these things. Many husbands are suggested for Princesses, but there is nothing binding in these suggestions."

"Nevertheless I am betrothed to Ferdinand of Aragon; and in view of this, marriage elsewhere is impossible."

Henry looked exasperated. His sister was going to be stubborn, and he was too weary of conflict to endure it. If he had been alone with her he would have agreed with her that she was betrothed to Ferdinand, that the King of Portugal's offer must be refused; and then, as soon as she had left him, he would have gone ahead with arrangements for the marriage, leaving someone else to break the news to her.

He could not do this, of course, in the presence of the Queen and his ministers.

"Dear Isabella!" cried Joanna. "She is but a child yet. She does not know that a great King like my brother cannot be refused when he asks her hand in marriage. You are fortunate indeed; you will be very happy in Lisbon, Isabella."

Isabella looked from Villena to the Archbishop and then appealingly at Henry. None of them would meet her gaze.

"The King of Portugal himself," said Henry, studying the rings on his fingers, "is coming to Castile. He will be here within the next few days. You must be ready to receive him, sister. I would have you show your pleasure and gratitude that he has chosen you for this high honour."

Isabella stood very still. She wanted to speak her protests but it seemed to her that her throat had closed and would not let the words escape.

In spite of that natural calm, that extraordinary dignity, standing here in the audience chamber with the eyes of all the leading ministers of Castile upon her, she looked like an animal desperately seeking a means of escape from a trap which it saw closing about it.

* * *

Isabella lay on her bed; she had the curtains drawn about it that she might be completely shut in. She had prayed for long hours on her knees, but she did not cease to pray every hour of the day.

She had talked to Beatriz; and Beatriz could only look sad and say that this was the fate of Princesses; but she had tried to comfort her. "This is an obsession you have built up for Ferdinand," she told her. "How can you be sure that he is the only one for you? You have never seen him. You know nothing of him except what has come to you through hearsay. Might it not be that the King of Portugal will be a kind husband?"

"I love Ferdinand. That sounds foolish to you, but it is as though he has grown up with me. Perhaps when I first heard his name I needed comfort, perhaps I allowed myself to build an ideal—but there is something within me, Beatriz, which tells me that only with Ferdinand can I be happy."

"If you do your duty you will be happy."

"I do not feel that it is my duty to marry the King of Portugal."

"It is what the King, your brother, commands."

"I shall have to go away from Castile . . . away from Alfonso . . . away from you, Beatriz. I shall be the most unhappy woman in Castile, in Portugal. There must be a way. They were determined to marry me to the Prince of Viana, but he died, and that was like a miracle. Perhaps if I prayed enough there might be another miracle."

Beatriz shook her head; she had little comfort to offer. She believed that Isabella must now leave her childish dreams behind her; she must accept reality, as so many Princesses had been obliged to do before her.

And since Beatriz could not help, Isabella wished to shut herself away, to pray, if not to be saved from this distasteful marriage, to have the courage to endure it.

There was a movement in her room and she sat up in bed, whispering: "Who is there?"

"It is I, Isabella."

"Alfonso!"

"I came to you quietly. I did not want anyone to disturb us. Oh . . Isabella, I am frightened."

The bed curtains divided and there stood her brother. He looked such a child, she thought, and she forgot her own misery in her desire to comfort him.

"What is it, Alfonso?"

"There are plots and intrigues all about us, Isabella. And I . . . I am the centre of them. That is what I feel. They are going to send you away so that I shall not have the comfort of your presence and advice. Isabella . . . I am afraid."

She held out her hand and he took it; then he threw himself into her arms and for a few seconds they clung together.

"They are going to make me the heir to the throne," said Alfonso. "They are going to say the little Princess has no right to it. I wish they would leave me alone, Isabella. Why cannot they leave us in peace . . . myself to be as other boys, you to marry where you wish."

"They will never leave us in peace, Alfonso. We are not as other boys and girls. The reason is that our half-brother is the King of Castile and that many people believe the child, who is known as his daughter, is not a child of his at all. That means that we are in the direct line of succession. There are some to support Henry and his Queen . . . and there are others who will use us in their quarrel with the King and Queen."

"Isabella . . . let us run away. Let us go to Arevalo and join our mother there."

"It would be of no use. They would not let us remain there."

"Perhaps we could all escape into Aragon . . . to Ferdinand."

Isabella considered this, imagined herself with her hysterical mother and her young brother arriving at the Court of Ferdinand's father John. In Aragon there was a state of unrest. It might even be that John had decided to choose another bride for Ferdinand.

She shook her head slowly. "Our feelings, our loves and hates . . . they are not important, Alfonso. We must try to see ourselves . . . not as people . . . but as pieces in a game, to be moved this way and that . . . whichever is most beneficial to our country."

"If they would leave me alone and not try to force the King to make me his heir, surely *that* would be beneficial to the country."

"Terrible things are happening in Castile, Alfonso. The roads are unsafe; the people have no protection; there is much poverty. It may be that it would be beneficial if you *were* made King of Castile with a Regency to rule until you are of age."

"I do not want it, I do not want it," cried Alfonso. "I want us to be together . . . quietly and at peace. Oh, Isabella, what can we do? I am frightened, I tell you."

"We must not be frightened, Alfonso. Fear is unworthy of us."

"But we are no different from other people," cried Alfonso passionately.

"We are. We are," insisted Isabella. "We make a mistake if we do not recognize this. It is not for us to harbour dreams of a quiet happiness. We have to face the fact that we are different."

"Isabella, people who are in the way of others with a wish to ascend the throne often die. Carlos, Prince of Viana, died. I have heard that was to make way for his young brother, Ferdinand."

Isabella said slowly: "Ferdinand played no part in that murder . . . if murder there was."

"It was murder," said Alfonso. He crossed his hands on his chest. "Something within me tells me it was murder. Isabella, if they made me heir . . . if they made me King . . ." He looked over his shoulder furtively; and Isabella thought of Carlos, the prisoner of his own father, feeling as Alfonso was now, looking over his shoulder as Alfonso looked, furtively, afraid of the greed and lust of men for power. "There was Queen Blanche too," went on Alfonso. "I wonder what she felt on her last day on Earth. I wonder what it felt like to be shut up in a castle, knowing that you have that which others want and only your death can give it to them."

"This is foolish talk," said Isabella.

"But they are marrying you into Portugal. You will not be here to see what happens. I know they are making plans concerning me, Isabella. Oh . . . how I wish that I were not the son of a King. Have you ever thought, Isabella, how wonderful it must be to be the child of a simple peasant?"

"To suffer hunger? To have to work hard for a cruel master?"

"There is nothing so much to be feared in your life," said Alfonso, "as the knowledge that men are planning to take it from you. I think if you could ask poor Queen Blanche to confirm this, she would do so. I know, you see, Isabella. Because . . . I have read the thoughts in men's eyes as they look at me. I know. They are sending you away because they fear you. I shall be left without a friend. For, Isabella, although the Archbishop tells me he loves me—and so does the Marquis of Villena—I do not trust them. You are the only one I can be sure of."

Isabella was deeply moved.

"Little brother," she said, and she seemed to draw strength and determination from Alfonso's melancholy words. "I will *not* go to Portugal. I will find some means of avoiding this marriage."

Alfonso, looking up at her and seeing the resolve in her face, began to believe that when Isabella made up her mind she could not be defeated.

* * *

It was when Alfonso had left her that inspiration came to Isabella.

She needed advice. She should discover whether she must inevitably accept this marriage with Portugal, or whether there was some way out of the situation.

She herself was a young girl, with little knowledge of the laws of the country, but she did suspect that the King and his adherents were endeavouring to rush her into this marriage and if this were so that they might have an ulterior reason for this haste.

She still believed that happiness for her lay in a marriage which had caught her childhood's imagination when she had made an ideal of Ferdinand; but common sense told her that a marriage between Castile and Aragon could bring the greatest good to Spain. During the revolt in Catalonia there had been strife between Castile and Aragon; and Isabella had begun to realize that one of the reasons why the Moors still governed a great part of Spain was because of the quarrels among Spaniards.

United they might defeat the Infidel. Warring among themselves they became weakened. How much more satisfactory it would be if Spaniards united and fought the Moors instead of each other.

A marriage between Castile and Aragon then must be of the greatest advantage to Spain; and Isabella believed that if she and Ferdinand were united that would be the first step towards driving the Moors from the country. Therefore their marriage must be the one to take place.

She was certain that the Prince of Viana had met his death by Divine interference. Perhaps that had come about by way of poisoned broth or wine. But who dared question the designs of Providence? God had decided that Aragon was for Ferdinand. Had He also decided that Isabella was for Ferdinand?

God was more inclined to consider those who sought to help themselves, they being more worthy of His support than those who idly accepted whatever fate was thrust upon them.

Isabella accordingly made up her mind that she would work with all her might to evade this marriage with Alfonso V of Portugal.

She had more than her own desires to consider. Her brother Alfonso needed her. To some he might appear as the heir to the throne; to Isabella he was her frightened little brother. His father was dead; his poor unbalanced mother was shut away from the world. Who was there to care for little Alfonso but his sister Isabella?

But they were children in a Court in which conflict raged. In such a Court, thought Isabella, the difficulty is to know who are your friends, who your enemies. Whom could she trust except Beatriz? It seemed that greater wisdom came to her and she understood that the only way to be sure whose side people were on was to consider their interests and motives.

She knew that the King and Queen wished to see her leave the country. The reason was plain. They had realized that differences of opinion concerning the rights of the Queen's baby daughter to the throne could bring the country to civil war. Therefore they wanted the little Princess's rivals out of the way. They could not remove Alfonso yet; that would be too drastic a step. But how easy it was to marry off Isabella and so remove her in a seemly way from the sphere of action.

The Marquis of Villena was against Isabella's marriage with Ferdinand for very strong personal reasons. A great deal of the property which he now held had once belonged to the House of Aragon, and he guessed that if Ferdinand attained influence in Castile, some means would be found of removing that property from the Marquisate of Villena and bringing it into the possession of its original owners.

There was, however, one person in Castile who Isabella believed would welcome the marriage between herself and Ferdinand. This was Don Frederick Henriquez, who was Admiral of Castile and father of the ambitious Joan Henriquez, Ferdinand's own mother.

The Admiral would naturally support the marriage between his grandson and one who was only separated from the throne of Castile by a few short steps.

There could be no doubt then where the Admiral's sympathies would lie; and, if anyone in Castile could help her now, this was the man.

Isabella had learned her first lesson in statecraft.

She would send for Frederick Henriquez, Admiral of Castile, a man of great experience; he would be able to tell her exactly how she stood in regard to the suggested marriage with Alfonso of Portugal.

* * *

In the great apartment lighted by a hundred torches which threw shadows on the tapestried walls, Isabella came to pay her respects to the visiting King of Portugal.

She held her head high as she walked towards the dais where the two Kings sat; and even though she felt that her wildly beating heart would leap into her throat and suffocate her, she yet managed to retain a certain serenity.

"I am for Ferdinand and Ferdinand is for me," she told herself even at this moment, as she had been telling herself while her women had prepared her for the interview.

Henry took her into his arms and she was held against his scented and jewel-decorated robes of state. He called her "our dearest sister"; and he was smiling with what most people would believe to be real affection.

Queen Joanna looked glitteringly beautiful; and of course Beltran de la Cueva was in attendance behind the chairs of the King and Queen, darkly handsome, dazzlingly clad, and . . . triumphant.

Now she saw the man whom they were eager to make her husband, and she shivered.

He seemed very old and repulsively ugly to the thirteen-year-old girl.

I will not, I will not, she told herself. If they force me, I will take a knife and kill myself rather than submit.

In spite of these wild thoughts her hand did not tremble as it was taken by the King of Portugal.

His eyes were a little glazed as they rested on her—this young virgin, with innocence shining in her eyes. A delectable morsel, thought the King of Portugal, and one who could conceivably bring a crown with her.

There was trouble in Castile. Wicked Joanna! What had she been about? He could guess. And this Beltran de la Cueva was such a handsome fellow that one could hardly blame Joanna. She should have arranged it, though, so that there were no suspicions. Yet why should he regret that! It was very possible that this delicious young girl would one day be the heiress of Castile. There was a young brother, but he might be killed in battle; for there would certainly be battles in Castile before long. And the baby Joanna? Oh, Isabella's chances were fair enough.

Isabella's eyes met his and she flinched. His lips were a little wet as though his mouth was watering at the sight of her.

Isabella's whole being called out in protest, but she respectfully returned the smiles of her brother, his Queen, and the Queen's brother, who so clearly was not averse to taking her as wife.

Henry said: "Our Isabella is overcome with joy at the prospect which awaits her."

"She has scarcely slept for excitement since we made her aware of her great good fortune," put in the Queen.

"She is conscious of the great honour done to her," went on Henry, "and now that she has seen you I know she will be doubly eager for the match. That is so, is it not, sister?"

"Highness," said Isabella earnestly, "would you not consider it indecorous of a young woman to discuss her marriage before she was betrothed?"

Henry laughed. "Isabella has been very carefully nurtured. She lived the life of a nun before she joined us here at Court."

"I know of no better upbringing," said Alfonso V of Portugal.

His eyes continued to wander over Isabella, so that she felt he was already picturing her in many different situations of intimacy which she could only vaguely imagine.

"My dear Isabella," said the Queen, "your brother and I will not be as strict with you as your mother was at Arevalo. We shall allow you to dance with the King of Portugal. You shall become friends before he takes you back with him to Lisbon."

Isabella forced herself to speak then. She said in a loud, clear voice, which could be heard by those courtiers who were in the room but some little distance from the royal group: "We cannot be sure yet that the betrothal will be agreed upon."

Henry looked surprised, the Queen angry, and the King of Portugal nonplussed.

But Isabella boldly resumed: "I know you have not forgotten that, as a Princess of Castile, my betrothal could not take place without the consent of the Cortes."

"The King gives his consent," said Joanna quickly.

"That is true," said Isabella, "but, as you are aware, it is essential that the Cortes also give consent."

"The King of Portugal is my brother," retorted Joanna haughtily. "Therefore we can dispense with the usual formality."

"I could not allow myself to be betrothed without the consent of the Cortes," Isabella affirmed.

It was the weariness in Henry's face, rather than the anger and astonishment in those of the Queen and the King of Portugal, which told Isabella how right the old Admiral had been when he assured her that the only way in which the King and Queen dare marry her off would be to do so at great speed, before the Cortes had time to remind them that they must have a say in the matter.

And, the Admiral had added, it was hardly likely that the Cortes would give their consent to Isabella's marriage with the Queen's brother. The people had little love for the Queen; they had always considered her levity most unbecoming, and now with the scandal concerning the parentage of her little daughter about to break, they would blame her more than ever.

The Cortes would never consent to a marriage repugnant to their Princess Isabella, and so desired by their weak and lascivious King and his less weak but hardly less lascivious wife.

When Isabella left the audience chamber she knew that she had planted dismay in the hearts of two Kings and a Queen.

How right the Admiral of Castile had been! She had learned a valuable lesson, and once again she thanked God for saving her for Ferdinand.

OUTSIDE THE WALLS OF AVILA

A BRILLIANT cavalcade was riding northwards to the shores of the River Bidassoa, the boundary between Castile and France, and a meeting-place close to the town of Bayonne.

In the centre of this procession rode Henry, King of Castile, his person glittering with jewels, and his Moorish Guard dazzling in their colourful uniforms.

His courtiers had done their utmost to rival the splendour of their King, although none, with the exception of Beltran de la Cueva, had been able to do so. Still, it was a splendid concourse that gathered to meet King Louis XI of France, his courtiers and his ministers.

This meeting had been arranged by the Marquis of Villena and the Archbishop of Toledo, the purpose of it being to settle the differences between the Kings of Castile and Aragon.

When John of Aragon had come into conflict with Catalonia over his treatment of his eldest son Carlos, Prince of Viana, Henry of Castile had thrown in certain men and arms to help the Catalans. Now, Villena had decided that there should be peace and that the King of France should be the mediator in a reconciliation.

Villena and the Archbishop had their own reasons for arranging this meeting between the Kings. Louis wished it and the two statesmen, having a profound respect for Louis' talents, had accepted certain favours from him in return for which they must not be unmindful of his wishes when at their master's Court.

Louis was a man who was eager to have a say in the affairs of Europe. He was determined to make France the centre of Continental politics, the most powerful of countries, and he deemed it necessary therefore to lose no opportunity of meddling in his neighbours' affairs if he could do so to the advantage of France.

He was interested in the affairs of Aragon, for he had lent the King of that Province three hundred and fifty thousand crowns, taking as security for the loan the provinces of Roussillon and Cerdagne. If there were to be peace between Castile and Aragon he was anxious that it should be brought about with no disadvantage to France. It was for this reason that he had his "pensioners"—such as Villena and the Archbishop of Toledo—in every country in which he could place them.

Louis was in his prime, for it was but some three years since he had ascended the throne at the age of thirty-eight, and he was already making good the ravages of the Hundred Years War. He knew Henry for a weak King growing more and more foolish as the years passed, and he could not but believe that, in conference, he would get the better of him, particularly as this King of Castile's two chief advisers were ready to accept bribes from himself, the King of France.

When Louis and Henry met there arose an immediate hostility between their followers.

Henry, magnificently attired, his company glittering in gold brocade and with the dazzle of their jewels, made a strange contrast to the sombrely-clad French King.

Louis had made no concession to the occasion and wore the clothes he was accustomed to wear at home. He delighted in making himself the least conspicuous of Frenchmen, and consequently favoured a short worsted coat with fustian doublet. His hat had clearly served him as well and as long as any of his followers; in it he wore a small image of the Virgin—not in glittering diamonds or rubies as might have been expected, but of lead.

French eyes smiled at the garments of the Castilians; there were suppressed guffaws and murmurs of "Fops! Popinjays!"

The Castilians showed their disgust of the French; and asked each other whether there had been a mistake, and it was the king of the beggars not the King of the French who had come to greet their King.

Tempers were hot and there was many a fracas.

Meanwhile the Kings themselves took each other's measure and were not greatly impressed.

Louis stated his terms for the peace, and these were not entirely favourable to Castile. Henry however, always eager to take that line which demanded the least exertion on his part, was eager for one thing only: to have done with the conference and return to Castile.

There was a great deal of grumbling among his followers.

"Why," they asked each other, "was our King ever allowed to make this journey? It is almost as though he must pay homage to the King of France and accept his judgment. Who is this King of France? He is a moneylender—and a seedy-looking one at that."

"Who arranged this conference? What a question! Who arranges everything at Court? The Marquis of Villena, of course, with that rascal, his uncle, the Archbishop of Toledo."

During the journey back to Castile Henry's adviser, the Bishop of Cuenca, and the Marquis of Santillana, who was head of the powerful Mendoza family, came to the King and implored him to re-consider before he allowed himself to enter into such humiliating negotiations again.

"Humiliating!" protested Henry. "But I should not consider my meeting with the King of France humiliating."

"Highness, the King of France treats you as a vassal," said Santillana. "It is unwise to have too many dealings with him; he is a wily old fox; and, as you will agree, the conference has brought little good to Castile. Highness, there is another matter which you should not ignore: Those who arranged this conference serve the King of France whilst feigning to serve Your Highness."

"That is a serious and dangerous accusation."

"It is a dangerous situation, Highness. We are certain that the Marquis and the Archbishop are in league with the King of France. Conversations between them have been overheard."

"It is difficult for me to believe this."

"Did they not arrange this conference?" asked Cuenca. "And what advantage has it brought to Castile?"

Henry looked bewildered. "Are you suggesting that I bring them before me and confront them with their villainies?"

"They would deny the accusation, Highness," Santillana put in. "That does not mean that they would speak the truth. We can bring you witnesses, Highness. We are assured that we are not mistaken."

Henry looked from his old teacher, the Bishop of Cuenca, to the Marquis of Santillana. They were trustworthy men, both of them.

"I will ponder this matter," he said.

They looked dismayed, and he added: "It is of great importance, and I believe that, if you are right, I should not continue to give these men my confidence."

* * *

The Archbishop of Toledo stormed into the apartments of his nephew.

"Have you heard what I have?" he demanded.

"I understand from your expression, Uncle, that you refer to our dismissal."

"Our dismissal! It is preposterous. What will he do without us?"

"Cuenca and Santillana have persuaded him that they will prove adequate substitutes."

"But why . . . why . . . ?"

"He objects to our friendship with Louis."

"Fool! Why should we not listen to Louis and give Henry our advice?"

Villena smiled at his fiery uncle. "It is a common failing among kings," he murmured, "and perhaps not only kings. They insist that those who serve them should serve no other."

"And does he think that we are going to lie down meekly under this . . . this insult?"

"If he does, he is more of a fool than we thought him."

"Your plans, nephew?"

"To call together a confederacy, to proclaim La Beltraneja illegitimate, to set up Alfonso as the heir to the throne . . . or . . ."

"Yes, nephew, or . . . what?"

"I do not know yet. It depends how far the King will proceed in this intransigent attitude of his. I can visualize circumstances in which it might be necessary to set up a new King in his place. Then, of course, we should put little Alfonso on the throne of Castile."

The Archbishop nodded, smiling. As a man of action he was impatient to go ahead with the scheme.

Villena smiled at him.

"All in good time, Uncle," he warned. "This is a delicate matter. Henry will have his supporters. We must act with care; but never fear, since Henry listens to others, he shall go. But the displacement of one King by another is always a dangerous operation. Out of such situations civil wars have grown. First we will test Henry. We will see if we can bring him to reason, before we depose him."

* * *

Queen Joanna paced angrily up and down the King's apartments.

"What are they doing, these ex-ministers of yours?" she demanded. "Oh, it was time they were dismissed from their posts. They are against us . . . do you not see? They are trying to push you aside and set up Alfonso in your place. Oh, it was folly not to force Isabella to go to Portugal. There she would at least have been out of the way. How do we know what she says to that brother of hers? You can be assured that she repeats the doctrines of her mad mother. She is priming Alfonso, telling him that he should be the heir to the throne."

"They cannot do this . . . they cannot do this," wailed Henry. "Have I not my own child!"

"Indeed you have your own child. I gave you that child. And there were not many women in Castile who could have managed that. Look at your trials and failures with your first wife. Now you have your child. Our little Joanna will remain heiress to the throne. We will not have Alfonso."

"No," said the King. "There is little Joanna. She is my heir. There is no law in Castile to prevent one of the female sex taking the crown."

"Then we must be firm. One of these days Villena will march to the executioner's knife, and he'll take that villainous old Archbishop with him. In the meantime we must be firm."

"We will be firm," echoed Henry uncertainly.

"And not forget those who are ready to stand firmly beside us."

"Oh yes, I wish there were more to stand firmly with us. I wish there need not be this strife."

"We shall be strong. But let us make sure of the strength of our loyal supporters. Let us give them our grateful thanks. You *are* grateful, are you not, Henry?"

"Yes, I am grateful."

"Then you must show your gratitude."

"Do I not?"

"Not sufficiently."

Henry looked surprised.

"There is Beltran," the Queen went on. "What honours has he had? The Count of Ledesma! What is that for one who has worked with us . . . for us . . . unflinchingly and devotedly? One to whom we should be for ever grateful. You must honour him further."

"My dear, what do you suggest?"

"That he be made Master of Santiago."

"Master of Santiago! But that is the greatest of honours. He would be endowed with vast estates and revenues. Why, he would have the largest armed force in the Kingdom put into his hands."

"And it is too much, you think?"

"*I* think, my dear? It is the people who will think it is too much."

"Your enemies?"

"It is necessary to placate our enemies."

"Coward! Coward! You have always been a coward! You fret over your enemies and forget your friends."

"I am willing to honour him, my dear. But to make him Master of Santiago . . . !"

"It is too much . . . too much for your friend! You would rather give it to your enemies!"

The Queen put her hands on her hips and laughed at him.

Now she was ready to begin pacing the apartment again. She was going to start once more on that diatribe which he had heard many times before. He was a coward; he deserved his imminent fate; when he was thrust from his throne he would remember that he had spurned her advice; he placated his enemies, and those who served him with every means at their disposal—like Beltran de la Cueva—were forgotten.

Henry lifted his hands as though to ward off this spate of accusation.

"That is enough," he said. "Let him have it. Let us bestow on Beltran the Mastership of Santiago."

* * *

Now the new party was in revolt. It was humiliating enough, they said, to be forced to suspect the legitimacy of the heiress to the throne, but to see the King so far forget his dignity as to heap honours on the man who was generally accepted as her father was intolerable.

Castile trembled on the edge of civil war.

Valladolid was entered by the rebels and several of Villena's party of confederates declared that they were holding the city against the King. However, the citizens of Valladolid, while deploring the weakness of the King, were not ready to ally themselves with Villena; and they expelled the intruders. But when Henry, travelling to Segovia, very narrowly escaped being kidnapped by the confederates, he was thoroughly alarmed. He, who had worked hard at nothing except avoiding trouble, now found himself in the midst of it.

Villena wrote to him. He was grieved, he said, that enemies had come between them. If the King would see him and the heads of his party he would do his utmost to put an end to the strife which trembled so near to civil war.

The King had deplored the loss of Villena's counsel. Villena had been the strong man Beltran could never be. Beltran was charming, and his company pleasant; but Henry needed the strength of Villena to lean on; and when he received this communication he was anxious to meet his ex-minister.

Villena, delighted at the turn of events, met Henry. With Villena came his uncle, the Archbishop, also the Count Benavente.

"Highness," Villena addressed Henry when they were gathered together, "the Commission, which has been set up to test the legitimacy of the Princess Joanna, has grave doubts that she is your daughter. In view of this we deem it wise that your half-brother Alfonso be proclaimed as your heir. You yourself must abandon your Moorish Guard and live a more Christian life. Beltran de la Cueva is to be deprived of the Mastership of Santiago. And finally your half-brother Alfonso is to be delivered into my hands that I may be his guardian."

"You ask too much," Henry told him sadly. "Too much."

"Highness," urged Villena, "it would be wise for you to accept our terms."

"The alternative?" asked Henry.

"Civil war, I greatly fear, Highness."

Henry hesitated. It was so easy to agree, but he had later to face an enraged Joanna, who was determined that her daughter should have the crown. Then Henry slyly thought of a way of pleasing both Joanna and Villena.

"I agree," he said, "that Beltran de la Cueva shall be deprived of the Mastership of Santiago and that you shall become the guardian of Alfonso. He shall be proclaimed heir to the throne, but there is a condition."

"What condition is this?" asked Villena.

"That he shall, in due course, marry the Princess Joanna."

Villena was startled. The heir to the throne marry the King's illegitimate daughter! Well, on consideration it was not a bad suggestion. There would always be some to declare that La Beltraneja had been falsely so called; there would also be others who, seeking a cause for which to make trouble, would choose hers. Moreover, it would be some years before La Beltraneja was of an age to marry. By that time, if necessary, other arrangements could be made.

"I do not see," said Villena, "why this should not be."

Henry felt pleased with his little effort of diplomacy. He could now more easily face the Queen.

* * *

Alfonso sat at his sister's feet, watching her as she worked at her embroidery. Beatriz de Bobadilla was with her.

Alfonso had lately made a habit of spending a great deal of time in his sister's apartments.

Poor Alfonso, mused Isabella; he is old enough to understand the intrigues which split the Court in two; and he knows that he—even more than I—is at their very core.

"Alfonso," she said. "You must not brood. It does no good."

"But I have a feeling that I shall not be allowed to stay here much longer."

"Why should they take you away?" asked Beatriz. "They know you are safe here."

"Perhaps they do not greatly care for my safety."

"You are wrong in that," said Isabella. "You are very important to them."

"I wish," said Alfonso, "that we were a more normal family. Why could not we all have been the children of our father's first wife! Then I think Henry would have loved us as you and I love each other. Why could not Henry have taken a wife who was more like a Queen, and had many sons about whose parentage there would have been no question!"

"You want everyone to be perfect in a perfect world," murmured Beatriz with a smile.

"No, not perfect . . . merely normal," said Alfonso sadly. "Do you know that the heads of the confederacy are meeting the King this day?"

"Yes," said Isabella.

"I wonder what they will decide."

"We shall soon know," said Beatriz.

"These confederates," went on Alfonso, "they have chosen me . . . me . . . as their figurehead. I do not want to be part of the confederacy. All I want is to stay here and enjoy my life. I want to go riding; I want to fence and play games. I want to sit with you two and talk now and then, not about unpleasant things . . . but about comfortable, cosy things."

"Well, let us do that," said Isabella. "Let us now be cosy . . . comfortable."

"How can we," demanded Alfonso passionately, "when we can never be sure what is going to happen next?"

There was silence.

What a pity, thought Isabella, it is that princes and princesses cannot always be children. What a pity that they have to grow up and that people often fight over them.

"Do the people hate Henry so much?" asked Alfonso.

"Some of them are displeased," Beatriz answered him.

"They have reason to be," Isabella spoke with some vehemence. "I have heard that it is unsafe to travel through the countryside without an armed escort. This is terrible. It is an indication of the corrupt state into which our country is falling. I have heard that travellers are captured and held to ransom, and that even noble families have taken up this evil trade and ply it shamelessly."

"There is the Hermandad, which has been set up to restore law and order," said Beatriz. "Let us hope it will do its work well."

"It does what it can," Isabella pointed out. "But it is a small force as yet; and everywhere in our country villainies persist. Oh, Alfonso, what a lesson this is to us. If ever we should be called upon to rule we must employ absolute justice. We must never install favourites; we must set good examples and never be extravagant in our personal demands; we must always please our people while helping them to become good Christians."

A page had come into the room.

He bowed before Isabella and said that the Marquis de Villena with the Archbishop of Toledo were below; they were asking to be received by the Infante Alfonso.

Alfonso looked sharply at his sister. His eyes appealed. He wanted to say that he could not be seen; for these were the two men whom he feared more than any others, and the fact that they had come to see him filled him with dread.

"You should receive them," said Isabella.

"Then I will do so here," said Alfonso almost defiantly. "Bring them to me."

The page bowed and retired, and Alfonso turned in panic to his sister.

"What do they want of me?"

"I know no more than you do."

"They have come from their audience with the King."

"Alfonso," said Isabella earnestly, "be careful. We do not know what they are going to suggest. But remember this: You cannot be King while Henry lives. Henry is the true King of Castile; it would be wrong for you to put yourself at the head of a faction which is trying to replace him. That would mean war, and you would be on the wrong side."

"Isabella . . ." Tears filled his eyes, but he dared not shed them. "Oh, why will they not let us alone! Why do they torment us so?"

She could have answered him. She could have said: Because in their eyes we are not human beings. We are lay figures placed at certain distances from the throne. They want power and they seek to obtain it through us.

Poor, poor Alfonso, even more vulnerable than she was herself.

The page was ushering in the Marquis of Villena and the Archbishop of Toledo, who seemed astonished to find Isabella and Beatriz there; but Alfonso immediately put on the air of an Infante and said: "You may tell me your business. These ladies share my confidence."

The Marquis and the Archbishop smiled almost obsequiously, but their respect could only disturb the others.

"We come from the King," said the Archbishop.

"And you have a message from His Highness for me?" Alfonso enquired.

"Yes, you are to prepare to leave your apartments here for new ones."

"Which apartments are these?"

"They are mine," said the Marquis.

"But I do not understand."

For answer the Marquis came forward, knelt and took Alfonso's hand.

"Principe, you are to be proclaimed heir to the throne of Castile."

A faint colour crept into Alfonso's cheeks.

"That is preposterous. How can I be? My brother will beget children yet. Moreover he has a daughter."

The Archbishop gave his short rasping laugh. He deplored wasting time.

"Your brother will never beget children," he said, "and a commission, set up to study the matter, has grave doubts that the young Joanna *is* his daughter. In view of this we have insisted that you be proclaimed the heir, and my nephew here has permission to take you under his guardianship that you may be trained in all the duties which, as King, will be yours."

There was a short silence, and when Alfonso spoke, his tone was bleak. "So," he said, "I am to settle under your wing."

"It shall be my greatest pleasure to serve Your Highness."

Then Alfonso smiled in momentary hopefulness. "I am capable of looking after myself, and I am very happy here in my apartments next to my sister's."

"Oh," laughed the Marquis, "there will not be much change. We shall merely look after you and see that you are prepared for your role. You will see much of your sister. There will be no attempt to curtail your pleasures."

"How can you know that?"

"Dear Highness, we will make sure of it."

"What if my pleasure is to stay as I am and not come under your guardianship?"

"Your Highness is pleased to joke. Could you leave at once?"

"No. I wish to be with my sister a little longer. We were talking together when you interrupted us."

"We crave Your Highness's pardon," said Villena in false concern. "We will leave you to finish your conversation with your sister, and we will await your pleasure in the ante-room. You should bring your most trusted servant with you. I have already given him instructions to prepare for your departure."

"But you . . . *you* gave instructions!"

"In matters like this one must act with speed," said the Archbishop.

Alfonso appeared resigned. He watched the two schemers retire, but when he turned to Isabella and Beatriz, they were both struck by the look of despair in his face.

"Oh, Isabella, Isabella," he cried, and she put her arms about him and held him close.

"You see," he went on, "it has come. I know what they will try to do. They will make me King. And I do not want to be King, Isabella. I am afraid of them. I shall have forced upon me that which is greatly coveted. All Kings should be wary, but none so much as those who are forced to wear the crown before it is theirs by right. Isabella, perhaps one day someone will do to me what was done to Carlos . . . to Blanche . . ."

"These are morbid fancies," Isabella chided him.

"I do not know," said Alfonso. "Isabella, I am afraid because I do not know."

* * *

Joanna stormed into her husband's apartments.

"So you have allowed them to dictate to you!" she cried. "You have allowed them to bring about the disinheritance of our daughter, and put up that sly young Alfonso in her place."

"But do you not see," cried Henry piteously, "that I have insisted on his betrothal to Joanna?"

The Queen laughed bitterly. "And you think they will allow that? Henry, are you a fool. Do you not see that, once you have proclaimed Alfonso your heir, you will have no say in deciding whom he shall marry? And the very fact that you allow him to be proclaimed your heir can only be because you accept these vile slanders against me and your daughter."

"It was the only way," murmured Henry. "It was either that or civil war."

He was thinking sadly of Blanche, who had been so meek and affectionate. Physically she had not excited him, but what a peaceful companion she had been. Poor Blanche! She had left this stormy life; she had been sacrificed to her family's ambition. One could almost say, Most fortunate Blanche, for there was no doubt that she would find a place in Heaven.

If I had never divorced her, he thought now, she might be alive at this time. And should I have been worse off? It is true there is a child now—but is she mine, and what a storm of controversy she is arousing!

"You are a coward," cried the Queen. "And what of Beltran? What will he think of this? He deserves to be Master of Santiago, and now you have agreed to deprive him of the title."

Henry spread his hands helplessly. "Joanna, would you see Castile torn in two by civil war?"

"Would it be if it had a King at its head instead of a lily-livered poltroon!"

"You go too far, my dear," said Henry mildly.

"At least I will not be dictated to by these men. As for Beltran, unless you wish to offend him mortally, there is only one thing you can do."

"What is that?"

"You have taken from him with one hand; therefore you must give with the other. You have sworn to deprive him of the Mastership of Santiago, therefore you should make him Duke of Albuquerque."

"Oh but . . . that would be tantamount to . . . to . . ."

"To opposing your enemies! Indeed it would. And if you are wise there is one other thing you will do. You will prevent your enemies from plotting your downfall. For, depend upon it, their scheme is not merely to set up an heir of their choosing in place of your own daughter, but to oust you from the throne."

"You may well be right."

"And what will you do about it? Sit on your throne . . . waiting for disaster?"

"What can I do? What would happen if we were plunged into civil war?"

"We should fight, and we should win. But at least you are the King. You could act quickly now. These people are not popular. Most hate the Marquis of Villena. Look what happened when he and his friends tried to seize Valladolid. You are not unpopular with the people, and you are the rightful King. Have these ringleaders of revolt quickly and quietly seized. When their leaders are in prison the people will not be so ready to rebel against their King."

The King gazed at his fiery wife. "My dear," he said, slowly, "I think perhaps you may be right."

* * *

The Marquis of Villena was alone when the man was shown into his presence.

The visitor was wrapped in a concealing cloak and, when he removed it, revealed himself as one of the King's Guards.

"Forgive the unceremonious intrusion, my lord," he said, "but the matter is urgent."

He then repeated the conversation which he had overheard between the King and Queen.

Villena nodded. "You have done your work well," he said. "I trust you were not recognized on your way here. Go back to your post and keep us informed. We shall find means to prevent these arrests which the King now plans."

He dismissed his spy and immediately called on the Archbishop.

"We are leaving at once," he said, "for Avila. There is not a moment to lose. I, with Alfonso, will meet you there. We shall take immediate action. De la Cueva is to be created Duke of Albuquerque in compensation for the loss of the Mastership of Santiago. This is the way the King observes his pledges!"

"And when we reach Avila with the heir to the throne, what then?"

"Alfonso will no longer be the heir to the throne. He will ascend it. At Avila we will proclaim Alfonso King of Castile."

* * *

Alfonso was pale, not with the strain of the journey, but with a fear of the future. He had spent long hours on his knees praying for guidance. He felt so young; it was a pitiable situation for a boy of eleven years to have to face.

There was no one whose advice he could ask. He could not reach those whom he loved. His mother's mind was becoming more and more deranged and sunk in oblivion, and, even if he were allowed to see her, it would be doubtful whether he would be able to explain to her his need. And when he thought of his childhood, his mother's voice seemed to come echoing down to him: "Do not forget that one day you could be King of Castile." So even if he could make her understand what was about to happen she would doubtless express great pleasure. Was this not what she had always longed for?

But Isabella—his dear, good sister—she would advise. Isabella was anxious to do what was right, and he had a feeling that Isabella would say: "It is not right for you to be crowned King, Alfonso, while our brother Henry lives, for Henry is undoubtedly the son of our father and is therefore the rightful heir to Castile. No good can come of a usurpation of the crown, for, if God had willed that you should be King, He would have taken Henry as He took Carlos that Ferdinand might be his father's heir."

"No good can come of it," murmured Alfonso. "No good . . . no good."

This city enclosed in its long grey walls depressed him. He looked out on the woods of oak and maple and those hardy trees which had been able to withstand the cruel winter.

Avila seemed to him a cruel city, a city of granite fortresses, set high above the plains, to receive the full force of the summer sun and the biting winds of a winter which was notoriously long and rigorous.

Alfonso was afraid, as he had never been afraid in his life.

"No good can come of this," he repeated.

* * *

The June sun was hot. From where he stood surrounded by some of the most important nobles of Castile, Alfonso could see the yellowish grey walls of Avila.

Here on the arid plain within sight of the city a strange spectacle was about to be enacted and he, young Alfonso, was to play an important part in it.

He experienced a strange feeling as he stood there. That clear air seemed to intoxicate him. When he looked at the city above the plain he felt an exultation.

Mine, he thought. That city will be mine. The whole of Castile will be mine.

He looked at those men who surrounded him. Strong men, all men who were eager for power; and they would come to him and take his hand, and when they took it they would offer him allegiance, for they intended to make him their King.

To be King of Castile! To save Castile from the anarchy into which it was falling! To make it great; perhaps to lead it to great victories!

Who knew, perhaps one day he might lead a campaign against the Moors. Perhaps in the years to come people would link his name with that of the Cid.

And as he stood there on the plain outside Avila, Alfonso found that his fear was replaced by ambition, and that he was now no unwilling participator in the strange ceremony which was about to take place.

Crowds had gathered on the plain. They had watched the cavalcade leave the gates of the city; at its head had been the Marquis of Villena and beside him was the young Alfonso.

On the plain there had been set up scaffolding and on this a throne had been placed. Seated on the throne was a life-sized dummy, representing a man, clad in a black robe; and on the head had been put a crown, in its hand a sceptre. A great sword of state was placed before it.

Alfonso had been led to a spot some distance from the scaffolding whilst certain noblemen, who had formed the procession which had been led by Villena and Alfonso, mounted the scaffolding and knelt before the crowned dummy, treating it as though it were the King.

Then one of the noblemen stepped to the front of the platform, and there was a tense silence among the multitude as he began to read a list of the crimes which had been committed by King Henry of Castile. The chaos and anarchy which persisted in the land were attributed to the King's evil rule.

The people continued to listen in silence.

"Henry of Castile," cried the nobleman, turning to the figure on the throne, "you are unworthy to wear the crown of Castile. You are unworthy to be given royal dignity."

Then the Archbishop of Toledo stepped on to the platform and snatched the crown from the head of the figure.

"You are unworthy, Henry of Castile, to administer the laws of Castile," went on the voice.

The Count of Plascencia then took his place on the platform and removed the sword of state.

"The people of Castile will no longer allow you to rule."

The Count of Benavente took the sceptre from the dummy's hand.

"The honour due to the King of Castile shall no longer be yours, and the throne shall pass from you."

Diego Lopez de Zuñiga picked up the dummy and threw it down on to the scaffolding, setting his foot upon it.

The people then were caught up in the hysteria which such words and such a spectacle aroused in them.

Someone in the crowd shouted: "A curse on Henry of Castile!" And the rest took up the cry.

Now the great moment had come for Alfonso to take his place on the platform. He felt very small, there under that blue sky. The town looked unreal with its granite ramparts, squat posterns and belfries.

The Archbishop lifted the boy in his arms as though he would show him to the people.

Alfonso appeared beautiful in the eyes of those watching crowds; this innocent boy appealed to them and tears came to the eyes of many assembled there because of his youth and the great burden which was about to be placed upon him.

The Archbishop announced that it had been decided to deprive the people of their feeble, criminal King, but in his place they were to be given this handsome, noble boy whom, now that they saw him, they would, he knew, be willing to serve with all their hearts.

And there on the plains before Avila there went up a shout from thousands of throats.

"Castile! Castile for the King, Don Alfonso!"

Alfonso was set upon the throne on which, shortly before, the dummy had been.

The sword of state was set before him, the sceptre placed in his hand, and the crown upon his head. And one by one those powerful nobles who had now openly declared their intention to make him King of Castile, came forward to swear allegiance as they kissed his hand.

The words echoed in Alfonso's brain.

"Castile for the King, Don Alfonso!"

DON PEDRO GIRON

ISABELLA was distraught. She was torn between her love for her brother Alfonso and her loyalty towards her half-brother Henry.

She was in her sixteenth year, and the problems which faced her seemed too complex for a girl of her limited experience to solve.

She could trust few people. She knew that she was watched by many, that her smallest gestures were noticed, and that even in her intimate circle she was spied upon.

There was one whom she could trust, but Beatriz herself had been a little absent-minded lately. It was understandable; she had been married to Andres de Cabrera, and it was inevitable that the pre-occupation of Beatriz with her new status should somewhat modify the devotion she was ready to give to her mistress.

I must be patient, thought Isabella; and she continued to dream of her own marriage, which surely could not be long delayed.

But this was not the time, when Alfonso had been placed in such a dangerous position, to think of her own selfish hopes.

There was civil strife in Castile, as there must be when two Kings claimed the throne. Sides must be taken, it seemed, by everybody; and although there were many in the kingdom who disapproved of Henry's rule, the theatrical ceremony outside the walls of Avila seemed to many to be revolutionary conduct in the worst taste. Henry was the King, and Alfonso was an impostor, declared many of the great nobles of Castile. At the same time there were many more who, not having been favourites of the King and Queen, were ready to seek their fortunes under a new monarch who must have a regency to help him govern.

Henry was almost hysterical with grief. He hated bloodshed and was determined to avoid it if possible.

"A firm hand is needed, Highness," his old tutor, the Bishop of Cuenca, warned him.

Henry turned on him with unusual anger. "How like a priest," he declared, "not being called upon to engage in the fight, to be very liberal with the blood of others!"

"Highness, you owe it to your honour. If you do not stand firm and fight your enemies, you will be the most humiliated and degraded monarch in the history of Spain."

"I believe that it is always wiser to settle difficulties by negotiation," Henry retorted.

News was brought to him of the unrest throughout the country.

In the pulpits and market squares the position was discussed. Was not a subject entitled to examine the conduct of his King? If the land was being drained of all its riches, if a state of anarchy had replaced that of law and order, had not the subject a right to protest?

From Seville and Cordova, from Burgos and Toledo, came the news that the people deplored the conduct of King Henry and were rallying to the support of King Alfonso and a regency.

Henry wept in his despair.

"Naked came I from my mother's womb," he cried. "And naked must I go down to the grave."

But he deplored war and let it be known that he would be very happy to negotiate a settlement.

* * *

There was at least one other who was not very happy about the turn of events, although he had been largely responsible for it. This was the Marquis of Villena.

He had believed that the youthful Alfonso would be his creature, and that he himself would be virtually ruler of Castile.

But this was not so. Don Diego Lopez de Zuñiga, the Counts of Benavente and Plascencia—those noblemen who had played a leading part in the charade which had been acted outside the walls of Avila—were also seeking power.

The Marquis wondered whether it might not be a good idea to seek some secret communication with Henry and thus, by some quick *volte-face*, score an advantage over his old allies who were fast becoming his new rivals.

He was brooding on this when his brother, Don Pedro Giron, came to him.

Don Pedro was still smarting under the rebuff which had been given him some time before by Isabella's mother. Grand Master of the Order of Calatrava though he was, he enjoyed the company of many mistresses; but there was not one who could make him forget the slight he had received at the hands of the Dowager Queen, nor could they collectively.

Don Pedro was a vindictive man; he was also a very vain man. The Dowager Queen had rejected his advances, and he often asked himself what he could do to anger her as much as she had angered him.

Poor mad thing, he said to himself. She did not know what was good for her.

It did soothe his vanity a little to remind himself that her madness was responsible for her rejection of him. It did please him a little to think of her living in retirement at Arevalo, sometimes, so he had heard, unaware of who she was and what was going on in the world.

He would like to get even with the girl too, that sedate little creature who had been hiding somewhere when he had made the proposals to her mother.

It was true that his brother, the great Marquis, sometimes talked to him of his plans.

"All is not going well, brother?" he asked on this occasion.

The Marquis frowned. "There are too many powerful men seeking more power. I found Henry easier to deal with."

"I have heard, brother, that Henry would give a great deal to have your friendship. He would be happy if you turned from Alfonso and his adherents back to him. Poor Henry, I have heard that he is ready to do a great deal for you if you would be his friend once more."

"Henry is a weak fool," said the Marquis.

"Alfonso is but a boy."

"That's true."

"Marquis, it is a pity that you cannot bind yourself more closely to Henry. Now, if you were not married already you might ask for the hand of Isabella in marriage. Such a connection would please the King, I am sure, and I do believe he would be ready to promise you anything to ensure your return."

The Marquis was silent for a while. He continued to study his brother through half-closed eyes.

* * *

The Queen and the Duke of Albuquerque were with the King. One on either side of him they explained to Henry what he must do.

"For," said the Queen, "you wish to end this strife. If you do not, there may be defeat for you. Alfonso is becoming more beloved of the people every day; which, my dear husband, is more than can be said for you."

"I know, I know," wailed Henry. "I am a most unhappy man, the most unhappy King that Spain has ever known."

"There must be an end to this strife, Highness," said the Duke.

"It *can* be brought about," the Queen added.

"Explain to me how. I would be ready to reward richly anyone who could put an end to our troubles."

The Queen smiled at her lover over the bowed head of her husband.

"Henry," she said, "there are two men who made the revolt, who lead the revolt. If they could be weaned from the traitors and brought to our side, the revolt would collapse. Alfonso would find himself without his supporters. Then our troubles would be over."

"You refer of course to the Marquis of Villena and the Archbishop," sighed Henry. "Once they were my friends . . . my very good friends. But enemies came between us."

"Yes, yes," said Joanna impatiently. "They must be brought back. They *can* be brought back."

"How so?"

"By making a bond, between our family and theirs, which is so strong that nothing can untie or break it."

"I repeat, how so?"

"Highness," said Beltran almost nervously, "you may not like what we are about to suggest."

"The King will like whatever is going to end his troubles," said the Queen scornfully.

"I pray you acquaint me with what you have in your minds," pleaded Henry.

"It is this," said the Queen. "The Archbishop and the Marquis are uncle and nephew. Therefore of one family. Let us unite the royal family of Castile with theirs . . . then both Archbishop and Marquis will be your most faithful adherents for ever."

"I do not understand."

"Marriage," hissed the Queen. "Marriage is the answer."

"But what marriage . . . with whom?"

"We have Isabella."

"My sister! And whom could she marry? Villena is married, and the Archbishop is a man of the Church."

"Villena has a brother."

"You mean Don Pedro?"

"Why not?"

"Don Pedro to marry a Princess of Castile!"

"The times are dangerous."

"Her mother would go completely mad."

"Let her. She is half way there already."

"And . . . the man . . . is a Grand Master of the Order of Calatrava, and sworn to celibacy."

"Bah! A dispensation from Rome would soon settle that."

"I could not agree to it. Isabella . . . that innocent child and that lecherous . . ."

"You do well to talk of *his* lechery!" The Queen laughed on a high note of scorn. "Isabella is grown up. She must know of the existence of lechers. After all, has she not been at Court for some time?"

"Isabella . . . marry that man!"

"Henry, you are as usual foolish. Here is an opportunity to right our troubles. Isabella must marry to save Castile from bloodshed and war. She must marry to save the throne for its rightful King."

Henry covered his face with his hands. Hideous pictures kept forming in his mind. Isabella, sedate and somewhat prim Isabella, whose upbringing had been so sternly pious . . . at the mercy of that coarse man, that notorious lecher!

"No," murmured Henry. "No. I'll not agree."

But the Queen smiled at her lover, and both knew that Henry could always be persuaded.

* * *

Isabella stood before her brother. The Queen was present and her eyes glittered—perhaps with malice.

"My dearest sister," said Henry, "you are no longer a child and it is time you married."

"Yes, Highness."

Isabella waited expectantly while Joanna watched her with amusement. The girl had heard fine stories of handsome Ferdinand, the young heir to Aragon. Ferdinand was a little hero and a handsome one at that. And Isabella believed that she was to have the pretty boy.

This, thought Joanna, will teach her to reject my brother, the King of Portugal! When she has had a taste of married life with Don Pedro she will wish she had not been so haughty, nor so foolish, as to reject the crown my brother offered her. Perhaps now she would wish to change her mind.

"I have decided," said Henry, "that you shall marry Don Pedro Giron, who is eager to become your husband. It is a match of which I . . . and the Queen . . . approve; and as you are of a marriageable age, we see no reason why there should be any delay."

Isabella had grown pale. Joanna was amused to see that the sedate dignity, for which she was now noted, had deserted her.

"I—I do not think I can have heard you correctly, Highness. You said that I was to marry . . ."

Henry's eyes were softened with pity. Not this innocent young girl to that coarse creature! He would not allow it.

But he said: "To Don Pedro Giron."

Don Pedro Giron! She remembered that scene in her mother's apartments: Don Pedro making obscene suggestions, her mother's indignation and horror—and her own. This was a nightmare surely. She could not really be in her half-brother's apartments. She must be dreaming.

There was a cold sweat on her forehead; her heart was beating uncertainly. Her voice was playing tricks and would not shout the protests which her brain dictated.

The Queen spoke then. "It is a good match and, my dear Isabella, you have rejected so many. We cannot allow you to reject another. Why, my dear, if you do that you will end with no husband at all."

"That would be preferable to . . . to . . ." stammered Isabella.

"Come, you were not meant to die a virgin." The Queen spoke gaily.

"But . . . Don Pedro . . ." began Isabella. "I think your Highnesses have forgotten that I am betrothed to Ferdinand, the heir of Aragon."

"The heir of Aragon!" laughed the Queen. "There will be little left for the heir of Aragon if the unhappy state of that country continues."

"And, Isabella," said Henry, "we, here in Castile, are not too happy, not too secure. The Marquis of Villena and the Archbishop of Toledo will be our friends when you are affianced to the brother of one and the nephew of the other. You see, my dear, Princesses must always serve their countries."

"I do not think any happy purpose could be served by such a . . . such a cruel and preposterous union."

"You are too young, Isabella, to understand."

"I am not too young to know that I would prefer death to marriage with that man."

"I think," said the Queen, "that you forget the respect due to the King and myself. We give you leave to retire. But before you go, let me say this: Suitors have been suggested to you and you have refused them. You should know that the King and I will allow no more refusals. You will prepare yourself for marriage, for in a few short weeks you are to be the bride of Don Pedro Giron."

Isabella curtsied and retired.

She still felt as though she were in a dream. That was her only comfort. This terrible suggestion could not be of this world.

It was too humiliating, too degrading, too heart-breaking to contemplate.

* * *

In her own apartment Isabella sat staring before her.

Beatriz, who drew authority from the fact that she was not only Isabella's maid of honour but her friend, dismissed everyone except Mencia de la Torre whom, next to herself, Isabella loved better than anyone in her circle.

"What can have happened?" whispered Mencia.

Beatriz shook her head. "Something has shocked her deeply."

"I have never seen her like this before."

"She has never been like this before." Beatriz knelt and took

Isabella's hand. "Dearest mistress," she implored, "would it not be easier if you talked to those who are ready to share your sorrows?"

Isabella's lips trembled, but still she did not speak.

Mencia also knelt; she buried her face in Isabella's skirts, for she could not bear to see that look of despair on the face of her beloved mistress.

Beatriz rose and poured out a little wine. She held this to Isabella's lips. "Please, dearest. It will revive you. It will bring back your power of speech. Let us share your trouble. Who knows, there may be something we can do to banish it."

Isabella allowed the wine to moisten her lips; and as Beatriz put an arm about her, she turned and buried her face against her friend's breast.

"Death," she muttered, "would I believe, be preferable."

Beatriz knew that what she had feared had now happened. The match with Ferdinand must have been broken off and a new suitor proposed.

"There must be some way of preventing this," said Beatriz.

Mencia raised her face and said passionately: "We will do anything . . . anything . . . to help, will we not, Beatriz?"

"Anything," Beatriz agreed.

Then Isabella spoke: "There is nothing you can do. This time they mean it. I saw it in the Queen's face. This time there will be no escaping it. Moreover, it is the wish of Villena, and that will decide it."

"It is a match for you?"

"Yes," said Isabella. "The most degrading match I could make. I think it has been chosen for me by the Queen as a deliberate revenge for having refused her brother and won the approval and sanction of the Cortes to do so. But this time . . ."

"Highness," whispered Mencia, "who?"

Isabella shuddered. "You will scarcely be able to believe it when I tell you. I cannot bear to say his name. I hate him. I despise him. I would rather be dead." She looked desperately from one to the other. "You see, I was trying to avoid saying his name, for even to speak of him fills me with such dread and disgust that I truly believe I shall die before the marriage ceremony can take place. But you will hear . . . if *I* do not tell you. The whole Court may be talking of it now. It is the brother of the Marquis of Villena—Don Pedro Giron."

Neither of her women could speak. Beatriz had turned pale with horror; Mencia rocked on her heels, forgetful of everything but this overwhelmingly distasteful news. The thought of her mistress, in the coarse hands of the man whose reputation was one of the most unsavoury in Castile, made Mencia put her hands over her face to prevent herself betraying the full force of her horror.

"I know what you are thinking," said Isabella. "Oh, Beatriz . . . Mencia . . . what shall I do? What *can* I do?"

"There must be some way out of this," Beatriz tried to soothe.

"They are determined. The Marquis naturally will do everything in his power to bring about the marriage. The Archbishop of Toledo will do the same. After all, this . . . this monster is his nephew. You see, my dear friends, they have taken Alfonso; they have forced him to call himself King of Castile while the King still lives. How do we know what that will cost him? And for myself I am to be the victim of the Queen's revenge, of Villena's and the Archbishop's ambition, and . . . the lust of this man."

Beatriz stood up; her face was hard and she, who Isabella had always known was possessed of a strong character, had never before looked so determined.

"There must be a way," she said, "and we will find it." Then suddenly her expression lightened. "But how can this marriage take place?" she demanded. "This man is a Grand Master of a religious Order and sworn to celibacy. Marriage is not for him."

Mencia clasped her hands together and looked eagerly at Isabella. "It's true, Highness, it's true," she cried.

"But of course it's true," insisted Beatriz. "He cannot marry. So that's an end to it. Depend upon it, this is merely a spiteful gesture of the Queen's. Nothing will come of it. And when you consider, how could it? It is too fantastic . . . too preposterous."

Isabella smiled at them wanly. She found a faint pleasure in the fact that they could comfort themselves thus, for they were two dear good friends who would suffer with her. She even allowed herself to be cheered a little. She must do something to lift herself from the blank despair into which she had fallen.

* * *

All through the night she had scarcely slept. She would awake from a doze, and the terrible knowledge would be there like a jailer sitting by her bed.

She dreamed of him; she saw him laying hands on her mother, making his obscene suggestions; and in her dream she ceased to be a looker-on, but the central figure in the repulsive scene.

She was pale when her women came to her. She asked that only Beatriz and Mencia should wait upon her. It would be unbearable to face any others, to see their pitying glances, for surely everyone would pity her.

Beatriz and Mencia were anxious. They talked together in her presence, because often when they addressed her she did not answer, for she did not hear.

"We shall hear no more of this," said Beatriz. "Of course Pedro Giron cannot marry."

"Of course he cannot!"

They did not tell Isabella that the news was spreading through the Court that the marriage was not to be long delayed, because it was going to be the means of luring Villena and the Archbishop from the side of the rebels. "Once the marriage is announced, the rebels will become of less importance. Once it is fact, Villena and the Archbishop will stand firmly with the King, who will be their kinsman."

They were glad that Isabella remained in her apartments; they did not wish her to hear what was being said.

The Queen came to see Isabella, and she was looking well pleased.

Isabella was lying on her bed when she entered. Beatriz and Mencia curtsied to the floor.

"What is wrong with the Infanta?" asked Joanna.

"She has been a little indisposed this day," Beatriz told her. "I fear she is too sick to receive Your Highness."

"That is sad," said Joanna. "She should be rejoicing at the prospect before her."

Beatriz and Mencia lowered their eyes; and the Queen went past them to the bed.

"Why, Isabella," she said, "I am sorry to see you sick. What is wrong? Is it something you have eaten?"

"It is nothing I have eaten," said Isabella.

"Well, I have good news for you. Perhaps you were a little anxious, eh? My dear sister, there is no need for further anxiety. I have come to tell you that a dispensation has arrived from Rome. Don Pedro is released from his vows. There is now no impediment to the marriage."

Isabella said nothing. She had known that there would be no difficulty in Don Pedro's obtaining his dispensation, because his powerful brother desired it.

"Well," coaxed Joanna, "does that not make you feel ready to leave your bed and dance with joy?"

Isabella raised herself on her elbow and looked stonily at Joanna.

"I shall not marry Don Pedro," she said. "I shall do everything in my power to prevent such an unworthy marriage for a Princess of Castile."

"Stubborn little virgin," said the Queen lightly. She put her face close to Isabella's and whispered: "There is nothing to fear, my dear, in marriage. Believe me, like so many of us, you will find much to delight you. Now, leave your bed and come down to the banquet which your brother is giving to celebrate this event."

"As I have nothing to celebrate, I shall stay here," Isabella replied.

"Oh come . . . come, you are being somewhat foolish."

"If my brother wishes me to come to his banquet, he will have to take me there by force. I warn you that should he do so, I shall then announce that this marriage is not only against my wishes but that the very thought of it fills me with dismay."

The Queen tried to hide her discomfiture and anger.

"You are sick," she said. "You must stay in your bed. Take care, Isabella. You must not over-excite yourself. Remember how your mother was affected. Your brother and I wish to please you in every possible way."

"Then perhaps you will leave me now."

The Queen inclined her head.

"Good day to you, Isabella. You need have no fear of marriage. You take these things too seriously."

With that she turned and left the apartment; and when Isabella called Beatriz and Mencia to her bedside she saw from the blank expression on their faces that they had heard all, and that now even they had lost all hope.

* * *

Preparations for the wedding were going on at great speed.

Villena and the Archbishop had brought their tremendous energy to the event. Henry was as eager. Once the marriage had taken place, the leaders of his enemies would become his friends.

Henry had always said that gifts should be bestowed on one's enemies to turn them into friends; he was following that policy now, for there was not a greater gift he could bestow, and on a more dangerous enemy, than the hand of his half-sister on Don Pedro.

There was murmuring in certain quarters. Some said that now Villena and his uncle would be more powerful than ever, and that was scarcely desirable; a few even deplored the fact that an innocent young girl was being given to a voluptuary of such evil reputation. But many declared that this was a way to put an end to civil war, and that such conflicts could only bring disaster to Castile.

Once the marriage had taken place and Villena and his uncle had transferred their allegiance from the rebles to the King's party, the revolt would collapse; Alfonso would be relegated to his position of heir to the throne, and there would no longer be this dangerous situation of two Kings 'reigning' at the same time.

As for Isabella, she felt numb with grief and fear as the days passed. She had lost a great deal of weight, for she could eat little. She had grown pale and drawn because she could not sleep.

She spent the days in her own apartments, lying on her bed, scarcely speaking; she prayed for long periods.

"Let me die," she implored, "rather than suffer this fate. Holy Mother of God, kill one of us . . . either him or myself. Save me from this impending dishonour and kill me that I may not be tempted to kill myself."

Somewhere in Spain was Ferdinand; had he heard of the fate which was about to fall upon her? Did he care? What had Ferdinand been thinking, all these years, of their betrothal? Perhaps he had not seen their possible union as she had, and to him she had been merely a match which would be advantageous to him. If he heard that he had lost her, perhaps he would shrug his shoulders, and look about him for another bride.

Ferdinand, fighting side by side with his father in his own turbulent Aragon, would have other matters with which to occupy himself.

She liked to imagine that he might come to save her from this terrible marriage. That was because she was a fanciful girl who had dreamed romantic dreams. She could not in her more reasonable moments hope that Ferdinand—a year younger than herself and as powerless as she was—could do anything to help her.

Her great comfort during these days of terror was Beatriz, who never left her. At night Beatriz would lie at the foot of her bed and, during the early hours of morning when sleep was quite impossible, they would talk together and Beatriz would make the wildest plans, such as flight from the Palace. This was impossible, they both knew, but there was a little comfort to be derived from such talk—or at least so it seemed in the dreary hours before dawn.

Beatriz would say: "It shall not be. We will find some means of preventing it. I swear it! I swear it!"

Her deep vibrating voice would shake the bed and, such was the power of her personality, she made Isabella almost believe her.

There was great strength in Beatriz; she had not the same love of law and order which was Isabella's main characteristic. There had been times in the past when Isabella had warned Beatriz against her rebellious attitude to life; now she was glad of it, glad of any mite of comfort which could come her way.

With the coming of each day, Isabella felt her load of misery growing.

"No escape," she murmured to herself. "No escape. And each day it comes nearer."

Andres de Cabrera came to visit his wife. He had scarcely seen her since Isabella had heard that she was to marry Don Pedro.

"I cannot leave her," Beatriz had told him, "no . . . not even for you. I must be with her all through the night, for I fear she might be tempted to do herself some injury."

Isabella received Andres with as much pleasure as she could show to anyone. He was very shocked to see the change in her. Gone was the serene Isabella. He felt saddened to see such a change; and he was doubly alarmed to see that Beatriz was almost equally affected.

"You cannot go on in this way," he remonstrated. "Highness, you must accept your fate. It is an evil one, I know, but you are a Princess of Castile. You will be able to extract obedience from this man."

"You can talk like that!" stormed Beatriz. "You can tell us to accept this fate! Look at her . . . look at my Isabella, and think of him . . . that . . . that . . . But I will not speak his name. Is it not enough that we are aware of him every hour of the day and night!"

Andres put his arm about his wife's shoulders. "Beatriz, my dearest, you must be reasonable."

"He tells me to be reasonable!" cried Beatriz. "It seems, Andres, that you do not know me if you can imagine I am going to stand aside and be reasonable while my beloved mistress is handed over to that coarse brute."

"Beatriz . . . Beatriz. . . ." He drew her to him and was aware of something hard in the bodice of her gown.

She laughed suddenly. Then she put her hand into her bodice and drew out a dagger.

"What is this?" cried Andres growing pale as her flashing eyes rested upon him.

"I will tell you," said Beatriz. "I have made a vow, husband. I have promised Isabella that she shall never fall into the hands of that crude monster. That is why I carry this dagger with me day and night."

"Beatriz, have you gone mad?"

"I am sane, Andres. I think I am the sanest person in this Palace. As soon as the Grand Master of Calatrava approaches my mistress, I shall be there between them. I shall take my dagger and plunge it into his heart."

"My dearest . . . what are you saying! What madness is this?"

"You do not understand. Someone must protect her. You do not know my Isabella. She, so proud, so . . . so pure . . . I think that she will kill herself rather than suffer this degradation. I shall save her by killing him before he has a chance to besmirch her with his foulness."

"Give me that dagger, Beatriz."

"No," said Beatriz, slipping it into the bodice of her dress.

"I demand that you give it to me."

"I am sorry, Andres," she answered calmly. "There are two people in this world for whom I would give my life if necessary. You are one. She is the other. I have sworn this solemn vow. There shall be no consummation of this barbarous marriage. That is the vow I have sworn. So it is no use your asking me for this dagger. It is for him, Andres."

"Beatriz, I implore you . . . think of *our* life together. Think of our future!"

"There could be no happiness for me if I did not do this thing for her."

"I cannot allow you to do it, Beatriz."

"What will you do, Andres? Inform on me? I shall die doubtless. Perhaps they will torture me first; perhaps they will say, This is a plot to assassinate Isabella's bridegroom. So, Andres, you will inform against your wife?"

He was silent.

"Andres, you will do no such thing. You must leave this to me. I have sworn he shall not deflower her. It is a sacred vow."

Her eyes were brilliant and her cheeks were scarlet; she looked very beautiful; and as powerful as a young goddess—tall, handsome and full of fire.

And he loved her dearly. He knew her well enough to understand that this was no wild talk. She was bold and completely courageous. He had no doubt that she would keep her word and, when the moment came, she would lift her hand and plunge the dagger into the heart of Isabella's bridegroom.

And when he murmured: "It must not be, Beatriz!" she answered: "It cannot be otherwise."

* * *

In his house at Almagro Don Pedro Giron was making preparations for his wedding. He had lost no time since the arrival of the dispensation from Rome.

He strolled about his apartment while his servants made ready his baggage. He put on the rich garments in which he would be married, and strutted before them.

"Look!" he cried to his servants. "Here you see the husband of a Princess of Castile. How does he look, eh?"

"My lord," was the answer, "there could not be a more worthy husband of a Princess of Castile."

"Ah!" laughed Don Pedro. "She will find me a worthy husband, I'll promise you."

And he continued to laugh, thinking of her—the prim young girl who had been in hiding when he had made certain proposals to her mother. He remembered her standing before them, her blue eyes scornful. He would teach her to be scornful!

He gave himself up to pleasant contemplation of his wedding night. Afterwards, he promised himself, she should be a different woman. She would never again dare show her scorn of him. Princess of Castile though she was he would show her who was her master.

He gave himself up to his sensual dreaming, to the contemplation of an orgy which would be all the more enticing because it would be shared by a prim and—oh, so sedate—Princess.

"Come on," he cried. "You sluggards, work harder. It is time we left. It is a long journey to Madrid."

"Yes, my lord. Yes, my lord."

How docile they were, how eager to please! They knew it would be the worse for them if they were not. She would soon learn also.

What a blessing it was to be the brother of a powerful man. But people must not forget that Don Pedro himself was also powerful—powerful in his own right.

One of the self-appointed tasks of Don Pedro was to assure those about him that, although he drew some of his power from his brother's high office, he was himself a man to be reckoned with.

He scowled at his servants. He was impatient to leave. He longed for the journey to be over; he longed for the wedding celebrations to begin.

* * *

With great pomp Don Pedro set out on the journey to Madrid. All along the road people came out to greet him; graciously he accepted their homage. Never had he been so pleased with himself. Why, he reckoned, he had come farther even than his brother, the Marquis. Had the Marquis ever aspired to the hand of a Princess? What glorious good fortune that he had joined the Order of the Calatrava and thus had escaped the web of matrimony. How disconcerting it would have been if this opportunity had come along and he had been unable to take advantage of it because of a previous entanglement. But no, a little dispensation from Rome had been all that was needed.

They would stay the first night at Villarubia, a little hamlet not far from Ciudad Real. Here members of the King's Court had come to greet him. He noticed with delight their obsequious manners. Already he had ceased to be merely the brother of the Marquis of Villena.

He had the innkeeper brought before him.

"Now, my man," he shouted, as he swaggered in his dazzling

garments, "I doubt you have ever entertained royalty before. Now's your chance to show us what you can do. And it had better be good. If it is not, you will be a most unhappy man."

"Yes, my lord . . . yes, Highness," stuttered the man. "We have been warned of your coming and have been working all day for your pleasure."

"It is what I expect," cried Don Pedro.

He was a little haughty with the officers of the King's Guard who had come to escort him on his way to Madrid. They must understand that in a few days' time he would be a member of the royal family.

The innkeeper's feast was good enough to satisfy even him; he gorged himself on the delicious meats and drank deep of the innkeeper's wine.

Furtive eyes watched him, and there were many at the table to think sadly of the Princess Isabella.

Don Pedro was helped to his bed by his servants. He was very drunk and sleepy, and incoherently he told them what a great man he was and how he would subdue his chaste and royal bride.

It was during the night that he awoke startled. His body was covered with a cold sweat and he realized that it was a gripping pain which had awakened him.

He struggled up in his bed and shouted to his servant.

* * *

Andres Cabrera came to Isabella's apartments and was greeted by his wife.

"Isabella?" he asked.

"She lies in her bed. She grows more and more listless."

"Then she has not heard the news. So I am the first to bring it to her."

Beatriz gripped her husband's arm and her eyes dilated. "What news?"

"Give me the dagger," he said. "You'll not need it now."

"You mean . . . ?"

"He was taken ill at Villarubia four days ago. The news has just been brought to me that he is dead. Soon all Madrid will know."

"Andres!" cried Beatriz, and there was a question in her eyes.

"Suffice it," he said, "that there will be no need for you to use your dagger."

Beatriz swayed a little, and for a few seconds Andres thought that the excess of emotion which she was undergoing would cause her to faint.

But she recovered herself. She gazed at him, and there was pride and gratitude in her eyes—and an infinite love for him.

"It is an act of God," she cried.

Andres answered: "We can call it that."

Beatriz took his hand and kissed it; then she laughed aloud and ran into Isabella's bedchamber.

She stood by the bed, looking down on her mistress. Andres had come to stand beside her.

"Great news!" cried Beatriz. "The best news that you could hear. There will be no marriage. Our prayers have been answered; he is dead."

Isabella sat up in bed and looked from Beatriz to Andres.

"Dead! Is it possible? But . . . but how?"

"At Villarubia," said Beatriz. "He was taken ill four days ago. I told you, did I not, that our prayers would be answered. Dearest Isabella, you see our fears were all for something which cannot happen."

"I cannot believe it," whispered Isabella. "It is miraculous. He was so strong . . . it seems impossible that he could . . . die. And you say he was taken ill. Of what . . . ? And . . . how?"

"Let us say," Beatriz answered, "that it was an Act of God. That is the happiest way of looking at this. We prayed for a miracle, Princesa; and our prayers have been granted."

Isabella rose from her bed and went to her *prie-Dieu.*

She knelt and gave thanks for her deliverance; and behind her stood Beatriz and Andres.

ALFONSO AT CARDEÑOSA

THE Archbishop of Toledo and his nephew the Marquis of Villena were closeted together, it was said, deep in mourning for Don Pedro.

The chief emotion of these ambitious men was however not sorrow but anger.

"There are spies among us," cried the militant Archbishop. "Worse than spies . . . assassins!"

"It is deplorable," agreed Villena sarcastically, "that they should have their spies and assassins, and that they should be as effective as our own."

"The whole of Castile is laughing at us," declared the Archbishop. "They are jeering because we presumed to ally our family with the royal one."

"And to think that we have been foiled in this!"

"I would have his servants seized, tortured. I would discover who had formulated this plot against us."

"Useless, Uncle. Servants under torture will tell any tale. And do we need to be led to the murderers of my brother? Do we not know that they are—our enemies? The trail would doubtless lead us to the royal Palace. That could be awkward."

"Nephew, are you suggesting that we should meekly accept this . . . this murder?"

"Meekly, no. But we should say to ourselves: Pedro, who could have linked our family with the royal one, has been murdered; therefore that little plan has failed. Well, we will show our enemies that it is dangerous to interfere with our plans. The marriage was accepted by Henry as an alternative to civil war. Very well, he has declined one, let him have the other."

The Archbishop's eyes were gleaming. He was ready now to play the part for which he had always longed.

He said: "Young Alfonso shall ride into battle by my side."

"It is the only way," said Villena. "We offered them peace and they retaliated by the murder of my brother. Very well, they have chosen. Now they shall have war."

* * *

On the plains of Almedo the rival forces were waiting.

The Archbishop, clad in armour, wore a scarlet cloak on which had been embroidered the white cross of the Church. He looked a magnificent figure, and his squadrons were ready to follow him into battle.

Alfonso, who was not quite fourteen years old at this time, could not help but be thrilled by the enthusiasm of the Archbishop. The boy Alfonso was dressed in glittering mail, and this would be his first taste of battle.

The Archbishop called Alfonso to him while they waited in the grey dawn light.

"My son," he said, "my Prince, this could be the most important day of your life. On these plains our enemies are gathered. What happens this day may decide your future, my future and, what is more important, the future of Castile. It may well be that after this day there will be *one* King of Castile, and that King will be yourself. Castile must become great. There must be an end to the anarchy which is spreading over our land. Remember that, when we go into battle. Come, let us pray for victory."

Alfonso pressed the palms of his hands together; he lowered his eyes; and with the Archbishop, in that camp on the plains of Almedo, he prayed for victory over his half-brother Henry.

* * *

In the opposing camp Henry waited with his men.

"How long the day seems in coming," said the Duke of Albuquerque.

Henry shivered; it seemed to him that the day came all too quickly.

Henry looked at this man who had played such a big part in his life. Beltran seemed as eager for the battle as he was for the revelries of the Court. Henry could not help feeling a great admiration for this man, who had all the bearing of a King and could contemplate going into battle without a trace of fear, although he must know that he would be considered one of the greatest prizes that could fall into the enemy's hands.

It was small wonder that Joanna had loved him.

Henry wished that there was some means of preventing the battle from taking place. He would be ready to listen to their terms; he would be ready to meet them. It seemed so senseless to fight and make terms afterwards. What could war mean but misery for those who took part in it?

"Have no fear, Highness," said Beltran, "we shall put them to flight."

"Ah, I wish I could be sure of that."

While he spoke information was brought to him that a messenger had arrived from the opposing camp.

"Give him safe conduct and send him in," said Henry.

The messenger was brought into the royal presence.

"It is a message I have from the Archbishop of Toledo for the Duke of Albuquerque, Highness."

"Then hand it to me," said Beltran.

Henry watched the Duke while he read the message and burst into loud laughter.

"Wait awhile," he said, "and I will give you an answer for the Archbishop."

"What message is this?" asked Henry hopefully. Could it be some offer of truce? But why should it be sent to the Duke, not the King? Surely the Archbishop knew that any offer of peace would be more eagerly accepted by the King than anyone else.

Beltran said: "It is a warning from the Archbishop, Highness. He tells me that I shall be foolish to venture on to the field this day. He says that no less than forty of his men have sworn to kill me. My chances of surviving the battle, he assures me, are very poor."

"My dear Beltran, you must not ride into battle today. There should be no battle. What good will it do any of us? Bloodshed of my subjects . . . that will be the result of this day's work."

"Highness, it is too late for such talk."

"It is never too late for peace."

"The Archbishop would not accept your peace offer except under the most degrading conditions. Nay, Highness. Today we go to do battle with our enemies. Have I permission to answer this note?"

Henry nodded gloomily, and the Duke smiled as he prepared his answer.

"What have you written?" he asked.

Beltran answered: "I have given him a description of my attire, so that those who have sworn to kill me shall have no difficulty in seeking me out."

* * *

Henry waited some miles from the battlefield. He had taken the first opportunity to retire when he had heard that the battle was going against his side.

For what good would it be, he reasoned with himself, to endanger the life of the King?

And he covered his face with his hands and wept for the folly of men determined to go to war.

Meanwhile the young Alfonso rode into battle side by side with the warlike Archbishop.

It was long, and the slaughter was great. Nor was it effective in forcing a decision. The courage of the Archbishop of Toledo was only matched by that of the Duke of Albuquerque, and after three hours of carnage such as had rarely been known before in Castile, the forces led by the Archbishop and Alfonso were forced to leave the battlefield in the possession of the King's men.

But Henry was not eager to take advantage of the fact that his army had not been routed; and Beltran, brave soldier that he was, was no strategist; and thus that which could have been called a victory was treated as a defeat.

Now Castile was a country divided. Each King ruled in that territory over which he held sway.

And following the advantage they had won on account of the King's refusal to regard the battle of Almedo as his victory, the Archbishop and the Marquis, with Alfonso as their figurehead, decided to march on Segovia.

* * *

Isabella, with Beatriz and Mencia, was eager for every item of news of Alfonso's progress.

"What is happening to our country?" she said one day as she sat with her friends. "In every town of Castile men of the same blood are fighting one another."

"What can be expected when our country is plunged in civil war!" Beatriz added.

"I dream of peace for Castile," murmured Isabella. "Here we sit stitching at our needlework, but, Beatriz, do you not think that if we were called upon to rule this land we could do it better than those in whose hands its government now rests?"

"Think!" cried Beatriz. "I am sure of it."

"If Castile could be ruled by you, Infanta, with Beatriz as your first minister," declared Mencia, "then I verily believe all our troubles would quickly be brought to an end."

"I shudder," said Isabella, "to think of my brother. It is long since I saw him. Do you remember the day the Archbishop called and told him he would be put under his care? I wonder . . . has all that has happened to him changed Alfonso?"

"It is hard to conjecture," Beatriz murmured. "In these last months he has become King."

"There can only be one King of Castile," Isabella reminded her. "And that is my half-brother Henry. Oh, how I wish that there was not this strife. Alfonso should be *heir* to the throne, because there is no doubt that the Queen's daughter is not the King's, but he should never have been proclaimed King. And to ride into battle against Henry . . . ! Oh, how I wish he had not done that."

"It was no fault of his," said Mencia.

"No," Beatriz agreed. "He is but a boy. He is only fourteen. How can he be blamed because they have caught him up in their fight for power!"

"Poor Alfonso. I tremble for him," murmured Isabella.

"All will be well," Beatriz soothed her. "Dearest Princesa, remember how on other occasions we have despaired, and how all has come right."

"Yes," said Isabella. "I was saved from a terrible fate. But is it not alarming to consider how a man . . . or a woman . . . can be alive and well one day and dead the next?"

"It has always been so," said the practical Beatriz. And she added significantly: "And sometimes it has proved a blessing."

"Listen!" cried Mencia. "I hear shouts from below. What can it be?"

"Go and see," said Beatriz.

Mencia got up to go, but before she had reached the door one of the men-at-arms rushed into the room.

"Princesa, ladies, the rebels are marching on the castle."

* * *

There was little resistance, for how could Isabella demand that resistance be shown against those at whose head rode her own brother.

As they stormed into the castle, she heard Alfonso's voice; it had changed since she had last heard it and grown deep, authoritative.

"Have a care. Remember, my sister, the Princess Isabella, is in the castle."

And then the door was flung open and there stood Alfonso—her little brother, seeming little no longer—not a boy but a soldier, a King, even though she would maintain he had no right to wear the crown.

"Isabella!" he cried; and he was young again. His face seemed to pucker childishly, and it was as though he were begging for her approval as he used to when he took his first tottering steps about the nursery.

"Brother . . . little brother!" Isabella was in his arms and for some seconds they clung together.

Then she took his face in her hands. "You are well, Alfonso, you are well?"

"Indeed yes. And you, dearest sister?"

"Yes . . . and so glad to see you once more, brother. Oh, Alfonso . . . Alfonso!"

"Isabella, we are together now. Let us stay together. I have rescued you from Henry. Henceforth it shall be you and I . . . brother and sister . . . together."

"Yes," she cried. "Yes . . ." And she lost her calm and was laughing in his arms.

* * *

And so she stayed with him, and on several occasions travelled with him through that territory which now considered him its King.

But she was perturbed. Her love of justice would not allow her to blind herself to the fact that he had usurped the throne, however unwillingly.

During those troublous months news came to Isabella of the disturbances which were rife throughout Castile. Old quarrels between certain noble families were renewed; nowhere was it safe for men or women to journey unescorted. Even men of the highest nobility took advantage of the situation to rob and pillage, and the Hermandad found itself almost useless against this tide of anarchy.

Alfonso's headquarters were at Avila, which had remained loyal to him since the occasion of that strange "coronation" outside its walls. On the Archbishop and Villena, to whom he owed his position, he bestowed the honours and favours they demanded.

Isabella remonstrated with him.

"While Henry lives you cannot be King of Castile, Alfonso," she told him, "for Henry is our father's eldest son and the only true King of Castile."

Alfonso had changed since those days when he had been afraid because he knew himself to be the tool of ambitious men. Alfonso had tasted the pleasures of kingship, and he was by no means prepared to relinquish them.

"But, Isabella," he pointed out, "a King rules by the will of his people. If he fails to please his people then he has no right to the crown."

"There are many in Castile who are still pleased to call Henry King," Isabella answered.

"Dear Isabella," replied her brother, "you are so good and so just. Henry has not been kind to you; he has tried to force you to a distasteful marriage—yet you would seem to support him."

"But it is not a question of kindness, brother. It is a matter of what is right. And Henry is King of Castile. It is you who are the impostor."

Alfonso smiled at her. "We must agree to differ," he said. "I am glad that, although you consider me an impostor, you still love me."

"You are my brother. Nothing can alter that. But one day I hope there will be a settlement and that you will be proclaimed heir to the throne. That is what I wish."

"The nobles would never agree."

"It is because they are seeking power rather than what is just and right, and they still use us, Alfonso, as puppets in their schemes. In supporting you they support that which they believe to be best for themselves, and those who support Henry do so for selfish reasons. It is only through what is just that good can come."

"Well, Isabella, although you would appear to be on the side of my enemies . . ."

"Never that! I am always for you, Alfonso. But your cause must be the just one, and you are now justly heir to the throne, but not the King."

"I would say, Isabella, that I would never force you to make a marriage which was distasteful to you. I would put nothing in the way of your match with Ferdinand of Aragon."

"Dear Alfonso, you wish me to be happy, as I wish you to be. For the moment let us rejoice in the fact that we are together."

"Shortly I leave for Avila, Isabella, and you must come with us."

"I would wish to do so," said Isabella.

"It is wonderful to have you with me. I like to ask your advice. And you know, Isabella, I take it often. It is merely this one great matter on which we disagree. Sister, let me tell you this: I do not wish to be unjust. If I were a little older I would tell these nobles that I would lay no claim to the crown until my half-brother dies or it is agreed by all that he should relinquish it. I would. Indeed, I would, Isabella. But you see, I am not old enough and I must obey these men. Isabella, what would become of me if I refused to do so?"

"Who shall say?"

"For you see, Isabella, I should be neither the friend of these men nor of my brother Henry. I should be in that waste land between them—the friend of neither, the enemy of both."

It was at such times that Isabella saw the frightened boy looking out from the eyes of Alfonso, the usurping King of Castile.

* * *

Isabella remained in Avila while Alfonso and his men went on to the little village of Cardeñosa, some two leagues away; for she had felt the need to linger awhile at the Convent of Santa Clara, where the nuns received her with Beatriz and Mencia.

Isabella had wanted to shut herself away, to meditate and pray. She did not ask that her marriage with Ferdinand might become a fact, because when she visualized leaving Castile for Aragon she reminded herself that that would mean leaving her brother.

"He needs me at this time," she told Beatriz. "Oh, when he is with his men, when he is conducting affairs of state, none would believe that he is little more than a child. But I know he is often a bewildered boy. I believe that, if it could be arranged that this wretched state of conflict could come to an end, none would be happier than Alfonso."

"There is some magic in a crown," mused Beatriz, "which makes those who feel it on their heads very reluctant to cast it aside."

"Yet Alfonso, in his heart, knows that he has no right to wear it yet."

"You know it, Princesa, and I verily believe that were it placed on your head before you felt it to be yours by right you would not accept it. But you are a woman in a million, dearest mistress. Have I not told you that you are good . . . as few are good?"

"You do not know me, Beatriz. Did I not rejoice at the deaths of Carlos and of Don Pedro? How can anyone be good who rejoices at the misfortune of others?"

"Bah!" said Beatriz, forgetting the deference due to a Princess. "You would have been inhuman not to rejoice on those occasions."

"A saint would not have rejoiced, so I pray you, Beatriz, do not endow me with saintliness, or you will be sadly disappointed. I would pray now for peace in our country, not because I am good, but because I know that the country's peace will make us all so much happier—myself, Henry and Alfonso."

There were special prayers in the Convent of Santa Clara, and these were for peace. Isabella had asked that these should be offered. She found life in the convent inspiring. She was ready to embrace its austerity; she was pleased to be able to give herself up to prayer and contemplation.

Isabella was to remember those days she spent in the convent as the end of a certain period of her life, but she could not know, as she walked the stone corridors, as she listened to the bells which called her to the chapel, and the chanting voices there, that events were taking shape which would force her to play a prominent part in the conflict which raged about her.

It was Beatriz who brought her the news.

They had asked Beatriz to do this because no other dared to do so.

And Beatriz came to her, her face blotched with the tears she had shed, for once unable to find words for what she had to say.

"What has happened, Beatriz?" asked Isabella, and her heart grew heavy with alarm.

When Beatriz shook her head and began to weep, Isabella went on: "Is it Alfonso?"

Beatriz nodded.

"He is ill?"

Beatriz looked at her with a tragic stare, and Isabella whispered: "Dead?"

Beatriz suddenly found words. "He retired to his room after supper. When his servants went to wake him they could not arouse him; he had died in his sleep."

"Poison . . ." murmured Isabella. She turned away and whispered: "So . . . it has happened to Alfonso."

She stared from the window. She did not see the black figures of the nuns hurrying to the chapel. She did not hear the tolling bell. In her mind's eye she saw Alfonso waking suddenly in the night, with the knowledge upon him. Perhaps he had called for his sister; for he would naturally call for her if he were in trouble.

And so . . . it had happened to Alfonso.

She did not weep. She felt too numb, too drained of feeling. She turned to Beatriz and said: "Where did it happen?"

"At Cardeñosa."

"And the news was brought . . . ?"

"A few minutes ago. Someone came to the convent from the town. They say that the whole of Avila knows of it, and that the town is plunged into mourning."

"We will go to Cardeñosa, Beatriz," said Isabella. "We will go at once and say our last farewells to Alfonso!"

Beatriz came to her mistress and put her arm about her. She shook her head sadly and her voice was poignant with emotion.

"No, Princesa, you can do no good. You can only add to your suffering."

"I wish to see Alfonso for the last time," stated Isabella blankly.

"You scourge yourself."

"He would wish me to be there. Come, Beatriz, we are leaving at once for Cardeñosa."

* * *

Isabella rode out from Avila, and as she did so the people in the streets turned their faces away from her. She was grateful to them for such understanding of her sorrow.

She had not yet begun to consider what the death of Alfonso would mean to her position; she had forgotten that those ambitious men, who had so ruthlessly terminated Alfonso's childhood to make him into a King, would now turn their attention to her. There was no room in her heart for more than this one overwhelming fact: Alfonso, little brother and companion of her early years, was dead.

She was surprised, when she rode into the little village of Cardeñosa, that there was no sign of mourning. She saw a group of soldiers cheerfully calling to each other; their laughter rang in her ears and it sounded inhuman.

When they noticed her they stopped their chatter, and saluted her, but she received their homage as though she were unaware of them. Was this all they cared for Alfonso?

Beatriz, in sudden anger, called out: "Is this the way you show respect for your King?"

The soldiers looked bewildered. One opened his mouth as though to speak, but Isabella with her little entourage had ridden on.

The grooms who took their horses wore the same cheerful looks as the soldiers they had seen in the streets.

Beatriz said impulsively: "You do not mourn in Cardeñosa as they do in Avila. Why not?"

"Mourn, my lady? Why should we mourn?"

Beatriz had to use great restraint to prevent herself giving the groom a slap across his face. "So you had no love for your King then?"

There was the same bewildered look on the groom's face as there had been on those of the soldiers in the village.

Then a voice from inside the inn which Alfonso had made his headquarters, called: "What is this? Has the Princess Isabella tired of convent life then, and come to join her brother?"

Beatriz saw Isabella turn pale; and she put out her arm to catch her, for she thought her mistress was about to faint. Could that have been the voice of a ghost? Could there be another who spoke with the voice of Alfonso?"

But there was Alfonso, full of health and vigour, running across the courtyard calling: "Isabella! So this is no lie. You are here then, sister."

Isabella slid from her horse and ran to her brother; she seized him in her arms and kissed him; then taking his face in her hands she stared into it.

"So it is you, Alfonso. It is really you. You are not a ghost. This is my brother . . . my little brother . . ."

"Well, I know of no one else it could be," said Alfonso, laughing.

"But I heard. . . . How . . . how could such wicked stories be spread abroad! Oh Alfonso . . . I am so happy."

And there, before the wondering eyes of grooms and soldiers, Isabella began to weep, not violently, but quietly; and they were tears of happiness.

Alfonso himself dried her eyes and, putting his arm about her, led her into the inn.

Beatriz walked beside them.

"It was an evil rumour," she said. "Avila is mourning your death. We heard that you had died in the night."

"These rumours!" said Alfonso. "How do they start? But let us not worry about that now. It is good to have you with me, Isabella. Now you will stay awhile? Tonight we shall have a special feast . . . as near a banquet as we can muster in this place." He called to his men: "My sister, the Princess Isabella, is here. Have them prepare a banquet worthy of her."

Alfonso was deeply moved by his sister's emotion. The fact that Isabella was usually so restrained made him aware of the depth of her feeling for him, and he was afraid he too would break down. He had to remind himself constantly that he was a King, and not a young boy any more.

He called to the innkeeper.

"A special banquet," he cried, "in honour of my sister's arrival! What can you put before us?"

"Highness, I have some chickens . . . very good, very tender; and there are some trout. . . ."

"Do your best, and let there be a banquet such as you have never served before, because my sister is come, and that is a very important matter to me."

Then he turned to Isabella and once more they embraced.

"Isabella," whispered Alfonso, "how glad I am that we are once more together. Let it be so as often as we can arrange it. Sister, I need you with me. Without you . . . I am still a little unsure."

"Yes, yes, Alfonso," she answered in the same quiet and tense tone, "we must be together. We need each other. In future . . . we must not be apart."

* * *

It was a merry supper that was served that night in the Cardeñosa inn.

The trout was delicious. Alfonso commented on its excellence and took a second helping.

Everyone was merry. It was pleasant, they said, to have been joined by the ladies, and they had heard that the Princess Isabella intended in future to accompany her brother on his journeys through his domain.

When they retired, Isabella and Beatriz talked about the day's doings and marvelled that they could have left Avila in such distress and have found such joy, the very same day, in Cardeñosa.

Beatriz, combing her mistress's hair, said: "Yet it surprises me how such rumours could be started."

"It is not difficult to understand, Beatriz. So many people in high places die suddenly that the story of another death is readily believed."

"That is so," agreed Beatriz and did not pursue the subject, for, she reasoned with herself, why spoil the day's pleasure?

Yet she was a little uneasy. Avila was only two leagues from Cardeñosa, and the rumour had a good hold on the former. How could it have happened . . . so close?

But she was not going to brood on that terrible moment, when the news had been brought to her and she realized it was her duty to break it to Isabella.

* * *

Isabella awoke early and for a few moments could not remember where she was. Then the events of the day before came back to her mind. That strange day which had begun in such sorrow and had ended in joy.

She was of course in the Cardeñosa inn.

She lay thinking of that moment when Alfonso had come out of the inn and for a few seconds she had thought she had seen his ghost. Now, she thought, I shall always be with him. I shall make it my duty to care for him, for after all he is but a boy and my own brother.

Perhaps she would be able to influence him, to persuade him that he could be no true King while Henry lived. If he were declared heir to the throne, she would be perfectly content; for she believed without doubt that the little Joanna had no right to that title. From now on, she told herself, Alfonso and I will be together.

There was a knocking at her door and she called to whoever was there to enter.

Beatriz came in. She was pale and she looked distraught.

"Highness," she said, "will you come to Alfonso's bedchamber?"

Isabella started up in dismay. "What has happened?"

"I have been asked to take you to him."

"He is ill!"

All the fears of yesterday were back with her.

"They cannot awaken him," said Beatriz. "They do not understand what can have happened."

Beatriz flung a robe about Isabella's shoulders and they went to Alfonso's chamber.

He lay in his bed, strangely unlike himself.

Isabella bent over him. "Alfonso . . . Alfonso, brother. It is Isabella. Wake up. What ails you?"

There was no response. The room was dark, for it had but one small window.

"I cannot see him clearly," said Isabella touching his forehead. Its coldness startled her. She took his hand; and it dropped lifelessly back to lie on the counterpane.

Isabella turned in horror to Beatriz who stood behind her.

Beatriz moved closer to the figure on the bed. She put her hand to the boy's heart and kept it there for some seconds while she wondered how she was going to say what she knew she must.

She turned to Isabella.

"No," cried Isabella. "*No!*"

Beatriz did not answer. But Isabella knew that there was no way of turning from the truth.

"But how . . . how?" she cried. "But why . . . ?"

Beatriz put an arm about her. "We will send for the doctors," she said. She turned angrily on his page. "Why did you not send for the doctors before this?"

"My lady, I came to wake him and he did not answer, and I was afraid; so I came for you. It is but a matter of ten minutes since I came into his room and found him lying thus. I came to you at once, knowing you would say how I should act."

"Fetch the doctors," Beatriz commanded.

The page went, and Isabella looked at her friend with heavy eyes.

"You know there is nothing the doctors can do, Beatriz?"

"Dearest, I fear it is so."

"So . . ." said Isabella, "I have lost him then. I have lost him after all."

Beatriz embraced her and for a little while Isabella remained passive.

The doctors came into the room. Isabella watched them listlessly as they stood about the bed, and they exchanged significant glances with each other.

Beatriz felt her control was snapping. "Well, say something!" she cried. "He is dead . . . dead . . . is he not?"

"We fear so, my lady."

"And . . . nothing can be done?"

"It is too late, my lady."

"Too late," whispered Isabella to herself. "How foolish I was to think I could help him, to think I could save him. How could I save him except by keeping him by my side day and night, by tasting every morsel of food before it touched his lips?"

Beatriz was crying: "But . . . how . . . *how* . . . ?"

That was a question they could not answer.

Isabella understood why she had heard the rumours in Avila. The planners had not been working in unison; something may have gone wrong at the inn while the carriers of the news went on and announced it in accordance with some preconceived plot.

Thus the news of Alfonso's death had been circulated *before* it happened.

How could Alfonso have died so suddenly unless someone had deliberately cut short his life? A few hours ago he had been full of life and health; and now he was dead.

Dear Alfonso, dear innocent Alfonso, this was what he had feared in those early days when he had talked so much of the fate of others. And it had come to him . . . even as he had feared it would.

She trusted that he had not suffered much. It was incredible that she should have been close by, and that he should have awakened in his need while she was sleeping peacefully unaware.

She saw Beatriz' smouldering eyes upon her. Beatriz would want to find those who had done this. She would want revenge.

But what would be the use? That would not bring Alfonso back to her.

THE HEIRESS TO THE THRONE

In the Convent of Santa Clara Isabella gave herself up to mourning.

She would sit thinking of the past when she and her mother had retired to Arevalo with little Alfonso. Now her mother lived, but could one call that existence living? And she, Isabella, was left to face a turbulent world.

There were times when she envied the young nuns who were about to take the veil and shut themselves off for ever from the world.

"I wish," she told Beatriz, "that I could so resign myself."

But Beatriz, who was always outspoken, shook her head. "No, my Infanta, you do not wish this. You know that a great future awaits you, and you would never turn your back on your destiny. Not for you the life of the cloistered nun. One day you will be a Queen. Your name will be honoured and remembered in the generations to come."

"Who can say?" murmured Isabella. "Might you not have made the same prophecy for my poor Alfonso?"

She had not been long at the convent when she had a visitor. The Archbishop of Toledo himself, representing the confederacy which was in revolt against the King, had travelled to the convent to see her. She received him with reserve and he was unusually humble.

"Condolences, Highness," said the Archbishop. "I know how you suffer through our great loss. I and my friends mourn with you."

"Yet," said Isabella, "had Alfonso never been acclaimed King of Castile he might be alive at this hour."

"It is true that he would not have been in Cardeñosa, and perhaps would not have contracted the plague."

"Or eaten trout!" said Isabella.

"Ah, these are dangerous times," murmured the Archbishop.

"That is why we need a firm government, a royal leader of integrity."

"The times must be dangerous in a country where two rulers are set up. I think that my brother might not have died if he had had God's blessing on his enterprise."

"But if, as you hint, Highness, his death was due to trout, that is the result of the criminality of man surely, not the justice of God."

"It may be," said Isabella, "that if God had looked with favour on Alfonso's accession, he would have prevented his death."

"Who shall say," said the Archbishop. "I come to remind Your Highness of the evil state of Castile and of the need for reform."

"There is no need to remind me of that," said Isabella, "for I have heard reports of the state of our country which fill me with such dismay that I could not forget them if I tried."

The Archbishop bowed his head. "Highness," he said, "we desire to proclaim you Queen of Castile and Leon."

"I thank you," said Isabella, "but while my brother Henry lives no one else has a right to wear the crown. Too long has there been conflict in Castile, which was largely due to the fact that it has two sovereigns."

"Highness, you cannot mean that you refuse to be proclaimed Queen!"

"That is exactly what I mean."

"But . . . this is incredible."

"I know it to be right."

"Why, Highness, were you Queen you could immediately begin to set right all that is wrong in Castile. My nephew and myself would be beside you. It could be the beginning of a new era for Castile."

Isabella was silent. She visualized all that she longed to do for her country. She had often planned how she would strengthen the Hermandad; how she would attempt to bring her people back to a more religious life, how she would establish a Court which would be in direct opposition to that of her brother.

"Our present Queen," murmured the Archbishop, "is becoming notorious on account of the lecherous life she leads. There was a time when she was content with one lover; now there must be many. Do you not see, Highness, what a bad example this sets our people?"

"Indeed I see," said Isabella.

"Then why do you hesitate?"

"Because, however good one's intentions, they will fail unless built on a foundation which is just. Were I to take what you offer me, I know I should be doing what is wrong. Therefore, I reject your offer."

The Archbishop was stunned; he had not believed in the true piety of Isabella, and he did not think she would be proof against this offer of the crown.

"What would please me," she went on, "would be to achieve reconciliation with my half-brother. It is the strife between two warring factions which is responsible for our troubles. Let us have peace and, since you believe the Queen's daughter to be illegitimate, I am next in the order of succession."

The Archbishop lifted his head.

"You agree with this?" she asked.

"Indeed I agree, Highness. It is at the root of all our troubles."

"Then, since you are assured of the Queen's adultery, I should be proclaimed heiress to the throne. Then there would be an end to this war, and matters would stand as it is proper that they should."

"But Highness, it is the throne itself that we are offering you."

"I shall never take it," Isabella told him firmly, "while my half-brother Henry lives."

And the astonished Archbishop was at length made to realize that she meant what she said.

* * *

His sister wanted to see him, mused Henry. Well, she had changed from the quiet little girl whose sedate manners had put a barrier of reserve between them.

She was an important person now. Villena and the Archbishop wanted to make her Queen—and it seemed that only Isabella's firm resolve that this should not be had prevented their crowning her as they had Alfonso.

Isabella had declared that she wanted peace.

Peace! thought Henry. None could want that more than I do.

He was ready to barter any of his possessions, ready to agree to whatever was suggested, for the sweet sake of peace.

He wanted Villena to be his friend again; he had great faith in Villena. The Cardinal Mendoza, who, from the time of that ceremony outside the walls of Avila, had supported Henry's cause with all the vigour of a strong nature, was not his friend as Villena had once been; he stood in awe of the Cardinal. As for Beltran de la Cueva, Duke of Albuquerque, he was more Joanna's friend than Henry's; they supported each other, those two; and often Henry felt they were not with him.

Now Villena and the Archbishop of Toledo, with Isabella replacing Alfonso as their figurehead, were asking for a meeting; and a meeting there should be.

He was surprised to receive a visit from Villena on the eve of the meeting. As soon as he was shown into Henry's presence, Villena begged to be left alone with the King.

Henry was only too willing to agree. The occasion reminded him of so many in the past.

"Highness," said Villena, kneeling before Henry, "I have great hopes that all may soon be as it once was between us."

Ready tears came to Henry's eyes. "Rise, my friend," he said. "Tell me what is in your mind."

"You are going to be asked to agree to certain proposals at Toros de Guisando. Highness, it may be difficult for you to agree to these proposals."

Villena had stood up and was smiling at the King as he used to in the days of their friendship.

A flicker of weariness crossed Henry's face.

"But," went on Villena, "would you take my advice?"

"Gladly I would consider it," said Henry.

"Highness, if there should be some condition which seems to you impossible, do not allow it to cause you too much concern."

"You mean?"

"That it is necessary to make peace now. If at a later date you feel that the conditions which were imposed upon you were unfair . . ." Villena lifted his shoulders.

Henry smiled. He was delighted to have Villena on his side again. Villena was a man who would take over the direction of state affairs completely, a man who struck fear into all who came into contact with him; it would be greatly desirable to place everything in his capable hands once more.

"It is desirable, Highness, that we should have peace at this time."

"Greatly desirable," agreed Henry.

"Then you will agree to these terms; and afterwards, if we decide they are untenable, we shall re-examine them."

"You mean . . . you and I will do so?" asked the King.

"If your Highness would graciously listen to my advice, how gladly would I give it."

Weak tears were in Henry's eyes. The long quarrel was over. The wily Villena had left the opposite camp and was his man once more.

* * *

The meeting took place at an inn which was known as the Venta de los Toros de Guisando. Toros de Guisando took its name from the stone figures of bulls which had been left on this spot by the invading armies of Julius Caesar, as their Latin inscriptions indicated.

Here Henry embraced Isabella with great warmth and was delighted to see that she was not unmoved by their meeting.

"Isabella," he said, "we meet in sorrow. The saints know I bore no resentment against Alfonso. It was not he who put the crown on his own head; others did that. Like you, I long for peace. Is it impossible for us to achieve that for which we so fervently long?"

"No, brother," said Isabella, "it shall not be impossible."

"I have heard, my dear," said Henry, "that you have refused to allow yourself to be proclaimed Queen of Castile. You are both wise and good."

"Brother," answered Isabella, "there could be only one monarch of Castile at this time, and you are by right that monarch."

"Isabella, I see that we shall come to terms."

This was very touching, thought the Archbishop, but it was time to discuss practical details.

"The first and most important item on our declaration is that the Princess Isabella be proclaimed heir to the crowns of Castile and Leon," he said.

"I agree to that," said Henry.

Isabella was astonished by his alacrity, for it could only mean that he accepted the fact that his wife's little daughter was not his.

"It would be necessary," went on the Archbishop, "that a free pardon be given to all who had taken part in the struggle."

"Gladly I give it," cried Henry.

"It grieves me to say this," went on the Archbishop, "but the conduct of the Queen is not that which can commend itself to her people."

The King shook his head sadly. Since Beltran had become so immersed in politics, it was true that Joanna had looked for lovers who had been more willing to make her the first consideration in their lives—and found them.

"We should require," went on the Archbishop, "that there be a divorce and the Queen sent back to Portugal."

Henry hesitated. He was wondering how he was going to face an enraged Joanna after agreeing to this. But he trusted in his ability to shift that responsibility on to other shoulders. After all, Joanna could find lovers in Portugal as readily as she did in Castile. He would assure her that it was none of his doing—if he had to tell her of the discussion.

He met Villena's gaze and a look of understanding passed between them.

"I . . . give my consent," said Henry.

"A Cortes should be invoked for the purpose of giving the Princess Isabella the title of heiress to the crowns of Castile and Leon."

"It shall be done," said Henry.

"And," went on the Archbishop, "the Princess Isabella shall not be forced to marry against her wishes; nor must she do so without the consent of yourself."

"I agree," said Henry.

"Then," cried the Archbishop, "is the Princess Isabella the heir to the crowns of Castile and Leon."

* * *

Beatriz could rejoice that her mistress had now been acclaimed as heiress to the crowns.

This was the surest way to soothe her grief, for Isabella was now suppressing her emotions in order that she might dedicate herself to the enormous task which, should she reach maturity, would almost certainly be hers.

Isabella was determined that under her rule Castile should become great.

She gave herself up to meditation and prayer; she was studying the history of her country and others. This dedication was, said Beatriz to Mencia, like a raft to a drowning creature.

Only thus could she grow away from the terrible shock of Alfonso's death, which had seemed doubly hard to bear because, after she had heard of his death, she had had the great joy of seeing him alive, only to lose him a few hours later.

Beatriz was determined to watch over her mistress. There would be many, she believed, ready to bring tasty trout to *her* table. There were the adherents of Queen Joanna and her daughter, who could wish for nothing which would serve them better than the death of Isabella.

But Isabella was not going to die. Beatriz had determined on that, and Beatriz was a very determined woman.

Isabella, heiress to the crowns of Castile and Leon, was not now merely the sister of the self-appointed King Alfonso. Now there were many to seek her hand in marriage.

Ambassadors from England arrived in Spain. They were seeking a bride for Richard of Gloucester, the brother of their King Edward IV, who himself, before his marriage to Elizabeth Grey, had considered Isabella as a possible Queen. Isabella would suit Richard very well.

"Why," said Beatriz, "if you made this match, it is possible that one day you might be Queen of England."

"But how could I serve Castile if I were England's Queen?" demanded Isabella.

There was a suitor from France. This was the Duke of Guienne, the brother of Louis XI; and he, since at this time Louis was without heirs, was next in succession to the throne of France.

"You would be Queen of France," said Beatriz.

But Isabella only shook her head and smiled.

"You still think of Ferdinand?"

"I have always considered myself betrothed to Ferdinand."

"You have made an image of him," Beatriz told her anxiously. "What if it should be a false one?"

"I do not believe that can be so."

"But, Princesa, how can you be sure? There are so many disappointments in life."

"Listen to me, Beatriz," said Isabella fervently. "Marriage with Ferdinand is the only marriage for me. By it we shall unite Castile and Aragon; do you not realize what that will mean for Spain? Sometimes I believe that it is part of a great design—a Divine design. You see how every obstacle in Ferdinand's progress to the throne of Aragon is being cleared away. And so, it would seem, is my way to the throne of Castile. Can that be a mere coincidence? I do not think so."

"You think then that you and Ferdinand are the elect of God."

Isabella clasped her hands together and lifted her eyes, and Beatriz caught her breath at the rapt expression she saw on her mistress's face.

Then Isabella said: "I believe it is God's will to make an all-Christian Spain. I believe that He wishes that to be a strong Spain. I believe that Ferdinand and I, when we are united, will do His Will and that we shall drive from this land all who do not belong to the Holy Catholic Church."

"You mean that together you and Ferdinand will convert or drive out every Jew and Moor from this country; that you will bring to the Christian Faith all those who follow other religions? What a mighty task! For centuries there have been Arabs in Spain."

"That is no reason why they should continue to remain here."

Beatriz was doubtful. Isabella, seeming so strong, was yet vulnerable. What if her Ferdinand were not the man she believed him to be? What if he were as lecherous as Don Pedro, as weak as her half-brother Henry?

"You will be strong. You will be capable of this, I know," said Beatriz. "But your partner must be equally strong and devoted to the Faith. How can we know that he is?"

"You doubt Ferdinand?"

"I know little of Ferdinand. Isabella, face the truth. What do *you* know of him?"

"I know this: that he is my betrothed husband and I will take no other."

Beatriz was silent awhile. Then she said: "Why do you not send a man to Aragon . . . that he may meet Ferdinand and tell you what you wish to know of him. Let him go there and let him go to France. Let him see the Duke of Guienne and discover what manner of man he is—and let him see Ferdinand and report on him. You could send your chaplain, Alonso de Coca. You could trust him."

Isabella's eyes sparkled.

"I will send him, Beatriz," she said. "But not because I need reassurance. I will send him that *you* may be assured that Ferdinand is the husband—and the only husband—for me."

* * *

The Marquis of Villena called on his uncle, the Archbishop of Toledo. Villena was a little uneasy, because he was unsure of his uncle's reaction to the turn in events.

Villena was a sly statesman; the Archbishop was a brave fighter and a man who, while seeking self-advancement, must believe in his cause. He was not the man—as his nephew was—to change his loyalties merely because they suited the immediate purpose.

Villena therefore began cautiously: "Isabella would never be the puppet that Alfonso was."

"It's true," said the Archbishop. "We have a real Queen here. One whom it will be our pleasure to serve. My only regret is that she refused to allow herself to be proclaimed Queen. She was right, of course, morally right. But I cannot help thinking that it would have been advantageous for our country if Isabella wore the crown which now is set so unbecomingly on Henry's head."

Villena remained silent. His uncle rejoiced in that quality of Isabella's which he deplored. Villena did not want a woman of purpose to rule Castile. He wanted a puppet whom he could direct. It was not easy to explain this to his fiery uncle.

"I do not think," went on the Archbishop, "that Alfonso's death is such a great calamity after all. I think that in Alfonso's sister we have our Queen. I give my allegiance to her and I believe she is beginning to understand that I wish to serve her." The Archbishop laughed. "She is inclined to distrust me. Was I not on the side of the rebels? And Isabella is so loyal to the crown, so determined to uphold its dignity, that she deplores rebels."

"Why, Uncle," said Villena, "you have allowed the young woman to bewitch you."

"I admit she impresses me deeply. I feel delighted to serve her."

"But, Uncle, what can a girl know of the governing of a country?"

"Depend upon it, nephew, she will never attempt to do that which is beyond her power. And I do assure you that the governing of the country is something she will quickly learn. Why, Isabella is dedicated to her task—and that is how all Kings and Queens should approach their duties."

"H'm," said Villena. "You have become mild, Uncle."

"Mild! Never! But I stand firmly beside our future Queen. And if any attack her, you will not have to complain of the mildness of Alfonso Carillo."

"Well, well, you are happy with this turn of events then."

"I feel more confident of the future of Castile than I ever did before."

Villena quickly took his leave of his uncle.

He had nothing to say to him; he knew they had arrived at a great divergence of opinion.

They would no longer work together; they were on opposite sides.

* * *

When Villena left the Archbishop, he made his way to Henry's apartments.

Henry received him eagerly. He could not show his gratitude sufficiently, so delighted was he to have Villena back in his camp.

Joanna the Queen had left him now. She had been so furious that he had agreed to divorce her that she had gone to Madrid, where she now lived scandalously, taking lover after lover as though in defiance of the verdict which had been passed on her at Toros de Guisando. It had been no use Henry's explaining to Joanna that he had no intention of keeping his word in regard to what had been laid down at the meeting with Isabella; Joanna was so furious, because he could even have *pretended* to agree to divorce her, that she had gone off in a rage.

That was of no great matter, for she had long brought him more uneasiness than pleasure; he was happy enough with his own mistresses, and he took care to choose those who would not dabble in politics.

And now here was his dear friend Villena, returned to be his friend and adviser, and so happily take charge of everything and instruct him as to what had to be done.

Villena explained that he had left his uncle and that the Archbishop had given his allegiance to Isabella, as he Villena had to Alfonso.

"He is a single-minded man," said Villena. "He can blind himself to his own advantages at times. After all, he is a man of the Church and he needs to have faith in something. He has now put that faith in Isabella. She has managed to appeal to his sense of righteousness. It is regrettable, Highness, for we have lost a useful ally."

"My dear Villena, I believe you will do very well without him."

"That may be. But I am a little disturbed about our Isabella. I was hoping a marriage with England or France would attract her. It would be comforting to know that she was no longer in Castile."

Henry nodded.

"It would be so very simple, if she were not here," went on Villena, "to proclaim the little Joanna heiress to the throne."

"So much easier," admitted Henry.

"Well, she declines England; she is preparing to decline France. You know why. She has set her heart on Ferdinand." Villena's face hardened. Not on any account was he going to allow the match with Aragon to become an accomplished fact. That would be the end of his ambitions, he knew. Isabella and Ferdinand together would be formidable opponents of his plans. Villena knew exactly what he wanted. A puppet King, a puppet heir, and himself the most powerful man in Castile. Where could he find a more suitable puppet King than Henry, where a more pliable puppet heiress than La Beltraneja? It was awkward to have to switch loyalties in this way, but he saw no help for it. Isabella had clearly shown that she would not be his puppet. Therefore Isabella must go.

"We cannot have meddlesome Ferdinand here. He would be ruling Castile in no time. That is why I propose to send an embassy into Portugal. Alfonso, I have reason to believe, will be ready to renew his suit."

"It is an excellent plan," said Henry. "If Isabella married him she would be Queen of Portugal."

"And that would take her finally from the Castilian scene," added Villena.

"Then let us send an embassy to Portugal."

"Highness, I have already forestalled your command. The embassy has left for Portugal."

"You always do exactly what I would do myself," said Henry.

"It is my greatest pleasure, Highness. And I have further news. Many powerful noblemen, including the Mendozas, disagree with the treaty of Toros de Guisando. They declare that the Infanta Joanna has not been proved illegitimate and that she, not Isabella, is the true heir to the throne."

"Oh?" said Henry mildly.

"I think," went on Villena slyly, "that when our Isabella has left for Portugal we shall have no difficulty in proclaiming your little daughter heir to the throne."

"It is what I would wish," said Henry. "Then, with Isabella in Portugal and Joanna proclaimed heiress of the throne of Castile, there would be no more strife. We should have peace."

* * *

Beatriz came hurrying to her mistress's apartment in the Castle at Ocaña, in which Isabella was resident.

"Highness, Alonso de Coca has returned."

"Then bring him to me at once," said Isabella.

The chaplain was brought to her presence and Isabella received him with affection.

"It seems long since you went away," she told him.

"Highness, it was only the desire to obey your command which kept me, so great was my longing for Castile."

Beatriz was chafing with impatience.

"Come, sit down," said Isabella, "and you shall tell me what you saw in the Courts of France and Aragon."

Alonso de Coca then began to tell his mistress of the manners of the French Court, and how the shabby King was so parsimonious that even his own courtiers were ashamed of him.

Beatriz cried. "And what of the Duke of Guienne?"

Alonso de Coca shook his head. "Why, Infanta, he is a feeble man, more like a woman than a man in manner. Moreover, his legs are weak so that he cannot dance, and he seems almost deformed. His eyes are weak also; they water continually, which gives the impression that he is always in tears."

"I do not think I should care much for such a husband," said Isabella looking demurely at Beatriz. "And what of your stay at the Court of Aragon? Did you set eyes on Ferdinand?"

"I did, Highness."

"Well, well," said the impatient Beatriz, "what of Ferdinand? Do his eyes water? Is he weak on his legs?"

Alonso de Coca laughed. "Ah, my Princesa, ah, my lady, Ferdinand bears no resemblance to the Duke of Guienne. His figure is all that the figure of a young Prince should be. His eyes flash; they do not water. His legs are so strong that he can do more than dance; he can fight beside his father and win the admiration of all by his bravery. He is fair of face and high of spirit. He is that Prince who could be most worthy of a young, beautiful and spirited Princess."

Isabella was looking in triumph at Beatriz, who grimaced and murmured : "Well, I rejoice. I rejoice with all my heart. It is not as I feared. I say now : 'Long life and happiness to Isabella and Ferdinand.' "

* * *

One of the pages came hurrying to the apartment of Beatriz, where she was chatting with Mencia de la Torre.

The page was white and trembling, and Beatriz was alarmed. She knew that, when anything disturbing happened, the servants always wished her to break the news to Isabella.

"What now?" she asked.

"My lady, a paper was nailed to the gates last night."

"What paper was this?"

"Shall I have it brought to you, my lady?"

"With all speed."

The page went out, and Beatriz turned to Mencia. "What now?" she murmured. "Oh, I fear that our Princess is far from the arms of her Ferdinand."

"She should send for him," said Mencia. "He would surely come."

"You forget that at Toros de Guisando she promised that she would not marry without the consent of the King, as he in turn promised that she should not be forced into marriage against her will. Do you not see that it could quite well be that Isabella will never marry at all, for such conditions, it seems, could produce a deadlock. It is for this reason that she does not communicate with Aragon. Isabella would keep her promise. But I wonder what has happened, and what paper this is."

The page returned and handed it to Beatriz.

She read it quickly and said to Mencia : "This is the work of her enemies. They declare that the proceedings at Toros de Guisando were not valid, that the Princess Joanna has not been proved illegitimate and is therefore heiress to the throne. They do not accept Isabella."

Beatriz screwed up the paper in her hands.

She murmured : "I see stormy days ahead for Isabella . . . and Ferdinand."

* * *

It was an angry Marquis of Villena who rode to Ocaña to visit Isabella.

He was determined to show her that she must obey the King's wishes—which were his own—and that she had offended deeply by her refusal of the King of Portugal.

She had received the Archbishop of Lisbon in her castle at Ocaña and, when he had put forward the proposals of his master, she had told him quite firmly that she had no intention of marrying the King of Portugal. The Archbishop of Lisbon had retired to his lodgings in Ocaña in great pique, declaring that this was a direct insult to his master.

It was for this reason that Villena came to Isabella.

She received him with dignity, yet she did not seek to hide the fact that she considered it impertinent of Henry, who at the meeting at Toros de Guisando had agreed that she should not be forced to marry without her consent, to send Villena to her thus.

"Princesa," said Villena when he was shown into her presence. His manner was almost curt, which was doubtless his way of telling her that he did not consider her to be heiress to the throne. "The King wishes you to know that he deeply deplores your attitude towards Alfonso, King of Portugal."

"I do not understand why he should," said Isabella. "I have explained with courtesy that I decline his suit. I could do no more nor less than that."

"You decline his suit! On what grounds?"

"That the marriage would not be one of my choosing."

"It is the wish of the King that you should marry the King of Portugal."

"I am sorry that I cannot fall in with the King's wishes in this respect."

"It is the King's *command* that you marry the King of Portugal."

"The King cannot so command me and expect me to obey. Has he forgotten our agreement at Toros de Guisando?"

"Your agreement at Toros de Guisando! That, my dear Princesa, is not taken very seriously in Castile."

"*I* take it seriously."

"That will avail you little, if no one else does. The King insists that you marry the King of Portugal."

"And I refuse."

"I am sorry, Infanta, but if you do not agree I may be forced to make you my prisoner. The King would have you remain in the royal fortress at Madrid until you obey his command."

Isabella's heart beat fast with alarm. They would make her a prisoner. She knew what could happen to prisoners whom they wanted out of the way. She looked calmly at Villena, but her outward appearance belied the fear within her.

She said: "You must give me a little time to consider this."

"I will leave you and return tomorrow," said Villena. "But then you must tell me that you consent to this marriage. If not . . ." He lifted his shoulders. "It would grieve me to make you my prisoner, but I am the King's servant and I must obey his commands."

With that he bowed and left her.

When he had gone she sent for Beatriz and told her all that had taken place.

"You see," she said, "they are determined to be rid of me. And they will be rid of me in one way or another. I have been offered a choice. I may go to Portugal as the bride of Alfonso, or I must go to Madrid as the King's prisoner. Beatriz, I have a feeling that, if I go to Madrid, one day my servants will come to me and find me as we found Alfonso."

"That shall not be!" declared Beatriz hotly.

"And the alternative . . . marriage with Alfonso? I swear I would prefer the Madrid prison."

"We have delayed too long," said Beatriz.

"Yes," said Isabella, and her eyes began to sparkle, "we have delayed too long."

"The King," went on Beatriz, "no longer carries out the vows he made at Toros de Guisando."

"So why should I?" demanded Isabella.

"Why indeed! A messenger could be sent into Aragon. It is time you were betrothed. I will go to the Archbishop of Toledo and Ferdinand's grandfather, Don Frederick Henriquez, and tell them you wish to see them urgently."

"That is right," said Isabella. "I will send an embassy into Aragon."

"This is no time," Beatriz declared, "for feminine modesty. This is a marriage of great importance to the state. Ferdinand's father has asked for your hand, has he not?"

"Yes, he has, and I shall send my embassy to tell him that I am now ready for marriage."

"It is time Ferdinand came to Castile. But, Isabella, Villena is here, and he is a determined man. It may well be that, before we have news from Ferdinand, he will have carried out his threat and you will be in that Madrid prison." Beatriz shuddered. "They will have to take me with you. I will taste everything before it touches your lips."

"Much good would that do!" cried Isabella. "If they were attempting to poison me, they would poison you. What should I do without you? No. We will *not* fall into their hands. We will stay out of their Madrid prison. And I think I know how."

"Then pray tell me, Highness, for I am in dreadful suspense."

"Villena would have to take me out of Ocaña, and the people of Ocaña love me . . . not the King. If we let it be known that I am threatened, they would rally to me and make it impossible for Villena to take me away."

"That is the answer," Beatriz agreed. "You may leave this to me. I shall see that it is known throughout the town that Villena is here to force you into a marriage which is distasteful to you, and that you have sworn to take as husband none other than handsome Ferdinand of Aragon."

* * *

The streets of Ocaña were crowded. People stood outside the castle and cheered themselves hoarse.

"Isabella for Castile!" they cried. "Ferdinand for Isabella!"

The children formed into bands; they made banners which they carried high. On some of these they had drawn grotesque figures to represent the middle-aged King of Portugal, and on others the young and handsome Ferdinand.

Sly songs were sung, extolling the beauty and bravery of Ferdinand, and jeering at the decrepit and lustful old man of Portugal.

And the purposes of these processions and their songs were: "We support Isabella, heiress to the crowns of Castile and Leon. And where Isabella wishes to marry, there shall she marry; and we will rise in a body against any who seek to deter her."

The Marquis of Villena, watching the processions from a window of his lodgings, ground his teeth in anger.

She had foiled him . . . as yet, for how could he convey her through those rebellious crowds—his prisoner? They would tear him to pieces rather than allow him to do so.

* * *

The Archbishop of Toledo and Don Frederick Henriquez were with Isabella.

The Archbishop had declared himself to be completely in favour of the Aragonese match.

For, as he explained, this would be the means of uniting Castile and Aragon, and unity was needed throughout Spain. Isabella's dream of an all-Catholic Spain had become the Archbishop's dream. He brought all his fire and fanaticism and laid them at her feet.

"The embassy," he said, "must be despatched into Aragon with all speed. Depend upon it, our enemies are growing restive. They will do all in their power to further the Portuguese match; and that, Highness, would be disastrous, as would any marriage which necessitated your leaving Castile."

"I am in entire agreement with you," said Isabella.

"Then," cried Don Frederick Henriquez, "why do we hesitate? Let the embassy set out at once, and I'll warrant that, in a very short time, my grandson will be riding into Castile to claim his bride."

Thus it was that when Villena and the Portuguese envoys rode disconsolately out of Ocaña, Isabella's embassy was riding with all speed to Aragon—and Ferdinand.

FERDINAND IN CASTILE

A GREAT sorrow had descended on the King of Aragon. His beloved wife was dying and he could not help but be aware of this.

Nor was Joan Henriquez ignorant of the fact. She had for several years fought against the internal disease which she knew to be a fatal one, and only her rare and intrepid spirit had kept her alive so long.

But there came a time when she could not ignore the warnings that she had but a few hours to live.

The King sat at her bedside, her hand in his. Ferdinand sat with them, and it was when the Queen's eyes fell on her son that mingling emotions moved across her face.

There he was, her Ferdinand, this handsome boy of sixteen, with his fair hair and strong features, in her eyes as beautiful as a god. For him she had become the woman she was, and even on her death-bed she could regret nothing.

She, the strong woman, was responsible for the existing state of affairs in Aragon. She had taken her place by the side of her son and husband in the fight to quell rebellion. She was wise enough to know that they were fortunate because Aragon was still theirs. She had risked a great deal for Ferdinand.

The Catalans would never forget what they called the murder of Carlos. They had refused to admit any member of the Aragonese Cortes into Barcelona; they had elected, in place of John of Aragon, René le Bon of Anjou to rule over them, in spite of the fact that he was an ageing man and could not fight, as he would have to, to hold what they had bestowed upon him.

But he had a son, John, Duke of Calabria and Lorraine, a bold adventurer who, with the secret help of sly Louis XI, came to do battle against the King of Aragon. King John of Aragon was no longer young. To help him there was his energetic wife and his brave son Ferdinand; but there were times when John felt that the ghost of his murdered son, Carlos, stood between him and final victory.

For some years John's eyesight had been failing him, and he lived in daily terror of going completely blind.

Now, beside his wife's bed, he could say to himself: "She will be taken from me, even as my eyesight. But the loss of her will mean more than the loss of my sight."

Was ever a man so broken? And he believed he knew why good fortune had forsaken him. The ghost of Carlos knew the answer too.

And so he sat by his wife's bed. He could not see her clearly, yet he remembered every detail of that well-loved face. He could not see the handsome boy kneeling there, yet the memory of that eager young face would never leave him.

"John," said Joan, and her fingers tightened on his, "it cannot be long now."

For answer he pressed her hand. He knew it was useless to deny the truth.

"I shall go," went on Joan, "with many sins on my conscience."

John kissed her hand. "You are the bravest and best woman who has ever lived in Aragon . . . or anywhere else."

"The most ambitious wife and mother," murmured Joan. "I lived for you two. All I did was for you. I remember that now. Perhaps because of that I may in some measure be forgiven."

"There will be no need of forgiveness."

"John . . . I sense a presence here. It is not you. It is not Ferdinand. It is another."

"There is no one here but ourselves, Mother," Ferdinand reassured her.

"Is there not? Then my mind wanders. I thought I saw Carlos at the foot of my bed."

"It could not be, my dearest," whispered John, "for he is long since dead."

"Dead . . . but perhaps not resting in his tomb."

Ferdinand raised his eyes and looked at his dying mother, at his aged and blind father. He thought: The end of the old life is near. She is going, and he will not live long after her.

It was as though Joan sensed his thoughts, as though she saw her beloved Ferdinand still but a boy. He was sixteen. It was not old enough to wage a war against Lorraine, against sly Louis. John must not die. If she had committed crimes—which she would commit again for Ferdinand—they must not have been committed in vain.

"John," she said, "are you there, John?"

"Yes, my dearest."

"Your eyes, John. Your eyes . . . You cannot see, can you?"

"Each day they grow more dim."

"There is a Hebrew doctor in Lerida. I have heard he can perform miracles. He has, it is said, restored sight to blind men. He must do that for you, John."

"My eyes are too far gone for that, my love. Do not think of me. Are you comfortable? Is there anything we can do to make you happier?"

"You must allow this man to perform the operation, John. It is necessary. Ferdinand . . ."

"I am here, my mother."

"Ah, Ferdinand, my son, my own son. I was speaking to your father. I would not forget that, though you be brave as a lion, you are young yet. You must be there, John, until he is a little older. You must not be blind. You must see this Jew. Promise me."

"I promise, my dearest."

She seemed contented now. She lay back on her pillows.

"Ferdinand," she whispered, "you will be King of Aragon. It is what I always intended for you, my darling."

"Yes, Mother."

"You will be a great King, Ferdinand. You will always remember what obstacles were in the way of your greatness and how I and your father removed them . . . one by one."

"I will remember, Mother."

"Oh Ferdinand, my son . . . Oh, John my husband, we are not alone, are we?"

"Yes, Mother, we are alone."

"Only the three of us here together, my love," whispered John.

"You are wrong," said Joan; "there is another. There is a presence here. Can you not see him? No, you cannot. It is because of your eyes. You must see that Jew, husband. You have promised. It is a sacred promise given on my death-bed. Ferdinand, you cannot see either for you are too young to see. But there is another here. He stares at me from the end of the bed. It is my stepson, Carlos. He comes to remind me. He is here that I may not forget my sins."

"She rambles," said Ferdinand. "Father, should I call the priests?"

"Yes, my son, call the priests. There is little time left, I fear."

"Ferdinand, you are leaving me."

"I will be back soon, Mother."

"Ferdinand, come close to me. Ferdinand, my son, my life, never forget me. I loved you, Ferdinand, as few are loved. Oh my son, how dear you have cost your mother."

"It is time to call the priests," said the King. "Ferdinand, delay no longer. There is so little time left. There is only time for repentance and departure."

So Ferdinand left the King and Queen of Aragon together, and the King bent over the bed and kissed the dying lips of the woman for love of whom he had murdered his first-born son.

* * *

King John of Aragon lay on his couch while the Jew performed the operation on his eye. The Jew had been reluctant. He was ready enough to try his skill on men of lesser rank, but he feared what would be his fate if an operation on the King should fail.

John lay still, scarcely feeling the pain, indeed being almost glad of it.

He had lost his wife and he no longer cared to live. For so long Joan had been everything to him. He saw her as the perfect wife, so handsome, so brave, so determined. He would not face the fact that it was due to her ambition for her own son that Aragon had suffered a long and bloody civil war. He had loved her with all the devotion of which he was capable; and now that she was gone, he could only find pleasure in carrying out her wishes.

That was why he now lay on this couch placing his life in the hands of the Hebrew doctor. If it were possible to save his eyes, this man would do it, he knew. There were no doctors in Spain to compare with the Jewish doctors, who had advanced far beyond the Spaniards in medical skill; and this man would know that his fortune would be made if he saved the eyes of the King.

And when I have the sight of one eye, thought John, I shall dedicate myself, as she would have wished, to making secure Ferdinand's succession to the throne of Aragon.

* * *

The operation was successful, and John had recovered the sight of one eye. He sent for the doctor and said: "Now you must perform the same operation on the other eye."

The man was afraid. He had done it once, but could he repeat it? Such operations were by no means always successful.

"Highness," he said, "I could not attempt to work on your second eye. The stars are against success."

"A plague on the stars!" cried John. "You will forget them and give my other eye its sight."

Everyone at Court trembled when they heard what was about to take place. They believed that, since the stars were against the performing of the operation, it could not succeed.

The doctor was in great fear, but he thought it more expedient to obey the King than the stars, and the operation was performed.

Thus John of Aragon, now almost eighty years of age, was cured of his blindness and, in obedience to the wishes of his dead wife, prepared himself to hold the crown of Aragon for Ferdinand.

* * *

With the return of his sight, John of Aragon regained a great deal of that energy which had been his chief characteristic in the past. John was shrewd and clever; his vulnerable spot had been his love for Joan Henriquez, and that in itself had been the stronger because of the strength of his character. His love for his wife had forced him to give to her son all the affection he had for his children, which meant robbing those by his first wife. John knew that the war, which had lasted so many years and had impoverished him and Aragon, was entirely due to his treatment of Carlos. Joan had demanded the sacrifice of Carlos, that her son Ferdinand might be his father's heir; and willingly had John given her all that she asked, because he found it impossible to deny her anything.

Now he did not regret what he had done. He was as determined as Joan had been that Ferdinand should rule Aragon.

The greatest pleasure left to him was to contemplate this handsome, virile youth, who had, under his mother's tuition, been trained for the great role which was being won for him.

If, thought John, before I was a father I had imagined a son who could be all that I looked for, he would have been exactly like Ferdinand.

Ferdinand was lusty; he was brave; he cherished what he had, because he had been fully aware that it had been won with blood and anguish, and he was as determined to hold it as his parents had been to give it to him.

How blessed am I in Ferdinand, his father often said.

And so to the Court of Aragon came the embassy led by Isabella's faithful servants, Gutierre de Cardenas and Alonso de Palencia.

John received them with great pleasure, for he knew their mission; his great regret was that Joan was not alive to share this triumph. He went to his son's apartment, and when they were alone together, he told him of the arrival of the embassy from Isabella.

"It is the best possible news," he said. "I could not imagine a match which would have given your mother greater pleasure."

"Isabella," mused Ferdinand. "I hear she is comely, though a little older than myself."

"A year! What is a year at your age?"

"It is not much perhaps. But I hear that she has a will of her own."

John laughed. "It will be for you to make your will hers. She is very ready to love you. Of that we are certain. She has refused many suitors, and on all these occasions has affirmed that she was betrothed to you."

"She will be faithful then," said Ferdinand.

"There are conditions," went on John. "It would seem that Castilians believe they are greatly honouring us in bestowing the hand of their future Queen upon us."

"Honouring us!" cried Ferdinand hotly. "We must make them understand that we are Aragon!"

"Ah, Aragon. In sorry state is Aragon at this time. By the saints, son, I wonder how we are going to fit you out for your wedding. Now, let us look at this matter calmly. Let us not quarrel with Castile. Let them believe for the present that they greatly honour us. We must get you married quickly, and then you will show your Isabella that you are lord and master."

"I will do that," said Ferdinand. "I hear she is handsome, yet haughty. She is a little prim." He smiled. "I shall teach her to cast aside her primness."

"You will remember that she is not a tavern girl."

"Yes, but tavern girls perhaps are not so very different from Queens in some respects."

"I would not have such remarks overheard and reported to Isabella. So have a care. Now listen. This Isabella is clearly a determined young woman. She has a year's advantage of you. You have been in battle, and have led to some extent a soldier's life, for all your tender years. She has lived a cloistered life but, make no mistake about it, she has been brought up to be a Queen. These are the conditions of the marriage agreement: You must live in Castile and not leave it without the consent of Isabella."

"What!" interrupted Ferdinand. "I should be as her slave."

"Hush, my son. Think of the richness of Castile and Leon; then think of poor Aragon. You will be the master—in time. At first it may be necessary to be a little more humble than you would wish to be."

"Well," said Ferdinand, "what next?"

"You are not to take property to yourself which belongs to the crown, nor make appointments without her consent. You shall jointly make decrees of a public nature; but she, personally, will nominate ecclesiastical benefices."

Ferdinand grimaced.

His father went on: "You will help her in every way to make war on the Moors."

"That I will do with all my heart and all my strength."

"You must respect the present King, and not ask for the return of that property in Castile which formerly belonged to us."

"She makes a hard bargain, this Isabella."

"But she comes with a handsome dowry. Moreover, she brings you Castile. Oh, my son, it cost your mother and myself a great deal to give you Aragon. Now comes Isabella to offer you Castile."

"Then, Father, shall we accept these conditions?"

"With great delight, my son. Come, you are not looking as pleased as you should."

"It would seem we must humble ourselves rather more than I like."

John put his arm about his son's shoulders.

"Come, come, my boy. I doubt not you will very soon have your own way. You are a handsome man, and Isabella—she may be the future Queen of Castile, but remember, she is also a woman."

Ferdinand laughed aloud.

He was completely confident of his power to rule both Aragon and Castile—and Isabella.

* * *

Isabella knew that her situation was dangerous and that the Marquis of Villena would sooner or later learn that she had sent an embassy to Aragon; she knew also that if it were discovered that she had gone as far as signing an agreement with Aragon, Villena would stop at nothing to prevent her marriage with Ferdinand.

Villena with Henry had gone to South Castile to deal with the last stronghold of the rebels; and Isabella, taking advantage of their absence, slipped quietly out of Ocaña to Madrigal.

Here she was received by the Bishop of Burgos; but she was somewhat alarmed, for he was the nephew of Villena and it occurred to her that he was probably more devoted to the Marquis than to that other relative, the Archbishop of Toledo.

She was right. The Bishop lost no time in sending a message to his uncle Villena telling him of Isabella's arrival.

Villena's reply came: "Have her watched. Bribe her servants, and if you should discover that she has been in touch with Aragon, lose no time in informing me."

The Bishop was eager to serve his powerful uncle, and in a very short time many servants in Isabella's entourage had been offered bribes to report Isabella's actions; and many letters which she wrote passed through the hands of the Bishop of Burgos before being sent on to their destination.

It was therefore not long before the Bishop discovered how far matters had gone between Isabella and Ferdinand.

* * *

Villena was furious. He raged against Isabella.

"This," he cried to Henry, "is your pious sister. She vows that she will not marry without your consent, but as soon as our backs are turned she is in communication with Aragon."

"We did break our part of the bargain," suggested Henry timidly.

Villena snapped his fingers. "There is one thing we can do now: make her our prisoner. We were foolish not to do so before."

"But we tried," said Henry. "And the people of Ocaña would not have it. I am afraid that Isabella, like young Alfonso, has that quality in her which arouses the loyalty of the people."

"The loyalty of the people!" snapped Villena. "We will put her where she cannot appeal to that—and where the gallant Ferdinand cannot reach her. We shall give orders at once for the Archbishop of Seville to go to Madrigal and take with him a strong enough force to seize and make her our prisoner."

"And what of the people of Madrigal? Will they allow her to be made a prisoner, any more than those of Ocaña did?"

"We shall make them aware of our displeasure, should they help her to resist arrest. We will strike such fear into them that they will not dare."

Henry looked worried. "She is, after all, my sister."

"Highness, are you prepared to leave this matter in my hands?"

"As ever, my dear friend."

* * *

Isabella was told that the leading citizen of Madrigal was asking to be admitted to her presence.

She received him at once.

"Highness," he said, "I come on behalf of my fellow citizens. We are in great peril, and so are you. We have received word from the King that you are about to be placed under arrest and that, should we attempt to help you, we shall suffer greatly. I have come to warn you to escape, for, in view of these threats, we of Madrigal dare do nothing to help you."

Isabella graciously thanked him for his warning and sent for two of her servants, both of whom she knew she could completely trust.

"I want you to take two messages for me—one to the Archbishop of Toledo and the other to Admiral Henriquez," she said. "This is a matter of the utmost urgency. There is not a second to lose. You will go at once, and with all speed."

As soon as they had gone she sent her page to summon Beatriz and Mencia to her presence, and when the women arrived she said calmly: "We are leaving Madrigal. I want you to go ahead of me. Go to Coca . . . it is not far; and wait for me there."

Beatriz was about to protest, but there were times when Isabella reminded her that she was the mistress, and Beatriz was always quick to appreciate her meaning.

A little hurt, the two women retired, and Isabella was uneasy until they had left. She knew that if the Bishop of Seville arrived to arrest her, he would take prisoner her confidential women also, and she wished to save Beatriz and Mencia even if she could not save herself.

They would be safe in Coca. She would not be. She needed to be under the safe protection of strong men.

Now began the anxious vigil when Isabella waited at her window. Soon she would hear the sound of advancing cavalry and shouts from below, and her future might depend upon this day's events. She did not know what would happen to her if she fell into the hands of the Bishop of Seville. She would be the King's prisoner—or more accurately, Villena's—and she did not think she would easily regain her freedom.

Then what would the future hold for her? An enforced marriage? With Alfonso of Portugal? With Richard of Gloucester? They would rid themselves of her in some way. They would wish to banish her either to Portugal or England. And if she refused?

Would it be the old familiar pattern? Would her servants find her one morning as Alfonso's had found him?

And Ferdinand? What of him? Eagerly he had accepted the marriage agreement. He understood, she was sure, even as she did, the glory that could come from the union of Castile and Aragon. But once she fell into the hands of the Archbishop of Seville, once Villena became the master of her fate, that would be the end of all their dreams and hopes.

And so she waited.

At length she heard what she listened for, and then . . . she saw him, the fiery, militant Archbishop of Toledo, now her loyal servant, ready to snatch her from under the very nose of the Bishop of Burgos who had meant to offer her up to his uncle, Villena.

She heard that resounding voice.

"Conduct me to the Princess Isabella."

He stood before her.

"Highness, there is little time to lose. I have soldiers below.

Enough to ensure our safe departure from this place, but it would be better if we left before Seville arrives with his troop. Come with all speed."

And so Isabella rode away from Madrigal only a little while before the Archbishop of Seville arrived to find the prize was gone.

"On!" cried Alfonso Carillo, Archbishop of Toledo, from now on Isabella's most firm supporter. "On to Valladolid, where we can be sure of a loyal welcome for the future Queen of Castile."

* * *

What joy it was to be received with acclaim by the citizens of Valladolid, and to know that they looked upon her as their future Queen.

But when the triumphant parade was over the Archbishop came to Isabella and reminded her—as she knew already—that this was no time for delay.

"I know my nephew, the Marquis of Villena," said the Archbishop. "He is a man of great resource, and he is as sly as a fox. I would meet him happily enough on the field of battle, but I would not care to have to match myself against his devious diplomacy. There is one thing we must do and that with all speed: hasten the marriage."

"I am willing that we should proceed with all haste," Isabella assured him.

"Then, Highness, I will despatch envoys at once to Saragossa, and this time we will inform Ferdinand that it is imperative that he set out for Castile with all speed."

"Let it be done," said Isabella.

* * *

When Villena heard that Isabella had escaped him he was furious.

"And to think," he said, "that it was due to my own uncle." Then he laughed, and there was a note of pride in his laughter. "Trust the old man to get there before that fool, Seville." And it amused him that members of his family should be deciding the fate of Castile even though they were now on opposite sides.

He went to the King.

"I know my uncle, and I'll swear that his first action will be to bring Ferdinand into Castile. He will marry him to Isabella, and thus we shall have not only Isabella's adherents but Aragon against us. Moreover, once Isabella is married we cannot hope to rid ourselves of her. It is imperative that Ferdinand and Isabella never meet."

"But how shall we prevent this?"

"By taking Ferdinand prisoner as soon as he sets foot in Castile."

"You can do this? But how?"

"Highness, we must do it. Let us make our plans. He will come through the frontier town of Osma. There he will receive the aid of Medina Celi. So he believes. We must make sure that Medina Celi is our man . . . not Isabella's."

"That will not be easy," said the King.

"But we will make sure of it," answered Villena. His eyes narrowed. "I will threaten our little Duke of Medina Celi with the direst penalties if he should aid Ferdinand. I assure Your Highness that Medina Celi will watch on our behalf, and the moment Ferdinand arrives we shall be informed. The King and Queen of Aragon went to great lengths to make him the heir to their crown. We will go to as great lengths to make sure he never touches that of Castile. Of course I have Your Highness's permission to deal with Medina Celi?"

"You must do as you wish, but how glad I shall be when all this strife is at an end."

"Leave this matter to me, Highness. Once we have curbed our haughty Isabella . . . once she is safely despatched to Portugal or . . . elsewhere . . . then, I promise you, there shall be peace in this land."

"I pray the saints it will be soon," sighed Henry.

* * *

When the embassy arrived at Saragossa, John of Aragon found himself in a quandary.

He sent for Ferdinand.

"Here is a pretty state of affairs," he said. "I hear from the Archbishop of Toledo that Villena is trying to prevent the match; and the Archbishop fears he will succeed unless the marriage takes place immediately. He suggests that you set out at once for Valladolid."

"Well, Father, I am ready."

John of Aragon groaned. "My son, how can you go into Castile as Isabella's bridegroom, when there are no more than three hundred *enriques* in the treasury? What sort of figure will you cut!"

Ferdinand looked grave. "I cannot go as a beggar, Father."

"I do not know how else you can go. I had hoped that there would be a little respite to enable me to get the money for your journey. I am making you King of Sicily so that you will enter Castile with the rank of King, but how can we possibly send you without the necessary pomp, the glittering garments and all that you will need for your wedding?"

"Then we must wait . . ."

"To delay could be to lose Isabella. Villena is working with all his might against the match. I believe his plan is to rid Castile of Isabella—perhaps by marriage, perhaps by other methods—and no doubt set up La Beltraneja in her place. My son, you may have to fight your way to Isabella. . . ." John stopped, and a smile spread across his face. "Why, Ferdinand, I think I have the solution to our problem. Listen to me. I will tell you briefly and then we will lay this plan before a secret council."

"I am eager to hear what you propose, Father," said Ferdinand.

"The frontier from Almazin to Guadalajara will be dangerous for you to cross. It is the property of the Mendoza family which, as you know, supports La Beltraneja. If you travelled as yourself, with the embassy, nobles and servants, you would find it impossible to cross that frontier unobserved. But what say you, my son, if you went with a party of merchants? What if you were disguised as one of their servants? I'll warrant then that you would travel to Valladolid unmolested."

Ferdinand wrinkled his nose in distaste. "In the attire of a servant, Father!"

John put his arm about the young man's shoulder.

"It is the answer," he cried. "You will remember, Ferdinand, that a kingdom is at stake. Now I consider this, I see that it is the only manner in which you could hope to reach Isabella in safety. And think! It provides us with the excuse we need. What folly to equip you as a King when you travel as a merchant's lackey!"

* * *

As soon as the innkeeper received the party of merchants he noticed their lackey. The fellow had an insolent air, and it was clear that he thought himself superior to the position he occupied.

"Here, fellow," cried the innkeeper when the merchants were being ushered to the table, "you'll need to go to the stables and see that your masters' mules are being watered and fed."

The arrogant fellow's eyes flashed, and for a moment the innkeeper thought he struck an attitude as though he would draw his sword—if he possessed one.

One of the merchants intervened. "My good host, let your grooms attend to our mules . . . water and feed them while we ourselves are at table. As for our servant here, he will wait upon us."

"As you wish, good sirs," was the answer.

"And," went on the merchant, "bring in the dishes. Our man will do the rest. We would be left in peace to eat our meal as we have business to discuss."

"I am at your service, my masters."

When the landlord had left them, Ferdinand grimaced.

"I fear I make an indifferent lackey."

"Considering that Your Highness has never played the part before, you do it very well."

"Yet I fancy the man believes me to be an unusual servant, and that is what we must avoid. I shall be glad when the role is ended. It becomes me not."

Ferdinand touched the rough cloth of his serving-man's doublet with distaste. He was young enough to be vain of his personal appearance, and because all through his life he had lived in fear of losing his inheritance, his dignity was especially dear to him. He was less philosophical than his father, and less able to stomach the indignity of creeping into Castile like a beggar. He had to accept the fact that Castile and Leon were of greater significance than Aragon; and it went hard with him that he, a man and prospective husband, should have to take second place with his future wife.

It should not continue to be so, he told himself, once he and Isabella were married.

"It will not be long, Highness," he was told, "that you have to masquerade thus. When we reach the castle of the Count of Treviño in Osma it will not be necessary for you to travel thus ignobly. And Treviño is waiting for us with a right good welcome."

"I can scarcely wait for our arrival at Osma."

The innkeeper had come in to usher into the room a servant who carried a steaming dish of *olla podrida*. It smelt good, and for a moment the men sniffed at it so hungrily that Ferdinand, who had been leaning against the table talking to the merchants, forgot to adopt the attitude of a servant.

So surprised was the innkeeper that he stopped and stared.

Ferdinand immediately understood and tried to put on a humble air, but he felt he had betrayed himself.

When he was again alone with his friends, he said: "I hope the innkeeper does not suspect that we are not what we pretend to be."

"We will soon deal with him, Highness, should he show too much curiosity."

Ferdinand said it would be better if he were not addressed as Highness until the journey was over.

As they were eating their meal, one of the men looked up suddenly and saw a face at the window. It disappeared immediately, so that he was not sure whether it had been that of the innkeeper or one of his servants.

"Look! The window," he said quietly; but the others were too late to see the face.

When he explained what he had seen dismay fell on the company.

"There can be no doubt," said Ferdinand, "that we are under suspicion."

"I will go out and slit the throat of the inquisitive innkeeper and all his servants," cried one member of the band.

"That would indeed be folly," said another. "Perhaps the same idle curiosity is shown here towards all travellers. Eat as fast as you can and we will be gone. It may well be that someone has already sent a message to our enemies, telling them of our arrival at this inn."

"They could not possibly see anything strange in a party of merchants . . . No, it is curiosity, nothing more. Come, let us eat in peace."

"Eat certainly," said Ferdinand, "but there is too much at stake to linger. Doubtless I have betrayed us by my manners. Let us hasten away from this place. We will pass the night out of doors or in some inn which we feel will be quite safe . . . but not here."

They ate hurriedly and in silence, and one of their party called in the innkeeper and settled the account.

They left the inn and rode on, but when they had gone some distance they began to laugh at their fears. The innkeeper and his servants were oafs who would know nothing of the coming of the heir of Aragon into Castile, and they had allowed themselves to be frightened without cause.

"Spend the night out of doors!" cried Ferdinand. "Certainly not. We will find an inn and have a good night's sleep there."

The man who had paid the innkeeper gave a sudden cry of dismay.

He had pulled up his mule, and the others pulled up with him.

"The purse," he said, "I must have left it on the dining table!"

They were all dismayed, for the purse contained the money to defray their expenses during the journey.

"I must go back for it," he said.

There was a short silence.

Then Ferdinand said: "What if they did suspect? What if they make you their prisoner? No. We are well away from that inn. We will go on, without money. Castile is too big a prize to be lost for the sake of a few *enriques*."

* * *

It was far into the night when they arrived outside the castle of the Count of Treviño.

Inside the castle there was tension.

The Count had given his instructions. "We must be prepared for an attack by our enemies. They know that we are for Isabella and that we shall offer shelter to the Prince of Aragon when he passes on his way to Valladolid. It may well be that the King's men will attempt to storm the castle and take possession of it so that they, not we, will be here when Ferdinand arrives. Therefore keep watch. Let no one enter. Guard well the drawbridge and be ready on the battlements with your missiles."

So the castle was bristling with defences when Ferdinand and his party arrived.

They were very weary and exhausted, for they had ridden through the night and the day without money to buy a meal; and when they came to the castle gates Ferdinand gave a great shout of joy.

"Open up!" he cried. "Open up! And delay not."

But one of the guards watching from the battlements, determined to defend the castle against the Count's enemies, believed that the King's men were below.

He dislodged one of the great boulders which had been placed on the battlements for this purpose and sent it hurtling down to kill the man who had advanced a few paces ahead of the group.

This was Ferdinand; and the guard's timing was sure.

Down came the massive boulder.

"Highness!" shouted one of the party who were watching Ferdinand, and there was such a shrill note of urgency in his voice that Ferdinand, alerted, jumped clear.

He was only just in time for the boulder landed on the spot where he had been standing, and Ferdinand had escaped death by only a few feet.

Startled into anger, Ferdinand called: "Is this the welcome that you promised us? I come to you, I, Ferdinand of Aragon, having travelled far in disguise, and you do your best to kill me after promising me succour!"

There was consternation in the castle. Torches appeared and faces were seen peering from the battlements.

Then there was shouting and creaking as the drawbridge was lowered, and the Count of Treviño himself hurried forward to kneel and ask pardon for the mistake which might so easily have turned the whole enterprise into tragedy.

"You shall have my pardon as soon as you give us food," cried Ferdinand. "We are starving, my men and I."

The Count gave orders to his servants; and across the drawbridge and into the great hall went Ferdinand's party; and there, at a table laden with food which had been prepared for them, the travellers refreshed themselves and laughed together at their adventures. For the most dangerous part of the journey was over. Tomorrow they would set forth with an armed escort supplied, at Isabella's command, by the Count of Treviño. Then it would be on to Dueñas, where Ferdinand would cease to be regarded as a humble lackey, and where he would find many noblemen rallying to his cause, eager to accompany him to Valladolid and Isabella.

THE MARRIAGE OF ISABELLA

In the house of Juan de Vivero, the most magnificent in Valladolid, which had been lent to Isabella on her triumphant entry into that city, she now waited.

This was, she believed, so far the most important moment of her life. For years she had dreamed of her marriage with Ferdinand. But for her own determination she would have long since been married elsewhere. And now Ferdinand was only a few miles from her, and this very night he would stand before her.

It was not easy to control her emotion. She must be calm; she must remember that she was not merely a Princess of Castile—she was its future Queen.

She had a large dowry to bring her husband, and on that account she rejoiced. But in spite of her dignity and position she was anxious as to whether she herself would appeal to Ferdinand, for this was to be the perfect marriage. Not only was it to be a welding together of Castile and Aragon, to make a stronger and all-Christian Spain; it was to be the mating of two people, whose interests and affections must be so entwined that they were as one person.

It was this second factor which gave her cause for anxiety.

I know I shall love Ferdinand, she told herself; but how can I be sure that he will love me?

He had lived the life of a man, although he was a year her junior; and she, although she had trained herself to understand state matters, had lived the sheltered life which had been necessary if she were not to be contaminated by her brother's licentious Court.

The Admiral and the Archbishop had talked seriously to her concerning the impending interview.

"Do not forget," said the Archbishop, "that while he can only make you Queen of Aragon, you can make him King of Castile and Leon. What is Aragon compared with Castile and Leon? You must never let him forget that you bring more to this marriage than he does, that it is you who will be Queen, and that his title of King will be one of courtesy."

"I do not think," said Isabella gently, "that a marriage such as this should begin by a jostling for position."

"I trust," said the Archbishop testily, "that you are not going to be overpowered by his good looks."

"I trust," replied Isabella, with a smile, "that I am going to be pleased with them."

The Archbishop regarded her with some sternness. He had admired her very much, and it was for this reason that he had decided to support her, but he wanted her to remember that it was he who was largely responsible for putting her where she was, and if she wanted to retain his co-operation she must listen to his advice—and take it.

He did not intend to allow Ferdinand to assume too much power, to take that place as chief adviser to Isabella which he, Alfonso Carillo, Archbishop of Toledo, had held.

"It might seem advisable," he said now, "that Ferdinand should be asked to perform some act of homage—merely to show that, as far as Castile and Leon are concerned, he is in an inferior position."

Isabella smiled, but her voice was firm. "I shall certainly not ask my husband for any such homage," she declared.

The Archbishop left her in a far from pleased frame of mind, and prepared himself to receive Ferdinand, who was shortly to arrive from Dueñas with as few as four of his attendants.

* * *

It was midnight when Ferdinand arrived at the house of Juan de Vivero.

Clothes had been lent to him, so he came not as the merchants' lackey but as King of Sicily.

The Archbishop received him and, when they met, Ferdinand was glad that his shrewd father had had the foresight to bestow the title of King upon him, for there was an arrogance about the Archbishop of Toledo which was not lost on Ferdinand. He hoped the man had not imparted the same quality to Isabella. Yet even as this thought entered his mind, Ferdinand smiled. He had a way with women—and Isabella, for all that she was the heiress of Castile and Leon, was a woman.

"The Princess Isabella is waiting to receive you," said the Archbishop. "I will conduct you to her presence."

Ferdinand inclined his head and the Archbishop led the way to Isabella's apartments.

"His Highness Don Ferdinand, King of Sicily and Prince of Aragon."

Isabella rose to her feet and stood for a few seconds, trembling with the force of her emotions.

And there he was—Ferdinand in the flesh, the dream become a reality, as handsome as she had imagined him (no, more so, she hastened to tell herself; for how could any person—imagined or real—compare with this young man who now stood before her?).

Ferdinand, seventeen years old, with fair hair and a complexion toned to bronze by exposure to the sun and air, a grown man in physique, slender and perfectly proportioned! His brow was high and broad, his expression alert; and he was too young and unmarked as yet for that alertness to be construed as cupidity.

Isabella was conscious of a great gladness, for the Ferdinand she saw before her had stepped right out of her dreams.

Ferdinand was gracious; he took her hand, bowed low over it; then he lifted his eyes to her face and there was a smile in them, for he too was not displeased.

What a joyous thing it was, he thought, when a royal person need not take someone who was aged and ugly. Here she was, his Isabella, the best possible match in Spain, and she was only one year older, and looked younger, than he was.

He saw a young woman somewhat tall, with a complexion as fair as his own, and bright hair with a gleam of red in it which was enchanting. And what pleased him most was the gentle manner, the almost mild expression in the blue eyes.

Charming Isabella, so suitable, so young and—he believed—so malleable.

Ferdinand, in his swaggering youth, told himself that he would very soon be master of Castile, Leon—and Isabella.

"I welcome you with all my heart," said Isabella. "Castile and Leon welcome you. We have long awaited your coming."

Ferdinand, who had retained her hand, with a swift gesture pressed an impassioned kiss upon it which brought a faint colour into Isabella's cheeks and a shine to her eyes. "I would," he said, "that I had come months ago . . . years ago. . . ."

"Suffice it that you are here. I pray you sit with me."

Together they went to the two ornate chairs which had been set side by side like two thrones.

"You have had a hazardous journey," said Isabella. And when he told her of his adventures at the inn and at the Count of Treviño's castle, Isabella turned pale at the thought of what could so easily have happened to him.

"It is of no importance," Ferdinand murmured. "You do not know it, but I have often with my father faced death in battle."

"But now you are safely here," said Isabella; and there was a note of exultation in her voice. She believed that this marriage had certainly been made in Heaven and that nothing on Earth could prevent its taking place.

The Archbishop, who was standing by listening to this conversation, was growing a little impatient.

"The marriage," he reminded them, "is not yet an accomplished fact. Our enemies will, even now, do all in their power to prevent it. It must take place at the earliest possible moment, and I suggest four days hence."

Ferdinand threw a passionate glance at Isabella who, taken off her guard by the prospect of such an early date for their marriage, returned it.

"There should," went on the Archbishop, "be a solemn betrothal immediately, and it is for this reason that Your Highness has ridden to Valladolid at this late hour."

"Then," said Isabella, "let us proceed with all speed."

The Archbishop then solemnly declared them betrothed, and there, before those very few witnesses, Ferdinand and Isabella ceremoniously joined hands.

So shall it be until death shall part us, Isabella told herself; and she was aware of a greater happiness than she had hitherto known.

* * *

There was great activity in the house of Juan de Vivero. Here was to be celebrated the marriage of the heiress of Castile to the heir of Aragon.

There was need of the utmost haste. There was so little time in which to prepare; and at any moment they might expect interruption by the King's soldiers, come to prevent the marriage which the Marquis of Villena had determined should not take place.

Isabella was alternately in a state of bliss and anxiety.

Four days seemed like four weeks; and every commotion in the courtyard, any shout from below, set her trembling with fear.

Apart from the fact that her half-brother's men might arrive at any moment, there were other causes for anxiety. She had very little money; Ferdinand had none at all. How could they celebrate a marriage without money?

And this was the most important marriage in Spain.

Celebration there must be, but how could they decorate the house, how could they provide a banquet without money?

There was only one thing to be done; they must borrow.

It was not a very happy start, thought Isabella.

She could not discuss this with Ferdinand, for after that midnight meeting and solemn betrothal he had gone back to Dueñas, there to await the day of his entry into Valladolid as bridegroom at the public ceremony.

But the money was found. That had not been so difficult after all.

Why, reasoned many to whom the problem was put, this is the heiress of Castile and Leon. One day she will be Queen, and then she will not forget those who provided the money for her wedding.

But there was a matter which gave even greater concern.

There was a degree of consanguinity between Isabella and Ferdinand, and therefore, before they could marry, it was necessary to procure a dispensation from the Pope.

Since this had not yet come to her, Isabella appealed to the Archbishop of Toledo.

"I fear," she said, "that we must postpone the marriage."

"Postpone the marriage!" cried the Archbishop in amazement. "That is impossible. If we postpone it, I can say with certainty it will never take place. Your brother and my nephew will take good care that we never again get as near to it as we are now."

"There is one thing of the utmost importance which you have forgotten. The dispensation has not yet come from the Pope."

The Archbishop was genuinely alarmed, but he gave no sign of this. He wondered whether it was possible to get a dispensation from the Pope, who was the friend of Henry and Villena.

"Would you marry Ferdinand if the Pope refused the dispensation?" asked the Archbishop cautiously.

"It would be impossible," replied Isabella. "How could I marry without it?"

"The marriage would be binding."

"We should be censured by Holy Church. How could we hope for a successful marriage if we began it by opposing the ecclesiastical canons?"

The Archbishop paused. Here was a new light on Isabella's character. Devout, he had always known her to be. Well, others were devout—inasmuch as they attended Mass regularly and did not ignore the tenets of the Church. But who would allow the rules of the Church to come between them and their desires? Isabella would, it seemed.

The Archbishop made a quick decision.

"Have no fear," he said. "We shall have the dispensation in good time. I have made all concerned aware of the urgency."

"My good friend," murmured Isabella, "what should I do without you?"

The Archbishop returned her smile. He hoped she would remember those words and not seek to take his power from him and bestow it on Ferdinand.

* * *

In his private apartments the Archbishop was writing. He wrote slowly and with the utmost care.

Eventually he laid down his pen and studied what he had written.

It was a perfect dispensation. Isabella would never doubt that it had come from the Pope.

The Archbishop shrugged his shoulders.

There were times when bold men had to take matters into their own hands. He had to lead the heiress of Castile and Leon the way she must go; and that way was through marriage with Ferdinand. And if Isabella was too scrupulous a woman of the Church, there must be times when a little deceit must be employed.

The Archbishop rolled up the scroll and went to Isabella's apartments.

"I have great joy in telling Your Highness that the dispensation has arrived."

"Oh, how happy that makes me!" Isabella held out a hand and the Archbishop handed her the scroll.

He watched her anxiously while she glanced at it; but she was too happy to study it with very much attention.

He took it from her and rolled it up.

"Is it not wonderful," she said, "how one by one obstacles are removed from our paths. I was afraid even at this late hour that something would happen to prevent the marriage. The Holy Father is very much the friend of my brother and the Marquis, and I was filled with fear that he might refuse the dispensation. But God has moved his heart—and we have it. It often seems to me that it is the Divine will that Ferdinand and I should marry, for it would appear that whenever we are faced with what might be insuperable obstacles, miracles happen."

The Archbishop bowed his head. He was a man who believed that when Divine Providence failed to provide the holy miracle, an earthly one devised by shrewd men could be substituted.

* * *

In the hall of the house of Juan de Vivero many had assembled to watch the wedding ceremony performed by the Archbishop of Toledo.

The hall had been as richly decorated as was possible, but this might have been the wedding of the daughter of a petty nobleman.

It seemed incredible that it could be that of the prospective Queen of Castile.

But it was the best that could be done on borrowed money and in such haste; and if the radiance of jewels and fine brocades was missing, its absence seemed unimportant on account of the shining happiness on the faces of the bride and groom.

They looked beautiful—so young, so healthy and handsome. Surely, said the observers, this hasty marriage was the most romantic that had ever taken place in Spain. And if there would not be the celebrations which usually heralded and followed such ceremonies, what did it matter? At last Castile and Aragon were united; and the townsfolk of Valladolid shouted themselves hoarse with delight when the handsome pair left the house to go to Mass and later dined in public that all might see them and bear witness to the joy they had in each other.

* * *

There came that time when they were alone together, and their contentment with each other was not abated.

Ferdinand, experienced young man of the world, and Isabella a little apprehensive, but so ready to follow where he should lead her!

Ferdinand believed that he would mould this woman to his way of thinking. His Isabella was a paragon of many virtues. She was virginal yet passionate; she was possessed of great dignity, yet she was his to command.

"I did not know," he said, "that such good fortune could be mine."

"I knew," said Isabella. And she smiled that slow dedicated smile, thinking of all the vicissitudes of her hazardous life which only her courage and her belief in her future had made victory over those circumstances possible.

No, Isabella was not surprised that at last she had married the man of her choice, and that he promised to be all for which she had hoped.

She believed firmly that it had always been intended that this should be so.

"Ferdinand," she said, "we will work together always. We shall be as one. All I have is yours; all you have is mine. Is that not wonderful to contemplate?"

Ferdinand kissed her with rising passion and said that it was indeed—for she had so much more to offer than he had.

"Isabella," he said, "my wife, my love! What a truly wonderful thing it is that in addition to all your beauty, all your virtue, you should also have . . . Castile. But," he added, "even if you were not the future Queen of Castile, if you were a serving-wench in a tavern, I should love you still, Isabella. Would you love me if I could not bring you Aragon?"

He did not wait for an answer. He was so sure of his ability to conquer her.

But Isabella was thoughtful. She loved him with all her heart, but she did not think it would be possible for the future Queen of Castile to love a tavern man.

Ferdinand had lifted her into his arms. He was so strong that he could do this easily; and his warm breath was on her cheek.

There was no need to answer Ferdinand's questions, for she was swept into a new adventure which overwhelmed her senses and subdued her dignity and her love of truth—temporarily.

Ferdinand, the adventurer, the man of action, believed himself to be the all-conquering male to whom the weak female must ever be subservient.

Isabella was subconsciously aware of this. Her marriage must be perfect; in the council and in the bedchamber there must be continued harmony.

Thus at the time she was pliant, so eager to learn, so earnestly anxious to please. It was certain that in the bedchamber Ferdinand must be master; he must be the one to lead her step by step along the diverse sensuous paths.

Ferdinand had often told himself that even though Isabella was the future Queen of Castile she was also a woman. He did not know that although she was a woman, she would never forget that she was the future Queen of Castile.

THE DEATH OF HENRY

THE first news of the marriage which reached Henry was brought by Isabella's messenger.

He read his half-sister's letter and trembled.

"But this," he moaned, "was exactly what we wished to prevent. Now we shall have Aragon against us. Oh, what an unlucky man I am! I wish I had never been born to be King of Castile."

He hesitated before showing Isabella's letter to Villena, dreading the storm that it would arouse.

He let the letter drop from his hands, and fell to dreaming. He wished that he had not rid himself of Blanche. He thought of poor Blanche. How dreadful her last days must have been in the château of Ortes. Did she know that plans to murder her were afoot?

"And if she had stayed in Castile, she would be alive now," he murmured. "And should I be worse off? I should not have my daughter . . . but is she mine? She is still known throughout the Court as La Beltraneja. Poor little girl! What trials await her!"

Henry shook his head. It was a sad fate to be born as she had been born, to be the centre of controversy over a throne. There had been Alfonso . . .

If he had not rid himself of Blanche, if he had tried to lead a better life, he would have been a happier man. Now there was nothing but scandal and conflict.

His Queen, Joanna, had left him and was living scandalously in Madrid. He was constantly hearing stories about her adventures. She had had many lovers and there were several illegitimate children of these unions.

Never had a man so urgently desired to live in peace; never had a man been so consistently denied it.

He could not postpone passing on the news to Villena. The Marquis would hear of it from some other source if he delayed.

He asked the page to bring Villena to his presence, and when the Marquis came, with a helpless shrug he handed him Isabella's letter.

Villena's face became purple with rage.

"The marriage has actually taken place!" he cried.

"That is what she says."

"But this is monstrous. Ferdinand in Castile! I know what we must expect from that young man. There is none more ambitious in the whole of Spain."

"I do not think Isabella would attempt to usurp the throne," said Henry mildly.

"Isabella! What say will she have in affairs does Your Highness think? She will be led into revolt. Holy Mother, on one side this ambitious young husband, and on the other my uncle Carillo who is thirsting for battle. This marriage should have been prevented at all costs."

"So far there is little harm done."

Villena scowled and averted his gaze from the King.

He said: "There is one thing we must do. The Princess Joanna is now nearly nine years old. We shall find a suitable bridegroom for her and she shall be declared the rightful heiress of Castile." He began to laugh. "Then our young gallant from Aragon may begin to wonder whether he has made such a brilliant marriage after all."

"But Isabella has many supporters. Valladolid is firmly behind her. So are many other towns."

"We have Albuquerque; we have the Mendozas. I doubt not that many others will rally to our cause. Would to God that your Queen would not create such scandal in Madrid! It lends some truth to the slander that the Princess Joanna is not your daughter."

"My dear Villena, do you believe she is?"

Villena's face grew a shade more purple.

"I believe the Princess Joanna to be the true heir to the crowns of Castile and Leon," he retorted; "and by God and all his saints, ill shall befall any who reject that belief."

Henry sighed.

Why, why, he pondered, were people so tiresome? Why must Villena be so fierce? Why must Isabella make this marriage which was so upsetting to them all?

"Is there never to be peace?" he demanded fretfully.

"Yes," said Villena contemptuously, "when Isabella and her ambitious Ferdinand learn that they must stand aside for the true heiress of Castile."

"That," said Henry peevishly, "they will never learn."

But Villena was not listening. He was already busy with plans.

* * *

It was an unusual little Court at Dueñas. There was so little money that it was often difficult to pay for their food and that of their servants. Yet Isabella had never been so happy in her life.

She was deeply in love with Ferdinand, and he was the most passionate and the most kind of husbands. He was delighted that her intelligence matched her physical charms and that she had a deep knowledge of political affairs.

Perhaps those months seemed so precious to them both because they knew that they were transient. They would not always live in such humble state. The day must come when they would leave their humble lodgings and take up residence in one of the castles, and all the pomp and ceremonies which surrounded the sovereigns of Castile and Leon be theirs.

Ferdinand longed for that day; and, in a way, so did Isabella. The delightful intimacies of this life would be lost perhaps, but for all her joy in it, Isabella must not forget that she and Ferdinand had been brought together, not for dalliance in sensuous pleasure, but to make of Spain a mighty country, to unite all Spaniards, to bring them to the true religion, to rid the country of its existing anarchy, to bring back law and order, and to release every acre of Spanish soil from the domination of the Infidel.

And a few months after her marriage, Isabella, to her great joy, discovered that she was pregnant.

Ferdinand embraced her with delight when he heard the news.

"Why, my Isabella," he said, "you are indeed possessed of all the virtues. You are not only beautiful and of great intellect, you are fruitful! It is more than I dared hope for. But you look complacent, my love!"

She *was* complacent. She knew that she would give birth to great rulers. It was her destiny to do so.

* * *

In the monastery of Loyola, not far from Segovia, the King with the Marquis of Villena, the Duke of Albuquerque and several members of the influential Mendoza family and other highly placed noblemen had gathered in the company of the French ambassadors.

There was one present who was not often seen at such assemblies; this was Joanna, the Queen of Castile, who had come from Madrid to play a special part in these proceedings.

Henry addressed the assembly, Villena on one side of him and his Queen on the other.

"My friends," said the King, "we are gathered here for a special purpose and I pray you listen to me and give me your support. We are beset by conflict which could at any moment break into civil war. My half-sister Isabella—as did her brother Alfonso before her—has set herself up as heiress of Castile and Leon. I do not forget that at one time I named her heiress to the throne. That was in the treaty of Toros de Guisando. There she agreed not to marry without my approval. She has broken her word. Therefore I declare that the treaty of Toros de Guisando becomes null and void, and my sister Isabella is no longer heiress to the throne of Castile and Leon."

There was a murmur of approval in the gathering, led by Villena, Albuquerque and the Mendozas; it quickly became a roar.

Henry lifted his hand.

"There is one whose place she usurps. This is my daughter, the Princess Joanna, now a child in her ninth year. Her mother has come here today to swear with me that the Princess is my daughter; and you will, when you have heard and accepted her testimony, agree with me that there can be only one heiress, the Princess Joanna."

"The Princess Joanna!" chanted the audience. "Castile for Joanna!"

"I am now going to ask the Queen to swear on oath that the Princess Joanna is the legitimate heiress of Spain."

Joanna rose to her feet. She was still a beautiful woman but the lines of depravity were firmly etched on her face now, and there was a certain insolence in her demeanour which was far from queenly. Joanna was aware that all present knew of the retinue of lovers who attended her in Madrid, and of the children who had been the result; and quite clearly she was indifferent to this.

Now she cried : "I swear the Princess Joanna is the daughter of the King and no other."

"Castile for Joanna !" cried the assembly.

Then the King rose and took his wife's hand. "I swear with the Queen that the Princess Joanna is my daughter and no other."

"Castile for Joanna !"

The King then turned to the French ambassadors, among whom was the Count of Boulogne. The Count came forward.

"It is our pleasure," said Henry, "formally to announce the betrothal of my daughter Joanna to the Duke of Guienne, brother of the King of France, and with the approval of the nobles of Castile the ceremony of betrothal will now take place, with the Count of Boulogne standing proxy for his master."

"Long live the Duke of Guienne !" was the cry. "Castile for Joanna !"

* * *

Meanwhile, in the house of Juan de Vivero, Isabella was preparing for her confinement.

She was in a state of bliss. She shut herself in with her happiness. She was reading history; it was necessary to profit from the experience of others. She was studying state matters; and as usual she spent a great deal of time with her confessor and at prayers. Her life was divided between the study, which she believed to be necessary for a ruler who had a mighty task before her, and the domestic affairs of a wife and mother. Isabella had determined that in neither role should she fail.

It was delightful to sit with Ferdinand and talk of the reforms she intended to bring to Castile. When she heard stories of the terrible state of affairs, which existed in the country districts as well as in the towns, she would work out plans for righting this state of affairs. She planned to bring a new order to Castile; and she would with the aid of Ferdinand.

These intimate little conferences were all the more delightful because they were shared only by the two of them. Previously all political discussions had been presided over by the Archbishop of

Toledo. Isabella had turned to him, trusting his loyalty and wisdom. But with the coming of Ferdinand it was with Ferdinand she wished to discuss affairs.

What could be more pleasant than a conference which was also a *tête-a-tête for* lovers!

The Archbishop found it far from pleasant.

On one occasion, when Ferdinand was on his way to Isabella's apartments, he met the Archbishop also bound for the same destination.

"*I* am going to the Princess," said Ferdinand, implying that the Archbishop must wait awhile.

Alfonso Carillo, always a hot-tempered man, reminded Ferdinand that he was Isabella's chief adviser. "She herself, I doubt not, will tell you that, but for me, she would never have been proclaimed heiress to the throne."

Ferdinand was young and also hot-tempered. He said: "My wife and I do not intend to be disturbed. We will send for you when we need you."

The eyes of the Archbishop widened with horror.

"I think, Highness," he said, "that you forget to whom you speak."

"*I* forget?"

"I would ask you to consult the Princess Isabella. She will tell you what she owes to my loyalty and advice."

Ferdinand retorted: "You will find that *I* am not to be put in leading strings as has been the case with some sovereigns of Castile."

The Archbishop bowed his head to hide his smouldering anger, and turned away to prevent an outburst which might have proved disastrous.

He muttered to himself: "Before you attempt to escape from leading strings, my young cockerel, make sure that you are a sovereign of Castile."

Ferdinand went on angrily to Isabella's apartment, where she was lying on her bed, her women about her.

Ferdinand stormed: "I have just left that insolent fellow. One would think he was King of Castile. He will have to learn a little humility if he is to hold his place."

"Ferdinand . . ." said Isabella, and anxiety showed in her eyes. She held out her hand. "It would be wise, I think, to go cautiously. He is much older than we are. He is wise, and he has been loyal."

"I care not!" blazed Ferdinand. "I would ask him to remember to whom he speaks."

"Nevertheless," replied Isabella, "our position is by no means stable."

Some of that indignation which Ferdinand had felt towards the Archbishop was now directed towards Isabella. Was she telling him what he should do? She was only a woman, and he was her husband.

"I think," began Ferdinand coolly, "that you may safely trust me to deal with such matters."

But Isabella had cried out.

"It is the pains, Highness," said one of the women, coming forward. "They grow more frequent now."

* * *

Isabella lay in her bed, her child in her arms.

Ferdinand stood by the bed, smiling down at her.

"A daughter, Ferdinand," she said. "It should have been a son."

"I would rather have this daughter than any son," declared Ferdinand in the first flush of parenthood.

"Then I am completely happy."

"We shall have sons."

"Oh yes, we shall have sons."

Ferdinand knelt by the bed in a sudden rush of emotion.

"There is one thing only that matters, my love. You have come through this ordeal."

Isabella touched his hair with her hand. "Did you doubt that I would?"

"Loving you as I did, I must needs fear."

"No," said Isabella. "Have no fear in future, Ferdinand. For something within me tells me that you and I will have many children and that there are long useful years before us."

"Oh, Isabella, you put me to shame. You think always of your duty."

"What a happy woman I am when it is my duty to love and serve you . . . and Castile."

He kissed her hand with mingling fervour and tenderness.

"We shall call this little one Isabella," he said; "and we shall hope that she will resemble her mother."

* * *

When King John of Aragon heard of Ferdinand's quarrel with the Archbishop of Toledo he was disturbed.

He wrote immediately to Ferdinand.

"Have a care, my son. You are unwise to offend a man of such influence. I advise you to placate him immediately, and in future act with great caution."

But John knew Ferdinand. He was impulsive and too young perhaps for the position in which he found himself. He would find it very difficult to placate the Archbishop, and it might well be that the prelate was beginning to waver in his loyalties.

I must be kept informed of affairs in Castile, John told himself.

The situation was full of dangers. Could it be that the young couple did not notice this? Many great families were supporting the claims of La Beltraneja, and Castile was divided on this matter of the succession. What could be more alarming? And here was Ferdinand jeopardizing the friendship of one of the most forceful and powerful of his supporters.

John himself was enjoying a little respite from his troubles.

The Duke of Lorraine, whom the Catalans had appointed as their ruler, had died and all his children were too young to take his place. Thus the Catalans were without a leader, and John saw his chance of settling their differences and restoring order; but the Catalans would not give in so easily. The result of their resistance was the rigorous blockade of Barcelona which eventually brought them to a mood for negotiations.

When John entered their city he was shocked by the terrible signs of famine which he saw, and being as eager for peace as the people of Barcelona themselves he went to the Palace and there swore to respect the constitution of Catalonia.

The ten-years-long civil war was over, and John felt as though the ghost of his first-born had at last been laid.

This peace was not achieved until the end of the year 1472, and during this time the situation in Castile had continued to give him cause for anxiety.

The daughter of Isabella and Ferdinand—little Isabella—was now two years old; poverty at the little Court at Dueñas was acute, and John was very anxious as to the fate of his son; he longed to have him with him, yet he realized the need for him to stay in Castile. Isabella had her adherents and John had heard that many of them had deserted the cause of the King and La Beltraneja when the Duke of Guienne had died in May of that year. At the same time the situation was alarming.

Then further conflict broke out in Aragon.

When John had borrowed money from Louis XI of France, Louis had taken as security the provinces of Roussillon and Cerdagne, the inhabitants of which now complained bitterly of their foreign masters and sent to John telling him that, if he would liberate them, they would very willingly become his subjects once more.

John immediately rallied to the cause, while Louis, incensed by what was happening, sent an army into Aragon.

* * *

The Archbishop of Toledo presented himself to Ferdinand and Isabella.

Ferdinand scarcely disguised the irritation the Archbishop aroused in him.

Ferdinand was worried and, because of this, so was Isabella. She had assured him that his father was the bravest of soldiers and the shrewdest of strategists, and he had no need to fear. But Ferdinand remembered the age of his father, and his uneasiness persisted. They were discussing the new turn of affairs in Aragon when the Archbishop was ushered in.

Carillo was secretly pleased with himself. He was seriously considering whether he would not abandon the cause of Isabella and join that of La Beltraneja. He felt that with the King and La Beltraneja there would be no interference in the conduct of affairs, except of course from his nephew the Marquis of Villena. But they understood each other; they were of a kind; the same blood ran in their veins; neither would interfere in the other's province. He, Carillo, would be immeasurably useful to the other side if he changed now.

Yet he was not eager to change sides again; he had not his nephew's easy conscience. Yet the need to lead was all-important. He was ready to support a failing cause, providing he might take the lead. He could not endure to be in a subordinate position, and since the coming of Ferdinand he had felt himself to be forced into one.

Now, as he stood before Ferdinand and Isabella, he expressed his deep concern regarding events in Aragon.

Ferdinand thanked him coolly: "My father is a seasoned warrior," he said. "I doubt not that he will be victorious."

"Yet the French are capable of throwing a powerful force into the field," answered the Archbishop.

Isabella looked alarmed and glanced at her husband, who had flushed and was beginning to grow angry.

"I would suggest," went on the Archbishop, "that if you should decide it was your duty to go to your father's help, we of Castile would provide you with men and arms." He turned to Isabella. "I know that Your Highness would put no obstacle in the way of this help to your father-in-law, and that I speak with your authority."

Ferdinand was torn between his emotions, and he was too young to hide them entirely—much to the amusement of the Archbishop.

He was delighted at the prospect of helping his father, and at the same time he was annoyed that the Archbishop should imply that he could only be provided with men and arms at Isabella's command.

Isabella drew a deep breath. She was so happy with her husband and her two-year-old little daughter; and the thought of Ferdinand's going into battle terrified her. She looked quickly at Ferdinand.

He had turned to her. "How could I bear to leave you?" he said.

Isabella answered: "You must do your duty, Ferdinand."

Ferdinand thought of riding into Aragon, where he would not be treated as the consort of the Queen but as the heir to the throne. It was tempting. Moreover he was fond of his father, who was too old to engage in battle.

There was the Archbishop smiling at them benignly. He would delay changing sides for a while. With Ferdinand out of the way he would feel much happier, and Ferdinand would go to Aragon.

"Yes," said Ferdinand slowly. "I must do my duty."

* * *

It was long since Beatriz de Bobadilla had seen Isabella, and she often thought of her and longed for the old companionship.

Life had changed for Beatriz since those days when she had been Isabella's most intimate maid of honour. She found herself in a difficult position, because her husband was an officer of Henry's household, and there was such a wide division in the country—on one side the supporters of the King, on the other those of Isabella.

Andres de Cabrera had been made Governor of the town of Segovia, and the Alcazar which he occupied there was the depository of the King's treasure. Andres was therefore in a very trusted position; so it was very difficult for his wife to communicate with Isabella.

Beatriz fumed incessantly about this state of affairs.

She was devoted to her husband, but she had a great affection for Isabella, and Beatriz never did anything by half-measures. She must be a devoted friend as well as a devoted wife.

Often she discussed the country's affairs with her husband and forced him to agree that there could be no prosperity in a land which, while there were two factions disagreeing as to who was the heiress to the throne, must continually be trembling on the brink of civil war.

On one occasion when Andres was smarting over the overbearing behaviour of the Marquis of Villena, Beatriz seized the opportunity for which she had been looking.

"Andres," she said, "it occurs to me that, were it not for this man

Villena, now Grand Master of St. James, there might be an end to this strife."

"Ah, my dear," replied Andres, shaking his head, "there are still the two heiresses. You cannot have peace when there is a division of opinion as to whether the Princess Isabella or the Princess Joanna has the right to the title."

"The Princess Joanna—La Beltraneja!" scoffed Beatriz. "Everyone knows she is a bastard."

"But the Queen swore . . ."

"The Queen swore! That woman would swear to anything, just for a whim. You know, Andres, that Isabella is the rightful heiress to the crown."

"Hush, my dear. Remember we serve the King, and the King has given the succession to his daughter Joanna."

"*Not* his daughter!" cried Beatriz, clenching her right fist and driving it into the palm of her left hand. "Nor does he believe it. Did he not at one time make Isabella his heiress? The people want Isabella. Do you know, I believe that if we could bring Isabella to Henry—in the absence of Villena—we could make him accept her as his heiress, and there would be no more nonsense about La Beltraneja. Would this not be a good thing for the country?"

"And for you, Beatriz, who would have your friend with you."

"I should like to see her again," mused Beatriz almost gently. "I should also like to see her little daughter. I wonder if she resembles Isabella."

"Well," said Andres, "what do you plot?"

"Henry comes here often," said Beatriz.

"He does."

"Sometimes without Villena."

"That is so."

"What if Isabella were here too? What if we arranged a meeting between them?"

"Isabella! Come here . . . into the enemy's camp!"

"You would call my house the enemy's camp? Any who sought to make her their prisoner in my house would have to kill me before they did so."

Andres laid his hand on his wife's shoulder. "You talk too lightly of death, my dear."

"It is Villena who rules this land. He rules the King. He rules you."

"That he does not. That he never shall do."

"Well, then, why should we not invite Isabella here? Why should she not meet Henry?"

"It would be necessary to ask Henry's permission first," warned Andres.

"Well, I would undertake to get that . . . provided he came here without Villena."

"You would play a dangerous game, my dear."

"That for danger!" cried Beatriz, snapping her fingers. "Have I your permission to speak to the King when he next comes here alone?"

Andres laughed. "My dear Beatriz," he said, "I know that when you ask for my permission it is merely a formality. So you have decided to speak to Henry at the first opportunity?"

Beatriz nodded. "I have decided," she said.

* * *

She knew it would not be difficult.

She asked the King for permission to talk with him when next he came to stay at the Segovia palace and Villena was busy in Madrid.

"Highness," she began, "will you forgive my boldness in raising a certain question?"

Henry was alarmed, immediately afraid that his peace was about to be disturbed.

Beatriz ignored his worried expression and hurried on. "I know Your Highness, like myself, loves peace beyond all things."

"You are right in that," agreed Henry. "I wish for no more conflict. I wish those about me would accept what is, and leave it at that."

"Some would, Highness, but there are others, close to you, who make strife. Yet it would be quite easy to have peace throughout Castile tomorrow."

"How so?" Henry wanted to know.

"Well, Highness, I am not skilled in politics but I know this: There are two sides in this quarrel. Part of the country supports Your Highness, and the other part, Isabella. If you made Isabella your heir you would placate those who are against you. Those who are with you would still remain with you. Therefore there would be an end to the conflict."

"But my daughter Joanna is the heir to the throne."

"Highness, the people will never accept her. As you know, I served Isabella and I loved her dearly. I know that she longs for an end of hostilities. She is truly your sister. There is not a doubt about that. But as to the Princess Joanna . . . at least there are great doubts as to her legitimacy. If you would only meet Isabella . . . talk to her . . . let her tell you how grieved she is by the conflict between you . . ."

"Meet her! But how? Where?"

"Highness, she could come here."

"It would not be permitted."

"But Your Highness would permit it—and those who would not, need not know of it."

"If I sent for her they would hear at once."

"Highness, if I fetched her and brought her to you they would not hear of it."

"If you set out for Aranda, where I understand she is now, the purpose of your mission would be surmised; all would know that you proposed bringing her to me."

Her eyes sparkled. "Oh, but, Highness, I would not go as myself. I would go disguised."

"This is a mad scheme of yours, my dear lady," said Henry. "Think no more of it."

"But if I could bring her to you . . . in secret . . . you would receive her, Highness?"

"I could not refuse to meet my sister. But have done."

Beatriz bowed her head and changed the subject.

Henry then seemed contented; but he did not know that Beatriz had begun to form her plans.

* * *

Isabella was lonely in the palace at Aranda. She was thinking of Ferdinand and wondering how long their separation must last.

Sitting by a great fire stitching with one of her women, and periodically glancing up, she saw through the windows the snow fluttering down. The roads would be icy; and she shivered, wondering what the weather was like in Aragon.

She was working on a shirt. She had been true to her vow to make all the shirts which Ferdinand wore. It was a little jest between them.

"Every shirt of yours must be stitched with my stitches," she had told him. "No other woman must make such a garment for you . . . only myself."

Ferdinand was delighted. He was always deeply touched by such feminine gestures. Isabella sighed. Ferdinand loved her feminity more than her predilection for governing. He would rather see her occupied with stitching than with state affairs.

One of her women, who was seated in the window seat, called out that a peasant with a pack on her saddle-bow had ridden into the courtyard.

"Poor woman, she looks so cold and hungry. I wonder if she has wares to sell."

Isabella laid aside her work and went to the window. She felt it her duty to take a great interest in all her subjects. She was teaching little Isabella to be considerate of all people. They might be her subjects one day, she reminded her; for if she and Ferdinand should have no sons, that little Isabella might be Queen of Castile.

"Poor woman indeed!" she said. "Go down, lest they turn her away. Have her brought in and fed. If she has goods to sell, perhaps she will have something that is needed in the house."

Her woman went away to do her bidding, but she soon came back, consternation on her face.

"The woman asks if she may see you, Highness," Isabella was told.

"What does she want?"

"She refused to say, Highness. She was very insistent. And, Highness, she does not speak like a peasant though she looks like one."

Isabella sighed. "Tell her that I am engaged," she said. "But ask her business and then come and tell me what she says."

Isabella paused, and held up a hand to stay her woman for she had heard a voice, protesting in loud tones, which held an unmistakable ring of authority. She knew that voice.

"Go," she said, "and bring this woman to me . . . at once."

In a few moments the woman was standing on the threshold of the room. She and Isabella looked at each other, and then Beatriz, throwing off her ragged cloak, held out her arms. This was no time for ceremony. Isabella ran to her and they embraced.

"Beatriz! But why? To come like this!"

"Could we be alone?" asked Beatriz.

Isabella waved her women away.

"It was the only way to come," Beatriz explained. "So I came thus . . . and alone. Had I come as myself, the news could have reached Villena. As it is, you shall come to Segovia, where the King now is, and until you have met and talked with him the meeting will be a secret. It is the only way."

"Henry has expressed a wish to see me?"

"Henry will see you."

"Beatriz, what does this mean?"

"We know, dearest Highness, that reconciliation between you and Henry would mean that the people of Castile could live without the daily threat of civil war."

"Henry knows this!"

"He longs for peace. It will not be difficult to persuade him to it . . . if we can keep him from Villena."

"Beatriz, you are asking me to go to Henry. Do you remember

how they tried to capture me, to imprison me? Do you remember what was done to Alfonso?"

"I ask you to come to the Alcazar of Segovia. No harm could come to you there. Andres guards it . . . and I guard Andres."

Isabella laughed.

"You were always a forceful woman. Does Andres love you the less for it?"

Beatriz looked hard at her friend. "You, too, are strong," she said. "And Ferdinand, does he love you less for that?"

Beatriz noticed that a slight shadow crossed Isabella's face as she said: "I do not know."

* * *

Isabella rode into Segovia with the Archbishop of Toledo beside her.

Henry received her with warmth, and his eyes filled with tears as he embraced her. "You know, my dear sister, that all this strife is none of my making."

"I do know that, Henry," answered Isabella; "and the state of our country brings as much grief to me as it does to you."

"I long for peace." Henry said this with unaccustomed vehemence.

"And I."

"Then, Isabella, why should we not have peace?"

"Because there are jealous nobles who surround us . . . who jostle each other for power."

"But if we are friends, what else should matter?"

"It is this affair of the succession, Henry. You know I am the true heiress of Castile. I am your half-sister . . . your only relation."

"But there is my daughter."

"You do not believe Joanna is that, Henry."

"Her mother swore it."

"You do not believe her, Henry."

"Who shall say? Who shall say?"

"You see," said Isabella, "if you would but accept me as heir to the throne there would be no more strife. If you and I were friends and were seen together, how happy all would be in Castile and Leon."

"I long to see all happy."

"Then Henry, we could begin to right these wrongs; we could bring back law and order to the country. There is this senseless conflict as to who is the heir, when there are so many important reforms to be considered."

"I know. I know."

The Archbishop came to them. He did not wait to be announced. He had assumed complete authority.

"If you would walk through the city holding the bridle of the Princess's palfrey, Highness, in an intimate manner, as brother to sister, it would give great joy to the people of Segovia."

"All I wish is to give them joy," Henry insisted.

* * *

The people of Segovia had vociferously expressed their delight at the sight of the King, walking through their streets and holding the bridle of his sister's palfrey. Here was good news. The threat of civil war was over. The King had cast off the yoke of Villena; he was thinking for himself; he was surely going to accept Isabella as his heir.

When they returned to the Alcazar, the people gathered outside and shouted: "Castilla! Castilla! Castilla for Henry and Isabella!"

Henry, with tears in his eyes, saluted the people.

It was long since he had been so cheered.

* * *

Late that night Beatriz hurried to Isabella's bedchamber.

Isabella had already retired.

"Isabella," whispered Beatriz in her ear, "wake up. Someone has arrived who is waiting to see you."

Isabella started up in bed. "What is this, Beatriz?"

"Hush," said Beatriz. "The palace is sleeping."

She then turned and beckoned, and Isabella saw a tall, familiar figure enter the apartment.

She gave a cry of gladness, for Ferdinand had thrown himself upon the bed, and she was in his arms.

Beatriz stood by, laughing.

"He has come at a good moment," she said.

"Any moment he comes is a good one," answered Isabella.

"My dear Isabella," murmured Ferdinand.

Beatriz said: "There will be plenty of time later to show each other your pleasure. At the moment there is one other matter of importance to settle. Henry has received you, Isabella, but will he receive your husband? That is what we have to consider. And it will soon be known that Ferdinand has returned and that you are both here with the King. Once this reaches Villena's ears, he will do his utmost to prevent the renewal of friendship between you all. Tomorrow morning early, you must seek an audience with Henry. You must persuade him to see Ferdinand."

"He will do so; I know he will."

"He must," said Beatriz. "It is imperative. He must be reconciled to you both. It will be Twelfth Day . . . is it tomorrow, or the next day? That is an excuse for a banquet. We shall give one—Andres and I and when it is seen how friendly the King is towards you two, all will know that he acknowledges your marriage and accepts you as his heirs. I shall leave you now. But until the King has received Prince Ferdinand it should not be known, except by those whom we can trust, that he is here."

* * *

Ferdinand had thrown off his travel-stained garments, and Isabella was in his embrace.

"It seems so long since I saw you," he said.

"There should not be these partings."

"Yet, if it is necessary, they must be. How is our daughter?"

"Well and happy. How delighted she will be to see her father!"

"Has she forgotten him?"

"No more than I could. And Aragon?"

"My father is a mighty warrior. He will always win."

"As you will, Ferdinand."

There was need for silence, and after a while she said: "Was it not courageous of Beatriz to arrange this meeting between the King and ourselves!"

"She is a courageous woman, I'll grant you—but . . ."

"You do not like Beatriz, Ferdinand. Oh, but that must not be. She is one of my dearest friends."

"She is unlike a woman. She has hectoring ways."

"That is her strength."

"I like not hectoring women," said Ferdinand.

The faintest alarm came to Isabella. In her life as a Queen there would be times when she must make her own decisions and all others must respect them.

But Ferdinand was home after a long absence; and she could not think of the difficulties which lay ahead. They were of the future and the present time had so much to offer.

* * *

Beatriz was exuberant. Her schemes for the re-union of Isabella and Ferdinand with the King had had as great a success as she had hoped for.

Henry was pliable, subject to be swayed by the prevailing wind; and here in Segovia with the guardian of his treasury, and the latter's forceful wife, he appeared to be the firm friend of Ferdinand and Isabella.

He had ridden to the Twelfth Night celebrations between Ferdinand and Isabella, smiling and chatting with them as they rode, to the intense joy of the people. Through the streets they had ridden thus to the Bishop's palace, between the Alcazar and the Cathedral, in which the Twelfth Night banquet was being held.

The banquet, supervised by the indefatigable Beatriz, was a success. Sweating serving men and women waited on the guests and minstrels played in the gallery. At the head of the table sat the King; on his right hand was Isabella, and on his left, Ferdinand.

Beatriz surveyed her beloved mistress and friend with beaming satisfaction, and Andres watched his wife.

He was aware of a certain tension, a certain watchfulness. It was inevitable, he told himself. All the conflict, all the strife, could not be dispersed by one brief meeting. Henry was eating and drinking with enjoyment, and his eyes were becoming a little glazed as they rested on one of the most sensuously beautiful of the women. Henry had not become a wise King in such a brief period of time; Isabella had not become secure in her place.

The banquet over, dancing began.

As Isabella was seated by the King, Beatriz hoped that he would lead the Princess in the dance. What could be more symbolic?

Yet Henry did not dance.

"My dear sister," he murmured, "I feel a little unwell. You must lead the dance—you and your husband."

So it was Isabella and Ferdinand who rose, and as they came into the centre of the hall others fell in behind them.

Beatriz hastened to the side of the King.

"All is well, Highness?" she asked anxiously.

"I am not sure," said Henry. "I feel a little strange."

"It is too hot for Your Highness, perhaps."

"I know not. I seem to shiver."

Beatriz beckoned to the beautiful young woman who had caught the King's notice during the banquet; but Henry now seemed to be unaware of her.

"Sit beside him," whispered Beatriz. "Speak to him."

But the King had closed his eyes and had slumped sideways in his chair.

* * *

All night long the King lay groaning on his bed. He was in great pain, he declared.

News spread through Segovia that the King was ill, and that the nature of his illness—vomiting, purging and stomach pains—pointed to poison.

There were silent men and women in the streets of Segovia; yesterday they had cheered; today they were solemn.

Could it be that the King had been lured to Segovia that he might be poisoned? And who was responsible for his condition?

There were many, who had helped at the banquet, who might wish him dead, for almost everyone present was a supporter of Isabella and Ferdinand.

The people of Segovia did not wish to believe that their beloved Princess could be guilty of such a crime.

When Isabella heard of the King's illness she was horrified.

"He must not die," she said to Beatriz. "If he does, we shall be blamed."

Beatriz recognized the good sense of that.

"Remember," said Isabella, "the conflict in Aragon when the people believed that Carlos was murdered. How many suffered and died during those ten years of civil war?"

"We must save the King's life," said Beatriz. "I must wait upon him. It would not be wise for you to be constantly in the sick room. If he died they would surely blame you then."

So Beatriz supervised the nursing of the King, and it seemed that because she so willed that he should not die, his condition began gradually to improve.

* * *

The Marquis of Villena rode with his troops into Segovia and imperiously presented himself at the Alcazar.

Isabella and Ferdinand received him calmly, but Villena was far from calm. He was enraged and alarmed.

The King was not to be trusted. As soon as his, Villena's, back was turned he was consorting with the opposite side. This would teach him a lesson.

Villena demanded that he be taken at once to the King.

"I fear," said Isabella, "that my brother is not well enough to receive visitors."

"I demand to be taken to him."

"You may not make your demands here," said Isabella.

"I wish to assure myself that he is receiving the best attention."

"I will send for our hostess and she will tell you that there is no need for alarm."

When Beatriz arrived she told Villena that the King's condition was improving, but that he was not well enough to leave Segovia for a while.

"I must be taken to him at once," said Villena.

"I am sorry, my lord," Beatriz answered, her voice placating but her eyes belying her tone. "The King is not well enough to receive visitors."

"I shall stay here until I see him," said Villena.

"We cannot deny you hospitality, since you ask it so graciously," answered Beatriz.

But even she could not keep Villena from the King. Villena had his men everywhere, and it was not an insuperably difficult task to get a message to Henry that Villena was in the Alcazar, and that if the King valued his life he must insist on seeing him without delay.

* * *

Villena sat by Henry's bed. He was shocked by the King's appearance. His illness had changed Henry. He had become gaunt and his skin was yellow.

Henry thought he saw a change in Villena. There was a certain lessening of that intense vitality, a certain greyish tinge to the skin.

"Your Highness should never have been so foolish as to come here," said Villena.

"I could not know that I should be smitten with this illness," murmured Henry peevishly.

"That you should be so smitten was the only reason why you were lured here."

"You think they tried to poison me?"

"I am sure of it. And they will continue to do so while you are in this place."

"I trust Isabella."

"Trust Isabella! She has a throne to gain. It cannot be hers while you live."

"She is certain that she is the true heiress, and she is ready to wait."

"But not to wait too long, it seems. No, Highness, we must remove you from here as soon as possible. And we must not allow this attempt on your life to be ignored."

"What do you suggest?" asked Henry wearily.

"We shall send forces to Segovia. They will enter the town stealthily and take possession of vital points. Then they shall make Isabella their prisoner on the ground that she tried to poison you. We could bring her to trial for that."

"I do not believe Isabella would try to poison me."

"Then you do not believe the evidence of your senses."

"Cabrera's wife has nursed me well."

"A poisonous woman."

"A good nurse. She seemed determined to save my life. And,

Marquis, do you not think that I should acknowledge Isabella as heir to the throne? She is the one the people want. And with Ferdinand's help she would bring Castile out of its present troubles."

"But your will, of which you have made me executor, clearly states that your daughter Joanna is heir to the throne."

"It's true. Little Joanna. She is but a child. She will be surrounded by wolves . . . wolves who seek power. I came to the conclusion, when I rode through the streets of the town with Ferdinand and Isabella, that matters would be simplified if I admitted that Joanna was not my daughter and made Ferdinand and Isabella my heirs."

"I see that some of the poison has been effective," said Villena. "As soon as you are well enough to travel we must leave this place for Cuellar. There we will make our plans for the capture of Isabella. We shall not be safe until she is under lock and key. And I tremble for *your* safety while you are in this place."

"I do not," said Henry. "I do not believe Isabella would allow any harm to befall me."

Villena looked with scorn on the King and, as he did so, he placed his hand to his throat.

"What ails you?" asked Henry. "You look as sick as I do myself."

"It is nothing. A certain dryness of the throat. A certain discomfort, nothing more."

"You have not the same colour that you had."

"I have scarcely slept since I heard the news that Your Highness was here at Segovia in the midst of your enemies."

"Ah, if I had but known who were my friends and who my enemies I should have had a happier life."

Villena looked startled. "You talk as though you had come to the end of it. No, Your Highness, you will recover from this attempt on your life. And it shall not be forgotten. Let us make certain of that."

"Well," said Henry, "if Isabella was behind a plot to poison me, she deserves imprisonment."

* * *

In the town of Cuellar, whither Villena had taken the King, plans were made for the capture of Isabella.

"Forces shall enter the town," said Villena. "Explosives will be thrown at the Alcazar; the inhabitants will be terror-stricken, and then it will be no difficult matter to secure the person of Isabella."

Several months had passed since the King's illness, but he had never fully recovered and was subject to attacks of vomiting.

As for Villena himself, that great energy which had sustained him seemed to be spent. He still planned; he still had ambitious schemes, but the pain in his throat persisted and he found it impossible to eat certain foods.

In the Alcazar at Segovia, Beatriz and her husband were aware of the plot to capture Isabella, and they doubled the guards at all vital points; thus when Villena's troops tried to make a stealthy entry into the town they were discovered and the plan was frustrated.

Villena received the news almost with indifference.

And the next day even his spirit broke and he accepted the advice of his servants and stayed in his bed. Within a few days he was suffering great pain, and was unable to swallow food. He knew that he had not long to live.

He lay back, considering all the ambitions of his life and wondering whether it had been worth while. He had achieved great power; he had been at times the ruler of Castile; and now it was over and he must lie on his bed, the victim of a malignant growth in his throat which would destroy him, as his enemies had not been able to do.

Isabella remained at large. The people were rallying about her. And he, Villena, who had sworn that she should never come to the throne, was dying helplessly.

* * *

Henry could not accept the fact when the news was brought to him. Villena . . . dead!

"But what shall I do?" he said. "What shall I do now?"

He prayed for his friend; he wept for his friend. He had always believed that he would die long before Villena. He had lost his master and his servant, and he was bewildered.

His secretary Oviedo came to him.

"Highness," said Oviedo, "there is a very important matter of which I must speak to you."

Henry nodded for him to proceed.

"On his death-bed the Marquis of Villena put this paper into my hand. It is your will, of which he was to be executor. I have glanced at it, Highness, and see it to be a document of the utmost importance, since it names the Princess Joanna as your heir."

"Take it away," said Henry. "How can I think of such matters when my dear friend has died and I am all alone?"

"Highness, what shall I do with it?"

"I care not what you do with it. I only wish to be left in peace."

Oviedo bowed and went away.

He looked at the will. He knew the explosive power of its contents if they became known; they were capable of plunging Castile into civil war.

He could not decide what to do with it, so as a temporary measure he put it in a box, which he locked.

* * *

Henry went back to Madrid. He felt not only ill but very weary. He knew that Villena had been self-seeking, a man of immense ambitions, yet without him the King felt lost. He believed that the most unhappy time of his life had been when Villena had sided with his enemies and given his support to young Alfonso. He remembered his delight when Villena had returned to him.

"And now," murmured Henry, "I am alone. He has gone before me, and I am sick and tired out with all the troubles about me."

He was often ill; there was a return of that sickness which had attacked him in Segovia. Indeed he had never fully recovered from it.

Tears of self-pity often filled Henry's eyes, and his doctors sought to rouse him from his lethargy. But there was nothing now which could give him the desire to live. His mistresses no longer interested him. There was nothing in life to sustain his flagging spirits.

It became clear to all in the immediate Court circle that Henry had not long to live. Ambitious noblemen began to court Isabella. The Cardinal Mendoza and the Count Benavente, who had supported first Alfonso and then turned to La Beltraneja, now began to turn again—this time towards Isabella.

Isabella was the natural successor. Her character had aroused admiration. She was of a nature to make a good Queen, and she had a strong husband in Ferdinand.

So, among others, Mendoza and Benavente came to Court, there to await the passing of the old sovereign and the nomination of the new.

* * *

On a cold December night in the year 1474, Henry lay on his death-bed.

Ranged round his bed were the men who had come to see him die, and among them was the Cardinal Mendoza and the Count Benavente. In the background hovered the King's secretary, Oviedo. He was uneasy, for he had something on his mind.

Mendoza whispered to Benavente: "He cannot last long. That was the death-rattle in his throat."

"He cannot have more than an hour to live. It is time he received the last rites."

"One moment. He is trying to say something."

The Cardinal and the Count exchanged glances. It might well be that what the King had to say had better not be heard by any but themselves.

The Cardinal bent over the bed. "Your Highness, your servants await your orders."

"Little Joanna," murmured the King. "She is but a child. What will become of her?"

"She will be taken care of, Highness. Do not fret on her account."

"But I do. We were so careless . . . her mother and I. She is my heiress . . . Little Joanna. Who will care for her? My sister Isabella is strong. She can look after herself . . . but little Joanna . . . she is my heiress, I tell you. She is my heiress."

The Cardinal said quickly: "The King's mind wanders." The Count nodded in agreement.

"I have left a will," went on Henry. "In it I proclaim her my heir."

"A will!" The Cardinal was startled, for this was an alarming piece of information. He and the Count were only waiting for the end of Henry that they might go and pay their homage to the new Queen Isabella. A will could complicate matters considerably.

"It is with Villena . . ." murmured the King. "I gave it to Villena."

"There is no doubt that the King's mind wanders," whispered the Count.

"It is with Villena," muttered Henry. "He will look after her. He will save the throne for Joanna."

One of the attendants came to the two men who stood by the bed, and asked if he should call the King's Confessor.

"The King's mind wanders," the Cardinal told him. "He believes the Marquis of Villena to be here in the palace."

The King's eyes had closed and his head had fallen a little to one side. His breathing was stertorous. Suddenly he opened his eyes and looked at the men about the bed. He obviously did not recognize them. Then he said, and the words came thickly through his furred lips: "Villena, where are you, my friend? Villena, come nearer."

"He is near the end," said the Cardinal. "Yes, call the King's Confessor."

* * *

As the Count and Cardinal left the chamber of death Oviedo hurried after them.

"My lords, may I have a word with you?"

They paused to listen to the secretary.

"The King has left in my keeping a document which greatly troubles me," said Oviedo. "It was in Villena's possession until he was dying. He then gave it to me to return to the King, but the King told me to lock it away; and this I have done."

"What document is this?"

"It is the King's last will, my lords."

"You should show it to us without delay."

Oviedo led them into a chamber in which he stored his secret documents. He unlocked the box, produced the will and handed it to the Cardinal.

Had the Cardinal been alone he might have destroyed it; at the moment Benavente was his friend; but men changed sides quickly in Castile at this time, and he dared not destroy such a document while there were witnesses to see him do so.

Benavente read his thoughts, for they were his also.

Then the Cardinal said: "Tell no one of this document. Take it to the curate of Santa Cruz in Madrid and tell him to lock it away in a safe place."

Oviedo bowed and retired.

The Count and Cardinal were silent for a few seconds; then the Cardinal said: "Come! Let us to Segovia, there to pay homage to the Queen of Castile."

ISABELLA AND FERDINAND

On the thirteenth day of December, in that year 1474, a procession consisting of the highest of the nobility and clergy of Castile made its way to the Alcazar of Segovia.

There, under a canopy of rich brocade, homage was paid to Isabella, Queen of Castile.

They had come to escort her to the city's square where a platform had been set up.

Isabella, in her royal robes, mounted her jennet and was led there by the magistrates of the city, while one of her officers walked before her carrying the sword of state.

When she reached the platform she dismounted and ascended the structure, there to take her place on the throne which had been set up for her.

When she looked out on that great assembly she was deeply moved. This, she felt, was one of the truly great moments in her life, and it was for this that she had been born.

She had two regrets—one disappointing, one very bitter. The first was that Ferdinand was not here to share this triumph with her because he had, only a few weeks before Henry's death, received an urgent call from his father and had joined him in Aragon; the other was that her mother could not be aware of what was happening to her daughter this day.

And as Isabella sat there on that throne, Queen of Castile by the desire of the people of Segovia, it was her mother's voice which she heard ringing in her ears: "Never forget, you could be Queen of Castile."

She had never forgotten.

She heard the bells peal out; she saw the flags fluttering in the breeze; she heard the guns boom forth. All these were saying: Here is the new Queen of Castile.

There were many to kneel before her, to kiss her hand and swear their loyalty; and she in her turn told them, in that sweet, musical, rather high-pitched young and almost innocent voice, that she would do all in her power to serve them, her subjects, to bring back law and order to Castile, and to be a worthy Queen.

The voices of the crowd rang out: "Castile! Castile for Isabella! Castile for the King Don Ferdinand and his Queen Doña Isabella, Queen Proprietor of the Kingdoms of Castile and Leon!"

She felt warmed by their mention of Ferdinand; she would be able to tell him how they had called his name. That would please him.

Then she descended from the platform and placed herself at the head of the procession, when it made its way to the Cathedral.

Isabella listened to the chanting of Te Deum; and earnestly she prayed for Divine guidance, that she might never falter in her duties towards her kingdoms and her people.

* * *

Ferdinand came with all speed from Aragon, and joyously Isabella received him.

Was it her fancy, or did he hold his head a little higher? Was he a little more proud, a little more masterful than before?

In the midst of his passion he whispered to her: "First you are my wife, Isabella. Do not forget that. Only second, Queen of Castile."

She did not contradict him, for he did not expect an answer. He had spoken as though he made a statement of fact. It was not true. If she had never known it before, it had become clear to her after the ceremony in the square and the Cathedral.

But she loved him tenderly and with passion. She was a wife and a mother, but the crown was her spouse, and the people of Castile—the suffering and the ignorant—they were her children.

She would not tell him now. But in time he must come to understand. He would, for he too had his duty. He was younger than she was, and for all his experience he was perhaps not so wise, though not for all the world would she tell him so.

He will understand, she assured herself, but he is younger than I—not only in years—and perhaps I am more serious by nature. It will take a little time before he understands as I do.

* * *

His grandfather, the Admiral Henriquez, was delighted at the turn of events.

He placed himself at the service of his grandson.

The day after Ferdinand's return he presented himself and embraced the young husband with tears in his eyes.

"This is the proudest moment of my life. You will be King of Aragon. You are already King of Castile."

Ferdinand looked a little sulky. "One hears much talk of the Queen of Castile, little of its King."

"That is a matter which should be set right," went on the Admiral. "Isabella has inherited Castile, but that is because the Salic law does not exist in Castile as it does in Aragon. If it were accepted here, you, as the nearest male claimant to the throne, through your grandfather Ferdinand, would be King of Castile—and Isabella merely your consort."

"That is so," agreed Ferdinand, "and it is what I would wish. But everywhere we go it is Isabella . . . Isabella . . . and they never forget to remind me that she is the *reina proprietaria*. It is almost as though they accept me on sufferance."

"It shall be changed," said the Admiral. "Isabella will do all that you ask of her."

Ferdinand smiled smugly. He was remembering her passionate reception of him, and he believed it to be true.

"It shall be done. She adores me. She can deny me nothing."

* * *

Isabella listened in dismay.

He was laughing, his arm about her, his lips against her hair. "So, my love, this shall be done. The King and his beloved consort, eh? It is better so. You, who are so reasonable, will see this."

Isabella felt dismay smite her, but her voice was firm, though sad, when she replied : "No, Ferdinand, I do not see it."

He released her, and his frown was ugly.

"But surely, Isabella . . ."

She wanted to cry out : Do not use that cold tone when you speak to me. But she said nothing. Instead she saw again the people in the square . . . the people who had suffered during the evil reign of her half-brother. And still she said nothing.

He went on : "So you hold me in such little esteem !"

"I hold you in the greatest esteem," she told him. "Are you not my husband and the father of my child?"

Ferdinand laughed bitterly. "Brought here as a stallion ! Is that what I mean to you? Let him do what he has been brought for—after that he is of little account."

"But how can you say this, Ferdinand? Do I not ask your advice? Do I not listen? Do we not rule these kingdoms together?"

Ferdinand stood up to his full height. For the first time she noticed the lights of cupidity in his eyes, the arrogance of his mouth; yet these faults in him did not make her love him less, although they confirmed her belief that she herself must rule Castile and Leon.

"I am your husband," he said. "It is you who should listen to my advice."

"In some matters, yes," she answered gently. "But have you forgotten that I am the Queen of Castile?"

"Forget it ! How can I? You will not allow me to do that. I can see that I demean myself by staying here. I can see that I am of no account whatsoever. Madam, Highness, I no longer wish to remain. Is it necessary for me to ask permission of the Queen of Castile to retire?"

"Oh Ferdinand . . . Ferdinand . . ." she cried; and the tears started to her eyes.

But he had bowed abruptly and left her.

* * *

It was the first quarrel, but she realized how easily there might have been others.

He had believed until this moment that he would have no difficulty in relegating her to second place.

She wanted to go and find him, to tell him that all that she possessed was his. She wanted to say : What do I care for power, if in gaining it I lose your love?

But she remembered his face as he had stood there. Ferdinand, a little vain, a little greedy. Handsome, virile Ferdinand who lacked the modesty, the dedicated desire to serve which were Isabella's.

There would only be one ruler of Castile from this moment until the end of her days; and that must be Isabella.

So she waited, fighting back her tears, trying to soothe her anguish.

It is not pleasure that is important; it is not happiness, she reminded herself. It is doing one's duty in that state of life to which God has called one.

* * *

The Court knew of the quarrel between Isabella and Ferdinand.

The Archbishop of Toledo smiled slyly and shrewdly. Here was a situation after his own heart. The Admiral had put these ideas into the head of that young bantam, and the Archbishop was going to vanquish the Admiral; and if it meant Ferdinand's retirement to Aragon in a sulk, that could not be helped.

The Archbishop was delighted at the prospect of dousing the arrogance of master Ferdinand.

"There is no law in Castile," he told the council, "to prevent a woman from inheriting the crown. Therefore there can be no question of Isabella's becoming merely the consort of King Ferdinand. It is Ferdinand who is the consort of Queen Isabella."

Ferdinand was furious.

"I shall not stay here to be so insulted," he declared. "I shall return to Aragon."

The news spread through the Palace, and reached Isabella.

"Ferdinand is preparing to return to Aragon . . . for ever."

* * *

Ferdinand was somewhat alarmed by the storm he had raised.

He was piqued and humiliated, but his father would call him a fool if he returned to Aragon. And a fool he would be.

He was hot-tempered and impulsive. He should never have declared his intention of returning. Now he would either have to go or make his position even more humiliating by remaining.

Already the news was spreading beyond the Palace. A rift between Isabella and Ferdinand, because Ferdinand wishes to take precedence and Isabella refuses to allow it!

He felt bewildered, for the first time realizing that he was after all only a very young man.

Outside the Palace little groups of people had gathered. They were waiting for the news that the marriage, which had seemed so ideal, was broken and that Ferdinand was to go back to Aragon.

He had seen them from the windows. He had seen the sneers on their faces. They would boo him out of Castile, for they were all firmly behind Isabella.

But what could he do?

His servants were waiting for orders.

"I shall return to Aragon," he had cried before them all. "I cannot wait to shake the dust of Castile from my shoes!"

And now . . . they were waiting.

Someone was coming into the room; he did not turn from the window.

"Ferdinand," said a voice, soft and very loving.

Then he turned and saw Isabella. She had waved all his servants out of the room and they were alone.

He looked at her sullenly for a few seconds, and her heart beat faster with her love for him, because he looked at that moment like a spoilt child, like their own little Isabella.

"Why, Ferdinand," she said, "we should not be bad friends."

He could not meet her eye. "It seems to be your wish," he mumbled.

She came to him and took his hand. "No, it is far from my wish. I was so happy, and now I am no longer so."

She knelt at his feet and was looking up at him.

For a few seconds he believed she had come to beg his pardon, to offer him all he asked, if he would stay with her.

Then he realized that until this moment he had not known Isabella. He had known a gentle woman, a woman who longed to please him, who loved with mingling tenderness and passion; and because he had been too much aware of Ferdinand to be aware of Isabella, he had thought he understood her.

She took his hand and kissed it. "Ferdinand," she said, "why should there be this trouble between us? We are quarrelling over power as children quarrel over sweetmeats. One day you will be King of Aragon, and it may be that you will sometimes ask me to help you with some problem in the governing of your country. I know I shall do the same as regards mine. Why, if you had your will in this matter and the Salic law was introduced into Castile, our little Isabella would no longer be heir to Castile and Leon. Think of that, Ferdinand. Come, my husband, do not, I beg you, I implore you, carry out your threat to leave me. For I need you. How can I rule these kingdoms without you? I shall need you a hundred times a day in our life together. Ferdinand, it is I, Isabella, who ask you . . . stay."

He looked at her then. There were tears shining in her eyes, and she knelt to him; but even as she knelt she remained Queen of Castile.

She was offering him a way out of his predicament. How could he return to Aragon except ignobly? She was saying : "How can I live happily without you, Ferdinand, I who need you so?"

He said : "Perhaps I have been hasty. It is not easy for a man . . ."

"No, it is not easy," she said eagerly, and she thought of him, Ferdinand, the beloved of his mother and father—and of herself. It was not easy for him to be merely the Queen's consort when he believed he should be King. "But you are King of Sicily now and one day, Ferdinand, you will be King of Aragon. And Aragon and Castile will be as one. Ferdinand, we must not allow the great happiness we have brought to each other to be spoilt. Think of the great happiness we shall bring to Castile and Aragon."

"I believe you are right," he said.

Then she smiled, and her smile was radiant.

"And since you say that you need me so much . . ."

"Ferdinand, I do, I do!" she cried.

Then she was on her feet and in his arms; and they clung together for a few moments.

She released herself and said : "You see, Ferdinand, we are so young and there is so much to do, and our lives lie before us . . ."

"It is true, Isabella," he said, and touched her cheek, looking at her as though he saw her afresh and that he had discovered something hitherto unknown to him.

"I want everyone to know that all is well," she said, "that everyone can be as happy as we are."

She drew him to the window and the people below saw them standing there.

Isabella put her hand in that of Ferdinand. He raised it to his lips and kissed it.

There was immediate understanding.

"Castile!" cried the people. "Castile for Isabella . . . and Ferdinand!"

Spain for the Sovereigns

© *Jean Plaidy 1960*

FERDINAND

It was growing dark as the cavalcade rode into the silent city of Barcelona on its way to the Palace of the Kings of Aragon. On it went, through streets so narrow that the tall grey houses—to which the smell of sea and harbour clung—seemed to meet over the cobbles.

At the head of this company of horsemen rode a young man of medium height and of kingly bearing. His complexion was fresh and tanned by exposure to the wind and sun; his features were well formed, his teeth exceptionally white, and the hair, which grew far back from his forehead, was light brown with a gleam of chestnut.

When any of his companions addressed him, it was with the utmost respect. He was some twenty-two years old, already a warrior and a man of experience, and only in the determination that all should respect his dignity did he betray his youth.

He turned to the man who rode beside him. "How she suffered, this city!" he said.

"It is true, Highness. I heard from the lips of the King, your father, that when he entered after the siege he could scarce refrain from weeping—such terrible sights met his eyes."

Ferdinand of Aragon nodded grimly. "A warning," he murmured, "to subjects who seek to defy their rightful King."

His companion replied: "It is so, Highness." He dared not remind Ferdinand that the civil war which had recently come to an end had been fought because of the murder of the rightful heir—Ferdinand's half-brother Carlos, his father's son by his first wife. It was a matter best forgotten, for now Ferdinand was very ready to take and defend all that his ambitious father, all that his doting mother, had procured for him.

The little cavalcade had drawn up before the Palace in which John of Aragon had his headquarters, and Ferdinand cried in his deep resonant voice: "What ails you all? I am here. I, Ferdinand, have come!"

There was immediate bustle within. Doors were flung open and grooms ran forward surrounding the party. Ferdinand leaped from his horse and ran into the Palace, where his father, who had heard his arrival, came to meet him, arms outstretched.

"Ferdinand! Ferdinand!" he cried, and his eyes filled with

tears as he embraced his son. "Ah, I knew you would not delay your coming. I knew you would be with me. I am singularly blessed. I was given the best of wives, and although she has now been taken from me, she has left me the best of sons."

The seventy-eight-year-old King of Aragon showed no signs of failing. Still strong and energetic—in spite of recent operations which had restored the sight of both eyes—he rarely permitted himself to show any weakness. But there was one emotion which he always failed to hide; that was the love he had for his dead wife and his son by her : Ferdinand.

His arm about Ferdinand's shoulder, John led his son into a small apartment and called for refreshment. When it was brought and they were alone Ferdinand said: "You sent for me, Father; that was enough to bring me hastening to your side."

John smiled. "But such a newly married husband, and such a charming wife!"

"Ah, yes," said Ferdinand, with a complacent smile. "Isabella was loth to lose me, but she is deeply conscious of duty, and when she heard of your need, she was certain that I should not fail you."

John nodded. "And all is well . . . in Castile, my son?"

"All is well, Father."

"And the child?"

"Healthy and strong."

"I would your little Isabella had been a boy!"

"There will be boys," said Ferdinand.

"Indeed there will be. And I will say this, Ferdinand. When you have a son, may he be so like yourself that all will say : 'Here is another Ferdinand come among us.' I cannot wish you better than that."

"Father, you think too highly of your son." But the young man's expression belied the charge.

John shook his head. "King of Castile! And one day . . . perhaps not far distant, King of Aragon."

"For the second title I would be content to wait all my life," said Ferdinand. "As for the first . . . as yet it is little more than a courtesy title."

"So Isabella is the Queen and you the Consort . . . for a time . . . for a time. I doubt not that very soon you will have brought her to understanding."

"Mayhap," agreed Ferdinand. "It is regrettable that the Salic law is not in force in Castile as in Aragon."

"Then, my son, you would be undoubted King and Isabella *your* Consort. Castile should be yours through your grandfather and namesake but for the fact that females are not excluded from the Castilian throne. But Isabella, the female heir, is your wife, my dearest son, and I am sure that this little difficulty is only a temporary one."

"Isabella is very loving," Ferdinand replied with a smile.

"There! Then soon all will be as we could wish."

"But let us talk of your affairs, Father. They are of greater moment, and it is for this purpose that I have come to you."

King John looked grave. "As you know," he said, "during the revolt of the Catalans it was necessary for me to ask help of Louis of France. He gave it to me, but Louis, as you know, never gives something for nothing."

"I know that the provinces of Roussillon and Cerdagne were placed in his custody as security, and that now they have risen in revolt against this foreign yoke."

"And have called to me for succour. Alas, the Seigneur du Lude has now invaded Roussillon with ten thousand infantry and nine hundred lances. Moreover, he has brought supplies that will keep his armies happy for months. The civil war has been long. You know how it has drained the exchequer."

"We must raise money, Father, in some way."

"That is why I have called you. I want you to go to Saragossa and by some means raise the money for our needs. Defeat at the hands of France would be disastrous."

Ferdinand was silent for a few seconds. "I am wondering," he said at length, "how it will be possible to wring the necessary funds from the estates of Aragon. How do matters stand in Saragossa?"

"There is much lawlessness in Aragon."

"Even as in Castile," answered Ferdinand. "There has been such strife for so long that civil affairs are neglected and rogues and robbers spring up all around us."

"It would seem," John told him, "that a certain Ximenes Gordo has become King of Saragossa."

"How can that be?"

"You know the family. It is a noble one. Ximenes Gordo has cast aside his nobility. He has taken municipal office and has put himself into a position of such influence that it is not easy, from this distance, to deal with him. All the important posts have been given to his friends and relations and those who offer a big enough bribe. He is a colourful rogue and has in some manner managed to win the popular esteem. He makes a travesty of justice and I have evidence that he is guilty of numerous crimes."

"His trial and execution should be ordered."

"My dear son, to do so might bring civil strife to Saragossa. I have too much on my hands. But if you are going to raise funds for our needs a great deal will depend on Ximenes Gordo."

"The King of Aragon dependent on a subject!" cried Ferdinand. "That seems impossible."

"Does it not, my son. But I am in dire need, and far from Saragossa."

Ferdinand smiled. "You must leave this matter to me, Father. I will go to Saragossa. You may depend upon it, I will find some means of raising the money you need."

"You will do it, I know," said John. "It is your destiny always to succeed."

Ferdinand smiled complacently. "I shall set off without delay for Saragossa, Father," he said.

John looked wistful. "So shortly come, so soon to go," he murmured. "Yet you are right," he added. "There is little time to lose."

"Tomorrow morning, at dawn, I shall leave," Ferdinand told him. "Your cause—as always—is my own."

* * *

On his way through Catalonia to Saragossa there was one call which Ferdinand could not deny himself the pleasure of making.

It must be as far as possible a secret call. There was one little person whom he longed to see and who meant a great deal to him, but he was determined to go to great lengths to conceal his existence from Isabella. He was beginning to realize that it was going to be somewhat difficult to live up to the ideal which his wife had made of him.

He and his followers had rested at an inn and, declaring that he would retire early, he with two of his most trusted attendants went to the room which had been assigned to him.

As soon as they were alone, he said: "Go to the stables. Have the horses made ready and I will join you when all is quiet."

"Yes, Highness."

Ferdinand was impatient when they had left him. How long his party took to settle down! He had to resist an impulse to go to them and demand that they retire to their beds immediately and fall into deep sleep.

That would be folly, of course, since the great need was for secrecy. He was not by nature impulsive. He knew what he wanted and was determined to get it; but experience had taught him that it was often necessary to wait a long time for success in one's endeavours. Ferdinand had learned to wait.

So now he did so, impatient yet restrained, until at last his servant was at the door.

"All is quiet, Highness. The horses are ready."

"That is well. Let us be off."

It was pleasant riding through the night. He had wondered whether to send a messenger ahead of him to warn her. But no. It should be a surprise. And if he found her with a lover, he did not greatly care. It was not she—beautiful as she was—who called him, it was not merely for her sake that he was ready to make this secret journey, news of which might be brought to the ears of Isabella.

"Oh, Isabella, my wife, my Queen," he murmured to himself, "you will have to learn something of the world one day. You will have to know that men, such as I am, who spend long periods away from the conjugal bed, cannot be denied a mistress now and then."

And from love affairs such as that which he had enjoyed with the Viscountess of Eboli there were often results.

Ferdinand smiled. He was confident of his powers to obtain what he would from all women—even his sedate, and rather alarmingly prim, Isabella.

He was remembering the occasion when he and the Viscountess had become lovers. It was during one of those spells when he was away from Castile, in Catalonia on his father's business. It was Isabella who had insisted that he leave her. "It is your duty to go to your father's aid," she had said.

Duty! he thought. It was a word frequently recurrent in Isabella's vocabulary.

She would never fail to do her duty. She had been brought up to regard it as of paramount importance. She would risk her life for the sake of duty; she did not know, she must not guess that, when she had allowed her husband to depart into Catalonia, she had risked his fidelity to their marriage bed.

It had happened. And now here he was at the Eboli mansion; the house was stirring and the cry went forth: "He is come! The Master is within the gates."

When he had given his horse to the waiting groom, he said: "Softly, I pray you all. This is an unofficial visit. I am passing on my way to Aragon and I but pause to pay a friendly call."

The servants understood. They knew of the relationship between their mistress and Don Ferdinand. They did not speak of it outside the household. They knew that it was the wish of Don

Ferdinand that this should be kept secret, and that it could be dangerous to offend him.

He had stepped into the house.

"Your mistress?" he asked of two women who had immediately dropped deep curtsies.

"She had retired for the night, Highness. But already she has heard of your coming."

Ferdinand looked up and saw his mistress at the head of the staircase. Her long dark hair fell in disorder about her shoulders; she was wearing a velvet robe of a rich ruby colour draped round her naked body.

She was beautiful; and she was faithful. He saw the joy in her face and his senses leaped with delight as he bounded up the stairs and they embraced.

"So . . . you have come at last . . ."

"You know that I would have been here before this, could I have arranged it."

She laughed, and keeping her arms about his neck, she said: "You have changed. You have grown older."

"A fate," he reminded her, "which befalls us all."

"But you have done it so becomingly," she told him.

They realized that they were being watched, and she took his arm and led him into her bedchamber.

There was a question which he wanted to ask above all others. Shrewdly he did not ask it . . . not yet. Much as she doted on the child, she must not suspect that it was for his sake that he had come and not for hers.

In her bedchamber he parted the velvet gown and kissed her body. She stood as though her ecstasy transfixed her.

He inevitably compared her with Isabella. Any woman, he told himself, would seem like a courtesan compared with Isabella. Virtue emanated from his wife. It surprised him that a halo was not visible about her head. Everything she did was done as a dedicated act. Even the sexual act—and there was no doubt that she loved him passionately—appeared, even in its most ecstatic moments, to be performed for the purpose of begetting heirs for the crown.

Ferdinand made excuses to himself for his infidelity. No man could subsist on a diet of unadulterated Isabella. There must be others.

Yet now, as he made love to his mistress, his thoughts were wandering. He would ask the all-important question at precisely the right moment. He prided himself on his calmness. It had been the admiration of his father and mother. But they had admired everything about him—good and bad qualities. And there had been times when he had been unable to curb his impetuosity. They would become fewer as he grew older. He was fully aware of that.

Now, satiated, his mistress lay beside him. There was a well-satisfied smile on her lips as he laced his fingers in hers.

"You are superb!" whispered Ferdinand. And then, as though it were an after-thought: "And . . . how is the boy?"

"He is well, Ferdinand."

"Tell me, does he ever speak of me?"

"Every day he says to me: 'Mother, do you think that this day my father will come?' "

"And what do you say to that?"

"I tell him that his father is the most important man in Aragon, in Catalonia, in Castile, and it is only because he is such an important man that he has not time to visit us."

"And his reply?"

"He says that one day he will be an important man like his father."

Ferdinand laughed with pleasure. "He is sleeping now?" he said wistfully.

"Worn out by the day's exertions. He is a General now, Ferdinand. He has his armies. You should hear him shouting orders."

"I would I could do so," said Ferdinand. "I wonder . . ."

"You wish to see him. You cannot wait. I know it. Perhaps if we were very quiet we should not wake him. He is in the next room. I keep him near me. I am always afraid that something may happen to him if I let him stray too far from me."

"What could happen to him?" demanded Ferdinand suddenly fierce.

"Oh, it is nothing, merely the anxieties of a mother." She had risen and put her robe about her. "Come, we will take a peep at him while he sleeps."

She picked up a candlestick and beckoned to Ferdinand, who threw on a few clothes and followed her to a door which she opened quietly.

In a small cot a boy of about three years was sleeping. One plump hand gripped the bedclothes, and the hair which curled about the well-shaped head had a gleam of chestnut in its brown.

This was a very beautiful little boy, and Ferdinand felt an immense pride as he looked down on him.

He and Isabella had a daughter, but this was his son, his first-born son; and the chubby charm and the resemblance to himself filled Ferdinand with an emotion which was rare to him.

"How soundly he sleeps!" he whispered; and he could not resist stooping over the bed and placing his lips against that soft head.

In that moment an impulse came to him to pick up the sleeping child and to take him from his mother, to take him into Castile, to present him to Isabella and say to her: "This is my son, my first-born son. The sight of him fills me with joy, and I will have him brought up here at Court with any children you and I may have."

He could never do such a thing. He imagined Isabella's reactions; and one thing he had learned since his marriage was the necessity of respecting Isabella in all her queenly dignity.

What a foolish thought when what he had to do was prevent Isabella's ever hearing of this child's existence.

The little boy awakened suddenly. He stared up at the man and woman by his bedside. Then he knew who the man was. He leaped up and a pair of small hot arms were about Ferdinand's neck.

"And what is the meaning of this?" cried Ferdinand in mock anger.

"It means my father is come," said the child.

"Then who are you?" asked Ferdinand.

"I am Alonso of Aragon," was the answer, and spoken like a Prince. "And you are Ferdinand of Aragon." The boy put his face close to Ferdinand's and peered into it; with his forefinger he traced the line of Ferdinand's nose.

"I will tell you something," he said.

"Well, what will you tell me?"

"We are something else too."

"What is that?"

"You are my father. I am your boy."

Ferdinand crushed the child in his arms. "It is true," he said. "It is true."

"You are holding me too tightly."

"It is unforgivable," answered Ferdinand.

"I will show you how I am a soldier now," the boy told him.

"But it is night and you should be asleep."

"Not when my father has come."

"There is the morning."

The boy looked shrewd and at that moment was poignantly like Ferdinand. "Then he may be gone," he said.

Ferdinand's hand stroked the glossy hair.

"It is his sorrow that he is not with you often. But tonight I am here and we shall be together."

The boy's eyes were round with wonder. "All through the night," he said.

"Yes, and tomorrow you will sleep."

"Tomorrow I will sleep."

The boy leaped out of bed. He was pulling open a trunk. He wanted to show his toys to his father. And Ferdinand knelt by the trunk and listened to the boy's chatter while his mother looked on and ambition gleamed in her eyes.

After a while the boy said: "Now tell me a story, Father. Tell me of when you were a soldier. Tell me about battles . . . and fighting and killing."

Ferdinand laughed. He sat down and nursed the boy in his arms.

And Ferdinand began to tell a story of his adventures, but before he was half-way through his son was asleep.

Ferdinand laid him gently in his bed, then with the boy's mother he tiptoed out of the room.

She said with a sudden fierceness: "You may have legitimate sons, princes born to be kings, but you will never have a child whom you can love as you love that one."

"I fear you may be right," said Ferdinand.

The door between the two rooms was fast shut, and Ferdinand leaned against it, looking at his mistress in the candlelight; she was no less beautiful when her eyes shone with ambition for her son.

"You may forget the love you once had for me," she went on, "but you will never forget me as the mother of your son."

"No," answered Ferdinand, "I shall never forget either of you."

He drew her to him and kissed her.

She said: "In the morning you will have gone. When shall I see you again?"

"Soon I shall be passing this way."

"And you will come," she answered, "to see the boy?"

"To see you both." He feigned a passion he did not altogether feel, for his thoughts were still with the child. "Come," he said, "there is little time left to us."

She took his hand and kissed it. "You will do something for him, Ferdinand. You will look after him. You will give him estates . . . titles."

"You may trust me to look after our son."

He led her to the bed and deliberately turned his thoughts from the child to his passion for the mother.

Later she said: "The Queen of Castile might not wish our son to receive the honours which you as his father would be ready to bestow upon him."

"Have no fear," said Ferdinand a little harshly. "I shall bestow them nevertheless."

"But the Queen of Castile . . ."

A sudden anger against Isabella came to Ferdinand. Were they already talking in Catalonia about his subservience to his wife? The Queen's Consort! It was not an easy position for a proud man to find himself in.

"You do not imagine that I will allow anything or anyone to come between me and my wishes for the boy!" he exclaimed. "I will make a promise now. When the Archbishopric of Saragossa falls vacant it shall be bestowed upon him . . . for a beginning."

The Viscountess of Eboli lay back, her eyes closed; she was the satisfied mistress, the triumphant mother.

* * *

Early next morning, Ferdinand took a hurried leave of the Viscountess of Eboli and kissed their sleeping son; then he sent one of his attendants back to the inn to tell his men who had slept there that he had gone on ahead of them and that they should overtake him before he crossed the Segre and passed into Aragon.

And as he rode on with his few attendants he tried to forget the son from whom he must part, and concentrate on the task ahead of him.

He called one of his men to ride beside him.

"What have you heard of this Ximenes Gordo who, it seems, rules Saragossa?"

"That he is a man of great cunning, Highness, and, in spite of his many crimes, has won the support of the people."

Ferdinand was grave. "I am determined," he said, "to countenance no other rulers but my Father and myself in Saragossa. And if this man thinks to set himself against me, he will discover that he is foolish."

They rode on in silence and were shortly joined by the rest of the party. Ferdinand believed that none of them was aware of the visit he had paid to the Viscountess of Eboli. Yet, he thought, when it is necessary to bestow honours on the boy there will be speculation.

He felt angry. Why should he have to pay secret calls on a woman? Why should he demean himself by subterfuge? He had never been ashamed of his virility before his marriage. Was he—Ferdinand of Aragon—allowing himself to be overawed by Isabella of Castile?

It was an impossible situation; and Isabella was like no other woman he had ever known. It was strange that when they had first met he had been most struck by her gentleness.

Isabella had two qualities which were strange companions—gentleness and determination.

Ferdinand admonished himself. He was dwelling on domestic matters, on love and jealousy, when he should be giving all his thoughts to the situation in Saragossa, and the all-important task of raising funds for his father.

* * *

Ferdinand was welcomed at Saragossa by its most prominent citizen—Ximenes Gordo. It was Gordo who rode through the streets at the side of the heir to the crown.

One would imagine, thought Ferdinand, that it was Ximenes Gordo who was their Prince, and Ferdinand his henchman.

Some men, young as Ferdinand was, might have expressed displeasure. Ferdinand did not; he nursed his resentment. He had noticed how the poor, who gathered in the streets to watch the procession, fixed their eyes admiringly on Gordo. The man had a magnetism, a strong personality; he was like a robber baron who held the people's respect because they both feared and admired him.

"The citizens know you well," said Ferdinand.

"Highness," was the bland answer, "they see me often. I am always with them."

"And I am often far away, of necessity," said Ferdinand.

"They rarely have the pleasure and honour of seeing their Prince. They must content themselves with his humble servant who does his best to see that justice is administered in the absence of his King and Prince."

"It would not appear that the administration is very successful," Ferdinand commented dryly.

"Why, Highness, these are lawless times."

Ferdinand glanced at the debauched and crafty face of the man who rode beside him; but still he did not betray the anger and disgust he felt.

"I come on an urgent errand from my father," he announced.

Gordo waited for Ferdinand to proceed—in a manner which seemed to the young Prince both royal and condescending. It was as though Gordo were implying: You may be the heir to

Aragon, but during your absence I have become the King of Saragossa.

Still Ferdinand restrained his anger, and continued: "Your King needs men, arms and money—urgently."

Gordo put his head on one side in an insolent way. "The people of Saragossa will not tolerate further taxation, I fear."

Ferdinand's voice was silky. "Will not the people of Saragossa obey the command of their King?"

"There was recently a revolt in Catalonia, Highness. There might be a revolt in Saragossa."

"Here . . . in the heart of Aragon! The Aragonese are not Catalans. They would be loyal to their King. I know it."

"Your Highness has been long absent."

Ferdinand gazed at the people in the streets. Had they changed? he wondered. What happened when men such as Ximenes Gordo took charge and ruled a city? There had been too many wars, and how could Kings govern their kingdoms wisely and well when they must spend so much time away from them in order to be sure of keeping them? Thus it was that scoundrels seized power, setting up their evil control over neglected cities.

"You must tell me what has been happening during my absence," said Ferdinand.

"It shall be my pleasure, Highness."

* * *

Ferdinand had been several days in the Palace of Saragossa, yet he had made no progress with his task. At every turn, it seemed, there were Ximenes Gordo and his friends to obstruct him.

They ruled the town, for Gordo had placed all his adherents in the important posts. All citizens who were possessed of wealth were being continually robbed by him; his power was immense, because wherever he went he was cheered by the great army of beggars. They had nothing to lose, and it delighted them to see the industrious townsfolk robbed of their possessions.

Ferdinand listened to all that his spies told him. He was astounded at the influence Gordo exercised in the town. He had heard of his growing power, but he had not believed it could be so great.

Gordo was not perturbed by the visit of the heir to the throne, so convinced was he of his own strength, and he believed that, if it came to a battle between them, he would win. His friends, who profited from his unscrupulous ways, would certainly not want a return to strict laws and justice. He had only to call to the rabble and the beggars to come to his aid and he would have a fierce mob to serve him.

Ferdinand said: "There is only one course open to me; I must arrest that man. I must show him and the citizens who is master here. Until he is imprisoned I cannot begin to raise the money my father needs, and there is no time for delay."

"Highness," he was told by his advisers, "if you arrest Gordo, the Palace will be stormed by the mob. Your own life might be in danger. The scum of Saragossa and his rascally friends stand behind him. We are powerless."

Ferdinand was silent; he dismissed his advisers, but his thoughts were not idle.

* * *

Gordo was with his family when the message arrived from the Prince.

He read it and cried: "Our haughty little Prince has changed his tune. He implores me to visit him at the Palace. He wishes to talk with me on an urgent matter. He has something to say to me which he wishes to say to no other."

Gordo threw back his head and laughed aloud.

"So he has come to heel, our little Ferdinand, eh! And so it should be. This young bantam! A boy! What more? They say that in Castile he is the one who wears the skirt. Well, as Doña Isabella can keep him in order in Castile, so can Ximenes Gordo in Saragossa."

He waved a gay farewell to his wife and children, called for his horse and rode off to the Palace.

The people in the streets called to him: "Good fortune, Don Ximenes Gordo! Long life to you!"

And he answered these greetings with a gracious inclination of the head. After all, he was King of Saragossa in all but name.

Arriving at the Palace he flung his reins to a waiting groom. The groom was one of the Palace servants, but he bowed low to Don Ximenes Gordo.

Gordo was flushed with pride as he entered the building. He should be the one who was living here. And why should he not do so?

Why should he not say to young Ferdinand: "I have decided to take up my residence here. You have a home in Castile, my Prince; why do you not go to it? Doña Isabella, *Queen* of Castile, will be happy to welcome her Consort. Why, my Prince, it may well be that there is a happier welcome awaiting you there in Castile than you find even here in Aragon."

And what pleasure to see the young bantam flinch, to know that he realized the truth of those words!

The servants bowed to him—he imagined they did so with the utmost obsequiousness. Oh, there was no doubt that Ferdinand was beaten, and realized who was the master.

Ferdinand was waiting for him in the presence chamber. He looked less humble than he had expected, but Gordo reminded himself that the young man was arrogant by nature and found it difficult to assume a humble mien. He must be taught. Gordo relished the thought of watching Ferdinand ride disconsolately out of Saragossa, defeated.

Gordo bowed, and Ferdinand said in a mild and, so it seemed, placating voice: "It was good of you to come so promptly at my request."

"I came because I have something to say to Your Highness."

"First," said Ferdinand, still mildly, "I shall beg you to listen to me."

Gordo appeared to consider this, but Ferdinand had taken his arm, in a most familiar manner, as though, thought Gordo, he accepted him as an equal. "Come," said Ferdinand, "it is more private in my ante-chamber, and we shall need privacy."

Ferdinand had opened a door and gently pushed Gordo before him into a room. The door had closed behind them before Gordo realized that they were not alone.

As he looked round that room Gordo's face turned pale; in those first seconds he could not believe that his eyes did not deceive him. The room had been converted into a place of execution. He saw the scaffolding, the rope and a masked man whom he knew to be the public hangman. Besides him stood a priest, and several guards were stationed about the room.

Ferdinand's manner had changed. His eyes glittered as he addressed Gordo in stern tones. "Don Ximenes Gordo, you have not long to make your peace, and you have many sins on your conscience."

Gordo, the bully, had suddenly lost all his swaggering arrogance.

"This cannot be . . ." he cried.

"It is to be," Ferdinand told him.

"That rope is for . . . for . . ."

"You have guessed right. It is for you."

"But to condemn me thus . . . without trial! Is this justice?"

"It is my justice," said Ferdinand coolly. "And in my father's absence I rule Aragon."

"I demand a trial."

"You would be better advised to concern yourself with the salvation of your soul. Your time is short."

"I will not submit. . . ."

Ferdinand signed to the guards, two of whom came forward to seize Gordo.

"I beg of you . . . have mercy," he implored.

"Pleasant as it is to hear you beg," said Ferdinand, "there will be no mercy for you. You are to die, and that without delay. This is the reward for your crimes." Ferdinand signed to the priest. "He has urgent need of you and the time is passing."

"There have been occasions," said Gordo, "when I have served your father well."

"That was before you became puffed up by your arrogance," answered Ferdinand, "but it shall not be forgotten. Your wife and children shall receive my protection as reward for the service you once gave my father. Now, say your prayers or you will leave this Earth with your manifold sins upon you."

Gordo had fallen to his knees; the priest knelt with him.

Ferdinand watched them.

And after an interval he signed to the hangman to do his work.

* * *

There was silence in the streets of Saragossa. The news was being circulated in the great houses and those haunts frequented by the rabble. There had been arrests, and those who had been seized were the more prominent of Gordo's supporters.

Then in the market-place the body of a man was hung that all might see what befell those who flouted the authority of the rulers of Aragon.

Gordo! It seemed incredible. There was the man who a few days before had been so sure of his ability to rule Saragossa. And now he was nothing but a rotting corpse.

The young Prince of Aragon rode through the streets of Saragossa; there were some who averted their eyes, but there were many to cheer him. They had been mistaken in him. They had thought him a young boy who could not even take first place in Castile. They had been mistaken. Whatever happened in Castile, he was, in the absence of his father, master of Aragon.

The volume of the cheers began to increase.

"Don Ferdinand for Aragon!"

Ferdinand began to believe that he would successfully complete the task which he had come to Saragossa to perform. He had been ruthless; he had ignored justice; but, he assured himself, the times were harsh and, when dealing with men such as Gordo, one could only attack with weapons similar to their own.

So far he had succeeded; and success was all that mattered.

The money so desperately needed was coming in, and if it was less than he and his father had hoped for that was due to the poverty of the people, not to their unwillingness to provide it.

Soon he would rejoin his father; and on the way he would call and see his little Alonso.

* * *

Messengers from Castile came riding into Saragossa. They had come in great haste, fearing that they might arrive to find Ferdinand had already left.

Ferdinand had them brought to him immediately.

He was thoughtful as he read what his wife had written. It was all the more effective because Isabella was by nature so calm.

She was asking him to return without delay. There was trouble about to break in Castile. An army was gathering to march against her, and many powerful nobles of Castile had gone over to the enemies' camp.

These men were insisting that she was not the rightful heir to the crown. It was true she was the late King Henry's half-sister, and he had no son. But he had a daughter—whom many believed to be illegitimate, and who was even known as La Beltraneja because her father was almost certainly Beltran de la Cueva, Duke of Albuquerque.

Those who had set themselves against Isabella now sought to place La Beltraneja on the throne of Castile.

There was a possibility that Portugal was giving support to their enemies.

Castile was in danger. Isabella was in danger. And at such a time she needed the military skill and experience of her husband.

"It may well be," wrote Isabella, "that my need of you at this time is greater than that of your father."

Ferdinand thought of her, kneeling at her *prie-Dieu* or with her advisers carefully weighing the situation. She would not have said that, had she not meant it with all her heart.

He shouted to his attendants.

"Prepare to leave Saragossa at once. I shall need messengers to go to my father and let him know that what he needs is on its way to him. As for myself and the rest of us, we must leave for Castile without delay.

ISABELLA

ISABELLA, Queen of Castile, looked up from the table at which she sat writing. There was a quiet pleasure in her serene blue eyes, and those who knew her very well wondered if what they suspected was true. She had been, these last weeks, a little more placid than usual, and through that placidity shone a certain joy. The Queen of Castile could be keeping a secret to herself; and it might be one which she would wish to remain unknown until she could share it with her husband.

The ladies-in-waiting whispered together. "Do you think it can be true? Is the Queen pregnant?"

They put their heads together and made calculations. It was only a few weeks since Ferdinand had ridden away to join his father.

"Let us pray that it is true," said these ladies, "and that this time it will be a son."

Even as she dealt with the papers on her table, Isabella too was saying to herself: "This time let it be a son."

She was very happy.

That destiny for which she had been prepared was being fulfilled; she was married to Ferdinand after years of waiting, after continual hazards and fears that the marriage which had been planned in their childhood might not take place.

But, largely due to her own determination—and that of Ferdinand and his family—the marriage had taken place; and on the death of Ferdinand's father, when Ferdinand would be King of Aragon, the crowns of Aragon and Castile would be united; and, apart from that small province still occupied by the Moors, Isabella and Ferdinand could then be said to rule over Spain.

It was certainly the realization of a dream.

And Ferdinand, her husband, a year younger than herself, handsome, virile, was all that she had hoped for in a husband—or almost. She had to admit that he did not accept with a very good grace the fact that she was Queen of Castile and he her Consort. But he would in time, for she had no intention of letting a rift grow between them. Theirs was to be a marriage, perfect in all respects. She was going to ask his advice in all matters; and if it should ever be necessary for her to make a decision with which he did not agree she would employ the utmost tact and try to persuade him in time to agree with her.

She smiled fondly.

Dear Ferdinand. He would hate this separation as much as she did. But it was his duty to go to his father's help when he was called upon to do so. And as her good confessor, Tomás de Torquemada, used to tell her—in those days when he had undertaken her religious instruction—no matter what the rank, duty came first.

Now she smiled, for her attendant was announcing that Cardinal Don Pedro Gonzalez de Mendoza was begging an audience.

She asked that he be brought to her without delay.

The Cardinal came to her and bowed low.

"Welcome," said Isabella. "You look disturbed, Cardinal. Is aught wrong?"

The Cardinal let his eyes rest on those of her attendants who remained in the apartment.

"I trust all is well with Your Highness. Then all will be well with me," he said. "Your Highness appears to be in excellent health."

"It is so," said Isabella.

She understood. Soon she would dismiss her attendants because she guessed that the Cardinal had something to say which could not be said before others; also he did not wish it to be known that his mission was one of great secrecy.

Isabella felt herself warming to this man, and she was surprised at herself.

He was Cardinal of Spain and, although he was the fourth son of the Marquis of Santillana, so talented was he, and to such a high position had he risen, that he was now at the head of the powerful Mendoza family.

To his Palace at Guadalaxara he could draw the most influential men in Spain, and there persuade them to act for or against the Queen.

These were dangerous times, and Isabella's great desire was to promote law and order in Castile. She had been brought up to believe that one day this duty might be hers; and she, with that conscientiousness which was a part of her nature, had determined to rule her country well. There was one condition which brought a country low and that was war. She wished with all her heart to be able to lead her country to peace; and she believed that she could do so through the support of men such as Cardinal Mendoza.

He was an exceptionally handsome man, gracious and charming. About forty years old, in spite of his association with the Church he had not lived the life of a churchman. He was too fond of the luxuries of life, and he deemed it unwise for a man to deny himself these.

Abstinence narrowed the mind and starved the soul, he had said. Hypocrisy was lying in wait for the man who denied his body the daily food it craved; and the man who indulged himself now and then was apt to be more lenient with other men; he would find a kindly tolerance growing within him to replace that fanaticism which could often find an outlet in cruelty.

Thus he soothed his conscience. He liked good food and wine, and he had several illegitimate children.

These sins, thought Isabella, sat lightly upon him. She deplored them, but there were times—and these would become more frequent—when she must compromise and suppress her natural abhorrence for the good of the country.

She knew that she needed this charming, tolerant and brilliant man on her side.

When they were alone, he said: "I have come to warn Your Highness. There is one who, while feigning to be your friend, is making plans to desert you for your enemies."

Isabella nodded slowly. "I think I know his name," she said.

Cardinal Mendoza took a step closer to her. "Alfonso Carillo, Archbishop of Toledo."

"It is hard to believe," Isabella spoke sadly. "I remember how he stood beside me. There was a time when I might have become the prisoner of my enemies. It would have meant not only incarceration but doubtless in time a dose of poison would have ended my life. But he was there to save me, and I feel I should not be alive, nor be where I am today but for the Archbishop of Toledo."

"Your Highness doubtless owes much to this man. But his object in helping you to the crown was that, although you wore it, he should rule through you."

"I know. Ambition is his great failing."

"Have a care, Highness. Watch this man. You should not share matters of great secrecy with him. Remember that he is wavering now. This time next week . . . perhaps tomorrow . . . he may be with your enemies."

"I will remember your words," Isabella assured him. "Now I pray you sit here with me and read these documents."

The Cardinal did so, and watching him, Isabella thought:

Have I gained the support of this man, only to lose that of one who served me so well in the past?

* * *

Impatiently, Alfonso Carillo, Archbishop of Toledo waited.

It was intolerable, he told himself that *he* should be kept waiting. It should be enough that the Queen knew he wished to see her for her to dismiss any other person that she might receive him.

"Ingratitude!" he murmured, as he paced up and down. "All that I have done in the past is forgotten. Since that young cockerel, Ferdinand, sought to show his power over me, he has poisoned her mind against me. And my place beside her has been taken by Mendoza."

His eyes narrowed. He was a man of choleric temper whose personality would have been more suited to the military camp than to the Church. But as Archbishop of Toledo he was Primate of Spain; he was determined to cling to his position; and although he prided himself on having raised Isabella to the throne, if she failed to recognize that the most important person in Castile was not its Queen, nor her Consort, nor Cardinal Mendoza, but Alfonso Carillo, he, who had helped her to reach the throne, would be prepared to dash her from it.

His eyes were flashing; he was ready for battle.

And so he waited; and, when at length he was told that the Queen was ready to receive him, he met Cardinal Mendoza coming from her apartments.

They acknowledged each other coolly.

"I have been waiting long," said the Archbishop reproachfully.

"I crave your pardon, but I had state matters to discuss with the Queen."

The Archbishop hurried on; it would be unseemly if two men of the Church indulged in violence; and he was feeling violent.

He went into the audience chamber.

Isabella's smile was apologetic.

"I regret," she said placatingly, "that you were forced to wait so long."

"I also regret," the Archbishop retorted curtly.

Isabella looked surprised, but the Archbishop considered himself especially privileged.

"The waiting is over, my lord. I pray you let us come to business."

"It would seem that Your Highness prefers to discuss state matters with Cardinal Mendoza."

"I am fortunate in having so many brilliant advisers."

"Highness, I have come to tell you that I can no longer serve you while you retain the services of the Cardinal."

"I suggest, my lord, that you go too far."

The Archbishop looked haughtily at this young woman. He could not help but see her as she had been when as a young Princess she asked for his help. He remembered how he had set up her young brother Alfonso as King of Castile while Henry IV still lived; he remembered how he had offered to make Isabella Queen on Alfonso's death, and how she had gently reminded him that it was not possible for her to be Queen while the true King, her half-brother Henry, still lived.

Had she forgotten what she owed to him?

"I pray," murmured the Archbishop, "that Your Highness will reconsider this matter."

"I should certainly not wish you to leave me," said Isabella.

"It is for your Highness to choose."

"But I choose that you should remain and curb your animosity towards the Cardinal. If you will be the Cardinal's friend I am assured that he will be yours."

"Highness, it is long since I visited my estates at Alcalá de Henares. I may shortly be asking your permission to retire there from Court for a while."

Isabella smiled sweetly. She did not believe that the Archbishop would willingly go into retirement.

"You are too important to us for that to be allowed," she told him; and he appeared to be placated.

* * *

But the Archbishop was far from satisfied. Every day he saw Cardinal Mendoza being taken more and more into his mistress's confidence and, a few weeks after that interview with the Queen, he made an excuse to retire from Court.

He had, however, no intention of retiring to his estates. He had decided that, since Isabella refused to be his puppet, he must set up one in her place who would be.

He was well aware that there were certain men in Spain who were dissatisfied with the succession of Isabella and would be ready to give their allegiance to the young Princess Joanna La Beltraneja, who many preferred to believe was not illegitimate—for if she were the legitimate daughter of the late King, then she, not Isabella, should be Queen of Castile.

He called to his house certain men whom he knew to be ready to rebel. Among these was the Marquis of Villena, son of the great Marquis, the Archbishop's nephew who, before his death, had played as big a part in his country's politics as the Archbishop himself. The present Marquis might not be a brilliant intriguer like his father, but he was a great soldier, and as such thirsted for battle. He was very rich, this young Marquis, and because he owned vast estates in Toledo and Murcia he could raise support from these provinces.

There were also the Marquis of Cadiz and the Duke of Arevalo.

When these men were gathered together the Archbishop, making sure that they were not overheard, announced his plans to them.

"Isabella has assumed the crowns of Castile and Leon," he said, "but there appears to be some doubt throughout this land as to whether she has a right to them. There are many who would rejoice to see the Princess Joanna in her place."

There were murmurs of approval. None of these men had received great honours from Isabella and, if the young Princess Joanna were accepted as Queen of Castile, since she was only twelve years old, there would be a Regency and high places for many of them.

Eyes glittered, and hands curled about sword hilts. A Regency would be a very desirable state of affairs.

"I strongly suspect these efforts to declare the Princess Joanna illegitimate," stated the Archbishop; and nobody reminded him that not very long ago he was one of the most fiery advocates of Joanna's illegitimacy and Isabella's right to the throne.

The circumstances had changed. Ferdinand had sought to curb his power; Isabella had transferred her interest to Cardinal Mendoza. Therefore the Archbishop had decided to change his mind.

"My lord Archbishop," said Villena, "I pray you tell us what plans you have for dethroning Isabella and setting up Joanna in her place."

"There is only one way of bringing this about, my friend," replied the Archbishop, "and that is with the sword."

"It would be necessary to raise an army," suggested Arevalo. "Is that possible?"

"It must be possible," said the Archbishop. "We cannot allow a usurper to retain the throne."

He smiled at the assembly. "I know what you are thinking, my friends. Isabella has won the allegiance of many. Ferdinand is related to many Castilian families. It might be difficult to raise an army, you are thinking. Yet we will do it. And I have other plans. They concern the Princess Joanna. Do not forget that young lady has her part to play in our schemes."

"I cannot see the young Princess riding into battle," said Villena.

"You take me too literally, my dear Marquis," answered the Archbishop. "You cannot believe that I would have brought you here unless I had something to put before you. The Princess will be the bait we have to offer. Then I think we can draw powerful forces into the field. I propose to despatch an embassy immediately. My friends, let us put our heads close together and lower our voices, for even here there may be spies. I will now acquaint you with my plans. They concern Portugal."

Many of those present began to smile. They could see whither the Archbishop's plans were leading.

They nodded.

How fortunate, they were thinking, that the Archbishop was on their side. How careless of Isabella to have lost his friendship, when such a loss could lead to a much greater one: that of the throne of Castile.

* * *

Alfonso V of Portugal had listened with great interest to the proposals which had been brought to him from the secret faction of Castile, headed by the Archbishop of Toledo.

He discussed this matter with his son, Prince John.

"Why, Father," said the Prince, "I can see that naught but good would come of this."

"It will mean taking war into Castile, my son. Have you considered that?"

"You have been successful in your battles with the Barbary Moors. Why should you not be equally so in Castile?"

"Have you considered the forces which could be put into the field against us?"

"Yes, and I have thought of the prize."

Alfonso smiled at his son. John was ambitious and greedy for the good of Portugal. If they succeeded, Castile and Portugal would be as one. There might be a possibility of the Iberian Peninsula's eventually coming under one ruler—and that ruler would be of the House of Portugal.

It was a tempting offer.

There was something else which made Alfonso smile.

There had been a time when he had thought to marry Isabella. His sister, Joanna, had married Isabella's half-brother, Henry IV of Castile. Joanna was flighty. He had often warned her about that. It was all very well for a Queen, married to a husband like

Henry, to take an occasional lover, but she should have made sure that there was no scandal until long after the birth of the heir to the throne. Joanna had been careless, and, as a result, his little niece—another Joanna—was reputed to be the daughter, not of Henry the King, but of Beltran de la Cueva, Duke of Albuquerque; and so strong was this belief that young Joanna had been dubbed "La Beltraneja", and the name still clung to her. And because Joanna had been declared illegitimate, Isabella was now Queen of Castile. But that state of affairs might not continue; and if he decided to go to war it should not prevail.

He had been very angry with Isabella. He recalled how he had gone to Castile to become betrothed to her, and she had firmly refused him.

It was an insult. On one occasion she had declared her unwillingness to accept him as a suitor and had sought the help of the Cortes in averting the marriage. It was too humiliating for a King of Portugal to endure.

Therefore it would be a great pleasure to turn Isabella from the throne and set the crown on the head of his little niece.

John was smiling at him now. "Think, Father," he said. "When little Joanna is Queen of Castile and your bride, you will be master of Castile."

"She is my niece."

"What of that! The Holy Father will readily give the dispensation; especially when he sees that we can put a strong army in the field."

"And but twelve years old!" added Alfonso.

"It is unlike a bridegroom to complain of the youth of his bride."

Alfonso said: "Let us put this matter before the Council. If they are in agreement, then we will give our answer to the Archbishop of Toledo and his friends."

"And if," said John, "they should be so misguided as to ignore the advantages of such a situation, it must be our duty, Father, to insist on their accepting our decision."

* * *

Little Joanna was bewildered. From her earliest childhood she had known there was something strange about herself. Sometimes she was called Highness, sometimes Infanta, sometimes Princess. She was never quite sure what her rank was.

Her father had been kind to her when they met, but he was dead now; and she had not seen her mother for a long time when the call came for her to go to Madrid.

When her father had died she had heard that her aunt Isabella had been proclaimed Queen of Castile; and Isabella had said that she, Joanna, was to have her own household and an entourage worthy of a Princess of Castile. Isabella was kind, she knew; and she would be good to her as long as she did not allow anyone to say that she was the King's legitimate daughter.

But how could a girl of twelve prevent people from saying what they wished to say?

Joanna lived in fear that one day important men would come to her, disturbing her quiet existence among her books and music; she was terrified that they would kneel at her feet, swear allegiance and tell her that they were going to serve her with their lives.

She did not want that and all it implied. She wanted to live in peace, away from these awe-inspiring men.

And now she was on her way to Madrid because her mother had sent for her.

She had heard many stories of her mother. She was very beautiful, it was said; and when she first came into Castile to be the wife of the King, although her manner had been frivolous by Castilian standards, no one had guessed that she would be responsible for one of the greatest and most dangerous controversies which had ever disturbed the succession of Castile.

And she, the Princess Joanna, was at the very heart of that controversy. It was an alarming thought.

She had often met the man who was reputed to be her father. He was tall and very handsome; a man of great importance and a brave soldier. But he was not her mother's husband, and therein lay the root of the trouble.

When she saw her mother on this occasion she would ask her to tell her sincerely the truth; and if Beltran de la Cueva, Duke of Albuquerque, was indeed her father she would make this widely known and in future refuse to allow anyone to insist on her right to the throne.

It was a big undertaking for a twelve-year-old girl, and Joanna feared that she was not bold or very determined; but there must be some understanding if she were ever to live in peace.

And, now that she was going to her mother's establishment in Madrid, she trembled to think what she might discover there. She had heard whispers and rumours from her servants of the life her mother led in Madrid. When she had left the King she had kept a lavishly extravagant house where, it was said, parties of a scandalous nature frequently took place.

Joanna had several brothers and sisters, she believed. They, however, were more fortunate than she was. They shared the stigma of illegitimacy, but nobody could suggest that they had even a remote claim to the throne.

She was alarmed to contemplate what sort of house this was to which she was going; and as she, with her little company, rode along the valley of the Manzanares the plain which stretched about them seemed gloomy and full of foreboding. She turned her horse away from the distant Sierras towards the town, and as they entered it they were met by a party of riders.

The man at the head of this party rode up to Joanna and, bowing his head, told her that he had been watchful for her coming.

"I am to take you to the Queen, your mother, Princess," he told her. "She has gone to a convent in Madrid, and it would be advisable for you to join her there with all speed."

"My mother . . . in a convent!" cried Joanna; for it was the last place in which she would expect to find her gay and frivolous mother.

"She thought it wise to rest there awhile," was the answer. "You will find her changed."

"Why has my mother gone to this convent?" she asked.

"She will explain to you when you see her," was the answer.

They rode into the town, and eventually they reached the convent. Here Joanna was received with great respect by the Mother Superior, who immediately said: "You are fatigued, Princess, but it would be well if you came to see the Queen without delay."

"Take me to her, I pray you," said Joanna.

The Mother Superior led the way up a cold stone staircase to a cell, which contained little more than a bed and a crucifix on the wall; and here lay Joanna, Princess of Portugal, Queen to the late Henry IV of Castile.

Joanna knelt by her mother's bed, and the older Joanna smiled wanly. Kneeling there, the Princess knew that it was the approach of death which had driven her mother to repentance.

* * *

Joanna sat by her mother's bed.

"So you see," said the Dowager Queen of Castile, "I have not long to live. Who would have thought that I should follow Henry so soon?"

"Oh, my Mother, if you lived quietly, if you rest here, you may recover and live for many more years."

"No, my child. It is not possible. I am exhausted. I am worn out. I have lived my life fully, recklessly. Now the price is demanded for such a life. I am repentant, yet I fear that if I were young again, if I felt life stirring within me, I should find the temptation which beckoned me irresistible."

"You are too young to die, Mother."

"Yet my life has been full. I have had lovers . . . my child . . . so many lovers that I cannot recall a half of them. It was an exciting life . . . a life of pleasure. But now it ebbs away."

"Mother, Castile has paid dearly for your pleasure."

Over the Dowager Queen's face there spread a smile of amusement and mischief.

"I shall never be forgotten. I, the wayward Queen, had a hand in shaping the future of Castile, did I not?"

Young Joanna shivered.

"Mother, there is a question I must ask you. It is important that I know the truth. So much depends on it."

"I know what is on your mind, my child. You ask yourself the same question which all Castile asks. Who is your father? It is the most important question in Castile."

"It is the answer that is important," said Joanna softly. "I would know, Mother. If I am not the King's daughter, I think I should like to go into a convent like this and be quiet for a very long time."

"A convent life! That is no life at all!"

"Mother, I beg of you, tell me."

"If I told you that Henry was your father what would you do?"

"There is only one thing I could do, Mother. I should be the rightful Queen of Castile, and it would be my duty to take the throne."

"What of Isabella?"

"She would have no alternative but to relinquish the throne."

"And do you think she would? You do not know Isabella, nor Ferdinand . . . nor all those men who are determined to uphold her."

"Mother, tell me the truth."

The Dowager Queen smiled. "I am weak," she said. "I will tell you later if I can. Yet, how could even I be sure? Sometimes I think you are like the King; sometimes you remind me of Beltran. Beltran was a handsome man, daughter. The handsomest at Court. And Henry. . . . Oh, it seems so long ago. I look back into mists, my child. I cannot remember. I am so tired now. Sit still awhile and I will try to think. Give me your hand, Joanna. Later it will come back to me. Who . . . who is my Joanna's father. Was it Henry? Was it Beltran?"

Joanna knelt by the bedside and her eyes were imploring. "I must know, Mother. I must know."

But the Dowager Queen had closed her eyes, and her lips murmured: "Henry, was it you? You, Beltran, was it you?"

Then she slipped into sleep; her face was so white and still that Joanna thought she was already dead.

* * *

The Dowager Queen of Castile had been laid in her tomb, and Joanna remained in the convent. The bells were tolling, and as she listened to their dismal notes she thought: I shall never know the answer now.

The peace of the convent seemed to close in around her, sheltering her from the outside world in which a mighty storm was rising; it was a storm which she could not escape. It was for this reason that the peace of the convent seemed doubly entrancing.

Each morning she thought to herself: Will this be the last day that I am allowed to enjoy this peace?

And as the weeks passed she began to wonder whether she had been unnecessarily anxious. Isabella had been proclaimed in many towns of Castile as Queen. The people admired Isabella; she, with Ferdinand, was so suited to become their Queen. Perhaps the people of Castile did not wish for trouble any more than she did. Perhaps they would now be content to forget that Joanna, wife of Henry IV of Castile, had had a daughter who might or might not be the King's.

One day two noblemen came riding to the convent. They came on a secret mission and they wished for an audience with the Princess Joanna.

As soon as they were brought to her and announced themselves as the Duke of Arevalo and the Marquis of Villena she knew that this was the end of her peace.

They bowed low and humbly.

"We have great news for you, Princess," they told her; and her heart sank, for she knew the purport of this news before they told her. She interpreted the ambitious glitter in their eyes.

"Princess," said Arevalo, "we have come to tell you that you are not forgotten."

She lowered her eyes lest they should read in them that it was her dearest wish to be forgotten.

"This is news to set Your Highness' heart soaring with hope," went on Villena. "There is a powerful force behind us, and we shall succeed in turning the impostor Isabella from the throne and setting you up in her place."

"There is great news from Portugal," added Arevalo.

"From Portugal?" Joanna asked.

"The King of Portugal, Alfonso V, asks your hand in marriage."

"My . . . mother's brother!"

"Have no fear. His Holiness will not withhold a dispensation if we can show him that we have the means to oust Isabella from the throne."

"But my uncle is an old man. . . ."

"He is the King of Portugal, Highness. Moreover, he has an army to put into the field. We cannot fail with Portugal behind us. Highness, we shall succeed, and in succeeding we shall bring you a crown and a husband."

Joanna felt unable to reply. She was struck dumb with horror. That ageing man, her uncle, as a husband! War . . . with herself as the reason for it!

She turned to these men, about to protest, but she did not speak, because, when she looked at their hard ambitious faces, she knew that it was useless. She knew her personal feelings were of no account. She was to be the figurehead, the symbol, and they would declare that they fought for her sake.

For my sake, she thought bitterly. To give me a throne which I do not want. To give me for a husband an ageing man who terrifies me!

* * *

Isabella was frowning over documents which were spread on a table before her in her private apartments in the Madrid Alcazar.

These documents told a desperate story, for to study them was to learn how ill-equipped for battle were the armies of Castile.

It seemed to her that, should there be a rising in Castile, she would not have more than about five hundred horse to attempt to quell it; and she was not even sure on which towns she could rely.

The Archbishop of Toledo had retired to his estates in Alcalá de Henares and she was not sure how far he was ready to go in order to betray her. The loss of his friendship wounded her deeply; and the practical side of her nature deplored it even more. In those stormy days which had preceded the death of her brother she had come to learn something of the resourcefulness of this man; and that at such a critical time he had ceased to be her friend hurt her. That he might become her active enemy horrified her.

War was what she dreaded more than anything. She needed long years of peace that she might restore order to Castile. She had taken over a bankrupt kingdom rent by anarchy, and she was determined to make it rich and law-abiding. Yet if at this stage she were plunged into war, how would she fare?

She had so little at her disposal. Her good friend Andres de Cabrera, who, in the Alcazar at Segovia, had charge of the treasury, had warned her that the royal coffers were almost empty. No war could be waged without men and equipment; and now it seemed that reckless men in her kingdom were ready to plunge Castile into war.

She needed strong men about her at this time; and most of all she needed Ferdinand.

Then even as she sat looking at these depressing figures, she heard the clattering of horses' hoofs below; she heard the shouts of voices raised in welcome and, forgetting her dignity, she leaped from her chair and ran to the window.

She stood there, clutching the hangings to steady herself, for the sight of Ferdinand after a long absence never failed to move her deeply. There he was, jaunty and full of vigour, coming to her as she had known he would, the moment he received her call for help.

She loved him so much, this husband of hers, that at times she was afraid of her own emotions, afraid that they would betray her into an indiscretion which would be unworthy of the Queen of Castile.

In a short time he was standing before her; and those attendants who knew something of the depth of her feelings for this man retired without orders, that Isabella might be alone with her husband.

At such times Isabella laid aside the dignity of queenship. She ran to Ferdinand and put her arms about him; and Ferdinand, never more delighted than at these displays of affection, embraced her with passion.

"I knew you would come without delay," she cried.

"As always when you needed me."

"We need each other at this time, Ferdinand," she told him quickly. "Castile is threatened."

He accepted the implication that the affairs of Castile concerned him as much as her.

"My love," he said, "joyous as I am to be with you, before we give ourselves to the pleasure of reunion we must explore this desperate situation in which we find ourselves."

"You have heard?" Isabella asked. "There are rumours that

Villena and Arevalo are rebelling in favour of La Beltraneja, and that they are gathering partisans throughout Castile."

"That child!" cried Ferdinand. "The people will never accept her."

"It will depend on what forces our enemies can muster, Ferdinand. Our treasury is depleted; I have discovered that we have no more than five hundred horse which we could put into the field."

"We must raise more men; we must find the means to fight these rebels. We shall do it, Isabella. Have no fear of that."

"I knew you would say that. Yes, Ferdinand, we shall do it. Oh, how glad I am that you have come. With you beside me, what seemed an insuperable task becomes possible."

"You need me, Isabella," said Ferdinand fiercely. "You need me."

"Have I ever denied it?" She was aware of a sudden fear within her. Was he going to demand once more that he be accepted in Castile on equal terms with herself? This was not the time for dissension between them. "Ferdinand," she said quickly, "I have news for you. I am with child."

She watched the frown change to a smile on Ferdinand's face.

"Why, Isabella, my Queen! That is great news. When will our son be born?"

"It is too early yet to say. But I am sure I am with child. I hope that by the time this child is born our troubles will be over and we shall have prevented this threatened rebellion from taking place."

Ferdinand had taken her hands in his; he bent swiftly to kiss them. When he was in Isabella's presence he could not help but admire her.

"Come," he said, "let us examine our position. What men could be put into the field?"

She answered: "I have been studying these matters." She led him to the table. "Ferdinand, my husband, I pray you examine these figures and tell me what, in your opinion, is best to be done."

She knew that Ferdinand was alert to the danger; that he would allow no friction to arise between them while it existed. She had been right to believe she could rely on him. There was not a man in Spain who was more suited to stand beside her in this fight for the crown. And if, on occasions, his desire for supremacy over her sullied their relationship, making it a little bitter, how could it be otherwise where a man as strong, as entirely masculine as Ferdinand was concerned.

While they worked a messenger arrived at the Alcazar. He came from the King of Portugal.

As soon as Isabella knew that he was in the Palace she had him brought to her. Ferdinand stood beside her and, as the man bowed and held out the despatches, he lifted a hand to take them. But Isabella, who had anticipated this move, was anxious to take them as unobstrusively as possible—for she knew that with regard to this matter of supremacy she dared not give way even in the smallest matters. She took them before it was evident to any others that Ferdinand had attempted to do so.

She dismissed the messenger and glanced at the papers.

Then she lifted her eyes to Ferdinand's face.

"He asks us to resign our crowns," she said, "that the Princess Joanna may ascend the throne."

"He must be an imbecile," retorted Ferdinand.

Isabella turned to the table on which the documents were still spread out.

"I am informed," she said, "that he could put five thousand six hundred horse and fourteen thousand foot into the field. Perhaps he would say that we were imbeciles to oppose him."

Ferdinand's eyes glittered. "Yet we *shall* oppose him, and we shall defeat him. You know that, Isabella."

"I do know it, Ferdinand."

"We have our daughter to fight for and our unborn son."

"And we have each other," she added, and smiled brilliantly. "I know, Ferdinand, that while we are together we cannot fail. And we must be together, Ferdinand, always. You feel that, as I do. Where is Isabella without Ferdinand? No matter what should befall, we shall always stand together."

"You speak truth," said Ferdinand, and his voice was gruff with emotion.

"And together we shall be invincible," she went on.

Then solemnly they embraced. Isabella was the first to withdraw.

"And now," she said, "to business. We shall ignore these demands; but we must decide how we, with the few resources at our disposal, can defeat the might of Portugal."

* * *

In spite of the ceremonial robes in which her women had dressed her, Joanna looked what she was, a child of barely thirteen.

There was an expression of mingled resignation and despair

on her face. She was to be affianced to a man who was thirty years older than herself, and the prospect terrified her. But this was even more than a distasteful marriage; it was a prelude to war.

Her women had chattered as they prepared her for this important ceremony.

"Why, Alfonso is the bravest of kings. They say he is called the African because of his exploits again the Moors of Barbary. He is a great soldier."

"He must be quite an old man," said Joanna.

"No, Princess, it is you who are so young. You will not think of his age. He is the King of Portugal and he comes here to make you his Queen."

"And to make himself King of Castile."

"Well, only because he will make you Queen."

"I do not wish . . ."

But what was the use of stating her wishes? Joanna had lived through so many conflicts that she had long realized the futility of words.

Her friends were imploring her to enjoy her prospects. A King was coming to claim her hand. She should be joyful, they told her; because they did not understand.

And when she was robed and made ready she was taken to meet the man who had come to this town of Placencia for the purpose of the betrothal, and to take Castile from Isabella and Ferdinand and bestow it upon herself.

All about the Palace were encamped the armies of her future husband, so that she could not be unaware of his might.

And when she stood before him and lifted her eyes to his eager ones, she saw a man in his forties; and that seemed to her very old. She was trembling, but she smiled and greeted him as though with pleasure. All the time she was aware of those two men who had determined to set her on the throne—the Duke of Arevalo and the Marquis of Villena.

Alfonso took her hand and led her to two ornate chairs which had been set side by side. As they took their seats he said: "My dear Princess, you must not be afraid of me."

"I am so young for marriage," Joanna answered.

"Youth is a blessing, compared with which the experience which comes with age is but a small compensation. Do not deplore your youth, my dear one, for I do not."

"Thank you, Highness," she whispered.

"You look uneasy. Do you so fear me?"

"We are very closely related. You are my mother's brother."

"Have no fear, my dear. A messenger is being despatched to the Pope. He will send us a dispensation without delay."

She could not endure his enquiring tender gaze, and she feigned relief.

Alfonso felt happy. He was a man who must for ever pursue some cause, and he preferred it to be a romantic one. He had had great success against the Moors, but fighting the Moors was a commonplace occupation in the Iberian Peninsula. Now here was a young girl—his own niece—in need of a champion. To some she was the rightful heiress to the throne; to others the late Queen's bastard. Her cause appealed to him because she was young and he, a widower, could make her his bride. This was the most romantic cause in which he had ever fought, and it delighted him—particularly as victory could bring such benefit to him.

He was not a man to bear a grudge, but he could not forget his meeting with the proud Isabella, who had shown so openly her distaste for marriage with him—King though he was.

It was not unpleasant therefore to contemplate the discomfiture of the haughty Isabella when she found herself ousted from the throne by the man whom once she had so recklessly refused.

He was smiling as he took Joanna's hand, and those assembled, led by Villena and Arevalo, proceeded to declare Alfonso and Joanna Sovereigns of Castile.

* * *

As soon as the dispensation from the Pope arrived they would be married. Joanna prayed that the dispensation might be delayed.

In the meantime, the betrothal was celebrated, and on this and all occasions she must sit side by side with Alfonso and accept his tender attentions.

After some days Alfonso and his army, Joanna travelling with them, left Placencia for Arevalo.

Being aware of the sad state of the Castilian armies and that Isabella and Ferdinand had inherited a bankrupt state, Alfonso anticipated a victory which would be easy to complete.

At Arevalo he paused in his journey, and it seemed as though he halted there to prepare himself for the attack.

* * *

Isabella and Ferdinand were together when news was brought to them of Alfonso's arrival at Placencia and of his betrothal to Joanna.

Ferdinand received the news gloomily. "This means he is prepared to risk his armies in her cause," he said.

"She is his niece," cried Isabella, "and but a child."

"What cares he for either fact! He thinks she will bring him Castile and, if he is successful, depend upon it the Pope will not long deny him the dispensation he needs."

"*If* he is successful. He shall not be successful! I promise you that."

"Isabella, what do you know of war? And how can we prevent him?"

"I know," she said, her eyes flashing, "that I was born to be Queen of Castile."

"Well, you have had your brief glory."

"I have done nothing of what I intend to do. I know I shall succeed."

Ferdinand took her gently by the arm and led her to a table on which a map was spread.

He pointed to South Castile. "Here," he said, "the friends of Alfonso are waiting. They are numerous and they have men and arms at their disposal. Arevalo, Villena, Cadiz . . . they are his men. They will give all they have to drive us from the throne and set up Joanna and Alfonso. He has only to turn south tomorrow and there traitors will be ready for him. Town after town will freely give itself into his hands. And we . . . we shall find ourselves unable to attack, for on his march through Castile he will grow richer and richer as important towns pass into his possession."

"Ferdinand," Isabella reproved him, "I do not understand you. Have we not *our* friends?"

"There are waverers."

"Then they shall cease to be waverers."

"They will cease to be when they see the might of Alfonso's army!"

"They must be converted to our cause."

"But who shall convert them?"

"I shall. I . . . their Queen."

Ferdinand looked at her with mild surprise; there were times when he felt that even now he did not know Isabella. She seemed so dedicated to her cause, so certain of her ability to fight and win in this unequal struggle, that Ferdinand believed her.

It was at times like this that he forgave her for insisting on her supremacy, when he was glad that he had not returned to Aragon in a fit of pique because she had been determined to be supreme in Castile.

"You forget, Isabella," he said gently, "you are in no fit state to conduct a campaign. You have our unborn son to think of."

"It is because of our unborn son that I must be doubly sure that none shall rob me of the throne," she told him.

* * *

Isabella had lived through many hazards, but she felt that never had she faced danger so great as that which threatened during the months that followed. The days were full and she worked far into the night. She spent a great deal of time at prayer, for she was sure that she had previously been granted Divine protection and that it would be afforded her again.

Yet, even while she prayed, she never forgot that if she were to win heavenly aid she must neglect nothing of which her human strength was capable.

She would sit during the night receiving from and sending messages to the pitiably few troops she possessed. That was not all. She had decided that she herself must visit those towns which, she feared, were waiting to see which was the stronger party before bestowing their allegiance.

She set out on a tour of these towns. Riding was difficult; the roads were rough and the hours she was forced to spend in the saddle were very irksome, as with each passing week her pregnancy became more apparent.

It was impossible for the townsfolk to see Isabella and listen to her without being deeply affected. Isabella was inspired; she believed in her destiny; she knew she could not fail, and she conveyed this certainty to many of those whom she had come to rally to her standard.

Ferdinand was with her army endeavouring to prepare it for the attack, which, for some strange reason, Alfonso was hesitating to make. Each day both Ferdinand and Isabella expected to hear that Alfonso was on the march; they dreaded to hear that news.

"Give us a few more weeks," prayed Isabella. "Then we shall not be so vulnerable."

"A month . . . two months of preparation," declared Ferdinand to his generals, "and, if the Queen continues to rally men to our cause as she has begun to do, I think we shall give a very good account of ourselves and soon send Alfonso marching back across the frontier. But we need those weeks . . . we need them desperately."

So while they worked they watched anxiously for Alfonso to

move; yet he remained at Arevalo awaiting, he said, the arrival of his Castilian supporters, so that when he attacked there should be one decisive battle.

"How could such a man have scored such successes against the Moors?" wondered Ferdinand. "He must be in his dotage. Castile lies open to him now—and he hesitates. If he will but hesitate a few weeks longer we have as good a chance as he has of winning this war."

And as Isabella neared Toledo on her journey through the kingdom she thought of that old ally, Alfonso Carillo, Archbishop of Toledo, without whose support she could never have attained the throne.

She believed that if she could meet him, if she could reason with him, she would win him back to her cause; and if the Archbishop were on her side she would have secured the most important man in Spain as her ally. It was difficult to believe that a man of his intelligence could desert her out of pique, yet first he had resented Ferdinand, and then Cardinal Mendoza. She had not realized that, although he was capable of great valour and possessed political skill, he could also be capable of petty jealousy.

She called to one of her servants and said to him: "We are near Alcalá de Henares, and the Archbishop of Toledo is in residence there. Go to him and tell him that I propose calling at his palace, as I wish to talk with him."

When her messenger returned from his visit to the Archbishop he came almost shamefacedly into Isabella's presence.

"What news?" she asked. "You saw the Archbishop?"

"Yes, Highness. I saw the Archbishop."

"I pray you do not hesitate," said Isabella gently. "Come, what is his answer?"

"The Archbishop replied, Highness, that even though your Highness wishes to see him, he does not wish to see you; and if you should enter his palace by one door he will go out by another."

Isabella's expression scarcely changed.

"I see that it was a fruitless errand. But perhaps not entirely so. We have discovered an enemy where we thought to have a friend. You have my leave to retire."

When she was alone she went to a chair and sat down heavily. She felt sick through her pregnancy and with fear for the future. Had the Archbishop believed she had the slightest chance of beating Alfonso he would never have dared send her such a message. Quite clearly he believed her to be on the brink of defeat.

She felt the child move within her, and with her awareness of this other life she longed to go to her bed and stay there, to give up this weary pilgrimage through her kingdom, to trust in God and her destiny and to be able to say to herself: If I lose the Kingdom of Castile I shall then be merely Queen of Aragon, and I shall devote myself to my husband, the child we already have and the children which will surely be ours. That would be so easy; and the churlish conduct of one who had once been so firm an ally filled her with such despair that she wanted nothing so much as the peace of her own apartments.

But there were despatches to be sent off to Ferdinand, telling him of her progress; there were more towns to be visited.

There was one important factor. Others would know of the rebuff she had received from the Archbishop; she must wear an even bolder face; she must be even more certain of success.

She ignored the stirring life within her, the great desire for rest.

Never for one moment must she forget her destiny, nor the fact that only if she were worthy to wear the crown of Castile could she hope for Divine favour.

* * *

Isabella was reading a despatch from Ferdinand.

"The position has changed for the better, thanks to your efforts. I now have at my disposal four thousand men-at-arms, eight thousand light horse and thirty thousand foot. We lack equipment, and many of these men know little of soldiering, but my confidence grows daily. And should Alfonso attack us now he will find he has missed the great chance which was his two months ago."

Isabella looked up and smiled.

They had worked a miracle. They had found men ready to fight for them; and if these men were as yet inexperienced that would be remedied. She had Ferdinand as the commander of her army, and Ferdinand was experienced in war; he was young and Alfonso was old. Ferdinand would win.

Isabella's smile became tender.

Her great friend, Beatriz de Bobadilla, wife of Andres de Cabrera, believed that she idealized Ferdinand, that she saw him as a god among men.

It was not entirely true nowadays. The years of marriage had changed that. Yet when he had first come to Castile she had thought him wonderful. She loved him no less; but she was aware of the vanity, the arrogance, the signs of cupidity which were all part of Ferdinand's character. She did not forget the sulkiness he had displayed when he had realized that, for all her love, she was not prepared to give him control of Castilian affairs. Yet these faults made her the more tender, even as did those of her young daughter Isabella. And if Ferdinand at times had the faults of a boy, he had also the attributes of a man. She trusted his generalship; she knew she could rely on him to fight her cause—perhaps because it was also his own—more than she could rely on any other man in the kingdom. But the disaffection of the Archbishop of Toledo had made her realize how unwise she would be to put complete trust in anyone.

She rose from her table, and as she did so her body was racked with a pain so violent that she could not repress a cry.

One of her women who had been in the apartment came hurrying to her side.

"Highness . . ." The woman gasped at the pallor of Isabella's face, and caught her in her arms, for she believed the Queen was on the point of fainting. She called to others, and in a few seconds Isabella was surrounded by her women.

She put out a hand to steady herself against the table. She knew the violent pain was coming again.

"Help me . . ." she murmured. "Help me to my bed. I fear my time has come . . . and it is so soon . . . too soon."

* * *

So it was over.

There would be no child. Isabella felt limp and defeated. Should she have considered the child? If she had done so there would not be that army under Ferdinand's generalship; Castile would lie open to the invader.

And because it had been necessary to rally men to her cause—and only she, the Queen, could do it—she had lost her child, the son she and Ferdinand were to have made the heir to Castile and Aragon.

She felt bitter.

It was time they had more children; but what chance had they of being parents while they lived this troubled life.

She lay thinking of the journeyings over rough roads, the jolting, the uncomfortable nights often spent in humble beds in roadside inns.

And so . . . she had lost her child. But in doing so she had formed an army.

She smiled briefly.

There would be other children. Once this weary matter of La

Beltraneja's right to the throne was settled, she and Ferdinand would be together always; they would have many children.

She dozed a little, and when her women came to see how she fared she was smiling peacefully. She murmured a little in her sleep, and when one of the women stooped to hear what she said she heard not the lament for the lost child but the words : "Eight thousand light horse."

THE PRINCE OF THE ASTURIAS

ISABELLA came riding to the Alcazar of Segovia.

More than a year had passed since she had lost her child and raised men and arms to fight the invading Alfonso. It had been an arduous period.

Yet Isabella had quickly recovered from her miscarriage; indeed, many said that it was her spirit which had proved the best doctor. There had been no time during that dark period to lie abed and woo back her health; Isabella had very soon to be on horseback, riding through her kingdom, calling a Cortes at Medina del Campo and by her eloquence moving all so deeply that she had raised the money she so badly needed.

That had been after the disasters at Toro and Zamora, which had both fallen to Alfonso, and when, had Alfonso been wise, he would have thrown in his full force against the inferior Castilian army of Ferdinand and Isabella.

But Alfonso had been timid; he had hesitated again, even when the Archbishop of Toledo, considering Alfonso's gains at Toro and Zamora to be decisive, not only openly allied himself with the King of Portugal but took with him five hundred lancers to join his new friend in the fight against his old one.

But now the Castilian army had been vastly improved and was ready to do battle with the enemy; and on her journeys through her kingdom Isabella gave herself up to the pleasure of a short respite where she would enjoy the hospitality of her dearest friend.

When the news was brought to Beatriz de Bobadilla that the Queen was in the Alcazar she hurried to greet Isabella, and the two women embraced without formality.

"This makes me very happy," said Beatriz emotionally. "I would I had known I might expect the honour."

"There would then have been no surprise," smiled Isabella.

"But think of the anticipation I have missed!"

"Beatriz, it is wonderful to see you. I would like to be alone with you as we used to be in the past."

"I will have food and wine sent to us, and we will take it in my small private chamber. I long to hear what has been happening to you."

"Pray lead me to that small private chamber," said Isabella.

Beatriz laid her hand on the Queen's arm as they went together to the small room of which Beatriz had spoken.

"I pray Your Highness sit down," said Beatriz. "Soon we shall be served, and then . . . we will talk in comfort." Beatriz called: "Food and wine, for the Queen and myself . . . with all speed."

Isabella, smiling, watched her. "You have not changed at all," she said. "They all hold you in great awe, I'll swear."

"Why should they not? They are my servants," said Beatriz, falling into the familiarity which had often existed between them.

"And your husband, Andrês too—do you still command him?"

Beatriz laughed. "Andres obeys me, he says, because he values peace and it is the only way to get it. And Ferdinand? He is well?"

"He is very well, Beatriz. What should I do without him?"

Beatriz looked at the Queen, her head on one side, a smile playing about her mouth. So, thought Beatriz, she continues to adore that man. But not completely. Beatriz knew that Ferdinand had been disappointed not to have taken full authority from Isabella. Beatriz applauded the Queen's resistance.

"He fights for his kingdom as well as yours," said Beatriz, "for although you are Queen of Castile, he is your Consort."

"He has been magnificent. Beatriz, I do not believe there has ever been a soldier in Spain to compare with Ferdinand."

Beatriz laughed aloud; then her servants appeared with refreshments and her manner changed. Now the utmost respect must be paid to the Queen, and Beatriz dropped the easy familiar manner.

But when they were alone again Beatriz said: "Isabella, you are looking a little tired. I hope you are going to stay here for some time that I may look after you, as I used to in the old days when we were together."

"Ah, those old days," sighed Isabella. "I was not a Queen then."

"But we had some anxious times, nevertheless." Beatriz smiled reminiscently. "At least we do not have to worry that you will be snatched from Ferdinand and given to some husband who would be unacceptable to you!"

"Thank God for that. Oh, Beatriz, I am a little worried about this battle that must soon take place."

"But you put your trust in Ferdinand."

"I do, indeed I do. But there are mighty forces against us."

"Ferdinand will succeed," said Beatriz. "He is a good soldier."

Beatriz was thoughtful for a few seconds. A better soldier than a husband, she was thinking; and he will be determined to succeed. He will not allow himself to be driven from Castile.

"I was very sad," went on Beatriz, "when I heard that you had lost your child."

"It seems long ago."

"But a bitter blow."

"As the loss of a child must be. But there was no time to brood. It was all-important that we should get an army together; and we did it, Beatriz, even though it may well be due to that that the child was lost."

"It might have killed you," said Beatriz gruffly.

"But I am strong, Beatriz; have you not yet learned that? Moreover, I am destined to be Queen of Castile."

"You *are* Queen of Castile."

"I have never really reigned yet. Since my accession there has been this trouble. Once it is settled I shall be able to do for Castile what I always longed to do."

"Castile will prosper when you are firmly on the throne, Isabella."

Isabella's eyes were shining with purpose. She looked full of vitality at such times, thought Beatriz; it was rarely that those outside her intimate circle saw her so unreserved.

"First," she was saying, "I shall abolish this disastrous anarchy. I shall bring law and order back to Castile. Then, when I have a law-abiding country, I shall do all in my power to make good Christians of my subjects. You remember Tomás de Torquemada, Beatriz?"

Beatriz grimaced. "Who could forget him?"

"You were harsh with him, Beatriz."

"He was too harsh with us all, including himself."

"He is a good man, Beatriz."

"I doubt it not. But I cannot forgive him for trying to suppress our laughter. He thought laughter was sinful."

"It was because he realized how necessary it was for me to avoid frivolous ways. I remember that one day, after confession, he made me promise that if ever it were in my power I would convert my kingdom to the true faith."

"Let us hope that in converting them you will not make them as lean and wretched looking as friend Tomás."

"Well, Beatriz, there is another task of mine when all is at peace. I will endeavour to free every inch of Spanish soil from Moslem rule; I will raise the flag of Christ over every Alcazar, over every town in Spain."

"I am sure you will do it," said Beatriz, "but only if you have some little regard for your health. Stay with me awhile, dear Isabella. Give me the pleasure of looking after you myself. Please. I beg of you."

"How I should enjoy that!" said Isabella. "But there is work to do. I have stolen these few short hours from my duty because I was in the neighbourhood of Segovia and could not resist the joy of seeing you. But tomorrow I must be on my way."

"I shall do my utmost to persuade you to stay."

But Isabella was not to be persuaded; the next day she set out for Tordesillas.

* * *

The battlefield was between Toro and Zamora, along the banks of the glittering Douro. The armies were now equally matched; Alfonso was old compared with Ferdinand, but his son, Prince John, had joined him and was in command of the cavalry.

Ferdinand, surveying the enemy, determined to succeed or die in the attempt. Alfonso lacked Ferdinand's zeal; it was characteristic of him to tire quickly of the causes for which he had originally been so enthusiastic. He had been long in Castile, and his presence was needed in his own country; his men were restive; they too had been a long time away from home. Alfonso had intended to make speedy war in Castile, drive Isabella, whom he called the usurper, from the throne and put his betrothed Joanna in her place. But the affair had been long drawn out; and already he was tiring of it. His son John was enthusiastic, but John had not much experience of war; and Alfonso longed for the end of this day's battle.

Ferdinand, riding between the Admiral of Castile and the Duke of Alva, cried aloud: "St. James and St. Lazarus!" which was the old cry of Castile; and those Castilians in the Portuguese ranks who heard it, trembled. It was as though Ferdinand were reminding them that they were traitors.

There was one riding furiously towards the enemy, who cared not for the old cry of Castile. The Archbishop of Toledo enjoyed battle, and he was determined to exploit this opportunity to the full.

The battle had begun, and furiously it raged; it was as though every soldier in those armies knew what depended upon its issue.

Ferdinand shouted to his men. They must fight. In the name of Isabella, they must fight. Their future and the future of their Queen, the future of Castile, depended on them.

There were many who remembered the Queen; they thought

of the pregnant woman who had endured great discomfort to come to them that she might move with them with her eloquence, that she might remind them of their duty to Castile. They remembered that these men who fought against them were their old enemies, the Portuguese, and those Castilians who had seen fit to fight against their own Queen.

Lances were shattered, and swords were drawn; and men grappled hand to hand with one another in the mêlée.

And Ferdinand's heart leaped with joy, for he knew that the outcome of this day's battle would be victory for him.

But there were a few men in the Portuguese Army who were determined that it should not be so. Edward de Almeyda, the Portuguese flag bearer, was an example to all. He had snatched the Portuguese Emblem from Castilian soldiers who were about to trample it in the dust and, with a shout of triumph, held it aloft, a sign to all Portuguese that the day was not lost for Alfonso.

But even as he rode away a Castilian soldier had lifted his sword and cut off the right arm which held the flag. But as it would have fallen, Almeyda, ignoring the loss of his right arm, had caught it in his left hand.

"Joanna and Alfonso!" he shouted as swords hacked at the arm which now held the flag aloft.

With both arms shattered and bleeding he managed to transfer the standard to his mouth; and he was seen riding among his defeated fellow countrymen, armless, the standard in his mouth, for some minutes before he was unhorsed.

Even such heroism could not save the day. Prince John was missing. Alfonso had also disappeared.

Ferdinand found himself master of the field.

* * *

In the castle of Castro Nuño, some miles from the battlefield, the young Joanna waited in apprehension. She knew that this battle would prove decisive, and she believed that her affianced husband would be the victor.

Then all hope of a peaceful existence for her would be over. She did not believe that Isabella would ever quietly stand aside and allow her to take the throne.

What would happen to her if Isabella's armies were victorious she could not imagine; all she knew was that neither solution could bring her much joy; and she greatly wished that she could have been allowed to stay in the Madrid convent, living a life which was governed by bells.

All day she had waited for news. She had placed herself at a window in the fortified castle where she could command a good view of the surrounding country.

Soon, she knew, a rider would appear, perhaps several; she would know then whether the result of the conflict was defeat or victory for Alfonso.

It was almost dusk when her vigil was rewarded, and she saw a party of riders coming towards the castle. She stood alert, her eyes strained, and as they came nearer she recognized the leader of the party. It was Alfonso, and with him were four of his men.

She knew what this must mean; for Alfonso did not come riding to Castro Nuño as a victor; it was obvious from his demeanour that he came as a fugitive.

She hurried down, calling as she went: "The King is riding to the castle. He will be here in a few minutes."

From all over the castle men and women came hurrying into the hall, and Joanna was in the courtyard when Alfonso and his party rode in.

Poor Alfonso! Indeed, he looked an old man today. He was dishevelled and dirty, his face grey; and for the first time she felt tender towards him.

He leaped from his horse and threw the reins to a groom, crying: "The army is routed. We must leave almost immediately for Portugal."

"I am to go to Portugal?" stammered Joanna.

Alfonso put a hand on her shoulder. His eyes were suddenly alight with that quixotic expression which was not unendearing.

"Do not despair," he said. "It is a defeat. A temporary defeat. I will win your kingdom for you yet."

Then he took her hand and they went into the castle.

A few hours later, when Alfonso and his party had refreshed themselves, they left Castro Nuño and rode westward over the border into Portugal; and Joanna went with them.

* * *

Isabella was at Tordesillas when the news was brought to her. Ferdinand triumphant! The King of Portugal and his son John in flight! Through great endeavour and fervent prayer she had overcome yet another ordeal which in the beginning had seemed impassable.

Never before had Isabella been so sure of her destiny as now.

At the Convent of Santa Clara she gave thanks to God for this further proof of His favour. There in that beautiful building which had once been the palace of a king's mistress she remained in her cell, on her knees, while she reminded herself that she owed this victory to the intervention of God. The atmosphere of the Convent of Santa Clara suited her mood. She, the triumphant Queen of Castile, was prostrated in humility, in that beautiful building with its Moorish baths which had once been the delight of Doña Maria de Padilla, who herself had delighted Pedro the Cruel; these walls, which must once have been the scene of voluptuous entertainments, now enclosed the refuge of silent-footed nuns.

Isabella wanted all to know that the victory was due to Divine guidance. All her subjects must understand that she was now the undoubted ruler of Castile.

The next day, in a loose and simple gown, her feet bare, Isabella led a procession to the Church of St. Paul, where, in the greatest humility, she gave thanks to God for this victory which could leave no doubt that she, and she alone, was Queen of Castile.

* * *

Although the battle which had been fought between Toro and Zamora was decisive, it did not bring complete peace to Castile.

Louis XI of France, who had come to the aid of Alfonso, was still giving trouble, and Ferdinand could not disband his army; and when Isabella studied the effect of the war, following on the disastrous reigns of her half-brother and her father, she knew that her task had hardly begun.

It was September before she was able to spend a few days in Ferdinand's company.

She was in residence at the Madrid Alcazar and, when messengers brought her news that he was on the way, she set her cooks to prepare a banquet worthy of the victor.

Isabella was not by nature extravagant and she knew that Ferdinand was not. How could they be when they considered the state of the exchequer; when they had had to work so hard to get together the means to fight their enemies? But although Isabella was cautious in spending money, she knew that there were times when she must put aside that caution.

Those about her must understand the importance of this victory. They must not whisper among themselves that the Queen of Castile and her Consort were a parsimonious pair who did not know how to live like royalty.

This would be the first real celebration she and Ferdinand together had had since the Battle of Toro, and everyone must be aware of its importance.

Ferdinand came riding in triumph to the Alcazar, and Isabella was waiting to receive him.

As she stood, surrounded by her ministers and attendants, and Ferdinand came towards her, her heart beat faster at the sight of him. He had aged a little; the lines were more deeply marked on his face; that alertness of his eyes was accentuated. But even in those first few seconds the rivalry was there between them. Ferdinand in battle was the supreme leader. Here in the Alcazar he was merely the Queen's Consort. He had to adjust himself, and the adjustment was somewhat distasteful.

He took Isabella's hand, bowed over it and put his lips against it.

"Welcome, my husband," she said, and her voice had lost its habitual calm. "Welcome, my dearest husband."

The heralds blew a few triumphant notes on their *trompas* and the drummers beat their *baldosas*.

Then Isabella laid Ferdinand's hand on her arm, and this was the signal for them to enter the castle.

There was feasting and music, and Isabella was happier than she had been for a very long time.

Ferdinand did not leave her side during the banquet and the ball which followed, and she believed that he had such an affection for her that he ceased to fret because in Castile she was supreme.

Isabella almost wished that she were not a queen on that night, and that she and Ferdinand could have retired in peace from their guests and spent an hour or so with their little seven-year-old Isabella.

When the ball was at last over and they had retired to their apartments she reminded him that it was eight years almost to the month since they had married.

"It is difficult to believe it is so long," said Isabella, "for in that eight years we have seen far too little of each other."

"When the kingdom is at peace," Ferdinand answered, "there will not be these separations."

"I shall be so much happier then. Oh, Ferdinand, what should I have done without you? You have brought victory to Castile."

"It is only my duty," he said. She saw the faintly sullen lines beginning to form about his mouth, and she went swiftly to him and put an arm about his shoulders.

"We have a great task before us, Ferdinand," she said, "but I thank God that we are together."

He was a little mollified. "Now it is our task to deal with the French," he told her.

"You think it will be difficult, Ferdinand?"

"No, I do not think so. Louis has his hands full with the trouble between himself and Burgundy, and now that we have driven Alfonso back where he belongs he'll have little heart for this fight."

"Soon, then, we shall have peace, and then, Ferdinand, begins our real task."

"I have news for you. Arevalo has made advances. I think he is prepared to forget the claims of Joanna and offer his allegiance to you."

"That is excellent news."

"It shows which way the wind blows, eh?"

"And the Archbishop of Toledo?"

"He will follow doubtless."

"Then victory will indeed be ours."

Ferdinand seized her hands and drew her to her feet. She was comely; she was a woman; and here in the bedchamber he was no longer merely the Consort of the Queen.

"Have we not fought for it, sacrificed for it?" he demanded. "Why, Isabella, you might have lost your life. You were very ill when you lost our child."

"It is a great grief to me . . . a continual grief. Yet our crown depended on the army I could raise."

"And all these months," went on Ferdinand, "I have scarcely seen you." He drew her towards him. "We are young, eh, Isabella. We are husband and wife. The quickest way to forget our sorrow is to have a son who will replace the child we lost. We have won a great victory, Isabella, and this should not be beyond our powers."

Then he laughed and lifted her in his arms. That cold dignity dropped from her as though it were a cloak which he had loosened. And there was Isabella, warm, loving, eager.

It was during Ferdinand's stay at the Madrid Alcazar that their son was conceived.

* * *

From his residence at Alcalá de Henares, Alfonso de Carillo, the Archbishop of Toledo, grimly reviewed the situation.

King Alfonso had fled with Joanna into Portugal. There were victories all over Castile for Ferdinand. Many of the Archbishop's possessions had already passed into the hands of Ferdinand, and very soon he himself would do so.

Ferdinand would have no mercy on him. Was this the end, then, of an exciting and glorious career?

His only hope lay with the Queen, and Isabella, after all, was the ruler of Castile.

He would write to her reminding her of all she owed him. It was true thât he had boasted of having raised her up and that he would cast her down. He had been wrong. He had not understood the force of her character. He had believed her to be steadfast and firm in her determination to support what she believed to be right. So she was. But she was shrewd also; or was it that her belief in her destiny was so strong that she forced others to share that belief even against their will?

The Archbishop of Toledo, statesman and soldier, was forced to admit that he had been foolish in allying himself with the wrong side.

Now he must humble himself. So he wrote to Isabella offering her his allegiance. He reminded her of all that he had done for her in the past. He asked pardon for his folly and arrogance.

Ferdinand, who was with Isabella when this plea arrived, laughed scornfully. "This is the man who, when you were risking your life to ride about the country pleading for funds, took five hundred lances and rode at the head of them to serve our enemy. He must think we are fools."

Isabella was thinking of that occasion when she had called at his palace and the Archbishop had said that if she entered by one door he would go out at the other. It was hard to forget such an insult. It was also hard to forget that occasion when she had been threatened with capture at Madrigal, and the Archbishop of Toledo had come galloping to her rescue.

She smiled. He was a fiery old man, whose dignity must be preserved at all costs. And he had been piqued by her reliance on Ferdinand and Cardinal Mendoza.

"We should not be too harsh with the old Archbishop," mused Isabella.

Ferdinand looked at her in amazement.

"Public execution should be his lot."

"Once he was my very good friend," she reminded him.

"He was also our very bad enemy. It will be good for the people to see what happens to those who work against us."

Isabella shook her head. "I should never agree to the execution of the Archbishop," she said.

"You are a sentimental woman."

"That may be, but I cannot forget all he once did for me."

Ferdinand snapped his fingers. "There was a time, Isabella, when defeat stared us in the face. If Alfonso had been a better general we should not be rulers of Castile at this moment. Fugitives we should be. Or you might. I should doubtless have died on the field of battle."

"Do not speak of it," said Isabella.

"Then I pray you be reasonable. This man is dangerous."

"This man is old and broken in spirit."

"Such as he is never accept age; their spirit is unbreakable."

"I would rather have him my friend than my enemy."

"Then send him where he can be neither."

"I could not do that, Ferdinand."

"Nevertheless . . ."

Gently she interrupted : "I *shall* not do it, Ferdinand."

She watched the slow flush spread over Ferdinand's face. He clenched his hands and said between his teeth : "I intrude. I had forgotten. *You* are the Queen. I ask Your Highness's permission to retire."

With that he bowed and left her.

It was not the first of such scenes. Isabella sighed. She feared it would not be the last. But she was right—she knew she was right.

She must rule Castile with that dignity and calm of which she—and so few others—was capable. Anger and resentment could never go hand in hand with justice.

The Archbishop had been her bitter enemy, she knew; but he had also been her friend.

She had decided how he should be dealt with. He should buy his pardon. He was rich, and the royal exchequer was low. He should remain in exile at Alcalá de Henares for the rest of his life.

He would be saddened, of course, by his exile from Court. But he was ageing, and he would find plenty to occupy him at Alcalá de Henares. He was an alchemist of some ability, and he would turn his immense energy into that field for the years that were left to him.

Isabella wrote the order which decided the future of the Archbishop of Toledo, and when she had despatched it she sat silent for a few moments, and a sad wistful smile touched her mouth.

She was thinking of Ferdinand.

* * *

Isabella was riding towards Arevalo. Beside her was her friend Beatriz de Bobadilla and a few of her attendants.

It was early spring, and soon Isabella would be too heavy to trust herself on horseback.

Beatriz would stay with her until after the confinement. Isabella turned to smile at her friend. Beatriz had declared her intention of resuming her old position with the Queen as chief maid of honour until the baby had been born; she was going to see that no undue exertion threatened the life of this one. And Beatriz was a forceful woman. Once she had stated her intention, Andres, her husband, must allow her to leave him; and Isabella, her Queen, must be ready to receive her.

"Your Highness is amused?" asked Beatriz.

"Only by your determination to look after me."

"Indeed I will look after you," said Beatriz. "And who better than one who loves you as I do?"

"I know, Beatriz. You are good, and it gives me great pleasure to have you with me. I am sorry though for poor Andres."

"Do not be. He has his work to do. Mayhap he is glad of a little respite from my tongue. This journey is too much for Your Highness."

"You tried hard to dissuade me from making it," said Isabella. "But I fear that in the next few weeks I shall feel still less inclined to do so."

"After this you must rest more frequently."

There was a frown between Beatriz's well-marked brows. She knew Isabella as well as anyone knew her; she was aware of that firm spirit behind the serene façade. She knew that she could only appear to persuade Isabella when the Queen had made up her own mind. That was why she had ceased to rail against this journey to Arevalo, once she realized that Isabella was quite determined to make it.

But Beatriz was not only worried by the effect this journey might have on Isabella; she was wondering how much the Queen would have to suffer during her stay at the castle of Arevalo.

Beatriz had made up her mind that their stay there should be as brief as she could make it.

Isabella turned to her friend. "I always feel deeply moved when I come to Arevalo," she said. "There are so many memories."

"Perhaps we should have delayed the journey until after the child is born."

"No, it is long since I have seen my mother. She may be growing anxious. It is very bad for her to be anxious."

"I would rather she was anxious because you were absent than that I and Ferdinand, and all who love you, should be because of your state of health."

"You fret too much, Beatriz. It is all in the hands of God."

"Who would have as little patience with us now as He had last time," retorted Beatriz.

"Beatriz, you blaspheme."

Isabella was really shocked, and Beatriz seeing the horror in the Queen's face, hastened to apologize.

"You see, Highness," she murmured, "I am as I always was. I speak without thinking."

A gentle smile crossed Isabella's face. "It is on account of your care for me, I know. But I would hear no more of the hazards of this journey and your disapproval of our visit to my mother."

"I see I have offended Your Highness, and crave pardon."

"Not offended, Beatriz, but please say no more."

It was an order and, as they rode on to Arevalo, Beatriz was silent for a while; and Isabella's thoughts went back to the day when she, with her mother and young brother, had hurried away from her half-brother's Court to live for so many years in obscurity in the castle of Arevalo.

* * *

Isabella knelt before the woman in the chair. This was her mother, also Isabella, Queen-widow of King John II of Castile.

And as Isabella knelt there she felt an urge to weep, for she remembered so well those days when she had watched her mother's face for a sign of the madness which could be terrifying to a small daughter.

The long thin fingers stroked her hair and the woman said: "Who is this who has come to see me?"

"It is Isabella."

"*I* am Isabella."

"It is that other Isabella, Highness. Your daughter."

"My daughter Isabella." The blank expression lifted and the eyes became more bright. "My little child, Isabella. Where is your brother, Isabella? Where is Alfonso?"

"He is dead, Mother," answered Isabella.

"One day he could be King of Castile. One day he shall be King of Castile."

Isabella shook her head and the tears stung her eyes.

The old Queen put her face close to her daughter's, but she did not seem to see her. She said in a husky whisper: "I must take them away while there is time. One day Alfonso could be King of Castile. And if aught should happen to him, my little Isabella would be Queen."

Isabella took the trembling fingers and laid her lips against them.

"Mother, so much time has passed. I am your Isabella and *I am* Queen of Castile. That makes you happy, does it not? Is it not what you always wanted?"

The old Queen rose in her chair, and Isabella stood up and quickly put her arms about her.

"Queen . . ." she murmured. "Queen of Castile?"

"Yes, Mother. I . . . your little Isabella. But little no longer. Mother, I am married to Ferdinand. It was the match we always wanted, was it not? And we have a daughter . . . yet another Isabella. A sweet and lively child. And, Mother, there is another soon to be born."

"Queen of Castile . . ." repeated the old Queen.

"She stands before you now, Mother, your own daughter."

There was a smile about the twitching lips. She had understood and she was happy.

How glad I am that I came, thought Isabella. She will be at peace now. She will remember.

"Come, Mother," she said, "let us sit down. Let us sit side by side, and I will tell you that the war is over and there is no more danger to my crown. I will tell you how happy I am with my kingdom, with my husband and my family."

She led her mother to her chair, and they sat side by side. They held hands while Isabella talked and the old woman nodded and from time to time said: "Isabella . . . my little daughter, Queen of Castile."

"So now, Mother, you know," said Isabella. "There is no need for you to be sad any more. As often as I can I will come to Arevalo and we will talk together. You can be happy now, Mother."

The old Queen nodded.

"I shall rest here for a few days," said Isabella, "then I shall go. I do not wish to stay too long at this time because of my condition. You understand, Mother?"

Old Isabella went on nodding her head.

Isabella put her lips to her mother's forehead. "While I am here we shall be together often. That makes me happy. Now I shall go to my apartment and rest awhile. It is necessary, you see, because of the child."

The old Queen put out a hand suddenly. She whispered: "Have a care."

"I will take great care," Isabella assured her.

"*He* will never get a child," said her mother. "It is the life he has led." She laughed suddenly. It was an echo of that wild laughter which had once terrified the young Isabella when she had first become aware of the taint of insanity in her mother. "He will try to foist the Queen's child on the people, but they'll not have it. No, they'll not have it."

She was talking of her stepson, King Henry IV, who had been dead for some years. She still at times lived in the past.

She gripped Isabella's hand. "I must keep the children away from him. A pillow over their mouths . . . that is what it would be. Poison mixed with their food. I do not trust them . . . neither Henry nor his Queen. They are evil . . . evil, and I have my babies to protect. My little Alfonso could be King of Castile . . . my little Isabella could be Queen."

So all that she had said had left only a momentary impression on that poor dazed mind.

Isabella felt the sobs about to choke her as she took a hurried leave of her mother.

* * *

She lay on her bed, and slowly the tears ran down her cheeks. This was weakness. She, the Queen of Castile, to be in tears! No one must see her thus.

It was so tragic. That poor woman, who had cared so much, who had planned for her children, whose unbalanced state had no doubt been aggravated by her anxieties for them, might now see one of her dearest dreams realized; but her poor mind could not grasp the truth.

"Poor sad Highness!" murmured Isabella. "Dearest Mother! Is there any sickness worse than that of the mind?"

Beatriz had come into the apartment.

"I did not send for you," said Isabella.

But Beatriz had thrown herself on her knees beside the bed.

"Highness, you are unhappy. When you are so, if I could comfort you in the smallest measure, nothing would keep me from you."

Beatriz had seen the tears; it was no use hiding the distress. Isabella put out a hand, and Beatriz took it.

"It makes me weep; it is so sad," said Isabella.

"It is not wise that you should upset yourself."

"You were right, I think, Beatriz. I should not have come. There is no good I can do her. Or is there? I fancy she was pleased to see me."

"The little good you may do her by your visit might mean a lot of harm to your health."

"I have been thinking about the child, Beatriz. I am a little upset this day, because my thoughts are melancholy."

"There is nothing to fear. You are healthy. The miscarriage was due to your exertions. There will be no more miscarriages."

"It was not a miscarriage that I feared, Beatriz."

"You feared for your own health. But you are strong, Highness. You are young. You will bear many children yet."

"It was seeing *her*, Beatriz. How did she become like that? Why was she born with a mind that could plunge into darkness? I can tell you the answer, my dear friend. It is because others in her family have suffered so."

"What are you thinking?" cried Beatriz aghast.

"That she is my mother . . . even as I am the mother of this life which stirs within me now."

"These are morbid thoughts. It is bad for a pregnant woman to harbour such."

"It is a sudden fear grown up within me, Beatriz, like an evil weed in a plot of beautiful flowers. There were others before her who were afflicted thus. Beatriz, I think of my child."

"It is folly. Forgive me, Highness, but I must say what I think. The Princess Isabella is a beautiful child, her mind is lively and quick. This darkness has come to your mother because of the sad life she led. It has nothing to do with her blood."

"Is that so, Beatriz? Do you believe it?"

"Indeed I do," lied Beatriz. "I will tell you something else. It will be a boy. I know it from the way you carry it."

"A boy, Beatriz. It is what Ferdinand wants. Do you know he would like our heir to be a boy? He thinks that sovereigns should be male."

"We ourselves have seen Castile under two kings, and we are not greatly impressed by masculine rule. Now we have a Queen, and I'll warrant that in a very short time Castile will have good reason to be thankful for that."

"Perhaps," said Isabella, "I should appoint you as my Primate."

"Nay," said Beatriz, "I would prefer to be the power behind the throne. Do you think we could leave tomorrow?"

"Our stay has been so short."

"Isabella, my dearest mistress, she does not know who you are nor why you are here. Let us leave tomorrow. It would be better for you . . . and the child."

"I believe you are right," said Isabella. "What good can we do by staying here? But when my child is born I shall come again and see her . . . I shall come often. There are times when her mind clears a little. Then she understands and is happy to see me."

"She is as happy here as she could be. You are her very dutiful daughter. It is enough, Isabella, that she is cared for. You must think of the child."

Isabella nodded slowly.

She *was* thinking of the child. A new dread had come into her life. She believed that it would always be haunted by a shadow.

She would think often of those wild fits of laughter which used to overtake her mother; she would think of the poor dazed mind, lost in a half-world of darkness; and in the future she would watch her children, wondering and fearful. Her mother had brought the seeds of insanity from Portugal. It was possible that they had taken root and would break into hideous flower in the generations to come.

* * *

Meanwhile Alfonso of Portugal had not been idle. No sooner had he returned to his country in the company of the young Joanna than he was eager to make another attempt to win for her and himself the crown of Castile, for although he had tired of the old campaign, he was very eager to begin a new one.

He discussed this with his son John.

"Are we to allow the crown of Castile to slip from our grasp?" he demanded. "What of our young Joanna—this lady in distress? Is she to be deprived of what is hers by right?"

"What do you propose to do, Father? We have lost the best of our army in Castile. We are not equipped to go to war again."

"We should need help," Alfonso agreed. "But we have our old ally. Louis will help us."

"At the moment he is deeply involved with Burgundy."

Alfonso's eyes were glittering with a new purpose.

"He will help if our ambassadors can persuade him of the justice of our cause."

"And the profit our success might bring to him," added John cynically.

"Well, Louis will see that there is profit in it for himself."

"Whom shall we send into France? You had someone in mind?"

Alfonso was restless. His desire for adventure did not leave him with advancing years. He wished to enjoy his youthful bride, but he could not marry a girl—however young, however charming—who might be illegitimate and have no claim to a crown whatsoever. There was only one way in which he could deal with this matter. He must set a crown on his little Joanna's head. Then he would marry her; then Castile would be under the sway of Portugal.

He could not bear to wait for what he wanted. He must be on the move all the time.

He thought of the long journey into France, of his ambassadors trying to set the case before Louis, whose mind would be on the threatened war with Burgundy.

There was only one man in Portugal, he felt sure, who could explain to Louis what great good could come to France and Portugal through an invasion of Castile and the setting up of Joanna in place of Isabella.

He looked as eager as a boy as he turned to John. "I myself will go to Louis," he said.

* * *

It was a triumphal progress which Alfonso made through France with the retinue of two hundred which he had taken with him.

Louis XI had given the order: "The King of Portugal is my friend. Honour him wherever he should go."

Thus the people of France gave a warm welcome to this friend of their King's, and those in the country villages threw flowers at his feet and cried "Long life" to him as he went on his way.

Louis himself, seeming so honest in his shabby fustian doublet and battered old hat, in which he wore a leaden image of the Virgin, took Alfonso in his arms and kissed him on both cheeks before a large assembly, to assure all those who did not know Louis of his friendship and esteem for his ally.

There was a meeting between the two kings, when they sat opposite each other in the council chamber surrounded by their ministers and advisers. Louis was as affable as ever, but his friendly words were couched in cautious phrases and he did not offer that which Alfonso had come to France to obtain.

"My dear friend and brother," said Louis, "you see me here in a most unhappy state—my kingdom plunged in war, my resources strained to their limit in this conflict with Burgundy."

"But my brother of France is master of great resources."

"Great!" The eyes of the King of France flashed with fire rarely seen in them. Then he smiled a little sadly, stroking his fustian doublet as though to call attention to his simple and shabby garments that the King of Portugal might compare them with his own finery. He shook his head. "Wars deplete our treasury, brother. I could not burden my poor people with more taxes than they already suffer. Nay, when I have brought this trouble with Burgundy to an end . . . then . . . why then I should be most happy to come to your help, that together we may defeat the usurper Isabella and set the rightful heiress on the throne of Castile. Until then . . ." Louis lifted his hands and allowed a helpless expression to creep over his cunning features.

"Wars have a way of dragging on," said Alfonso desperately.

"But until this conflict has been brought to a satisfactory conclusion you will stay in my kingdom as my guest . . . my very honoured guest."

Louis had leaned forward in his chair, and certain of the Portuguese retinue shivered with distaste. Louis reminded them of a great spider in his drab garments, his pale face brightened only by those shrewd, alert eyes.

"And it may well be," went on the King of France, "that by that time His Holiness can be persuaded to give you the dispensation you need for marriage with your niece."

It was a further excuse for delay. The marriage could not take place without the dispensation from the Pope, and was he likely to give it while Isabella was firmly on the throne of Castile?

If the journey through France had delighted the King of Portugal, his meeting with France's King could only fill him with foreboding.

* * *

Alfonso had been right to feel apprehensive. As the months passed, although the French continued to treat him with respect, Louis, on every occasion when the purpose of his visit was mentioned, became evasive.

Burgundy! was the answer. And where was the dispensation from the Pope?

A whole year Alfonso lingered in France, for, having made the long journey, how could he face a return without having achieved what he had come for?

The unhappy figure of the King of Portugal at the Court of France had become a commonplace. He was looked upon as a hanger-on whose prestige waned with each passing week.

The Duke of Burgundy had died and Louis had invaded his dominions. The Pope had given the dispensation.

Still there was no answer for Alfonso.

He began to grow melancholy and to wonder what he should do, for he could not stay indefinitely in France.

And one day, after he had been a year in Louis' dominions, one of his retinue asked to speak to Alfonso privately; and when they were alone he said to the King: "Highness, we are being deceived. Louis has no intention of helping us. I have proof that he is at this time negotiating with Ferdinand and Isabella, and seeking a treaty of friendship with them."

"It is impossible!" cried Alfonso.

"There is proof, Highness."

When he was assured that he had been told the truth Alfonso was overcome with mortification.

What can I do? he asked himself. Return to Portugal? There he would become the object of ridicule. Louis was not to be trusted, and he, Alfonso, had been a fool to think he could bargain with such a man. Louis had never intended to help him; and it was obvious that, since he sought the friendship of Isabella and Ferdinand, he believed them to be secure on the throne of Castile.

He called to three of his most trusted servants.

"Prepare," he said, "to leave the Court immediately."

"We are returning home, Highness?" asked one eagerly.

"Home," murmured the King. "We can never go home again. I could never face my son, nor my people."

"Then where shall we go, Highness?"

Alfonso looked in a bewildered fashion at his servants.

"There is a little village in Normandy. We will make for that place, and there we shall live in obscurity until I have made up my mind what I had best do."

* * *

Alfonso stared out of the window of the inn at the fowls which scrabbled in the yard.

I, he mourned, a King of Portugal to come to this!

For several days he had lived here, like a fugitive, incognito, afraid to proclaim his identity lest even these humble people should be laughing at him.

At the Court of France his retinue would be asking themselves what had become of him; he did not care. All he wanted now was to hide from the world.

In Portugal Joanna would hear of his humiliation; and what would become of her? Poor child! A sad life hers, for what hope had she now of ever attaining the throne of Castile?

He had dreamed of a romantic enterprise. A fair young girl in distress, a gallant king to her rescue, who should become her bridegroom; and here he was, an ageing man in hiding, perhaps already known to the world as a fighter of lost causes.

What is left to me? he asked himself. What is left to Joanna? A convent for her. And for me?

He saw himself in coarse robe and hair shirt. He saw himself barefoot before some shrine. Why not a pilgrimage to the Holy Land and, after that, return home to the monastic life? Thus if he could not procure the crown of Castile he could make sure of his place in heaven.

He did not pause long to consider. When had he ever done so?

He called for pen and paper.

"I have a very important letter to write," he said.

"My son, [he wrote] I have decided to retire from the world. All earthly vanities which were once within me are dead. I propose to go on a pilgrimage to the Holy Land and after that devote myself to God in the monastic life.

"It is for you to hear this news as though it were of my death, for dead I am to the world. You will assume the sovereignty of Portugal. When you receive this letter Alfonso is no longer King of Portugal. I salute King John. . . ."

* * *

Isabella lay in her bed awaiting the birth of her child. It would not be long now, and she was glad that Beatriz was with her. The Queen's journeyings had brought her to Seville. It was the month of June, the heat was intense and the sweat was on Isabella's brow as the intermittent pain tortured her body.

"Beatriz," she murmured, "are you there, Beatriz?"

"Beside you, my dearest."

"There is no need to worry, Beatriz. All will be well."

"Indeed all will be well!"

"The child will be born in the most beautiful of my towns. Seville, *La Tierra de Maria Santisima*. One understands why it is so called, Beatriz. Last night I sat at my window and looked out on the fertile vineyards. But how hot it is!"

Beatriz leaned over Isabella, moving the big fan back and forth.

"Is that better, my dearest?"

"Better, Beatriz. I am happy to have you with me."

A frown had puckered Isabella's brow, and Beatriz asked herself: "Is she thinking of the woman in the castle of Arevalo? Oh, not now, my dearest, not at this time. It would be wrong. It might work some evil. Not now . . . Isabella, my Queen, when the child is about to come into the world."

"It is the pain," said Isabella. "I should be able to endure it better than this."

"You are the bravest woman in Castile."

"When you think what it means! Our child is about to be born . . . mine and Ferdinand's. This child could be King or

Queen of Castile. That was what my mother used to say to us. . . ."

Isabella had caught her breath, and Beatriz, fanning more vigorously, said quickly: "The people are already gathering outside. They crowd into the *patios* and in the glare of the sun. They await news of the birth of your child."

"I must not disappoint them, Beatriz."

"You will never disappoint your people, Isabella."

* * *

Beatriz held the child in her arms. She laughed exultantly. Then she handed it to a nurse and went to kneel by Isabella's bed.

"The child?" said Isabella.

"Your Highness has borne a perfect child."

"I would see the child."

"Can you hear the cries? Loud . . . healthy . . . just as they should be. Oh, this is a happy day! Oh, my dearest mistress, your son is born."

Isabella lay back on her pillows and smiled.

"So it is a son."

"A Prince for Castile!" cried Beatriz.

"And he is well . . . quite well . . . in all ways?"

"He is perfect. I know it."

"But . . ."

She was thinking that, when her mother had been born, doubtless there had been no sign of the terrible affliction which was to come to her.

"Put unhappy thoughts from your mind, Highness. They are doubly bad at such a time. All is well. This is a beautiful child, a fine heir for Castile. Here he is." She took him from the nurse and laid him in Isabella's arms.

And as she looked at her son, Isabella forgot her fears.

He was born at last—the son for whom she and Ferdinand had longed.

"He shall be John . . . Juan," she said, "after Ferdinand's father. That will delight my husband."

She kissed the baby's brow and whispered: "Juan . . . my little son, born in the most beautiful of my towns, welcome . . . welcome to Castile."

ISABELLA AND THE ARCHBISHOP OF SARAGOSSA

ALFONSO gave himself up to dreaming. He would sit in the room overlooking the inn yard, dreaming of the life he would lead in the monastery of his choosing. He had decided that he would become a Franciscan because their simple way of life best fitted his present mood. How different would existence at a Franciscan monastery be compared with that of a royal court!

First there would be his pilgrimage. He closed his eyes and saw himself, pack on back, simply clad in a flowing garment, the sun beating upon him, suffering a hundred discomforts. Imaginary discomforts were so comforting.

And as he sat dreaming there he heard the clatter of horses' hoofs in the lane and started out of his world of imagination to see that several members of his retinue, whom he had left behind at the Court of France, had arrived at the inn.

He went down to greet them.

They bowed before him. "God be praised, Highness," said their leader, "that we have found you."

"Call me Highness no more," said the King. "I have relinquished my rank. Very soon I shall be nothing more than the humblest friar."

His followers looked aghast, but he saw that they were already aware of his intended abdication; and it was for this reason that they, discovering his hiding-place, had come to him with all haste.

"Highness," said one, "it is imperative that you return to Portugal with all speed. If there is any delay it may well be that the Prince, your son, will have become King."

"It is what I intended."

"There is also the Princess Joanna, who expects to be your bride."

Alfonso looked pained. He had allowed the thought of Joanna to slip from his mind. But she was so young, so helpless. She would be a charmingly innocent bride.

The Franciscan robe lost some of its charm then; thinking of the soft body of the Princess Joanna, he was reminded of the hardship of the hair shirt.

A princess in distress, and he was sworn to rescue her! How could he desert her?

He remembered the Court—its balls and banquets, its fêtes, all its pleasures. The life of a King was his life; he had been brought up to expect it.

"It is too late," he said. "I have already written to my son. When he receives my letter he will make ready for his coronation. Once he is crowned King of Portugal, there will be no place there for me."

"Highness, it is not too late. Louis has offered a fleet of ships to carry you back to Portugal. We should leave without delay. And if we are fortunate we may reach Portugal before the coronation of Prince John."

Alfonso shook his head. "But no," he said. "I have decided." He smiled. This would be the most quixotic adventure of them all. The charms of Joanna were appealing; the court life had its attractions; but he could not abandon the Franciscan habit as easily as this.

"Highness," went on the chief of his advisers, "you cannot give up your crown. The Princess Joanna awaits you. She will be longing for your return. All Portugal will wish to see their King again. You cannot abandon the Princess Joanna. You cannot abandon your people."

He told himself they were right.

My beautiful Joanna, my little niece-bride. Of course I could not abandon you.

Yet he remained aloof from their argument, for his dignity would not allow him to give way too easily.

They knew that; they also knew that in time they would persuade him to give up this dream of retirement; they would make him see it as the chimera it was.

* * *

Ferdinand faced Isabella in that apartment where they were alone with their children. Ferdinand was dressed for a long journey.

"It grieves me to leave you," he was saying, "but you understand that it must be so."

"Indeed I understand. You must always go to your father when he needs you . . . as I must to my mother."

Ferdinand thought that the one was not to be compared with the other. His father, the great warrior statesman, and Isabella's mother, the insane creature of the Castle of Arevalo! But he did not comment on this. Isabella was, of course, referring to their duty.

"At least," she said, "you have happier news for him than when you were last with him. Although we must not forget that we are not yet completely safe."

"I shall always be wary of Alfonso," he said. "How can one know what mad scheme he will think of next? The idea of giving up his throne to his son! He talks of going into a monastery!"

Isabella smiled. "He has been humiliated by Louis, and he cannot face his countrymen. Poor Alfonso! He is unfit to wear a crown."

"You will take care of yourself and our children while I am away."

Isabella smiled at him fondly. "You can trust me to do so, Ferdinand."

"Care for them as assiduously as you care for Castile."

"I will, Ferdinand."

"There is a large enough force on the frontier to withstand an attack from Portugal should it come."

"Have no fear."

"You are a wise woman, Isabella. I regret I must leave my family. But the time is passing."

"You must say goodbye to the children," Isabella reminded him. She called to her daughter. "Isabella, my dear. Come. Your father has to leave us now."

The eight-year-old Infanta Isabella came running at her mother's call. She was a pretty though delicate child, and in her abundant hair was that hint of red which she had inherited from her Plantagenet ancestors. Even at eight she lacked the serenity of her mother.

She knelt before Ferdinand and Isabella, but Ferdinand swung her up in his arms and, holding her tightly against him, kissed her.

"Well, daughter," he said, "are you going to miss me?"

"So much, dear Father," she answered.

"I shall soon be with you again."

"Please come back soon, Father."

Isabella looked at them fondly.

"You will not," said the Infanta, "look for a husband for me, Father."

"That had not been my intention."

"Because," said young Isabella, playing with the ornament on his doublet, "I shall never wish to leave you and the Queen to go to France and be the daughter of the French King."

"You shall not leave us for many years," Ferdinand promised.

And Isabella threw her arms about her father's neck and hugged him tightly.

The Queen, watching them, found herself praying silently. "Preserve them both. Bring them happiness . . . the greatest happiness in life. If there are afflictions to be borne I will bear them. But let these two know perfect happiness."

They seemed to her like two children. Ferdinand, who was so often like a spoilt boy, for all his valour in battle, for all his dignity; and dear Isabella, whose desire at this time was never to leave the heart of her family.

Isabella thrust away her emotion and said: "You should not forget your son, Ferdinand. He will wish to take his leave of you."

"He is too young to know our father," said young Isabella, pouting slightly, not wishing to share her parents' attention with the baby who, she considered, usually had an unfair portion of it.

"Yet your father will wish to take his leave of him," said the Queen.

So they went to the royal nursery. The nurses curtsied as they approached and stood back from the cradle, where little Juan crowed and smiled as though to show off his prowess to the spectators.

Ferdinand lifted him in his arms and kissed the small forehead, young Juan showing a mild protest; but he was a healthy, happy baby. A quiet baby, thought Isabella exultantly.

And so the farewells were said and Ferdinand left his wife and children to ride into Aragon.

* * *

He was shocked to see how his father had aged. John of Aragon was almost eighty-three years old, but, although he looked ill, his mental powers had not diminished in the least; moreover, his agility belied his years.

Ferdinand had no need to complain of any lack of respect shown to him in Aragon. Here his father insisted on treating him not only like a king, but a greater king than he was himself.

"Ferdinand, King of Castile!" cried John as he embraced his son. "It does my heart good to see you. Oh, no . . . no. I shall walk on your left. Castile should take precedence over Aragon."

"Father," said Ferdinand, deeply moved, "you are my father and always should take precedence."

"Not in public any more, my son. And I pray you do not kiss my hand. It is I who shall kiss yours on all public occasions. Oh, it does me good to see you thus. King of Castile, eh?"

"Consort to the Queen, Father."

"That little matter? It is of no account. King of Castile you are, and as such worthy of the utmost respect."

It was a delight to John to be alone with his son. He would hear all the news. So he was grandfather to two children now. That delighted him. And Ferdinand had a son. Juan! They had thought to delight him to the utmost by giving him that name. "May it be long before he comes to the throne of Castile," cried John emotionally.

He wanted news of Isabella. "She still refuses to allow you equal rights then? She is a strong woman."

"To understand Isabella one must be with her constantly," mused Ferdinand. "And even then perhaps one does not know her really well. She has the strongest character in Castile and the mildest manners."

"She is highly respected throughout all Spain, and France too, I believe. It is of France that I wish to speak to you, my son. I have been in communication with Louis, and he is prepared to relinquish his friendship with Portugal, to give no more support to the cause of La Beltraneja and to make an alliance with you and Isabella, that there shall be perpetual peace between France and Castile."

"If this could be effected, Father, it would lift great anxieties from our minds."

"If it should be effected! Do you not know your old father? It *shall* be effected."

* * *

Ferdinand felt happy to be in Aragon.

"There is something in one's native air," he said to his attendants, "that lifts the spirits. How I miss my family! I long to see the Queen and my children. But nevertheless I could not be entirely unhappy while I am in Aragon."

There were certain delights in Saragossa, but Ferdinand must enjoy them in secret.

He left his father's palace and rode out at dusk. His destination was a house in the city, where he was received by a dignified lady who gave way to expressions of pleasure when she saw who her visitor was.

"I have business," said Ferdinand, "with the Archbishop of Saragossa. I pray you take me to him."

The lady bowed her head and led the way up a staircase. Ferdinand noted the expensive furnishings of the house and said: "It delights me that my lord Archbishop lives in a manner fitting to his rank."

"My lord is happy to enjoy the benefits of his rank," was the answer.

She opened a door on to a room where a boy of about seven years old was taking a fencing lesson.

He did not look up as the two stood in the doorway, but his tutor turned.

"On guard!" cried the boy.

"Pray continue," said Ferdinand; and he smiled to watch the boy's skill with the sword.

The tutor, no doubt thinking that the lesson should be brought to an end, with a flick of his wrist sent the boy's sword spinning out of his hand.

"How dare you! How dare you!" cried the boy. "One day I will run you through for that."

"Alonso, Alonso," said the lady. She turned to Ferdinand. "He has such high spirits. He excels at most sports and cannot bear not to shine." She signed to the tutor to leave them, and when they were alone she said: "Alonso your father has come."

The boy stood for a few seconds, staring at Ferdinand; then he came forward, knelt, took Ferdinand's hand and kissed it.

"So my lord Archbishop is glad to see his father?"

"The Archbishop has great pleasure in welcoming the King."

Ferdinand's lips twitched at the corners. This boy, with his flashing dark eyes and bold manners, was very dear to him. For his sake he had risked unpleasant scandal by bestowing on him, when he was only six years old, the Archbishopric of Saragossa, with all its attendant revenues, so the child was one of the richest people in Aragon.

"He would wish," went on the boy, "that he was more often given the opportunity of doing so."

Ferdinand smiled at the boy's mother, who was clearly delighted with her son's precocity.

"It is a matter of deep regret to the King also," said Ferdinand. "But let us endure it, for the time being. There may come a day when we shall be more frequently in each other's company."

The boy's eyes sparkled. His dignity deserted him and he was an eager child begging for a treat. He had seized Ferdinand's arm and was shaking it. "When, Father, when?" he demanded.

"One day. Have no fear of that." Ferdinand pictured this boy at the Court of Castile. Isabella would have to know. Well, she must accept the fact that kings such as Ferdinand must be expected to have an illegitimate son here and there. He would insist on Isabella's accepting this fact. Here, under the admiring gaze of his mistress and his son, he did not doubt that he would be capable of dealing with Isabella.

"I shall come to Court."

"Certainly you shall come to Court. By the saints, what a dashing courtier you will make, eh?"

"I shall be brave," said the boy. "And I shall be very important. All men will tremble at my approach."

"Will you be as fierce as all that?"

"I shall be the King's son," said Alonso simply.

Ferdinand replied solemnly: "You have learned much, Alonso —to strut like a courtier, to fence a little. But there is one thing you have not learned, and that is humility."

"Humility? You mean you would have me humble?"

"It is a lesson we all have to learn at some time or other, whether we be archbishops or king's sons. You lost your temper when your tutor showed more skill with the sword than you. Come, let me take his place."

The Viscountess of Eboli stood aside, watching her son and lover fencing together.

Again and again Ferdinand sent the boy's sword spinning out of his hand. Alonso was disconsolate, yet Ferdinand noticed with pleasure that the boy returned again and again to the play, always with the hope that this time it would not happen.

At last Ferdinand said: "That is enough." He threw aside his sword and put a hand on the boy's arm. "You will be a great swordsman one day, my son," he said, "providing you learn your lesson. I want you to excel in all things which you attempt. But I would have you understand that while you must have complete confidence in your ability to succeed, you must always be prepared to learn from those who have greater experience. That is the true humility, Alonso—and the only sort worth having."

"Yes, Father," said the boy, a little subdued.

"Now you shall tell me what you have been doing during my absence. There is little time left to us. My visit, as usual, must be brief."

The boy's face puckered in distress, and Ferdinand put his arm about him impulsively and embraced him.

"Perhaps, my son," he said fervently, "it will not always be so."

* * *

Alfonso of Portugal had arrived in his own country. Like most of his ventures, his arrival was ill-timed. As he set foot on the shores of his native land two items of news were brought to him, both of them disturbing.

His son John had been crowned King of Portugal five days before; and Pope Sixtus IV had been induced by Isabella and Ferdinand, and the conduct of Alfonso himself, to withdraw the dispensation which he had previously given to make the marriage between Alfonso and Joanna possible.

"What an unhappy man I am," mourned Alfonso. "You see, my friends, the hand of God is turned against me. I promised myself that I would return to my country, that I would marry the Princess Joanna, that I would rule more wisely than I have in the past. You see, I am not to marry nor to rule. What is left to me? Oh, why did I allow myself to be dissuaded from living the monastic life! What is left to me . . . but that!"

He travelled to Lisbon, and he felt that, as he passed through the towns, people watched him furtively. They did not know how to receive him. He was a king and yet not a king. He had brought poverty to Portugal with his wild enterprises; he had brought more than poverty—humiliation.

His son John received him with affection.

"You are the King of Portugal now," said Alfonso, kissing his hand. "You take precedence of your father. I was wrong to have come back to Court. I think I shall soon be leaving it."

John answered: "Father, if it were possible to retrace our steps, would you have kept the crown for yourself?"

Alfonso looked sadly at his son. "There is no place at Court for a king who has abdicated. He only makes trouble for his successor."

"Then what will you do, Father?"

"I think the monastery is the only answer."

"You would not long be happy in a monastery. The novelty would soon disappear, and you have been used to such an active life. How could you endure it?"

"I should learn to live a new life."

"Father, you regret abandoning the crown to me, do you not?"

"My son, I wish you all success."

"There comes a day when a son should take the crown from his father, and that is when his father is in his tomb."

"What do you mean, John?"

"I mean, Father, that as you gave your crown to me, I now abdicate and give it back to you. My time to wear it has not yet come. I trust it will not come for many years."

Alfonso smiled at John with tears in his eyes.

John felt relieved. He had been alarmed when his father had bestowed the crown upon him. He considered what often happened when there were two kings with only one crown between them. His father had abdicated, but there would almost certainly arise a faction which desired to put him back on the throne, whether he wished it or not.

John was happier waiting to inherit the crown on his father's death than wearing it while he was still alive.

So Alfonso forgot his humiliating adventure in France and accepted the crown at the hands of John.

As for the people of Portugal, they had grown accustomed to the eccentricities of their King, and after a while they ceased to talk of the two abdications.

* * *

Alfonso sent for the Princess Joanna.

She was growing into a charming young woman, and it distressed him that Sixtus had withdrawn the dispensation.

"My dear," he said, taking her hand and making her sit beside him, "how very unsettled life is for you."

"I am learning to be happy here, Highness," Joanna told him.

"I am glad. But I cannot be happy while our marriage is delayed."

Highness, we accept what is."

"Nay, my dear, we will not accept it. We will marry. I am determined on that."

Joanna drew back in alarm. "We could not," she said, "without the dispensation."

"The dispensation!" cried Alfonso. "Sixtus declares that he withdrew it because we did not give him the true facts. We know how much truth there is in that! He withdrew it because Isabella and Ferdinand insisted that he should; and they are supreme in Castile . . . at the moment."

"Yes," said Joanna, "the people accept Isabella as their Queen. They want no other."

"They are successful at the moment," said Alfonso. "But remember I say at the moment. This does not mean that they will always be so."

"We have tried," said Joanna, "and we have failed."

"My dear, your future husband never accepts failure. I have a plan."

"Not . . . not to go into Castile again?" stammered Joanna.

"We have failed once. But he wins who is successful in the last battle. That is the important one, my dear."

"You could not thrust the people of Portugal into war again."

The dreamlike expression was creeping over Alfonso's face.

"We must fight," he said, "we must fight for the right."

* * *

Ferdinand had returned from Aragon, and Isabella had prepared a banquet to welcome him.

She had wished it to be an elaborate feast. Not that Ferdinand was given to excessive eating or drinking any more than she was; not that he would care to see so much money spent, any more than she would; but he would appreciate the fact that his return was of such importance to herself and Castile.

Isabella carefully watched the expenditure of the treasury, but she was the first to admit that there were occasions when it was wise to spend; and this was one of them.

Ferdinand looked well, but she noticed a change in him. He was experiencing mingling anxiety and excitement. She felt she understood. His father's health must be giving him that cause for anxiety, while it gave him equal cause for excitement.

Ferdinand was fond of his father; he would never cease to be grateful to him; but at the same time King John's death would make Ferdinand King of Aragon; and, once that title was bestowed upon him, he would feel that he could stand in equality beside Isabella.

Isabella knew that all Ferdinand's emotions must be mingled with his love of possessions, so that even the death of a beloved parent could not be entirely deplored if it brought him a crown.

When she had received him and they were at last alone she said to him: "And your father, Ferdinand? How fares your father?"

"He is pleased with what we have done here in Castile; but he is ailing, I fear. He forgets that he is nearly eighty-three. And I think we forget it too."

"He has caused you to worry, Ferdinand."

"I cannot help feeling that his end is near."

"Yet it is largely due to him that this treaty of St. Jean de Luz, between ourselves and the French, has been made."

"His mind will be active till the end, Isabella. But I fear I may never see him again."

"Come, Ferdinand, I will call our daughter. She will turn your thoughts from this melancholy subject."

But even as Isabella called for her daughter she knew that the subject was not an entirely melancholy one; and the thought disturbed her.

* * *

It was early in the following year when the news came from Aragon.

The fierce winds of January, sweeping across the plain from the Guadarramas, penetrated the Palace, and in spite of huge fires it was difficult to keep it warm.

As soon as the messenger entered his presence, Ferdinand knew the nature of the news he had brought. It was evident, in the man's attitude as he presented the message, that he was not merely in the presence of the heir to the throne but in that of the monarch himself.

The colour deepened in Ferdinand's bronzed cheeks.

"You bring news of the King of Aragon?"

"Long live Don Ferdinand, King of Aragon!" was the answer.

"It is so?" said Ferdinand, and he drew himself up to his full height while he tried to think of his sorrow and all that the loss of one of the best friends he could ever have would mean to him. He turned away as though to hide his emotion. But the emotion was not entirely grief, and he did not want the man to see how much it meant to him to have inherited the throne of Aragon.

He turned back and put his hand over his eyes. "I pray you leave me now," he said quietly.

He waved his hand, and those who had been with him retired also.

He sat down at a table and buried his face in his hands. He was trying to think of his father, who had schemed for him—murdered for him—and all those occasions when John of Aragon had given him advice and help. He remembered his father at his mother's bedside when she had been afraid because she believed that the ghost of Carlos, Ferdinand's murdered stepbrother, had been there at the bedside. Carlos had died, it was generally believed, at the hands of his father and stepmother, so that their son Ferdinand might find no one to stand in his way to the throne.

This man was dead now. Never again could Ferdinand turn to him for guidance. The father who had loved him, surely as few were loved, was now no more. Every action of his had been for the advancement of Ferdinand; not only was Ferdinand his idolized son but the son of the woman whom he had loved beyond all else in the world.

Even in dying he gave Ferdinand a crown.

Isabella had heard the news and came in haste to the apartment.

He glanced up as she approached. She looked grave; and he thought then that there could not be a woman in the world who disguised her feelings as successfully as Isabella.

She knelt at his feet; she took his hand and kissed it. She was offering him solace for the loss of his father and at the same time homage to the King of Aragon.

"It has come, Isabella," he said, "as I feared." He might have added, and as I hoped. For he had certainly longed to feel the crown upon his head.

He felt a flicker of irritation against her because, being aware of his own mercenary feelings at this time, he could blame Isabella for them. It was Isabella's determination to remain supreme in Castile that made it so necessary for him to be a King in his own right—not merely of Sicily, but of the great province of Aragon.

Now that had happened and, when he should be grieving for his father, he found himself elated.

"You must not grieve," said Isabella. "He would not have it so. Ferdinand, this is a great occasion. I am Queen of Castile; you are King of Aragon. All that I have is yours; all that you have is mine. Now almost the whole of Spain is united."

"The whole of Spain—apart from that accursed Moorish kingdom—ours . . . ours, Isabella."

"We have a son who will be King of Spain, Ferdinand. I remind you of this, because I know how you suffer at this moment."

Ferdinand was suddenly aware of his loss. He said: "He was so good to me. No one ever had a better father."

"I know," she said; and she lifted her kerchief to her eyes.

But she was thinking: Castile and Aragon—we reign over almost the whole of Spain. Our destiny is being fulfilled. We are God's chosen rulers.

And he was thinking: I am a king . . . a king in my own right. King of Aragon, to stand side by side with the Queen of Castile.

* * *

The King of Aragon was no longer quite so insistent on the deference which must be paid to him. It was clear that he was the King . . . the King in his own right. He had a crown which he did not owe to his wife.

Isabella was delighted to see this change in him. She believed it augured well for their future. Ferdinand would not now grudge her her power in Castile.

If the war for the Succession could only be settled once and for all, Isabella would be ready to set her kingdom in order; but as long as Alfonso boasted of his intention to set Joanna on the throne of Castile in place of Isabella there could be no peace.

Yet her hopes for the future were high. She had her family—her charming Isabella, her healthy little Juan, so normal, both of them—and she for a brief spell had Ferdinand with her, a contented Ferdinand no longer looking for slights: Don Ferdinand, the King of Aragon.

It was during those spring months that Isabella once more discovered that she might expect a child.

* * *

Isabella found it necessary to visit the fortified towns on the borders of Castile and Portugal.

As she travelled from place to place she brooded on the sad state of her kingdom. Robbers were still numerous on the road. The Hermandad was doing good work, but while war threatened it was impossible to find the necessary funds to keep the organization going. The position was not as serious as it had once been, but there must be continual vigil in the frontier towns.

Beatriz came from Segovia to be with her.

"You should rest," said Beatriz. "Eight months after the birth of Juan and you become pregnant again!"

"It is a Queen's duty, Beatriz," Isabella reminded her friend with a smile, "to ensure that the royal line is continued."

"And to take care of herself that she may perform this duty," retorted Beatriz. "Has Your Highness forgotten another occasion, when you lost your child?"

Isabella smiled. She allowed Beatriz to speak to her in this rather hectoring manner because she knew that it was the outward sign of a great affection. Perhaps no one in Castile loved her, reflected Isabella, as did this forthright, bold Beatriz de Bobadilla.

"It is not for me to think of the peril to myself," she said calmly. "If I am timid, how can I expect my friends to be otherwise?"

Beatriz attempted once more to dissuade Isabella from making these journeys, which were not only arduous but dangerous; but Isabella firmly implied that she wished to hear no more; and although Beatriz was by nature overbearing and Isabella so calm, Beatriz always realized when the moment had come to say no more and to drop the role of privileged friend for that of humble confidante.

It was while Isabella was inspecting the border fortifications that she received a communication from the Infanta Doña Beatriz of Portugal. The Infanta, who was Isabella's maternal aunt, deplored the fact that Castile and Portugal, whose sovereigns were so closely related, should be continually at war. She would be grateful, she wrote, if Isabella would meet her, and if together they could discuss some means of making peace between the two countries.

Isabella was eager for the meeting, and she immediately agreed to it.

Meanwhile, with Ferdinand and her counsellors, she drew up the peace terms.

* * *

Isabella, not yet incapacitated by pregnancy, rode to the border town of Alcantara, where Doña Beatriz of Portugal was waiting for her.

The ladies embraced and, because each was so eager to bring about peace, they wasted no time in celebrations but began their discussions immediately.

"My dear Doña Beatriz," said Isabella, as they sat together in the council chamber, "the Portuguese Army was beaten in the field, and should it come against us once more we should be confident of annihilating it."

"That is true," said Doña Beatriz, "but let us not consider the possibility of war. Let us turn our thoughts to peace."

"By all means," was the answer. "The first clause that we should insist on would be that Alfonso gives up the title and armorial bearings of Castile which he has assumed."

"That is reasonable. I feel sure he will agree to that."

"There must be no more claims from or on behalf of Joanna, and the King must no longer consider himself betrothed to her. Moreover, he must never again aspire to her hand."

Doña Beatriz frowned. "He has a great fondness for Joanna," she said.

"And for the crown of Castile," replied Isabella dryly, "to which he pretends to believe she has a claim."

"I can put this clause before him," said Beatriz. "It will be for me to persuade him to accept it."

"You are convinced of the justice of it?"

"I am convinced that there must be peace between Castile and Portugal."

"Between Castile *and* Aragon and Portugal," said Isabella with a smile. "We are stronger now."

"I will remind the King of that also."

"As for Joanna," went on Isabella, "she must either leave Portugal or be betrothed to my son, Juan."

"Juan! He is not yet a year old . . . and she . . . she is now a young woman."

"It is a condition," said Isabella. "We will give her six months to decide whether she will leave Portugal or be betrothed to my son. If, when he reaches a marriageable age, she prefers to enter a convent, I shall not stand in her way. If she did enter a convent it would be necessary for her to take the veil."

Beatriz looked long into the smiling face of Isabella, and she thought: We are discussing the life of a young girl who, although she has been a menace to Isabella, is in herself innocent. Yet Isabella, herself so happy in her marriage and her family, is so determined to be secure upon the throne, that she is not only denying this girl any hope of the crown but of the normal life of a woman. The face Isabella showed to the world was completely enigmatic. It would be well not to be deceived by that gentle façade.

"It is a hard choice for a young girl," mused Beatriz. "Betrothal to a baby—or the veil!"

"It is an important condition," said Isabella.

"I can put these terms before Joanna," said Beatriz, "and before the King. I can do no more."

"That is understood," said Isabella. "All Castilians who have fought with the King of Portugal for Joanna will be pardoned and, to show that I and my husband wish for friendship with Portugal, my daughter, the Infanta Isabella, shall be betrothed to Alonso, son of the Prince of Portugal."

"So these are your conditions," said Beatriz. "I do not think it will be easy to obtain the King's consent to all of them."

"I deplore war," Isabella told her. "But it will be necessary for the King to agree to *all* these conditions if we are to have peace. He must remember that he was defeated in the field. He will know that, eager as Castile is for peace, it does not need it so desperately as does Portugal."

The two ladies took their leave of each other, Beatriz travelling westward to Lisbon, Isabella eastward to Madrid.

Isabella waited. The conditions were hard, but they were necessarily so, she told herself, to secure lasting peace. She was sorry for Joanna, who had been a helpless puppet in the hands of ambitious men; but the comfort and happiness of one young woman could not be considered when the prosperity of Castile was at stake.

Isabella was large with her child when news came that Alfonso had accepted her terms.

Her spirits were high. The War of the Succession, which had lasted four years, was over.

And very soon another child would be born to her and Ferdinand.

* * *

The city of Toledo was set high on a plateau of stone which appeared to have been carved out of the surrounding mountains in the gorge of the Tagus. Only on the north side was it accessible by a narrow isthmus which connected it with the plain of Castile. In no other city in Isabella's Castile was there more evidence of Moorish occupation.

Isabella could never visit her city of Toledo without reiterating the vow that one day she would wrest from the Moors those provinces of Spain which were still under their domination, and that the flag of Christian Spain should float over every city.

But, to remind her of the state of her country, not far from this very palace of Toledo in which she now lay was that great rock, from which it was the custom to hurl alleged criminals. Many would meet their fate at the rock of Toledo before Castile would be safe for honest men and women to live in.

A tremendous task lay before her, and as soon as she had left this childbed she must devote herself to stabilizing her country. Nothing should be spared, she had decided. She would be harsh if harshness were needed, and all her honest subjects would rejoice. She had sworn to rid Castile of its criminals, to make the roads safe for travellers by imposing such penalties on offenders that even the most hardened robber would think twice before offending.

But now there was the child about to be born.

It would be soon, and she was unafraid. One grew accustomed to child-bearing. The pains of birth she could bear stoically. She had a daughter and son, and she no longer had any uneasy feelings regarding a child she would bear. Her mother was living in a dark world of her own at Arevalo, and the dread that the children should be like her had disappeared. Why should they be? Isabella was in full possession of her mental powers. No one in Castile was more balanced, more controlled than the Queen. Why, then, should she fear?

The pains were becoming more frequent. Isabella waited awhile before she called to her women.

It was some hours later when, in the fortress town of Toledo, Isabella's second daughter and third child was born.

She called her Juana.

* * *

Joanna knew herself to be deserted. Alfonso had agreed to Isabella's terms, and she had been offered her choice: marriage with a boy who was still a baby, or the veil.

Joanna knew that only would that marriage take place if by the time Prince Juan was in his teens there were still people to remember her cause in Castile. She wondered what sort of marriage she could hope for with a partner so many years younger than herself.

The peace of the cloister seemed inviting; but to take the veil, to shut herself off from the world for ever! Could she do that?

Yet what alternative was Isabella offering her? Shrewd Isabella who, so gently and with seeming kindness, could drive a poor bewildered girl into a prison from which there was no escape!

She must resign herself. She would take the veil. It was the only way to end conflict. How unhappy were those who, by an accident of birth, could never be allowed to live their lives as they would choose to do.

"I think," she said to her attendants, "that I will prepare myself to go to the convent of Santa Clara at Coimbra."

The visiting embassy called upon her when her decision was made known.

The leaders of this embassy were Dr. Diaz de Madrigal, a member of Isabella's Council, and Fray Fernando de Talavera, her confessor.

Talavera gave Joanna his blessing.

"You have chosen well, my daughter," he said. "In the convent of Santa Clara you will find a peace which you have never known outside the convent walls."

Joanna smiled wanly.

She knew then how fervent had been Isabella's wish that she would take this course.

* * *

Alfonso came to her to take his last farewell.

"My dearest," he said, taking both her hands and kissing them. "So this is the end of all our hopes."

"It is perhaps better so," said Joanna. "Many seem to be of that opinion."

"It leaves me desolate," declared Alfonso. "My dearest Joanna, I had made so many dreams."

"Too many dreams," said Joanna wistfully.

"What shall I do when you are immersed in your convent? What shall I do when there is an impenetrable barrier between us?"

"You will govern your country and doubtless make another marriage."

"That I shall never do," cried Alfonso. His eyes kindled, and Joanna guessed that he was conceiving a new plan to marry her in spite of the Pope, in spite of the agreement he had made with Isabella.

Joanna shook her head. "You have agreed to these terms," she said. "There can be no going back. That would result in a war which might prove disastrous to Portugal."

"Must I let you go?"

"Indeed you must."

Alfonso's looks became melancholy. He had abandoned the idea of defiance. He now said: "Since you are to incarcerate yourself in a convent, I shall spend the rest of my days in a monastery. As it must be the veil for you, it must be the Franciscan habit for me."

She smiled at him sadly. "You remember, Alfonso," she said, "that on a previous occasion you came near to entering a monastery. On that occasion, you changed your mind."

"This time I shall not change," said Alfonso, "for this is the only way I can bear the loss of my lady Joanna."

* * *

Never before had Isabella felt so confident, never so sure of her powers.

She had summoned a Cortes to meet at Toledo, and here new laws had been discussed and introduced. Isabella had made it clear that she intended to crush the power of the nobles and to eliminate crime in her dominions as far as possible.

The Santa Hermandad must be extended; only if it were efficient could crime be dealt with, and Isabella was certain that only harsh punishment, meted out to proved offenders, could deter others from following their example. Officers of the Hermandad were sent to every village in Castile, where they took up residence so that order there might be maintained. Two *alcaldes* were set up in every village. This had to be paid for, and a house tax of 18,000 *maravedis* was imposed on every hundred householders.

But Isabella was fully aware of the fact that she could not punish with great severity those who carried out their crimes in a small way and allow those who offended on a larger scale to escape.

During the reigns of her father and half-brother many sinecures had been created, and those men who had supported these kings had received large incomes as a reward. Isabella was determined that such drains on the exchequer should cease. Those who supported her must do so for love of their country, not for monetary reward. Thus Isabella deprived Beltran de la Cueva of a yearly income of a million and a half *maravedis*, in spite of the fact that he had turned from Joanna, alleged to be his daughter, to offer his services to Isabella; the Duke of Alva lost 600,000 *maravedis*, the Duke of Medina Sidonia 180,000 and Ferdinand's relative, Admiral Henriquez, 240,000.

This caused discontent among these nobles, but they dared not protest; and thus these large sums, which they had been squandering, helped to support the Santa Hermandad; and the effect of Isabella's stern rule soon began to be noticed throughout the land.

She was confident that in a few years' time she would transform the anarchical kingdom, which Castile had been when she had become its Queen, into a well-ordered state; she believed that the empty coffers of the treasury would be filled.

And once she had set her own house in order she would look farther afield.

Her eyes were on the Kingdom of Granada, and Ferdinand was beside her in this. He yearned to go into battle against the Moors, but she, the wiser one, restrained him for a while.

When they went into battle there should be victory for them. But they would not engage in war until there was peace and prosperity at home.

In spite of her preoccupation with state affairs, Isabella tried not to forget that she was a wife and mother. She deplored her own lack of education. Often she thought of those years at Arevalo, where she lived with her mother and her brother Alfonso, and where she was taught that one day she might be Queen, but little Latin, Greek or any other language which would have been useful to her. Her children should not suffer similarly; they should have the best of tutors. Most important of all was their religious instruction. That should certainly not be neglected.

There were occasions when she liked to escape to the nursery to forget the magnitude of the task of governing a kingdom which until recently had been on the verge of decay.

She liked to sit and sew with a few of her women as though she were a simple noblewoman, and talk of matters other than those concerned with the state. There was little time for this, and greatly she treasured those brief hours when she could indulge in it.

It was on one of these occasions, when her women were chattering together, that one of them who had recently come from Aragon talked of a ceremony she had seen there.

Isabella listened idly to the conversation. ". . . such a ceremony! The churchmen, brilliant in their vestments. And the one who attracted most attention was, of course, the Archbishop of Saragossa. An Archbishop only ten years old . . . certainly little more. Such a handsome little fellow . . . with all the dignity required of his rank."

"An Archbishop, ten years old?" said Isabella.

"Why yes, Highness, the Archbishop of Saragossa. He cannot be much more."

"He is very young to have attained such a post. The Archbishop of Saragossa must be a remarkable person indeed."

Isabella changed the subject, but she kept in mind the young Archbishop of Saragossa.

* * *

Isabella was discussing that ever-present problem with Ferdinand—the state of the treasury; and she said : "I am determined to divert the wealth of the great Military and Religious Orders to the royal coffers."

"What?" cried Ferdinand. "You will never do that."

"I think I shall."

"But how?"

"By having you elected Grand Master of each of them when those offices fall vacant."

Ferdinand's eyes took on that glazed look which the contemplation of large sums of money always brought to them.

"Calatrava, Alcantara, Santiago . . ." he murmured.

"All shall fall gradually into our hands," said Isabella. "When I contemplate the wealth in the possession of these Orders—the armies, the fortresses—it is inconceivable that they should exist to threaten the crown. We should be able to rely on the loyalty of these Orders without question, to use their arms and their wealth as we need it. Therefore they should be the property of the crown. And when you are Grand Master that will be achieved."

"It is a brilliant idea," agreed Ferdinand gleefully, and he gave his wife a glance of admiration. At such times he did not resent her determination to stand supreme as ruler of Castile.

"You shall see it achieved," she told him. "But it will be when the time is ripe."

"I believe," said Ferdinand, "that our struggles are behind us. A glorious future will be ours, Isabella, if we stand together."

"And so we shall stand. It was what I always intended."

He embraced her, and she drew back from his arms to smile at him.

"Castile and Aragon are ours! We have three healthy children," she said.

Ferdinand caught her hands and laughed. "We are young yet," he reminded her.

"Our little Isabella will be Queen of Portugal. We must arrange grand marriages for the others."

"Never fear. There will be many who will wish to marry with the children of Ferdinand and Isabella."

"Ferdinand, I am glad they are young yet. I shall suffer when they are forced to go from us."

"But they are still children as yet. Why, our little Isabella is but eleven years old."

"Eleven years old," mused Isabella. "But perhaps that is not so young. I hear you have an Archbishop in Saragossa of that age."

Ferdinand's face grew a little pale and then flushed. His eyes had become alert and suspicious.

"An Archbishop . . ." he murmured.

"You must have had your reasons for sanctioning the appointment," she said with a smile. "I wondered what great qualifications one so young could have."

She was unprepared for Ferdinand's reaction. He said: "You have made the affairs of Castile yours. I pray you leave to me those of Aragon."

It was Isabella's turn to grow pale. "Why, Ferdinand . . ." she began.

But Ferdinand had bowed and left her.

Why, she asked herself, should he have been so angry? What had she done but ask a simple question?

She stared after him and then sat down heavily. Understanding had come to her.

To have made a boy of that age an Archbishop, Ferdinand must have a very special reason for favouring him. What reason could Ferdinand have?

She refused to accept the explanation which was inevitably forcing itself into her mind.

He would have been born about the same time as their . . . first-born, little Isabella.

"No!" cried Isabella.

She, who had been so faithful to him in every way, could not tolerate this suspicion. But it was fast becoming no longer a suspicion. She now knew that Ferdinand was the lover of other women, that they had given him children—children whom he must love dearly to have risked exposure by making one of them Archbishop of Saragossa.

There was nothing that could have hurt her more. And this discovery had come to her at a time when all that she had hoped for seemed to be coming her way.

Her marriage was to have been perfect. She had known that he was jealous of her authority, but that she had understood. This was different.

She felt numb with the pain of this discovery. She felt a longing to give way to some weakness, to find Ferdinand, to rail against him, to throw herself on to her bed and give way to tears—to rage, to storm, to ease in some way the bitterness of this knowledge which wounded her more deeply than anything had ever done before.

Her women were coming to her.

She set her face in a quiet smile. None would have guessed that the smiling face masked such turbulent emotions and jealous humiliation.

TOMÁS DE TORQUEMADA

In a cell in the Monastery of Santa Cruz in the town of Segovia, a gaunt man, dressed in the rough garb of the Dominican Order, was on his knees.

He had remained thus for several hours, and this was not unusual for it was his custom to meditate and pray alternately for hours at a time.

He prayed now that he might be purged of all evil and given the power to bring others to the same state of exaltation which he felt that he himself—with minor lapses—enjoyed.

"Holy Mother," he murmured, "listen to this humble supplicant. . . ."

He believed fervently in his humility and, if it had been pointed out to him that this great quality had its roots in a fierce pride, he would have been astonished. Tomás de Torquemada saw himself as the elect of Heaven.

Beneath the drab robe of rough serge he wore the hair-shirt which was a continual torment to his delicate skin. He revelled in the discomfort it caused; yet after years of confinement in this hideous garment he had grown a little accustomed to it and he fancied that it was less of a burden than it had once been. The thought disturbed him, for he wanted to suffer the utmost discomfort. He slept on a plank of wood without a pillow. Soft beds were not for him. In the early days of his austerity he had scarcely slept at all; now he found that he needed very little sleep and, when he lay on his plank, he fell almost immediately into unconsciousness. Thus another avenue of self-torture was closed to him.

He ate only enough to keep him alive; he travelled barefoot wherever he went and took care to choose the stony paths. The sight of his cracked and bleeding feet gave him a similar pleasure to that which fine garments gave to other men and women.

He gloried in austerity with a fierce and fanatical pride—as other men delighted in worldly glitter.

It was almost sixty years ago that he had been born in the little town of Torquemada (which took its name from the Latin *turre cremata*—burnt tower) not far from Valladolid in North Castile.

From Tomás' early days he had shown great piety. His uncle, Juan de Torquemada, had been the Cardinal of San Sisto, a very distinguished theologian and writer on religious subjects.

Tomás had known that his father, Pero Fernandez de Torquemada, hoped that he would make the care of the family estates his life work, as he was an only son, and Pero was eager for Tomás to marry early and beget sons that this branch of the family might not become extinct.

Tomás had inherited a certain pride in his family, and this may have been one of the reasons why he decided so firmly that the life he had been called upon to lead, by a higher authority than that of Pero, should be one which demanded absolute celibacy.

At a very early age Tomás became a Dominican. With what joy he cast aside the fine raiment of a prosperous nobleman! With what pleasure he donned the rough serge habit, even at that age refusing to wear linen so that the coarse stuff could irritate his skin! It was very soon afterwards that he took to wearing the hair-shirt, until he discovered that he must not wear it continually for fear that he should grow accustomed to it and the torment of it grow less.

He had become Prior of Santa Cruz of Segovia, but the news of his austere habits had reached the Court, and King Henry IV had chosen him as confessor to his sister Isabella.

He had refused at first; he wanted no soft life at Court. But then he had realized that there might be devils to tempt him at Court who could never penetrate the sanctity of Santa Cruz; and there would be more spiritual joy in resisting temptation than never encountering it.

The young Isabella had been a willing pupil. There could rarely have been a young Princess so eager to share her confessor's spirituality, so earnestly desirous of leading a rigidly religious life.

She had been pleased with her confessor, and he with her.

He had told her of his great desire to see an all-Christian Spain and, in an access of fervour, had asked that she kneel with him and swear that, if ever it were in her power to convert to Christianity the realm over which she might one day rule, she would seize the opportunity to do so.

The young girl, her eyes glowing with a fervour to match that of her confessor, had accordingly sworn.

It often occurred to Tomás de Torquemada that the opportunity must soon arise.

Torquemada had kept the esteem of the Queen. She admired his piety; she respected his motives; in a Court where she was surrounded by men who sought temporal power, this ascetic monk stood out as a man of deep sincerity.

As Torquemada prayed there was a thought at the back of his mind: now that Castile had ceased to be tormented by civil war, the time had come when the religious life of the country should be examined, and to him it seemed that the best way of doing this was to reintroduce the Inquisition into Castile, a new form of the Inquisition which he himself would be prepared to organize, an Inquisition which should be supervised by men like himself—monks of great piety, of the Dominican and Franciscan orders.

But another little matter had intruded into Torquemada's schemes, and he had been diverted. It was because of this that he now prayed so earnestly. He had allowed himself to indulge in pleasure rather than duty.

A certain Hernan Nuñez Arnalt had recently died, and his will had disclosed that he had named Tomás de Torquemada as its executor. Arnalt had been a very rich man, and had left a considerable sum for the purpose of building a monastery at Avila which should be called the Monastery of Saint Thomas.

To Tomás de Torquemada had fallen the task of carrying out his wishes and he found great joy in this duty. He spent much time with architects and discovered a great love of building; but so great was this pleasure that he began to be doubtful about it. Anything that made a man as happy as the studying of plans for this great work made him, must surely have an element of sin in it. He was suspicious of happiness; and as he looked back to that day when he had first heard of the proposed endowment, and that he had been entrusted to see the work carried out, he was alarmed.

He had neglected his duties at Santa Cruz; he had thought only occasionally of the need to force Christianity on every inhabitant of Castile; he had ceased to consider the numbers who, while calling themselves Christians, were reverting to the Jewish religion in secret. These sinners called for the greatest punishment that could be devised by the human mind; and he, the chosen servant of God and all his saints, had been occupying himself by supervising the piling of stone on stone, by deciding on the exquisite line of the cloisters, by taking sensuous enjoyment in planning with sculptors the designs for the chapel.

Torquemada beat his hands on his breast and cried: "Holy Mother of God, intercede for this miserable sinner."

He must devise some penance. But long austerity had made him careless of what his body suffered. "Yet," he said, "the Monastery will be dedicated to the glory of God. Is it such a sin to erect a building where men will live as recluses, a spiritual life, in great simplicity and austerity, and so come close to the Divine presence? Is that sin?"

The answer came from within. "It is sin to indulge in any earthly desire. It is sin to take pleasure. And you, Tomás de Torquemada, have exulted over these plans; you have made images of stone, works of exquisite sculpture; and you have lusted for these earthly baubles as some men lust for women."

"Holy Mother, scourge me," he prayed. "Guide me. Show me how I can expiate my sin. Shall I cut myself off from the work on the monastery? But it is for the glory of God that the monastery will be built. Is it such a sin to find joy in building a house of God?"

He would not visit the site of Avila for three weeks; he would look at no more plans. He would say: "My work at Santa Cruz demands all my energy. Castile is an unholy land, and I must do all in my power to bring sinners back to the Church."

He rose from his knees. He had decided on the penance. He would shut his beautiful monastery from his mind for three weeks. He would live on nothing but dry bread and water; and he would increase his hours of prayer.

As he left his cell a monk came to him to tell him that two Dominicans from Seville had arrived at Santa Cruz, and they had come to speak with the Sacred Prior, Tomás de Torquemada.

* * *

Torquemada received the visitors in a cell which was bare of all furniture except a wooden table and three stools. On a wall hung a crucifix.

"My brothers," said Torquemada in greeting, "welcome to Santa Cruz."

"Most holy Prior," said the first of the monks, "you know that I am Alonso de Ojeda, Prior of the monastery of Saint Paul. I would present our fellow Dominican, Diego de Merlo."

"Welcome, welcome," said Torquemada.

"We are disturbed by events in Seville and, knowing of your great piety and influence with the Queen, we have come to ask your advice and help."

"I shall be glad to give it, if it should be in my power," was the answer.

"Evil is practised in Seville," said Ojeda.

"What evil is this, brother?"

"The evil of those who work against the Holy Catholic Church. I speak of the *Marranos*."

Torquemada's face lost its deathlike pallor for an instant, and his blood showed pale pink beneath his skin; his eyes flashed momentarily with rage and hatred.

"These *Marranos,*" cried Diego de Merlo, "they abound in Seville . . . in Cordova . . . in every fair city of Castile. They are the rich men of Castile. Jews! Jews who feign to be Christians. They are *Conversos.* They are of the true faith; so they would imply. And in secret they practise their foul rites."

Torquemada clenched his fists tightly and, although his face was bloodless once more, his eyes continued to gleam with fanatical hatred.

Ojeda began to speak rapidly. "Alonso de Spina warned us some years ago. They are here among us. They jeer at all that is sacred . . . in secret, of course. Jeer! If that were all! They are the enemies of Christians. In secret they practise their hideous rights. They spit upon holy images. You remember what Spina wrote of them?"

"I remember," said Torquemada quietly.

But Ojeda went on as though Torquemada had not spoken: "They cook their food in oils, and they stink of rancid food. They eat *kosher* food. You can tell a Jew by his stink. Should we have these people among us? Only if they renounce their beliefs. Only if they are purified by their genuine acceptance of the Christian faith. But they cheat, I tell you."

"They are cheats and liars," echoed Diego de Merlo.

"They are murderers," went on Ojeda. "They poison our wells; and worst of all they show their secret scorn of the Christian faith by committing hideous crimes. Only recently a little boy was missing from his home . . . a beautiful little boy. His body was discovered in a cave. He had been crucified, and his heart cut out."

"So these outrages continue," said Torquemada.

"They continue, brother; and nothing is done to put an end to them."

"Something must be done," said de Merlo.

"Something *shall* be done," replied Torquemada.

"There should be a tribunal set up to deal with heretics," cried Ojeda.

"The Inquisition is the answer," replied Torquemada; "but a new Inquisition . . . an efficient organization which would in time rid the country of heresy."

"There is no Inquisition in Castile at this time," went on Ojeda. "And why? Because, brother, it is considered that there are not enough cases of heresy existing in Castile to warrant the setting up of such an institution."

Torquemada said: "There are Inquisitors in Aragon, in Catalonia and in Valencia. It is high time there were Inquisitors in Castile."

"And because of this negligence," said Ojeda, "in the town of Seville these knaves flourish. I would ask for particular attention to the men of Seville. Brother, we have come to ask your help."

"Readily would I give it in order to drive heresy from Spain," Torquemada told them.

"We propose to ask an audience of the Queen to lay these facts before her. Holy Prior, can we count on your support with Her Highness?"

"You may count on me," said Torquemada. His thin lips tightened, his eyes glistened. "I would arrest those who are suspect. I would wring confessions from them that they might implicate all who are concerned with them in their malpractices; and when they are exposed I would offer them a chance to save their souls before the fire consumed them. Death by the fire! It is the only way to cleanse those who have been sullied by partaking in these evil rites." He turned to his guests. "When do you propose to visit the Queen?"

"We are on our way to her now, brother, but we came first to you, for we wished to assure ourselves of your support."

"It is yours," said Torquemada. His eyes were shining. "The hour has come. It has been long delayed. This country has suffered much from civil war, but now we are at peace and the time has come to turn all men and women in Castile into good Christians. Oh, it will be a mighty task. And we shall need to bring them to their salvation through the rack, hoist and faggot. But the hour of glory is about to strike. Yes, yes, my friends, I am with you. Every accursed Jew in this kingdom, who has returned to the evil creed of his forefathers, shall be taken up, shall be put to the test, shall feel the healing fire. Go. Go to the Queen with my blessing. Call on me when you wish. I am with you."

* * *

When his visitors had gone, Torquemada went to his cell and paced up and down.

"Holy Mother," he cried, "curse all Jews. Curse those who deny the Christ. Give us power to uncover their wickedness and, when they are exposed in all their horror, we shall know how to deal with them in your holy name and that of Christ your son. We will take them. We will set them on the rack. We will tear their flesh with red-hot pincers. We will dislocate their limbs on the hoist. We will torture their bodies that we may save their souls.

"A curse on the *Marranos*. A curse on the *Conversos*. I hate all practising Jews. I suspect all those who call themselves New

Christians. Only when we have purged this land of their loathsome presence shall we have a pure Christian country."

He fell to his knees and one phrase kept hammering in his brain : I hate all Jews.

He shut his mind to thoughts which kept intruding. It was not true. He would not accept it. His grandmother had *not* been a Jewess. His family possessed the pure Castilian blood. They were proud of their *limpieza*.

Never, never would Alvar Fernandez de Torquemada have introduced Jewish blood into the family. It was an evil thought; it was like a maggot working in his brain, tormenting him.

It was impossible, he told himself.

Yet, during the period in which his grandfather had been married, persecution of the Jews was rare. Many of them occupied high posts at Court and no one cared very much what blood they had in their veins. Grandfather Alvar Fernandez had carelessly married, perhaps not thinking of the future trouble he might be causing his family.

Tomás de Torquemada refused to believe it. But the thought persisted.

He remembered early days. The sly knowledge and sidelong looks of other boys, the whispers : "Tomás de Torquemada—he boasts of his Castilian blood. Oh, he is so proud of his *limpieza*—but what of his old Grandmother? They say she is a Jewess."

What antidote was there against this fear? What but hatred?

"I hate the Jews!" he had said continually. He forced himself to show great anger against them. Thus, he reasoned, none would believe that he was in the slightest way connected with them. Thus he could perhaps convince himself.

Alonso de Spina, who, almost twenty years before, had tried to arouse the people's anger against the Jews, was himself a *Converso*. Did he, Tomás de Torquemada, whip himself to anger against them for the same reason?

Torquemada threw himself on to his knees. "Give me strength," he cried, "strength to drive all infidels and unbelievers to their death. Give me strength to bring the whole of Castile together as one Christian state. One God. One religion. And to the fire with all those who believe otherwise."

Torquemada—who feared there might be a trace of Jewish blood in his veins—would emerge as the greatest Catholic of Castile, the punisher of heretics, the scourge of the Jews, the man who worked indefatigably to make an all-Christian Castile.

*　　*　　*

Ferdinand was with Isabella when she received Alonso de Ojeda and Diego de Merlo.

Isabella welcomed the monks cordially and begged them to state their business.

Ojeda broke into an impassioned speech in which he called her attention to the number of *Conversos* living in Seville.

"There are many *Conversos* throughout Castile," said Isabella quietly. "I employ some of them in my own service. I rejoice that they have become Christians. It is what I would wish all my subjects to be."

"Highness, my complaint is that while many of these *Conversos* in Seville profess Christianity they practise the Jewish religion."

"That," said Isabella, "is a very evil state of affairs."

"And one which," put in Diego de Merlo, "Your Highness would doubtless wish to end at the earliest possible moment."

Isabella nodded slowly. "You had some project in mind, my friends?" she said.

"Highness, the Holy Office does not exist in Castile. We ask that you consider installing it here."

Isabella glanced at Ferdinand. She saw that the pulse in his temple had begun to hammer. She felt sad momentarily, and almost wished that she did not understand Ferdinand so well. He was possessed by much human frailty, she feared. It had been a great shock to discover that not only had he an illegitimate son but that he had appointed him, at the age of six, Archbishop of Saragossa. That boy was not the only child Ferdinand had had by other women. She had discovered that a noble Portuguese lady had borne him a daughter. There might be others. How should she hear of them?

Now his eyes glistened, and she understood why. The Inquisition had been set up in Aragon and because of it the riches of certain condemned men had found their way into the royal coffers. Money could make Ferdinand's eyes glisten like that.

"Such procedure would need a great deal of consideration," said Isabella.

"I am inclined to believe," said Ferdinand, his eyes still shining and with the flush in his cheeks, "that the installation of the Holy Office in Castile is greatly to be desired."

The monks had now turned their attention to Ferdinand, and Ojeda poured out a storm of abuse against the Jews. He spoke of ritual murders, of Christian boys, three or four years old, who had been kidnapped to take part in some loathsome rites which involved the crucifixion of the innocent child and the cutting out of his heart.

Ferdinand cried: "This is monstrous. You are right. We must have an enquiry immediately."

"Have the bodies of these children been discovered?" asked Isabella calmly.

"Highness, these people are crafty. They bury the bodies in secret places. It is a part of their ritual."

"I think it would be considered necessary to have proof of these happenings before we could believe them," said Isabella.

Ferdinand had turned to her. She saw the angry retort trembling on his lips. She smiled at him gently. "I am sure," she said quietly, "that the King agrees with me."

"An enquiry might be made," said Ferdinand. His voice sounded aloof, as it did when he was angry.

"An enquiry, yes," said Isabella. She turned to the monks. "This matter shall have my serious consideration. I am indebted to you for bringing it to my notice."

She laid her hand on Ferdinand's arm. It was a command to escort her from the chamber.

* * *

When they were alone, Ferdinand said: "My opinion would appear to count for little."

"It counts for a great deal," she told him.

"But the Queen is averse to setting up the Inquisition in Castile?"

"I have not yet given the matter sufficient consideration."

"I had always believed that it was one of your dearest wishes to see an all-Christian Castile."

"That is one of my dearest wishes."

"Why, then, should you be against the extirpation of heretics?"

"Indeed I am not against it. You know it is part of our plans for Castile."

"Then who is best fitted to track them down? Surely the Inquisitors are the men for that task?"

"I am not sure, Ferdinand, that I wish to see the Inquisition in Castile. I would wish first to assure myself that, by installing the Inquisition here, I should not give greater power to the Pope than he already has. We are the sovereigns of Castile, Ferdinand. We should share our power with no one else."

Ferdinand hesitated. Then he said: "I am sure we could set up our Inquisition—our own Inquisition which should be apart from Papal influence. I may tell you, Isabella, that the Inquisition can bring profit to the crown. Many of the *Conversos* are rich men, and it is one of the rules of the Inquisition that those who are found guilty of heresy forfeit land . . . wealth . . . all possessions."

"The treasury is depleted," said Isabella. "We need money. But I would prefer to replenish it through other means."

"Are the means so important?"

She looked at him almost coldly. "They are of the utmost importance."

Ferdinand corrected himself quickly. "Providing the motive is a good one . . ." he began. "And what better motive than to bring salvation to poor misguided fools? What nobler purpose than to lead them into the Catholic Church?"

"It is what I would wish to see, but as yet I am inclined to give this matter further consideration."

"You will come to understand that the Inquisition is a necessity if you are to make an all-Catholic Castile."

"You may be right, Ferdinand. You often are." She smiled affectionately. Come, she seemed to be saying, let us be friends. This marriage of ours has brought disappointments to us both. I am a woman who knows she must rule in her own way; you hoped I would be different. You are a man who cannot be faithful to his wife; I hoped *you* would be different. But here we are—two people of strong personalities which we cannot change, even for the sake of the other. Let us be content with what we have been given. Do not let us sigh for the impossible. For our marriage is more than the union of two people. What matters it if in our hearts we suffer these little disappointments? What are they, compared with the task which lies before us?

She went on: "I wish to show you our new device. I trust it will please you, for it gives me so much pleasure. I am having it embroidered on a banner, and I did not mean to show you until it was finished; but soon it will be seen all over Castile, and when the people see it they will know that you and I stand together in all things."

He allowed himself to be placated; and she called to one of her pages to bring the piece of embroidery to her.

When it was brought she showed him the partly finished pattern.

She read in her quiet voice, which held a ring of triumph: "*Tanto monta, monta tanto—Isabel como Fernando.*"

She saw a slow smile break out on Ferdinand's face. As much as the one is worth, so much is the other—Isabella as Ferdinand.

She could not say more clearly than that how she valued him, how she looked upon him as her co-ruler in Castile.

Still he knew that in all important matters she considered herself the sole adjudicator. Whatever their device, whatever her gentleness, she still remained Queen in her own right. She held supreme authority in Castile.

As for the installation of the Inquisition, thought Ferdinand, in time she would agree to it. He would arrange for Torquemada to persuade her.

With Ferdinand on one side to show what material good the Inquisitors could bring them, with Torquemada on the other to speak of the spiritual needs of Castile—they would win. But it would not be until they had convinced Isabella that the Inquisition was necessary to Castile.

* * *

Isabella sent for Cardinal Mendoza and commanded that it should be a completely private audience.

"I pray you sit down, Cardinal," she said. "I am deeply disturbed, and I wish you to give me your considered opinion on the matter I shall put before you."

The Cardinal waited respectfully; he guessed the matter was connected with the visit of the two Dominicans.

"Alonso de Ojeda and Diego de Merlo," began Isabella, "are deeply concerned regarding the behaviour of *Marranos* in Seville. They declare that there are many men and women who, proclaiming themselves to be Christians, cynically practise Jewish rites in secret. They even accuse them of kidnapping and crucifying small boys. They wish to set up the Inquisition in Castile. What is your opinion of this, Cardinal?"

The Cardinal was thoughtful for a few seconds. Then he said: "We have fanatics in our midst, Highness. I am deeply opposed to fanaticism. It warps the judgment and destroys the peace of the community. Through the centuries the Jewish communities have been persecuted, but there is no evidence that such persecution has brought much good to the countries in which it was carried out. Your Highness will remember that in the fourteenth century Fernando Martinez preached against the Jews and declared that they were responsible for the Black Death. The result —pogroms all over Spain. Many suffered, but there is no evidence of any good that this brought. From time to time rumours spring up of the kidnapping and crucifixion of small boys, but we should ask ourselves what truth there is in these rumours. It was not very long ago that Alonso de Spina published his account of the evil doings of *Conversos*. Strange, when he himself was a *Converso*. One feels that he wished it to be widely known that he was a good Catholic . . . so good, so earnest that he was determined to expose his fellows. Very soon afterwards rumours of kidnappings and crucifixions occurred again. I think, Highness, knowing your desire for justice, that you would wish to examine these rumours with the utmost care before accepting them as truth."

"You are right. But should they not be examined? And in that case, who should be the examiners? Should this task not be the duty of Inquisitors?"

"Can we be sure, Highness, that this desire to set up the Inquisition in Castile does not come from Rome?"

Isabella smiled faintly. "It is as though you speak my thoughts aloud."

"May I remind you of the little controversy which recently occurred?"

"There is no need to remind me," answered Isabella. "I remember full well."

Her thoughts went to that recent incident, when she had asked for the appointment of one of her chaplains, Alonso de Burgos, to the bishopric of Cuenca; but because the nephew of Pope Sixtus, Raffaele Riario, had desired the post it had gone to him. As Isabella had on two previous occasions asked for appointments for two of her protégés—which had gone to the Pope's candidates—she was angry and had recalled her ambassador from the Vatican. With Ferdinand's help she had proposed to get together a council, that the conduct of the Pope might be examined. Sixtus, alarmed that his nepotism would be exposed in all its blatancy, gave way to Isabella and Ferdinand, and bestowed the posts they had demanded on their candidates.

It was quite reasonable to suppose therefore that Sixtus would have his alert eyes on Isabella and Ferdinand and would seek some means of curbing their power. How could this be done with greater effect than by installing the Inquisition—an institution which was apart from the state and had its roots in Rome? The Inquisition could grow up side by side with the state, gradually usurping more and more of its power. It could be equivalent to a measure of Roman rule in Spain.

Isabella looked with grateful affection at the Cardinal, who had been thinking on the same lines and who saw the issues at stake as clearly as she did herself.

"I know Your Highness will agree with me that we must be continually watchful of the power of Rome. Here in Castile Your Highness is supreme. It is my urgent desire that you should remain so."

"You are right as usual," answered Isabella. "But I am disturbed that some of my subjects should revile the Christian faith."

The Cardinal was thoughtful. In his heart—although this was something he could never explain to Isabella, for he knew she would never understand him—he believed in taking his religion lightly. He was aware that belief—to be real belief—must be free. It was something which could not be forced. This was contrary to the accepted notion, he was fully aware, and for this reason he must keep his thoughts to himself. He wished life to be comfortably pleasant and, above all, dignified. The Inquisition in Aragon, Valencia and Catalonia was, he realized, at this stage a lethargic institution. Its officers lived easily and did not much concern themselves with the finding of heretics. If such were discovered they could, no doubt, by the means of a little bribery and diplomacy, escape disaster.

But when he thought of this earnest young Queen who, by her single-minded purpose and strict punishment of all offenders, had changed a state of anarchy into one of ever-growing law and order, he could imagine what such a new and terrifying institution as the Inquisition could become under the sway of Isabella and such men as Tomás de Torquemada, whom it was almost certain, Isabella would nominate—perhaps with himself—as her chief adviser if she should establish the Inquisition in Castile.

Isabella and Torquemada were stern with themselves; they would be more dreadfully so with others.

To a man who loved luxury, who cared for good living, who was devoted to the study of literature and enjoyed translating Ovid, Sallust and Virgil into verse, the thought of forcing opinions on men who were reluctant to receive them, and would only do so under threat of torture and death, was abhorrent.

Cardinal Mendoza would have enjoyed calling to his presence those men of different opinion, discussing their views, conceding a point, setting forth his own views. To *force* his opinions on others was nauseating to a man of his culture and tolerance. As for the thought of torture, it disgusted him.

This he could not explain to Isabella. He admired Isabella. She was shrewd; she was earnest; she was determined to do what was right. But, in the Cardinal's opinion, she was uneducated; and he deplored her lack of education, which had resulted in a narrow mind and a bigotry which prevented her from meeting the Cardinal on his own intellectual level.

The Cardinal was going to fight against the installation of the Inquisition with certain enthusiasm. He could not, however, bring to bear the fervour of a Torquemada, for he was not of the same fervent nature. But he would certainly attempt to lead Isabella away from that line of action.

He said: "Highness, let us give a great deal of thought to this matter. Before we decide to bring in the Inquisitors, let us warn the people of Seville that they place themselves in danger by denying the faith."

Isabella nodded. "We will prepare a manifesto . . . a special catechism in which we will explain the duties of a true Christian. This could be set up in all churches in Seville and preached from all pulpits."

"Those who do not conform," said the Cardinal, "will be threatened with the fires of hell."

"It may well be," said Isabella, "that this will be enough to turn these men and women of Seville from their evil ways."

"Let us pray that it will serve," said the Cardinal. "Is it Your Highness's wish that I should prepare this catechism?"

"None could do it so well, I am sure," said Isabella.

The Cardinal withdrew, well pleased. He had—for the time at least—foiled the attempt of the Dominicans to install the Inquisition in Castile. Now he would produce his catechism, and he hoped that it would bring about the required effect.

Shortly afterwards Mendoza's *Catecismo de la Doctrina Cristiana* was being widely circulated throughout the erring town of Seville.

* * *

When Torquemada heard that Mendoza's *Catecismo* was being circulated in Seville he laughed aloud, and laughter was something he rarely indulged in. But this laughter was scornful and ironical.

"There is a great deal you have to learn about the wickedness of human nature, Cardinal Mendoza!" he murmured to himself.

Torquemada was sure that the heretics of Seville would pretend to study the catechism; they would feign belief in the Christian faith; then they would creep away and jeer at Mendoza, at Isabella, at all good Christians while they practised their Jewish rites in secret.

"This is not the way to cleanse Seville!" cried Torquemada; and he was on his knees asking for Divine help, imploring the Virgin to intercede for him, that he might be given the power to cleanse not only Seville but the whole of Castile of the taint of heresy.

In time, he told himself, understanding will dawn on the

Queen—even on the Cardinal who, though a good Catholic himself, leads a far from virtuous life. Scented linen, frequent baths, *amours* . . . indulgence in the sensuous enjoyment of music and literature! The Cardinal would on his death-bed have to ask remission of many sins.

Torquemada embraced himself, pressing his arms round his torso so that the hair-shirt came into even more painful contact with his long-suffering body. Secretly he thanked God and the saints that he was not as other men.

It seemed to him then that he had a glimmer of the Divine will. His time would come. The Cardinal would fail, and into the hands of Torquemada would be placed the task of bringing Castile to repentance.

Until then he might concern himself with the building of the monastery of St. Thomas. So to Avila he travelled with a good conscience. He was sure that soon he would receive the call to desert pleasure for duty.

* * *

Isabella had journeyed to Seville.

It had been the custom of the Kings of Castile to sit in the great hall of the Alcazar and pronounce judgment on offenders who were brought before them.

Each day Isabella attended in the great hall. Occasionally Ferdinand accompanied her and they sat side by side administering justice.

These sessions were conducted in a ceremonial manner, and Isabella was sumptuously dressed for the purpose. She took little delight in fine clothes, but was always ready to see the need for splendour. It was imperative that she be recognized in this turbulent city as the great Queen of Castile; and in this place, where the inhabitants had lived among the remains of Moorish splendours, it was necessary to impress them with her own grandeur.

Isabella proved herself to be a stern judge.

Determined as she was to eradicate crime in her kingdom, she showed little mercy to those who were found guilty. She believed that the slightest leniency on her part might send certain of her subjects back to a life of crime, and that, she was determined, should not happen. If she could not make them reform for the love of virtue she would make them do so from the fear of dire punishment.

Executions were numerous, and a daily ceremony.

The people were beginning to understand that this woman, who was their Queen, was far stronger than the male rulers of the past years. Four thousand robbers escaped across the frontiers, while Isabella dealt with those who had been caught and found guilty. They would suffer as they had made others suffer, and they should be an example to all.

It was in the great hall of the Seville Alcazar that a party of weeping women, led by the church dignitaries of Andalucia, came to her and implored her for mercy.

Isabella received them gravely. She sat in regal state, her face quite impassive, while she watched those women in their anguish.

They were the mothers and daughters of men who had offended against the laws of the land.

"Highness," cried their spokesman, "these people admit that their loved ones have sinned and that the Queen's rule is just, but they implore your mercy. Grant them the lives of their husbands and fathers on condition that they swear never to sin again."

Isabella considered the assembly.

To her there was only wrong and right—completely clear cut. She could condemn malefactors to great suffering and be quite unmoved; Isabella had not much imagination, and it would never occur to her to see herself in another's place. Therefore she could contemplate the utmost suffering unperturbed.

But her aim was not punishment in itself, but only as a means to law and order; and, as she studied these weeping women, it occurred to her that if they would be responsible for the good conduct of their men she had no wish to punish them.

"My good people," she said, "you may go your way in peace. My great desire is not to inflict harsh punishment on you and your folk, but to ensure for you all a peaceful land. I therefore grant an amnesty for all sinners—except those who have committed serious crimes. There is a condition. Those who are freed must give an undertaking to live in future as peaceful citizens. If they do not, and are again brought before myself or any of the judges, their punishment will be doubly severe."

A great cry went up in the hall. "Long live Isabella!" In the streets, the cry was taken up; and as a tribute to her strength they added: "Long live *King* Isabella!"

* * *

From Andalucia to Galicia, went Ferdinand and Isabella. Galicia was a turbulent province, ready to give trouble to Isabella as Catalonia had given trouble to Aragon.

But how different was the state of the country! Already there were signs of prosperity where there had been desolation.

Travellers no longer had their fear of robbers which had once made travelling a nightmare. The inns were looking prosperous and almost gay.

Isabella felt a wave of exultation as she rode through the countryside and received the heartfelt gratitude of her subjects.

Ferdinand, riding beside her, said: "We see a prosperous country emerging from the chaos. Let us hope that soon it will be not only a prosperous but an all-Christian country."

Isabella knew that this was a reference to her refusal to establish the Inquisition in Castile, but she feigned ignorance of the meaning behind his words. "I share that hope," she said gently.

"It will not be until we have defeated Muley Abul Hassan and have set the holy banner flying over Granada."

"I fear not, Ferdinand."

"He showed his defiance of us when he asked for a peace treaty and refused to pay the tribute I demanded on your behalf. Because he had paid none to your brother, that did not mean that we should allow him to pay none to you. You remember his insolent answer."

"I remember it very well," answered Isabella. " 'Tell the Queen and King of Castile that we do not coin gold but steel in Granada.' "

"An insolent threat," cried Ferdinand, "made by Muley Abul Hassan because he knew that we were not in a position to chastise him for it. But the position is changing, eh, Isabella."

She smiled at him. He was restive, always eager for action. It was as though he said : Since we cannot have the Inquisition installed in Castile let us make immediate war on Granada.

She said, continuing her thoughts aloud: "We have recently emerged from one war. There is nothing that saps a country's resources so surely as war, there is nothing so fraught with danger."

"This would be a holy war," said Ferdinand piously. "We should have Heaven on our side."

"A holy war," mused Isabella.

She was thinking of herself as a young Princess, kneeling with Tomás de Torquemada, who had said : "You must swear that if ever you have the power you will work with all your might to make an all-Christian Spain." And she had replied : "I swear."

"I swear," now said Isabella the Queen.

* * *

In Galicia Isabella dispensed justice with the same severity as she did in Castile. For those who had robbed and murdered she showed little mercy; and she dealt justice alike to rich and poor.

Often Ferdinand would be on the point of making suggestions to her. She did her utmost to avoid this; one of the things she hated most was to have to deny Ferdinand what he asked; yet she never hesitated to do so if she felt that justice demanded it.

It was thus in the case of Alvaro Yañez de Lugo. De Lugo was a very wealthy knight of Galicia who had been found guilty of turning his castle into a robber's den; travellers had been lured there to be robbed and murdered; and Isabella had judged that his punishment should be death.

She had left the judgment hall for her apartments when she heard that a man was imploring an audience with her on a matter of extreme importance.

Ferdinand was with her, and she asked that the man be brought to her presence immediately.

When he came, he looked furtively about him, and Isabella gave the order for all except Ferdinand to retire.

The man still looked apprehensive, and Isabella said: "I pray you tell me your mission. Have no fear, none but the King and myself will hear what you have to say."

"Highnesses," said the man falling on his knees, "I come from Don Alvaro Yañez de Lugo."

Isabella frowned. "The robber," she said coldly, "who is under sentence of death?"

"Yes, Highness. He has rich and powerful friends. They offer you a large sum of money if you will spare his life."

Isabella indignantly replied: "How could his life be spared when he has been justly sentenced to death?"

"How much money?" Ferdinand had found it impossible to prevent himself asking that question.

The answer same promptly. "Forty thousand *doblas* of gold."

"Forty thousand *doblas*!" Ferdinand echoed the words almost unbelievingly. "Have his friends so large a sum?"

"Indeed yes, Highness. And it is at your disposal. All that is asked in return is the life of Alvaro Yañez de Lugo."

"His is a very valuable life," said Ferdinand with a smile, and to her horror Isabella saw the acquisitive light in his eyes.

"In gold, Highness," whispered the man. "Half to be delivered on your Highnesses' promise, the other half when Don Alvaro is free."

Isabella spoke then. She said: "It seems to have been forgotten that this man is guilty of crimes so great that the death penalty has been imposed on him."

"That is why," explained Ferdinand, not without some impatience, "a great sum is offered for his release."

"It would seem to me," said Isabella quietly, "that this money, which is doubtless stolen property, would be highly tainted."

"We would wash it free of all taint," said Ferdinand, "if . . ."

"We shall not put ourselves to such pains," answered Isabella decisively. "You may return to your friends," she went on, addressing the man, "and tell them that this is not the way the Queen of Castile dispenses justice."

"Highness . . . you refuse!"

"The friends of Alvaro Yañez de Lugo do not know me, or they would not have dared bring such a dishonourable proposal to me. You should leave immediately before I decide to have you arrested for attempted bribery."

The man bowed and hurried from the apartment.

Ferdinand's face was white with anger.

"I see that you do not wish to pursue this holy war against the Moors."

"I wish it with all my heart," Isabella replied mildly.

"And as we are debarred from fighting this war because of the low state of the treasury you turn your back on forty thousand gold *doblas!*"

"I turn my back on bribery."

"But forty thousand *doblas* . . ."

"My kingdom shall be built on justice," Isabella told him simply. "How could that be if I brought to justice only those who could not buy their release?"

Ferdinand lifted his hands in an exasperated gesture. "We need money . . . desperately."

"We need honour more," she told him with dignity.

Ferdinand turned away from her. He could not trust himself to speak. Money . . . gold was in question; and Isabella was learning that her husband loved gold with a fervour he rarely bestowed on anything else.

* * *

Alonso de Ojeda had returned to the Monastery of St. Paul in Seville a disappointed man. He had hoped by this time to have seen the Inquisition flourishing in Seville; and he feared that since Torquemada—who he knew desired, as much as he did himself, to see the Inquisition set up—could not persuade the Queen to it, there was little hope that anyone else could.

The fiery Ojeda stormed at his fellow Dominicans; he harangued the saints in his prayers. "How long, how long," he demanded, "must you look on at the sin of this city? How long before to us there is given a means of punishing these heretics that they may have a chance of salvation? Give me a sign . . . a sign."

Then—so Ojeda believed—came the sign, when there arrived at the monastery a young man who asked that he might be allowed an interview with the Prior, as he was deeply disturbed by something he had witnessed. He needed immediate advice.

Ojeda agreed to see him.

The man was young and good looking, and Ojeda, recognizing him immediately as a member of the noble house of Guzman, took him into a small cell-like apartment.

"Now, my son," said the Prior, "you look distraught. What is this you want to confess, and why did you not take the matter to your own confessor?"

"Most Holy Prior, I feel this matter to be more than a confession. I feel it could be of the utmost importance. I know that you journeyed to Court recently and saw the Queen. For this reason, I believed I should come to you."

"Well, let me hear the nature of this confession."

"Holy Prior, I have a mistress."

"The lusts of the flesh must be subdued. You must do penance and sin no more."

"She is a *Marrano*."

Ojeda's lids fell over his eyes, but his heart leaped with excitement.

"If she is a true Christian her Jewish blood should be of small account."

"Holy Prior, I believed her to be a true Christian. Otherwise I should never have consorted with her."

Ojeda nodded. Then he said: "She lives in the Jewish quarter?"

"Yes, Holy Prior. I visited her father's house in the *judería*. She is very young, and it is naturally against the wishes of her family that she should take a lover."

"That is understandable," said Ojeda sternly. "And you persuaded her to defy her father's commands?"

"She is very beautiful, Holy Prior, and I was sorely tempted."

"How was it that you visited her father's house when he had forbidden her to take a lover?"

"I went in secret, Holy Prior."

"Your penance must be harsh."

"It may be, Holy Prior, that my sin will be readily forgiven me because had I not gone in secret I should never have discovered the evil that was going on in the house of my mistress."

Ojeda's voice shook with excitement. "Pray continue," he said.

"This is Holy Week," went on the young man. "I had forgotten that it was also the eve of the Jewish Passover."

"Go on, go on," cried Ojeda, unable now to suppress his eagerness.

"My mistress had secreted me in her room, and there we made love. But, Holy Prior, I became aware of much bustle in the house. Many people seemed to be calling, and this was not usual. There were footsteps outside the room in which I lay with my mistress, and I grew alarmed. It occurred to me that her father had discovered my presence in the house and was calling together his friends to surprise us and perhaps kill me."

"And this was what they were doing?"

"They had not a thought of me, Holy Prior, as I was to discover. I could no longer lie there, so I rose hastily and dressed. I told my mistress that I wished to leave as soon as I could, and she, seeming to catch my fear, replied that the sooner I was out of the house the better. So we waited until there was quietness on the stairs, and then we slipped out of her room. But as we reached the hall we heard sounds in a room near by, and my mistress, in panic, opened a door and pushed me into a cupboard and shut the door. She was only just in time, for her father came into the hall and greeted friends who had just arrived. They were close to the cupboard in which I was hidden, and they did not lower their voices; so I heard all that was said. The friends had arrived at the house to celebrate the Passover. My mistress's father laughed aloud and jeered at Christianity. He laughed because he, a professing Christian, in secret practised the Jewish religion."

Ojeda clenched his fists and closed his eyes. "And so we have caught them," he cried; "we have caught them in all their wickedness. You did right, my friend; you did right to come to me."

"Then, Holy Prior, I am forgiven?"

"Forgiven! You are blessed. You were led to that house that you might bring retribution on those who insult Christianity. Be assured the holy saints will intercede for you. You will be forgiven the sin you have committed, since you bring these evil doers to justice. Now tell me, the name of your mistress's father? The house where he lives? Ah, he will not long live in his evil state!"

"Holy Prior, my mistress . . ."

"If she is innocent all will be well with her."

"I would not speak against her."

"You have saved her from eternal damnation. Living in such an evil house, it may well be that she is in need of salvation. Have no fear, my son. Your sins are forgiven you."

* * *

The *Marrano* family was brought before Ojeda.

"It is useless," he told them, "to deny your sins. I have evidence of them which cannot be refuted. You must furnish me with a list of all those who took part with you in the Jewish Passover."

The head of the house spoke earnestly to Ojeda. "Most Holy Prior," he said, "we have sinned against the Holy Catholic Church. We reverted to the religion of our Fathers. We crave pardon. We ask for our sins to be forgiven and that we may be taken back into the Church."

"There must have been others who joined in these barbarous rites with you. Who were these?"

"Holy Prior, I beg of you, do not ask me to betray my friends."

"But I do ask it," said Ojeda.

"I could not give their names. They came in secrecy and they were promised secrecy."

"It would be wiser for you to name them."

"I cannot do it, Holy Prior."

Ojeda felt a violent hatred rising in his heart. It should be possible now to take this man to the torture chambers for a little persuasion. Oh, he could stand there very nobly defending his friends. How would he fare if he were put on the rack, or had his limbs dislocated on the hoist? That would be a very different story.

And here am I, thought Ojeda, with a miserable sinner before me; and I am unable to act.

"Your penance would be less severe if you gave us the names of your friends," Ojeda reminded him.

But the man was adamant. He would not betray his friends.

Ojeda imposed the penance, and since these *Marranos* begged to be received back into the Christian Church, there was nothing to be done but admit them.

When he was alone Ojeda railed against the laws of Castile. Had the Inquisition been effective in Castile, that man would have been taken to a dungeon; there he would have been questioned; there he would have betrayed his friends; and instead of a few penances, a few souls saved, there might have been hundreds. Nor would they have escaped with a light sentence. They would have been found guilty of heresy, and the true punishment of heresy was surely death . . . death by fire that the sinner might have a foretaste of hell's torment for which he was destined.

But as yet the Inquisition had not been introduced into Castile.

* * *

Ojeda set out for Avila, where Torquemada was busy with the plans for the monastery of Saint Thomas.

He received Ojeda with as much pleasure as it was possible for him to show, for Ojeda was a man after his own heart.

Ojeda lost no time in coming to the point.

"I am on my way to Cordova, where the sovereigns are at this time in residence," he explained. "I have uncovered certain iniquity in Seville which cannot be passed over. I shall ask for an audience and then implore the Queen to introduce the Inquisition into this land."

He then told Torquemada what had happened in the house in the *judería.*

"But this is deeply shocking," cried Torquemada. "I could wish that the young Guzman had gone to the house on a different mission—but the ways of God are inscrutable. In the cupboard he heard enough to condemn these people to death—if as much consideration had been given here in Spain to spiritual life as has been given to civil laws. The facts should be laid before the Queen without delay."

"And who could do that more eloquently than yourself? It is for this reason that I have come to you now. I pray you accompany me to Cordova, there to add your pleas to mine."

Torquemada looked with some regret at the plans he had been studying. He forced his mind from a contemplation of exquisite sculpture. This was his duty. The building of a Christian state from which all heresy had been eliminated—that was a greater achievement than the finest monastery in the world.

* * *

Torquemada stood before the Queen. A few paces behind her stood Ferdinand, and behind Torquemada was Ojeda.

Ojeda had recounted the story of what the young man had heard in the cupboard.

"And this," cried Torquemada, "is an everyday occurrence in your Highness's city of Seville."

"I cannot like the young man's mission in that house," mused Isabella.

"Highness, we deplore it. But his discovery is of the utmost importance; and who shall say whether or not this particular young man was led to sin, not by the devil, but by the saints? Perhaps in this way we have been shown our duty?"

Isabella was deeply shocked. To her it seemed sad that certain of her subjects should not only be outside the Christian faith but that they should revile it. Clearly some action must be taken.

She did not trust Sixtus. Yet Ferdinand was eager for the setting up of the Inquisition. She knew, of course, that his hope was that by its action riches would be diverted, from those who now possessed them, to the royal coffers. She knew that many of the New Christians were rich men, for the Jews had a way of enriching themselves. She needed money. But she would not so far forget her sense of honour and justice as to set up the Inquisition for the sake of monetary gain.

She hesitated. Three pairs of fanatical eyes watched her intently while the fate of Spain hung in the balance.

Ojeda and Torquemada believed that torture and death should be the reward of the heretic. Isabella agreed with them. Since they were destined for eternal hell fire, what was a little baptismal burning on Earth? Ferdinand was a fanatic too. When he thought of money and possessions his eyes flashed every bit as fiercely as Torquemada's did for the faith.

Isabella remembered the vow she had once made before Torquemada; he was reminding her of it now.

An all-Christian Spain. It was her dream. But was she to give the Pope more influence than he already had?

Yet, considering her recent victories over him, she believed she—and Ferdinand with her—could handle him, should the occasion arise. Therefore why should she hesitate to set up the Inquisition in Castile that the land might be purged of heretics?

She turned to Ferdinand. "We will ask His Holiness for permission to set up the Inquisition in Castile," she said.

The waiting men relaxed.

Isabella had decided the fate of Spain, the fate of thousands.

LA SUSANNA

It was spring in Toledo. Isabella rode through the streets between the Moorish buildings, and with her was Ferdinand and her two-year-old son, Prince Juan.

This was an important occasion. The Cortes was assembled in Toledo.

Isabella, so simple in her tastes on ordinary occasions, displayed the utmost splendour when she took her place at affairs of state. Now she was dressed in crimson brocade which was embroidered with gold, cut away to show a white satin petticoat encrusted with pearls; and seated on her horse she made a beautiful picture.

The people cheered her. They did not forget that she had brought justice into the land. They recalled the reigns of her father and half-brother, when favouritism had ruled in the palace and anarchy on the highway. Yet this young woman with the serene and gentle smile had been responsible for the change.

The sight of the little Prince in brocade and satin, as fine as that worn by his parents, warmed their hearts. There he sat on his pony, smiling and accepting the applause of the crowd as though he were a man instead of a very small boy.

"Long live Isabella and Ferdinand! Long live the Prince of the Asturias!" cried the people.

The citizens of Toledo were sure that this little one, when he reached manhood, would be as wise as his parents.

Into the great hall they went, and the first duty of that Cortes was to swear allegiance to the young Prince and proclaim him heir to the throne.

Isabella watched her son, and her smile became even more gentle. She was so proud of him. Indeed, she was proud of all her children. She wished that she had more time to spend with them. It was one of her greatest regrets that her duties called her so continually from the company of her children.

But she was dedicated to a great task. She was already achieving that which she had set out to do; she had made of Castile a law-abiding state. Galicia and Leon were following Castile. Once she had made them a *Christian* state, perhaps she would be able to think a little more frequently of her own family. For the time being she must leave them in the care of others; and only on rare occasions could she be with them.

Now little Juan was the recognized heir to the thrones of Castile and Aragon. Isabella determined that, before he reached these thrones, she and Ferdinand would have done their duty, so that it would not only be Castile and Aragon that he inherited but the whole of Spain, including the kingdom of Granada.

The Cortes then discussed the finances of the country; and it was agreeable to realize that these had been placed on a much firmer foundation than had existed when Isabella had inherited the throne.

But the most important edicts of that Cortes were the rules against the Jews, which were being reinforced.

These were unanimously adopted.

"All Jews in the kingdom to wear a red circle of cloth on the shoulders of their cloaks that they may be recognized as Jews by all who behold them.

"All Jews to keep within the *juderías*, the gates of which shall be locked at nightfall.

"No Jew is to take up a profession as innkeeper, apothecary, doctor or surgeon."

The persecution had been renewed.

* * *

Alonso de Ojeda was on the scent. As he walked through the streets of Seville he promised himself that very soon these carefree citizens would see sights to startle them.

The Jews did not believe that the laws were to be taken seriously. They had found living easy for too many years, thought Ojeda grimly.

They were to be seen without their red circles; they continued to practise as surgeons and doctors, and many people patronized them—for they were noted as being very skilled in these professions. They were not keeping to their ghettos.

They shrugged aside the new law. They could be seen sunning themselves under the palms and acacias, or strolling with their families along the banks of the Guadalquivir.

They had not realized that the old sun-drenched life was fast coming to an end.

One of Ojeda's fellow Dominicans brought a pamphlet to him and, as Ojeda read it, he smiled cynically.

Some Jew who was a little too sure of himself had written this.

What, he demanded, were these new laws but an attack on the Jewish community? The country was under the spell of priests and monks. Was that the way to prosperity? The Christian religion sounded impressive in theory; but how was it in practice?

"Blasphemy! Blasphemy!" cried Ojeda, and hurried with all speed to Torquemada, who, when he had read the pamphlet, was in full agreement with Ojeda that something must be done immediately.

He went to see Isabella.

* * *

Isabella, reading the pamphlet, shared the horror of the Dominicans.

She sent for Cardinal Mendoza and Torquemada.

"You see, Cardinal," she said, "your plan of persuasion has failed."

The Cardinal answered: "Highness, dire punishment will prove no more effective than persuasion, I feel sure."

Torquemada's fiery eyes blazed in his emaciated face. "Persuasion has undoubtedly failed," he cried. "We will at least try dire punishment."

"I fear, Cardinal," said Isabella, "that the time has come to do so."

"What are Your Highness's orders?" Mendoza asked.

"I desire," said Isabella, "that you and Tomás de Torquemada appoint Inquisitors; and as the town of Seville would appear to be more tainted with heresy than any other in our dominion, I pray you begin there."

Tomás de Torquemada flashed a glance of triumph at the Cardinal. His way was to be the accepted one. The catechism had proved fruitless.

The Cardinal was resigned. He saw that there was nothing he could do to hold back the tide of persecution. That Jew and his pamphlet had caused his race a great deal of harm.

The Cardinal had no alternative but to go with the stream.

"My lord Cardinal," said Torquemada, "let us obey the Queen's command and appoint Inquisitors for Seville. I suggest two monks of my order—Miguel Morillo and Juan de San Martino. Do you agree?"

"I agree," said the Cardinal.

* * *

In the narrow streets of Seville, dominated by the buildings of a Moorish character, the people lounged. It was warm on that October day, and ladies wearing high combs and black mantillas sat on the balconies overlooking the crowds gathering in the streets.

This was in the nature of a feast day, and the people of Seville loved feast days.

A man and his family sat on the balcony of one of the handsomest houses in the town, overlooking the streets. With them sat a young boy strumming a lute and another with a flute.

People paused to glance at the balcony as they passed along the street. They had been looking at Diego de Susan, who was known as one of the richest merchants in Seville.

They whispered of him : "They say he owns ten million *maravedis.*"

"Is there so much money in all Spain?"

"He earned it himself. He is a shrewd merchant."

"Like all these Jews."

"He has something besides his fortune. Is it true that his daughter is the loveliest girl in Seville?"

"Take a look at her. There she is, on the balcony. La Susanna, we call her here in Seville. She is his natural daughter and he dotes on her, they tell me. She is well guarded; and needs to be. She is not only full of beauty but full of promise, eh?"

And those who glanced up at the balcony saw La Susanna beside her father. Her large black eyes were slumbrous; her small face an enchanting oval, her heavy black hair caught up with combs which sparkled in the sunshine; her white, ringed hands waved the scarlet and gold fan before her exquisite features.

Diego de Susan was much aware of his daughter. She was his delight, and his great regret was that she was not his legitimate child. He had not been able to resist the temptation to take her into his household and bring her up with all the privileges of one born in wedlock.

He was afraid for La Susanna. She was so beautiful. He feared that the fate of her mother might befall her; and so he guarded her well. This he intended to do until he could make a brilliant marriage for her, which he was sure he would do, since she was so beautiful and he was so rich.

But now his attention was turned to the events of this day.

He had felt a little uneasy when he had heard the proclamation read in the streets.

Great suspicion had been aroused concerning the secret habits of certain New Christians—those Jews who had embraced the Christian religion only to revert in secret to their own faith. This, went on the proclamation, was the worst sort of heresy, and Inquisitors had been appointed to stamp it out. It was the duty of all citizens to watch their neighbours and if they discovered aught that was suspicious they must report it to the Inquisitors or their servants with all speed.

That made Diego de Susan feel vaguely uncomfortable; and

when he recalled that it was added that those who did not report such suspicious conduct would themselves be considered guilty, his fear took on a more definite shape.

Were neighbours being asked to spy on each other? Were they being told: "Report heretics, for if you do not you in your turn will be considered guilty!"

Diego tried to shrug aside such uneasy thoughts. This was Seville—this beautiful and prosperous town which had been made prosperous by men such as himself and his fellow merchants. Many of them were New Christians, for it was the Jewish community who by their industry and financial genius had brought prosperity to the town.

No, these priests could do no harm in Seville.

He looked at his daughter. Automatically the white hand worked the vivid fan back and forth. Her long lashes drooped. Did she look a little secretive? Was all well with La Susanna?

La Susanna was thinking: What will he say when he knows? What will he do? He will never forgive me. It is what he feared would happen to me.

She grew suddenly angry. She had a fiery temper which could rise within her and madden her temporarily. It is his own fault, she told herself. He should not have shut me away. I am not the kind to be shut away. Perhaps I take after my mother. I must be free. If I wish for a lover, a lover I must have.

Her expression did not change as she went on moving the fan.

She adored Diego, but her emotions were too strong to be controlled. She hated herself because she had deceived him, and because she hated herself she hated him.

It is his fault, all his fault, she told herself. He has no one to blame but himself.

Soon, she thought, I shall be unable to hide the fact from him that I am pregnant. What then?

She had been well guarded, but, with the help of her sympathetic maid, it had not been impossible to have her lover smuggled into the house. He was young and handsome, a member of a noble Castilian family, and she had been unable to repress her desire for him. She had not thought of the consequences. She had never thought of the consequences of her actions. She had been impulsive. Thus must her mother have been.

Now she sat on the balcony, only vaguely hearing the shouts in the streets, unaware of the new tension which was creeping over the city. She was thinking of her father, who had loved her so tenderly during the years of her childhood, who was so proud of the daughter known throughout Seville as *la hermosa hembra.*

Oh, yes, she was indeed beautiful, but she was no longer a child; now she was a woman who must live her life as she wished to, who must escape from the rule of a father who, out of his very love for her, treated her with a strictness which, to one of her wild nature, was intolerable.

And what will he say, she asked herself again and again, when I present myself to him and say, "Father, I am with child"?

And where was her lover? She did not know. She had tired of him, and he had no longer been smuggled into her room. There was only the child within her to remind herself how much she had loved him.

A procession was now coming through the street, and the sight of it sent a shiver through the most thoughtless of the spectators. It was as though a warning cloud hung over the sunny streets.

On it came, headed by the Dominican monk who carried the white cross. There were the Inquisitors in their white robes and black hoods. With them walked their familiars, the *alguazils*, who would assist them in their work, and the Dominican friars, in their coarse habits, their feet bare.

It was a mournful procession, funereal and depressing. On it went to the Convent of St. Paul, where the Prior, Alonso de Ojeda, was ready to instruct these men in the duties which lay before them, to whip them to fierce enthusiasm by his fiery denunciation of those who did not accept the rigid tenets of his own faith.

Even La Susanna, her mind full of her own impending tragedy, sensed the foreboding inspired by that grim band of men. She looked at her father and saw that he was sitting tense, watching.

Crowds of gipsies, beggars and children followed the procession to the convent, but they, who previously had been chattering, shouting and dancing as they went, had fallen silent.

A visitor had stepped on to the balcony. It was a fellow merchant and friend of Diego de Susan.

He was looking grave. He said: "I do not like the look of that, my friend."

Diego de Susan seemed to rouse himself and throw off his depression. "Why, they are trying to bring the Inquisition to Seville. They will not succeed."

"Who will prevent them?"

Diego had risen and laid his hand on the shoulder of his friend. "Men like you and myself. Seville prospers. Why? Because we have brought trade to it. Men such as ourselves rule Seville. We have only to stand together, and we shall soon make it clear that we will have no inquisitors enquiring into our private lives."

"You think this possible?"

"I am sure of it."

Diego de Susan spoke in strong ringing tones; and one of the musicians on the balcony began to strum his lute.

La Susanna forgot the procession. She was saying to herself: How shall I tell him? How shall I dare?

* * *

In a back room of Diego de Susan's house many of the most important citizens of Seville were gathered together. Among them were Juan Abolafio, who was the Captain of Justice and Farmer of the Royal Customs, and his brother Fernandez Abolafio, the licentiate. There were other wealthy men, such as Manuel Sauli and Bartolomé Torralba.

Diego had all the doors closed and had posted servants whom he could trust outside, that none might overhear what was said.

Then he addressed the gathering. "My friends," he said soberly, "you know why I have asked you to assemble here this day. We have seen the procession on its way to the Convent of St. Paul, and we know what this means. Hitherto we have lived happily in this town. We have enjoyed prosperity and security. If we allow the Inquisitors to achieve the power for which they are clearly aiming that will be the end of our security, the end of our prosperity.

"At any hour of the night we may hear the knock on the door. We may be hurried away from our families before we even have time to dress. Who can say what will happen to us in the dark dungeons of the Inquisition? It may be that, once taken, we should never see our friends and families again. My friends, it need not be. I am convinced it need not be."

"Pray tell us, friend Diego, how you propose to foil these plots against us?" asked Juan Abolafio.

"Are they plots against *us?*" interrupted his brother.

Diego shook his head sadly. "I fear they may well be directed against us. We are the New Christians; we have wealth. It will be easy to bring a charge against us. Yes, my friends, I am certain that these plots are directed against ourselves. The Inquisitors have been shown great respect by the people of Seville; but their invitation to come forward and expose those whom they call heretic has not been taken up. Therefore they themselves will begin to look for victims."

"It has been announced that it is a sin for the people not to pass on any information that comes their way . . . in other words, the citizens are being subtly threatened that they must become spies, or themselves be suspected," said Bartolomé Torralba.

"You are right, Bartolomé," Diego replied. "We must consider the fate of those New Christians who fled from Seville and took refuge with the Marquis of Cadiz, the Duke of Medina Sidonia and the Count of Arcos."

"It is because you are considering these people," put in Sauli, "that you have asked us to come here this day, is it not, Diego?"

Diego nodded sadly. "You know, my friends, that these noblemen, who gave the fugitives refuge on their estates, have been ordered to hand them over to the Inquisitors of our town."

All the men looked grave.

He went on: "They have been threatened with ecclesiastical displeasure if they do not obey. More than that . . . they themselves will incur the displeasure of the Queen, and we know what this could mean. But do not let us be downhearted. Seville is our town. We will fight to preserve our rights and dignities."

"Can we do this?"

"I think we can. Once we show our determination to be strong, the people of Seville will be with us. We have their high regard. They know that we have brought prosperity to the town, and they ask that they may go on in that prosperity. Yes, if we show that we are strong and ready to fight for our liberty—and the liberty of conscience for all—they will be on our side. We are not poor men. I have brought you here to ask you how much money, how many men and arms you can put into this enterprise."

Diego drew papers towards him, and the conspirators watched him tensely.

* * *

From then on the conspirators met in the house of Diego de Susan.

There was great need, Diego impressed upon them, to preserve secrecy. Since the Inquisitors were continually reminding the people that it was their duty to spy, how could they be sure who, even among those servants whom they considered loyal, might not be on the alert?

It was a few days later when Diego came into his daughter's room without warning; he saw her sitting with her embroidery in her hand, staring before her with an expression on her face which Diego could only construe as fearful apprehension.

His mind was full of the conspiracy which was coming to its

climax, and he thought: My dearest child, she has sensed what is about to happen and she is terrified of what will become of me.

"My darling," he cried, and he went to her and embraced her.

She threw herself into his arms and began to sob passionately.

He stroked her hair. "All will be well, my daughter," he murmured. "You should have no fear. No harm will come to your father. They frightened you, did they not . . . with their black hoods and their mournful chanting voices! I grant you they are enough to strike terror in any heart. But they shall not harm us. Your father is safe."

"Safe?" she murmured, in a bewildered voice. "You, safe . . . Father?"

"Yes, yes, daughter. This is our secret . . . not to be spoken of outside these walls. But you, who know me so well, have sensed what is happening. You know why the Captain of Justice and his friends come to the house. You have heard the injunctions from the Convent of St. Paul. Yes, my child, we are going to rise against them. We are going to turn them out of Seville."

La Susanna had been so occupied with her personal tragedy that she had not given much thought to the new laws which had been brought to Seville. The conspiracy, of which her father was the head, seemed to her, in her ignorance—for she had always lived in the utmost comfort and luxury, sheltered in her father's house—a trivial affair. She could not conceive that her father, the rich and influential Diego de Susan, could ever fail in his dealings with the authorities; and this conspiracy seemed to her a childish game compared with her own dilemma.

She had never been able to restrain her feelings. Her wild and passionate nature broke forth at that moment, and she burst into loud laughter.

"Your conspiracy!" she cried. "You are obsessed with that and give no thought to me and what may be happening to me. I am in dire trouble . . . and you are concerned only with your conspiracy!"

"My dearest, what is this?"

She stood up, drew herself to her full height and, as he looked at her body, in which the first signs of pregnancy were beginning to be apparent, he understood.

She saw him turn pale; he was stunned with horror; she realized with triumph that for a moment she had made him forget his conspiracy.

"It is impossible," he cried out, angry and pathetic at the same time. He was refusing to believe what he saw; he was imploring her to tell him he was mistaken.

La Susanna's uncontrolled emotions broke out. She loved him so much that she could not bear to hurt him; and because she was self-willed, defiant and illogical she now hated herself for having brought this tragedy on him; and since she could not continue to hate herself, she must hate him because his pain made her suffer so.

"No!" she cried. "It is not impossible. It is true. I am with child. My lover visited me at night. You thought you had me guarded so well. I deceived you. And now he has gone and I am to have a child."

Diego groaned and buried his face in his hands.

She stood watching him defiantly. He dropped his hands and looked at her; and his face, she saw, was distorted with rage and grief.

"I have loved you," he said. "I could not have loved you more if you had been my legitimate daughter. I have cared for you . . . I have watched over you all these years, and this is how you repay me."

La Susanna thought: I cannot endure this. I am going mad. Is it not enough that I must bear my child in shame? How can he look at me like that? It is as though he no longer loves me. He thinks to rule me . . . to rule Seville . . . me with his strict rules; Seville with his conspiracy. I cannot endure this.

"So you regret taking me into your house! Have no fear. I shall ask nothing of you that you do not want to give."

She was laughing and crying as she ran from the room and out of the house. She heard his voice as he called her: "Daughter, daughter, come back."

But she went on running; she ran through the streets of Seville, her beautiful black hair escaping from its combs and flying out behind her.

She was thinking of her father whom she had loved so dearly. She could not forget the expression of rage and sorrow on his face.

"I love him no longer . . . I hate him. I hate him. I shall punish him for what he has made me suffer."

And, when she stopped running, she found herself outside the Convent of St. Paul.

* * *

It was dusk, and still La Susanna had not returned to the house.

Diego was frantic. He had searched for her in the streets of Seville and beyond; he had wandered along the banks of the Guadalquivir calling her name, imploring her to come home.

But he could not find her.

He thought of her wandering in the country in the darkness of the night, at the mercy of robbers and bold adventurers who would have no respect for her womanhood. It was more than Diego could bear. His anxiety for her had made him forget temporarily the plan which was about to come to fruition to oust the Inquisitors from Seville.

He returned to the house, and when he heard that she had not come home he wandered out into the streets again, calling her name.

And at last he found her.

She was quiet now, and she walked through the streets as though she were unaware of everything, even herself.

He ran to her and embraced her; she was trembling and she could not find words to speak to him. But she was coming home.

He put his arm about her. "My little one," he said, "what anxiety you have caused me! Never run away from me. This has happened, but we will weather it together, my darling. Never run away from me again."

She shook her head and her lips framed the words: "Never . . . never . . ."

Yet she seemed distrait, as though her mind wandered; and Diego, who knew the wild impetuosity of her nature, feared that some harm had been done to her mind by the shock she had suffered.

He murmured tenderly as they came towards the house: "All is well now, my little one. Here we are at home. Now I shall nurse you back to health. We will overcome this trouble. Have no fear. Whatever happens, you are my own dear daughter."

They entered the house. It seemed unusually quiet. One of the servants appeared. He did not speak, but at the sight of his master and La Susanna he turned and hurried away.

Diego was astonished. He strode into the small parlour, and there he found that they had visitors, for several men rose silently as he entered.

They were the *alguazils* of the Inquisition.

"Diego de Susan," said one of them, "you are the prisoner of the Inquisition. You will accompany us to the Convent of St. Paul for questioning."

"I!" cried Diego, his eyes flashing. "I am one of the leading citizens of Seville. You cannot . . ."

The *alguazil* made a sign to two guards, who came forward and seized Diego.

As they dragged him out of the house, Diego saw that La Susanna had fainted.

* * *

The news spread through Seville. Its leading citizens were lodged in the cells of St. Paul's. What was happening to them there could be guessed. The Inquisitors were determined to show the citizens of Seville that a mistake had been made if it was thought they did not mean to carry out their threats.

Others were arrested. Did this mean that the cells of St. Paul's had been turned into torture chambers?

La Susanna, who had collapsed at the sight of the *alguazils* who had come to arrest her father, had been lying on her bed in a dazed condition. When at length she arose, her grief was terrible. It was the grief of remorse.

It was she who had brought the *alguazils* to the house; it was she who, in a sudden uncontrollable rage, had run to the Convent of St. Paul's and told the eager Inquisitors of the conspiracy which was brewing in her father's house and of which her father was the leader.

What were they doing to him and his friends now in the Convent of St. Paul? There were terrible hints of torture, and if these were true, she and she alone was responsible.

There was only one way to cling to her sanity. She would refuse to believe these stories of the methods of Inquisitors. There would merely be gentle questionings; the plot would be unmasked; and then her father would return home.

She went out and stood in the shadow of the Convent of St. Paul looking up at those stone walls.

"Father," she sobbed, "I did not mean to do it. I did not know. I did not think . . ."

Then she went to the gate and asked to be admitted.

"Let my father be freed," she implored. "Let me take his place."

"This girl is mad," was the answer. "Tell her to go away. There is nothing we can do for her here."

Then she beat with her hands on the stone walls, and she wept until she was exhausted and slumped down in her misery, her dark hair falling about her face so that she, *la hermosa hembra*, had the appearance of a beggar rather than of the one-time pampered daughter of the town's richest man.

As she crouched there a man who was passing took pity on her.

"Rise, my child," he said. "Whatever your sorrow, you cannot wash it away with tears."

"I deserve death," she answered, and she lifted her beautiful eyes to his face.

"What crime have you committed?"

"The greatest. That of betrayal. I have betrayed the one whom I loved best in the world, who has shown me nothing but kindness. He is in there and I do not know what is happening to him, yet some sense tells me that he is suffering greatly. I brought this suffering to him—*I* who have received nothing but good at his hands. That is why I weep and pray for death."

"My child, you should go home and pray for the man you have betrayed, and pray for yourself. Only in prayer can you find consolation."

"Who are you?" she asked.

"I am Reginaldo Rubino, Bishop of Tiberiades. I know who your father is. He is Diego de Susan, who has been guilty of plotting against the Holy Office. Go home and pray, my child, for he will need your prayers."

A great despair came to her then.

She knew this man spoke the truth. She knew that a tragedy had come to Seville which made her own problems but trifles in comparison.

In awe she returned to the house; and although she believed that she had reached the very depth of despair, she was silent and no longer wept.

* * *

The day had come.

It was to be as a feast day . . . a grim holiday when all the people must go into the streets to see the show.

The bells were tolling. This was the occasion of the first *auto de fé* in Seville.

La Susanna had not slept for several nights. She had awaited this day with a terror which numbed her. Yet she would be there; she would witness the results of her treachery.

She listened to the bells, and she wrapped her shawl tightly about her, for she did not wish to be recognized. All Seville knew who would be the chief victims in today's grizzly spectacle; and they would know who was the wicked one who had made this possible—the girl who had betrayed her own father.

But I did not know, she wanted to cry out. I did not understand. Did any of you understand what the coming of the Inquisition would mean to Seville? Once we were free. Our doors were left open and we did not dread a knocking on them. We had no fear that suddenly the *alguazils* would be among us . . .

pointing at our loved ones. You . . . you and you . . . *You* are the prisoners of the Inquisition. You will come with us. And who could realize that that would be the last one saw of the dear familiar face.

For when one saw it again, the face would appear to be different. It would be unfamiliar. It would not be the face of one who had lived at peace for years among his family. It would be that of a man who had been torn from the family life he had once known, by a terrible experience of physical and mental pain and the brutal knowledge of the inhumanity of men towards their fellows. No, it would not be the same.

"I cannot look. I dare not look," she murmured. But she must look.

There was the Dominican monk leading the procession; he looked sinister in his coarse robes. He carried the green cross high, and about it had been draped the black crêpe. This meant that the Holy Church was in mourning because it had discovered in its midst those who did not love it.

La Susanna looked up at the sky and asked herself: "Perhaps it is all Heaven that is in mourning because men can act with such cruelty towards other men?"

Here they were—the dreary monks, the familiars of the Holy Office; and then the halberdiers guarding the prisoners.

"I cannot look, I cannot look," murmured La Susanna yet she continued to look; and she saw him—her beloved father, barefoot and wearing the hideous yellow *sanbenito,* and she saw that on it was painted the head and shoulders of a man being consumed by flames; there were devils with pitchforks, and the flames were pointing upwards.

With him were his fellow conspirators, all men whom she had known throughout her childhood. She had heard them laugh and chat with her father; they had sat at table with the family. But now they were strangers. Outwardly they had changed. The marks of torture were on them; their faces had lost their healthy colour; they were yellow—although a different shade from that of the garments they wore; and in their eyes was that look of men who had suffered horror, before this undreamed of.

The prisoners passed on, and following them were the Inquisitors themselves with a party of Dominicans, at the head of which was the Prior of St. Paul's, Alonso de Ojeda . . . triumphant.

* * *

Ojeda looked down on the prisoners as he preached his sermon in the Cathedral.

His expression was one of extreme fanaticism. His voice was high-pitched with mingled fury and triumph. He pointed to the prisoners in their yellow garments. These were the sinners who had defiled Holy Church. These were the men who would undoubtedly burn for ever in hell fire.

All must understand—all in this wicked city of Seville—that the apathy of the past was over.

Ojeda, the avenger, was among them.

* * *

From the Cathedral the procession went to the meadows of Tablada.

La Susanna followed.

She felt sick and faint, yet within her there burned a hope which she would not abandon. This could not be true. This could not happen to her father. He was a rich man who had always been able to buy what he wanted; he was a man of great influence in Seville. He had so few enemies; he had been the friend of the people and he had brought prosperity to their town.

Something will happen to save him, she told herself.

But they had reached the meadows; and there were the stakes; and there were the faggots.

"Father!" she cried shrilly. "Oh, my father, what have they done to you?"

He could not have heard her cry; yet it seemed to her that his eyes were on her. It seemed that for a few seconds they looked at each other. She could scarcely recognize him—he who had been so full of dignity, he who had been a little vain about his linen—in that hideous yellow garment.

"What have they done to you, my father?" she whispered. And she fancied there was compassion in his eyes; and that he forgave her.

The fires were lighted. She could not look. But how could she turn away?

She heard the cries of agony. She saw the flames run up the hideous yellow; she saw her father's face through the smoke.

"No!" she cried. "*No!*"

Then she slid to the ground, and knelt praying there, praying for a miracle while the smell of burning flesh filled her nostrils.

"Oh God," she whispered, "take me. . . . Let me not rise from my feet. Strike me dead, out of your mercy."

She felt a hand on her shoulder and a pair of kindly eyes were looking into hers.

It was the Bishop of Tiberiades who had spoken to her outside the Convent of St. Paul.

"So . . ." he said, "it is La Susanna. You should not have come here, my child."

"He is dying . . . cruelly dying," she moaned.

"Hush! You must not question the sentence of the Holy Office."

"He was so good to me."

"What will you do now?"

"I shall not go back to his house."

"All his goods will be confiscated by the Inquisition, my child; so you would not be able to stay there long if you went."

"I care not what becomes of me. I pray for death."

"Come with me."

She obeyed him and walked beside him through the streets of the city. She did not notice the strained faces of the people. She did not hear their frightened whispers. She was unaware that they were asking themselves whether this terrible scene, which they had witnessed this day, could become a common one in Seville.

There was nothing for La Susanna but her own misery.

They had reached the door of a building which she knew to be one of the city's convents.

The Bishop knocked and they were admitted.

"Take care of this woman," said the Bishop to the Mother Superior. "She is in great need of your care."

And he left her there, left her with her remorse and the memory of her father at the stake, with the sound of his cries of anguish as the flames licked his body—all of which were engraved upon her mind for ever.

* * *

In the Convent of St. Paul Ojeda planned more such spectacles. They had begun the work. The people of Seville had lost their truculence. They understood now what could happen to those who defied the Inquisition. Soon more smoke would be rising above the meadows of Tablada.

Seville should lead the way, and other towns would follow; he would show Torquemada and the Queen what a zealous Christian was Alonso de Ojeda.

He sent his Dominicans to preach against heresy in all the pulpits of the city. Information must be lodged against suspected heretics. Anyone who could be suspected of the slightest heresy must be brought before the tribunals and tortured until he involved his neighbours.

There were friars at St. Paul's whose special duty it was on the Jewish Sabbath to station themselves on the roof of the convent and watch the chimneys of the town. Anyone who did not light a fire was suspect. Those whose chimneys were smokeless would be brought before the tribunal; and if they did not confess, the torture could be applied; it was very likely that, on the rack or the hoist or subjected to a taste of the water torture, these people would be ready not only to confess their own guilt but to involve their friends.

"Ah!" cried Ojeda. "I will prove my zeal to Tomás de Torquemada. The Queen will recognize me as her very good servant."

And, even as he spoke, one of his monks came hurrying to him to tell him that plague had struck the city.

Ojeda's eyes flashed. "This is the Divine will," he declared. "This is God's punishment for the evil-living in Seville."

* * *

The stricken people were dying in the streets.

"Holy Prior," declared the Inquisitor Morillo, "it is impossible to continue with our good work while the plague rages. It may be that men who are brought in for questioning will sicken and die in their cells. Soon we shall have plague in St. Paul's. There is only one thing we can do."

"Leave this stricken city," agreed Ojeda. "It is the Divine Will that these people shall be punished for their loose living; but God would not wish that we, who do His work, should suffer with them. Yes, we must leave Seville."

"We might go to Aracena, and there wait until the city is clean again."

"Let us do that," agreed Ojeda. "I doubt not that Aracena will profit from our visit. It is certain that it contains some heretics who should not be allowed to sully its purity."

"We should travel with all speed," said Morillo.

"Then let us leave this day."

When he was alone Ojeda felt a strange lethargy creep over him; he felt sick and dizzy.

He said to himself: It is this talk of the plague. It is time we left Seville.

He sat down heavily and tried to think of Aracena. The edict should be read immediately on their arrival, warning all the inhabitants that it would be advisable for them to report any acts of heresy they had witnessed. Thus it should not be difficult to find victims for an *auto de fé*.

One of the Dominicans had come into the room; he looked at the Prior, and his startled terror showed on his face.

He made an excuse to retire quickly, and Ojeda tried to rise to his feet and follow him, but he slipped back into his chair.

Then Ojeda knew. The plague had come to St. Paul's; it embraced not only those who defied the laws of the Church but also those who set out to enforce them.

Within a few days Ojeda was dead; but the *Quemadero*—the Burning Place—had come to stay; and all over Castile the fires had begun to burn.

THE BIRTH OF MARIA AND THE DEATH OF CARILLO

CHRISTMAS had come and Isabella was enjoying a brief respite from her duties, with her family. It was rarely that they could all be together, and this union made the Queen very happy.

She could look back over the years of her reign with a certain pride.

There was peace in the kingdom. Alfonso of Portugal had died in the August of the previous year. He had been making preparations to resign the throne in order to go into residence at the monastery of Varatojo, and was travelling through Cintra when he was attacked by an illness which proved to be fatal. He had caused her a great deal of anxiety and she could only feel relieved that he could cause her no more.

She had punished criminals so harshly that she had considerably reduced their number; and she now proposed to punish heretics until none was left in her country.

She saw her friend Tomás de Torquemada infrequently now; he was obsessed by his work for the Holy Office. Her present confessor was Father Talavera, who was almost as zealous a worker for the Faith as Torquemada himself.

She knew she must not rest on her triumphs. Always she must remember the work that was left to be done. There was yet another great task awaiting her, for the setting up of the Inquisition, and the ridding her country of all heretics, was not all. There, she told herself, like a great abscess on the fair form of Spain, was the Kingdom of Granada.

But for this Christmas she would indulge herself. She would be as an ordinary woman in the heart of her family.

She went to the nurseries to see her children.

As they stood before her and curtsied she felt a sadness touch her. She was a stranger to them, and she their mother. She suppressed a desire to take them in her arms and caress them, to weep over them, to tell them how she longed to be a gentle mother to them.

That would be unwise. These children must never forget that, although she was their mother, she was also their Queen.

"And how are my children this day?" she asked them.

Isabella, who was eleven years old, naturally spoke for the

others. "They are all well, Highness; and they hope they see Your Highness in like state."

A faint smile curved Isabella's lips. What a formal answer to a mother's question! But it was the correct answer of course.

Her eyes dwelt on her son—her little three-year-old Juan. How could she help his being her favourite? Ferdinand had wanted a boy, because he had felt it was fitting that there should be a male heir to the throne; and for Ferdinand's sake she was glad.

And there was little Juana, a charming two-year-old, with a sparkle in her eyes.

"I am very happy, my dears," said Isabella, "because now your father and I can spare a little time from our duties to spend with our family."

"What duties, Highness?" asked young Juana.

The Infanta Isabella gave her sister a stern look, but the Queen said: "Nay, let her speak."

She sat down and lifted her youngest daughter on to her knee. "You would know what the duties of a King and Queen are, my child?"

Juana nodded.

The Infanta Isabella nudged her. "You must not nod when the Queen speaks to you. You must answer."

Juana smiled enchantingly. "What must I say?"

"Oh, Highness," said the Infanta Isabella, "she is but two, you know."

"I know full well," said Isabella. "And now we are in our close family circle we need not observe too strictly the etiquette which it is necessary to maintain on all other occasions. But of course you must remember that it is only at such times as this that we can relax."

"Oh, yes, Highness," the young Isabella and Juan replied together.

Then the Queen told her children of the duties of King and Queen, how they must travel from place to place; how it was necessary to call a Cortes to govern the country, how it was necessary to set up courts to judge evil doers—those who broke the civic law and the laws of God.

The children listened gravely.

"One day," said Isabella, "Juan will be a King, and I think it very possible that you, my daughters, may be Queens."

"Queens?" asked young Isabella. "But Juan will be King, so how can we be Queens?"

"Not of Castile and Aragon, of course. But you will marry,

and your husbands may be Kings; you will reign with them. You must always remember this and prepare yourselves."

Isabella stopped suddenly. She had had a vivid reminder of the past. She remembered those days at Arevalo where she and her young brother Alfonso had spent their childhood. She remembered her mother's hysteria and how the theme of her conversation was always : You could be King—or Queen—of Castile.

But this is different, she hastened to assure herself. These children will ascend thrones without trouble. It is not wild hysteria which makes *me* bid them prepare.

But she changed the subject abruptly and wished to know how they were progressing with their lessons. She would see their books and hear them read.

Then young Isabella read and, while she was doing so, the child began to cough.

"Do you cough often?" the Queen asked.

"Now and then, Mother."

"She is always coughing," Juan told his mother.

"Not always," Isabella contradicted. "At night sometimes, Mother. Then I am given a soothing syrup, and that makes me go to sleep."

Isabella looked grave. She would consult the Infanta's governess about the cough.

The two younger children were clearly healthy; she wished that Isabella did not look so fragile.

"Highness," said little Juana, "it is my turn to read."

"She cannot," said the Infanta Isabella.

"She points to the page and pretends to," Juan added.

"I do read. I do," cried Juana. "I do, Highness. Highness, I do! I do! I *do!*"

"Well, my little one, you must not become so excited; and you must not tell lies, you know. If you say you can read, and you cannot read, that is a lie."

"People who tell lies go to hell and burn for ever," announced Juan. "They burn here too. There are lots of people who burn here. *They* tell lies. They don't believe in God . . . our God . . . so we burn them to death."

"So you hear these things?" the Queen asked.

"They are always listening to gossip, Highness," the Infanta Isabella told her.

"It does not matter that they burn," Juan announced. "They are going to burn for ever, so what do a few minutes on Earth matter? The priest told me so."

"Now, my children," said Isabella, "you must not talk of these matters, for they are not for children. Juana has told me she can read, and I shall be very disappointed in her if she has told me a lie."

Juana's face puckered, and Juan, who was very kind, put his arm about her shoulder.

"She learns some words, Highness, and knows them by heart. She points to the book and *thinks* she is reading."

Juana stamped her foot. "I do not *think* I read. I *do* read."

"Silence, my child!" commanded Isabella.

"You forget," said the Infanta, to her little sister, "that you are in the presence of Her Highness the Queen."

"I can read. I *can* read!" sobbed the child.

Isabella tried to catch her, but she wrenched herself free; she began to run round the room shouting: "I can read. I can. I can . . ."

The elder children watched her in dismay and amazement.

Then little Juana began to laugh, and as she laughed her laughter turned to tears.

The Queen stared at her youngest child, and a terrible fear had come to her.

* * *

Ferdinand burst on the domestic scene. Isabella started up at the sight of him, because she saw from his expression that some disaster had come to them.

Juan ran to his father and threw himself into his arms, but although Ferdinand lifted the boy up and kissed his cheek, he was not thinking of his children.

"Now that the King has come, you must go back to your nursery," Isabella told the children.

"No!" cried the naughty Juana. "No! We wish to stay with Papa."

"But you have heard Her Highness's command," said young Isabella horrified.

"And she will obey them," put in Ferdinand, smiling down at his little daughter, who was pulling at his doublet, murmuring:

"My turn, Papa. It was my turn to be kissed."

"This little one," said Ferdinand, "reminds me of my mother."

Those words delighted Isabella so much that she forgot to wonder what ill news Ferdinand had to impart to her. Like *his* mother, she thought—calm, shrewd, practical Joan Henriquez. Not like Isabella's own mother, the poor sad Queen living in darkness at Arevalo.

"Come little mother-in-law," said Isabella, "you must go now to your nursery."

"What is a mother-in-law?" Juana asked.

"It is the mother of a wife's husband or a husband's wife," Isabella told her daughter.

Juana stood very still, her bright eyes wide, repeating to herself: *"Suegra. Suegra* . . . the mother of a wife's husband."

"Go along, Suegra, at once, I said," the Queen reminded her daughter; and young Isabella took her sister's hand and forced her to curtsey.

Ferdinand and Isabella stood looking after the children as they retired.

"You have bad news, Ferdinand," she said.

"The Moors have surprised our fortress of Zahara; it has fallen into their hands."

"Zahara! But that is serious."

Ferdinand nodded. "It was my own grandfather who recovered it from the Infidel," he said, "and now it is theirs once more."

"It must not remain so," Isabella replied.

"It shall not, my dear. If we had funds at our command I would wage a mighty war against the Infidel; and I would not cease to fight until every Mussulman had been driven from our land."

"Or converted to our faith," said Isabella.

"I would see the Christian flag flying over every town in Spain," went on Ferdinand. And his eyes were brilliant, so that Isabella knew that he was thinking of the riches of Moorish cities; he was thinking of their golden treasures.

"It shall come to pass," she told him.

Ferdinand turned to her then and laid his hands on her shoulders.

"You are tired, Isabella. You should rest more."

"No," she told him, "I am but in my third month of pregnancy. You know how it is with me. I work up to the end."

"Have a care, my wife. Although we have three children, we do not wish to lose any newcomers."

"I will take care, Ferdinand. Have no fear of that. You consider the loss of this fortress very damaging to our cause?"

"I consider it as the beginning of the Holy War."

"There have been many beginnings of that war which has been waged over our land periodically for centuries."

Ferdinand's grip on her shoulders tightened. "This, my Queen, is the beginning of that Holy War which is to end all such wars. This is the beginning of a united Spain."

* * *

It was three months after the loss of Zahara, when Isabella was in the town of Medina. She was now six months pregnant and was finding journeys irksome indeed. Again and again she reminded herself—and her friends did also—of that time when, undertaking similar journeys, she had suffered a miscarriage.

When she passed through villages and saw mothers in the fields and vineyards with their children about them she was a little envious. She loved her children dearly, and one of the greatest sorrows of her life was that she saw so little of them.

But as long as they were in good health and well cared for she must not think too constantly of them; perhaps when she had completed her great tasks she would be able to spend more time with them.

By then, she admitted ruefully, they would probably be married. For the magnitude of the two tasks which lay before her she well understood: To purge her country of all heretics, to set the Christian flag flying over all Spanish territory—these were the meaning of life to her; and she did not forget that they had been attempted before in the past centuries. But no one, as yet, had succeeded in completing them.

"Yet, with God's help, I will," declared Isabella. "And Ferdinand and such men as Torquemada will make my task easier."

Her confessor, Fray Fernando de Talavera, came to her, and she greeted him with pleasure.

Devoted to piety as she was, she had always had a special friendship for her confessors, and when she was on her knees with them, she rarely sought to remind them that she was the Queen.

The influence of Torquemada would always be with her; and Talavera equally enjoyed her esteem.

Talavera was a much milder man than Torquemada—indeed it would have been difficult to find anyone who could match his zeal with that of the Prior of Santa Cruz—yet he was fervent in his piety. Like Torquemada, he did not hesitate to reprimand either Isabella or Ferdinand if he felt it was right to do so; and, although Ferdinand might resent this, Isabella never did if she believed that she deserved that reprimand.

She remembered now the first time Talavera had come to her to hear her confess. She had knelt, and had been astonished that he remained seated.

"Fray Fernando de Talavera," she had said, "you do not kneel with me. It is the custom for my confessors to kneel when I kneel."

But Talavera had answered: "This is God's Tribunal. I am

here as His minister. Thus it is fitting that I should remain seated—as I represent God—while Your Highness kneels before me to confess."

Isabella had been surprised to be so addressed; but considering this matter, she came to agree that, as God's minister, her confessor should remain seated while she, the Queen, knelt.

From that day she had begun to believe that she had found a singularly honest man in Talavera.

Now she confessed that she longed for a simpler life, so that she might take a larger part in the bringing up of her children, that she envied mothers in humbler stations, that on occasion she asked herself what she had done to be condemned to a life of continual endeavour.

Talavera took her to task. She was God's chosen instrument. She did wrong to complain or to rail against such a noble vocation.

"I know it," she told him. "But there is a continual temptation for a mother who loves her husband and children to long for a more peaceful life with them at her side."

She prayed with Talavera for strength to do her duty, and for humility that she might accept with grace this life of sacrifice which had been demanded of her.

And when they had prayed, Ferdinand came to them.

He said : "I come to you with all speed. There is exciting news. The fortress of Alhama has been captured by Christian troops."

Isabella stood very still, her eyes closed, while she thanked God for this victory.

Ferdinand looked at her with some impatience. Her piety at times irritated him. Isabella never forgot it; as for himself, he had long decided that his religion was meant to serve him, not he his religion.

"The place," said Ferdinand, his eyes agleam, "is a treasure house. Ponce de Leon, the Marquis of Cadiz, attacked the fortress, and it succumbed after a struggle. He and his men stormed the town. The carnage was great; bodies are piled high in the streets, and the booty is such as has rarely been seen."

Isabella said : "And Alhama is but five or six leagues from Granada."

"There is wailing throughout the Arab kingdom," Ferdinand told her gleefully. "I shall prepare to leave at once and go to the assistance of brave Ponce de Leon, who has entered Alhama and is now being besieged by the Moors."

"This is a great victory," said Isabella. She was thinking of wild Ponce de Leon, who was an illegitimate son of the Count of Arcos, but who, on account of his many attributes, had been legitimized and given the title of Marquis of Cadiz. He was one of the boldest and bravest soldiers in Castile.

"Alhama must never be allowed to fall again into Moorish hands," said Ferdinand. "We have it and we will hold it. It shall be the springboard for our great campaign."

He left Isabella with Talavera and, when they were alone, Isabella said: "Let us give thanks for this great victory." And confessor and Queen knelt side by side.

When they arose, the Queen said: "My dear friend, when an opportunity arises I shall reward you for your services to me."

"I ask for no reward but to remain in Your Highness' service," was the answer.

"But I am determined to reward you," said the Queen, "for the great good you have done me. I shall bestow upon you the bishopric of Salamanca when it falls vacant."

"Nay, Highness, I should not accept it."

Isabella showed faint surprise. "So you would disobey my orders?"

Talavera knelt and, taking her hand, put his lips to it. "Highness," he said, "I would not accept any bishopric except one."

"And that one?"

"Granada," he said.

Isabella replied firmly: "It shall be yours . . . before long, my friend."

Her voice rang with determination. There would be no holding back now. The war against the Moors must begin in earnest.

* * *

It was April, and Isabella had journeyed from Medina to Cordova, where Ferdinand was stationed. She was now large with her child and she knew that she could do little more travelling before it was born.

Yet she wished to be with Ferdinand at this time.

But when she arrived, Ferdinand had already left, as the siege of Alhama had now been raised and Ponce de Leon freed.

Ferdinand had gone into Alhama with members of the Church and there had taken place a ceremony of purification. The mosques were turned into Christian churches, and bells, altar-cloths and such articles which were so much a part of the Christian Church were pouring into the town.

There was great rejoicing throughout Castile; there was great wailing throughout Granada.

"What treatment must we expect at the hands of these Christians?" the Moors asked themselves; for when they had ridden to the defence of Alhama they had found the bodies of the conquered Moors of that town, lying outside the walls, where they had been thrown by the conquerors; and those bodies lay rotting and naked, half devoured by vultures and hungry dogs.

"Is there to be no decent burial for an honourable enemy?" demanded the Moors.

The Christian answer was: "But these are Infidels. What should honourable burial mean to them?"

Furious with rage and humiliation, the Moors had again gone savagely to the attack, but by this time more Christian troops had appeared, and their efforts were futile.

Thus the victory of Alhama was complete, and Moors as well as Christians believed that this might well be a turning point in the centuries-long war.

To the church of Santa Maria de la Encarnacion Isabella sent an altar-cloth which she herself had embroidered; and she announced her regret that she could not go barefoot in person to give thanks for this victory. She dared not risk danger to her child, even in such a cause.

* * *

June had come and Isabella lay in childbed.

Beatriz de Bobadilla had come to be with her at this time. "For," said Beatriz, "I trust no other to care for you."

Isabella could always smile at her forthright friend, and only to Beatriz could she speak of her innermost thoughts.

"I long to be up and active again," she told Beatriz; "there is so much of importance to be done."

"You are a woman, not a soldier," grumbled Beatriz.

"A Queen must often be both."

"Kings are fortunate," said Beatriz. "They may give themselves to the governing of their kingdom. A Queen must bear children while she performs the same tasks as a King."

"But I have Ferdinand to help me," Isabella reminded her. "He is always there . . . ready to take over my duties when I am indisposed."

"When this one is born you will have four," said Beatriz. "Perhaps that is enough to ensure the succession."

"I would I had another boy. I feel there should be more boys. Ferdinand wishes for boys."

"The conceit of the male!" snorted Beatriz. "Our present Queen shows us that women make as good rulers as men—nay, better."

"Yet I think the people feel happier under a King."

"Clearly they do not, since they will not have the Salic law here."

"Never mind, Beatriz. The next ruler of Castile and Aragon—and perhaps all Spain—will be my Juan."

"That," answered Beatriz, "is years away."

"Beatriz . . ." Isabella spoke quietly. "Have you noticed anything . . . unusual about my little Juana?"

"She's a lively little baggage. That's what I have noticed."

"Nothing more, Beatriz?"

Beatriz looked puzzled. "What should I have noticed, Highness?"

"A certain wildness . . . a tendency to be hysterical."

"A spirited little girl with a brother who is a year older, and a sister who is several years older! She would need to be spirited, I think. I should say she is exhibiting normal tendencies."

"Beatriz . . . are you telling me the truth?"

Beatriz threw herself on to her knees beside her mistress. "Pregnant women are notorious for their fancies," she said. "I am learning that Queens are no exception."

"You are my comforter, Beatriz."

Beatriz kissed her hand. "Always at your service . . . ready to die there," she answered brusquely.

"Let us not talk of death, but of birth. I do not think it will be long now. Pray for a boy, please, Beatriz. That would delight Ferdinand. We have two girls and but one boy. Families such as ours grow nervous. Our children must be more than children; and they do not belong entirely to us but to the state. So . . . pray for a boy."

"I will," said Beatriz fervently.

A few days later, Isabella's fourth child was born. It was a girl: Maria.

* * *

In a convent in the town of Seville a young woman was on her knees in her cell. She listened to the tolling bells and thought: I shall go mad if I stay here.

There was no way of forgetting in this quiet place. Every time she heard the bells, she thought of a grim procession passing through the streets; she could hear the voice of the preacher in the Cathedral; she could see, among the yellow-clad figures, the face of one whom she had loved and betrayed, she could smell the hideous odour which she had smelt for the first time in the meadows of Tablada.

Assuredly, she told herself a thousand times, I shall go mad if I stay here.

But where should she go? There was nowhere. The house which had been her father's had been confiscated. All that he had possessed had passed into the hands of the Inquisition; they had taken his goods when they had taken his life; and they had taken his daughter's peace of mind.

If she had her child. . . . But what could a nun in a convent do with a child? She had lost her child. She had lost her father; she was losing her freedom.

How can I forget? she asked herself. Perhaps there was a way. She thought of fine glittering garments to replace the coarse serge of the nun's habit. She thought of a soft bed shared with a lover, to take the place of a hard pallet in a cell.

Perhaps in a life of gaiety she could forget her unhappiness.

I must escape, she told herself, for I shall go mad if I stay here.

She was passing out of her novitiate. Soon she must take the veil, and that would be the end of her hopes. Her days would be passed in silent solitude. A nun's life for *la hermosa hembra*, a life of solitude for one who had been the most beautiful woman in Seville?

She ran her hand through her short curls. They would grow again in all their beauty. But she must act quickly, before it was too late.

It was dusk as she slipped out of the convent.

On an errand of mercy, it was believed. They did not know her secret thoughts.

And when she was outside those grey walls she made her way to her father's house.

It was a foolish thing to do. There was no one belonging to him there.

She stood looking at the house and, as she looked, a man passed by. He stared at her. Her hood had fallen back, showing her short, glistening curls; and her face was no less beautiful than it had been in the days when she had sat on her father's balcony and fanned herself.

"Forgive me," said the man. His voice and manner told her he was of the nobility. "You are in distress?"

"I have escaped from a convent," she told him. "I have nowhere to go."

"But why did you escape? Do you mean you have simply walked out and decided not to go back again?"

"I escaped because the life of a nun is not the life for me."

Then he looked at her face, at the slumberous dark eyes, at the sensual lips.

He said: "You are very beautiful."

"It is long since I was told so," she answered.

"If you come with me I will give you shelter," he told her. "Then you can tell me your story and make your plans. Will you come?"

She hesitated for a moment. His eyes, though courteous, were bold. She knew she was taking a step along a certain path. She must make up her mind now whether she would continue on that road to which he was beckoning her.

Her hesitation was brief.

It was for this that she had left her convent. This man pleased her; and he was offering to be her protector.

"Yes," she said. "I will come with you."

She turned her back on the house which had been her father's, and she was smiling as she walked beside her new protector.

* * *

In his residence at Alcalá de Henares, Alfonso Carillo, the Archbishop of Toledo, had left his laboratories and retired to his own apartments.

He said to his servants: "I will go to my bed, for I am very tired."

They were astonished because they had never before seen him so resigned. It was as though all the militancy had gone out of him and that he had no longer any interest in the affairs of the country, nor in the discoveries he might make through the scientific experiments in the pursuit of which he had squandered his vast fortunes.

"I think it is time," he said, "for me to make my peace with God, for I am an old man and I do not think there is much time left to me."

So his servant hurried away to arrange for the last rites, and the old Archbishop lay back on his bed thinking of the past.

"She is a great Queen, this Isabella of ours," he murmured to himself. "She has set the fires burning all over Castile. She will rid Castile of heretics and, it may well be, of all infidels, for she is determined to drive the Moors from Granada, and I have a feeling that what our Isabella sets out to achieve she will.

"And but for me she would never have attained the throne. Yet here I live in disgrace, cut off from the affairs which were once the whole meaning of life to me. I have been foolish. I should have taken no offence at Ferdinand's treatment of me. I should have shown no rancour towards Mendoza, the sly old fox! They are only waiting for my death to make him Primate of Spain.

"Yes, I have been foolish. After raising her up, I thought I could dash her down. But I was mistaken. I did not know Isabella. I could not guess the strength of this woman. And who can blame me? Was there ever such gentleness disguising such strength?"

He fell into a doze and, when he awoke, he saw the priests at his bedside. They had come to administer Extreme Unction.

The end of his turbulent life was near.

* * *

Isabella was with her month-old baby, Maria, when news from Loja was brought to her.

Muley Abul Hassan, the King of Granada, had taken fright at the loss of Alhama, and throughout the city of Granada there had been great mourning. But the Arabs were a warlike people and they remembered defeats of the past which had been turned into victories.

So they rallied and met the Christians at Loja.

Perhaps the Christians had allowed the success of Alhama to go to their heads; perhaps they had underestimated the resourcefulness of their enemies.

At Loja, that July, there was such a rout of the Christian armies that, had reinforcements come more quickly from Granada, Muley Abul Hassan would have wiped out all that was left of Ferdinand's army.

Isabella received the news without changing her expression, although her heart was filled with anxiety.

She sent for Cardinal Mendoza and, when he was with her, she told him the news.

He bowed his head and there were a few seconds of silence.

Then Isabella spoke. "I think this may be sent as a warning to us. We were too confident; we believed that we owed our victories to our own arms and skill, and not to God."

Mendoza gave the Queen a look which she construed as conveying his agreement with her. But in fact Mendoza was marvelling at her ability to see the guiding hand of God in all that befell her.

All over Castile the dread Inquisition was establishing itself. In many towns the atmosphere had changed almost overnight. The people walked the streets, furtive and afraid. The Cardinal guessed that their nights were uneasy. For who could know when there would be that knock at the door, those dreaded words: "Open in the name of the Inquisition."

Yet if he asked her what had happened to her towns she would have answered: "They are being cleansed of heretics." And she would believe that she was carrying out the wishes of God by setting up the Inquisition in Spain.

She will succeed in all she does, pondered Mendoza. There is a fire and fervency beneath that gentle façade which is unbeatable. She does not question the rightness of what she does. She is Isabella of Castile, and therefore rules by Divine Will.

"The Moors are strong," said the Cardinal. "The task before us would seem insuperable—except by our brave and wise Queen."

Isabella accepted the compliment. Mendoza was too gallant, too courteous. He lacked the honesty of men such as Talavera and Torquemada; but his company was perhaps more pleasant, and she must forgive him his light-mindedness. He was a wise man in spite of the life he led; and disapproving of that as she did, she was still ready to accept him as her leading minister.

In affairs of state, she told herself, one must not overlook people because of their licentious habits. This man was a statesman, shrewd and wise, and she had need of him.

She said: "We shall prosecute the war with success. And now, my friend, I have news from Alcalá de Henares for you. Alfonso Carillo is dead. Poor Alfonso Carillo, he has died deeply in debt, I fear. He could never restrain himself—neither in politics nor in his scientific experiments. It was always so. He did me great harm, yet I am saddened because I remember those days when he was my friend."

"Your Highness should not grieve. He was your friend when he felt it expedient to be so."

"You are right, Archbishop."

The Cardinal looked at her, and she smiled at him in her gentle way.

"Who but you should be Archbishop of Toledo, and Primate of Spain? Who else could be trusted at the head of affairs in the years before us?"

Mendoza knelt and took her hand.

He was an ambitious man and was overcome with admiration and respect for a Queen as bigoted as herself, who could choose a man of his reputation because she knew he was her ablest statesman.

* * *

Ferdinand was pacing up and down the Queen's apartment. The defeat at Loja had greatly upset him. He had believed that victory over the Moors was almost within their grasp; and he could not face set-backs with the calm which was his wife's.

But Isabella herself—although she did not show this—was uneasy on account of the latest item of news which had now been brought to them.

They had thought La Beltraneja safe in her convent. Had she not taken the veil?

Ferdinand cried: "How can one be sure what Louis will do next? He has his eyes on Navarre. Make no mistake about that. Navarre shall belong to us. It is mine . . . through my father."

Isabella considered the position. The first wife of Ferdinand's father, Blanche, daughter of Charles III of Navarre, had on her death left Navarre to her son Carlos, who had been murdered to make way for Ferdinand. Navarre had then passed to Blanche, elder sister of Carlos and repudiated wife of Henry IV of Castile. Poor Blanche, like her brother, had met an untimely death; this was at the instigation of her sister Eleanor, who wanted Navarre for her son, Gaston de Foix.

On the death of John of Aragon, who had retained the title of King of Navarre, Eleanor had greedily seized power, but her glory was short-lived, for she died three weeks after her father.

Eleanor had arranged the murder of her sister Blanche, that her son, Gaston de Foix, might inherit Navarre, but Gaston had been killed during a tourney at Lisbon some years before the death of Eleanor, and the next heir was Gaston's son, Francis Phoebus.

Gaston's wife had been the Princess Madeleine, sister of Louis XI of France; thus Louis had his eye on Navarre and was determined that it should not go back to the crown of Aragon.

Ferdinand now told Isabella the cause of his alarm.

"Who can guess what Louis plans next? He now suggests a marriage between Francis Phoebus, King of Navarre, and La Beltraneja!"

"That is quite impossible," cried Isabella. "La Beltraneja has taken the veil and will spend the rest of her days in the convent of Santa Clara at Coimbra."

"Do you think the vows of La Beltraneja will stop Louis' making this marriage if he wishes it?"

"You may be right," said Isabella. "Doubtless he wishes to put Navarre under French rule and then, if La Beltraneja were the wife of his nephew, Francis Phoebus, he would support her claims to my crown."

"Exactly!" agreed Ferdinand. "We plan to make war on the

Moors. Louis knows this. Doubtless he has heard of what happened at Loja. The crafty old man is choosing the right moment to strike at us."

"We must stop him, Ferdinand. Nothing should now stand in the way of our campaigns in this Holy War."

"Nothing shall," said Ferdinand.

INSIDE THE KINGDOM OF GRANADA

The most beautiful and the most prosperous province of Spain was Granada. It contained rich resources; there were minerals in its mountains; its Mediterranean ports were the most important in the whole of Spain; its pasture lands were well watered; and the industry of its people had made it rich.

The most beautiful city in Spain was the capital of the kingdom, Granada itself. Enclosed in walls with a thousand and thirty towers and seven portals, it appeared to be impregnable. The Moors were proud of their city and had reason to be. Its buildings were exquisite; its streets were narrow and the lofty houses were decorated with metal which shone in sun and starlight, giving the impression that they were jewelled.

The most handsome building in Granada—and in the whole of Spain—was the mighty Alhambra, fortress and palace, set on a hill. Not only was this enchanting to the eye, with its brilliant porticos and colonnades, not only did it, with its *patios* and baths, speak of luxury and extravagance, it was also useful and could house, should the need arise, an army of forty thousand.

Granada had been the centre of Moorish culture since 1228, when a chieftain of the tribe of Beni Hud had decided to make himself ruler of this fair city and had received rights of sovereignty from the Caliph of Baghdad, that he might reign under the titles of Amir ul Moslemin and Al Mutawakal (the Commando of the Moslems and the Protected of God).

There had been many to come after him, and their reigns had been turbulent; there were continual affrays with the Christian forces, and in 1464 a treaty was made with Henry IV in which it was arranged that Mohammed, the reigning King, should put Granada under the protection of Castile, and for this protection should pay to the Kings of Castile an annual tribute of 12,000 gold ducats. It was this sum that the acquisitive Ferdinand had sought to bring to the Castilian coffers, for, when the affairs of Castile became anarchical during the latter years of the disastrous reign of Henry IV, the Moors had allowed the tribute to lapse, and the Castilians had not been in a position to enforce it.

Mohammed Ismail died in 1466, and when his son Muley Abul Hassan came to the throne the affairs of Granada were becoming almost as turbulent as those in the nearby province of Castile.

Even so, the Moors were a warlike people and determined to defend what they considered to be theirs. It was seven hundred years since the Arabs had conquered the Visigoths and settled in Spain. After seven hundred years the Moors felt that they could call Granada their own country.

Unfortunately for the Moorish population of Spain they faced defeat, not only because of the enemy without but on account of their troubles within.

There was treason in the very heart of the royal family.

* * *

From behind the hangings the Sultana Zoraya, the Star of the Morning, looked out on to the *patio* where the Sultan's favourite slave sat trailing her fingers in the water. Zoraya was full of hatred.

The Greek was beautiful, with a strange beauty never seen before in the harem; and the Sultan visited her often.

Zoraya was not disturbed by this. Let the Sultan visit the Greek when he wished. Zoraya was no longer young, and she had lived long enough in the harem to know that the favour of Sultans passed quickly.

The great ambition of the Sultan's wives should be to have a son, and Zoraya had her son, her Abu Abdallah, known as Boabdil.

Her fear was that the Greek's son should be put above Boabdil; and that she would never allow. She would be ready to kill any who stood between her son and his inheritance, and she was determined that the next Sultan of Granada should be Boabdil.

It was for this reason that she watched the Greek; it was for this reason that she intrigued within the Alhambra itself—a difficult feat for a woman who, a wife of the Sultan, must live among women guarded by eunuchs.

But Zoraya was no humble Arab woman, and she did not believe in the superiority of the male.

She had been educated in her home in Martos, when she had been intended for a brilliant marriage, so it was surprising that she should have lived so many years of her life in a Sultan's palace.

Yet it had not been a bad life. She would have no regrets once she had set Boabdil on the throne of Granada.

It was not difficult to arrange for messages to be passed from the harem to other parts of the palace. She who had been such a beautiful woman in her youth was now a forceful one. And Muley Abul Hassan was growing old and feeble. It was his brother, who was known by the name of El Zagal, the Valiant One, whom she feared.

Zoraya was proud. She had had her way often enough with the old Sultan. She had demanded special privileges from the moment when she had been brought before him in chains, and Muley Abul Hassan had denied her little in those days.

She was allowed to visit her son, Boabdil, though it should have been clear to the old Sultan that she sought to set a new Sultan in his place.

She despised Muley Abul Hassan as much as she feared his brother.

Now, as she watched the Greek slave, she asked herself what she had to fear. The Greek was beautiful, but Zoraya had more than beauty.

She thought of the day she had been brought to the Alhambra. She, the proud daughter of the proud governor of the town of Martos.

A strange day of heat and tension, a day which stood out in her life as one in which everything had changed, when she had stepped from one life to another—from one civilization to another. How many women were destined to live the life of a sheltered daughter of a Castilian nobleman and that of one of several wives in the harem of a Sultan!

But on that day Doña Isabella de Solis had become Zoraya, the Star of the Morning.

All through the day the battle had raged, and it was in the late afternoon when the Moors had stormed her father's residence. In a room in one of the towers, which could only be reached by a spiral staircase, she had cowered with her personal maid, listening to the shouts of the invaders, the death-cries of men, the screams of the women.

"We cannot escape," she had said again and again. "How is it possible for us to escape? Will they not search every room, every corner?"

She was right. There was no escape. And when she heard footsteps on the spiral staircase she pushed her trembling maid behind her and confronted the intruder. He was a man of high rank in the Moorish army. He stood looking at her, his bloody scimitar in his hand, and he saw that she was beauitful. Her dignity—that ingrained Castilian quality—was not lost on her captor. He took her maid. She would be for him, but when he set the chains on the wrists of Doña Isabella de Solis, he said to her: "You are reserved for the Sultan himself."

And so she was taken in chains to Granada, into the mighty

fortress which was to be her home. And there, she stood before Muley Abul Hassan, as proud as a visiting Queen.

This amused him. He had taken her to his harem. She should be one of his wives. It was clearly an honour due to a high-born lady of such dignity.

Then she became his Star of the Morning and she bore him Boabdil; and from that time she determined that the next Sultan of Granada should be her son.

She had no fear that this would not be so. But the Greek had come, and the Greek was full of wiles. She also had a son.

* * *

Boabdil stood before his mother. He had the face of a dreamer. He wished that life would run more peacefully.

"Boabdil, my son," said Zoraya, "you seem unmoved. Do you not understand that that woman plots against us?"

"She will not succeed, oh my Mother," said Boabdil. "For I am the eldest son of my father."

"You do not know how women will fight for their children."

Boadbil smiled at her. "But do I not see you, my Mother, fighting for yours?"

"I will find a means of removing her from the palace. We will trick her. We will lure her into a situation from which she cannot escape. She shall be slain in the manner of an unfaithful woman. Boabdil, where is your manhood? Why do you not wish to fight for what is yours?"

"When Allah decides, I shall be Sultan of Granada, my Mother. If Allah wished me to be Sultan at this time, he would make me so."

"You accept your fate. That is your Moorish blood, my son. My people take what they want."

"Yet it was they who were taken," said Boabdil gently.

"You anger me," said Zoraya. She came closer to him: "Boabdil, my son, there are men in Granada who would take up arms for you if you set yourself in opposition to your father."

"You would ask me to take up arms against my father?"

"There is your uncle, El Zagal, whose plan it is to take the crown from you. Your father is weak. But you would have your supporters. You do not ask me how I know this, but I will tell you. I have my spies in the streets. Messages are brought to me. I know what we could do."

"You endanger your life by such action, my Mother."

She stamped her foot and threw back her still handsome head.

Boabdil looked at her with affection, admiration and exasperation. He had never known a woman like his mother.

She narrowed her eyes and whispered : "If I thought that any might succeed in taking the throne from you, I would put you at the head of an army . . . this very day."

"My Mother, you talk treason."

Her eyes flashed. "I owe loyalty to none. I was taken from my home against my will. I was brought here in chains. I was forced to lead the life of an Arab slave. I . . . the daughter of a proud Castilian. I owe no loyalty to any. Others ruled my life; now I say my reward is a crown for my son. You shall be Sultan of Granada even if we must make war on your father to put the crown on your head."

"But why should we fight for that which must, when Allah wills it, be ours?"

"My foolish son," answered Zoraya, "do you not understand that others intrigue to take the crown of Granada instead of you? The Greek wants it for her son. She is sly. How can we know what promises she wrings from a besotted old man? Your uncle looks covetously towards the crown. He wants it for himself. Allah helps those who help themselves. Have you not yet learned that, Boabdil?"

"I hear voices."

"Go then and see who listens to us."

"I beg of you, my Mother, do not speak treasonably in case any should hear."

But even as he spoke guards had entered the apartment.

Zoraya was shocked. She demanded : "What do you here? Do you not know what the punishment is for forcing your way into the apartments of the Sultana?"

The guards bowed low. They spoke to Boabdil. "My lord, we come on the command of Muley Abul Hassan, Sultan of Granada. We must humbly request you to allow us to put these chains upon you, for it is our unhappy duty to conduct you and the Sultana to the prison in the palace."

Zoraya cried : "You shall put no chains on me."

But it was useless; the guards had seized her. Her eyes flashed with contempt when she saw her son Boabdil meekly hold out his hands to receive the chains.

* * *

In her prison Zoraya did not cease to intrigue. As Sultana and mother of Boabdil, recognized heir to the crown of Granada, there were many to work for her. The rule of Muley Abul Hassan was not popular. It was well known throughout the Kingdom that the Christian armies were gathering against Mussulmans and that the Castile of today was a formidable province—no less so because, through the marriage of Isabella with Ferdinand, it was allied with Aragon.

"The Sultan is old. He is finished. Can an old man defend Granada against the growing danger?" That was the message which Zoraya had caused to be circulated through Granada. And in the streets the people whispered: "We are a kingdom in peril and a kingdom divided against itself. Old men are set in old ways. Our future is in the hands of our youth."

Zoraya and her son, although prisoners, did not suffer any privations. They were surrounded by servants and attendants. Thus Muley Abul Hassan had made it easy for Zoraya to continue to work for his dethronement and the succession of her son, Boabdil.

She sent her spies into the streets to spread abroad the scandals of the palace, to whisper of the bravery of Zoraya and Boabdil whom others sought to rob of their inheritance. Here was a brave mother fighting for the rights of her son; they could depend upon it that Allah would not turn his back upon her.

News was brought to her that the people in the streets were no longer whispering but saying aloud: "Have done with the old Sultan. Give us the new!" And Zoraya judged the moment had come. She summoned all her servants and attendants to her. She made the women take off their veils, the eunuchs their *haiks*.

Then she, with Boabdil and a very few of her most trusted servants, tied these end to end, making a long rope, which they secured and hung from a window.

First she descended the rope, followed by Boabdil.

She had arranged that they should be expected. No sooner had Boabdil reached the ground than several of their supporters were on the spot greeting Boabdil as their Sultan, honouring Zoraya as the great Sultana and mother, a woman whose name, they believed, would be a legend in the history of the Mussulmans, because she, in her maternal love, by her bravery and resource, had delivered their new Sultan from the tyranny of the old one.

* * *

There was war in Granada. Thousands rallied to the cause of Boabdil.

In the streets of the beautiful city of Granada, Moor fought Moor and the battle was fierce.

Muley Abul Hassan was taken by surprise, first by the treachery of his family, then by the force of their supporters. And although the fortress of the Alhambra itself remained faithful to him, the city was against him. Chivalry turned the men of Granada to the brave Sultana and her young son. Prudence weighed the matter and decided that Muley Abul Hassan had had his day and that the times needed the vigour of a young Sultan; and Muley Abul Hassan was driven from Granada, whence he fled to the city of Malaga, which had declared itself for him.

Thus while the Christian armies were gathering against them there was civil strife in the Kingdom of Granada.

* * *

Isabella was thoughtful as she sat at her needlework. This was one of the rare occasions when she could find a brief hour's escape from state duties; and it was pleasant to have Beatriz with her at such a time.

Beatriz had her duties to her husband and was not in constant attendance on Isabella, so that those opportunities of being together were especially precious.

Isabella was now thinking of Ferdinand, who had seemed to be brooding on some secret matter. She wondered if his thoughts were with the events in Granada as hers were; but perhaps they were with some woman, some family of his, which existed unknown to her. It seemed strange that Ferdinand might have other families, women who loved him, children who aroused his affection even as her Isabella, Juan, Juana and little Maria did—a strange, disturbing and unhappy thought.

She looked at Beatriz, who, not with any great pleasure, was working on a piece of needlework. Beatriz was too active a woman to find delight in such a sedentary occupation. Isabella would have enjoyed talking of these matters which disturbed her to a sympathetic friend like Beatriz; but she refrained from doing so; not even to Beatriz would she speak of matters, so derogatory, she believed, to the dignity of herself and Ferdinand as sovereigns of Castile and Aragon.

Beatriz herself spoke, for on these occasions Isabella had asked her friend to dispense with all ceremony, and that they should behave as two good wives come together for a friendly gossip.

"How go affairs in Navarre?" asked Beatriz.

"They give us cause for anxiety," answered Isabella. "One can never be sure what tortuous plan is in Louis' mind."

"Surely even he could not arrange that the vows La Beltraneja has taken should be swept aside."

"He is very powerful. And I do not trust Pope Sixtus. We have had our differences. And bribes can work wonders with a man such as he is, I fear."

"Bribes or threats," murmured Beatriz. "Francis Phoebus is, I hear, a beautiful creature. They say that he is rightly called Phoebus and that his hair is like golden sunshine."

"Doubtless," answered Isabella, "they exaggerate. Phoebus is a family name. It may well be that he is handsome, but he is also a King, and the beauty of Kings and Queens often takes its lustre from their royalty."

Beatriz smiled at her friend. "My Queen," she said, "I believe your natural good sense is equal to your beauty—and you are beautiful, Isabella, Queen or not!"

"We were talking of Francis Phoebus," Isabella reminded her.

"Ah, yes, Francis Phoebus, who is as beautiful as his name. I wonder what he feels about marrying the released nun of doubtful parentage."

"If that marriage is made," said Isabella grimly, "there will be many to assure him that there is no doubt whatsoever of her parentage. Oh, Beatriz, the tasks before us seem to grow daily. I had hoped that ere long we should be making war . . . real war . . . on Granada. But now that it would seem favourable to do so, there is trouble in Navarre. If Louis suggests removing La Beltraneja from her convent, having her released from her vows and married to his nephew of Navarre, make no mistake about it, his first plan will be to take Navarre under the protection of France, and his second to win my crown for La Beltraneja."

"Even Louis would never succeed."

"He would not succeed, Beatriz, but there would be another bitter war. A War of the Succession has already been fought and won. I pray hourly that there may not be another."

"That you may devote your energies to the war against the Moors."

Isabella thoughtfully continued with her needlework.

It was shortly afterwards that Ferdinand entered her apartment. He came without ceremony, but Beatriz, realizing that he would not wish her to greet him with the informality which Isabella allowed, was on her feet and gave him a deep curtsey.

Isabella saw that Ferdinand was excited. His eyes shone in his bronzed face and his mouth twitched slightly.

"You have news, Ferdinand, good news?" she asked. "Please do not consider the presence of Beatriz. You know she is our very good friend."

Beatriz waited for his dismissal, but it did not come.

He sat down on the chair beside the Queen, and Isabella signed to Beatriz that she might return to her chair.

Ferdinand said: "News from Navarre."

"What news?" asked Isabella sharply.

"The King of Navarre is dead."

An almost imperceptible look of triumph stole across Ferdinand's face.

Beatriz caught her breath. She had visualized so clearly the young man known as Francis Phoebus who had been likened to the Sun God himself, and only a few moments ago she had considered him in his golden beauty; now she must adjust the picture and see a young man lying on his bier.

"How did he die?" Isabella asked.

"Quite suddenly," said Ferdinand; and, try as he might to look solemn, he could not manage it. The triumph remained on his face.

Beatriz' eyes went to Isabella's face, but as usual the Queen's expression told her nothing.

What does she think of murder? wondered Beatriz. How can I know, when she does not betray herself? Does she accept the murder of a young man, as beautiful as his name implies, because his existence threatens the throne of Castile? Will she say Thank God? Or in her prayers will she ask forgiveness because, when she hears that murder has been done at the instigation of her husband, she has rejoiced?

"Then," said Isabella slowly, "the danger of a marriage between Navarre and La Beltraneja no longer exists."

"That danger is over," agreed Ferdinand.

He folded his arms and smiled at his Queen. He looked invincible thus, thought Beatriz. Isabella realizes this; and perhaps she says to herself: Unfaithful husband though you are, murderer though you may be, you are a worthy husband for Isabella of Castile!

"Now who rules Navarre?" asked Isabella.

"His sister Catharine has been proclaimed Queen."

"A child of thirteen!"

"Her mother rules until she is older."

"There is one thing we must do with all speed," said Isabella. "Juan shall be betrothed to Catharine of Navarre."

"I agree," said Ferdinand. "But I have news that Louis has not been idle. He is making preparations to seize Navarre. In which case it may very well be that they will not accept our son for Catharine."

"We must act against Louis at once," said Isabella.

"Your short respite is over," Ferdinand told her ruefully.

"I will leave at once for the frontier," Isabella replied. "We must show Louis that, should he attempt to move into Navarre, we have strong forces to resist him."

Isabella folded up her needlework as though, thought Beatriz, she were a housewife, preparing to perform some other domestic duty.

She handed the work to Beatriz. "It must be set aside for a time," she said.

Beatriz took the work, and understanding that they wished to discuss plans from which she was excluded, she curtsied and left Ferdinand and Isabella alone together.

* * *

Boabdil rode into battle against the Christian army.

Muley Abul Hassan and his brother El Zagal were fighting their own war, also against the Christians. They had made several attacks near Gibraltar and had had some success.

The people of Granada were beginning to say: "It may be that Muley Abul Hassan grows old and feeble, but with El Zagal beside him he can still win victories. Perhaps it is not the will of Allah that we throw him aside for the new Sultan, Boabdil."

"Boabdil must go into action," cried Zoraya. "He must show the Arab kingdom that he can fight as poor Muley Abul Hassan, and even El Zagal, never could."

So it was that Boabdil rode into action against the Christians. He was confident of success. Brilliantly clad in a mantle of crimson velvet embroidered with gold, he was an impressive figure, for beneath the cloak his damascened steel armour caught and reflected the light and glistened.

Out of the town of Granada he rode to the cheers of the people; and those cheers were still ringing in his ears when he took the road to Cordova.

He met the Christian forces on the banks of the Xenil, and the fighting was fierce.

Boabdil had not been born to be a fighter. He was a man who longed for peace; and but for his forceful mother he would never have found himself in the position he was in that day. His men sensed the lack of resolution in their leader; and the Christians were determined.

And there on the banks of the Xenil, Boabdil saw his Moors defeated and, realizing that he himself in his rich garments and on his milk-white horse was conspicuous as their leader, he sought a way to hide himself and escape death or what would be more humiliating, capture.

He saw his men mowed down, his captains slaughtered; and he knew the battle was lost.

The river had risen during the night, and it was impossible for him to ford it; so he dismounted and, abandoning his horse, hid himself among the brush which bordered the river.

As he cowered there among the reeds, a passing soldier caught a glimpse of the bright scarlet of his cloak and came to investigate.

Boabdil stood up, his scimitar in his hand, and prepared to fight for his life. But his discoverer, a soldier named Martin Hurtado, realizing that here was a man of high rank, yelled to his comrades and, at once, Boabdil was surrounded.

Now his scimitar was of no use against so many and, in an endeavour to save his life, he cried: "I am Boabdil, Sultan of Granada."

That made the soldiers pause. Here was a prize beyond their wildest hopes.

"Stay your swords, my friends," cried Martin Hurtado. "We will take this prize to King Ferdinand. I'll warrant we'll be richly rewarded for it."

The others agreed, although it went against the grain to relinquish that scarlet velvet cloak, that shining armour and all the other treasures which, it was reasonable to believe, such a personage might have upon him.

So in this way was Boabdil brought to Ferdinand a prisoner.

* * *

Isabella was at the frontier town of Logroño, when news was brought to her of the death of Louis.

She fell on her knees and gave thanks for this deliverance.

The King of France, she heard, had died in great fear of the hereafter, for he had committed many sins and the memory of these tortured him.

Yet, thought Isabella, he worked for his country. France was put first always. Perhaps his sins would be forgiven because of that one great virtue.

His son, Charles VIII, was a minor and there would be troubles enough in his country to keep French eyes off Navarre for some time.

It is yet another miracle, pondered Isabella. It is further evidence that I have been selected for the great tasks before me.

Now she need no longer stay on the borders of Navarre. She

could join Ferdinand; they could prosecute the war against the Infidel with all their resources.

As she travelled towards Cordova more exhilarating news was brought to her.

The Moors had been routed on the banks of the Xenil, and Boabdil himself was Ferdinand's prisoner.

"Let us give thanks to God and his saints," cried Isabella to her attendants. "The way is being made clear to us. Our Inquisitors are bringing the heretic to justice. Now we shall drive the Infidel from Granada. If we do this we shall not have lived in vain, and there will be rejoicing in Heaven. Our sins will be as molehills beside the mountain of our achievements."

And she was smiling. For the first time since she had heard of it she was no longer disturbed by the thought of bright and beautiful Francis Phoebus, lying dead at the hand of a poisoner.

THE DREAM OF CHRISTOFORO COLOMBO

IN a small shop in one of the narrow streets of the town of Lisbon a man waited for customers, and on his face was an expression of frustration and sorrow.

"Will it always be thus?" he asked himself. "Will my plans never come to fruition?"

He had asked the question again and again of Filippa, his wife, and she had always replied in the same way: "Have courage, Christoforo. One day your dreams will be realized. One day you will find those who will believe you, who will make it possible for you to carry out your plan."

And he had said in those days: "You are right, Filippa; one day I shall succeed."

He had smiled at her because he had known that in her heart she was not displeased. When the great day came she would stand at the door of the shop, little Diego in her arms, waving to a husband who was going away on his great adventure, an adventure which would, more likely than not, end in death.

Yet she need not have feared on that account. She was the one who had gone to meet death—not on the high seas, but in the back room of this dark little shop which was crowded with charts and nautical instruments.

Little Diego came and stood beside him. Patient little Diego, who now had no mother to care for him, and tried so hard to understand the meaning of the dreams he saw in his father's eyes.

Few people came into the shop to buy. Christoforo was not a good salesman, he feared. If they came, if they were interested in sailing the seas, he would invite them into the room beyond and there, over a bottle of wine, they would talk while Christoforo forgot the need to sell his goods that he might provide food for himself and his son.

It was nearly ten years since he had come to Lisbon from Genoa. He was even then nearly thirty years old. He often talked now to little Diego, who had been his chief companion since Filippa had died.

Diego would stand, his hands on his father's knees, listening.

Diego thought his father the most handsome man in Lisbon, indeed in the world, for Diego knew nothing of the world beyond

Lisbon. When his father talked his eyes would glow with a luminosity which Diego did not understand—and yet it thrilled his small body. His father talked as no others talked; and his talk was all of a land that lay somewhere across the oceans, a land which existed and yet about which no one on this side of the world knew anything.

Diego looked into the face of a man who saw visions. A tall man, a broad man, with long legs, blue eyes which seemed made for looking over long distances, and thick hair which had a touch of red and gold in it.

"Father," Diego would say, "tell me about the great voyage of discovery."

Then Christoforo would talk, and as he talked those light, luminous eyes swept across the past to the present and on into the future, and it was as though he saw clearly what had happened, what was happening and what the future held.

"I came to Lisbon, my son," he would begin, "because I believed that here in this country I might find more sympathy for my schemes than was given me in Italy. In Italy . . . they laughed at me. My son, I think they begin to laugh at me here."

Diego listened intently. They laughed at his father because they were fools. They did not believe in the existence of the great land across the water.

"Fools! Fools!" cried Diego, clenching his fists and bringing them down on his father's knees.

Then Christoforo remembered the youthfulness of his son and he was unhappy again, for he thought: What if they listened to me with serious attention? What if they smiled on me? What would become of this small boy?

It had been different when Filippa was alive. He could no longer see himself setting out while Filippa waved farewell with their son in her arms.

He would take the boy on his knee and tell him of the journeys he had made. He would talk of voyages to the coast of Guinea and Iceland, to the Cape de Verd Islands. He talked of the time when he had first come to Lisbon. Filippa had come with him; and she had known what he planned; he had made no secret of his ambitions. She had understood. She was her father's daughter and *he* had sailed the seas; *he* understood the desire of men to discover new lands. So Filippa Muñiz de Palestrello understood also.

She had watched her husband and her father bending over the charts, growing excited, talking of what lay beyond the wastes of water so far unexplored by Europeans.

When her father died all his charts and all his instruments were left to Christoforo, who had by then married Filippa.

One day Christoforo, who had vainly been trying to interest influential men in his projects, heard that an adventurer was more likely to get a sympathetic understanding in the maritime port of Lisbon than anywhere else, for King John II of Portugal was interested in expeditions into the unknown world.

"Pack up what we have, Filippa," he had said. "This day we leave for Lisbon."

And so to Lisbon they had come, and found a home here among its seven hills. But Filippa had died, leaving him only Diego to remind him of her—Diego, that precious and beloved creature, who because of the dream must be an anxiety.

Wandering along the banks of the Tagus, walking disconsolately through the Alfama district, gazing up to the Castle of São Jorge set on the highest of the hills, he dreamed continually of the day when he would leave Lisbon; for his dream had become an obsession which tormented him, and had grown to such proportions that it obliterated even the love of his wife and child.

"But one day, Diego, my son," said Christoforo, "they will not laugh. One day they will honour your father. Mayhap they will make him an Admiral and I shall ask a place at Court for you, my little son."

Diego nodded; he had no idea what a place at Court would mean to him, but he was pleased that his father did not forget him; for young as he was, Diego understood the force of his father's ambition.

"Father," he said, "will it be soon that you sail away?"

"Soon, my son. It must be soon. I have waited long. And while I am away, you will be good?"

"I will be good," said the boy, "but I shall long for your return."

Christoforo was smitten with remorse afresh. He lifted the boy in his arms and held him tightly. Little Diego had such confidence in his father who was preparing to leave him, and indeed longing to do so. He did not doubt that provision would be made for him during his father's absence, and in the event of his father's not returning at all.

And it shall be! Christoforo assured himself. Even if I have to take him with me.

Yet what sort of a father was he, to expose a tender child to the hazards of the sea!

I am not a father, Christoforo told himself, any more than I was a husband. I am an explorer-adventurer—and there is little space in one lifetime to be more than that. Yet, I swear, Diego shall be cared for.

He set the boy on his knee and took out one of the charts which had been left to him by his father-in-law. He showed the boy where he believed the new land to lie, and as he talked he was railing against this fate which prevented him from making the voyage of his dreams. If he were but a rich man. . . . But he was a poor adventurer who had to depend on the wealth of others to finance his venture; and in some ways he was a practical man; he knew that great wealth would have to be expended on an expedition such as he wished to lead. Only great nobles could help; only kings.

But nothing could be done without the approval of the Church; and the Church was inclined to laugh at his proposals. The Bishops wanted verification of his assumptions. What were the chances of success? Could they put their trust in the dream of an adventurer? They did not believe in the existence of this great undiscovered land.

Yet they had allowed him to hope.

It was while he sat with his son that a visitor called to see him. Christoforo's heart leaped as the man entered the shop. He knew that he had not come to buy nautical instruments, for he was in the service of the Bishop of Ceuta.

Christoforo rose hastily and pushed Diego from his knee.

"Leave us, my son," he said.

And Diego ran up the spiral staircase, but he did not enter the room above the shop; he sat on the top stair listening to the voices below. He could not hear what was said but he would know by the sound of his father's voice whether the news was good. Good news would be that his father might prepare immediately to make the voyage, and although Diego knew that would mean separation, no less than his father he longed to hear this news. For Diego, like Christoforo, there could only be real satisfaction when the dream became reality; and like his father, the boy was ready to endure any hardship if this should come to pass.

Meanwhile Christoforo had taken his visitor into the dark little room beyond the shop.

Christoforo's heart had sunk at the sight of the man's face; he had seen that expression on faces before, the faintly suppressed smile of superiority which men of small understanding, who thought themselves wise, gave to those who in their opinion bordered on imbecility.

"I come from my lord Bishop of Ceuta," said the man.

"And your news?"

The man shook his head. "Nothing more can be done. The voyage is impossible."

"Impossible!" cried Christoforo rising, his blue eyes blazing. "How can any say this of that which has not been proved?"

"It had been proved." The man's smile widened. "The Ecclesiastical Council decided that your project would be a hopeless one, but his lordship, the Bishop of Ceuta, did not dismiss your claims as lightly as did the others."

"I know," said Christoforo, "he promised me that ere long I should be equipped with all I needed to make the voyage."

"Meanwhile his lordship decided to put your theories to the test."

"But he has not done so. I have been here in Lisbon these many months . . . waiting . . . waiting, eternally waiting."

"But he has done this. He sent his own expedition. He equipped a vessel and sent her out in search of this new world which you are so sure exists."

Christoforo was fighting hard to restrain himself. He was not a meek man, and he wanted to crash his fist into the smiling face. They had cheated him. They had listened to his plans; they had studied his charts. It had been necessary to convince them that he had something to support his theories. Then they had deceived him. They had equipped a vessel for someone else.

"The ship returned, battered and almost unseaworthy. It is a miracle that she arrived back safely in Lisbon. She encountered such storms in the Saragossa Sea that it was impossible to continue the journey. In fact, the discovery has been made that the journey is impossible."

Christoforo's rage was tempered with relief. The failure of others did not affect his dream.

He held it intact, but he had made one important discovery. He could expect no help in Lisbon. He had wasted his time.

"You are now convinced that what you propose is impossible, I hope?" he was asked.

Christoforo's eyes were as hard and brilliant as aquamarines.

"I am convinced of the impossibility of getting help from Portugal," he said.

Now the visitor was smiling broadly. "I trust business is good?"

Christoforo lifted his hands in a gesture of despair. "What do you think, my good sir? Do you think that Lisbon is a city of adventurers who would be interested in my charts and instruments?"

"Sailors need them on their journeys, do they not?"

"But in Lisbon!" said Christoforo, his anger rising. "Perhaps the sale of such articles would be more profitable in towns where men do not set out to sea and then allow a storm or two to drive them back to port."

"You are an angry man, Christoforo Colombo."

"I should be less angry if I were alone."

The visitor rose abruptly and left him.

Christoforo sat down at the table and stared ahead of him. Little Diego crept down and stood watching him.

Diego longed to run to his father and comfort him, but he was afraid. He could understand and share the terrible disappointment.

Then Christoforo saw the small figure standing there, and he smiled slowly. He beckoned, and the boy ran to him. Christoforo took him into his arms, and for a while neither spoke.

Then Christoforo said: "Diego, let us start packing the charts and a few things that we shall need for a journey."

"A long journey, Father?"

"A very long journey. We are leaving Lisbon. Lisbon has cheated us. I shall not rest until I have shaken its dust from off my feet."

"Where shall we go, Father?"

"We have little money. We shall go on foot, my son. There is only one place we can make for."

Diego looked expectantly into his father's face. Then he saw the disappointment fade; he saw the rebirth of hope.

"They say Isabella, the Queen of Castile, is a wise woman. My son, let us prepare with all speed. We shall go to Spain and there attempt to interest Isabella in our new world."

* * *

The journey was long and arduous. They were often hungry, always footsore. But their spirits never flagged. Christoforo knew with absolute certainty that one day he would interest some wealthy and influential person in his schemes; as for eight-year-old Diego, he had been brought up with the dream and he too never doubted.

In his scrip Christoforo carried his charts; he also wore a dagger, for the way through the Alemtejo district was wild and infested with robbers.

It was late afternoon; they had left the province of Huelva behind them and were approaching the estuary of the Rio Tinto.

The month was January, and a cold wind was blowing in from the Atlantic.

"Diego, my son," said Christoforo, "you are weary."

"I am weary, Father," the boy admitted.

They had left the small town of Palos two or three miles behind, and Diego had wondered why they did not stop there and ask for shelter. Christoforo, however, had walked purposefully on.

"Soon we shall have a roof over our heads, my son. Can you keep up your spirits for another mile?"

"Why, yes, Father."

Diego threw back his shoulders and walked on beside his father. Then, as they trudged on in the direction of Cadiz and Gibraltar, and the wind caught the sand and flung it among the pine trees which grew sparsely here and there, he understood, for in the distance he saw the walls of a monastery and he knew that this was the place to which his father was taking him.

"There we will ask for food and shelter for the night," said Christoforo. He did not add that he hoped for more. He was now inside Spain; and in the monasteries were learned men who might listen to his talk of an undiscovered world.

If, however, he could interest no one at the Franciscan Monastery of Santa Maria de la Rabida he must pass hopefully on.

They approached the gate, and Christoforo addressed the lay brother whose duty it was to guard it.

"I come to beg food and shelter for myself and my child," he said. "We have come far; we are poor, weary and hungry. I believe you will not deny us charity."

The lay brother looked at them—the travel-stained man and the weary little boy. He said: "You are right, traveller, to expect charity from us. It is our boast that we never turn the weary and hungry from our gates. Enter."

Christoforo took Diego by the hand and they entered the monastery of Santa Maria de la Rabida.

They were taken to wash off the travel stains in the great trough, and when this was done they were led to the kitchens and set at a table where hot soup and bread were given them.

They fed ravenously; and while they ate, a young monk who was passing paused to look with curiosity at the man and boy and said: "Good day to you, travellers. Have you come far?"

"From Lisbon," answered Christoforo.

"And you have a long journey ahead of you?"

"We travel hopefully," answered Christoforo, "and it may be, if we are fortunate, to the Court of Isabella, the Queen."

The monk was interested. Occasionally travellers stopped at the monastery, but never before had he encountered a man with that almost fanatical light in his eyes; never had he seen such a shabby traveller on his way to visit the Queen.

Christoforo was determined to exploit the interest of the monk. It was not by chance that he had come to this monastery. He was aware that the Prior, Fray Juan Perez de Marchena, was a man of wide interests and a friend of Fernando de Talavera, who was confessor to, and in high favour with, the Queen herself.

So he talked to the monk of his ambitions; he patted his scrip and told him: "In here I have plans, I have charts. . . . If I could find the means to equip an expedition, I would find a New World."

It was fascinating talk to the monk who lived life within the quiet walls of the monastery, and he listened entranced while Christoforo entertained him with tales of his adventures off the coast of Guinea and Iceland.

Diego had finished his soup, and his father's was growing cold. The boy anxiously tugged his father's sleeve and nodded at the soup, whereupon Christoforo smiled and finished it.

The monk said: "And the child, he is to go with you to this New World?"

"There are hazards, and he is young," said Christoforo. "But if other provision cannot be made for him . . ."

"You are a man of dreams," said the monk.

"Many of us are, and those who are not, should be. All that is accomplished on Earth must begin as a dream."

The monk rose and hurried away to his duties, but he could not forget the strange talk of the traveller; he sought out the Prior and told him of the unusual guests who had sought comfort within their walls.

* * *

Diego lay on a pallet in a small cell. He was so tired that he was soon fast asleep.

Meanwhile the Prior of Santa Maria de la Rabida had sent for Christoforo.

In the small room with bare walls apart from a large crucifix, and by the light of two candles, Christoforo spread his charts on the table and talked to the Prior of his ambitions.

Fray Juan believed he understood men. He looked at that weather-beaten face with the bright seaman's eyes and he said to himself: This man has genius.

Fray Juan was fascinated. It was late, but he could not release the traveller. He must hear more.

And when they had talked for many hours he said suddenly:

"Christoforo Colombo, I believe in you. I believe in your New World."

Then Christoforo covered his face with his hands and there were tears in his eyes. He was ashamed of himself, but so intense was his relief that he could not hide his emotion.

"You will help me to obtain an audience with the Queen?" he asked.

"I will do all in my power," answered Fray Juan. "You know it is not easy. She has little time. There has been trouble in Navarre, and it is the great wish of the Queen to see a Christian Spain. The war with Granada is imminent . . . in fact it has already begun. It may be that the Queen, with so much to occupy her thoughts, will have little patience with . . . a dream."

"You hold out little hope, Fray Juan."

"I implore you to have patience," was the answer. "But listen. I have a plan. I will not approach Fernando de Talavera. He is a good man, the Queen's confessor, and I know him well, but he is so anxious to make war on the Infidel that he might be impatient of your schemes. I will, however, give you an introduction to the Duke of Medina Sidonia, who is rich and powerful and could bring your case to the notice of the Court."

"How can I show my gratitude?"

"By discovering your New World. By justifying this faith I have in you."

"It shall be done," said Christoforo as though he were taking an oath.

"There is one matter which needs consideration," said Fray Juan. "I refer to the boy, your son."

Christoforo's face changed and anxiety took the place of exhilaration.

Fray Juan was smiling. "I wish to set your mind at rest concerning him. Go to the Queen, go and find your New World. While you do these things I will undertake the charge of your son. He shall remain with us here at Rabida, and we will clothe and feed him, we will shelter and educate him until your return."

Christoforo rose. He could not speak. The tears were visible in his eyes now.

"Do not thank me," said Fray Juan. "Let us get to our knees and thank God. Let us do that . . . together."

THE ROYAL FAMILY

THROUGHOUT the Kingdom of Granada there was mourning. Never before had a Moorish Sultan fallen captive to a Christian army. Nor was Boabdil the only prisoner in the hands of the enemy. Many of the captured were powerful men and, as the character of Ferdinand was beginning to be known throughout Granada, it was calculated that large ransoms would be demanded before they were allowed to return.

"Allah has turned his face from us," mourned the people. "The hostile star of Islam is scattering its malignant influences upon us. Can this mean the downfall of the Mussulman Empire?"

* * *

Muley Abul Hassan discussed the position with his brother, El Zagal.

"Boabdil must be released without delay. The effect of his captivity on the people is becoming disastrous."

El Zagal agreed with his brother. He was certain that Boabdil should be returned to them so that they might quash his rebellion.

"Offer a ransom," he said. "Offer a sum which Ferdinand will find it difficult to refuse."

"It shall be done," said Muley Abul Hassan.

* * *

The Sultana Zoraya was torn between anger and anxiety. Her son, the captive of the Christians! He must be released at once.

She raged against Boabdil, who had never been a warrior. When all was well she would devote herself to the upbringing of Boabdil's young son and make a warrior out of him.

It was imperative that Boabdil should not be allowed to remain in the hands of his captives. If he were, the people of Granada would forget they had called him their Sultan. She foresaw a return to the undisputed rule of Muley Abul Hassan. The Moors might, in their adversity, forget their differences. Then what would happen to Boabdil? Would he be left to fret in his Christian prison? What would happen to her?

When she heard that Muley Abul Hassan had offered a ransom she was determined that further delay would be dangerous. Boabdil must not be delivered into the hands of his father.

"What ransom has Muley Abul Hassan offered?" she demanded to know. "No matter what it is, I must offer a greater."

* * *

Ferdinand was gleeful. This was an unexpected stroke of good fortune. Boabdil was in the hands of General the Count of Cabra, having been captured by some of his men.

"Highness," ran the Count's message, "Boabdil, King of Granada, is now a prisoner in my castle of Baena. Here I am according him all the courtesy which his rank demands while I await Your Highness's instructions."

Ferdinand sat with Isabella in the Royal Council Chamber, and the fate of Boabdil was considered.

Isabella knew that Ferdinand was thinking of the large ransoms offered by Muley Abul Hassan and the Sultana Zoraya, and that he longed to lay his hands on their gold.

Ferdinand addressed the Council, saying that the ransom should be accepted and Boabdil sent back to his people.

There was an immediate outcry. Send back such a valuable prisoner! The King of Granada himself in their hands, and he to be sent back on the payment of a certain sum!

Isabella listened to the impassioned pleading, to the clash of opinion.

The Marquis of Cadiz rose and said: "Your Highnesses and Gentlemen of the Council, our one thought should be to weaken our enemy, to prepare him to our advantage for the final battle. What we have to consider is whether Boabdil is of more use to us here as our prisoner than there, free to cause trouble in his own Kingdom."

"He is our captive!" was the answer. "He, the leader, the King! What is an army without a leader?"

The Marquis answered: "But there were two leaders, other than Boabdil, in Granada—Muley Abul Hassan and El Zagal."

Ferdinand had begun to speak and, as she listened to him, Isabella rejoiced in his shrewdness.

"It is clear what must be done," said Ferdinand. "If Boabdil remains here there will soon be peace within Granada. Muley Abul Hassan will return to the throne with the support of his brother. There will only be one ruler . . . no longer the Old King and the Little King. By our capture of Boabdil we shall have ended civil war in Granada, and one of the greatest aids to our cause *is* the civil war in Granada."

Isabella lifted her hand then and said: "I am sure that the path we must take is clear to us all now. The King is right. Boabdil must be returned to his people. We must not help to make peace within the Kingdom of Granada. Return Boabdil to his people, and once more there, civil war will be intensified."

"And we shall have the ransom money," added Ferdinand with a gay smile. "Zoraya's ransom money, for naturally he must be returned to his mother, who will help him to reorganize his forces against his father and uncle. And by God's good grace the ransom money which she offers is greater than that suggested by Muley Abul Hassan. Heaven is with us." The Council then declared itself to be in agreement with Ferdinand' suggestion; and Ferdinand took the Queen's hand and they, with a few of their highest ministers, retired to draw up the treaty with Boabdil.

* * *

Ferdinand received Boabdil at Cordova, determined to charm his captive into a ready acceptance of his proposals.

When Boabdil would have knelt, Ferdinand put out his hand to prevent his doing so.

"We meet as Kings," said Ferdinand.

The two Kings sat side by side in chairs which had been set for them.

"You are blessed with a mother who gives all she has for your sake," said Ferdinand.

"It is true," Boabdil replied.

"And, because she has pleaded with us so touchingly, the Queen and myself are inclined to grant her request."

"Your Highness is munificent," Boabdil murmured.

Ferdinand did not deny it. "I will tell you briefly what terms we have drawn up, and when you have agreed to them, and your mother has sent the ransom, we shall hold you here no longer, but shall allow you to depart; for if you give us your word that you will accept these terms we shall trust you."

Boabdil bowed his head in grateful thanks.

"We grant a truce of two years' standing to such territory within the Kingdom of Granada which is under your dominion."

"I gratefully accept that," answered Boabdil.

"You have been captured in battle, and it will be necessary for you to make some reparation," said Ferdinand smoothly. "Our people would not be pleased if you did not."

"It is understandable," agreed Boabdil.

"Then you shall return to us four hundred Christian slaves for whom we shall pay no ransom."

"They shall be yours."

"You shall pay annually twelve thousand gold *doblas* to the Queen and myself."

Boabdil looked less pleased, but he had known that Ferdinand would require some such reward for his clemency, and there was nothing to be done but to grant it.

"We must ask you for a free passage through your Kingdom, should we wish it while making war on your father and your uncle."

Boabdil was taken aback by this suggestion. Ferdinand was calmly suggesting that he should play the traitor to his own country; and although Boabdil was ready to make war on his father, he hesitated before agreeing to allow the Christians a free passage through his land.

Ferdinand passed on quickly: "Then you may go free; but should I wish to see you at any time to discuss the differences between our kingdoms, you must come immediately to my command; and I shall require you to give your son into my possession together with the sons of certain of your nobles, that we may hold them as sureties for your good faith."

Boabdil was stunned by these terms. But he saw the need to escape from captivity, and that there was nothing to be done but to accept them.

So Ferdinand took the ransom offered by the Sultana, and Boabdil returned to his people, bewildered, humiliated, aware that he had agreed to act as Ferdinand's pawn to be moved at his will; and he could be certain that those moves would be made for the aggrandizement of the Sovereigns and the detriment of his own people.

Boabdil, saddened and chastened, wished that he had never listened to his mother's advice, wished that he was now fighting the Christians on the side of his father.

* * *

Ferdinand was saying his farewell to Isabella before he set out on his journey to Aragon.

Isabella was doing her best to be patient, but it was not easy. They had made great strides in the war against the Moors; Boabdil could be said to be their creature, yet they lacked the means to continue the war against the Moors in a way which could be conclusive.

"Always," cried Ferdinand, "we are faced with this lack of money."

Isabella agreed that this was so and, agreeing, forgave

Ferdinand his preoccupation with possessions. She knew there was a reproach in his words. She was in a position to replenish the royal coffers, yet she steadfastly refused to act. She was determined that her rule should be just, and that she would give no favours in exchange for bribes. Even though the moment seemed ripe for the attack on the Moors, she would not resort to dishonourable means of raising money. She was certain that God would turn His favour from her if she did.

"What can we do?" he demanded now. "Merely destroy their crops, merely attack their small hamlets, lay waste their land, set fire to their vineyards! This we will do, but until we have the means of raising a mighty army we can never hope for complete conquest."

"We shall raise that army," said Isabella. "Have no doubt of that."

"It is to be hoped that, by the time we do, we shall not have lost the advantage we now hold."

"If so, we shall gain others," answered Isabella. "It is the will of God that we shall rule over an all-Christian Spain, and I have never for a moment doubted it."

"And in the meantime we must tarry. We must show ourselves as being too weak, too poor, to prosecute the war."

"Alas that it should be so!"

"But it need not be."

Isabella gave him that firm yet affectionate smile. "When the time comes God and all Heaven will be beside us," she said. "Why, now your presence is needed in Aragon, so it is no bad thing that we had not planned to make our great attack on Granada."

Ferdinand was inclined to be sullen. This was one of those occasions when he blamed her methods as the cause of their inability to prosecute the war.

But she was convinced that she was right. She must act honourably and according to her own lights, or she would lose that belief in her destiny. God was with her, she was sure, and He would only support that which was just. If He had been slow in giving her the means of attacking the Moors, she must wait in patience, telling herself that the ways of Heaven were often inscrutable.

She wondered now whether she should tell Ferdinand that she hoped she was pregnant once more. It was early yet, and perhaps it would be unwise to raise his hopes. He would begin to plan for another son. And of her four children only one was a boy, so perhaps her fifth would also be a girl.

No, she would keep this little matter to herself. She would

watch him ride away with Torquemada into Aragon, whence reports had come that heretics abounded; Torquemada had been denouncing them and was eager that the methods which were being used in Castile should be put into force in Aragon. Away with the old easy-going tribunals! Torquemada's Inquisition should be taken to Aragon.

"It may well be," she told Ferdinand, "that God wishes to see how we bring tormented souls back to His kingdom, before He helps us to take possession of those of the Moors."

"It may be so," agreed Ferdinand. "Farewell, my Queen and wife."

Once more he embraced her, but even as he did so she wondered whether, when he reached Aragon, he would make his way to the mother of that illegitimate son, of whom he had been so besottedly fond that he had made him an Archbishop at the age of six.

* * *

During that summer Isabella found time to be with Beatriz de Bobadilla.

"It would seem," she said to her friend, "that it is only when I am about to have a child that I have an opportunity of being with my family and my friends."

"Highness, when the Holy War is over, when the Moors have been driven from Spain, then you will have a little more time for us. It will be a great joy and pleasure to us all."

"To me also. And, Beatriz, I believe that day is not so far off as I once feared it might be. Now that the Inquisition is working so zealously throughout Castile, I feel that one part of our plan is succeeding. Beatriz, bring the altar-cloth I am working on. I will not waste time while we talk."

Beatriz sent a woman for the needlework and, when it was brought, they settled down to it.

Isabella worked busily with the coloured threads. She found the work very soothing.

"How do matters go in Aragon?" asked Beatriz.

Isabella frowned down at her work. "I hear that there is opposition there to the Inquisition, but Ferdinand and Torquemada are determined that it shall be established and that it shall become as effective as it is here in Castile."

"There are many New Christians in Aragon."

"Yes, and I believe they have been practising Jewish rites in private. Otherwise why should they fear the coming of the Inquisition?"

Beatriz murmured: "They fear that accusations may be brought against them, and that they may not be able to prove their innocence."

"But," said Isabella mildly, "if they are innocent, why should they not be able to prove it?"

"Perhaps torture might force a victim to confess not only what is true but what is completely untrue. Perhaps it is this they fear."

"If they tell the truth immediately, and name those who have shared their sins, the torture will not be applied. I expect we shall have a little trouble in Aragon, although I do not doubt that it will be promptly quelled, as the Susan affair was in Seville."

"Let us hope so," said Beatriz.

"My dear friend, Tomás de Torquemada, has sent two excellent men into Aragon. I know he has the utmost confidence in Arbués and Juglar."

"Let us hope that they are not over-stern—at first," said Beatriz quietly. "It is the sudden change from lethargy to iron discipline that seems to terrify the people."

"They cannot be too stern in the service of the Faith." Isabella spoke firmly.

Beatriz thought it might be wise to change the subject, and after a slight pause asked after the health of the Infanta Isabella.

The Queen frowned slightly. "Her health does give me cause for anxiety. She is not as strong, I fear, as the other three. In fact, our baby, young Maria, seems to be the healthiest member of the family. Do you think so, Beatriz?"

"I think that Maria has perfect health, but so have Juan and Juana. As for Isabella, she certainly has this tendency to catch cold. But I think that will pass as she grows older."

"Oh, Beatriz," said Isabella suddenly, "I do hope this one will be a boy."

"Because Ferdinand wishes it?" asked Beatriz.

"Yes, perhaps that is so. For myself, I would be content with another girl. Ferdinand wants sons."

"He has one."

"He has more than one," said Isabella after some hesitation. "And that is a great sorrow to me. I know of one illegitimate son. It is the Archbishop who succeeded to the See of Saragossa when he was but six years old. Ferdinand dotes on him. I have heard it whispered that there is another son. And I know there are daughters."

"These things will happen, Highness. They have always been so."

"I am foolish to think too much of them. We are often apart, and Ferdinand is not a man who could remain faithful to one woman."

Beatriz laid her hand on that of the Queen.

"Highness, may an old friend speak frankly?"

"You know you may."

"My thoughts are taken back to the days before your marriage. You made an ideal of Ferdinand. You made an image—a man who had all the virtues of a great soldier, king and statesman, and yet was as austere in his nature as you are yourself. You made an impossible ideal, Highness."

"You are right, Beatriz."

"Such a person as you conjured up is not to be found in Christendom."

"Then I should be content with what I have."

"Highness, you should be content indeed. You have a partner who has many qualities to bring to this governing of your country; you have children. Think of the kings who long for children and cannot get them."

"Beatriz, my dear, you have done me much good. I will be thankful for what I have. I will not ask for more. If God sees fit to give me another girl, I shall be happy. I shall forget that I longed for a son."

Isabella was smiling. She had decided that for the next few months she would give herself up to the enjoyment of her family; she would spend much time in the nurseries with her children; and it would be as though she were not Queen of Castile but merely the mother of a boy and three girls, awaiting the arrival of a new baby.

* * *

Ferdinand had returned from Aragon, reluctantly, Isabella believed.

It was natural, Isabella told herself, that his first thoughts should have been for Aragon, and she believed his presence had been needed there.

When he returned to her after a long absence he was always the passionate lover: A state of affairs which had delighted her in their earlier relationship, but which she now knew to be due to Ferdinand's love of change.

He was an adventurer in all respects. And she accepted him not as the embodiment of an ideal, but as the man he was.

He had risen from their bed, although only the first streaks of dawn were in the sky. He was restless, she saw, and found it difficult to lie still.

He sat on the bed, his embroidered robe about him, while she sat up and studied him gravely.

"Ferdinand," she said, "do you not think it would be better if you confided your troubles to me?"

He smiled at her ruefully. "Ours is a troublous realm, Isabella," he said. "We are sovereigns of two states, and it would seem that in order to serve one we must neglect the other."

Isabella said firmly: "Events in Castile are moving towards a climax. Since the capture of Boabdil we have made such great strides towards victory that surely it cannot be long delayed."

"Granada is a mighty kingdom which I have likened to a pomegranate. I have sworn to pluck the pomegranate dry, but there are still more juicy seeds to be taken. And meanwhile the French hold my provinces of Rousillon and Cerdagne."

Isabella was startled. "Ferdinand, we cannot face a war on two fronts."

"A war against the French would be a just one," urged Ferdinand.

"The war against the Moors is a holy one," Isabella replied.

Ferdinand was a little sullen. "My presence is needed in Aragon," he said.

She wondered then whether it was herself whom he wanted to leave for some other woman, whether he longed to be with another family, not the one he had through her. She felt sick at heart to contemplate his infidelity; yet as she looked at him, so handsome, so virile, she remembered Beatriz' words. She had greatly desired marriage with him. Young and handsome, he had appealed to her so strongly when she compared him with other suitors who had been selected for her.

No, she thought, it is not some other woman, some other family which calls him: It is Aragon. He is too firm a ruler, too clever a diplomatist ever to allow his personal emotions to interfere with his ambitions.

Not another woman, not the mother of the Archbishop of Saragossa, nor the Archbishop himself, nor any of those other mistresses whom he had doubtless found more to his taste than his chaste wife Isabella—it was Aragon.

As for herself, she longed to please him. There were times when she almost wished that she could have changed her nature, that she could have been more like what she imagined the others to be—voluptuously beautiful, as brimming over with sensual passion as he was himself. But she would suppress such thoughts.

Such a life was not for her. She was a Queen—the Queen of Castile—and her duty came before any such carnal pleasure, the safety of her kingdom before a contented life.

She resisted an impulse to put out a hand and take his, to say to him: "Ferdinand, love me . . . me only; you may have anything in exchange that I could give you."

She thought then of Christ's temptation in the wilderness, and she said coldly: "The Holy War must be continued at the expense of all else."

And Ferdinand rose from the bed. He walked to the window and looked out, watching the dawn encroach on the darkness.

His back was towards her, but she saw that there was an angry gesture in the way he held his head.

It was a scene which had been repeated so many times in their life together. It was the Queen of Castile in command, not only of her own nature, but of the lesser ruler of Aragon.

* * *

The children, with the exception perhaps of Juana, were delighted to have their mother with them. Juana was the wild one, the one who could not conform to the high standard set by her mother, the one who fidgeted during church services, who refused to confess *all* her sins to her confessor, the one who struck a certain cold fear into her mother's heart on many occasions.

Isabella was six months pregnant, and it was during her pregnancies that she relaxed her stern hold upon herself to some extent.

I am, after all, a mother, she excused herself, and these children of mine will one day be rulers of some part of this Earth. I must treat them as a very important part of my life.

If at this time it had been possible to continue with the war against the Moors with vigour, she would have neglected everything to do so. But it was not possible; it would take several years to build up the army they needed. There was nothing she could do at present to speed up matters in that direction. What she must think of was having a healthy pregnancy and recovering her strength as soon as possible. So for these few months she gave herself to domesticity more wholeheartedly than she usually could.

She loved her children devotedly. She wanted to make sure that they were receiving the best education which could be provided for them—remembering how she herself had missed it. At the same time their spiritual education must not be neglected.

She wanted the girls to be both good rulers and good wives and parents; she insisted that they sit with her and learn to embroider; and there was nothing which made her more contented than to have her children with her while she and the girls worked on an altar-cloth, and Juan sat on a stool close by and read aloud to them.

This they were now doing, and again and again her eyes would stray from her work to rest on one or other of her children. Her pale and lovely daughter, Isabella, her first-born, who still coughed a little too frequently for her mother's comfort, was beautiful, bending over her work. They would have to find a husband for her soon.

It will be more than I can bear, to lose her, thought Isabella.

And there was Juan—perhaps the best loved of them all. Who could help loving Juan? He was the perfect child. Not only was he the boy for whom Ferdinand had longed, he had the sweetest nature of all the children; he was docile, yet excelled in all those sports in which Ferdinand wished to see him excel. His tutors discovered in him a desire to please, which meant that he learned his lessons quickly and well. He was beautiful—at least in the eyes of his mother. She felt her love overflowing as she looked at him. In her thoughts she had long called him Angel. She had even done so openly, and consequently he was beginning to be known in the family circle by that name.

There was Juana—little Suegra. Almost defiantly Isabella insisted on the nickname. It was as though she wished to emphasize the resemblance between this child and her grandmother, Ferdinand's sprightly and clever mother. Isabella tried not to see a subtler resemblance, that between her own sad mother and this child.

It was difficult to avoid this comparison. If there was trouble Juana would be in it. She had charm; it was in her very wildness. The others were serene children; perhaps they took after their mother. Yet little Juana, though she might have the features of Ferdinand's mother, had that in her—at least, so Isabella often told herself—which bore a terrifying similarity to the frailty of the poor sick lady at Arevalo.

And little Maria, the plain one, stolid, reliable, good little Maria! She would give her parents little concern, Isabella guessed. Strangely enough—for this very reason—she did not give her mother the same delight as did the others.

Isabella wondered whether she herself, when a child, had been rather like Maria—quiet, serene, docile . . . and not very attractive.

She saw that Juana was not working, and that her part of the altar-cloth was not as neat as that of the others.

Isabella leaned forward and tapped the child on her knee.

"Come, Suegra," she said, "there is work to be done."

"I do not like needlework," said Juana, which made young Isabella catch her breath in horror. Juana went on: "It is no use scowling at me, sister. I do not like needlework."

"This, my child," said the Queen, "is for the altar. Do you not wish to work for a holy purpose?"

"No, Highness," said Juana promptly.

"That is very wrong," said the Queen sternly.

"But Your Highness asked me what I wanted," Juana pointed out. "I must tell the truth, for if I did not that would be a lie, and I should have to confess it, and do a penance. It is very wrong to tell lies."

"Come here," said Isabella; and Juana came to her. Isabella held the child by her shoulders and drew her close to her. "It is true," she went on, "that you must not tell lies. But it is true also that you must discipline yourself. You must learn to like doing what is good."

Juana's eyes, which now bore a strong resemblance to those of Ferdinand, flashed in rebellion. "But Highness, if you do not like . . ." she began.

"That is enough," said Isabella. "Now you will work on this cloth tomorrow until you have completed your share of it, and if it is badly done you will unpick your stitches and do them again until it is well done."

Juana's lower lip protruded and she said defiantly: "I shall not be able to go to Mass if I must sit over my needlework."

The Queen was aware of a tension among the children, and she said: "What has been happening here?"

Her eldest daughter looked uncomfortable; so did Juan.

"Come," said Isabella, "I must know the truth. You, Angel, you tell me."

"Highness, I do not know of what you speak."

"I think you do, my son. Your sister Juana has been wicked in some way. I pray you tell me what she has done."

"I . . . I could not say, Highness," said Juan; but his beautiful face had turned a shade paler and he was afraid that he was going to be forced to say something which he would rather not.

Isabella could not bear to hurt him. His kindly nature would not allow him to betray his sister; and at the same time he was anxious not to disobey his mother.

She turned to Isabella; Isabella also did not wish to betray her sister.

The Queen was faintly irritated and yet proud of them. She would not have them tellers of tales against each other. She respected this family loyalty.

And fortunately she was saved from forcing an answer, by Juana herself—bold, fearless Juana, with the wild light in her eyes.

"I will tell you, Highness," she said. "I often do not go to church. I run away and hide, so that they cannot find me. I do not like to go to church. I like to dance and sing. So I hide . . . and they cannot find me, and so they go without me."

Isabella surveyed this defiant child with a stern expression which would have filled the others with terror. But Juana merely stood her ground, her handsome little head held high, her eyes brilliant.

"So," said Isabella slowly, "you have been guilty of this wickedness. I am ashamed that a child of mine could behave thus. You, the daughter of the Sovereigns of Castile and Aragon! You whose father is the greatest soldier in the world and who has brought peace within these kingdoms! You are a Princess of the royal house. You would seem to forget this."

"I do not forget," said Juana, "but it does not make me want to go to church."

"Juan," said the Queen to her son, "go and bring to me your sister's governess."

Juan, white-faced obeyed. As for Juana, she stood regarding her mother with eyes that dilated with a certain fear. She believed that she was to be beaten, and she could not endure corporal punishment; not that she feared the pain; it was the attack upon her dignity which was so upsetting.

She turned and would have run from the room, but the Queen had caught her skirt. This was a very embarrassing situation for the Queen to encounter, and she felt a physical sickness which she found it difficult to control.

She told herself that it was due to her pregnancy; but there was a deep fear within her; and as she held the struggling child in a firm grip she felt a great love for this wild daughter come over her. She wanted to hold the child to her breast and weep over her; she wanted to comfort her, to soothe her, to beg the others to kneel with her and pray that Juana might not go the way of her grandmother.

"Let me go!" cried Juana. "Let me go! I don't want to stay here. I don't want to go to Mass."

Isabella held the child's head against her; she was aware of the shocked and wondering eyes of Isabella and Maria.

"Be quiet, my daughter," she warned. "Be still. It will be better for you if you are."

The quiet tones of her mother soothed the little girl somewhat, and she laid her head against the Queen's breast and stayed there. Isabella thought she was like an imprisoned bird, a wild bird who knew that it was hopeless to struggle.

Juan had returned with the governess, who looked very frightened to have been summoned thus to the presence of the Queen.

Isabella, still holding her daughter against her, acknowledged the governess's deep curtsey and said in a clear expressionless voice: "Is it true that the Infanta Juana has not been attending church?"

The governess stammered: "Highness, it was unavoidable."

"Unavoidable! I do not understand how that can be. It must not happen again. It must be avoided."

"Yes, Highness."

"How many times has this occurred?" asked the Queen.

The governess hesitated, and the Queen went on quickly: "But it is enough that it has occurred once. The soul of the Infanta has been put in jeopardy. It must never occur again. Take the Infanta away now. She is to be beaten severely. And if she attempts to absent herself from church again, I wish to be told. Her punishment then will be even more severe."

Juana had lifted her head and was staring at her mother pleadingly: "No!" she cried. "Please, Highness, no!"

"Take the Infanta away now and do my bidding. I shall satisfy myself that my orders have been carried out."

The governess dropped a deep curtsey and laid her hand on Juana's arm. Juana clung to the chair and would not move. The governess took her arm and pulled and Juana's face grew scarlet with exertion as she clung to the chair.

The Queen smartly slapped the small hand. Juana let out a great wail; then the governess seized her and dragged her from the room.

There was silence in the nursery as the door closed on them.

The Queen said: "Come, my daughters, we have this cloth to finish. Juan, continue to read to us."

And Juan obeyed, and the girls sewed, while in the distance they heard the loud protesting screams as Juana's strokes were administered.

The children took covert looks at their mother, but she was placidly sewing as though she did not hear.

They did not know that she was praying silently, and the words which kept repeating themselves in her brain were: "Holy Mother of God, save my darling child. Help me to preserve her from the fate of her grandmother. Guide me. Help me to do what is right for her."

* * *

A rider had come galloping to Cordova from Saragossa. There was news which he must impart immediately to Ferdinand.

Isabella knew of his arrival, but she did not seek out Ferdinand; she would wait until he told her what was happening. She herself was determined to remain the ruler of Castile; she left the governing of Aragon to him.

She knew that this trouble might well be concerned with the setting up of the Inquisition in Aragon. The first *auto de fé*, under the new Inquisition over which Torquemada presided, had taken place in May; this had been followed by another in June. She had heard that the people of Aragon regarded these ceremonies with the same sentiments as the people of Castile had done. They looked on in horrified bewilderment; they seemed stunned; they accepted the installation of the Inquisition almost meekly. But in Seville their meekness had been proved to be part of their shock; and, when that had subsided, men, such as Diego de Susan, had sought to rise against the Holy Office.

Isabella had warned Ferdinand that they must be equally watchful in Aragon.

She discovered that she had been right, for Ferdinand came quickly to tell her the news. She knew he was anxious and she always rejoiced that in times of crisis they stood together, all differences forgotten.

"Trouble," said Ferdinand, "trouble in Saragossa. A plot among the New Christians against the Inquisition."

"I trust that the Inquisitors are safe."

"Safe!" cried Ferdinand. "Murder has been done. By the Holy Mother of God, these criminals shall pay for their crimes."

He then told her the news which had been brought to him from Saragossa. It appeared that, as in Seville, the wealthy New Christians of Saragossa had believed that they could drive the Inquisition out of their town. Their plan was to assassinate the Inquisitors, Gaspar Juglar and Pedro Arbués de Epila, who had been working so zealously to provide victims for the hideous spectacles which had taken place in the town.

Several attempts had been made to murder these two men and they, being aware of this, had taken special precautions. They wore armour under their robes, but this had not saved them.

The conspirators had planned to murder their victims in the church, and had lain in wait for them there. Gaspar Juglar had not attended the church because he had become suddenly and mysteriously ill. It was evident that another plan had been put into action concerning him. So Arbués went to the Metropolitan church alone.

"It was quiet in the church," cried Ferdinand in anger, "and they waited as bloodthirsty wolves wait for the gentle lamb."

Isabella bowed her head in sorrow, and it did not occur to her that it was a little incongruous to describe as a gentle lamb, the man who had been hustling the people of Saragossa into the prisons of the Inquisition, into the dungeons where their bodies were racked and their limbs dislocated that they might inform on their friends.

She would have replied had this been put to her: The Inquisitors are working for Holy Church and the Holy Inquisition, and everything they do is in the name of the Christian Faith. If they find it necessary to inflict a little pain on those who have offended against Holy Church, of what importance can this be, since these people are destined for eternal damnation? The body suffers transient pain, but the soul is in danger of eternal torment. Moreover, there is always the hope that the heretic's soul may be saved through his earthly torments.

She said to Ferdinand: "I pray you tell me what evil deed was done in the church."

"He came into the church from the cloisters," said Ferdinand, his face working with emotion. "It was dark, for it was midnight, and there was no light except that from the altar lamp. These wicked men fell upon Arbués, and although he wore mail under his robes, although there was a steel lining to his cap, they wounded him . . . to death."

"They have been arrested?"

"Not yet, but we shall discover them."

A messenger came to the apartment to tell them that Tomás de Torquemada was outside and implored immediate admission.

"Bring him to us," said Ferdinand. "We need his help. We shall bring these criminals to justice. We will show them what punishment will be meted out to those who lay hands on God's elected."

Torquemada's emaciated face was twisted with emotion.

"Your Highnesses, this terrible news has been brought to me."

"The Queen and I are deeply distressed and determined that these murderers shall be brought to justice."

Torquemada said: "I am despatching three of my most trusted Inquisitors to Saragossa with all speed. Fray Juan Colvera, Doctor Alonso de Alarcon and Fray Pedro de Monterubio . . . all good men. I trust this meets with Your Highnesses' approval."

"It has our approval," said Ferdinand.

"I fear," said Isabella, "that there will be some delay, and that these good servants cannot hope to arrive in time to prevent the escape of all the criminals."

"I shall discover them," said Torquemada, his lips tightly compressed. "If I have every man and woman in Saragossa on the rack, I'll discover them."

Isabella nodded.

Torquemada went on: "The people of Saragossa have been deeply shocked by this murder. The whole town is in an uproar."

"Yes," said Ferdinand; and quite suddenly all the anger went out of his voice, and it was soft, almost caressing. "I hear that riots were avoided by the prompt action of one of its citizens."

"Is that so?" said Isabella. "An important citizen, he must have been."

"Yes," said Ferdinand. "He left his palace and summoned the justices and grandees. He placed himself at the head of them and rode bravely to meet those who threatened to burn and pillage the city. He is but seventeen, and I fear he endangered his life; but he was very brave."

"He should be rewarded," Isabella declared.

"So shall he be," answered Ferdinand.

He had moved towards the window as though deep in thought, and that tender smile still curved his mouth.

Isabella turned to Torquemada. "You know who this young man is?" she asked.

"Why, yes, Highness. It is the young Archbishop of Saragossa."

"Oh," said Isabella. "I believe I have heard of this young man. It was a brave action and one which delights the King of Aragon."

And she thought: How he loves his son! Rarely have I seen his face so gentle as when he spoke of him; never have I seen him so quickly turned from anger.

She felt an impulse to ask questions about this young man, to demand of Ferdinand how often they met, what further honours he had showered upon him.

It is because of the child within me, she told herself. I am a very weak woman at these times.

Then she began to talk to Torquemada of this terrible occurrence in Saragossa, and how she was in complete agreement with his determination to meet opposition with greater severity.

Ferdinand joined them; he had recovered from the emotion which the mention of his beloved natural son had caused him.

The three of them talked earnestly of the manner in which they would deal with the rebels of Saragossa.

CRISTOBAL COLON AND BEATRIZ DE ARANA

In the nursery of the Palace at Cordova, Isabella sat holding a child a few months old, on her lap.

This was her daughter, Catalina, who had been born in the December of the preceding year. Her hopes had been in some way disappointed, for she had longed to present Ferdinand with another boy. But Juan was still her only son, and here was her fourth daughter.

Isabella could not continue to feel this disappointment as she looked at the tiny creature in her arms. She loved the child dearly and, on the birth of little Catalina, she had made up her mind that she would not allow herself to be so continually separated from her family.

She glanced up at Beatriz de Bobadilla, who was with her once more, bustling about the apartment as though she were mistress of it.

Isabella smiled at her friend. It was very pleasant to know that Beatriz was willing to leave everything to come to her when she was called. There was no one whom she could trust as she trusted Beatriz; and she realized that it was rare for one in her position to enjoy such a disinterested friendship.

She fancied today that Beatriz had something on her mind, for she was somewhat subdued—a rare state for Beatriz; Isabella waited for her friend to tell her what was the cause of her thoughtfulness, but Beatriz was evidently in no hurry to do so.

She came and knelt by Isabella's side and put out a hand to touch the baby's cheek.

"I declare," said Beatriz, "already the Infanta Catalina bears some resemblance to her august mother."

Isabella gave way to a rare gesture of affection; she lifted the child in her arms and kissed her forehead.

"I was thinking, Beatriz," she said, "how quickly time passes. Soon we shall be thinking of a husband for this little one, as we are for my dear Isabella."

"It will not be for many years yet."

"For this one," said Isabella. "But what of my young Isabella? I cannot bear to part with one of them. Beatriz, I think I love my children more fiercely than most mothers do because, since I have had them, I have been able to spend so little time with them. That will not be the case in future. When I go on my travels I shall take my family with me. It is a good thing that the people should know them, as they know their King and Queen."

"The children will enjoy it. They hate these partings as much as you do."

"Isabella will be leaving us soon," said the Queen.

"But now you have Catalina to take her place."

"Once Isabella is married we must think of marriages for the others. I fear they will take them far from us."

"The Infanta Isabella will go into Portugal, dearest Highness, but Portugal is not far away. Who will be next? Juan. Well, you will keep him here in Castile, will you not. You will not lose your son, Highness. Then Juana will have a husband and go away, I suppose."

A shadow crossed the Queen's face, and Beatriz, following her thoughts, said quickly: "But she is only six years old. It will be years yet."

The Queen was wondering what the years ahead held for wild Juana, and she tried hard to fight her rising fear.

"As for Maria and this little one," went on Beatriz, "marriage is far . . . far away. Why, Highness, you are indeed fortunate."

Isabella said: "Yes, I am fortunate. Isabella will be but a few miles across the border. She will be Queen of Portugal, and thus a very desirable alliance will be forged between our countries. Yet . . . her health worries me sometimes, Beatriz. She has that cough."

"It will pass. When she begins to bear children she will grow healthy. It happens so with some women."

Isabella smiled. "You are my comforter."

The baby began to whimper, and Isabeila rocked her soothingly. "There, my little one. Perhaps you will go away from your home. . . . Perhaps you will go to some country across the seas . . . but not yet . . . not for years . . . and here is your mother to love you."

Beatriz was thinking that now was the time to put her request. The Queen's mood was softened when she was with her children. Indeed, few were allowed to see her displays of tenderness.

Now is the time, thought Beatriz.

"Highness," she began tentatively.

"Yes," said Isabella, "you should tell me, Beatriz. I see there is something on your mind."

"I have had news from the Duke of Medina Sidonia, Highness."

"What sort of news? Good, I hope."

"I think it might be good . . . very good. It concerns a strange adventurer. A man who has impressed him deeply. He begs an audience with Your Highness. The Duke tells me that his attention was called to this man by Fray Juan Perez de Marchena, who is guardian of the convent of La Rabida. He has approached Your Highness's confessor, but doubtless Talavera has been unimpressed by the man's story. Talavera has his mind on one thing —ridding this country of heretics."

"And what could be better?" demanded Isabella. She was thinking placidly of the punishment which had been carried out on the murderers of Arbués in Saragossa. Six of them had been dragged through Saragossa on hurdles, and had had their hands cut off on the Cathedral steps before they had been castrated, hanged, drawn and quartered for the multitude to see. One of the prisoners had committed suicide by eating a glass lamp. A pity, thought Isabella, smoothing the down on her baby's head, for thus he had evaded punishment.

Beatriz said quickly: "Highness, this man has a fantastic story to tell. As yet it is but a dream; but I have seen him, Highness, and I believe in his dreams."

Isabella wrinkled her brows in some puzzlement. Beatriz was by nature a practical woman; it was unlike her to talk of dreams.

"He came originally from Italy and went to Lisbon in the hope of interesting the King of Portugal in his schemes. Apparently he considers he was cheated there and, because he believes you to be the greatest ruler in the world, he wishes to lay his gift at your feet."

"What is this gift?"

"A new world, Highness."

"A new world! What can this mean?"

"A land of great riches as yet undiscovered. He is certain that it exists beyond the Atlantic Ocean, and that he can find a new route to Asia without crossing the Eastern continent. Time and money would be saved if this were accomplished. The riches of Cathay could be easily brought to Spain. This man speaks so convincingly, Highness, that he convinces me."

"You have been caught in the dreams of a dreamer, Beatriz."

"As I feel sure Your Highness would be if you would receive him in audience."

"What does he ask of me?"

"In exchange for a new world, he asks for ships which will take him there. He needs three carvels, fitted out for a long journey. He needs the patronage and approval of yourself."

Isabella was silent. "This man has impressed you deeply," she said at length. "What manner of man is he?"

"He is tall, long limbed, with eyes which seem to look into the future. Red-haired, blue-eyed. Near your Highness's own colouring. But it is not his physical features which impress me; it is his intensity, his certainty that his dream can be realized."

"His name, Beatriz?"

"It was Christoforo Colombo, but since he has been in Spain he has changed it to Cristobal Colon. Highness, will you receive him? I implore you to."

"My dear Beatriz, since you ask it, how could I refuse?"

* * *

Cristobal Colon was preparing to present himself to the Sovereigns, and in the small house in which he had lived since he came to Cordova, impatiently he awaited the moment to depart. It had been impressed upon him by his patrons that this was a great honour which was being bestowed upon him. Cristobal did not accept this. It was he who was bestowing the honour.

There was a knock on his door. A high feminine voice said: "Señor Colon, you have not left yet, then?"

Cristobal's face softened slightly. "No, I have not yet left. Pray come in, Señora."

She was a pretty little woman, and the fact that now there was a great anxiety in her eyes endeared her to the adventurer.

"I prayed for you last night and this morning, Señor Colon. May all go well. May they give you what you ask."

"That is good of you."

"And, Señor, when you return, would it be asking too much of you to step into my house? I will prepare a meal for you. You will be hungry after your ordeal. Oh, I know you will not be thinking of food. But you should, you know, You will need a good meal, and I will have it waiting for you."

"You have been a good neighbour to me, Señora de Arana."

"I was about to say that I hope I shall always be so, but of course I do not: I hope that you will be successful and that soon you will be sailing away. Pray let me look at you." She had a brush with her, and began brushing his coat. "Why, have you forgotten that you are to be in the presence of the King and Queen?"

"It is not my clothes I am taking to show them."

"Whatever else you show, you must first show respect."

She put her head on one side and smiled at him. Then he stooped and kissed her cheek.

She flushed a little and turned away. He took her chin in his hands and looked into her face. There were tears in her eyes.

He thought of this woman who had been his neighbour for some months; he thought of the pleasantness of their friendship. Then he understood; she had treated him with a certain motherly devotion; but she was a young woman, younger than he was.

His head had been so full of his schemes that he had not realized until this moment that those long months of waiting had only been made tolerable by this woman.

He said: "Señora de Arana, Beatriz . . . why . . . when I leave I shall be very sad because I must say goodbye to you."

"It will be some time before you are able to leave," she answered quickly. "So . . . the parting will not be yet."

He hesitated for only a second. He was a man of strong passions. Then he caught her to him, and the kiss he gave her was long and demanding.

She had changed subtly; she was flushed and happy.

"What now, Señor Colon!" she said. "At any moment you must leave for your audience at the Palace. That is what you have been waiting for."

He was astonished at himself. He was certain that he was about to achieve that for which he had longed for many years; and here, on the brink of achievement, he was dallying with a pretty woman.

He stood still while she continued to brush his coat. Then he knew the time had come.

He said a somewhat brusque farewell and left for the Palace.

* * *

Cristobal stood before the Queen.

Behind her stood Beatriz de Bobadilla, who encouraged him by her warm looks; seated beside the Queen was the King, her husband; and by the side of the King stood the Queen's confessor, Fernando de Talavera.

Cristobal held his head high. Even Isabella and Ferdinand were not more dignified than he, not more proud. His looks were impressive and, because he believed that he had a great gift to offer, he was lacking in humility.

This was noted by all present. On Ferdinand and Talavera it had an adverse effect. They would have preferred a humble supplicant. Isabella was as impressed by him as Beatriz had been. The man, it seemed, did not behave with the decorum to which she was accustomed in her Court, but she recognized the fine spirit in him, which had so impressed Beatriz, and she thought:

This man may be mistaken, but he believes in himself; and in such belief lie the seeds of genius.

"Cristobal Colon," said Isabella, "you have a plan to lay before us. I pray you tell us what it is you think you can do."

"Your Highness," said Cristobal, "I would not have you think that I have no practical knowledge with which to back up my schemes. I was instructed at Pavia in the mathematical sciences, and since the age of fourteen I have led a seafaring life. I came to Portugal because I had heard that in that country I was more likely to receive a sympathetic hearing. It was said to be the country of maritime enterprise."

"And you did not find that sympathy," said Isabella. "Tell us what you hope to discover."

"A sea route to Cathay and Zipango. Highnesses, the great Atlantic Ocean has never been crossed. No one knows what lies beyond it. There may be rich lands as yet undiscovered. Highnesses, I ask you to make this expedition possible."

The Queen said slowly: "You speak with some conviction, yet the King of Portugal was unconvinced."

"Highness, he set up an ecclesiastical council. He asked monks to decide regarding a voyage of discovery!" Colon had drawn himself up to his great height, and his eyes flashed scorn.

Talavera's indignation rose. Talavera, whose life had been lived in the cloister, was afraid of new ideas. He was fanatically religious and deeply superstitious. He was telling himself that if God had wished man to know of the existence of certain continents He would not have made them so inaccessible that over many centuries they had remained unheard of. Talavera was wondering whether this foreigner's suggestions did not smack of heresy.

But Talavera was on the whole a mild man; it would give him no pleasure—as it would have given Torquemada—to put this man on the rack and make him confess that his suggestions came from the devil. Talavera showed his scepticism by cold indifference.

"So you failed to convince the King of Portugal," said the Queen. "And for this reason you come to me."

Ferdinand put in: "Doubtless you have charts which might help us to decide whether this journey would be a profitable one."

"I have certain charts," said Cristobal cautiously. He was remembering that the Bishop of Ceuta, having been made aware of nautical details, had despatched his own explorers. Cristobal was not going to allow that to happen again. His most important charts he would keep to himself.

"We should have to give this mattter great thought before committing ourselves," said Ferdinand. "We are engaged in a holy war at the moment."

"But," said Isabella, "rest assured that your suggestions shall have our serious consideration. I shall appoint a council to consider them. They will be in touch with you; and if the report they bring to me is hopeful, I will then consider what can be done to provide you with what you need." She inclined her head. "You will be informed, Señor Colon, of the findings of the committee which I shall set up."

From beside the Queen, Beatriz de Bobadilla was smiling encouragement at him.

Cristobal knelt before the Sovereigns.

The audience was over.

* * *

The Señora Beatriz de Arana was waiting for him on his return. She looked at him expectantly; his expression was noncommittal.

"I do not know what will be the outcome," he said. "They are going to set up a commission."

"But that is hopeful, surely."

"They set up a commission in Lisbon, my dear lady. An ecclesiastical commission. The Queen's confessor was present at this interview. I did not much like his looks. But there was one there—a maid of honour of the Queen—and she . . . she seemed to think something of me."

"Was she handsome?" asked the Señora earnestly.

Cristobal smiled at her. "Very handsome," he said. "Very, very handsome."

Beatriz de Arana looked a little sad, and he went on quickly: "Yet haughty, forceful. I prefer a gentler woman."

She said: "I have a meal waiting for you. Come into my house and we will eat together. We will drink to the success of your enterprise. Come now, for the food is hot, and I would not have it spoilt."

So he followed her into her house and, when they had eaten the excellent food she had cooked and were flushed with the wine she provided, he leaned his arms on the table and talked to her of voyages of the past and voyages of the future.

He felt then what a comfort it was to have someone to talk to, as once he had talked to Filippa. This homely, comfortable widow reminded him of Filippa in many ways. She came and looked over his shoulder, for he had taken a chart from his pocket and was describing the routes to her; and as he felt her hair against his cheek, he turned to her suddenly and took her into his arms.

She lay across his knees smiling at him gently and hopefully. She had been lonely for so long.

He kissed her and she responded.

It was a strange day for Cristobal—the audience with the King and Queen, the acquisition of a mistress. It was the happiest day he had lived through for years. Diego was being well cared for in the Monastery of Santa Maria de la Rabida, and his mind was at rest concerning Filippa's son; and here was a woman ready to comfort him. For once in his life he would cease to dream of the future and for a very short time enjoy the present.

Later, Beatriz de Arana said to him: "Why should you go back to your lonely house? Why should I be lonely in mine? Give up your house and let my house be our house during the weeks of waiting."

* * *

Ferdinand snapped his fingers when Colon had left and Beatriz de Bobadilla and Talavera had been dismissed.

"This is a dream," he said. "We have no money to finance a foreigner's dreams."

"It is true that there is little to spare," Isabella agreed.

Ferdinand turned to her, his eyes blazing. "We should prosecute the Holy War with every means at our disposal. Boabdil is ours to command. Never has the position been so favourable, yet we are prevented from making war by lack of money. Moreover, there are the affairs of Aragon to be considered. I have given all my energies to this war against the Infidel, when, were I able to work for Aragon, I should make myself master of the Mediterranean. I could defeat the French and win back that which they have taken from me."

"If we dismiss this man," said Isabella, "he will go to France and in that country ask for the means to make his discoveries."

"Let him!"

"And if he should be right? If his discoveries should bring great wealth to our rivals, what then?"

"The man is a dreamer! He'll discover nothing."

"I think you may be right, Ferdinand," said Isabella quietly, "but I have decided to set up a commission to consider the possibilities of his success in this enterprise."

Ferdinand lifted his shoulders. "That could do no harm. And whom will you put in charge of this commission?"

"I think Talavera is the man to conduct it."

Ferdinand smiled. He felt certain that if Talavera were at the head of the commission the result would be the refusal of the foreign adventurer's request.

* * *

Talavera sat at the head of the table; about him were ranged those who had been selected to help him arrive at a decision.

Cristobal Colon had stood before them; he had eloquently argued his case; he had shown them charts which were in his possession, but he had held back certain important details, remembering the perfidy of the Portuguese.

Then he had been dismissed, while the judges made their decision.

Talavera spoke first. "I believe this man's claims to be fantastic."

Cardinal Mendoza put in quickly: "I would not be so bold as to say that anything on this Earth was fantastic until I had proved it to be."

Talavera looked with mild exasperation at the Cardinal, who had become Primate of Spain and who took such a large part in state affairs that he was beginning to be known as the Third King of Spain. It was like Mendoza to side with the adventurer. Lackadaisical in his religion, Talevera believed that, for all his undoubted talents, Mendoza was a menace to Castile. The Inquisition was firmly established, but Mendoza was not in favour of it. He was no zealot for either side, and he made no attempt to pit his love of toleration against the burning fanaticism of men such as Torquemada. He merely turned distastefully from the subject and devoted himself to state affairs.

Friar Diego Deza, a Dominican, who was of the commission, also spoke up in favour of the adventurer.

"The man has a zeal about him, a determination, which it is impossible to ignore," said Deza. "I believe he knows more than he tells us. I believe that if he were supported he would at least discover new sea routes, if he did not discover new lands."

Talavera said: "I sense the devil in his proposals. Had God wished us to know of this land, do you doubt that He would have told us? I am not certain that we should not pass this man over to the Holy House for questioning."

Mendoza inwardly shivered. Not that, he thought. That bold man, stretched on the rack, hanging on the pulley, subjected to the water torture . . . forced to admit . . . what! That he had strayed from the tenets of the Church, that he had committed the mortal sin of heresy?

Mendoza pictured him—boldly facing his accusers. No, no! It must not happen. Mendoza would bestir himself for such a man.

He rejoiced, for the sake of Cristobal Colon, that it was the comparatively mild Talavera and not the fanatical Torquemada who was at the head of this commission, as he, Mendoza, had decided what he would do. He would not press his point here. He would let Talavera have his way. He would agree that the voyage was impracticable and have a word with the Queen quietly afterwards, for Talavera would be contented if he prevented the Sovereigns' spending money on the enterprise. This unimaginative man would feel he had done his duty, and Cristobal Colon would then be of no more importance to him.

So Mendoza, subduing Deza with a look which conveyed that they would talk together later of this matter, allowed Talavera to carry the day.

The other members, mostly ecclesiastics of the same type as Talavera, were ready to follow him, and the news was taken to the Sovereigns. "The Commission has questioned Cristobal Colon; they have weighed up the possibilities of success and have found them wanting. It would be quite impracticable to finance such a fantastic voyage which, it is the considered opinion of the commission, could only end in failure."

* * *

Beatriz de Bobadilla put aside her decorum and stormed into the Queen's apartment.

"That fool Talavera!" she cried. "So he has turned you against this adventurer."

"Beatriz!" Isabella exclaimed in pained surprise.

Beatriz' answer was to fling herself at Isabella's feet. "Highness, I believe he should be given a chance."

"My dear friend," said Isabella, "what can you know about this? A commission of learned men has decided that it would be a waste of money we need so badly to finance this man's expedition."

"A commission of idiots!" cried Beatriz.

"Beatriz, my dear, I suggest you retire and calm yourself," said Isabella quietly and firmly, in that tone which implied that immediate obedience was expected.

When Beatriz had left, the Cardinal of Mendoza arrived.

"Highness," he said, "I have come to tell you that I am not in entire agreement with the findings of the commission."

"You mean you have given way to Talavera?"

"I felt the bulk of opinion against me, Highness. May I tell you exactly what I feel?"

"That I expect you to tell me."

"I feel this, Highness. It may well be an impracticable dream, but it is equally certain that it may not be. If we dismiss this man he will go to another country . . . probably France or England. I ask Your Highness to consider what would happen if the King of France or England provided this man with what he asks. If he were successful, if he discovered a world of great riches for them . . . instead of for us . . . our position would be changed considerably. That is what I wish to avoid."

"But, my dear Cardinal, the commission does not believe this voyage would be a success."

"The commission is largely composed of ecclesiastics, Highness."

"Of whom you are one!"

"I am also a statesman; and I beg Your Highness to consider the possibility of the man's discoveries passing into hands other than your own."

"Thank you, Cardinal," she said. "I will consider this."

* * *

Cristobal Colon was summoned once more to the presence of the Sovereigns.

Ferdinand was delighted.

"I knew," he told Isabella, "that the man was a fanatic, from the moment I saw him. Three carvels! Men to man them! He asked us to provide these that we may waste our substance. So the Commission has proved me right."

"There were a few voices raised in opposition," Isabella reminded him.

"The majority saw through my eyes," retorted Ferdinand.

Isabella said softly: "Ferdinand, can you visualize the riches that may exist in lands as yet undiscovered?"

Ferdinand was silent for a few moments; then he snapped his fingers. "Better to seek to regain the riches which we have lost than look for those which may not even exist. There are riches within Granada which we know to exist. Let us make sure of the substance before we seek to grasp the shadow."

Talavera and Mendoza arrived with the members of the commission, and news was brought that Cristobal Colon had arrived at the Palace and was seeking audience with the Sovereigns.

"Let him be brought to us at once," said Isabella.

Cristobal came in. With the air of a visiting King he bowed before the Sovereigns. His eyes were alight with fervour. He could not believe that they would be so foolish as to deny him the money he asked, in exchange for which he would bring them great riches.

"The commission has given us its answer concerning your project," said Isabella slowly.

He lifted those brilliant blue eyes to her face and she felt herself soften towards him. When he stood before her thus he could make her believe in his promises. She understood why he had produced the effect he had on Beatriz and Mendoza.

She said gently: "At this time we are greatly occupied with a grievious war; and it is for this reason that we find ourselves unable to embark on this new undertaking."

She saw the light die out of his eyes. She saw the droop of his shoulders; she saw the frustration on his face, and she went on quickly: "When our war is won, Señor Colon, we shall be ready to treat with you."

He did not answer. He was not aware of the amazement in Talavera's eyes, of the triumph in Mendoza's. He only knew that once again he had been bitterly disappointed.

He bowed and left the presence of the Sovereigns.

* * *

It was Beatriz de Arana who comforted him.

"At least," she said, "they have promised to do something."

"My dear," he answered, "I have heard such promises before. They come to nothing."

She told him then that she could not understand her feelings. She wept because she loved him and she could not bear to see his bitter disappointment; yet how could she help but rejoice that he was left to her a little longer!

But even as she spoke she saw the speculation in his eyes.

She knew he was wondering whether he might not find more sympathy at the Court of France.

Yet he turned to her and caressed her, and he too would have been sad if they had to part. But she understood. This dream of a great voyage was a part of himself; it must come to fruition. He had parted with his beloved son, Diego, for its sake. So would he part from Beatriz if and when the time should come.

There was at least this respite, she told herself; and as she felt his hands stroking her hair, she knew that all the comfort he could feel at this moment must come from her.

* * *

There was a visitor to the little house, and Beatriz ushered him in and called to Cristobal.

Beatriz left the two men together.

"Let me introduce myself," said the man. "I am Luis de Sant'angel and I am the Secretary of Supplies in Aragon to King Ferdinand."

"I am glad to know you," said Cristobal, "but what can your business be with me?"

"I come to tell you that you have friends at Court; there are many of us who believe in your enterprise and are going to do our utmost to persuade the Sovereigns to support you."

Cristobal smiled wanly. "I thank you. And if I seem ungrateful, let me tell you that for many years I have sought to make this journey, and again and again I have suffered the same frustration. I have had friends at Court, but they have not been able to persuade my detractors that I can achieve what I say I can."

"Do not despair. Let me tell you, Señor Colon, that you have friends in very high places. The great Cardinal Mendoza believes you should be given a chance. And he is said to be the most important man at Court, and to wield great influence over the Queen. Fray Diego de Deza, who is tutor to the Prince Don Juan, is also in your favour. And there is one other—a lady of great power. You see, Señor, you have your friends and supporters."

"I rejoice to hear this, but I would rejoice more if I might be allowed to fit out my carvels and make my plans."

"Come to the Palace this day. We have news for you."

He left shortly afterwards, and Cristobal hurried to tell Beatriz what had happened.

She stood at the window watching him as he left for the Palace; there was a spring in his step. The Aragonese Jew, Luis de Sant'angel, had revived his hopes.

Beatriz turned hurriedly away from the window.

* * *

When Cristobal presented himself at the Palace he was taken to the apartments of Beatriz de Bobadilla.

Beatriz, who was now Marchioness of Moya, was not alone. With her were Fray Diego de Deza, Alonso de Quintanilla the Queen's secretary, Juan Cabrero Ferdinand's chamberlain and Luis de Sant'angel.

Beatriz studied the man who stood before her, and she felt her spirits lifted. She wished in that moment that she could accompany him on his voyage, that she might be the one to stand beside him when he had his first sight of the new lands which he would discover.

I am being foolishly emotional, she thought. Merely because the man has such dignity, such character, such handsome looks; merely because he is a man of purpose, am I to forget my position, my common sense on his account?

It was so unlike her to be foolishly romantic. Yet this man moved her deeply as few men ever had; and she had determined that his cause should be her cause.

She had already begun to work for him, and it was for this reason that she had sent for him.

"Señor Colon," she said, "I would have you know that those of us who are gathered here today believe in you. We are sorry that there must be this delay, but in the meantime we would have you know that we are your friends and that we intend to help you."

"You are gracious, my lady," said Colon, inclining his head slightly.

"We have no doubt," said Beatriz, "that many have said these words to you."

"It is true."

"Yet," said Luis de Sant'angel, "we intend to show you our regard with more than words. That is so, my friends, is it not?"

"It is," agreed the others.

"We have therefore," went on Beatriz, "persuaded the Queen to give you some token of her regard during the waiting period. She has agreed that you shall receive a sum of 3,000 *maravedis*. It is not to be considered as something towards your expedition. That would be useless, we know. But while you remain here you must live, and this money is to help you, and to show that the Queen does not forget you."

"I am grateful to Her Highness."

Sant'angel touched his elbow. "Be grateful to the Marchioness," he murmured. "It is she who has the ear of the Queen. It is she who will work for you."

Beatriz laughed. "It is true," she said. "I shall see that in a few months' time more money is given you. Nor shall I allow the Queen to forget you."

"How can I express my thanks?"

Beatriz smiled almost gently. "By remaining firm in your resolve. By holding yourself in readiness. It may be necessary for you to follow the Court when it leaves Cordova. I shall arrange that you shall suffer no expense from these journeys. The Queen has given her consent to the proposal that you shall be provided with free lodging. You see, Señor Colon, we are your friends."

Cristobal looked from one to the other.

"My friends," he said, "your faith in me makes me a happy man."

* * *

For a few months his spirits were high. He had friends in high places. More money was paid to him; but the war with Granada went on in a series of sharp attacks and skirmishes. Cristobal knew that it would be long before it was brought to an end.

He would sit at dusk with Beatriz de Arana, looking out on the little street, always hoping that there would be a knock on the door to summon him to Court.

Once as they sat in the darkened room he said to her: "This is how it has always been. I wait here as I waited in Lisbon. Here I am happier because you are here, because I know my little Diego is being well cared for in his monastery. Sometimes I think I shall spend my whole life waiting."

"And if you do, Cristobal, could you not be happy? Have you not been happy here with me?"

"It is my destiny to sail the seas," he said. "It is my life. It sounds ungrateful to you who have been so good to me. Let me say this, that there is only one thing that has made these months of waiting tolerable: my life with you. But for this urge within me I could settle here and live happily with you for the rest of my days."

"But the time will come when you will go away, Cristobal."

"I shall come back to you."

"But you will be long away, and how can I be sure that you will come back? There are dangers on the seas."

"You must not be unhappy, Beatriz. I could not bear to think that I have brought unhappiness to you who have brought so much happiness to me."

"No," she said, "remember this. When you sail away—as you must—I shall not be alone."

He started and sought to look into her face, but it was too dark for him to see it clearly.

"I shall have my child then, Cristobal," she said softly, "your child, our child."

BEFORE MALAGA

ISABELLA sat at her sewing with her eldest daughter, the Infanta Isabella. She was conscious that now and then the girl was casting covert glances at her, and that she was on the verge of tears.

Isabella herself was fighting back her emotion. She does not know it, she told herself, but the parting is going to be even harder for me to bear than it is for her. She is young and will quickly adjust herself to her new surroundings . . . whereas I . . . I shall always miss her.

"Mother . . . " said the Infanta at length.

"My dear," murmured Isabella; she put aside her needlework and beckoned to her daughter. The Infanta threw hers aside and ran to her mother to kneel at her feet and bury her face in her lap.

Isabella stroked her daughter's hair.

"My dearest," she said, "you will be happy, you know. You must not fret."

"But to go away from you all! To go to strangers. . . ."

"It is the fate of Infantas, my darling."

"You did not, Mother."

"No, I stayed here, but many efforts were made to send me away. If my brother Alfonso had lived, doubtless I should have married into a strange country. So much hangs on chance, my dearest; and we must accept what comes to us. We must not fight against our destinies."

"Oh, Mother, how fortunate you were, to stay in your home and marry my father."

Isabella thought fleetingly of the first time she had seen Ferdinand; young, handsome, virile. She thought of the ideal she had built up and the shock of discovering that she had married a sensual man. She had come to her marriage hoping for a great deal and had received less than she hoped for. She prayed that her daughter would find in marriage something more satisfying than she had thought possible.

"Your Alonso will be as beloved by you as Ferdinand is by me," Isabella told her daughter.

"Mother, must I marry at all? Why should I not stay here with you?"

"It is very necessary that you should marry, my darling. A marriage between you and the heir to the throne of Portugal could bring great stability to our two countries. You see, not very long ago there was war between us. It was at the time when I came to the throne and Portugal supported the claims of La Beltraneja. The threat of La Beltraneja has always been with us, for she still lives in Portugal. Now Alonso will one day be King of Portugal, and if you marry him, my darling, you will be its Queen; our two countries would be united and this threat removed. That is what we have to think of when making our marriages—not what good it will bring to us, but what good it will bring to our countries. But do not fret, my child. There is much to be arranged yet, and these matters are rarely settled quickly."

The Infanta shivered. "But they are settled . . . in time, Mother."

"Let us enjoy all the time that is left to us."

The Infanta threw her arms about her mother and clung to her.

As she embraced her daughter, Isabella heard the sounds of arrival below, and she put the Infanta from her, rose and went to the window. She saw a party of soldiers from Ferdinand's army, and she prepared to receive them immediately because she guessed that they brought news from the camp.

Ferdinand had taken possession of Velez Malaga, which was situated some five or six leagues from the great port of Malaga itself; and the King was now concentrating all his forces on the capture of this town.

The Christian armies were before Malaga, which was perhaps the most important town—next to Granada itself—in Moorish territory. It was a strongly defended fortress, rich and prosperous. The Moors were proud of Malaga, this beautiful city of handsome buildings with its fertile vineyards, olive groves and gardens of oranges and pomegranates.

They were determined to fight to the death to preserve it; thus Isabella knew that it would be no easy task for Ferdinand to take it.

Therefore she was impatient to hear what news these messengers brought from the front.

She commanded that they be brought to her presence immediately, and she did not dismiss the Infanta. She wished her daughter to know something of state matters; she did not want to send her, an ignoramus, into a strange country.

She took Ferdinand's letters and read that the siege of Malaga had begun and that he feared it would be long and arduous. There was no hope of an easy victory. If the Moors lost the port it would be a turning point in the war, and they knew this. They were therefore as determined to hold Malaga as the Christians were to take it.

The city had been placed in the hands of a certain Hamet Zeli, a general of outstanding courage and integrity, and he had sworn that he would hold Malaga for the Moors to the death.

Ferdinand wrote: "And I have determined to take it, no matter what the cost. But this will give some indication of the man we have to deal with. It was brought to my notice that many of the rich townsfolk were ready to make peace with me, in order to save Malaga from destruction. I sent Cadiz to offer concessions to Hamet Zeli and the most important of the citizens if they would surrender Malaga to me. I know that many of the burghers would have accepted my offer, but Hamet Zeli intervened. 'There is no bribe the Christians could offer me,' he retorted, 'which would be big enough to make me betray my trust.' That is the kind of man with whom we have to deal.

"Isabella, there is certain friction in our camp which causes me anxiety. There have been rumours of plague in some of the surrounding villages. These are unfounded, but I believe them to have been set in motion to distract our troops. There has been a shortage of water; and, I regret to say, several of the men have deserted.

"I can think of only one person who could stop this decadence. Yourself. Isabella, I am asking you to come to the camp. Your presence here will lift the spirits of the soldiers. You would give heart to them and, when the news reaches the people of Malaga that you are with us, I feel sure that their anxieties would be increased. They will know that we are determined to take Malaga. Isabella, leave everything and come to our camp before Malaga with all speed."

Isabella smiled as she read this despatch.

She looked at the Infanta, who was watching her with curiosity.

"I am leaving immediately for the Camp before Malaga," she said. "The King requests my presence there."

"Mother," said the Infanta, "you said that we should not be parted . . . that there may not be much time left to us. Dearest Mother, please stay here with us."

Isabella looked at her eldest daughter and said: "But of course I must go. There is work to do in the camp; but do not fret, my daughter. We shall not be parted, for you are coming with me."

* * *

Isabella arrived at the camp, accompanied by the Infanta and several of the ladies of the Court, among whom was Beatriz de Bobadilla.

They were greeted with enthusiasm, and the effect on the morale of the army was immediate.

Isabella's dignity never failed to have its effect, and when she turned several tents into a hospital and, with her women, cared for the sick and wounded, there was no doubt that her coming had saved a dangerous situation. Those soldiers who were wearying of the long war, who had been telling themselves that they could never conquer the well-fortified city of Malaga, now changed their minds. They were eager to perform feats of valour in order to win the respect of the Queen and her ladies.

Ferdinand had been right. What the army needed was the presence of its Queen.

There was little peace, for there were continual forays by the Moors who crept out of the besieged city under cover of darkness and made raids on the encamped army.

It might well have been that the Christian armies would have been defeated before Malaga, for El Zagal sent forces to help the town. Unfortunately for the Moors, and to the great advantage of the Christians, Boabdil's troops encountered the relieving force on its way, a battle ensued and there were so many casualties that it was impossible for El Zagal's men to come to the relief of Malaga.

When Isabella heard this she thanked God for the shrewdness of Ferdinand, who had insisted, instead of keeping Boabdil in captivity, on sending him back that he might do great damage to the Moorish cause.

Poor Boabdil was a bewildered young man. He hated war; he wished to end it as quickly as possible. He sought to placate the Christian Sovereigns by sending them presents, almost as though to remind them that through the recent treaty he was their vassal.

"We owe a great deal to Boabdil," said Ferdinand. "This war would have been longer and more bloody for us but for him. I will make him some return to show him that I am his friend. I shall allow his supporters to cultivate their fields in peace. After all, soon this land will be ours. It would be wise therefore to leave some of it in cultivation and at the same time reward Boabdil."

So the siege continued, and Ferdinand was confident of victory. He trusted his own shrewdness and his ability to get the best of any bargain; he had called his Master of Ordnance, Francisco Ramirez, to the front; this clever inventor with his powder mines could work miracles until now never used in warfare; and there was Isabella, with her dignity, piety and good works.

We cannot fail, thought Ferdinand; we have everything which makes for success.

* * *

It was afternoon when the prisoner was brought in. He was dragged before the Marquis of Cadiz; and he fell to his knees and begged the Marquis to spare his life. As the man could not speak Castilian, the Marquis spoke to him in the Moorish tongue.

"I come as a friend. I come as a friend," repeated the Moor. "I pray you listen to what I have to say. I will lead you into Malaga. I am the friend of the Christian King and Queen, as is my King, Boabdil."

The Marquis of Cadiz, who was about to order the Moor's execution, paused.

He signed to the two guards who stood on either side of the Moor to seize him.

"Follow me," said the Marquis, "and bring him with you."

He made his way to the royal tent, where Isabella was with Ferdinand. She came to the entrance, for she had heard the man shouting in his own language.

"Highness," said the Marquis. "this man was captured. He says he has escaped from the city because he has something he wishes to tell you. Will you and the King see him now?"

Isabella looked back into the tent, where Ferdinand, worn out with his recent exertions, was fast asleep.

"The King is asleep," she said. "I do not wish to waken him. He was quite exhausted. This man's story can wait. Take him into the next tent. There let him remain until the King awakes, when I will immediately tell him what has happened."

She indicated the tent next to her own, in which Beatriz de Bobadilla sat with Don Alvaro, a Portuguese nobleman, and son of the Duke of Braganza, who had joined the Holy War, as so many foreigners had, since they looked upon it as a crusade.

They were discussing the siege and, when Beatriz heard the Queen's words, she went to Isabella.

"I wish this man to be detained until the King awakes," said Isabella. "He says that he has news for us."

"We will detain him until it is your pleasure to receive him," said Beatriz; and when the guards, after having brought the Moor to her tent, stationed themselves outside, she continued her conversation with the Duke.

The Moor watched them. She was a very handsome woman and far more magnificently dressed than Isabella had been. He had glimpsed the sleeping Ferdinand, his doublet lying beside his pallet, and he had not thought for one moment that this could be the great King of whom he had heard so much.

But here was a courtly man in garments of scarlet and gold; and here was a lady, queenly in her bearing, with jewels at her throat and on her hands, her gown stiff with silken embroidery.

The Moor remained motionless, watching them slyly as they continued to talk together as though he were not there. He believed they were discussing how they would treat him, what questions they would ask.

He began to make soft moaning noises, and when they looked at him he gazed towards a jar of water with pleading eyes.

"The man is thirsty," said Beatriz. "Let us give him a draught of water."

The Duke poured water into a cup and handed it to the Moor, who drank it eagerly. As the Duke turned away, to put the cup by the jar, the Moor knew that the moment he had been waiting for had come.

He knew that death would doubtless be his reward, but he did not care. This day he was going to perform a deed which would make his name glorious in Arab history for evermore. There were two whose names struck terror into every citizen within the walls of Malaga—and of Granada also: Ferdinand, the great soldier, Isabella, the dedicated Queen.

He slipped his hand beneath his *albornoz* and his fingers closed round the dagger which he had secreted there.

The man should be first because, when he was dead, it would be easy to deal with the woman. He lifted the dagger as he sprang, and in a few seconds Don Alvaro, bleeding profusely from the head, sank to the floor. Beatriz screamed for help as the Moor then turned to her. Again he lifted the dagger, but Beatriz' arm shot up and the blow he struck at her breast was diverted.

"Help!" Beatriz shouted. "We are being murdered."

Again the Moor lifted the dagger, but Beatriz was ready for him. She slipped aside and the blow glanced off the encrusted embroidery of her gown. She was calling for help at the top of her voice. There was an answering shout and the guards entered the tent.

Again the Moor sought to strike at the woman whom he believed to be Isabella. But he was too late. He was caught by the guards, who seized him and dragged him from the tent.

Beatriz followed them shouting: "Send help at once. Don Alvaro has been badly wounded."

Then she turned back and knelt by the wounded man seeking to stem his bleeding.

Isabella came into the tent.

"Beatriz, what is this?" she asked; and she gasped with horror as she looked at the wounded man.

"He is not dead," said Beatriz. "With God's help we shall save him. It was the Moor, who said he had news for you."

"And I sent him to your tent!"

"Thank God you did."

Ferdinand had now appeared in the tent; he was pulling on his doublet as he came.

"An attempt, Highness," said Beatriz, "on the life of the Queen and yourself."

Ferdinand stared down at the wounded man.

* * *

"You see," said Beatriz later, "you are in danger here, Highness. You should not be in camp. It is no place for you."

"It is the only place for me," answered Isabella.

"That might have been the end of your lives. If you had taken that man into your tent he could have killed the King while he slept."

"And what should I have been doing to allow that?" asked Isabella with a smile. "Do you not think that I should have given as good an account of myself as you did?"

"I was fortunate. I am wearing this dress. I think his knife would have pierced me but for the heavy embroidery. You, Highness, are less vain of your personal appearance than I am. The knife might have penetrated your gown."

"God would have watched over me," said Isabella.

"But, Highness, will you not consider the danger, and return to safety?"

"Not long ago," said Isabella, "the King was reproved by his soldiers because he took great risks in battle and endangered his life. He told them he could not stop to consider the risk to himself while his subjects were putting their lives in peril for his cause, which was a holy one. That is the answer I make to you now, Beatriz."

Beatriz shivered. "I shall never cease to thank God that you sent that murderer into my tent."

Isabella smiled at her friend and, taking her hand, pressed it affectionately.

"We must take care of the Infanta," she said. "We must remember the dangers all about us."

All over the camp there was talk of the miraculous escape of the King and Queen, and the incident did much to lift the spirits of the soldiers. They believed that divine power was guarding their Sovereigns, and this, they told themselves, was because the war they were prosecuting was a holy war.

The Moor had been done to violent death by those guards who had dragged him from the tent, and there were cheers of derision as his mutilated body was taken to the cannon.

A great shout went up as the corpse was propelled by catapult over the walls and into the city.

* * *

Inside the city, faces were grim. Hunger was the lot of everyone and the once-prosperous city was desolate.

From the mosques came the chant of voices appealing to Allah, but despair was apparent in those chants.

Some cursed Boabdil, who had been the friend of the Christians; some murmured against El Zagal, the valiant one, who waged war on Boabdil and the Christians. Some whispered that peace should be the aim of their leaders . . . peace for which they would be prepared to pay a price. Others shouted : "Death to the Christians ! No surrender !"

And as they lifted the mangled remains of the intrepid Moor, an angry murmur arose.

One of their Christian prisoners was brought out. They slew him most cruelly; they tied his mutilated body astride a mule, which they drove out from Malaga into the Christian camp.

* * *

Inside the city the heat was intense. There was little to eat now. There were few dogs and cats left; they had long ago eaten their horses. They existed on vine leaves; they were emaciated, and in the streets men and women were dying of exhaustion or unspecified diseases. And outside the walls of the city the Christians still waited.

Several of the town's important men formed themselves into a band and presented themselves before Hamet Zeli.

"We cannot much longer endure this suffering," they told him.

He shook his head. "In time, help will come to us."

"When it comes, Hamet Zeli, it will be too late."

"I have sworn to El Zagal never to surrender."

"In the streets the people are dying of hunger and pestilence. No help will come to us. Our crops have been destroyed; our cattle stolen. What has become of our fertile vineyards? The Christians have left our land desolate and we are dying a slow death. Allah has turned his face against us. Open the gates of the city and let the Christians in."

"That is the wish of the people?" asked Hamet Zeli.

"It is the wish of all."

"Then I will take my forces into the Gebalfaro, and you may make your peace with Ferdinand."

The burghers looked at each other. "It is what we wished to do weeks ago," said one of them.

"That is true," said another. "You, Ali Dordux should lead a deputation to Ferdinand. He offered us special concessions some weeks ago if we would surrender the town to him. Tell him that we are now ready to do so."

"I will lead my deputation to him with all speed," said Ali Dordux. "It may be that the sooner we go, the more lives we shall save."

"Go from me now," said Hamet Zeli. "This is no affair of mine. I would never surrender. I would die rather than bow to the Christian invader."

"We are not soldiers, Hamet Zeli," said Ali Dordux. "We are men of peace. And no fate which the Christian can impose upon us could be worse than that which we have endured."

"You do not know Ferdinand," answered Hamet Zeli. "You do not know the Christians."

* * *

Ferdinand heard that the deputation had called upon him.

"Led, Highness," he was told, "by Ali Dordux, the most prominent and wealthy citizen. They beg an audience that they may discuss terms for surrendering the city to you."

Ferdinand smiled slowly.

"Pray return to them," he said, "and tell them this : I offered them peace and they refused it. Then they were in a position to bargain. Now they are a conquered people. It is not for them to make terms with me but to accept those on which I shall decide."

The deputation returned to Malaga, and when it was learned what Ferdinand had said there was loud wailing throughout the city.

"Now," the people whispered to each other, "we know that we can expect no mercy from the Christians."

There were many to exhort them to stand firm. "Let us die rather than surrender," they cried. They had a wonderful leader in Hamet Zeli; why did they not put their trust in him?

Because their families were starving, was the answer. They had seen their wives and children die of disease and hunger. There must be an end to the siege at any price.

A new embassy was sent to Ferdinand.

They would surrender their city to him in exchange for their lives and freedom. Let him refuse this offer and every Christian in Malaga—and they held six hundred Christian prisoners—should be hanged over the battlements. They would put the aged and the weak, the women and the children, into the fortress, set fire to the town and cut a way for themselves through the enemy. So that Ferdinand would lose the rich treasure of Malaga.

But Ferdinand was aware that he was dealing with a beaten people. He felt no pity; he would give no quarter. He was a hard man completely lacking in imagination. He saw only the advantage to his own cause.

He was making no compacts, he replied. If any Christian within the city was harmed he would slaughter every Moslem within the walls of Malaga.

This was the end of resistance. The gates of the city were thrown open to Ferdinand.

* * *

Isabella, richly gowned, rode beside Ferdinand into the conquered city of Malaga.

It had been purified before their arrival, and over all the principal buildings floated the flag of Christian Spain.

The great mosque was now the church of Santa Maria de la Encarnacion; and bells could be heard ringing throughout the city.

Isabella's first desire was to visit the new cathedral and there give thanks for the victory.

Afterwards she rode through the streets, but she did not see the terror in the eyes of the people; she did not see the cupidity in those of Ferdinand as he surveyed these rich treasures which had fallen into his hands. She heard only the bells; she could only rejoice.

Another great city for Christ, she told herself. The Moorish kingdom was depleted afresh. This was the greatest victory they had yet achieved, for the Moors in Granada would be seriously handicapped by the loss of their great port.

A cry of anger went up from the assembly as the Christian slaves tottered out into the streets; some could scarcely see, because they had been kept so long in darkness. They limped and dragged themselves along, to fall at the feet of the Sovereigns in order to kiss their hands in gratitude for their deliverance.

The sound of their chains being pulled along as they walked was audible, for as they approached the Sovereigns there was a deep silence among the spectators.

"No," cried Isabella; and she slipped from her horse and placed her hands on the shoulders of the blind old man who was seeking to kiss her hand. "You shall not kneel to me," she went on. And she raised him up. And those watching saw the tears in her eyes, a sight which moved those who knew her, as much as the spectacle of these poor slaves.

Ferdinand had joined her. He too embraced the slaves; he too wept; but he could weep more easily than Isabella, and he quickly allowed indignation to dry his tears.

Isabella said: "Let these people be taken from here. Let their chains be taken from them. Let a banquet be prepared for them. They must know that I shall not allow their sufferings to be forgotten. They shall be recompensed for their long captivity."

Then she mounted her horse and the procession continued.

Hamet Zeli was brought before them, proud, bold, though emaciated, and in heavy chains.

"You should have surrendered long ere this," Ferdinand told him. "You see how foolish you have been. You might once have bought concessions for your people."

"I was commanded to defend Malaga," said Hamet Zeli. "Had I been supported, I would have died before giving in."

"Thus you show your folly," said Ferdinand. "Now you will obey my commands. I would have the whole of the population of Malaga assembled in the courtyard of the *alcazaba* to hear the sentence I shall pass upon them."

"Great Ferdinand," said Hamet Zeli, "you have conquered Malaga. Take its treasures. They are yours."

"They are mine," said Ferdinand smiling; "and certainly I shall take them."

"But, Christian King, spare the people of Malaga."

"Should they be allowed to go free for all the inconvenience they have caused me? Many of my men have died at their hands."

"Do what you will with the soldiers, but the citizens played no part in this war."

"Their obstinacy has angered me," said Ferdinand. "Assemble them that they may hear their fate."

* * *

In the courtyard of the *alcazaba*, the people had assembled. All through the day the sound of wailing voices had filled the streets.

The people were calling on Allah not to desert them. They begged him to plant compassion and mercy in the heart of the Christian King.

But Allah ignored their cries, and the heart of the Christian King was hardened against them.

He told them what their fate would be in one word : Slavery.

Every man, woman and child was to be sold or given in slavery. They had defied him and, because of this, they must pay for their foolishness with their freedom.

Slavery ! The dreaded word fell on the still, hot air.

Where was the proud city of Malaga now? Lost to the Arabs for evermore. What would befall its people? They would be scattered throughout the world. Children would be torn from their parents, husbands from their wives. This was the decree of the Christian King : Slavery for the proud people of Malaga.

* * *

In the *alcazaba* Ferdinand rubbed his hands together. He could scarcely speak, so excited was he. He could only contemplate the treasures of this beautiful city which were now his . . . all his.

Then a certain fear came to him. How could he be sure that all the treasure would be handed to him? These Arabs were a cunning people. Might they not hide their most precious jewels, their richest treasures, hoping to preserve them for themselves?

It was an alarming thought. Yet how could he be sure that this would not happen?

Isabella was calculating what they would do with the slaves.

"We shall be able to redeem some of our own people," she told Ferdinand.

Ferdinand was not enthusiastic. He was thinking of selling the slaves. They would help to fill the treasury, he pointed out.

But Isabella was determined. "We must not forget those of our people who have been taken into slavery. I propose that we send one-third of the people of Malaga into Africa in exchange for an equal number of our people held there as slaves."

"And sell the rest," said Ferdinand quickly.

"We might sell another third," Isabella replied. "This should bring us a goodly sum which will be very useful for prosecuting the war."

"And the remainder?"

"We must not forget the custom. We should send some to our friends. Do not forget that those who have worked with us and have helped us to win this great victory will expect some reward. The Pope should be presented with some, so should the Queen of Naples. And we must not forget that we hope for this marriage between Isabella and Alonso; so I would send some of the most beautiful of the girls to the Queen of Portugal."

"So," said Ferdinand, somewhat disgruntled, "we shall only sell a third of them for our own benefit."

But what was really worrying him was the thought that he could not be sure that all the treasures of Malaga would come to him, and he feared that some might be secreted away and he not know of their existence.

* * *

Hope suddenly sprang up in the desolate town of Malaga.

"There is a chance to regain our freedom!" The words were passed through the streets from mouth to mouth. A chance to evade this most dreadful of fates.

King Ferdinand had decreed that if they could pay a large enough ransom he would sell them their freedom.

And the amount demanded?

It was a sum of such a size that it seemed impossible that they could raise it. Yet every man, woman and child in Malaga must help to do so.

Nothing must be held back. Everything must be poured into the great fund which was to buy freedom for the people of Malaga.

The fund grew big, but it was still short of the figure demanded by Ferdinand.

In the streets the people called to each other: "Hold nothing back. Think of what depends upon it."

And the fund grew until it contained every treasure, great and small, for all agreed that no price was too great to pay for freedom.

* * *

Ferdinand received the treasure.

"Oh, great Christian King," he was implored, "this is not the large sum you asked. It falls a little short. We pray you accept it, and out of your magnanimity grant us our freedom."

Ferdinand smiled and accepted the treasure.

"Alas," he said, "it is not the figure I demanded. I am a man who keeps his word. This is not enough to buy freedom for the people of Malaga."

When he had dismissed the Arabs he laughed aloud.

Thus he had made sure that the people of Malaga would hold nothing back from him. Thus he had defeated them utterly and completely. He had all their wealth, and still they had not regained their freedom.

The capture of Malaga was a resounding victory.

There remained the last stronghold: Granada.

MARRIAGE OF AN INFANTA

THE Queen crept into the bedchamber of her daughter, the Infanta Isabella. As she had expected, the girl was lying on her bed, her eyes wide open, staring into space.

"My dearest child," said the Queen, "you must not be unhappy."

"But to go far away from you all," murmured the Infanta.

"It is not so very far."

"It is too far," said the girl.

"You are nineteen years old, my daughter. That is no longer young."

Young Isabella shivered. "If I could only stay with you!"

The Queen shook her head. She was thinking how happy she would be if it were possible to find a husband for her eldest daughter here at the Court, and if they might enjoy the preparations for marriage together; if after the wedding, she, the mother, might be beside her daughter, advising, helping, sharing.

It was a foolish speculation, and they should be rejoicing. For years Portugal had represented a menace. It would always be so while La Beltraneja lived. And John, the King, had allowed her to live outside her convent! In Portugal there had been times when La Beltraneja had been known as Her Highness the Queen.

This could have been a cause for war. She and Ferdinand might have deemed it wise to make war on Portugal, had they not been so busily engaged elsewhere.

And now John saw the advantages of a match between his son Alonso and the Infanta of Castile. If this marriage took place he would no longer allow La Beltraneja to be called Her Highness the Queen, he would stop speculating as to whether it would be possible to put her back on the throne of Castile, and instead send her back to her convent.

"Oh, my darling," said the Queen, taking her daughter's limp hand and raising it to her lips, "with this marriage you are bringing great good to your country. Does that not comfort you?"

"Yes, dear Mother," said the Infanta faintly. "It brings me comfort."

Then Isabella kissed her daughter's forehead and crept away.

* * *

It was April in Seville and there was *fiesta* in the streets.

The people had gathered to watch the coming and going of great personages. These were the streets which so frequently saw the grim processions of Inquisitors, and condemned men in their yellow *sanbenitos*, making their way to the Cathedral and the fields of Tablada. Now here was a different sort of entertainment; and the people threw themselves into it with an almost frenzied joy.

Their Infanta Isabella was to be married to the heir of Portugal. There were to be feasts and banquets, bull-fights and dancing. This was a glorious occasion which would not end in death.

Tents had been set up along the banks of the Guadalquivir for the tourneys which were to take place. The buildings were decorated with flags and cloth of gold. The people had grown accustomed to seeing groups of horsemen magnificently caparisoned—the members of their royal family and that of Portugal.

They saw their King distinguish himself in the tournaments, and they shouted themselves hoarse in approval of the stalwart Ferdinand, who had recently won such resounding victories over the Moors and was even now preparing for what he hoped would be the final blow.

And there was the Queen, always gracious, always serene; and the people remembered that she had brought law and order to a state where it had been unsafe for travellers to ride out on their journeys. She had also brought this new Inquisition. But this was a time of rejoicing. They were determined to forget all that was unpleasant.

The Infanta, who looked younger than her nineteen years, was tall and stately, rather pale and delicate but very lovely, full of grace and charm—the happy bride.

The bridegroom did not come to Seville, but the news had spread that he was young, ardent and handsome. In his place was Don Fernando de Silveira, who appeared at the side of the Infanta on all public occasions—a proxy for his master.

Yes, this was a time of rejoicing. The marriage was approved by all. It was going to mean peace for ever with their western neighbours, and peace was something for which everybody longed.

So they tried to forget their friends and relations who were held by the Holy Office. They danced and sang in the streets, and cried: "Long live Isabella! Long live Ferdinand! Long life to the Infanta!"

* * *

To go from one's home to a new country! How often it had happened. It was the natural fate of an Infanta.

Does everyone suffer as I do? young Isabella asked herself.

But we have been so happy here. Our mother has been so kind, so gentle, so just to us all. Our father has loved us. Ours has been such a happy home. Am I now regretting that this has been so? Am I saying that, had we been a less happy family, I should not be suffering as I am now?

No. Any daughter should rejoice to have such a mother as the Queen.

They were dressing her in her bridal robes, and her women were exclaiming at her beauty.

"The Prince Alonso will be enchanted," they told her.

But will he? she asked herself. Can I believe them?

She had heard certain scandal at the Court concerning her own father. He had sons and daughters whom she did not know. Her mother must have heard this, yet she gave no sign of it. How could I ever be like her? the Infanta Isabella asked herself. And if *she* does not satisfy my father, how could I hope to satisfy Alonso?

There was so little she knew, so much she had to learn; she felt that she was being buffeted into a world of new sensations, new emotions, and she was unsure whether she would be able to deal with them.

"It is time, Infanta," she was told.

And she left her apartments to be joined by the seventy ladies, all brilliantly clad, and the hundred pages in similar magnificent attire, who were waiting to conduct her to the ceremony.

She placed her hand in that of Don Fernando de Silveira and the solemn words were spoken.

The ceremony was over; she was the wife of the heir of Portugal, the wife of a man whom she had never seen.

Out in the streets they were shouting her name. She smiled and acknowledged their applause in the manner in which she had been taught.

On to the banquets, on to the balls and fêtes and tourneys—all given in honour of a frightened girl whose single prayer was that something would happen which would prevent her leaving the heart of the family she loved.

* * *

There was respite. All through the summer the festivities continued, and it was not until autumn that she rode out of Castile.

The people lined the roads to see her pass and cheer her.

It was said that Portugal had prepared to welcome her in a royal manner. They were delighted to receive her. She brought with her a larger dowry than that usually accorded to the Infantas of Castile, and it was said that she had such magnificent gowns which alone had cost twenty thousand golden florins.

And so, on she rode over the border, away from her old country into the new.

* * *

She was bewildered by the pomp which awaited her.

She saw one man standing by the throne of the King who smiled at her encouragingly. He was young and handsome, and his eyes lingered on her.

She thought: There is my husband. There is Alonso. And she averted her eyes because she was afraid that, out of her inexperience, she might betray her emotion.

She approached King John, and knelt before him, but he raised her up and embraced her. "Welcome, my daughter," he said. "We have long awaited your coming. I rejoice that you are safely with us."

"I thank Your Highness," she answered.

"There is one who waits most impatiently to greet you! My son, who is also your husband."

And there he was, Alonso—not the man she had at first noticed—young and handsome; and because she sensed that he also was a little nervous, she felt happier.

He embraced her before the Court and the people cried: "Long live the Prince and Princess of Portugal!"

* * *

And so she came to happiness. Her mother had been right. If one grasped one's duty firmly, one was rewarded. She knew she was particularly fortunate, because she had been given a young and handsome husband, a kindly gentle husband, who admitted that marriage alarmed him even as it alarmed her.

Now they could comfort each other, they could laugh at their fears. And out of the intensity of their relief in having found each other, was born a great affection.

Isabella wrote home of her happiness.

Her mother wrote of her intense joy to receive such glad news from her daughter.

All was well. The important link had been forged between two old enemies, and at no cost to the happiness of the Queen's beloved daughter.

Now that she was away from her mother's supervision, the character of the Princess began to change. She discovered a love of dancing, a love of laughter. This was shared by Alonso.

One day Isabella woke up to the realization that she had begun to live in a way which she had not thought possible. She had realized that life could be a gay affair, that one need not think all the time of the saving of one's soul.

"We are young," said Alonso, "we have our lives before us. There is plenty of time, twenty years hence, for us to think of the life to come."

And she laughed with him at what, such a short time ago, would have shocked her deeply.

She grew less pale; her cough worried her less, for she was spending a great deal of time out of doors. Alonso loved to hunt, and he was unhappy unless she accompanied him.

She understood that these months, since she had been the wife of Alonso, were the happiest she had ever known. It was a startling and wonderful discovery.

Her beauty was intensified. Many people watched her unfold. She was like a bud that opened to become a beautiful flower, slightly less fragile than had been expected.

"You are beautiful," she was often told; and she had learned to accept such compliments with grace.

"No one at Court is more beautiful than you," she was assured by Emmanuel, Alonso's cousin, the young man whom she had noticed when she had first come to the Court.

"When I arrived," she told him, "I thought you were Alonso."

Emmanuel's face glowed with sudden passion. "How I wish that had been so," he said.

* * *

Afterwards she said to herself that it was folly to expect such happiness to last.

A day arrived which began as other days began.

She awoke in the morning to find Alonso beside her . . . handsome Alonso who woke so suddenly and in such high spirits, who embraced her and made love to her and then said: "Come, I want to hunt while the morning is young. We will leave as soon as we are ready. Come, Isabella, it is a beautiful morning."

So they summoned their huntsmen, mounted their horses and rode away into the forest.

Indeed it was a beautiful morning; the sun shone on them and they exchanged smiles and jokes as they rode along.

They were separated for a while in the hunt, so she did not see it happen.

She had been aware of a sudden stillness in the woods—a brief stillness, yet it seemed to her to last a long time, for it brought to her, like the scent of an animal on the wind, the consciousness of evil.

The silence was broken by shouting voices, by cries of alarm.

When she arrived on the scene of the accident the huntsmen had improvised a stretcher, and on it lay her beautiful, her beloved Alonso.

* * *

He was dead when they reached the Palace. She could not believe it. It was too sudden, too tragic. She had entered her new life, had learned to understand it and to find it contained more happiness than she had believed possible, only to lose it.

The Palace was plunged into mourning. The King's only son, the heir to the throne, was dead. But none mourned more sincerely, none was more broken-hearted than Alonso's young widow.

Now the young Emmanuel was treated with greater respect than had ever before come his way, for who would have believed that one so healthy and vital as Alonso would not live to take the crown.

But he had died in the space of a few hours, and now the more intellectual Emmanuel was heir to the throne.

Isabella was unaware of what was going on in the Palace. Everything else was obscured by this one overwhelming fact: she had lost Alonso.

The King sent for her, for her grief alarmed him. He had been warned that if she continued to shut herself away and mourn, she herself would soon join her husband.

What would Isabella and Ferdinand have to say to that? The Princess was a precious commodity. It was important that she be kept alive.

"My dear," he said to her, "you must not shut yourself away. This terrible thing has happened, and you cannot change it by continually grieving."

"He was my husband, and I loved him," said Isabella.

"I know. We loved him also. He was our son and our heir. We knew him longer than you did, so you see our grief is not small either. Come, I must command you to take more care of your health. Promise me you will do this."

"I promise," said Isabella.

She walked in the Palace gardens and asked that she might be alone. She looked with blank eyes at terraces and statues. There she had walked with Alonso. There they had sat and planned how they would spend the days.

There was nothing but memories.

Emmanuel joined her and walked beside her.

"I would rather be alone," she said.

"Forgive me. Allow me to talk with you for a minute or two. Oh, Isabella, how it grieves me to see you so unhappy."

"Sometimes I blame myself," she said. "I was too happy. I thought only of my happiness; and perhaps we are not meant to be happy."

"You suffered ill fortune, Isabella. We *are* meant to be happy. When you have recovered from this shock, I would implore you to give me a chance to make you happy."

"I do not understand you."

"I am heir to my uncle's throne. Therefore your parents would consider me as worthy a match as Alonso."

She stood very still in horror.

"I could never think of marrying anyone else," she said. "Alonso is the only husband I shall ever want."

"You say that because you are young and your grief is so close."

"I say it because I know it to be true."

"Do not dismiss me so lightly, Isabella. Think of what I have said."

* * *

She was always conscious of him. He was so often at her side.

No, no, she cried with all her heart. This cannot be.

And she fretted and continued to mourn, so that the King of Portugal's alarm increased.

He wrote to the Sovereigns of Castile, to tell them how their daughter's grief alarmed him.

"Send our daughter home to us," said Isabella. "I myself will nurse her back to health."

So a few months after she had left her country Isabella returned to Castile.

And when she felt herself enfolded in her mother's embrace she cried out that she was happy to come home. She had lost her beloved husband, but her beloved mother was left to her—and only through the Queen and a life devoted to piety could she want to live.

THE LAST SIGH OF THE MOOR

THE time had come for the onslaught on the capital of the Moorish Kingdom, and Ferdinand's army was now ready to begin the attack.

He and Isabella were waiting to receive Boabdil. They had sent a messenger to him, reminding him of the terms he had agreed to in exchange for his release, and they now commanded him to leave Granada and present himself before them, that the terms of surrender might be discussed.

Ferdinand hoped that the people of Granada would remember the terrible fate which had overtaken Malaga, and that they would not be so foolish as to behave in such a way that Ferdinand would have no resort but to treat them similarly.

"He should be here ere this," Ferdinand was saying. "He should know better than to keep us waiting."

Isabella was silent. She was praying that the surrender of the last Moorish stronghold might be accomplished without the loss of much Christian blood.

But the time passed and Boabdil did not come.

Isabella looked at Ferdinand, and she knew that he was already making plans for the siege of Granada.

* * *

The messenger stood before the Sovereigns.

He handed the despatch to Ferdinand, who, with Isabella, read what Boabdil had written.

"It is impossible for me to obey your summons. I am no longer able to control my own desires. It is my wish to keep my promises, but the city of Granada refuses to allow me to depart. It is full now, not only with its own population, but those who have come from all over the kingdom to defend it. Therefore I regret that I cannot keep my promise to you."

Ferdinand clenched his fists and the veins stood out at his temples.

"So," he said, "they will not surrender."

"It is hardly to be expected that they would," Isabella replied mildly. "When we have taken Granada, consider, Ferdinand, we shall have completed the reconquest. Could we expect it to fall into our hands like a ripe fruit? Nay, we must fight for this last, this greatest prize."

"He has spoken," said Ferdinand. "He has chosen his own fate and that of his people. We shall no longer hesitate. Now it shall be . . . to Granada!"

The Sovereigns called together the Council and, while it was sitting, news was brought that fresh revolts had broken out in many of the cities which had been captured from the Moors. There had been Moorish forays into Christian territory, and Christians had been slaughtered or carried away to be prisoners or slaves.

This was the answer to Ferdinand's imperious command to the Moorish king.

The war was not yet won. The Moors were ready to defend the last stronghold of the land which they had called their own for seven hundred years.

* * *

In the little house in Cordova, Cristobal continued to wait for a summons to Court. None came. From time to time he saw some of his friends at Court, particularly Luis de Sant'angel. Beatriz de Bobadilla sent messages to him, and occasionally he received sums of money through her, which she said came from the Queen.

But still there was no summons to Court, no news of the fitting out of the expedition.

Little Ferdinand, the son of Cristobal and Beatriz de Arana, would sit on his knee and be told tales of the sea, as once little Diego had.

Beatriz watched Cristobal uneasily. Once she had been secretly glad that the summons did not come; but she was glad no longer. How could she endure to see her Cristobal grow old and grey, fretting continually against the ill fortune which would not give him the chance he asked.

One day a friend of his early days called at the house.

Cristobal was delighted to see him, and Beatriz brought wine and refreshments. The visitor admired sturdy little Ferdinand—also Beatriz.

He came from France, he said; and he brought a message from Cristobal's brother, Bartholomew.

Bartholomew wished to know how Cristobal was faring in Spain, and whether he found the Spanish Sovereigns ready to help him in his enterprise.

"He says, if you do not find this assistance, you should consider coming to France, where there is a growing interest in maritime adventures."

"France," murmured Cristobal, and Beatriz saw the light leap into his eyes once more. "I had thought once of going to France."

When the visitor had left, Beatriz brought her chair close to that of Cristobal; she took his hand and smiled at him fondly.

"What is the use of waiting?" she said. "You must go, Cristobal. It is the whole meaning of life to you. Do not think I do not understand. Go to France. Perhaps you will be fortunate there. And if you must wait upon the French Sovereign as you have on those of Spain, then will I join you. But if they give you what you want, if you make your voyage, you will come back to us here in Cordova. Ferdinand and I can wait for you."

Then Cristobal rose and drawing her to her feet kissed her solemnly.

She knew that he had made his decision.

* * *

Ferdinand's troops were encamped on the banks of the Xenil, and before them lay the city of Granada. A natural fortress, it seemed impregnable, and even the most optimistic realized that its storming would be long and hazardous.

They could see the great walls which defended it on the side which faced the Christian armies; and on the east side the peaks of the Sierra Nevada made a natural barrier.

Ferdinand looked at that great fortress, and he swore to take it.

From the battlements the Moors looked down on the Christian armies; they saw that the fertile land before the city had been burned and pillaged, the crops destroyed; and they vowed vengeance on the Christians.

So the two combatants—Arab and Christian—stood face to face, and both decided to fight to the death.

* * *

Ferdinand, who had seen the effect Isabella could have on the troops at the time of the siege of Malaga, had suggested that she should accompany the army. Isabella's reply was that she had had no intention to do otherwise. This was her war, even more than it was Ferdinand's. It was she who had made her early vows that, should it ever be in her power to do so, she would make an all-Christian Spain.

So to the battle-front came Isabella. The Prince of the Asturias, although only thirteen years old, was with his father. He already considered himself to be a warrior, for in the spring of the previous year Ferdinand had conferred the honour of knighthood upon him, and the ceremony had been performed on the battlefield.

Isabella had brought with her her children and some of her ladies, for she had determined that she would not be parted from her family again. She believed that the presence of the entire royal family in camp was an inspiration to the army; as indeed it seemed to be.

Isabella herself was indefatigable. She nursed the sick, and even her youngest, the five-year-old Catalina, was given tasks to do. Her eldest, Isabella, worked with fervour; for since the death of Alonso, the piety of the young Isabella had rivalled that of the elder.

Ferdinand was delighted to have his family with him, for where the Queen was, dignity and decorum were not forgotten. There was neither gambling nor swearing in the camp when the Queen was present; instead there were continual prayers. Ferdinand was quick to realize the importance of a disciplined army, and the dignity of the Queen was more effective in ensuring this than any strict rules he could have enforced.

The weeks passed, but the great battle for Granada did not take place. There was deadlock between the two forces.

The great fortress remained impregnable.

* * *

Cristobal had said his farewells. He had left Cordova and travelled westward.

But before he could find his way to France there was one call he must make.

It was six years since he had seen Diego, and he could not leave Spain without seeing his son once more and explaining that he was leaving the country.

Thus it was that on a July day he arrived at the Monastery of Santa Maria de la Rabida, to find at the gate the lay brother who had been there on that day when Cristobal had come there with Diego. "I seek shelter," he said.

"Enter, my friend," was the answer. "It is denied no traveller within these walls."

And when he had entered, he said: "Tell me, is Fray Juan Perez de Marchena at the Monastery?"

"He is here, my friend."

"I greatly wish to speak with him."

Fray Juan embraced him and took him into the room where they had previously talked.

"You see a defeated man," said Cristobal. "Spain treats me

even as Portugal has done. I have come to see my son, and to ask you if you will keep him here a little longer, or whether I should take him with me into France."

"You are leaving us, Cristobal Colon?"

"There is no point in staying."

"I did not think you were a man who would give in so easily."

"I am a man determined to embark on an enterprise."

"And you have decided to leave Spain."

"I am going to lay my proposition before the French. I have heard from my brother who is there. He tells me that there is some hope that there I might find more willing ears."

"This grieves me."

"You have been so good to me."

"I will send for Diego," said Fray Juan.

* * *

Cristobal beheld the tall youth with astonishment.

"Can it be?" he cried with emotion.

"I do not ask the same," answered the youth. "I know you, Father."

They embraced, and the bright blue eyes of the adventurer were misty with tears.

Finally, Cristobal released his son. He laid his hands on his shoulders and looked into his face.

"So, Father, you did not succeed."

"I do not give up hope, my son. I am leaving Spain. Will you come with me?"

Fray Juan had come forward. He said: "We have taken good care of Diego. We have educated him, as you will learn, Señor Colon. If he left us his education would be interrupted. I could wish that you had not decided to leave Spain for a while, and that Diego would stay with us."

"My mind is made up," said Cristobal.

"This day I feel prophetic," said the Friar. "Señor Colon, will you stay with us for a week . . . two weeks? Will you give me your company for that time?"

"You are hospitable; you have done much for me. One day I shall reward you. If the French support me, one day I shall be a rich man. I shall not forget your kindness."

"If you give me riches it would not be what I asked; and of what use is a gift which is not acceptable? I have cared for your son for six years. Give me this now. Stay here with us . . . two weeks . . . three . . . This is all I ask."

"For what reason do you ask this?"

"Obey me unquestioningly. I believe one day you will not regret it."

Diego said: "Father, you cannot deny Fray Juan this."

Cristobal looked at the earnest face of the Prior.

"If you would tell me . . ." he began.

"I will tell you this. I believe it is God's will that you stay here. Señor Colon, do not deny me what I ask."

"Since you put it like this, I will stay," said Cristobal.

* * *

Fray Juan was satisfied.

He left father and son together and went to his cell.

He wrote for some time; then destroyed what he had written.

He paced his cell. He knelt and prayed.

Then he made a sudden decision.

He went to Cristobal and Diego and said: "I have to leave the monastery on a most urgent matter. You have given me your word, Cristobal Colon, that you will stay here. I want you to promise me now that you will not leave until I return."

He looked so earnest that Cristobal gave his promise.

And that very day the Prior set out on his mule for the two-hundred-mile journey to Granada.

* * *

Isabella lay sleeping in her pavilion. These elaborate sleeping quarters were very different from the tents used by the soldiers, and had been provided for her by the Marquis of Cadiz.

She was weary, for the days in camp were exhausting. She was continually going among the troops, talking to them of their homes, urging them to valour; and as there were constant skirmishes, there were many wounded to be attended to.

But now the night was still, and she slept.

She awoke suddenly to a sense of alarm; it was some seconds before she realized that what had awakened her was the smell of burning.

She hastened from her bed, calling to her women, and as she ran from the pavilion she saw that draperies at one side of it were ablaze and that the fire had spread to the nearby tents.

Isabella immediately thought of her children, who were sleeping near the pavilion, and she found time in those seconds to visualize a hundred horrors which might befall them.

"Fire!" called Isabella. "Fire in the camp!"

Immediately the camp was awake, and Isabella made with all

speed to those tents in which the royal children were sleeping; she found to her immense joy that the fire had not yet touched them, so she roused the children hastily and, throwing a few clothes about them, they hurried with her into the open.

There she found Ferdinand giving instructions.

"Be watchful," he called to the sentinels. "If the enemy see what is happening they might attack."

As Isabella, with her daughters, watched the soldiers dealing with the fire, she noticed that Juana's eyes were dancing with excitement and that the child seemed even a little disappointed when the fire was under control. Maria looked on with an expression which was almost one of indifference, while little Catalina grasped her mother's hand and clung to it tightly. Their sister Isabella seemed listless, as she had habitually become since the death of Alonso.

The Marquis of Cadiz joined Isabella and explained that a lamp had evidently caught the draperies of the pavilion and the wind had carried the flame to the nearby and highly inflammable tents.

At length Isabella led the children into one of the tents which had been prepared for them. She lifted Catalina into her arms and the child was almost immediately asleep.

She kept them with her for the rest of the night.

* * *

The elaborate pavilion and many of the costly tents and their furnishings had been destroyed; and in the morning Ferdinand estimated the damage with a frown. The loss of valuable property always upset him more than any other calamity.

"Ferdinand," said Isabella slowly, "this might have been a great disaster. We might have lost our lives, if the Saints had not watched over us. How ironical if, on the eve of victory, we should have died through a fire caused accidentally."

Ferdinand nodded grimly. "The loss must amount to a small fortune," he grumbled.

"I have been thinking, Ferdinand. It is now July. Very soon the summer will be over. Suppose we do not take Granada before the winter is upon us?"

Ferdinand was silent.

"The advantage," she went on, "will be all on the side of our enemies. They will be in warm winter quarters in their town, while we shall be exposed to the weather in our encampment."

"You and the children will have to leave us."

"And what effect will that have, do you think? I prefer to

remain with the army, Ferdinand. I think it is essential that I remain with the army."

"Then we shall have to retire and come back in the spring."

"And lose the advantage we now have! No! I have a plan. We will build ourselves a town here . . . here on the plain before Granada."

"A town! You cannot mean that."

"But I do mean it, Ferdinand. We will build houses of stone which will not take fire so easily as our tents. We will build a great garrison—houses, quarters for the soldiers and stables. And we shall not retreat from our position, but stay here all through the winter as comfortably housed as our enemies!"

"Is this possible?"

"With God's help everything is possible," she answered.

"It would have to be completed in three months."

"So shall it be."

Ferdinand looked at her with admiration. The previous day she had been exhausted by her work in the camp; her night had been disturbed by this disastrous fire; and here she sat, looking fresh and as energetic as ever, calmly proposing a plan which, had anyone but Isabella suggested it, he would have declared to be absurd.

* * *

Before Granada the work went on. The town grew up with a speed which astonished all who beheld it.

The Moors looked on in despair.

They understood the meaning of this. The Christians would remain there throughout the winter. The respite for which they had longed would be denied them.

"Allah has turned his face from us," wailed the people of Granada. And they cursed Boabdil, their King, who had brought civil war among them when he had challenged the rule of Muley Abul Hassan.

Isabella moved about among her workmen. They must work harder. The task was tremendous, but it must be accomplished. They must ignore the sporadic sallies of the Moors. They must build their town by winter.

There were two avenues traversing this new town as Isabella had planned that there should be.

"Thus," she said, "my new town is in the form of the cross—that cross for which we fight. It shall be the only town in Spain which has not been contaminated by Moslem heresy."

The town must have a name, it was decided; and a deputation

of workers came to her and asked if she would honour the town by bestowing her name upon it.

She smiled graciously. "I thank you for the honour you have done me," she said. "I thank you for the good work you have done in this town. But I have decided on a more appropriate name than my own. We shall call this town Santa Fé."

And there was the town in the shape of a cross—a monument to the determination of the Christians not to rest until they had brought about the reconquest of every inch of Spanish soil.

* * *

Beatriz de Bobadilla was in her quarters within the fortifications of Santa Fé when one of her women came to her and told her that a friar had arrived and wished to speak to her on the most urgent business.

Beatriz received him at once.

"My lady," said Fray Juan, "it is kind of you to receive me so promptly."

"Why," she said, "you have made a long journey and you are exhausted."

"I have travelled two hundred miles from La Rabida, but the matter is one which needs urgent attention, and I beg you to give it. It concerns the explorer, Cristobal Colon."

"Ah," said Beatriz, "the explorer." She smiled almost tenderly. "How fares it with him?"

"He is frustrated, my lady; indignant and angry with Spain and himself. He is no longer a young man, and he bitterly resents the wasted years."

"There has been so much to occupy the mind of the Queen," she answered.

"It is true, and a tragedy for Spain. Unless something is done immediately, he will leave the country, and some other monarch will have the benefit of his genius."

"That must not be," said Beatriz.

"It will be, my lady, unless there is no more delay."

Beatriz made a quick decision. "I am going to see that you are given refreshment and an opportunity to wash the travel-stains from your person. I will go to the Queen immediately and, when I have returned, I will let you know whether Señor Colon is to be given help from Spain. I promise to let you know how I have fared with all speed."

The Prior smiled. He had done his part, and there was no more he could do.

* * *

Beatriz begged an audience with the Queen. Ferdinand was with Isabella, a fact which dismayed Beatriz.

But Ferdinand was friendly. He was pleased with the way events were moving, and was very much aware of the important part the women were playing before Granada.

"Highness," said Beatriz, "I come to you in great haste. Fray Juan Perez de Marchena has arrived in Santa Fé from La Rabida. Cristobal Colon is on the point of leaving Spain."

"I am sorry to hear this," said the Queen. "Was he not told to wait awhile, and that his schemes would have our attention when we had the time to devote to them?"

"Yes, Highness, he was, but he will wait no longer. He thinks that his expedition is of the greatest importance; and frankly, if your Highnesses will not help him, he has decided to find a Sovereign who will do so. He plans to go to France."

At the mention of the great enemy of Aragon, Ferdinand flushed with anger. His eyes narrowed, and with a certain delight Beatriz noticed the lights of cupidity shining there.

She went on to talk of the riches which he would bring back if he were successful. "For, Your Highnesses, even if he should fail in his discovery of a New World, he will have shown us a new route to the riches of Cathay and the East, of which Marco Polo wrote so glowingly.

"I thought," she finished, "that Your Highnesses would wish to stop him before he has an opportunity of bringing to another the riches which, would you but equip his expedition, he would lay at your feet."

"Willingly," said Isabella, "would we equip him for this expedition, but everything we possess must go into the prosecution of the war."

She looked at Ferdinand.

"Highness," pleaded Beatriz, "would it be so costly? It is unbearable to think that all that he might discover may go to another country."

"I was impressed by the man," said Isabella. She looked at Ferdinand as though expecting him to speak against asking the man to return, but Ferdinand said nothing; his eyes had that glazed look, and she realized that he was seeing the return of the explorer, his ships laden with treasures—gold, jewels, slaves.

Isabella continued: "I would be prepared to reconsider what might be done." She smiled towards Ferdinand. "Perhaps the King would agree with me in this."

Ferdinand was thinking: The man must be stopped from taking his plans to France. Even if he and the Queen did not fit out his expedition, they must stop him from taking his plans to the enemy.

Ferdinand smiled at Isabella. "As usual, Your Highness speaks good sense. Let us recall this man and reconsider what he has to tell us."

Beatriz cried: "Thank you, Your Highnesses. I am sure your munificence will be rewarded." She turned to Isabella. "Highness, this man is poor. Would you agree that he might be sent money for his journey here, money to buy garments which would make him fit to appear before Your Highnesses?"

"By all means let that be done," said Isabella.

* * *

Within Granada conditions were deteriorating rapidly. The effect of the building of Santa Fé was disastrous to the morale of the besieged. The blockade, which the people had hoped would be lifted by the retirement of the Christian army during the winter, continued.

There were some who declared that there must be no surrender, that their fellow Moslems in Africa would never allow them to lose their grip on Spanish soil. But there were others who gazed out on the bustling and efficient fortifications of Santa Fé, who considered the destruction of the crops and knew that the end was near.

One of these was Boabdil. He called on Allah; he prostrated himself in his grief. He felt responsible for the plight into which his people had fallen, and he longed to save his country from the terrible fate which had befallen Malaga.

Under cover of darkness he sent messengers from the city to Ferdinand to ask what terms would be offered for the surrender of the town.

* * *

Ferdinand wrote:

> "I am prepared to be magnanimous. Surrender the city, and the inhabitants of Granada shall keep possession of their mosques and shall be allowed to retain their own religion. They shall also retain their own laws and be judged by their own *cadis*, although there will be a Castilian governor of the town. They may continue to use their own language and the Arab dress. If they wish to leave the country they may dispose of their property on their own account. There would be no extra taxes for three years. King Boabdil would abdicate, but he should be given a territory in the Alpujarras which would

be a protectorate of the Castilian crown. All the fortifications and artillery must be handed over to the Christians, and the surrender must take place in no more than sixty days."

Ferdinand stopped writing and smiled. If Boabdil and his counsellors accepted these terms he would be content. Lives and —what was more important to Ferdinand—money would be saved by a quick surrender. It was by no means certain how long the war would last, even though at the moment the Christians had all the advantages.

Eagerly he awaited the reply.

* * *

In his private apartments of the Alhambra, Boabdil read the Sovereigns' terms and rejoiced. He had saved the people of Granada from the fate which had befallen those of Malaga, and he believed that that was the best he could hope for.

The Sultana Zoraya was going about the town urging the people to stand firm. With flashing eyes and strong words she assured them that the battle against the Christian armies was not yet lost.

"You lose heart," she cried, "because you see them encamped outside our walls. But you should not lose heart. Allah will not desert us in our hour of need."

"Boabdil deserts us," was the answer. "So how can we expect Allah to smile upon us?"

They whispered among themselves. "Boabdil is a traitor. He is the friend of the Christian Sovereigns. He seeks concessions for himself, and will betray us to get them."

Revolt was stirring in the city, for it was rumoured that Boabdil was carrying on secret negotiations with the enemy.

Zoraya stormed into her son's apartment. She told him that the people were murmuring against him.

"They talk foolishly. They say you are negotiating with the enemy. These rumours do our cause great harm."

"They must be stopped, my Mother," he said.

And later he sent word to Ferdinand.

All his terms were accepted; but there should be no delay. They must come with all speed to prevent revolt within the walls of Granada. If they did not, they might arrive to find their friend Boabdil assassinated, and the treaty flung in their faces.

* * *

There was rejoicing throughout Santa Fé.

Preparations had begun for the entry into Granada.

The Cardinal Mendoza, surrounded by troops, rode into the city that he might occupy the Alhambra and prepare it for the entry of the Sovereigns.

He ascended the Hill of Martyrs and to meet him rode Boabdil surrounded by fifty Moorish noblemen.

The vanquished Boabdil rode past the Cardinal towards Ferdinand, who, surrounded by his guards, had taken up a position in the rear of the Cardinal and his men.

On his black horse Boabdil was a pathetic figure; his tunic was green decorated with gold ornaments, his white *haik* flowed about his shoulders, and his gentle face wore an expression of infinite sadness.

He dismounted when he reached Ferdinand, and would have thrown himself at the conqueror's feet. Ferdinand, however, leaped from his horse and embraced Boabdil; he veiled the triumph in his eyes and assumed an expression of great sympathy.

Boabdil said that all might hear: "I bring you the keys of the Alhambra. They belong to you, O King of the Christians. Allah decrees that it should be so. I beg you to show clemency to my sorrowing people."

Boabdil then prostrated himself before Ferdinand, and turning went to Isabella, who was some short distance behind Ferdinand, and made similar obeisance to her.

He then left her and rode towards the sad group who were waiting for him. This was his family, at the head of which was the angry Zoraya.

"Come," said Boabdil. "Now is the time to say farewell to Granada and greatness."

Zoraya was about to speak, but, with a gesture full of dignity, Boabdil signed for all to fall in behind him; and spurring his horse, he galloped away in the direction of the Alpujarras.

On he rode, followed by his family and those of his courtiers and troops whom he had been allowed to take with him.

At the hill called Padul he stopped. This was the last point from which he could hope to see Granada in all its glory.

He looked back to that most beautiful of cities—the city which had once been the capital of his kingdom and was now lost to him.

His emotions overcame him, and the tears began to flow down his cheeks.

Zoraya pushed her horse beside his.

"Weep!" she cried. "Weep! It is what we expect of you. Weep like a woman for the city you could not defend like a man!"

Boabdil turned his horse, and the melancholy cavalcade moved on. Boabdil did not look back on the city he would never see again.

* * *

Meanwhile Isabella and Ferdinand, side by side, made their triumphant entry into the city, where the streets had already been anointed with holy water that it might be washed clean of the contamination of Infidels.

Magnificently clad, the Sovereigns rode at the head of the cavalcade. They both realized the need to impress with their grandeur the people of Granada, who had been used to the splendour of their Sultans. And although neither Isabella nor Ferdinand cared for fine clothing and outward displays of riches, they were determined to appear at their most magnificent on this progress through the city.

Christian troops lined the hill-road leading to the Alhambra and, raising her eyes, Isabella saw that which she had determined to see since, as a girl, she had made her solemn vows. The flag of Christian Spain was flying over the Alhambra; the last Moorish stronghold in Spain had capitulated, and the reconquest was complete.

Joyous shouts filled the air.

"Granada! Granada for the Kings—Isabella and Ferdinand!"

TRIUMPH OF THE SOVEREIGNS

CRISTOBAL COLON had arrived at Santa Fé in time to see the triumphant procession.

A day after the Sovereigns had made their entry and taken formal possession of the city he was brought to their presence by Beatriz de Bobadilla.

Cristobal's hopes were high, for the war was over, and it was the war which had made them hesitate.

Again he described all that he hoped to do; to Isabella he stressed the importance of conquering new lands that poor ignorant savages might be brought into the Christian fold; to Ferdinand he talked of the riches which these countries must contain.

The Sovereigns were excited.

"Your Highnesses will understand," said Cristobal, "that I must be granted certain concessions."

"These concessions are?" Ferdinand demanded.

"I should ask to be made Admiral of the lands I discover during my life-time, and that on my death this title should be the right of my heirs."

Isabella, shocked, caught her breath. The title of Admiral was only bestowed on members of the nobility, and the Admiral of Castile was now Don Alonso Enriquez, Ferdinand's own uncle. Yet here was this humble sailor asking for a noble title!

Ferdinand's face had hardened also. It seemed to the Sovereigns that this man was insolent.

Cristobal went on serenely: "I should be Governor and Viceroy of the discovered lands."

"You do not know," said Ferdinand coldly, "but how could you—not being conversant with the ways of the Court—that it is the Sovereign's prerogative to choose and dismiss governors and viceroys."

"I know it, Highness," went on Cristobal stubbornly. "I should also need one-tenth of all the treasure I bring back, and one-eighth share in every expedition which leaves Spain for the Indies. If any dispute should arise concerning this, the right should be mine to appoint judges to try the case, and their decision should be final. I would also ask for a place at Court for my son."

The Sovereigns were dumbfounded. Isabella recovered her composure first.

"Señor Colon," she said, "these demands astonish us. You may leave us now, and we will discuss them; and in time you will hear our decision."

Cristobal bowed low. He said : "Highness, I would beg you not to delay the decision, for I have news that I should be very welcome at the Court of France."

He then left the presence of the Sovereigns.

* * *

"Impudence !" cried Ferdinand.

Talavera, who had been present, said : "Your Highnesses, the man should be sent about his business. Clearly he comes from the devil. Perhaps it would be advisable to hand him over to the Holy Office. They would discover what evil prompts him."

"He is a very bold man," commented Isabella, "but I think this boldness grows out of his certainty. I should like a little time to consider his claims, which we might induce him to modify."

"Your Highness heard what he said about the Court of France?" cried Talavera.

"Yes," answered Isabella. "But he will wait awhile, I think."

Ferdinand's anger seemed to abate suddenly, and Isabella, who knew him so well, realized that he was considering all the treasure which might be his.

"There is little money to spare for such an expedition," she said.

"Highness," insisted Talavera, "God has given a city of Infidels into our care. Should we not devote ourselves to bringing them to the true faith, rather than waste time and money on an adventurer?"

"I do not think it would be easy to find the money to equip the expedition," said Isabella. "But Cristobal Colon should be told that we still consider the matter."

* * *

The case of Cristobal Colon was temporarily forgotten by the Sovereigns, for another matter of the greatest importance had arisen.

Torquemada's campaign against the Jews had been relentlessly pursued since he had established his new form of Inquisition with himself as Inquisitor General, and the time had now come, he said, to make the supreme gesture against the Jews.

He wanted every Jew who would not accept Christianity to be driven from Spain.

Now, he declared, was the moment to do this. The Sovereigns had clearly been selected by the divine will to create an all-Christian Spain. After seven hundred years they had recaptured the land from the Moors, so that the conquest was complete.

"This is a sign," said Torquemada.

Public opinion was ready. The Jews had never been so hated as they were at this time.

This was due to a case which had excited much public attention.

A year or so before, a Jew, named Benito Garcia, was travelling in the course of his business, when he had been robbed; and in his knapsack was found a consecrated wafer.

The robbers took this wafer to the magistrate and told him where they had found it. They were immediately forgiven *their* crime, and Garcia was arrested for what was considered an even greater one. He was cruelly tortured; in his agony he mentioned the names of other Jews, and a story emerged. It was the old story of a Christian boy who was kidnapped by Jews, taken to a cave where he had been subjected to ritual murder, his heart having been cut out, after which he was crucified in the manner in which Christ had been.

The case had excited public opinion, and Torquemada and his officials had seen that it received the utmost publicity. The Christian boy's body could not be found, but this, it was explained, was due to the fact that he had ascended to heaven as Christ had done. He became known then as Santo Niño, and miracles were said to have been performed in his name. Hysteria and superstition were intensified.

All those who were accused of being concerned in the case were tortured and met death at the stake. Two of them, however, had been considered too evil even for death by burning. These were an old man of eighty and his young son, who refused to accept the Christian faith and remained loyal to that of their forefathers to the end. Their flesh was torn with red-hot pincers, but before they died they were set over faggots which had been dampened that they might not burn too quickly, and these two—the old man and the youth—were finally killed by roasting over a slow fire.

Torquemada now believed the moment was ripe for the banishment of the Jews, and for this reason he came to Granada to see the Sovereigns.

* * *

Ferdinand's greed was now well known and, as the fury of the people had been whipped up against them, the anxious Jews met together to discuss what could be done.

It was suggested that they should collect a large sum of money which they would offer to Ferdinand in exchange for permission to keep their homes.

So, shortly after Torquemada reached Granada to obtain the consent of Ferdinand and Isabella to his plan, a deputation of Jews arrived and asked for an audience with the Sovereigns.

Ferdinand and Isabella received this deputation.

"Highnesses," they were told, "we could raise a sum of thirty thousand ducats which we would present to you in exchange for permission to stay in Spain and keep our homes. We implore your Highnesses to allow us to set about collecting this money and to give us your sacred promise that when it is yours we shall be unmolested."

Even Isabella hesitated. The exchequer was perilously low, for the war had cost so much more than she had believed possible and there was still a great deal to be done. The need for money was desperate.

Thirty thousand ducats! The words were the sweetest music in Ferdinand's ears. And all they had to do was refuse to sign the Edict which Torquemada was preparing.

"I see that you are eager to become good citizens," said Ferdinand. "I believe that we might come to some arrangement."

The members of the deputation were almost weeping with relief; and Isabella felt a certain pleasure that she could agree to please both them and Ferdinand at the same time.

* * *

Meanwhile one of Torquemada's lieutenants had sought out his master.

"Holy Prior," he said, "a deputation is now in the presence of the Sovereigns. I have made it my business to discover theirs, and I have learned that they are offering thirty thousand ducats in exchange for the Sovereigns' promise that they may remain in Spain."

Torquemada's face was paler than usual.

He snatched up a crucifix and made his way to the royal apartments.

He did not ask for an audience but stormed into the chamber, where Ferdinand and Isabella sat at a table while the Jewish deputation stood by, presenting documents which the Sovereigns were about to sign.

Ferdinand looked at the Prior with astonishment.

"What means this?" he demanded.

"I will tell you what it means!" cried Torquemada. "The Angels are weeping this day. And the reason? Judas Iscariot sold his Master for thirty pieces of silver. The Sovereigns of Christian Spain are preparing to sell him for thirty thousand!"

He took the crucifix from under his robe and, holding it up, he raised his eyes to Heaven.

"Holy Mother of God," he went on, "you have interceded for us. Great victories have been granted us. Now you look down and see our unworthiness. I pray you do not hesitate to take our greatness from us. We have been granted grace, and in return we desecrate the holy name of God."

Then he threw the crucifix on to the table, and continued: "You are bartering Christ for your pieces of silver. Here He is. Barter Him away!"

Torquemada then strode out of the apartment.

Isabella and Ferdinand looked at each other, then at the crucifix on the table, and a terrible fear came to them.

They saw themselves as guilty of the great betrayal.

Isabella said: "Pray leave us. The Prior is right. The Edict shall go forth."

Thus was the fate of the Jews settled.

* * *

Meanwhile Cristobal waited.

Beatriz de Bobadilla and Luis de Sant'angel both implored the Queen not to allow him to go away again, while Talavera, on the other hand, was pointing out to the Sovereigns that the arrogance of Cristobal Colon was insupportable.

Luis de Sant'angel talked to Ferdinand of the explorer's prospects.

"Why, Highness," he said, "it is true the man demands a high price, but if he makes no discovery he receives nothing; and if he succeeds in making this discovery Spain will receive wealth as yet undreamed of."

Ferdinand listened intently. He had made up his mind that Cristobal Colon must make his discoveries for Spain and no other country.

"It is, however," he said to Luis de Sant'angel, "a question of providing the means. You know how the exchequer has been depleted since the Moorish wars. Where could we find the money to finance such an expedition?"

Luis was staring carefully ahead of him, for he knew that

Ferdinand did not wish to meet his eyes. As Aragonese Secretary of Supplies, Luis knew that there were ample funds in the Aragonese Treasury to finance the expedition. But the affluence of the Aragonese Treasury was a close secret which Ferdinand did not wish to be made known at the Court of Castile—and more especially to the Queen.

Ferdinand did not forget for a moment his Aragonese ambitions, which meant as much to him as the conquest of Granada itself. Therefore while Castile groaned in poverty, and the Queen had wondered how they could continue to prosecute the war, Ferdinand's Aragonese Treasury had been in possession of these ample funds.

"I see," said Luis slowly, "that the Queen could not find the means to fit up this expedition."

"Alas, it is so," said Ferdinand, but he was thoughtful.

* * *

Ferdinand had now become convinced that there was too much at stake to allow Cristobal to offer his plans elsewhere.

He said to Isabella: "The man's demands are arrogant, but if he is unsuccessful he gets nothing. What harm would there be in making him our Admiral and Viceroy of lands he discovers? For if he discovers nothing the title is an empty one."

Isabella was pleased; she had always been in favour of the man and was delighted as always when Ferdinand veered round to her way of thinking.

"Then," she said, "when we can muster the money we will send him out on his voyage of discovery."

"When will that be?" asked Ferdinand. "I do not think this man will remain here much longer. He has as good as said that if there is any more delay he will begin his journey into France."

The thought of the French's benefiting by new discoveries so agitated Ferdinand that Isabella said: "If I had not already pawned my jewels to pay for the war, readily would I do so to finance this expedition. The treasury is very low. I doubt whether there is enough money in it for what he will need."

Ferdinand, who had been walking agitatedly about the room, stopped short as though he had come to a sudden decision.

"There is something I have to tell you, Isabella," he said. He called to one of the pages: "Send for Don Luis de Sant'angel at once," he said.

"You think you know of a means to obtain this money?" Isabella asked him.

Ferdinand lifted a hand and slowly nodded his head. But he did not speak, and Isabella did not press him.

Within a few minutes Luis de Sant'angel was standing before them.

"You are very interested in this man, Cristobal Colon," said Ferdinand. "You feel certain that his voyage will be successful."

"I do, Highness," said Luis.

"You talked to me recently about money . . . money you have in Aragon."

Luis looked rather puzzled, but Ferdinand hurried on: "You would be prepared to help in financing this expedition which Colon wishes to make?"

Ferdinand was now looking intently into the face of his Secretary of Supplies, and Sant'angel, after long experience of his master, understood.

Ferdinand wished this voyage to be made; he knew that delay was dangerous. He was going to finance it from the treasury of Aragon, but Isabella and Castile must not know that, during the time they had been urgently in need of money, Ferdinand had kept amounts of money separate from those of Castile to be used in the service of Aragon.

Any discoveries Cristobal Colon made would be for the good of Aragon as well as Castile. Therefore what Ferdinand was suggesting was that the money should be provided by Aragon, but that it should be advanced in the name of Luis de Sant'angel.

Luis felt a great uplifting of his spirits.

Cristobal Colon, he thought, at last you are about to have your chance!

* * *

"Since," said Ferdinand, "you are so generous, Sant'angel, you had better send Colon to us with all speed. We will grant his request, and he shall set about his preparations without further delay."

Luis retired as quickly as he could and went in search of Cristobal; but the explorer was nowhere to be found.

All through Granada, all through Santa Fé the question was being asked: "Have you seen Cristobal Colon?"

At last it was discovered that he had packed his few belongings and had left. He had said that he would not be back; he was leaving Spain, since Spain had no use for him.

Luis was nonplussed. It must not be that, when success was about to come to Cristobal after so many years of waiting, he was to lose it through giving in a day or so too soon. Luis was determined that it should not be so.

He wondered which way Colon had gone. He would go, he believed, in the direction of La Rabida, as he would certainly wish to see Diego before he left Spain. His other son, Ferdinand, had a mother to care for him, but he would want to make some provision for Diego.

Yet perhaps he had decided he could not afford to waste more time and was hurrying northwards to France!

Luis therefore despatched riders in several directions, and one of these overtook Cristobal six miles from Granada at the Puente de Piños.

Cristobal heard the sound of horses' hoofs thudding behind him as he made his way towards the bridge. He slackened his pace, and hearing his own name called, stopped.

"Cristobal Colon," he was told, "you must come back to the Court with all speed. You are to be granted all that you ask, and can make your preparations at once."

A smile touched Cristobal's face, and it was so dazzling that it made of him a young man again.

At last . . . success. The long waiting was over.

* * *

The roads to the coast were thick with bands of refugees. Old and young, those who had been accustomed to the utmost luxury, those who had been bred in poverty, now walked wearily together; they had been stripped of all they possessed, for although they had been allowed to sell their property, they had been cynically forbidden to take money out of the country.

This was the exodus of the Jews of Spain. Onward they trudged, hoping to find some human creatures who would be kinder to them than those in the land which for centuries had been the home of their ancestors.

It was forbidden to help them. It was no crime to rob them.

The shipmasters looked upon them as legitimate prey. Some took these suffering people aboard, extracted payment for the voyage and then threw their passengers, who had trusted them, into the sea.

From all parts of this all-Christian Spain those Jews who refused to conform to the Christian Faith wandered on their wretched way to an unknown future.

Thousands died on many a perilous journey; some of plague, but many of barbaric murder. The rumour, that it had become a practice of these Jews to swallow their jewels in the hope of preserving them, was circulated and numbers of them, on arriving in Africa, were ripped up by barbarians, who hoped in this way to retrieve the jewels from their hiding-places.

Some, however, found refuge in other lands, and a few managed to survive the horror.

Torquemada was satisfied. He had had his way.

He knelt with the Sovereigns and they prayed together for the continued greatness of their all-Christian state.

* * *

In a room over a grocer's shop in the town of Seville a woman saw the Jews gathering together to leave their homes.

She looked from her window upon them, for she was too ill to leave her room, and she knew that only a few more weeks of life were left to her.

Those faces, on which were depicted blank despair and bewildered misery, took her mind back to the days when she, a Jewess, had lived in her father's luxurious house; and with a sudden, terrible fear she began to wonder what part she herself had played in bringing about this terrible crime which was taking place all over Spain.

What if she had not taken a lover; what if she had not been in fear that her father would discover her pregnancy? What if she had not betrayed him and his friends to the Inquisition—would this be happening now?

It was a terrible thought. She had not allowed herself to think of it before, although it had always been there hovering in her mind, hanging over her life like a dark shadow of doom which she could not escape for ever.

If Diego de Susan had not been betrayed by La Susanna, if his conspiracy against the Inquisition had succeeded, who knew, the Inquisition might not have taken hold in Spain as it had this day.

She clenched her hands and beat them against her wasted breasts.

And what a life had been hers, passing from one protector to another, moving down the scale as *la hermosa hembra* lost her beauty little by little.

At last she had found a man who really loved her—this humble grocer who had known her in the days of her pride, and was happy to be the protector of Diego de Susan's daughter—he who had been a millionaire of Seville—even though that man had been burned alive through La Susanna's betrayal of him.

He had looked after her, this little grocer, looked after her and the children she had had. And now this was the end. She could hear the suppressed sobbing of children in the crowd, little ones who sensed tragedy without understanding it.

Then she could bear no more. She stumbled back to her bed, but the effort of leaving it and the agony of remorse had been too much for her. She had shortened her life—but only by a few weeks.

Her lover came into the apartment, and there was anguish in his eyes. Ah, she thought, it is because he does not see me as I am; to him I am still the young girl who sat on the balcony of the house of Diego de Susan, then far out of the reach of a humble grocer.

"I am dying," she told him.

He helped her back to bed and sat beside her. He did not deny the truth of what she said, for he realized it would be futile to do so.

"Do something for me," she said. "When I die, put my skull over the door of this house, that all may know it is the skull of one whose passions led her to an evil life, and that she wishes a part of her to be left there as a warning to all. The skull of a woman who was a bawd and betrayer of those who loved her best."

The grocer shook his head. "You must not fret," he said. "I will take care of you till the end."

"This is the end," she said. "Promise me. Swear it on your Faith."

So he promised.

And, before the Jews had all left Spain, the skull of the woman who had once been judged the most beautiful in Seville was set up over the door of the grocer's house.

* * *

The reconquest secure, Isabella and Ferdinand appointed Talavera Archbishop of Granada, and the Count of Tendilla its Governor, and set off on a progress through the country, with their children, to receive the grateful thanks of the people.

They rode with all the splendour of royalty, and always beside them was Juan, the Prince of the Asturias. Isabella felt that all her subjects must agree that one of her greatest gifts to them was this bright and beautiful boy, the heir to a united Spain.

Ferdinand had said: "Castile is with us to a man, so is Aragon; but there has always been trouble in Catalonia since . . . the death of my half-brother. Now is the time to show the Catalans that we include them in our kingdom, that they mean as much to us as the Castilians and the Aragonese."

Isabella agreed that this was so and that now, in the full flush of their triumph, was the time to make the Catalans forget for ever the mysterious death of Carlos, Prince of Viana, who had been removed to make way for Ferdinand to take the throne of Aragon.

So into Catalonia rode the procession.

* * *

Ferdinand had been presiding at the hall of justice in Barcelona, and was leaving the building to rejoin Isabella at the Palace.

He was pleased, for never had he been so popular in Catalonia as he was at this time. Congratulations were coming to him from all over the world. He and Isabella were accepted as the hero and heroine of this great victory for Christianity. He was to be henceforth known as Ferdinand the Catholic, and Isabella as Isabella the Catholic. Even Catalonia, which had for so long set itself against Ferdinand, now cheered him wherever he went.

But no doubt there were some who did not share the general opinion. Ferdinand came face to face with one as he left the hall of justice, and suddenly he found himself looking into the face of a fanatic, while a knife gleamed before his startled eyes.

"Die . . . murderer!" cried a voice.

Ferdinand fell forward, and there was a shout of triumph from the man who held up the bloodstained knife.

* * *

Isabella was with her children when she received the news. Her daughter, Isabella, covered her face with her hands; the Prince was as one struck dumb; and the little girls ran to their mother and clung to her in terror.

"Highness, the King is being brought here to you. It was a madman outside the hall of justice."

Isabella felt her heart leap in fear.

"Not now," she prayed. "Not this. We have come through so much together. There is so much for us yet. . . ."

Then she recovered her serenity.

She put the frightened children from her and said: "I will go to the King at once."

* * *

She was at his bedside, for she was determined that no one should nurse him but herself.

She prayed constantly, but she did not neglect to nurse him during those days while his life was in danger.

The would-be assassin had been captured, and had suffered the most cruel torture; but he could not be made to confess that he had had accomplices.

There was one fact which emerged from the torture chamber; the man was a lunatic, for he declared that he was the true heir to the throne of Aragon and that he expected to gain this on Ferdinand's death.

There came the day when Isabella knew that Ferdinand was out of danger and that this was not the end of their life together, as she had feared it might be. Outside the Palace the people were waiting for news. Never had Ferdinand been so popular in Catalonia as he was at this time. The people saw him as the hero of the reconquest, and they saw also a new life for themselves and their country through the greatness of their rulers.

Isabella was of Castile, and they had at first been suspicious of her; they believed that it was her careful nursing, her constant prayer, which had saved the life of Ferdinand.

The news was conveyed to them: "The King will live." And Isabella appeared on the balcony before the sick-room while the people shouted themselves hoarse with delight.

"Isabella and Ferdinand! Ferdinand and Isabella!" No longer for Castile, for Aragon, for Catalonia. But "Isabella and Ferdinand for Spain!"

* * *

She returned to Ferdinand's bed. He was smiling at her, for he had heard the shouts outside the Palace.

"It would seem," he said, "that they love us both with an equal fervour."

"They know," said Isabella, "that we are as one."

"It is true," said Ferdinand. "We are as one." And as he took her hand, he thought of the humiliation he had suffered when he had been forced to take second place in Castile; he thought of the women he had loved, so many of them, so much more accomplished in the arts of love than Isabella could ever be. But even as he considered them and all the differences of the past—and all those which no doubt were to come in the future—he knew that the most important person in his life was Isabella, and that in generations to come, when his name was mentioned, that of Isabella would be for ever linked with it.

She understood his thoughts and she was in complete harmony with them.

She said: "They are demanding the most painful death for your would-be assassin. It is to be in public that they all may see, that all may gloat over the agonies of one who might have caused the death of their beloved King."

Ferdinand nodded.

She went on: "I have given orders that he shall be strangled first. Secret orders. They will see his body taken out. They will not know that he is past pain, for he has been greatly tortured. But now I would let him die in peace."

Ferdinand restrained an oath. *She* had given orders in Catalonia . . . *his* province!

Again she read his thoughts, and for a moment that old hostility hovered between them.

Then she said: "Can you hear what they are shouting? It is 'Ferdinand and Isabella. Isabella and Ferdinand . . . for Spain!' "

The irritation vanished from his face and he smiled at her.

"We have done so much," Isabella said gently. "There is so much to do. But we shall do it . . . together."

* * *

Crowds had gathered in the streets of Barcelona, to take part in one of the great occasions in Spanish history.

It was April and the sun shone brilliantly as through the streets to the Palace came a brilliant procession.

Nuggets of gold were carried by brown-skinned men in robes decorated with gold ornaments; there were animals such as none had ever seen before.

And in the midst of this procession came the Admiral of the New World, Cristobal Colon, his head held high, his eyes gleaming, because now his dream of discovery had become a reality.

Among the crowd was a woman who held a young boy in her arms that he might see the hero of this occasion.

"See, Ferdinand," Beatriz de Arana whispered with pride, "there is your father."

"I see, Mother," cried the boy excitedly. "Mother, I see my father."

Isabella and Ferdinand were waiting to receive their Admiral, and with them were their family. There was one page, in the service of the Prince of the Asturias, who could scarcely bear to look, so strong was his emotion.

This was Diego, that other son of the explorer, who had waited so many years for the return of his father, first in the monastery of La Rabida, then at the Court.

Cristobal Colon knelt before the Sovereigns, and when

Isabella offered him her hand to kiss, she knew that what he was offering her—and Spain—was a New World.

How happy I am in this moment, thought Isabella. Ferdinand has fully recovered his strength. I have all my beloved children with me. I have made not only a united Spain but a Christian Spain.

I have all this. I should be singularly blessed, even were this all.

But it was not all. And here is this adventurer, returned from his long journey with strange tales to tell. Here he comes, to lay a new world at my feet.

Isabella's smiling gaze embraced her beloved family; but she looked beyond them all into a future when men and women who were gathered together to discuss the greatness of a mighty Empire would say: "It was Isabella who made Spain great—Isabella . . . and Ferdinand."

* * *

Daughters of Spain

© *Jean Plaidy 1961*

THE ROYAL FAMILY

CATALINA KNELT on a window-seat looking out from the Palace to the purple slopes and the snowy tips of the Sierra de Guadarrama.

It would soon be Easter and the sky was cobalt, but the plain stretching out before the mountains was of a tawny bleakness.

Catalina enjoyed studying the view from the nursery window. Out there the scene always seemed a little frightening. Perhaps this was because she, who had seen bitter fighting outside Granada when she was a few years younger, was always afraid that her parents' rebellious subjects would rise again and cause distress to her beloved mother.

Here within the granite walls of the Madrid Alcazar there was a feeling of security, which was entirely due to the presence of her mother. Her father was also in residence at this time, so that they were a united family, all gathered together under this one roof.

What could be more pleasant? And yet even now her brother and sisters were talking of unpleasant matters, such as the marriages which they would have to make at some time.

"Please," murmured Catalina to herself, "do not do it. We are all together. Let us forget that one day we may not be so happy."

It was no use asking them. She was the youngest and only ten years old. They would laugh at her. Only her mother would have understood if she had spoken her thoughts, although she would immediately have reminded her daughter that duty must be faced with fortitude.

Juana, who was laughing in her wild manner as though she would not in the least mind going away, suddenly noticed her young sister.

"Come here, Catalina," she commanded. "You must not feel left out. You shall have a husband too."

"I don't want a husband."

"I know. I know." Juana mimicked her young sister: "I want to stay with my mother all the time. I only want to be the Queen's dear daughter!"

"Hush!" said Isabella, who was the eldest and fifteen years older than Catalina. 'You must curb your tongue, Juana. It is unseemly to talk of marriage before one has been arranged for you."

Isabella spoke from knowledge. She had already been married and had lived in Portugal. Lucky Isabella, thought Catalina, for she had not remained long there. Her husband had died and she had come home again. She had done her duty but had not had to go on doing it for long. Catalina wondered why Isabella always seemed so sad. It was as though she regretted being brought back home, as though she still pined for her lost husband. How could any husband ever make up for the companionship of their mother, the delights of being all together and part of one big happy family?

"If I wish to talk of marriage, I will," announced Juana. "I will, I tell you, I will!" Juana stood up to her full height, tossing back her tawny hair, her eyes ablaze with that wildness which it was so easy to evoke. Catalina watched her sister in some trepidation. She was a little afraid of Juana's moods. This was because she had often seen her mother look worried when her eyes rested on Juana.

Even the mighty Queen Isabella was anxious about her second daughter. And Catalina, whose feelings for her mother were close to idolatry, was conscious of every mood, every fear, and she passionately longed to share them.

"One day," said the Princess Isabella, "Juana will learn that she has to obey."

"I may have to obey some people," cried Juana, "but not you, sister. Not you!"

Catalina began to pray silently. "Not a scene now . . . please, please, not a scene now when we're so happy."

"Perhaps," said Juan who always tried to make peace, "Juana will have such an indulgent husband that she will always be able to do as she wishes."

Juan's beautiful face framed in fair hair was like that of an angel. The Queen's favourite name for her only son was Angel. Catalina could well understand why. It was not only that Juan looked like an angel, he acted like one. Catalina wondered whether her mother loved Angel better than all the rest of them. Surely she must, for he was not only the heir to the crown but the most beautiful, gentle and kind person it was possible to know. He never sought to remind people of his important position; the servants loved to serve him and considered it a pleasure as well as an honour to be of his household. Now he, a seventeen-year-old boy, who, one would have thought, would have wished to be with companions of his own sex, hunting or at some sport or another, was here in the old nursery with his sisters—perhaps because he knew they liked to have him or, as Catalina did, he appreciated the pleasure of belonging to a family such as theirs.

Juana was smiling now; the idea of having an indulgent husband on whom she could impose her will pleased her.

Their sister Isabella watched them all a little sadly. What children they were! she was thinking. It was a pity they were all so much younger than she was. Her mother of course had had little time for childbearing in the early part of her reign. There had been the great war and so many state matters to occupy her; so it was not surprising that Juan, who was the next in the family, was eight years younger than herself.

Isabella wished they would not talk of marriage. It brought back such bitter memories. She saw herself five years ago, clinging to her mother even as Catalina did now, terrified because she must leave her home and go into Portugal to marry Alonso, heir of the crown of that country. Then the promise of a crown had held no charm for her. She had cried for her mother even as poor little Catalina undoubtedly would when her turn came.

But she had found her young husband as terrified of marriage as she was herself, and very soon a bond had grown between them which in its turn burgeoned into love—so deep, so bittersweet, so short-lived.

She told herself that she would be haunted for ever by the sight of the bearers carrying his poor broken body in from the forest. She thought of the new heir to the throne, the young Emanuel who had tried so hard to comfort her, who had told her that he loved her and who had invited her to forget her dead husband and marry him, to stay in Portugal, not to return, a sad widow, to her parents' dominions, but to become the bride of her late husband's cousin who was now heir to the King of Portugal.

She had turned shuddering from handsome Emanuel.

"No," she had cried. "I wish never to marry again. I shall continue to think of Alonso . . . until I die."

That had happened when she was twenty; and ever since she had kept her vow, although her mother sought to persuade her to change her mind; and her father, who was so much less patient, was growing increasingly irritated with her.

She shuddered at the thought of returning to Portugal as a bride. Memories would be too poignant to be borne.

She felt tears in her eyes, and looking up she saw the grave glance of little Catalina fixed upon her.

Poor Catalina, she thought, her turn will come. She will face it with courage—that much I know. But what of the others?

Thirteen-year-old Maria was working on a piece of embroidery. She was completely unruffled by this talk of marriage. Sometimes Isabella thought she was rather stupid, for whatever happened she showed little excitement or resentment, but merely accepted what came. Life would be much less difficult for Maria.

And Juana? It was wiser not to think of Juana. Juana would never suffer in silence.

Now the wild creature had leapt to her feet and held out her hand to Juan.

"Come, let us dance, brother," she commanded. "Maria, take up your lute and play for us."

Maria placidly put down her embroidery, took up the lute and played the first plaintive notes of a *pavana*.

The brother and sister danced together. They were well matched and there was only a year's difference in their ages. But what a contrast they made! This thought occurred both to Isabella and Catalina. It was so marked and people often referred to it when they saw Juan and Juana together. Their names were so much alike; they were of the same height; but one would never have guessed that they were brother and sister.

Even Juana's hair seemed to grow rebelliously from her forehead; that touch of auburn was like their mother's yet it was more tawny in Juana's, so that she looked like a young lioness; her great eyes were always restless; her mood could change in a second. Juana gave the impression of never being tranquil. Even in sleep she had the appearance of restlessness.

How different was Juan with his fair face which resembled that of angels. Now he danced with his sister because she asked him to, and he knew that the thoughts of marriage and the husband she might have, had excited her. The dance would calm her; her physical exertion would help to allay the excitement of her mind.

If Juan did not want to dance when he was asked to do so, he immediately changed his mind. That was characteristic of Juan. He had a rare quality in not only wishing to please others but in finding that their wishes became his own.

Catalina went back to the window-seat, and looked out once more at the plain and the mountains and the arrivals and departures.

She found her sister Isabella standing beside her. Isabella put an arm about her as Catalina turned to smile. She had felt in that moment a need to protect the child from the ills which could befall the daughters of the House of Spain. Memories of Alonso always made her feel like this. Later she would seek out her mother's confessor and talk to him of her sorrow. She preferred to talk with him because he never gave her easy comfort, but scolded her as he would scourge himself if necessary; and the sight of his pale, emaciated face never failed to comfort her.

There were times when she longed to go into a convent and spend her life in prayer until death came to unite her with Alonso. If she were not a daughter of Spain that would have been possible.

"Look," said Catalina, pointing to a gaunt figure in a Franciscan robe, "there is the Queen's confessor."

Isabella looked down at the man who with his companion was about to enter the Alcazar. She could not clearly see the emaciated features and the stern expression of the monk, but she was deeply aware of them.

"I am glad he is here," she said.

"Isabella, he . . . he frightens me a little."

Isabella's face grew sterner. "You must never be afraid of good men, Catalina; and there is not a better man in Spain than Ximenes de Cisneros."

* * *

In her apartments the Queen sat at her writing-table. Her expression was serene but it was no indication of her thoughts. She was about to perform an unpleasant duty and this was painful to her.

Here I am, she thought, with my family all about me. Spain is more prosperous than she has been for many a year; we now have a united Kingdom, a Christian Kingdom. In the past three years, since together Ferdinand and I conquered the last Moorish stronghold, the Christian flag has flown over every Spanish town. The explorer Christobal Colon has done good work and Spain has a growing Kingdom beyond the seas. As Queen I rejoice in my country's prosperity. As a mother I know great happiness because at this moment I have my entire family with me under one roof. All should be well and yet . . .

She smiled at the man who was sitting watching her.

This was Ferdinand, her husband; a year younger than herself he was still a handsome man. If there was a certain craftiness in the eyes, Isabella had always refused to recognize it; if his features were touched with sensuality Isabella was ready to tell herself that he was indeed a man and she would not have him otherwise.

He was indeed a man—a brave soldier, a wily statesman; a man who loved little on this Earth as he loved gold and treasure. Yet he had affection to spare for his family. The children loved him. Not as they loved their mother of course. But, thought Isabella, it is the mother who bore them who is closer to them than any father could be. That was not the answer. Her children loved her because they were aware of the deeper devotion which came from her; they knew that, when their husbands were chosen, their father would rejoice at the material advantages those marriages would bring; his children's happiness would rank only as secondary. But their mother, who would also wish grand marriages for them all, would suffer even as they did from the parting.

They loved their mother devotedly. They alone knew of the tenderness which was so often hidden beneath the serenity, for it was only for them that Queen Isabella would lift the veil with which she hid her true self from the world.

Now she was staring at the document which lay on the table before her and she was deeply conscious of Ferdinand's attention which was riveted on it.

They must speak of it. She knew that he was going to ask her outright to destroy it.

She was right. His mouth hardened and for a moment she could almost believe that he hated her.

"So you intend to make this appointment?"

Isabella was stung by the coldness of the tone. No one could convey more hatred and contempt in his voice than Ferdinand.

"I do, Ferdinand."

"There are times," went on Ferdinand, "when I wish you would listen to my advice."

"And how I wish that I could take it."

Ferdinand made an impatient gesture. "It is simple enough. You take the document and tear it in two. That could be an end to the matter."

He had leaned forward and would have taken it, but Isabella's plump white hand was immediately spread across it, protecting it.

Ferdinand's mouth was set in a stubborn line which made him look childish.

"I am sorry, Ferdinand," said Isabella.

"So once again you remind me that you are Queen of Castile. You will have your way. And so . . . you will give this . . . this upstart the highest post in Spain, when you might . . ."

"Give it to one who deserves it far less," said the Queen gently; "your son . . . who is not my son."

"Isabella, you talk like some country wife. Alfonso is my son. I have never denied that fact. He was born when you and I were separated . . . as we were so often during those early days. I was young . . . hot blooded . . . and I found a mistress as young men will. You must understand."

"I have understood and forgiven, Ferdinand. But that does not mean that I can give your bastard the Archbishopric of Toledo."

"So you're giving it to this half-starved monk . . . this simple man . . . this low . . ."

"He is of good family, Ferdinand. It is true he is not royal. But at least he is the legitimate son of his father."

Ferdinand brought his fist down on the table. "I am weary of these reproaches. It has nothing to do with Alfonso's birth. Confess it. You wish to show me . . . as you have so often . . . that you are Queen of Castile and Castile is of greater importance to Spain than is Aragon; therefore you stand supreme."

"Oh Ferdinand, that has never been my wish. Castile . . . Aragon . . . what are they compared with Spain? Spain is now united. You are its King; I its Queen."

"But the Queen will bestow the Archbishopric of Toledo where she wishes."

Isabella looked at him sadly.

"Is that not so?" he shouted.

"Yes," said Isabella, "that is so."

"And this is your final decision on the matter?"

"It is my final decision."

"Then I crave your Highness's permission to retire." Ferdinand's voice was heavy with sarcasm.

"Ferdinand, you know . . ." But he would not wait. He was bowing now and strutting from the room.

Isabella remained at her table. This scene was reminiscent of so many which had occurred during their married life. There was this continual jostling for the superior position on Ferdinand's part; as for herself, she longed to be the perfect wife and mother. It would have been so easy to have said: Have it your own way, Ferdinand. Give the Archbishopric where you will.

But that gay young son of his was not suited to this high post. There was only one man in Spain whom she believed to be worthy of it, and always she must think first of Spain. This was why she was now determined that the Franciscan Ximenes should be Primate of Spain, no matter how the appointment displeased Ferdinand.

She rose from the table and went to the door of the apartment.

"Highness!" Several of the attendants who had been waiting outside sprang to attention.

"Go and discover whether Fray Francisco Ximenes de Cisneros

is in the Palace. If he is, tell him that it is my wish that he present himself to me without delay."

* * *

Fray Francisco Ximenes de Cisneros was praying silently as he approached the Palace. Beneath the rough serge of his habit the hair shirt irritated his skin. He took a fierce delight in this. He had eaten nothing but a few herbs and berries during his journey to Madrid from Ocaña, but he was accustomed to long abstinence from food.

His nephew, Francisco Ruiz, whom he loved as dearly as he could love anyone, and who was closer to him than his own brothers, glanced anxiously at him.

"What," he asked, "do you think is the meaning of the Queen's summons?"

"My dear Francisco, as I shall shortly know, let us not waste our breath in conjecture."

But Francisco Ruiz was excited. It had so happened that the great Cardinal Mendoza, who had occupied the highest post in Spain—that of the Archbishop of Toledo—had recently died and the office was vacant. Was it possible that such an honour was about to be bestowed on his uncle? Ximenes might declare himself uninterested in great honours, but there were some honours which would tempt the most devout of men.

And why not? Ruiz demanded of himself. The Queen thinks highly of her confessor—and rightly so. She can never have had such a worthy adviser since Torquemada himself heard her confessions. And she loves such men, men who are not afraid to speak their minds, men who are clearly indifferent to worldly riches.

Torquemada, suffering acutely from the gout, was now an old man with clearly very little time left to him. He was almost entirely confined to the monastery of Avila. Ximenes on the other hand was at the height of his mental powers.

Ruiz was certain that it was to bestow this great honour on his uncle that they were being thus recalled to Madrid.

As for Ximenes, try as he might, he could not thrust the thought from his mind.

Archbishop of Toledo! Primate of Spain! He could not understand this strange feeling which rose within him. There was so much about himself which he could not understand. He longed to suffer the greatest bodily torture, as Christ had suffered on the cross. And even as his body cried out for this treatment, a voice within him asked: "Why, Ximenes, is it because you cannot endure that any should be greater than yourself? None must bear pain more stoically. None must be more devout. Who are you, Ximenes? Are you a man? Are you a God?

"Archbishop of Toledo," the voice gloated within him. "The power will be yours. You will be greater than any man under the Sovereigns. And the Sovereigns may be swayed by your influence. Have you not had charge of the Queen's conscience; and is not the Queen the real ruler of Spain?

"It is for your own vanity, Ximenes. You long to be the most powerful man in Spain; more powerful than Ferdinand whose great desire is to fill his coffers and extend his Kingdom. Greater than Torquemada who has set the holy fires scorching the limbs of heretics throughout the land. More powerful than any. Ximenes, Primate of Spain, the Queen's right hand. Ruler of Spain?"

I shall not take this post if it is offered to me, he told himself.

He closed his eyes and began to pray for strength to refuse it, but it was as though the Devil spread the kingdoms of the Earth at his feet.

He swayed slightly. There was little nourishment in berries, and when he travelled he never took food or money with him. He relied on what he could find growing by the wayside, or the help from the people he met.

"My Master did not carry bread and wine," he would say, "and though the birds had their nests and the foxes their lairs there was no place in which the Son of Man might lay his head."

What his Master had done Ximenes must do also.

When they entered the Palace the Queen's messenger immediately called to him.

"Fray Francisco Ximenes de Cisneros?"

"It is I," answered Ximenes. He felt a certain pride every time he heard his full title; he had not been christened Francisco but Gonzalo, and had changed his first name that he might bear the same one as the founder of the Order in which he served.

"Her Highness Queen Isabella wishes you to wait upon her with all speed."

"I will go to her presence at once."

Ruiz plucked at his sleeve. "Should you not wipe away the stains of the journey before presenting yourself to the Queen's Highness?"

"The Queen knows I have come on a journey. She will expect me to be travel-stained."

Ruiz looked after his uncle in some dismay. The lean figure, the emaciated face with the pale skin tightly drawn across the bones were in great contrast to the looks of the previous

Archbishop of Toledo, the late Mendoza, sensuous, good-natured epicure and lover of comfort and women.

Archbishop of Toledo! thought Ruiz. Surely it cannot be!

Isabella gave a smile of pleasure as her confessor entered the apartment.

She waved her hand to the attendant and they were alone.

"I have brought you back from Ocaña," she said almost apologetically, "because I have news for you."

"What news has Your Highness for me?"

His manner lacked the obsequiousness with which Isabella was accustomed to being addressed by her subjects, but she did not protest. She admired her confessor because he was no great respecter of persons.

But for the truly holy life this man led, it might have been said that he was a man of great pride.

"I think," said Isabella, "that this letter from His Holiness the Pope will explain." She turned to the table and took up that document which had caused such displeasure to Ferdinand, and put it into the hands of Ximenes.

"Open it and read it," urged Isabella.

Ximenes obeyed. As he read the first words a change passed across his features. He did not grow more pale—that would have been impossible—but his mouth hardened and his eyes narrowed; for a few seconds a mighty battle was raging within his meagre frame.

The words danced before his eyes. They were in the handwriting of Pope Alexander VI himself, and they ran as follows:

"To our beloved son, Fray Francisco Ximenes de Cisneros, Archbishop of Toledo . . ."

Isabella was waiting for him to fall on his knees and thank her for this great honour; but he did no such thing. He stood very still, staring before him, oblivious of the fact that he was in the presence of his Queen. He was only aware of the conflict within himself, the need to understand what real motives lay behind his feelings.

Power. Great Power. It was his to take. For what purpose did he want power? He was unsure. He was as unsure as he had been years ago when he had lived as a hermit in the forest of Castañar.

Then it seemed to him that devils mocked him. "You long for power, Ximenes," they said. "You are a vain and sinful man. You are ambitious, and by that sin fell the angels."

He put the paper on to the table and murmured: "There has been a mistake. This is not for me." Then he turned and strode from the room, leaving the astonished Queen staring after him.

Her bewilderment gave way to anger. Ximenes might be a holy man but he had forgotten the manner in which to behave before his Queen. But almost immediately her anger disappeared. He is a good man, she reminded herself. He is one of the few about me who do not seek personal advantage. This means he has refused this great honour. What other man in Spain would do this?

* * *

Isabella sent for her eldest daughter.

The young Isabella would have knelt before her mother but the Queen took her into her arms and held her tightly against her for a few seconds.

Holy Mother of God, thought the Princess, what can this mean? She is suffering for me. Is it a husband that I shall be forced to take? Is that why she is so sorry for me?

The Queen put the Princess from her and composed her features.

"My dearest," she said, "you do not look as well as I would wish. How is your cough?"

"I cough now and then, Highness, as I always have."

"Isabella, my child, now that we are alone together, let us throw aside all ceremony. Call me Mother. I love to hear the word on your lips."

The Princess began: "Oh, my Mother . . ." and then she was sobbing in the Queen's arms.

"There, my precious child," murmured Isabella. "You still think of him then? Is it that?"

"I was so happy . . . happy. Mother, can you understand? I was so frightened at first, and when I found that . . . we loved . . . it was all so wonderful. We planned to live like that for the rest of our lives. . . ."

The Queen did not speak; she went on stroking her daughter's hair.

"It was cruel . . . so cruel. He was so young. And when we went out into the forest that day it was like any other day. He was with me but ten minutes before it happened . . . laughing . . . with me. And then there he was . . ."

"It was God's will," said the Queen gently.

"God's will? To break a young body like that! Wantonly to take one so young, so full of life and love!"

The Queen's face set into stern lines. "Your grief has unnerved you, my child. You forget your duty to God. If it is His wish to make us suffer we must accept suffering gladly."

"Gladly! I will never accept it gladly."

The Queen hastily crossed herself, while her lips moved in prayer. Isabella thought: She is praying that I may be forgiven my wicked outburst. However much *she* suffered she would never give way to her feelings as I have done.

She was immediately contrite. "Oh, Mother, forgive me. I know not what I say. It is like that sometimes. The memories come back and then I fear . . ."

"You must pray, my darling, for greater control. It is not God's wish that you should shut yourself away from the world as you do."

"It is not my father's wish, you mean?" demanded Isabella.

"Neither the wish of your heavenly nor your earthly father," murmured the Queen soothingly.

"I would to God I could go into a convent. My life finished when his did."

"You are questioning the will of God. Had He wished you to end your life He would have taken you with your husband. This is your cross, my darling; think of Him and carry it as willingly as He carried His."

"He had only to die. I have to live."

"My dearest, have a care. I will double my prayers for you this night and every night. I fear your sufferings have affected your mind. But in time you will forget."

"It is four years since it happened, Mother. I have not forgotten yet."

"Four years! It seems long to you because you are young. To me it is like yesterday."

"To me it will always be as though his death happened yesterday."

"You must fight against such morbid thoughts, my darling. It is a sin to nurse a grief. I sent for you because I have news for you. Your father-in-law has died and there is a new King of Portugal."

"Alonso would have been King had he lived . . . and I his Queen."

"But he did not live, yet you could still be Queen of Portugal."

"Emanuel . . ."

"My dear daughter, he renews his offer to you. Now that he has come to the throne he does not forget you. He is determined to have no wife but you."

Emanuel! She remembered him well. Kindly, intelligent, he was more given to study than his gay young cousin Alonso had been; but she had known that he envied Alonso his bride. And now he was asking for her hand once more.

"I would rather go into a nunnery."

"We might all feel tempted to do that which seems easier to us than our duty."

"Mother, you are not commanding me to marry Emanuel?"

"You married once, by the command of your father and myself. I would not command you again; but I would have you consider your duty to your family . . . to Spain."

Isabella clenched her hands tightly together. "Do you realize what you are asking of me? To go to Lisbon as I did for Alonso . . . and then to find Emanuel waiting for me and Alonso . . . dead."

"My child, pray for courage."

"I pray each day, Mother," she answered slowly. "But I cannot go back to Portugal. I can never be anything but Alonso's widow as long as I live."

The Queen sighed as she drew her daughter down to sit beside her; she put an arm about her and as she rested her face against her hair she was thinking: In time she will be persuaded to go to Portugal and marry Emanuel. We must all do our duty; and though we rebel for a while it avails us little.

* * *

Ferdinand looked up as the Queen entered. He smiled at her and his expression was slightly sardonic. It amused him that the Franciscan monk who, in his opinion so foolishly, had been offered the Archbishopric of Toledo, should merely have fled at the sight of his title in the Pope's handwriting. This should teach Isabella to think before bestowing great titles on the unworthy. The fellow was uncouth. A pleasant prospect! The Primate of Spain a monk who was more at home in a hermit's hut than a royal Palace. Whereas his dear Alfonso—so handsome, so dashing—what a Primate he would have made! And if he were unsure at any time, his father would have been at hand to help him.

Ferdinand could never look at his son Alfonso without remembering voluptuous nights spent with his mother. What a woman! And her son was worthy of her.

Fond as he was of young Juan he almost wished that Alfonso was his legitimate son. There was an air of delicacy about Juan, whereas Alfonso was all virility. Ferdinand could be sure that this bastard of his knew how to make the most of his youth, even as his father had done.

It was maddening to think that he could not give him Toledo. What a gift that would have been from father to son.

Still, he did not despair. Isabella might admit her folly now that the monk had run away.

"I have spoken to Isabella," said the Queen.

"I hope she realizes her great good fortune."

"She does not call it such, Ferdinand."

"What! Here's Emanuel ready to do a great deal for her."

"Poor child; can you expect her to *enjoy* returning to the place where she has once been so happy?"

"She'll be happy there again."

Isabella studied her husband quizzically. Ferdinand would be happy were he in his daughter's place. Such marriage would mean to him a kingdom. He could not see that it made much difference that the bridegroom would be Emanuel instead of Alonso.

The Queen stifled the sorrow which such a thought roused. It was not for her to feel regrets; she was entirely satisfied with her fate.

"You made our wishes known to her, I hope?" went on Ferdinand.

"I could not command her, Ferdinand. The wound has not yet healed."

Ferdinand sat down at the polished wood table and beat his fist on it. "I understand not such talk," he said. "The alliance with Portugal is necessary for Spain. Emanuel wants it. It can bring us great good."

"Give her a little time," murmured Isabella; but in such a way that Ferdinand knew that, whatever he wished, their daughter would be given a little time.

He sighed. "We are fortunate in our children, Isabella," he said. "Through them we shall accomplish greatness for Spain. I would we had many more. Ah, if we could have been together more during those early years of our marriage. . . ."

"Doubtless you would have had more legitimate sons and daughters," agreed Isabella.

Ferdinand smiled slyly, but this was not the moment to bring up the matter of Alfonso and the Archbishopric of Toledo. Instead he said: "Maximilian is interested in my proposals."

Isabella nodded sadly. At such times she forgot she was ruler of a great and expanding country; she could only think of herself as a mother.

"They are young yet . . ." she began.

"Young! Juan and Juana are ready for marriage. As for our eldest, she has had time enough in which to play the widow."

"Tell me what you have heard from Maximilian."

"Maximilian is willing for Philip to have Juana and for Juan to have Margaret."

"They would be two of the grandest marriages we could

arrange for our children," mused Isabella. "But I feel that Juana is as yet too young . . . too unsteady."

"She will soon be too old, my dear; and she will never be anything but unsteady. No, the time is now. I propose to go ahead with my plans. We will tell them what we propose. There is no need to look gloomy. I'll warrant Juana will be excited at the prospect. As for your angel son, he'll not have to leave his mother's side. The Archduchess Margaret will come to Juan. So it is only your poor unsteady Juana who will have to go away."

"I wish we could persuade Philip to come here . . . to live here."

"What, Maximilian's heir! Oh, these are great matches, these marriages of our son and daughter to Maximilian's. Have you realized that Philip's and Juana's offspring will hold the harbours of Flanders, and in addition will own Burgundy and Luxembourg, to say nothing of Artois and Franche Comté? I would like to see the face of the King of France when he hears of this match. And when Isabella marries Emanuel we shall be able to relax our defences on the Portuguese frontier. Oh yes, I should like to see the French King's face."

"What do you know of Maximilian's children . . . Philip and Margaret?"

"Nothing but good. Nothing but good." Ferdinand was rubbing his hands together and his eyes gleamed.

Isabella nodded slowly. Ferdinand was right, of course. Both Juan and Juana were due for marriage. She was allowing the mother to subdue the Queen when she made wild plans to keep her children with her for ever.

Ferdinand had begun to laugh. "Philip will inherit the Imperial crown. The house of Hapsburg will be bound to us. France's Italian projects will have little success when the German dominions stand with us against them."

He is always a statesman first, thought Isabella, a father second. To him Philip and Margaret are not two human beings—they are the House of Hapsburg and the German Dominions. But she had to admit that his plan was brilliant. Their empire overseas was growing, thanks to their brilliant explorers and adventurers. But Ferdinand's dream had always been of conquests nearer home. He planned to be master of Europe; and why should he not be? Perhaps he would be master of the world.

He was the most ambitious man she had ever known. She had watched his love of power grow with the years. Now she asked herself uneasily whether this had happened because she had found it necessary so often to remind him that she was the Queen of Castile, and in Castile her word should be law. Had his *amour propre* been wounded to such a degree that he had determined to be master of all the world outside Castile?

She said: "If these marriages were made it would seem that all Europe would be your friend with the exception of that little island—that pugnacious, interfering little island."

Ferdinand kept his eyes on her face as he murmured: "You refer to England, do you not, my Queen. I agree with you. That little island can be one of the greatest trouble spots. But I have not forgotten England. Henry Tudor has two sons, Arthur and Henry. It is my desire to marry Arthur, Prince of Wales, to our own little Catalina. Then, my dear, the whole of Europe will be bound to me. And what will the King of France do then? Tell me that."

"Catalina! She is but a child."

"Arthur is young also. This will be an ideal match."

Isabella covered her face with her hands.

"What is the matter with you?" demanded her husband. "Will you not congratulate your children on having a father who makes such good matches for them?"

Isabella could not speak for a moment. She was thinking of Juana—wild Juana whose spirits no amount of discipline had been able to subdue—of Juana's being torn from her and sent to the flat, desolate land of Flanders, there to be wife of a man whom she had never seen but who was so suitable because he was the heir of the Hapsburgs. But chiefly she thought of Catalina . . . tender little Catalina . . . taken from her family to be the bride of a foreign Prince, to live her life in a bleak island where, if reports were true, the sun rarely shone, and the land was frequently shrouded in mists.

It had to come, she told herself. I always knew it. But that does not make it any easier to bear now that it is upon me.

* * *

The Queen had finished her confession and Ximenes enumerated her penances. She was guilty of allowing her personal feelings to interfere with her duty. It was a weakness of which she had been guilty before. The Queen must forget she is mother.

Isabella meekly accepted the reproaches of her confessor. He would never stray from the path of duty, she was sure. She looked at his emaciated face, his stern straight lips which she had never seen curved in a smile.

You are a good man, Ximenes, she was thinking; but it is easier for you who have never had children. When I think of my little Catalina's eyes fixed upon me I seem to hear her pleading with me: Don't send me away. I do not want to go to that island of fogs and rains. I shall hate Prince Arthur and he will hate me. And for you, Mother, I have a love such as can never be given to any other person.

"I know, my love, I know," Isabella whispered. "If it were in my power . . ."

But her thoughts were straying from her sins and, before she had earned forgiveness, she was falling into temptation once more.

When she next saw Catalina she would remind the child of her duty.

She rose from her knees. Now she was no longer a penitent but the Queen. Regality fell like a cloak about her and she frowned as her eyes rested on the monk.

"My friend," she said, "you still refuse the honour I would give you. How much longer will you hold out?"

"Your Highness," answered Ximenes, "I could not take office for which I felt myself to be unfitted."

"Nonsense, Ximenes, you know that the position fits you as a glove. I could command you to accept, you know."

"If Your Highness should adopt such a measure there would be nothing for me to do but retire to my hut in the forest of Castañar."

"I believe that is what you wish to do."

"I think I am more suited to be a hermit than a courtier."

"We do not ask you to be a courtier, Ximenes, but Archbishop of Toledo."

"They are one and the same, Your Highness."

"If *you* took the office I am sure they would be quite different." Isabella smiled serenely. She was certain that within the next few days Ximenes would accept the Archbishopric of Toledo.

She dismissed him and he went back to the small chamber which he occupied in the Palace. It was like a monk's cell. There was straw on the floor; this was his bed, and his pillow was a log of wood. There would be no fire in this room whatever the weather.

It was said in the Palace: Fray Francisco Ximenes enjoys punishing himself.

As he entered this cell-like apartment he found a Franciscan monk awaiting him there and, as the hood of this newcomer fell back, Ximenes saw that his visitor was his own brother Bernardín.

The grim face of Ximenes was as near to expressing pleasure as it could be. It delighted him that Bernardín had entered the

Franciscan brotherhood. Bernardín had been a wild boy and the last thing to have been expected of him was that he should enter the Order.

"Why, brother," he said, "well met. What do you do here?"

"I come to pay a call on you. I hear that you are highly thought of at Court."

"The man who is highly thought of at Court one day is often in disgrace the next."

"But you are not in disgrace. Is it true that you are to be Archbishop of Toledo?"

Bernardín's eyes sparkled with pleasure, but Ximenes said quickly: "You have been misinformed. I am not to be Archbishop of Toledo."

"It can't be true that the post has been offered to you and you refused it! You wouldn't be such a fool."

"I have refused it."

"Ximenes! You . . . idiot! You crass . . . stupid . . ."

"Have done. What do you know of these matters?"

"Only what good you could have brought to your family if you had become the most important man in Spain."

"I feared they had not made a monk of you, Bernardín. Tell me, what advantages should a good Franciscan hope for from the most important man in Spain?"

"You don't expect an answer to such a stupid question. Any man would hope for the highest honours. Whom should an Archbishop honour if not his own family?"

"Is this my brother speaking?"

"Don't be an old hypocrite!" burst out Bernardín. "Do you think you can hide your true feelings from *me*? You've refused this, have you not? Why? So that you can be pressed more strongly. You'll take it. And then, when you see what power is yours, perhaps you'll give a little something to a needy fellow Franciscan who also happens to be your own brother."

"I should prefer you to leave me," said Ximenes. "I do not like the way you talk."

"Oh, what a fool I have for a brother!" wailed Bernardín. His expression changed suddenly. "You have forgotten, have you not, that there are so many wrongs that you can put right. Why, even within our own Order there is much that you dislike. Some of our fellows love luxury too much. You would like to see us all tormenting our bodies with our hair shirts; you would like to see us all using planks as our pillows; starvation should be our lot. Well, it is in your power to bring all these discomforts to us, oh holy brother."

"Get you gone," cried Ximenes. "You are no brother of

mine . . . nay, even though our mother bore us both and you wear the habit of the Franciscans."

Bernardín bowed ironically. "Even though you are a hypocrite, even though you are so holy that you will not take the honours which would enable you to help your family, it is not a bad thing to be the brother of Francisco Ximenes de Cisneros. Men already are wary how they treat me, and seek my favour." Bernardín came closer to his brother and whispered: "They all know that in good time you will not be able to resist this honour. They all know that I, Bernardín de Cisneros, will one day be the brother of the Archbishop of Toledo."

"They shall not have that gratification," Ximenes told him.

Bernardín laughed slyly and left his brother. When he was alone Ximenes fell to his knees and began to pray. The temptation was very great.

"Oh Lord," he murmured, "if I accepted this great honour there are so many reforms I could bring about. I would work in Thy name. I would work for Thy glory and for that of Spain. Might it not be my duty to accept this honour?"

"No, no," he admonished himself. "It is temporal power which you are seeking. You want to wear the robes of the Archbishop, to see the people kneel before you."

But that was not true.

What did he want? He did not know.

"I will never accept the Archbishopric of Toledo!" he said aloud.

It was but a few days later when he was summoned to the Queen's apartment.

Isabella received him with a gracious smile which held a hint of triumph.

She put a document into his hand. "It is for you, Fray Francisco Ximenes," she said. "You will see it is from His Holiness and addressed to you."

Once more the Pope had addressed Ximenes as Archbishop of Toledo, and this document contained direct instructions from Rome.

There must be no more refusals. Alexander VI wrote from the Vatican that Fray Francisco Ximenes de Cisneros was henceforth Archbishop of Toledo, and any refusal on his part to accept the post would be regarded as disobedience to the Holy See.

The decision had been made for him.

Ximenes wondered whether the feeling he experienced was exultation. The Kingdoms of the world were no longer merely shown to him. He was forced by the Holy Father himself to accept his destiny.

* * *

Isabella sat with her children. Whenever she could spare the time from her state duties she liked to be with them, and it was comforting to know that they enjoyed this intimacy as she did.

Juan put a shawl about her shoulders. "There is a draught coming from the window, dear Mother."

"Thank you, Angel." She offered a silent prayer of thankfulness because, whoever else was taken from her, Angel would always be near.

Catalina was leaning against her knee, dreamily happy. Poor defenceless little Catlina, who was the baby. Isabella remembered well the day the child had been born, a miserably cold December day in Alcalá de Henares. Little did she think then that this, her fifth child, would be her last.

Juana could not cease chattering. "Mother, what are the women like in Flanders? They have golden hair, I hear . . . most of them. They are big women with great breasts."

"Hush, hush!" said the Princess Isabella. She was sitting on her stool, her fingers caressing her rosary. The Queen believed she had been praying. She was constantly praying. And for what? A miracle which would bring her young husband back to life? Was she praying that she would not have to leave home and go once more as a bride to Portugal? Perhaps that would be as much a miracle as the return to life of Alonso would have been.

"But," cried Juana, "the Queen said there was to be no ceremony. There never is ceremony when we are together thus."

"That is so, my daughter," said the Queen. "But it is not seemly to discuss the size of the breasts of the women in your future husband's country."

"But Mother, why not? Those women might be of the utmost importance to me."

Has she been hearing tales of this handsome philanderer who is to be her husband? the Queen wondered. How could she? Has she second sight? What strangeness is this in my Juana? How like her grandmother she grows . . . so like that I never look at her without feeling this fear twining itself about my heart like ivy about a tree . . . strangling my contentment.

"You should listen to your sister, Juana," the Queen said. "She is older than you and therefore it is very possible that she is wiser."

Juana snapped her fingers. "Philip will be a greater King than Alonso ever could have been . . . or Emanuel will be."

The younger Isabella had risen to her feet; the Queen noticed how she clenched her hands, and the colour flooded into her pale cheeks.

"Be silent, Juana," commanded the Queen.

"I will not. I will not." Juana had begun to dance round the room while the others watched her in dismay. None of them would have dreamed of disobeying the Queen. Juana must be bordering on one of her odd moods or she would not have dared.

The Queen's heart had begun to beat wildly but she smiled outwardly serene. "We will ignore Juana," she said, "until she has learned her manners. Well, Angel, so soon you are to be a husband."

"I hope I shall be a satisfactory one," he murmured.

"You will be the most satisfactory husband there ever was," said Catalina. "Will he not, Mother?"

"I believe he will," answered the Queen.

Juana had danced up to them. She had flung herself at her mother's feet and now lay on her stomach, propping her face in her hands.

"Mother, when shall I sail? When shall I sail for Flanders?"

The Queen ignored her and, turning to Catalina, she said: "You are looking forward to the festivities of your brother's wedding, eh, my child?"

Juana had begun to beat her fist on the floor. "Mother, when . . . when. . . ?"

"When you have apologized to your sister for what you have said, we shall be ready to talk to you."

Juana frowned. She glared at Isabella and said: "Oh I'm sorry. Philip will be as great a King as Alonso would have been if he had lived. And I'll be as good a Queen as you would have been if Alonso's horse had not kicked him to death."

The Princess Isabella gave a little cry as she went to the window.

"My dear child," the Queen patiently said to her wild daughter, "you must learn to put yourself into the place of others, consider what you are about to say and ask yourself how you would feel if it were being said to you."

Juana's face crinkled up and she burst out: "It is no use, Mother. I could never be like Isabella. I don't think Philip could ever be like Alonso either."

"Come here," said the Queen and Juana came to her mother. The Queen put her arms about this daughter who had caused her many a sleepless night. How can I part with her? she asked herself. What will happen to her in a strange country where there will be no one to understand her as I do?

"Juana," she said, "I want you to be calm. Soon you will be going among people who do not know you as we do. They may not make allowances as we do. Soon you will be travelling to

Flanders with a great fleet of ships. There you will meet your husband Philip, and the ships which take you to him will bring his sister Margaret home for Juan."

"I shall be left behind in Flanders where the women have big breasts . . . and Philip will be my husband. He will be a great ruler, will he not, Mother . . . greater than Father. Is that possible?"

"It is only at the end of a ruler's life that his greatness can be judged," murmured the Queen. Her eyes were on her eldest daughter and she knew by the rigid position of her body that she was fighting back her tears.

She took Juana's hand and said: "There is much you will have to be taught before you go away. It is regrettable that you cannot be as calm as your brother."

Catalina spoke then. "But Mother, it is easy for Angel to be calm. He is not going away. His bride will come *here* for him."

The Queen looked down at the solemn little face of her youngest daughter; and she knew then that the parting with Catalina was going to be the most heartbreaking of them all.

I will not tell her just yet that she is to go to England, she mused. It will be years before she must leave us. There is no point in telling her now.

Ferdinand came into the room and the effect of his presence was immediate. He could not even regard his children without betraying his thoughts of the brilliant future he had planned for them. Now, as his eldest daughter came first to greet him, the Queen knew that he saw her as the link to friendship with Portugal . . . a peaceful frontier which would enable him to continue with greater ease his battles against his old enemies, the French. Now Juan—and Juana. The Hapsburg alliance. And Maria. He scarcely glanced her way, for no grand schemes for a profitable alliance had yet formed in his mind regarding her.

The Queen put her hand on Catalina's arm, as though to protect her. Poor little Catalina! She would mean to her father, friendship with England. She had been chosen as the bride of Arthur, Prince of Wales, because she was only a year older than he was, and therefore more suitable than Maria who was four years Arthur's senior.

Ferdinand surveyed his family. "I see you merry," he said.

Merry! thought the Queen. My poor Isabella with the grief on her face; the resignation of my Angel; the wildness of Juana; the ignorance of Catalina. Is that merriment?

"Well," went on Ferdinand, "you have good reason to be!"

"Juana is eager to learn all she can about Flanders," the Queen said.

"That is well. That is well. You must all be worthy of your good fortune. Isabella is fortunate. She knows Portugal well. How singularly blessed is my eldest daughter. She thought to lose the crown of Portugal and finds it miraculously restored to her."

The Princess Isabella said: "I cannot return to Portugal, Father. I could not . . ." She stopped, and there was a short but horrified silence in the room. It was clear that in a few moments the Princess Isabella was going to commit the terrible indiscretion of weeping before the King and Queen.

The Queen said gently: "You have our leave to retire, daughter." Isabella threw her mother a grateful glance and curtsied.

"But first . . ." Ferdinand was beginning.

"Go now, my dear," interrupted the Queen firmly, and she did not look at the angry lights which immediately shot up in Ferdinand's eyes.

For the sake of her children, as for her country, Isabella was ready to face the wrath of her husband.

Ferdinand burst out: "It is time that girl was married. The life she leads here is unnatural. She is continually at her prayers. What does she pray for? Convent walls! She should be praying for children!"

The children were subdued with the exception of Juana, in whom any conflict aroused excitement.

"I am praying for children already, Father," she cried.

"Juana," warned her mother; but Ferdinand gave a low laugh. "That's well enough. You cannot start your prayers too early. And what of my youngest daughter? Is she eager to learn the manners of England?"

Catalina was staring at her father in frank bewilderment.

"Eh, child?" he went on, looking at her lovingly. Little Catalina, the youngest, only ten years old—and yet so important to her father's schemes.

Isabella had drawn her little daughter close to her. "Our youngest daughter's marriage is years away," she said. "Why, Catalina need not think of England for many a year."

"It will not be so long," declared Ferdinand. "Henry is an impatient man. He might even ask that she be educated over there. He'll be wanting to turn her into a little Englishwoman at the earliest possible moment."

Isabella felt the tremor run through her daughter's body. She wondered what she could do to appease her. That it should have been broken like this! There were times when she had to restrain her anger against this husband who could be so impetuous in some matters, so cold blooded in others.

Could he not see the stricken look in the child's face now? Could he not understand its meaning?

"I have a little matter to discuss with your mother," he went on. "You may all leave us."

The children came forward in order of seniority and took their leave of their parents. The coming of Ferdinand into the apartment had brought with it the return of ceremony.

Little Catalina was last. Isabella leaned towards her and patted her cheek. Those big dark eyes were bewildered; and the fear was already beginning to show in them.

"I will come to you later, my child," whispered the Queen, and for a moment the fear lifted. It was as it had been in the days of the child's extreme youth when she had suffered some slight pain. "Mother will come and make it well." It was always so with Catalina. Her mother's presence had such an effect on her that its comfort could always soothe her pain.

Ferdinand was smiling the crafty smile which indicated that he had some fresh scheme afoot and was congratulating himself on its shrewdness.

"Ferdinand," said Isabella when they were alone, "that is the first indication that Catalina has had that she is to go to England."

"Is that so?"

"It was a shock to her."

"H'm. She'll be Queen of England one day. I can scarcely wait to get those marriages performed. When I think of the great good which can come to our country through these alliances I thank God that I have five children and wish I had five more. But it was not of this that I came to speak to you. This man Ximenes . . . this Archbishop of yours . . ."

"And yours, Ferdinand."

"Mine! I'd never give my consent to setting up a humble monk in the highest office in Spain. It has occurred to me that, as a humble man who will suddenly find himself a very rich one, he will not know how to manage great riches."

"You can depend upon it, he will not change his mode of life. He will give more to the poor, I'll swear, and I believe it has always been a great dream of his to build a University at Alcalá and to compile a polyglot Bible."

Ferdinand made an impatient gesture. There came into his eyes that acquisitive gleam which Isabella now knew so well and which told her that he was thinking of the rich revenues of Toledo, and she guessed that he had some scheme for diverting them from the Archbishop to himself.

"Such a man," said Ferdinand, "would not know what to do with such a fortune. It would embarrass him. He prefers to live his hermit's life. Why should we prevent him? I am going to offer him two or three *cuentos* a year for his personal expenses, and I do not see why the rest of the revenues of Toledo should not be used for the good of the country generally."

Isabella was silent.

"Well?" demanded Ferdinand impatiently.

"Have you put this matter before the Archbishop?" she asked.

"I thought it would be wiser if we did so together. I have sent for him to come to us. He should be here very shortly. I shall expect you to support me in this."

Isabella did not speak. She was thinking: I shall soon need to oppose him with regard to Catalina. I shall not allow him to send my daughter away from home for some years. We must not continually pull one against the other. The Archbishop, I am sure, is more able to fight his battles than my little Catalina.

"Well?" repeated Ferdinand.

"I will see the Archbishop with you and hear what he has to say on this matter."

"I need money . . . badly," went on Ferdinand. "If I am going to pursue the Italian wars with any success I must have more men and arms. If we are not to suffer defeat at the hands of the French . . ."

"I know," said Isabella. "The question is, is this the right way to get the money you need?"

"Any way to get the money for such a purpose is the right way," Ferdinand sternly told her.

It was shortly afterwards when Ximenes came to the apartment.

"Ah, Archbishop!" Ferdinand stressed the title almost ironically. Anyone looking less like an Archbishop there could not possibly be. Why, in the day of Mendoza the title had carried much dignity. Isabella was a fool to have bestowed it on a half-starved holy man.

"Your Highnesses," murmured Ximenes, making obeisance before them.

"His Highness the King has a suggestion to make to you, Ximenes," said the Queen.

The pale eyes were turned on Ferdinand, and even he felt a little disturbed by their cold stare. It was disconcerting to come face to face with someone who was not in fear of one. There was nothing this man feared. You could strip him of office and he would shrug his shoulders; you could take him to the faggots and set them alight and he would delight in his agony. Yes, it was certainly disturbing for a King, before whom men trembled, to find one so careless of his authority as Ximenes.

"Ah," Ferdinand was blustering in spite of himself, "the Queen and I have been speaking of you. You are clearly a man of simple tastes, and you find yourself burdened with great revenues. We have decided that you shall not be burdened with these. We propose to take them from you and administer them for the good of the country. You shall receive an adequate allowance for your household and personal expenses . . ."

Ferdinand stopped, for Ximenes had lifted a hand as though demanding silence; he might have been the sovereign and Ferdinand his subject.

"Your Highness," said Ximenes, addressing himself to Ferdinand, for he knew that this was entirely his idea, "I will tell you this. It was with great reluctance that I accepted my Archbishopric. Nothing but the express orders of the Holy Father could induce me to do so. But I have accepted it. Therefore I will do my duty as I see it should be done. I know that I shall need these resources if I am to care for the souls in my charge. And I must say this without more ado: If I remain in this post I and my Church must be free; and what is mine must be left to my jurisdiction in much the same way as Your Highness has charge of your kingdoms."

Ferdinand's face was white with anger. He said: "I had thought that your mind was on holy matters, Archbishop, but it seems it is not unaffected by your revenues."

"My mind is on my duty, Your Highness. If you persist in taking the revenues of Toledo you must also remove its Archbishop from his post. What has Her Highness the Queen to say of this matter?"

Isabella said quietly: "It must be as you wish, Archbishop. We must find other means for meeting the requirements of the state."

Ximenes bowed. "Have I your leave to retire, Your Highnesses?"

"You have our leave," answered Isabella.

When he had gone she waited for the storm to break. Ferdinand had gone to the window; his fists were clenched and she knew that he was fighting to control his anger.

"I am sorry, Ferdinand," she said, "but you cannot rob him of his rights. The revenues are his; you cannot take them merely because he is a man of holy habits."

Ferdinand turned and faced her. "Once again, Madam," he said, "you give an example of your determination to thwart and flout me."

"When I do not fall in with your wishes it is always with the utmost regret."

Ferdinand bit his lips to hold back the words which were struggling to be spoken. She was right of course. She was indeed happy when they were in agreement. It was her perpetual conscience which came between them. "Holy Mother," he murmured, "why did you give me such a *good* woman for my wife? Her eternal conscience, her devotion to duty, even when it is opposed to our good, is the cause of continual friction between us."

It was no use being angry with Isabella. She was as she always had been.

He said in such a low voice that she could scarcely hear him: "That man and I will be enemies as long as we live."

"No, Ferdinand," pleaded Isabella. "That must not be. You both wish to serve Spain. Let that be a bond between you. What does it matter if you look at your duty from different angles when the object is the same?"

"He is insolent, Archbishop of Toledo!"

"You must not blame Ximenes because he was chosen instead of your natural son, Ferdinand."

Ferdinand snapped his fingers. "That! That is forgotten. Have I not grown accustomed to seeing my wishes disregarded? It is the man himself . . . the holy man, who starves himself . . . and walks the Palace in his grubby serge. I think of Mendoza's day . . ."

"Mendoza is dead now, Ferdinand. This is the day of Ximenes."

"The pity of it!" murmured Ferdinand; and Isabella was wondering how she was going to keep her husband and her Archbishop from crossing each other's paths.

But her mind was not really on Ximenes, nor on Ferdinand. From the moment Catalina had left the apartment with her brother and sisters she had been thinking of the child.

She must go to her without delay. She must explain to her that marriage into England was a long way off.

"I do not believe," said Ferdinand, "that you are giving me your attention."

"I was thinking of our daughter, of Catalina. I am going to her now to tell her that I shall not allow her to leave us until she is much older."

"Do not make rash promises."

"I shall make none," said Isabella. "But I must comfort her. I know how badly she needs such comfort."

With that she left him, frustrated as he so often was, admiring her as he had such reason for doing, realizing that although she often exasperated him beyond endurance he owed a great deal to her of what was his.

He thought ruefully that she would seek to protect Catalina from his marriage plans in the same way as she had stubbornly refused to give Toledo to his son Alfonso. Yet he was bound to her as she was to him. They were one; they were Spain.

Isabella was thinking only of her daughter as she hastened to the children's apartments. It was as she had expected: Catalina was alone. The child lay on her bed and her face was buried in the pillows as though, thought Isabella tenderly, by hiding her eyes she need not see what was too unpleasant to be borne.

"My little one," whispered the Queen.

Catalina turned, and her face was illumined with sudden joy.

Isabella lay down and took the child in her arms. For a few moments Catalina clung childishly to her mother as though by doing so she could bind them together for ever.

"I did not mean you to know for a long, long time," whispered the Queen.

"Mother . . . when shall I go away from you?"

"My dearest, it will not be for years."

"But my father said . . ."

"Oh, he is an impatient man. He loves his daughters so much and is so happy in the possession of them that he longs to see them with children of their own. He forgets how young you are. A little girl of ten to be married!"

"Sometimes they are taken away from their mothers to live in foreign courts . . . the courts of their bridegrooms."

"You shall not leave me for many years. I promise you."

"How many, Mother?"

"Not until you are grown up and ready for marriage."

Catalina snuggled closer to her mother. "That is a long, long time. That is four years, or five years perhaps."

"It is indeed. So you see how foolish it would be to worry now over what may happen in four or five years' time. Why, by then you will be almost a woman, Catalina . . . wanting a husband of your own perhaps, not so eager to cling to your mother."

"I shall always cling to my mother!" Catalina declared passionately.

"Ah," sighed Isabella, "we shall see."

And they lay silently side by side. Catalina was comforted. To her, four or five years seemed an eternity. But to her mother it seemed a very little time.

But the purpose was achieved, the blow was softened. Isabella would talk to her young daughter about England. She would discover all she could about the Tudor King who, some said, had usurped the throne of England. Though of course it would be well if the child did not hear such gossip as that. She would talk to her about the King's children, the eldest of whom was to be her husband . . . a boy a year younger than herself. What was there to fear in that? There was another boy, Henry; and two girls, Margaret and Mary. She would soon learn their ways and in time forget about her Spanish home.

That was not true, she knew. Catalina would never forget.

She is closer to me than any of the others, I believe, thought Isabella. How happy I should be if this English marriage came to nothing and I were able to keep my little Catalina at my side until the day I die.

She did not mention such a thought. It was unworthy of the Queen of Spain and the mother of Catalina. At this time it seemed that Catalina's destiny lay with the English. As a daughter of Spain, Catalina would have to do her duty.

XIMENES AND TORQUEMADA

The cavalcade had come to rest at last in the port of Laredo which stood on the eastern borders of the Asturias. During the journey from Madrid to Laredo the Queen's anxieties had kept pace with her daughter's increasing excitement.

Isabella had determined to remain with Juana until that moment when she left Spanish soil. She would have liked to accompany her all the way to Flanders, for she was very fearful of what would await her wild daughter there.

Isabella had left her family and her state duties to be with her daughter, and during that long and often tedious journey she had never ceased to pray for Juana's future and to ask herself continually: What will become of her when she reaches Flanders?

Isabella had spent a night on board that ship in which Juana would sail. She now stood on deck with her daughter, awaiting the moment of departure when she must say farewell to Juana. About them was a fine array of ships, a fleet worthy of the Infanta's rank which would carry her to Flanders and bring back the Archduchess Margaret to be Juan's bride. There were a hundred and twenty ships in this magnificent armada, some large, some small. They carried means of defending themselves, for they had been made ready to fight against the French. Ferdinand, however, had been willing to put them to this use, because in conveying his unstable daughter to Flanders they were prosecuting the war against the French as certainly as if they went into battle.

Ferdinand himself was not with them on this occasion. He had gone to Catalonia to make ready for an attack on the French. Isabella was rather pleased that she was alone to say goodbye to Juana. So great were her anxieties that she could not have borne to see the pleasure which she knew would shine from her husband's eyes as he watched their daughter's departure.

Juana turned to her mother, her eyes sparkling, and cried: "To think that all that is for me!"

Isabella continued to look at the ships, because she could not bear to look into her daughter's face at that moment. She knew that she was going to be reminded of her own mother, who was living out her clouded existence at the castle at Arevalo, unable to distinguish between past and present, raging now and then against those who were long since dead and had no power to harm her. There had been times when Isabella had dreaded her mother's outbreaks of violence, even as she now dreaded those of her daughter.

How will she fare with Philip? was another question she asked herself. Will he be kind to her? Will he understand?

"It is a goodly sight," murmured the Queen.

"How long before I reach Flanders, Mother?"

"So much will depend on the weather."

"I hope there will be storms."

"Oh, my child, no! We must pray for calm seas and a good wind."

"I should like to be delayed a little. I should like Philip to be waiting for me . . . rather impatiently."

"He will be waiting for you," murmured the Queen.

Juana clasped her hands across her breasts. "I long for him, Mother," she said. "I have heard that he is handsome. Did you know that people are beginning to call him Philip the Handsome?"

"It is pleasant to have a handsome bridegroom."

"He likes to dance and be gay. He likes to laugh. He is the most fascinating man in Flanders."

"You are fortunate, my dear. But remember, he is fortunate too."

"He must think so. He *shall* think so."

Juana had begun to laugh; it was the laughter of excitement and intense pleasure.

"Soon it will be time to say goodbye," said the Queen quickly. She turned impulsively to her daughter and embraced her, praying as she did so: "Oh God, let something happen to keep her with me. Let her not go on this long and hazardous journey."

But what was she thinking! This was the grandest marriage Juana could have made. It was the curse of Queens that their daughters were merely lent to them during their childhood. She must always remember this.

Juana was wriggling in the Queen's arms. It was not her mother's embrace that she wanted; it was that of her husband.

Will she be too eager, too passionate? wondered the Queen. And Philip—what sort of man is he? How I wish I could have met him, had a word with him, warned him that Juana is not quite like other girls.

"Look!" cried Juana. "The Admiral is coming to us."

It was true. Don Fadrique Enriquez, Admiral of Castile, had appeared on deck and Isabella knew that the moment was at hand when she must say goodbye.

"Juana," she said, grasping her daughter's hands and forcing the girl to look at her, "you must write to me often. You must never forget that my great desire is to help you."

"Oh no, I will not forget." But she was not really listening. She was dreaming of "Philip the Handsome", the most attractive man in Europe. As soon as this magnificent armada had carried her to Flanders she would be his wife, and she was impatient of everything that kept her from him. She was already passionately in love with a bridegroom whom she had never seen. The desire which rose within her was driving her to such a frenzy that she felt that if she could not soon satisfy it she would scream out her frustration.

The ceremony of the farewell was almost more than she could endure. She did not listen to her mother's gentle advice; she was unaware of the Queen's anxiety. There was only one need within her: this overwhelming hunger for Philip.

Isabella did not leave Laredo until the armada had passed out of sight. Then only did she turn away, ready for the journey back to Madrid.

"God preserve her," she prayed. "Give her that extra care which my poor Juana so desperately needs."

* * *

Young Catalina was watching for her mother's return.

This, she thought, is what will happen to me one day. My mother will accompany me to the coast. Perhaps not to Laredo. To what town would one go to embark for England?

Juana had gone off gaily. Her shrill laughter had filled the Palace during her last days there. She had sung and danced and talked continually of Philip. She was shameless in the way she talked of him. It was not the way Catalina would ever talk of Arthur, Prince of Wales.

But I will not think of it, Catalina told herself. It is far away. My mother will not let me go for years and years . . . even if the King of England does say he wishes me to be brought up as an English Princess.

Her sister Isabella came into the room and said: "Still watching, Catalina?"

"It seems so long since Mother went away."

"You will know soon enough when she returns. Watching will not bring her."

"Isabella, do you think Juana will be happy in Flanders?"

"I do not think Juana will be happy and contented anywhere."

"Poor Juana. She believes she will live happily for ever when she is married to Philip. He is so handsome, she says. They even call him Philip the Handsome."

"It is better to have a good husband than a handsome one."

"I am sure Prince Arthur is good. He is only a boy yet. It will be years before he marries. And Emanuel is good too, Isabella."

"Yes," agreed Isabella, "Emanuel is good."

"Are you going to marry him?"

Isabella shook her head and turned away.

"I am sorry I mentioned it, Isabella," said Catalina. "It reminds you, doesn't it?"

Isabella nodded.

"Yes," said Catalina, "you were happy, were you not? Perhaps it was better to have found Alonso such a good husband even though he died so soon . . . better than to have married a husband whom you hated and who was unkind to you."

Isabella looked thoughtfully at her young sister. "Yes," she said, "it was better than that."

"And you have seen Emanuel. You know him well. You know he is kind. So, Isabella, if you should have to marry him, perhaps you will not be so very unhappy. Portugal is near home . . . whereas . . ."

Isabella suddenly forgot her own problems and looked into the anxious eyes of her little sister. She put her arm about her and held her tightly.

"England is not so very far away either," she said.

"I have a fear," Catalina answered slowly, "that once I am there I shall never come back . . . never see you all again. That is what I think would be so hard to bear . . . never to see you and Juan, Maria and our father . . . and mother . . . never to see *Mother* . . ."

"I thought that. But, you see, I came back. Nothing is certain, so it is foolish to say 'I shall never come back.' How can you be sure?"

"I shall not say it. I shall say: 'I *will* come back,' because only if I did could I bear to go."

Isabella put her sister from her and went to the window. Catalina followed.

They saw two men riding fast up the slope to the Palace.

Catalina sighed with disappointment, because she knew they were not of the Queen's party.

"We shall soon discover who they are," said Isabella. "Let us go to Juan. The messengers will have been taken to him if they have important news."

When they reached Juan's apartments, the messengers had already been conducted to him and he was ordering that they be taken away and given refreshments.

"What is the news?" Isabella asked.

"They come from Arevalo," said Juan. "Our grandmother is very ill and calls constantly for our mother."

* * *

The Queen entered the familiar room, the memory of which she felt would haunt her with sadness for as long as she lived.

As soon as she had arrived at Madrid she had set out for Arevalo, praying that she would not be too late and yet half hoping that she would be.

In her bed lay the Dowager Queen of Castile, Isabella's ambitious mother, that Princess of Portugal who had suffered from the scourge of her family and whose mental aberrations had darkened her daughter's life.

It was because of her mother that Isabella felt those shocks of terror every time she noticed some fresh wildness in her daughter Juana. Had this madness in the royal blood passed one generation to flower in the next?

"Is that Isabella. . . ?"

The blank eyes were staring upwards, but they did not see the Queen, who leaned over the bed. They saw instead the little girl Isabella had been when her future was the greatest concern in the world to this mother.

"Mother, dear Mother. I am here," whispered Isabella.

"Alfonso, is that you, Alfonso?"

One could not say: Alfonso is dead, Mother . . . dead these many years. We do not know how he died, but we believe he was poisoned.

"He is the true King of Castile. . . ."

"Oh, Mother, Mother," whispered Isabella, "it is all so long ago. Ferdinand and I rule all Spain now. I became more than the Queen of Castile."

"I do not trust him . . ." the tortured woman cried.

Isabella laid a hand on her mother's clammy forehead. She called to one of the attendants. "Bring scented water. I would bathe her forehead."

The sick woman began to laugh. It was hideous laughter, reminding Isabella of those days when she and her young brother, Alfonso, had lived here in this gloomy palace of Arevalo with a mother who lost a little more of her reason with the passing of each day.

Isabella took the bowl of water from the attendant.

"Go now and leave me with her," she said; and she herself bathed her mother's forehead.

The laughter had lost its wildness. Isabella listened to the harsh breathing.

It could not be long now. She would call in the priests who would administer the last rites. But what would this sadly deranged, dying woman know of that? She had no idea that she was living through her last hours; she believed that she was a young woman again, fighting desperately for the throne of Castile that she might bestow it upon her son Alfonso or her daughter Isabella.

Still it was just possible that she might realize that it was Extreme Unction that was being administered; she might for a few lucid seconds understand the words of the priest.

Isabella stood up and beckoned one of the attendants who had been hovering in a corner of the apartment.

"Your Highness . . ." murmured the woman.

"My mother is sinking fast," said Isabella. "Call the priests. They should be with her."

"Yes, Highness."

Isabella went back to the bed and waited.

The Dowager Queen Isabella was lying back on her pillows, her eyes closed, her lips moving; and her daughter, trying to pray for her mother's soul, could only find the words intruding into her prayers: "Oh God, You have made Juana so like her. I pray You, take care of my daughter."

* * *

Catalina was eagerly awaiting the return of her mother from Arevalo, but it was long before she could be alone with her.

Since the little girl had learned that she was to go to England she could not spend enough time in her mother's company. Isabella understood this and made a point of summoning Catalina to her presence whenever this was possible.

Now she dismissed everyone and kept Catalina with her; the joy on the face of the child was rewarding enough; it moved Isabella deeply.

Isabella made Catalina bring her stool and sit at her feet. This, Catalina was happy to do; she sat leaning her head against her mother's skirts, and Isabella let her fingers caress her youngest daughter's thick chestnut hair.

"Did it seem long that I was away then?" she asked.

"So long, Mother. First you went away with Juana, and then as soon as you had returned you must leave for Arevalo."

"We have had little time together for so long. We must make up for it. I rejoiced to be with my mother for a little while before she died."

"You are unhappy, Mother."

"Are you surprised that I should be unhappy now that I have no mother? You who, I believe, love your own mother, can understand that, can you not?"

"Oh yes. But your mother was not as *my* mother."

Isabella smiled. "Oh, Catalina, she has caused me such anxieties."

"I know it, Mother. I hope never to cause you one little anxiety."

"If you did it would be solely because I loved you so well. You would never do aught, I know, to distress me."

Catalina caught her mother's hand and kissed it fiercely. Such emotion frightened Isabella.

I must strengthen her, this tender little child, she thought.

"Catalina," she said, "you are old enough to know that my mother was kept a prisoner, more or less, at Arevalo because . . . because her mind was not . . . normal. She was unsure of what was really happening. She did not know whether I was a woman or a little girl like you. She did not know that I was the Queen but thought that my little brother was alive and that he was the heir to Castile."

"Did she . . . frighten you?"

"When I was young I was frightened. I was frightened of her wildness. I loved her, you see, and I could not bear that she should suffer so."

Catalina nodded. She enjoyed these confidences; she knew that something had happened to make her relationship with her mother even more poignantly precious. This had taken place when she had discovered she was destined to go to England; and she believed that the Queen did not want her to go as an ignorant child. She wanted her to understand something of the world so that she would be able to make her own decisions, so that she would be able to control her emotions—in fact, so that she would be a grown-up person able to take care of herself.

"Juana is like her," said Catalina.

The Queen caught her breath. She said quickly: "Juana is too high spirited. Now that she is to have a husband she will be more controlled."

"But my grandmother had a husband; she had children; and she was not controlled."

The Queen was silent for a few seconds, then she said: "Let us pray together for Juana."

She took Catalina's hand and they went into that small anteroom where Isabella had set up an altar; and there they knelt and prayed not only for the safe journey of Juana but for her safe and sane passage through life.

Afterwards they went back to the apartment and Catalina sat once more on her stool at the Queen's feet.

"Catalina," said Isabella, "I hope you will be friends with the Archduchess Margaret when she comes. We must remember that she will be a stranger among us."

"I wonder whether she is frightened," Catalina whispered, trying not to think of herself setting out on a perilous journey across the sea to England.

"She is sixteen years old, and she comes to a strange country to marry a young man whom she has never seen. She does not know that in our Juan she will have the kindest, dearest husband anyone could have. She has yet to learn how fortunate she is. But while she is discovering this I want you and your sisters to be very kind to her."

"I shall, Mother."

"I know you will."

"I would do anything you asked of me . . . gladly I would do it if you commanded me."

"I know it, my precious daughter. And when the time comes for you to leave me you will do so with good courage in your heart. You will know, will you not, that wherever I am and wherever you are, I shall never forget you as long as I live."

Catalina's lips were trembling as she answered: "I will never forget it. I will always do my duty as you would have me do it. I shall not whimper."

"I shall be proud of you. Now take your lute, my dearest, and play to me awhile; for very soon we shall be interrupted. But never mind, I shall steal away from state duties and be with you whenever it is possible. Play to me now, my dearest."

So Catalina brought her lute and played; but even the gayest tunes sounded plaintive because Catalina could not dismiss from her mind the thought that time passed quickly and the day must surely come when she must set out for England.

* * *

Those were sad weeks for the Queen. She was in deep mourning for her mother, and there had been such tempests at sea that she feared for the safety of the armada which was escorting Juana to Flanders.

News came that the fleet had had to put into an English port because some of the ships had suffered damage during the tempest. Isabella wondered how Don Fadrique Enriquez was managing to keep the wild Juana under control. It would not be easy and the sooner she was married to Philip the better.

But travelling by sea was a hazardous affair and it might well be that Juana would never reach her destination.

A storm at sea might rob Ferdinand of his dearest dream. If Juana were lost on her way to Flanders, and Margaret on her way to Spain, that would be the end of the proposed Hapsburg alliance. Isabella could only think of the dangers to her children, and her prayers were constant.

She tried to concentrate on other matters, but it was not easy to shut out the thought of Juana in peril; and since the recent death of her mother she had had bad dreams in which the sick woman of Arevalo often changed into the unstable Juana.

She was fortunate, she told herself, in her Archbishop of Toledo. Others might rail against him, criticize him because he had taken all the colour and glitter from his office, because he was as stern and unrelenting in his condemnation of others as he was of himself. But for him Isabella had that same admiration which she had had—and still had—for Tomás de Torquemada.

Tomás had firmly established the Holy Inquisition in the land, and Ximenes would do his utmost to maintain it. They were two of a kind and men whom Isabella—as sternly devout as they were themselves—wished to have about her.

She knew that Ximenes was introducing reforms in the Order to which he belonged. It had always seemed deplorable to him that many monks, who appeared in the Franciscan robes, did not follow the rules which had been set down for them by their Founder. They loved good living; they feasted and drank good wine; they loved women, and it was said that many of them were the fathers of illegitimate children. This was something to rouse fury in a man such as Ximenes and, like Torquemada, he was not one to shrug aside the weaknesses of others.

Therefore Isabella was not entirely surprised when, one day while she mourned her mother and waited anxiously for news of Juana's safe arrival in Flanders, she found herself confronted by the General of the Franciscan Order who had come from Rome especially to see her.

She received him at once and invited him to tell her his grievance.

"Your Highness," he cried, "my grievance is this: the Archbishop of Toledo seeks to bring reforms into our Order."

"I know it, General," murmured the Queen. "He would have you all following the rules laid down by your Founder. He himself follows those rules and he deems it the duty of all Franciscans to do the same."

"His high position has gone to his head, I fear," said the General.

The Queen smiled gently. She knew that the General was a Franciscan of the Conventual Order, while Ximenes belonged to the Observatines, a sect which believed it should follow the ways of the Founder in every detail. The Conventuals had broken away from these rigid rules, believing that they need not live the lives of monks to do good in the world. They were good-livers, some of these Conventuals, and Isabella could well understand and sympathize with the desire of Ximenes to abolish their rules and force them to conform with the laws of the Observatines.

"I crave Your Highness's support," he went on. "I ask you to inform the Archbishop that he would be better employed attending to his duties than making trouble within the Order of which he is honoured to be a member."

"The Archbishop's conduct is a matter for his own conscience," said Isabella.

The General forgot he was in the presence of the Queen of Spain. He cried out: "What folly is this! To take such a man and set him up in the highest position in Spain! Archbishop of Toledo! The right hand of the King and Queen. A man who is more at home in a forest hut than in a Palace. A man without ability, without noble birth. Your Highness should remove him immediately from this high office and put someone there who is worthy of the honour."

"I think," said Isabella quietly, "that you are mad. Have you forgotten to whom you speak?"

"I am not mad," replied the General. "I know I am speaking to Queen Isabella—she who will one day be a handful of dust . . . even as I or anyone else."

With that he turned from her and hurried out of the room.

Isabella was overcome by astonishment, but she did not seek to punish this man.

She was astounded though at the hatred which Ximenes engendered, but she was more certain than she had ever been that, in making him Archbishop of Toledo, she had made a wise choice.

* * *

Francisco Ximenes de Cisneros lay in his bed in his house at Alcalá de Henares. He preferred this simpler dwelling to the palace which could have been his home at Toledo, and there were often times when he yearned for his hermit's hut in the forest of Our Lady of Castañar.

His thoughts were now on Bernardín, that erring brother of his who would come to him soon; he had sent for him and he did not believe even Bernardín would dare disobey.

It was disconcerting to have to receive his brother while in bed, but he was now enduring one of his spells of illness, which some said were due to his meagre diet and the rigorous life he led. He spent most of his time in a cell-like room, the floor of which was uncovered and which he kept unheated during the coldest weather. He felt great need to inflict punishment on himself.

It was true that he now lay in this luxurious bed, because here he must receive those who came to see him on matters of State and Church. At night he would leave this luxury and lie on his hard pallet bed with a log for his pillow.

He longed to torture his body, and deplored the fact that orders had come from the Pope commanding him to accept the dignity of his office. There had been many to lay complaints against him. They complained because he was often seen in his shabby Franciscan robe, which he had patched with his own hands. Was this the way for the Archbishop of Toledo to conduct himself? many demanded.

It was useless to tell them that it was the way of a man who wished to follow in the footsteps of his Master.

But instructions had come from Rome.

"Dear brother," Alexander had written, "the Holy and Universal Church, as you know, like heavenly Jerusalem, has many and diverse adornments. It is wrong to seek them too earnestly, so it is also wrong to reject them too contemptuously. Each state of life has its appropriate conditions, which are pleasing to God and worthy of praise. Everyone, therefore, especially prelates of the Church, must avoid arrogance by excessive display, and superstition by excessive humility; for in both cases the authority of the Church will be weakened. Wherefore we exhort and advise you to order your life suitably to the rank which you hold; and since the Holy Father has raised you from humble station to that of Archbishop, it is reasonable that as you live in your conscience according to the rules of God (at which we feel great joy), so in your external life you should maintain the dignity of your rank."

That was the command of the Pope and not to be ignored. So Ximenes had since worn the magnificent garments of an Archbishop, though beneath them had been the robe of the Franciscan, and beneath that the hair shirt itself.

Ximenes felt that there was something symbolic about the manner in which his emaciated body appeared to the public. The people saw the Archbishop, but beneath the Archbishop was the real man, the Franciscan friar.

But which was the real man? Often his fingers itched to deal with problems of State. He longed to see Spain great among the nations and himself at the helm guiding the great ship of state from one triumph to another until the whole world was under the domination of Spain . . . or Ximenes.

"Ah," he would cry swiftly when such a thought came to him. "It is because I wish to see the Christian flag flying over all the Earth." He wished all lands to be governed as Spain was being governed since Torquemada had set the fires of the Inquisition burning in almost every town.

But now his thoughts must turn to Bernardín, for soon his brother would be with him and he would have to speak to him with the utmost sternness.

He rehearsed the words he would say: "You are my brother, but that does not mean that I shall treat you with especial leniency. You know my beliefs. I hate nepotism. I shall never allow it to be used in any of my concerns."

And Bernardín would stand smiling at him in that lazy cynical way of his, as though he were reminding his powerful brother that he did not always live up to his own rigid code.

It was true that he had made exceptions. There was the case of Bernardín for one. He had taken him into his household with a lucrative post as steward. What folly!

"Yet this was my brother," said Ximenes aloud.

And how had Bernardín shown his gratitude? By giving himself airs, by stirring up trouble, by extricating himself from those difficult situations which were of his own making, by truculently reminding those who sought justice: "I am the brother of the Archbishop of Toledo. I am greatly favoured by him. If you dare to bring any complaints against me, it will go ill with you."

"Oh shame!" cried Ximenes. "This was the very weakness I deplore in others."

And what had he done with Bernardín? Banished him to a monastery, and there Bernardín had drawn up complaints against his brother in which he had been supported by the Archbishop's enemies—who were numerous.

There had been nothing to do but send Bernardín to prison. And how his conscience had suffered. "My own brother . . . in prison!" he had demanded of himself. "Yes, but he deserves his fate," was the answer. "Your own brother! Oh, it is only little Bernardín who was always one for mischief."

So he had brought him out of prison and taken him back as a

steward, and had talked to him sternly, imploring him to lead a better life.

But what had been the use? Bernardín would not mend his ways. It had not been long before news had come to Ximenes that his brother had interfered with the justice of the Courts, threatening that if a judge did not give a certain verdict he would incur the displeasure of the Archbishop of Toledo.

This was the final disaster. For this reason he had sent for Bernardín, for all his peccadilloes of the past seemed slight compared with this interference with the justice of the Courts.

Ximenes raised himself and called Francisco Ruiz.

His nephew came hurrying to his bedside. How he wished that his brother were like this trustworthy man.

"Francisco, when Bernardín comes, have him brought to me at once and leave us together."

Ruiz bowed his head and, when Ximenes waved a hand, immediately left the sickroom.

"I would be alone," Ximenes said gently as he went. "I want to pray."

He was still praying when Bernardín was brought to him.

Ximenes opened his eyes and regarded his wayward brother, looking in vain for a sign of penitence in Bernardín's face.

"Well, brother," said Ximenes, "as you see I have been forced to take to my bed."

"I pray you do not ask for my sympathy," cried Bernardín. "You are ill because of this ridiculous life you lead. You could be well and strong if you allowed yourself to live in comfort."

"I have not summoned you to me that you may advise me on *my* way of life, Bernardín, but to remonstrate with you regarding your own."

"And what sins have I committed now?"

"You will know so much better than I."

"In your eyes, brother, all human actions are sin."

"Not all, Bernardín."

"All mine. Your own, of course, are virtues."

"I found it necessary recently to have you imprisoned."

Bernardín's eyes glittered and he came nearer to the bed. "Do not attempt to do such a thing again. I swear to you that if you do you will live to regret the day."

"Your threats would never make me swerve from my duty, Bernardín."

Bernardín leaned over the bed and seized Ximenes roughly by the shoulder. Ximenes tried to throw him off but failed to do so and lay panting helplessly on his pillows.

Bernardín laughed aloud. "Why, 'tis not I who am at your

mercy, but you at mine. What is the Archbishop of Toledo but a skin full of bones! You are sick, brother. Why, I could put these two hands of mine about your neck and press and press . . . In a matter of seconds the Sovereigns would find themselves without their Archbishop of Toledo."

"Bernardín, you should not even think of murder."

"I will think what I will," cried Bernardín. "What good will you ever do me? What good have you ever done? Had you been a normal brother to me I should have been a Bishop by now. And what am I? Steward in your household! Brought before my Lord Archbishop to answer a charge. What charge? I ask you. A charge of getting for myself what most brothers would have given me."

"Have a care, Bernardín."

"Should I have a care? I . . . the strong man? It is you who should take care, Gonzalo Ximenes . . . I beg your pardon . . . The name our parents gave you is not good enough for such a holy man. Francisco Ximenes, you are at my mercy. I could kill you as you lie there. It is you who should plead with me for leniency . . . not I with you."

A lust for power had sprung up in Bernardín's eyes. What he said was true. At this moment his brilliant brother was at his mercy. He savoured that power, and longed to exercise it.

He will never do anything for me, he told himself. He is no good to our family . . . no good to himself. He might just as well have stayed in the hermitage at Castañar. A curse on him! He has no natural feeling.

All Bernardín's dreams were remembered in that second. Ximenes could have made them come true.

Ximenes had recovered his breath and was speaking.

"Bernardín, I sent for you because what I heard of your conduct in the Courts distressed and displeased me . . ."

Bernardín began to laugh out loud. With a sudden movement he pulled the pillow from under his brother's head and laughing demoniacally he held it high. Then he pushed Ximenes back on the bed and brought the pillow down over his face and held it there.

He could hear Ximenes fighting for his breath. He felt his brother's hands trying to pull at the pillow. But Ximenes was feeble and Bernardín was strong.

And after a while Ximenes lay still.

Bernardín lifted the pillow; he dared not stop to look at his brother's face, but hurried from the room.

* * *

Tomás de Torquemada had left the peace of his monastery of St. Thomas in Avila and was travelling to Madrid. This was a great wrench for him as he was a very old man now and much of the fire and vitality had gone from him.

Only the firm belief that his presence was needed at Court could have prevailed upon him to leave Avila at this time.

He loved his monastery—which was to him one of the greatest loves in his life. Perhaps the other was the Spanish Inquisition. In the days of his health they had fought together for his loving care. What joy it had been to study the plans for his monastery; to watch it built; to glory in beautifully sculptured arches and carvings of great skill. The Inquisition had lured him from that love now and then; and the sight of heretics going to the *quemadero* in their hideous yellow *sanbenitos* gave him as much pleasure as the cool, silent halls of his monastery.

Which was he more proud to be—the creator of St. Thomas in Avila or the Inquisitor General?

The latter was more or less a title only nowadays. That was because he was growing old and was plagued by the gout. The monastery would always stand as a monument to his memory and none could take that from him.

He would call first on the Archbishop of Toledo at Alcalá de Henares. He believed he could rely on the support of the Archbishop for the project he had in mind.

Painfully he rode in the midst of his protective cavalcade. Fifty men on horseback surrounded him, and a hundred armed men went on foot before him and a hundred marched behind.

The Queen herself had implored him to take adequate care when he travelled. He saw the wisdom of this. People whose loved ones had fed the fires of the Inquisition might consider revenge. He could never be sure, as he rode through towns and villages or along the lonely roads, whether the men and women he met bore grudges against him.

Fear attacked him often, now that he was growing infirm. A sound in the night—and he would call to his attendants.

"Are the doors guarded?"

"Yes, Excellency," would be the answer.

"Make sure to keep them so."

He would never have anyone with Jewish blood near him. He was afraid of those with Jewish blood. It was but a few years ago that all Jews who would not accept the Christian faith had been mercilessly exiled from Spain on his decree. Many Jews remained. He thought of them sometimes during the night. He dreamed they stole into his room.

He had every dish which was put before him first tasted in his presence before he ate.

When a man grew old he contemplated death often, and Torquemada, who had sent thousands to their deaths, was now afraid that someone who had suffered through him would seek to hurry him from life.

But duty called; and he had a plan to lay before the Sovereigns.

He reached Alcalá in the late afternoon. The residence of Ximenes was very sombre.

Ruiz received Torquemada in the place of his master.

"Does aught ail Fray Francisco Ximenes de Cisneros?" Torquemada asked.

"He is recovering from an illness which has been most severe."

"Then perhaps I should not delay but continue my journey to Madrid."

"Let me tell him that Your Excellency is here. If he is well enough he will certainly wish to see you. Allow me to inform him of your arrival after I have shown you to an apartment where you can rest while I have refreshment sent to Your Excellency."

Torquemada graciously agreed to this proposal and Ruiz hurried to the bedside of Ximenes who had not left his bed since that horrifying encounter with Bernardín.

He opened his eyes and looked at Ruiz as he entered. To this nephew he owed his life. Ruiz had dashed into the apartment as Bernardín had hurried out because Ruiz, who knew Bernardín well, had feared he might harm his brother. It was Ruiz who had revived his half-dead uncle and brought him back to life.

Ximenes had since been wondering what action to take. Clearly he could not have Bernardín back in his household, but justice should be done. There should be punishment for such a crime. But how could he denounce his own brother as a would-be murderer?

Ruiz came to stand by the bed.

"Uncle," he said, "Tomás de Torquemada is with us."

"Torquemada! Here!" Ximenes attempted to raise his weakened body. "What does he want?"

"To have a word with you if you are well enough to see him."

"It must be some important business which brings him here."

"It must be. He is a sick man and suffering greatly from the gout."

"You had better bring him to me, Ruiz."

"If you do not feel strong enough I can explain this to him."

"No. I must see him. Have him brought to me."

Torquemada entered Ximenes' bedchamber and coming to the bed embraced the Archbishop.

They were not unlike—both had the stern look of the man who believes himself to have discovered the righteous way of life; both were ascetic in the extreme, emaciated through hardship; both were well acquainted with semi-starvation and the hair shirt—all of which they believed necessary to salvation. Both had to fight with their own particular demon, which was a pride greater than that felt by most men.

"I am sad to see you laid low, Archbishop," said Torquemada.

"And I fear you yourself are in no fit state to travel, Inquisitor." Inquisitor was the title Torquemada enjoyed hearing more than any other. It was a reminder that he had set up an Inquisition the like of which had never been seen in Spain before.

"I suffer from the gout most cruelly," said Torquemada.

"A strange sickness for one of your habits," answered Ximenes.

"Strange indeed. And what is this latest illness of yours?"

Ximenes answered quickly: "A chill, I suspect."

He was not going to tell Torquemada that he had been almost suffocated by his own brother, for if he had Torquemada would have demanded that Bernardín should be brought to trial and severely punished. Torquemada would doubtless have behaved with rigorous justice if he had been in the place of Ximenes.

Perhaps, thought Ximenes, I lack his strength. But he has had longer in which to discipline himself.

Ximenes went on: "But I believe you have not come here to talk of illness."

"No, I am on my way to Court and, because I know I shall have your support in the matter which I have decided to bring to the notice of the Sovereigns, I have called to acquaint you with my mission. It concerns the Princess Isabella, who has been a widow too long."

"Ah, you are thinking that with the Hapsburg marriages, the eldest daughter should not be forgotten."

"I doubt she is forgotten. The Princess is reluctant to go again into Portugal."

"Such reluctance is understandable," said Ximenes.

"*I* cannot understand it," Torquemada retorted coldly. "It is clearly her duty to make this alliance with Portugal."

"It has astonished me that it has not been made before," Ximenes put in.

"The Queen is a mother who now and then turns her face from duty."

They, who had both been confessors to Isabella the Queen, exchanged nods of understanding.

"She is a woman of great goodness," Torquemada acceded, "but where her children are concerned she is apt to forget her duty in her desire to please them."

"I know it well."

"Clearly," Torquemada went on, "the young Isabella should be sent immediately into Portugal as the bride of Emanuel. But there should be one condition, and it is this which I wish to put before the Sovereigns."

"Condition?"

"When I drove the Jews from Spain," said Torquemada, "many of them found refuge in Portugal." His face darkened suddenly; his eyes gleamed with wild fanaticism; they seemed like living things in a face that was dead. All Torquemada's hatred for the Jewish race was in his eyes, in his voice at that moment. "They pollute the air of Portugal. I wish to see them driven from Portugal as I drove them from Spain."

"If this marriage were made we should have no power to dictate Emanuel's policy towards the Jews," Ximenes pointed out.

"No," cried Torquemada triumphantly, "but we could make it a condition of the marriage. Emanuel is eager for this match. He is more than eager. It is not merely to him a grand marriage . . . union with a wealthy neighbour. This young King is a weak and emotional fellow. Consider his tolerance towards the Jews. He has strange ideas. He wishes to see all races living in harmony side by side in his country following their own faiths. You see he is a fool; he is unaware of his duty to the Christian Faith. He wishes to rule with what he foolishly calls tolerance. But he is a love-sick young man."

"He saw the Princess when she went into Portugal to marry Alonso," murmured Ximenes.

"Yes, he saw her, and from the moment she became a widow he has had one plan: to make her his wife. Well, why not? Isabella must become the Queen of Portugal, but on one condition: the expulsion of the Jews from that country as they have been expelled from our own."

Ximenes lay back on his pillows exhausted and Torquemada rose.

"I am tiring you," he said. "But I rely on your support, should I need it. Not that I shall." All the fire had come back to this old man who was midway in his seventies. "I shall put this to the Queen and I know I shall make her see her duty."

When Torquemada had taken his leave of Ximenes the Archbishop lay back considering the visit.

Torquemada was a stronger man than he was. Neither of them thought human suffering important. They had sought to inflict it too often on themselves to be sorry for others who bore it.

But at this time Ximenes was more concerned with his own problem than that of Isabella and Emanuel. He had decided what he must do with Bernardín. He would send his brother back to his monastery; he would give him a small pension; but it should be on condition that he never left his monastery and never sought to see his brother again.

I am a weak man where my own are concerned, thought Ximenes. And he wondered at himself who could contemplate undisturbed the hardships which would certainly befall the Jews of Portugal if Emanuel accepted this new condition, yet must needs worry about a man who, but for chance, might have committed fratricide—and all because that man happened to be his own brother.

* * *

The Princess Isabella looked from her mother to the stern face of Torquemada.

Her throat was dry; she felt that if she had tried to protest the words would not come. Her mother had an expression of tenderness yet determination. The Princess knew that the Queen had made up her mind—or perhaps that this stern-faced man who had once been her confessor had made it up for her as he had so many times before. She felt powerless between them. They asked for her consent, but they did not need it. It would be as they wished, not as she did.

She tried once more. "I could not go into Portugal."

Torquemada had risen, and she thought suddenly of those men and women who were taken in the dead of night to his secret prisons and there interrogated, until from weariness—and from far worse, she knew—agreed with what he wished them to say.

"It is the duty of a daughter of Spain to do what is good for Spain," said Torquemada. "It is sinful to say 'I do not wish that.' 'I do not care to do that.' It matters not. This is your duty. You must do your duty or imperil your soul."

"It is you who say it is my duty," she answered. "How can I be sure that it is?"

"My daughter," said the Queen, "that which will bring benefit to Spain is your duty and the duty of us all."

"Mother," cried the Princess, "you do not know what you are asking of me."

"I know full well. It is your cross, my dearest. You must carry it."

"You carry a two-edged sword for Spain," said Torquemada. "You can make this marriage which will secure our frontiers, and you can help to establish firmly the Christian Faith on Portuguese soil."

"I am sure Emanuel will never agree to the expulsion of the Jews," cried Isabella. "I know him. I have talked with him. He has what are called liberal ideas. He wants freedom of thought in Portugal. He said so. He will never agree."

"Freedom for sin," retorted Torquemada. "He wishes for this marriage. It shall be our condition."

"I cannot do it," said Isabella wearily.

"Think what it means," whispered her mother. "You will have the great glory of stamping out heresy in your new country."

"Dearest Mother, I do not care . . ."

"Hush, hush!" It was the thunderous voice of Torquemada. "For that you could be brought before the tribunal."

"It is my daughter to whom you speak," the Queen put in with some coldness.

"Highness, it is not the first time I have had to remind *you* of your duty."

The Queen was meekly silent. It was true. This man had a more rigorous sense of duty than she had. She could not help it if her love for her family often came between her and her duty.

She must range herself on his side. Ferdinand would insist on this marriage's taking place. They had indulged their daughter too long. And, if they could insist on this condition, that would be a blow struck for Holy Church, so she must forget her tenderness for her daughter and put herself on the side of righteousness.

Her voice was stern as she addressed her daughter: "You should cease to behave like a child. You are a woman and a daughter of the Royal House. You will prepare yourself to accept this marriage, for I shall send a despatch to Emanuel this day."

Torquemada's features were drawn into lines of approval. He did not smile. He never smiled. But this expression was as near to a smile as he could come.

When her mother spoke like that, Isabella knew that it was useless to protest; she lowered her head and said quietly: "Please, may I have your leave to retire?"

"It is granted," said the Queen.

* * *

Isabella ran to her apartment. She did not notice little Catalina whom she passed.

"Isabella, Isabella," called Catalina, "what is wrong?"

Isabella took no notice but ran on; she had one concern—to reach her bedroom before she began to weep, for it seemed to her in that moment the only relief she could look for was in tears.

She threw herself on to her bed and the storm burst.

Catalina had come to stand by the side of her bed. The child watched in astonishment, but she knew why Isabella cried. She shared in every sob; she knew exactly how her sister felt. This was like a rehearsal of what would one day happen to her.

At length she whispered very softly: "Isabella!"

Her sister opened her eyes and saw her standing there.

"It is Catalina."

Catalina climbed on to the bed and lay down beside her sister.

"It has happened then?" asked the little girl. "You are to go?"

"It is Torquemada. That man . . . with his schemes and his plots."

"He has made this decision then?"

"Yes. I am to marry Emanuel. There is to be a condition."

"Emanuel is a kind man, Isabella. He loves you already. You will not be unhappy. Whereas England is a strange place."

Isabella was silent suddenly; then she put her arms about Catalina and held her close to her.

"Oh Catalina, it is something we all have to endure. But it will be years before you go to England."

"Years do pass."

"And plans change."

Catalina shuddered, and Isabella went on: "It is all changed now, Catalina. I wish I had gone before. Then Emanuel would have loved me. He did, you know, when I was Alonso's wife."

"He will love you now."

"No, there will be a shadow over our marriage. You did not know what happened here when the Jews were driven out. You were too young. But I heard the servants talking of it. They took little children away from their parents. They made them leave their homes. Some died . . . some were murdered. There was great suffering throughout the land. Emanuel will hate to do in his country what was done in ours . . . and if he does not do it there will be no marriage."

"Who said this?"

"Torquemada. He is a man who always has his way. You see,

Catalina, if I go to Portugal it will not be the same any more. There will be a great shadow over my marriage. Perhaps Emanuel will hate me. They cursed us . . . those Jews, as they lay dying by the roadside. If I go to Portugal they will curse me."

"Their curses cannot hurt you, for you will be doing what is good."

"Good?"

"If it is what our mother wants, it will be good."

"Catalina, I'm frightened. I think I can hear their curses in my ears already."

They lay in silence side by side. Isabella was thinking of the roads of Portugal filled with bands of exiles, broken-hearted men and women looking for a home, prepared to find death on the highway, at the hands of murderers or from exposure.

"This is my marriage with Emanuel," she whispered.

Catalina did not hear her; she was thinking of a ship which would sail away to a land of fogs and strangers; and she was a passenger on that ship.

THE ARCHDUCHESS MARGARET

THE ARCHDUCHESS MARGARET clung to the ship's bulwarks. The wind was rising; the storm clouds loured.

Was the middlc of winter a good time to make a perilous sea journey? She was sure that it was not. Yet, she thought, what would it have availed me had I asked to wait for the spring?

There had already been much delay, and her father was anxious for her marriage; so, it seemed, were the King and Queen who were to be her parents-in-law.

"It is their will, not mine," she murmured.

Some girls of sixteen might have been terrified. There were so many events looming ahead of her which could be terrifying. There was to be a new life in a strange country, a new husband; even closer, was a threatening storm at sea.

But the expression on the face of the Archduchess was calm. She had been sufficiently buffeted by life to have learned that it is foolish to suffer in anticipation that which one may or may not have to suffer in fact.

She turned to the trembling attendant at her side and laid a hand on the woman's arm.

"The storm may not touch us," she said. "It may break behind us. That can happen at sea. The strong wind is carrying us fast to Spain."

The woman shuddered.

"And if we are to die," mused Margaret, "well then, that is our fate. There are worse deaths, I believe, than drowning."

"Your Grace should not talk so. It is tempting God."

"Do you think God would change His plans because of the idle chatter of a girl like myself?"

The woman's lips were moving in prayer.

I should be praying with her, thought Margaret. This is going to be a bad storm. I can feel it in the air. Perhaps I am not meant to be a wife in reality.

Yet she did not move, but stood holding her face up to the sky—not with defiance but with resignation.

How can any of us know, she asked herself, when our last hour will come?

She turned her comely face to the woman. "Go to my cabin," she said. "I will join you there."

"Your Grace should come with me now. This is no place for you."

"Not yet," said Margaret. "I will come when the rain starts."

"Your Grace . . ."

"That was an order," said Margaret with a quiet firmness, and a few seconds later she was smiling to see with what alacrity the woman left her side.

How terrified people were of death, mused Margaret. Was it because they remembered their sins? Perhaps it was safer to die when one was young. At sixteen a girl, who had been watched over as she had been, could not have committed a great many sins.

She held up her face to the rising anger of the wind.

How far are we from the coast of Spain? she wondered. Can we reach it? I have a feeling within me that I am destined to die a virgin.

It was unusual that a young girl could feel so calm when she was leaving her home for a strange country. But then her father's dominions had not been home to her for so long. She scarcely knew Maximilian, for he was a man of many engagements. His children were to him as counters in a great game to be used in winning him possessions in the world. He was fortunate to have a son and a daughter—both strong and healthy, both comely enough; in the case of Philip extremely so. But it was not the appearance of men that was so important. Nevertheless Maximilian had nothing of which to complain in his children. He had a worthy son and a daughter with whom to bargain in the markets of the world.

Margaret smiled. The men were the fortunate ones. They did not have to leave their homes. Arrogant Philip had merely to wait for his bride to be delivered to him. It was the women who must suffer.

And for that, thought Margaret, I should be grateful, since I suffer scarcely at all. Does it matter to me whether I am in France, in Flanders or in Spain? None has seemed to be home to me. I am too young to have had so many homes, and as I quickly learned that my hold on any of them lacked permanence, I learned also not to attach myself too tenderly to any one of them.

She faintly remembered her arrival in France. She had been barely three years old at the time and had been taken from her home in Flanders to be brought up at the French Court because, through her mother, Mary of Burgundy, she had inherited Burgundy; and the French King, Louis XI, had sought to bring Burgundy back to France by betrothing her to his son, the Dauphin Charles.

So to Amboise she had come. She often thought of the great château which had been her home for so many years. Even now, with the storm imminent, she could imagine that she was not on this deck but within those thick walls. She recalled the great buttresses, the cylindrical towers and the rounded roofs, which looked as if they could defy the wind and rain to the end of time.

Within those walls she had been prepared to meet her betrothed—a rather terrifying experience for a little girl of three and a half whose bridegroom was a boy of twelve.

That ceremony of betrothal was an occasion which would never be obliterated from Margaret's memory. Clearly she could recall meeting her bridegroom at a little farm near the town of Amboise, which was afterwards called *La Métairie de la Reyne*, whither she had been carried in a litter. It was a strange ceremony, doubtless considered fitting for children of such tender years. She remembered being asked if she would take Monsieur le Dauphin in marriage, and how the Grand Sénéchal, who stood close to her, prodded her and told her she must say that she would.

Then she had been put into the arms of young Charles and told to kiss him. She was to be a wife to the future King of France, and the people of Amboise showed their pleasure by hanging scarlet cloth from their windows and putting up banners which were stretched across the streets.

After that she had been taken back to the château, and her sister-in-law, Anne, the Duchess of Bourbon who was the eldest daughter of the reigning King and past her twentieth birthday, had been her guardian.

Margaret had quickly adjusted herself and had pleased her tutors by her love of learning. She will make a good Queen of France, they often said; she is the best possible wife for the Dauphin.

Charles had very soon become King, and that meant that she, Margaret, was an even more important person than before.

Yet she had never been Charles' wife in reality, for eight years after her arrival in France, while she was still a child, Charles decided that he preferred Anne, Duchess of Brittany, to be his wife.

So, to the wrath of Margaret's father, Charles sent her back to Flanders, ignoring the vows he had taken in the *Métairie de la Reyne* on that day eight years before.

Maximilian was infuriated by the insult, but Margaret had felt philosophical.

She thought of Charles now. He was far from the handsome

husband a girl might long for. He was short and, because his head was enormous, his lack of inches was accentuated. His expression was blank and his aquiline nose so enormous that it overpowered the rest of his features. He seemed to find it difficult to keep his mouth closed, for his lips were thick and coarse and he breathed heavily and took a long time to consider what he was going to say; whereas Margaret herself was quick-witted and fluent.

He was kind enough; but he had little interest in books and ideas, which made him seem dull to her; she could not share his interest in sport and jousting.

So, she thought, perhaps it was not such a tragedy that he shipped me back to Flanders.

And now she was being shipped to Spain. "If I ever reach there," she murmured.

Two of the ship's high-ranking officers had approached her, and so deep was she in her thoughts that she had not noticed them.

"Your Grace," said one, bowing low, "it is unsafe for you to remain on deck. The storm is about to break and we must ask you to seek the shelter of your cabin."

Margaret inclined her head. They were anxious about her, she knew. She was the most important cargo they had ever carried. She represented all the advantages that union with a daughter of Maximilian could bring to Spain.

They were right too. She was almost blown off her feet as she started across the deck. The two men held her, and laughing, she accepted their assistance.

* * *

The ship tossed and rolled, and the din was terrific. As she sheltered in her cabin with two of her attendants she occasionally heard the shouts of the sailors above the roar of the wind.

She saw two of her attendants clinging together. They were terrified. Their orders had been not to leave her if there was any danger, and their fear of Maximilian was greater than their fear of the storm.

She saw the tears on their faces as their fingers clutched their rosaries and their lips moved in continual prayer.

"How frail a thing is a ship," said Margaret. "How fierce is an ocean!"

"You should pray, Your Grace. I fear some of the smaller ships will have been lost and we shall never come out of this alive."

"If it is the end, then it is the end," said Margaret.

The two women looked at each other. Such calmness alarmed them. It was unnatural.

"We shall die without a priest," sighed one of the women, "with all our sins on us."

"You have not sinned greatly," Margaret comforted her. "Pray now for forgiveness, and it will be granted you."

"You pray with us."

"I find it difficult to ask God to spare my life," said Margaret, "for, if He has decided to take it, I am asking Him to go against His wishes. Perhaps we shall hate living so much that it will be more intolerable than death."

"Your Grace! Do not say such things!"

"But if we are to find bliss in Heaven why should we be so distressed at the thought of going there? I am not distressed. If my time has come, I am ready. I do not think that my new father and mother-in-law are going to be very pleased with me. Perhaps they will already have heard of the manner in which Philip is treating their daughter."

She was thinking of Philip—golden haired and handsome. What a beautiful boy he had always been. Everyone had made much of him, especially the women. She suspected that he had been initiated into the arts of love-making at a very early age, for some lusty young serving girl would surely have found the good looks of Philip impossible to resist; and Philip would be so eager to learn; he had been born to philander.

At an early age he had had his mistresses and had not been greatly interested in the wife he was to have. He had accepted her in his free and easy Flemish way—for Philip had the Flanders easy manners—as one of a group. Margaret knew he would not give up his mistresses merely because he had a wife.

And it was said that the Spaniards were a dignified people. Their ways would certainly not be the ways of Flanders. Poor Juana. Her future was not an enviable one. But perhaps, thought Margaret, she has a temperament like my own. Then she will accept what is, because it must be, and not ask for what it is impossible for life to give her.

Did they know in Spain that Philip had made no haste to greet his bride, that he had dallied with his gay friends—so many of them voluptuous women—and had laughingly declared that there was time enough for marriage?

I am afraid Juana is not getting a good husband, mused Margaret. I must say this even though that husband is my own brother.

So perhaps there would not be a very enthusiastic welcome for Philip's sister when she reached Spain; and if she never did, who could say at this stage that that would not be a fortunate outcome?

The women in her cabin were moaning.

"Our last hour has come," whispered one of them. "Holy Mother of God, intercede for us."

Margaret closed her eyes. Surely the ship was being rent asunder.

Yes, she thought, this is the end of my father's hopes through me. Here on the ocean bed will lie the bones of Margaret of Austria, daughter of Maximilian, drowned on her way to her wedding with the heir of Spain.

She began to compose her epitaph. It helped her not to catch the fear of those about her; she had discovered that it was all very well to talk lightly of death when it was far off; when you felt its breath in your face, when you heard its mocking laughter, you could not resist a certain fear. How could anyone be sure what was waiting on the other side of that strange bridge which joined Life with Death?

"*Ci gist Margot*," she murmured, "*la gentil' damoiselle*
Qu'a deux maris, et encore est pucelle."

THE MARRIAGE OF JUAN

On a bright March day what was left of the battered fleet came into the port of Santander.

Waiting to greet it were Ferdinand the King and by his side his son, Juan, the bridegroom to be.

Juan was nervous. His thoughts were for the young girl who had come perilously near to death at sea and had been miraculously brought to him. He must try to understand her; he must be gentle and kind.

His mother had talked to him about her, although she knew of course that she had no need to ask her son to show indulgence. Kindness came naturally to him. He hoped that she was not a flighty, senseless girl. Although if she were he would try to understand her ways. He would try to be interested in her interests. He would have to learn to enjoy dancing perhaps; he would have to pay more attention to sports. It was hardly likely that she would share his interests. She was young and doubtless she was gay. One could not expect her to care for books and music as he did.

Well then, he must suppress his inclinations. He must try above all to put her at ease. Poor child! How would she feel, leaving her home?

Ferdinand was smiling at him.

"Well, my son, in a short while now you will see her," he said.

"Yes, Father."

"It reminds me of the first day I saw your mother." Ferdinand wanted to say: If she does not please you, you should not take it to heart. There are many women in the world and they'll be ready enough to please the heir to my crown.

But of course one would not say such things to Juan. He was quite unlike the gay Alfonso on whom Ferdinand had wished to bestow the Archbishopric of Toledo. Ferdinand felt a little wistful. It would have been pleasant had this son of his been a little more like himself. There was too much of Isabella in him. He had too strong a sense of duty. He looked almost frail in the spring sunshine. We should try to fatten him up, harden him, thought Ferdinand. And yet he was always a little abashed in the presence of his son; Juan made him feel earthy, a little uneasy about the sins he had committed throughout a long and lusty life. Angel was a good name for him; but the company of an angel could sometimes be a little disconcerting.

Even now Ferdinand guessed that, instead of impatiently waiting to size up the girl's personal attributes—which was all he need concern himself with, her titles and inheritance being good enough even for the heir to Spain—he was thinking how best he could put her at ease.

Odd, thought Ferdinand, that such as I should have a son like that.

"She is coming ashore now," said Juan; and he was smiling.

* * *

They rode side by side on their way to Burgos where Queen Isabella and the rest of the royal family would be waiting to greet them.

They were pleased with each other, and they made a charming pair. The people, who had lined their route to watch them pass, cheered them and called out their blessings.

They loved their heir. He was not so much handsome as beautiful, and his sweet expression did not belie the reports they had heard of him. It was said that any petition first submitted to Juan would be certain to receive attention, no matter if it came from the most humble. Indeed the more humble the petitioner, the more easily the Prince's sympathies were aroused.

"Long live the Prince of the Asturias!" cried the people. "Long live the Archduchess Margaret!"

Ferdinand, riding with them, had graciously hung back. He was ready on this occasion to take second place to his heir and the bride. He would not have had it otherwise. He was congratulating himself. The girl looked healthy and none would guess she had been almost drowned at sea a week ago.

Margaret wished to talk to Juan. His Spanish manners were to her somewhat dignified, and she, after some years in Flanders, knew no such restraint.

"The people love you," she said.

"They love a wedding," he answered. "It means feasting and holidays."

"Yes, no doubt they do. But I think they have a special regard for you personally. Is my Spanish intelligible to you?"

"Completely. It is very good."

She laughed. "You would say it was good, no matter how bad it was."

"Nevertheless it is very good indeed. I trust my sister Juana speaks her husband's language as well as you speak that of the man who will be yours."

"Ah . . . Juana," she said.

"Did you see much of my sister?" he asked anxiously.

"No. She travelled to Lille, you know, for the wedding. I had to prepare myself to return with the fleet."

He was quick to notice that she found the subject of Juana disconcerting, so changed it immediately although he was anxious to hear news of Juana.

"Tell me, what pastimes please you most?"

She gave him a grateful look. "I'm afraid you will find me rather dull," she said.

"I cannot believe it."

She laughed aloud again, and he noticed—though she did not—that the attendants were astonished at her displays of mirth. Flemish manners! they were thinking. It was not fitting to show such lack of dignity in Spain.

But Juan liked that laughter; it was fresh and unaffected. "Yes," she said, "I do not greatly care for games and dancing and such diversions. I spend a great deal of time reading. I am interested in the history of countries and the ideas of philosophers. I think my brother deemed me a little odd. He says that I have not the right qualities to please a husband."

"That is not true." She saw the sudden gleam in Juan's eyes. "I am not good at sport and games either. I frankly dislike hunting."

Margaret said quickly: "I too. I cannot bear to hunt animals to the death. I picture myself being hunted to death. My brother laughs at me. He said that you would."

"I would never laugh at you nor scorn your ideas if they differed from my own. But, Margaret, I think that you and I are going to think alike on many things."

"That makes me happy," she said.

"And you are not afraid . . . coming to a strange land . . . to a strange husband?"

"No," she answered seriously, "I am not afraid."

Juan's heart began to beat wildly as he looked at her clean-cut young profile and her fair, fine skin.

She has all that I could have wished for in a wife, he told himself. Surely I am the luckiest of Princes. How serene she is! She looks as though she would never be ruffled. It is going to be so easy . . . so pleasant . . . so wonderful. I need not have been afraid. I shall not be shy and awkward with her. She is so young, and yet she has a calmness almost equal to that of my mother. What a wonderful person my wife will be.

"You are smiling," she said. "Tell me what amuses you."

He answered seriously: "It is not amusement which makes me smile. It is happiness."

"That," she replied, "is the best possible reason for smiling."

So, thought Juan, I am beginning to love her already.

Margaret also began to smile. She was telling herself that she had been fortunate as she remembered the flabby lips of Charles VIII of France.

She was glad that she had been sent to France and affianced to Charles. It was going to make her realize how lucky she was to have come to Spain to marry Juan.

So on they rode to the shouts of "Long live the Prince! Blessings on him and his bride!"

They were already serenely contented as they thought of the years ahead.

* * *

In the Palace at Burgos the arrival of the cavalcade, headed by Ferdinand, his son and the bride, was awaited with eagerness.

In the children's apartments the Princess Isabella watched the servants busy at the toilet of her sisters, Maria and Catalina.

How quiet they were! It would have been so different if Juana had been with them. She would have been speculating about the bride, shouting her wild opinions to them all.

Isabella felt rather pleased that Juana was no longer with them.

She was praying—she spent a great deal of time praying—that this young girl would make Juan happy. She hoped that she would be a gentle, religious girl. It would be heartbreaking if she were a wanton; and Isabella knew that stories were already reaching Spain of this girl's brother's conduct.

The Queen was very anxious about Juana, and the Flemish marriage was her greatest concern at the moment. Their father of course was only congratulating himself because the alliance had been made, and that Juana would be the mother of the Hapsburg heirs. It would seem unimportant to him if she were wretchedly unhappy while she was producing them.

Maria was placidly relaxed while her attendants dressed her. She was as emotionless as ever. Stolid Maria, who lacked the imagination to wonder what Margaret felt on coming into a new country, to wonder whether she herself would not be doing the same in a future which was not really very distant!

How different it was with Catalina. Her little face was set and anxious, and it was not difficult to guess at the thoughts which went on behind those big dark eyes.

Poor little Catalina! She was going to suffer a terrible wrench if she ever went to England.

An attendant came to the apartment and whispered to Isabella that the Queen's Highness wished to see her without delay, and she was to present herself in the Queen's bedchamber.

Young Isabella left her sisters at once and went to her mother's apartment.

The Queen was waiting for her, and Isabella's heart sank as she looked at her, for she guessed what she had to say.

The Queen kissed the Princess and said: "There is news from Portugal. I wanted to tell you myself. I wanted to prepare you. Your father will doubtless be speaking of this matter when he sees you."

Isabella's mouth had gone dry. "Yes, Mother," she said.

"Emanuel writes that since we insist on this condition he is ready to accept it."

Isabella's pale cheeks were suddenly flushed. She cried out: "You mean he will drive all those people out of his country just because . . ."

"Just because he is so eager for this marriage. So, my dear, you should really begin to plan your departure for Portugal."

"So . . . soon?" stammered Isabella.

"I'm afraid your father wishes the marriage to take place this year."

"Oh . . . no!"

"It is so. Dear Isabella, I shall insist that we meet again soon after you leave us. If you do not come to me here in Spain, I will come to you in Portugal."

"Mother, do you promise this?"

"I swear it."

Isabella was silent. Then she burst out: "Is there nothing I can do. . . ? I did not think he would agree to this. . . ."

"He wants this marriage. You should rejoice. It is more than a good marriage. On his side it is a love-match."

"But there is my side, Mother."

"You will love him in time. I know, my child. I am sure of it. He is a good and gentle man and he loves you dearly. You have nothing to fear."

"But, Mother, this condition . . ."

"But shows how much he loves you."

"I know that he does it against his will."

"That is because, good as he is, he has a certain blindness. That holy man, Tomás de Torquemada, sees in this the hand of God."

Isabella shuddered. She wanted to shout that she did not like Torquemada, that she feared him, and when her cough kept her awake at night she fancied she heard the curses of the exiled Jews.

Her mother would not understand such flights of fancy. How could she explain to her? Her emotions seemed to choke her, and she feared that if she did not calm herself one of her bouts of coughing would overtake her.

She tried not to cough in front of her mother, because she knew how it worried the Queen. It was enough that Juana gave her such anxieties.

She said: "Mother, if you will excuse me, I will go back to my apartment. I have some more preparations to make if I am to be ready when the party arrives."

The Queen nodded assent and, when her daughter had gone, murmured to herself: "All will be well. This is the best thing that could happen to my Isabella."

* * *

Isabella the Queen took the daughter of Maximilian in her arms and embraced her.

There were tears in Isabella's eyes. The girl was charming; she was healthy; and it seemed to her that Juan was already very happy with his bride.

Ferdinand looked on, his eyes agleam. It was very pleasant to be able to share in the general delight.

"We welcome you to Burgos," said the Queen. "I could not express how eager we have been for your coming."

"I am happy to be here, Your Highness."

The girl's smile was perhaps too warm, too friendly.

I must remember, the Queen told herself, that she has lived long in Flanders and the Flemish have little sense of decorum.

The Princesses Isabella, Maria and Catalina came forward and formally welcomed Margaret.

They thought her strange with her Flemish clothes, her fresh complexion and her familiar manners; but they liked her. Even Maria seemed to grow a little animated as she watched her. As for Catalina, she took great courage from this girl, who seemed quite unperturbed that she had come to a land of strangers to marry a man whom she had only recently met.

A banquet had been prepared, and Juan and his bride sat with the King and Queen; and they talked of the jousting and festivities which had been arranged to celebrate the marriage.

"It is a pity that it is Lent," said the Queen. "But as soon as it is over the nuptials shall be solemnized. We think that the third of April shall be the day of the wedding."

Catalina looked quickly at the face of the Flemish Archduchess;

she was relieved to see that the mention of a date for her wedding did not seem to disturb her.

* * *

It was the most magnificent spectacle seen in Spain for many years.

This was, after all, the wedding of the heir to the throne. It seemed more than the celebrations of a wedding. Spain had never seemed to hold out such hopes of a prosperous future for her people. The prospects for peace were brighter than they had been for many years. No more taxes to pay for useless battles! No more forcing men from their peaceful labours to fight in the armies! Peace meant prosperity—and it seemed that here it was at last.

The charming young bridegroom would be the first heir of the whole of Spain, and the people had come to realize that a united Spain was happier to live in than a country divided into kingdoms which were continually warring with each other.

Even the frugal Isabella was determined that this marriage of her only son should be an occasion which all should remember, and she was therefore ready to spend a great deal of money in making it so.

All over the country there were tourneys and fêtes. Towns were gaily decorated throughout the land. Across the narrow streets in the smallest villages banners hung.

"Long life to the heir!" cried the people. "Blessings on the Prince of the Asturias and his bride!"

The marriage was celebrated with the greatest dignity and ceremony. The Archbishop of Toledo performed it, and with him were the grandees of Castile and the nobility of Aragon. It was a sight of great magnificence and splendour.

And as Margaret made her vows once more she compared her bridegroom with that boy of twelve to whom she had been betrothed in a farmhouse near the château of Amboise, and again she rejoiced in her good fortune.

* * *

Juan had dreaded the moment when they would be alone together. He had imagined the terrors of a young girl who might not fully understand what would be required of her, and himself explaining as gently as he could; he had not relished the task.

When they lay in the marriage bed it was Margaret who spoke first.

"Juan," she said, "you are afraid of me."

"I am afraid that I might distress you," he answered.

"No," she told him. "I shall not be distressed."

"Are you never distressed, Margaret?"

"Not by that which must be."

Juan lifted her hand and kissed it. "I am sorry," he said. "As you say, what must be, must be."

Then she laughed suddenly and, pulling her hand away from him, she put her arms about him.

"I am so glad that you are as you are, Juan," she said. "I am sure nothing you do could possibly distress me. When I think that it might have been Charles lying beside me at this moment . . ." She shivered.

"Charles? The King of France?"

"He has thick lips, and he grunts. He is not unkind but he would be coarse and . . . he would never understand me."

"I hope to understand you, Margaret."

"Call me Margot," she said. "It is my special name . . . the name I like those whom I love to call me by."

"Do you love me then, Margot?"

"I think so, Juan. I think I must, because . . . I am not afraid."

And so the difficulty was soon over, and that which had alarmed them became a pleasure. She taught him to laugh in her gay Flemish way, and he found himself fascinated by her familiar talk which might have seemed coarse on some lips, never on hers.

"Oh Juan," she cried, "I thought my bones would now be lying on the sea bed and the big fishes would have eaten my flesh, and the little ones sport about my skeleton and swim in and out of the sockets of my eyes."

"Don't say such things," he said, kissing her eyes.

"I said, 'Here lies Margot. She was twice married but she died a virgin.' " Then she began to laugh afresh. "That can never be my epitaph now, Juan. For here lies Margot . . . beside you . . . but she is no longer a virgin . . . and she is not displeased."

So they made love again, this time without fear or shame.

And in the morning Juan said: "We have given our parents what they wanted."

Margaret interrupted: "The crown of Spain."

Juan chanted: "The Hapsburg inheritance."

Then they laughed and began to kiss in a sudden frenzy of passion. Margaret drew herself away from him and kneeling on the bed bowed her head as though before the thrones of the King and Queen.

"We thank Your Gracious Majesties. You may keep the crown of Spain. . . ."

"And the Hapsburg inheritance . . ." added Juan.

"Because . . ." began Margaret, smiling at him.

"Because," added Juan, "you gave us each other."

* * *

The wedding celebrations continued. The most popular person in the whole of Spain was the young Prince Juan. It was said of him that since the coming of Margaret he looked more like a man than an angel, but his sweetness of expression had not grown less. His bride was clearly a happy girl. It was small wonder that wherever they went there was rejoicing.

The Queen discussed with her husband her pleasure in this marriage.

"You see," said Ferdinand, "how well it has turned out. This was a marriage of my making. You will admit that I knew what I was about."

"You have acted with the utmost wisdom," Isabella agreed. "You have given our Juan a share in the Hapsburg inheritance—and happiness."

"Who would not be happy with a share in the Hapsburg inheritance?" demanded Ferdinand.

Isabella's face was anxious. "I do not like these rumours I hear about Juana. She is so far from home and . . ."

"Nonsense! All will be well. She will adjust herself. The Flemings have different manners from our own. *I* have heard that she is passionately attached to her husband."

"Too passionately attached."

"My dear Isabella, can a wife love her husband too much?"

"If he is not kind to her it would be easier for her to bear if she did not love him dearly."

"Strange words on your lips! You seem to imply it is a virtue that a wife should not love her husband dearly."

"You misunderstand me."

"Ah, have no fear for Juana. Rumour often lies."

The Queen knew that he could not think of their daughter, Juana, without remembering all the advantages her marriage had brought to Spain. It was no use expecting him to see the personal view. He was quite incapable of that. He had hardened with the years. Have I softened? Isabella asked herself. No, it is merely that having so many loved ones I have become more vulnerable.

Ferdinand said abruptly: "Why should there be this delay with our daughter Isabella? Emanuel grows impatient."

"Should she not wait until her brother's wedding celebrations are over?"

"But we planned that these ceremonies should continue for a long time. The people expect it. Soon however I want Juan and Margaret to go on a long pilgrimage through the country, showing themselves in the various towns. There will be feasting and celebrations wherever they halt. There is nothing like a progress for winning the devotion of the people. And when you have a pair like Juan and Margaret . . . young, handsome and in love . . . the people will be their devoted slaves for ever." Ferdinand's eyes blazed. "When I think of all that young man of ours is heir to, I could sing for joy."

"Perhaps Isabella could accompany them on their pilgrimage."

"And thus delay her departure for Portugal?"

"It would remind the people of all that we are doing for them with these alliances."

"Quite unnecessary. Isabella must prepare to leave Spain for Portugal at once."

The Queen was about to protest, but Ferdinand's mouth was stubborn.

These are my children as well as yours, he was reminding her. You may be Queen of Castile, but I remain the head of the family.

It was useless to protest, the Queen decided. And a short postponement would make little difference to Isabella in the long run. She was sure that when her daughter was in Portugal she would be as happy with Emanuel as Margaret was with Juan.

* * *

The coming of Margaret to Spain had brought an immense relief to Catalina. It seemed to her that here she saw, played out before her eyes, that drama which had begun to dominate her life. The transference of a foreign Princess to the home of her bridegroom could be a happy event.

It was exhilarating therefore to watch the happiness of Margaret and Juan.

Margaret was very friendly with her husband's sisters. She was amusing and clever, and her manner of never hesitating to say what she meant was extraordinary.

Catalina knew that the Princess Isabella was a little shocked by her sister-in-law. But Isabella could not share in the general rejoicing, because her own departure was imminent.

"How cruel of us," said Catalina to Maria, "to be happy when soon Isabella is going to leave us."

Maria looked astonished. Like her father she could not understand why Isabella should be so distressed. She was going to have a wedding, as Juan had; she was going to be the centre of attraction. That seemed a very fine thing to Maria.

Catalina often left the company, which Margaret was enlivening with some story of the manners of the Flemish, that she might sit with her sister, Isabella.

Isabella had changed in the last weeks. She had become resigned. She seemed a little thinner than usual but there was a hectic flush on her cheeks which made her look very pretty. Her cough worried her still but she continually sought to control it.

One day Catalina crept to her sister's apartments and found her at the window, looking out wistfully on the scene below.

"May I come in, Isabella?"

"But of course."

Isabella held out her hand and Catalina took it.

"Why do you come to me?" Isabella asked. "Is it not more fun to be with the others?"

Catalina was thoughtful. Yes, it was more fun. Margaret was amusing and it was pleasant to watch her and remind oneself that this was what it was like going to a strange country to be married; but Catalina could not enjoy the stories of Margaret while she must be thinking of Isabella.

"I wished to be with you," she explained.

"There will not be many more days when we can be together, for I shall soon be setting out for Portugal. Juan and Margaret will be starting on their journey, so you will miss them also. But of course they will be coming back."

"You will come back too."

"Yes. Our mother has promised that I shall return to see you all or she will come to me. If she does I hope she will bring you with her, Catalina."

"I will implore her to."

They were silent for a while and then Isabella said: "Catalina, you are the youngest, yet I think you are the wisest. You understand my feelings more than any of the others."

"It is because one day I too shall have to go away."

"Why yes, Catalina. How selfish I am, to think of myself all the time. But it will be different for you. Catalina, how I wish that I had gone before."

"Then you would not have been here now."

"You are too young to remember what happened in this country; and because of me it will happen in Portugal. Emanuel has agreed that it shall."

"They will drive out the Jews, Isabella; but is that not a good thing? Then Portugal will be an all-Christian country, even as Spain is."

"I think of those men, women and children driven from their homes."

"But they are Jews, Isabella. I have heard the servants talking about them. They poison wells. They destroy the crops with their incantations and, do you know, Isabella, they do something far worse. They kidnap Christian boys and crucify them as Christ was crucified."

"I have heard these stories too, but I wonder if they are true."

"Why should you wonder?"

"Because when people do great injustice they always seek to convince themselves that what they have done is just."

"But it is surely just to bring all people to the Christian Faith. It is for their good."

"I believe that, but I am haunted by them, Catalina. I see them in my dreams. Terrible things happen to them. When they reached barbarous foreign countries they were robbed and murdered. Little girls like you were violated before the very eyes of their parents. And when they had raped them they slit open their bodies because it was rumoured that they had swallowed their jewels that they might take them away with them. You see, they were not allowed to take what belonged to them."

"Isabella, you must pray. You must be serene, as Margaret is. You must not think of these things."

"It is easy for her. She does not come to her husband with this guilt upon her."

"Nor should you, Isabella."

"But I do, Catalina. I hear their voices in my dreams. I see them . . . rows and rows of angry, frightened faces. I see terrible things in my dreams, and I feel that a curse is upon me."

There was little that Catalina could do to comfort Isabella.

TRAGEDY AT SALAMANCA

JUAN AND Margaret had started on their triumphal journey, and the time had come for the Princess Isabella to set out for the meeting with Emanuel.

She was glad that her mother was travelling with her. Ferdinand also accompanied them, but the Princess had little to say to her father; she was aware of his impatience for the marriage to take place.

The Queen understood her daughter's reluctance to return as a bride to the country of the man she had loved so tenderly; but she had no idea of the horrors which filled her daughter's mind. It was inconceivable to the Queen that young Isabella could be so concerned about the fate of a section of the community who refused the benefits of Christianity.

The marriage was to be performed without the pomp which usually accompanied royal marriages. Isabella was a widow. The people were still rejoicing over the marriage of Juan and Margaret. A great deal had been spent on that ceremony, and important as this marriage with Portugal was, it must be performed with the minimum outlay. Neither Ferdinand nor Isabella were spendthrifts and they were not eager to spend unless it was necessary.

So the ceremony which was to take place at Valencia de Alcantara would be a quiet one. In this little town Emanuel was waiting for his bride.

Strange emotions filled the young Isabella's heart as she lifted her eyes to her bridegroom's face. Memories came back to her of the Palace in Lisbon where she had first seen him standing beside the King, and she remembered thinking at that moment that he was Alonso.

He had been her friend afterwards; he had shown clearly his desire to be in Alonso's place; and after that unhappy day when Alonso had died he had been the kindest and most sympathetic of her friends. It was then that he had suggested that she stay in Portugal as his wife.

Now he was the King of Portugal—an honour which could never have come to him but for that accident in the forest, for had Alonso lived she and he would have sons to come before Emanuel.

But it had happened differently, tragically so. And here she was, the bride of Emanuel.

He lifted her hand to his lips and kissed it. He loved her still. How wonderful that this young man should have remained faithful to her all those years. While she had mourned in her widowhood and declared that she would never marry again, he had waited.

And so she had come to him at last, but now it was with a hideous burden about her neck, the misery of thousands of Jews.

There was pain behind his smile. He too was thinking that it was a terrible price—the denial of his own beliefs—which he had to pay for her.

The ceremony was performed, while Ferdinand exulted, and the Queen smiled graciously. All was well. The Infanta Isabella of Spain was now the Queen of Portugal.

* * *

Isabella was glad that it had not been the usual exhausting ceremony. That was something she could not have endured.

When she was with Emanuel, when she was aware of his tenderness for her, his gentleness, his determination to make her happy, she felt a quiet contentment. She thought, I am fortunate, even as Margaret has been in Juan.

She had been foolish in delaying so long. She could have married him a year . . . two years . . . why, three years before. If she had done so she might have had a child by now.

"What a faithful man you are," she told her husband, "to wait all those years."

"Did you not understand that, once I had seen you, I should be faithful?" he answered.

"But I am not young any more. I am twenty-seven. Why, you could have married my sister Maria. She is twelve years younger than I, and a maiden."

"Does it seem strange to you that it was Isabella I wanted?"

"Oh, yes," she said, "very strange."

He took her hands and kissed them. "You will soon learn that it is not strange at all. I loved you when you first came to us. I loved you when you went away; and I love you more than ever now that you have come to me."

"I shall try to be all that you deserve in a wife, Emanuel."

He kissed her then with passion, and she had a feeling that he was trying to shut something from his mind. She knew what it was. He had not mentioned "the condition", but it was there between them, she felt, between them and complete happiness.

To lie beside Emanuel, to know that she had a husband once

more, did not bring back the bitter memories of Alonso which she had so feared. She realized now that this was the quickest way to obliterate the memory of that long ago honeymoon which had ended in tragedy.

Emanuel was not unlike his dead cousin. And if she could not feel the wild exultation which she had enjoyed with Alonso she believed that this quieter contentment was something to which she and Alonso would have come in time.

In those first days of marriage, Alonso and Emanuel had begun to mingle strangely in her mind. They had become as one person.

During those first days they forgot. Then she noticed that one of Emanuel's attendants had a Jewish cast of feature, and when it seemed to her that she caught this man's gaze fixed upon her malevolently, a terrible fear shot through her.

She said nothing of this at the time, but that night she woke screaming from a frightening dream.

Emanuel sought to comfort her but she could not remember what the dream was.

She could only sob out her terror in Emanuel's arms.

"It is my fault," she said. "It is my fault. I should have come to you earlier. I should never have let this happen."

"What is it, my dearest? Tell me what is on your mind."

"It is what we are going to do to those people. It is the price you had to pay for our marriage."

She felt his body stiffen, and she knew that this terrible thing was on his mind as surely as it was on her own.

He kissed her hair and whispered: "You should have come before, Isabella. You should have come long ago."

"And now?"

"And now," he answered, "the deed must be done. I have given my word. It is a condition of the marriage."

"Emanuel, you hate this. You loathe it. It haunts you . . . even as it does me."

"I wanted you so much," he said. "It was the price that was asked of me and I paid it . . . because I wanted you so much."

"Is there no way out?" she whispered.

It was a stupid question. As she asked it, she saw the stern face of Torquemada, the serene one of her mother, the shrewd one of her father. They had made this condition. They would insist on its being carried out.

They were silent for a while, then she went on: "It is like a blight upon us. Those strange people, with their strange religion, will curse us for what we have done to them. They will curse our House. Emanuel, I am afraid."

He held her tightly against him and when he spoke his voice sounded muffled: "We must do the deed and then forget. It was not our fault. I was weak in my need of you. But we are married now. We will do this thing and then . . . we will begin again from there."

"Is it possible?"

"It is, my Isabella."

She allowed herself to be comforted; but when she slept her dreams were haunted by a thousand voices—voices of men, women and children who, because of their faith, would be driven from their homes. These voices cursed her, cursed the united Houses of Spain and Portugal.

* * *

Salamanca was celebrating the arrival of the heir of Spain and his bride. The people had come in from miles around; men, women and children moved like ants across the plain on their way to the town of the University.

The students were *en fête*; they were of all nationalities for, next to Paris, this was the foremost seat of learning in the world. The town was rich, as many noblemen had bought houses there that they might live near their student sons and watch over them during their years at the University.

Through the streets the students swaggered in their stoles, the colour of which indicated their faculties. Salamanca was often gay, but it had never seen anything to equal this occasion. The bells of the churches rang continually; its streets and courtyards were filled with laughter; the bulls were being brought in—there must always be bulls; and in the Plaza Mayor the excitement was at its height. On the balconies of the houses sat beautiful women, and the students watched them with gleaming eyes. Now and then a brilliant cavalcade would sweep through the streets, and the crowd would cheer because they knew this was part of the Prince's retinue.

On their way to the balls and banquets, which were given in their honour, the Prince and his bride would pass through the streets, and the people of Salamanca were given an opportunity to show their delight in the heir to the throne.

In Salamanca there was nothing but gaiety and loyalty to the royal pair.

Margaret looked on with serene eyes.

It was pleasant to know that the people loved her and her husband. She suspected that they loved the excitement of ceremony even more, but she did not tell Juan this. She was perhaps a little more cynical than he was.

He delighted in the people's pleasure, not because he wanted adulation—this worried him because he did not think himself worthy of it—but because he knew that his parents would hear of the reception which was being given them and how much it would please them.

They had danced at the ball given in their honour and were now in their own apartment.

Margaret was not tired; she could have danced all night because she was happier than she had ever been in her life. She looked at Juan and thought: Now this is the time to share this happiness with him, for it is his as well as mine and will please him as much as it pleases me.

She had not wanted to tell him until she was sure, but now she believed there could not be a doubt.

She sat down on the bed and looked at him. She had waved away the attendants who would have helped them to bed, wanting none of their ceremonies. She shocked them, she knew; but it was not important. Juan accepted her free Flemish manners and others must do the same. Those attendants who had come with her from Flanders found it difficult to settle happily in Spain. "The continual ceremonies," they complained, "they are not only wearying but ridiculous." She had answered: "You must understand that to them our customs seem coarse, which is perhaps worse than ridiculous. There is a saying: When you are in Rome you must do as the Romans do. I would say to you, the same applies to Spain."

Yet she thought, if they cannot adapt themselves to Spanish ways they must go home. I, who am so happy, would not have them otherwise.

"Juan," she said, "I fancy I shocked the company a little tonight."

"Shocked them?"

"Oh come, did you not notice raised eyebrows? My Flemish ways astonished them."

"What does it matter as long as you pleased them?"

"Did I please them?"

"You pleased me—let us leave it at that."

"But Juan, you are so easy to please. Perhaps I shall have to learn to be more solemn, more of a Spaniard, more like the Queen. I must try to model myself upon your mother, Juan."

"Stay as you are," he said, kissing her lips. "That will please me best."

She leaped up and began to dance a *pavana* with the utmost solemnity. Then suddenly her mood changed.

"This," she said, "is how we should dance it in Flanders."

She performed such a wild travesty of the Spanish dance that Juan burst out laughing.

"Come, dance with me," she said, and held out her hands to him. "If you dance very nicely I will tell you a secret."

As he stood beside her she noticed that he looked exhausted and that his face was unusually flushed.

"Juan," she said, "you are tired."

"A little. It was hot in the ballroom."

"Your hands are burning."

"Are they?"

"Sit down. I shall help you to bed. Come, I will be your valet."

He said, laughing: "Margaret, what will your attendants think of your mad ways?"

"That I am Flemish . . . merely that. Did you not know that the people of Flanders are people who love to joke and laugh rather than stand on ceremony? They'll forgive me my oddities simply because I'm Flemish. And when *they* know my news they'll be ready to forgive me everything."

"What news is this?"

"Come, can you not guess?"

"Margot!"

She leaned towards him and kissed him gently on the forehead.

"Long life and happiness to you, little father," she whispered.

* * *

That was a never-to-be-forgotten night.

"I shall always love Salamanca," said Margaret.

"We'll bring him to Salamanca as soon as he is old enough," Juan told her.

"We will send him to the University here and we will tell the people that we love their town because there we spent some of the happiest days and nights of our honeymoon."

"There I first knew that he existed."

They laughed and made love again; they felt more serious, more responsible people. They were no longer merely lovers; they were almost parents, and felt awed at the prospect.

It was dawn when Margaret awoke. It was as though something had startled her. She did not know what. The city was wakening to life. The students were already in the streets.

Margaret had a feeling that something was wrong.

She sat up in bed. "Juan!" she cried.

He did not answer her at once, and she bent over him calling him again.

The flush was still in his cheeks and as she laid her face against his she was struck by the heat of it.

"Juan," she whispered, "Juan, my dearest. Wake up."

He opened his eyes and she felt that she wanted to sob with relief to see him smile at her.

"Oh Juan, for the moment I thought something was wrong."

"What could be wrong?" he asked, taking her hand.

His fingers seemed to scorch her flesh.

"How hot you are!"

"Am I?" He began to raise himself but, even as he did so, he fell back on the pillows.

"What is wrong, Juan? What ails you?"

He put his hand to his head. "It is a dizziness," he said.

"You are sick," she cried. She sprang from the bed and wrapped a robe about her trembling body. She ran to the door calling: "Come quickly. The Prince is ill."

* * *

The physicians stood at his bedside.

His Highness had contracted a fever, they said. He would soon recover with their remedies.

All that day Margaret sat by his bedside. He watched her tenderly, trying hard to assure her with his glances that all was well.

But she was not deceived; and all through the next night she sat with him.

In the early morning he was delirious.

The physicians conferred together.

"Highness," they said to her, "we think that a message should be sent to the King and Queen without delay."

"Let it be done, with all speed," said Margaret quietly.

While the messengers galloped to the frontier town of Valencia de Alcantara, Margaret sat at the bedside of her husband.

* * *

Ferdinand received the messengers from Salamanca.

He read the letter from Margaret. Juan ill! But he had been perfectly well when he set out on his honeymoon. This was the hysterical fear of a young bride. Juan was a little exhausted; perhaps being married could be exhausting to a serious young man who, before his wedding, had lived an entirely virtuous life. Ferdinand's marriage had presented no such problems; but he was ready to concede that Juan was different from himself in that respect.

But there was another letter. This was signed by two physicians.

The Prince's health was giving them cause for alarm. They believed he had contracted a malignant fever and that he was so ill that his parents should come immediately to his bedside.

Ferdinand looked grave. This was no hysteria; Juan must be really ill.

It was inconvenient. Emanuel and his daughter Isabella were still celebrating their marriage, and it would give rise to great anxiety if both he and the Queen left them abruptly to go to Juan's bedside.

Ferdinand went to Isabella's apartment, wondering how best he could break the news. She smiled as he entered, and he felt a tenderness towards her. She looked a little older; the sorrow of parting with Juana, and now Isabella, had etched a few more lines on her face. When Ferdinand had his own way, as he had over this matter of Isabella's marriage, he had time to feel affection for his Queen. She was a good, devoted mother, he reminded himself, and if she erred in her conduct towards her children it was on the side of over-indulgence.

He decided to suppress the physicians' letter and show her only that of Margaret. Thus he could avoid arousing too much anxiety at this moment.

"News," he announced, "from Salamanca."

Her face lit up with pleasure.

"I heard," she said, "that the people have given them a welcome such as they have rarely given any before."

"Yes, that is true," answered Ferdinand, "but . . ."

"But . . . ?" cried the Queen and the alarm shot up in her eyes.

"Juan is a little unwell. I have a letter here from Margaret. The poor child writes quite unlike the calm young lady she pretends to be."

"Show me the letter."

Ferdinand gave it to her, and put his arm about her shoulders while she read it.

"You see, it is the hysterical outburst of our little bride. If you ask me, our Juan finds being a husband to such a lively girl a little exhausting. He is in need of a rest."

"A fever!" said the Queen. "I wonder what that means . . .?"

"Over-excitement. Isabella, you are getting anxious. I will go at once to Salamanca. You remain here to say your farewell to Isabella and Emanuel. I will write to reassure you from Salamanca."

Isabella considered this.

"I know," went on Ferdinand, "that if I do not go you will continue anxious. And if we both go, we shall have all sorts of ridiculous rumours spreading throughout the country."

"You are right, Ferdinand. Please go to Salamanca with all speed. And write to me . . . as soon as you have seen him."

Ferdinand kissed her with more tenderness than he had shown her for a long time. He was very fond of her when the submissive wife took the place of the Queen.

* * *

As Ferdinand rode through the town of Salamanca he was greeted with silence. It was almost as though the university town was one of mourning.

The physicians were waiting for him, and he had but to look at them to sense their alarm.

"How is my son?" he asked brusquely.

"Highness, since we wrote to you his fever has not abated, but has in fact grown worse."

"I will go to his bedside at once."

He found Margaret there and noticed that several of the women in the room were weeping, and that the expressions on the faces of the men were so doleful that it appeared as though Juan were living through his last hours.

Ferdinand glowered at them, anger swamping his fear. How dared they presume that Juan was going to die. Juan must not die. He was the heir to united Spain, and there would be trouble in Aragon if there was not a male heir. He and Isabella had only daughters beside this one son. After all their hopes and plans Juan must not die.

Margaret's face was white and strained but she was composed, and Ferdinand felt a new affection for his daughter-in-law. But the sight of Juan's wan face on the pillow frightened him.

He knelt by the bed and took Juan's hand.

"My son, what is this bad news I hear?"

Juan smiled at him. "Oh, Father, so you have come. Is my mother here?"

"Nay. Why should she come because you have a little indisposition. She is at the frontier, speeding your sister on her way to Portugal."

"I should have liked to have seen her," said Juan faintly.

"Well, you will see her soon enough."

"She will have to come soon, I think, Father."

Ferdinand's angry voice boomed out: "But why so?"

"You must not be angry with me, Father, but I think I feel death close to me."

"What nonsense! Margaret, it is nonsense, is it not?"

Margaret said stonily: "I do not know."

"Then I do!" cried Ferdinand. "You are going to recover . . .

and quickly. By God, are you not the heir to the throne . . . the only male heir? There would be a pretty state of affairs if you left us without a male heir."

Juan smiled faintly. "Oh, Father, there will be others. I am not so very important."

"I never heard such nonsense. What of Aragon? Tell me that. They will not have a female sovereign, as you know. You must therefore consider your duty and not talk of dying and leaving us without a male heir. I will see your physicians at once. I will command them to cure you of this . . . honeymoon fever . . . at once."

Ferdinand rose and stood glowering affectionately at his son. How he had changed! he thought uneasily. Juan had never been a strong boy as he himself had been, as young Alfonso was. Holy Mother, what a pity that boy was not his legitimate son. Action was needed here . . . drastic action.

Ferdinand stalked from the room, beckoning the physicians to follow him; and in the ante-room before the bedchamber he shut the door and demanded: "How sick is he?"

"Very sick, Highness."

"What hope is there of his recovery?"

The physicians did not answer. They were afraid to tell Ferdinand what they really thought. As for Ferdinand, he was afraid to probe further. He had as much affection for his son as he was capable of, but mingled with it was the thought of the part that son had to play in his own ambitions. "I think," he said, "that my son has overtaxed his strength. He has had his duty to do both day and night. He has had to be a good Prince to the people and a good husband to the Archduchess. It has been too much for him. We will nurse him back to health."

"Highness, if this sickness has been brought on through his exhaustion perhaps it would be well to separate him from his bride. This would give him a chance to grow strong again."

"Is that the only remedy you can suggest?"

"We have tried every other remedy, and the fever grips him the more firmly."

Ferdinand was silent for a while. Then he said: "Let us go back to the sickroom."

He stood at the foot of Juan's bed and tried to speak jocularly.

"The doctors tell me that you have become exhausted. They propose keeping you very quiet, and even Margaret shall not visit you."

"No," said Margaret, "I must stay with him."

Juan put out a hand and gripped that of his wife. He held it tightly and, although he did not speak, it was clear that he wished her to remain with him.

Ferdinand stared at his son's hand and noticed how thin his wrist had become. He must have lost a great deal of weight in a very short time. Ferdinand was realizing at last that his son was very ill indeed.

Yes, he thought, he is very attached to Margaret. They must stay together, for ill as he is there might yet be time to beget an heir. A child conceived in the passion of fever was still a child. If Juan could give Margaret a child before he died, his death would not be such a tragedy.

"Have no fear," he said. "I could never find it in my heart to separate you."

He turned and left them together. He was now more than uneasy; he was decidedly worried.

* * *

He could not sleep that night. Juan's condition had worsened during the day and Ferdinand found that he was sharing the general opinion of all those about the Prince.

Juan was very seriously ill.

When he had said good night to him Juan had put his burning lips to his father's hand and had said: "Do not grieve for me, Father. If I am to die, and I think I am, I shall go to a better world than this."

"Do not say such things," Ferdinand had answered gruffly. "We need you here."

"Break the news gently to my mother," whispered Juan. "She loves me well. Tell her that her Angel will watch over her if it is possible for him to do so. Tell her that I love her dearly and that she has been the best mother anyone ever had. Tell her this for me, Father."

"You shall tell her such things yourself," retorted Ferdinand.

"Father, you must not grieve for me. I shall be in the happier place. Grieve more for those I leave. Comfort my mother and care for Margaret. She is so young and she does not always understand our ways. I love her very dearly. Take care of her . . . and our child."

"Your child!"

"Margaret is with child, Father."

Ferdinand could not hide the joy which illumined his face. Juan saw it and understood.

"You see, Father," he said, "if I go, I shall leave you consolation."

A child! It made all the difference. Why had they not told

him before? The situation was not so cruel as he had feared, since Margaret carried the heir to Spain and her Hapsburg inheritance.

For the moment Ferdinand forgot to fear that his son might be dying.

But now that he was in his own room he thought of Juan, his gentle son, and how Isabella had doted on her "angel". Juan had never caused them anxiety except over his health. He had been a model son, clever, kindly and obedient.

Ferdinand found that even the thought of the heir whom Margaret carried could not compensate for the loss of his son.

What was he going to tell Isabella? He thought tenderly of his wife who had given such love and devotion to their family. How was he going to break the news to her? She had wept bitterly because she was losing Isabella; she suffered continual anxiety over Juana in Flanders. She was thinking now of the days when Maria and Catalina would be torn from her side. If Juan died . . . how could he break the news to Isabella?

There was a knock at his door. He started forward and flung it open.

He knew what this message meant even before the man spoke.

"The physicians think you should come to the Prince's bedside to say goodbye to him, Highness."

Ferdinand nodded.

Juan lay back on his pillows, a faint smile on his lips. Margaret was kneeling by his bed, her face buried in her hands. Her body looked as still as that of her dead husband.

* * *

Ferdinand faced his daughter-in-law. She seemed much older than the girl who only a few months before had married Juan. Her face was expressionless.

Ferdinand said gently: "There is the child to live for, my dear."

"Yes," answered Margaret, "I have the child."

"We shall take great care of you, my dear daughter. Let us comfort each other. I have lost the best of sons; you have lost the best of husbands. Your fortitude wins my admiration. Margaret, I do not know how to send this terrible news to his mother."

"She will wish to know the truth with all speed," Margaret said quietly.

"The shock would kill her. She has no idea that he was suffering from anything but a mild fever. No, I must break this news gently. I am going to write to her now and tell her that Juan is ill and that you are with child. Two pieces of news, one good one bad. Then I will write again saying that Juan's condition is giving cause for anxiety. You see, I shall gradually break this terrible news to her. It is the only way she could bear it."

"She will be heartbroken," Margaret murmured, "but I sometimes think she is stronger than any of us."

"Nay. At heart she is only a woman . . . a wife and mother. She loves all her children dearly, but he was her favourite. He was her son, the heir to everything we have fought for." Ferdinand suddenly buried his face in his hands. "I do not know how she will survive this shock."

Margaret did not seem to be listening. She felt numb, telling herself that this had not really happened and that she was living through some hideous nightmare. She would wake soon to find herself in Juan's arms and they would rise from their bed, go to the window and look out on the sunlit *patio*. They would ride again through the cheering crowds in the streets of Salamanca. She would laugh and say: "Juan, last night I had a bad dream. I dreamed that the worst possible thing which could befall me happened to me. And now I am awake, in the sunshine, and I am so happy to be alive because I know how singularly my life has been blessed since I have you."

* * *

Ferdinand felt better when he was taking action. No sooner had he dispatched the two messengers than he called a secretary to him.

"Write this to Her Highness the Queen," he commanded.

And the man began to write as the King dictated:

"A terrible calamity has occurred in Salamanca. His Highness the King has died of a fever."

The man stopped writing and stared at Ferdinand.

"Ah, my good fellow, you look at me as though you think I am mad. No, this is not madness. It is good sense. The Queen will have to learn sooner or later of the death of the Prince. I have been considering how best I can break this news. I fear the effect it will have on her, and in this way I think I can soften the terrible blow. She will have had my two letters telling her of our son's indisposition. Now I will ride with all speed to her. I shall send a messenger on ahead of me with the news of my death. That would be the greatest blow she could sustain. While she is overcome with the horror of this news I will stride in and confront her. She will be so overjoyed to see me that the blow of her son's death will be less severe."

The secretary bowed his head in melancholy understanding, but he doubted the wisdom of Ferdinand's conduct.

However, it was not for him to criticize the action of his King, so he wrote the letter and, shortly afterwards, left Salamanca.

* * *

Isabella had said her last farewells to her daughter and Emanuel; the Infanta of Spain, now the Queen of Portugal, had set out with her husband and her retinue on the way to Lisbon.

How tired she was! She was becoming too old for long journeys, and taking leave of her daughter depressed her. She was extremely worried by the news of Juana which filtered through from Flanders. And now Juan was unwell.

The first of the messages arrived. Margaret was with child. The news filled her with joy; but the rest of the message said that Juan was unwell. The health of her children was a continual anxiety to her, and the two elder ones had always been delicate. Isabella's cough had caused her mother a great deal of misgiving; Juan had been almost too frail and fair for a young man. Perhaps she had been so concerned about Juana's mental condition that she had worried less about the physical health of the two elder children than she otherwise would have done. Maria and Catalina were much stronger; perhaps because they had been born in more settled times.

The second letter came almost immediately after the first. It appeared that Juan's condition was more serious than they had at first thought.

"I will go to him," she said. "I should be at his side at such a time."

While she was giving orders to the servants to make ready for the journey to Salamanca another messenger arrived.

She was bewildered as she read the letter he brought. Ferdinand . . . dead! This could not be. Ferdinand was full of strength and vitality. It was Juan who was ill. She could not imagine Ferdinand anything but alive.

"Hasten," she cried. "There is not a moment to lose. I must go with all speed to Salamanca to see what is really happening there."

Ferdinand! Her heart was filled with strangely mingling feelings. There were so many memories of a marriage which had lasted for nearly thirty years.

She was bewildered and found it difficult to collect her thoughts.

Was it possible that there had been some mistake? Should she read Juan for Ferdinand?

She was sick with anxiety. If Juan were dead she would no longer wish to live. He was her darling whom she wished to keep by her side for as long as she lived. He was her only son, her beloved Angel. He could not be dead. It would be too cruel.

She read the message again. It clearly said the King.

Juan . . . Ferdinand. If she had lost her husband she would be sad indeed. She was devoted to him. If that great love which she had borne in the beginning had become a little battered by the years, he was still her husband and she could not imagine life without him.

But if Juan were spared to her she could rebuild her life. She would have her children, whose affairs would be entirely hers to manage as she would. She was experienced enough to rule alone.

"Not Juan . . ." she whispered.

And then Ferdinand strode into the room.

She stared at him as though he were a ghost. Then she ran to him and clasped his hands, pressing them in her own as though she wished to reassure herself that they were flesh and blood.

"It is I," said Ferdinand.

"But this . . ." she stammered. "Someone has played a cruel trick. This says . . ."

"Isabella, my dearest wife, tell me you are glad to know that paper lied."

"I am so happy to see you well."

"It is as I hoped. Oh, Isabella, fortunate we are indeed to be alive and together. We have had our differences, but what should we be without each other?"

She put her head against his chest and he embraced her. There were tears in his eyes.

"Isabella," he continued, "now that you are happy to see me restored to you I have some sad news which I must break to you."

She drew away from him. Her face had grown deathly pale and her eyes were wide and looked black with fear.

"Our son is dead," he said.

Isabella did not speak. She shook her head from side to side.

"It is true, Isabella. He died of a malignant fever. The physicians could do nothing for him."

"Then why . . . why . . . was I not told?"

"I thought to protect you. I have tried to prepare you for this shock. My dearest Isabella, I know how you suffer. Do I not suffer with you?"

"My son," she whispered. "My angel."

"Our son," he answered. "But there will be a child."

She did not seem to hear. She was thinking of that hot day in Seville when he had been born. She remembered holding him in her arms and the feeling of wild exultation which had come to her. Her son. The heir of Ferdinand and Isabella. She had been deeply concerned about the state of her country then; anarchy was in full spate, and there was the chaos which had followed on the disastrous reigns preceding her own; she had been setting up the Santa Hermandad in every town and village. And in her arms had lain that blessed child, so that at that time in spite of all her trials, she had been the happiest woman in Spain.

She could not believe that he was dead.

"Isabella," said Ferdinand gently, "you have forgotten. There is to be a child."

"I have lost my son," she said slowly. "I have lost my angel child."

"There will be grandsons to take his place."

"No one will ever take his place."

"Isabella, you and I have no time for looking backwards. We must look forward. This tragedy has overcome us. We must be brave. We must say: This was the will of God. But God is merciful. He has taken our son, but not before he has left his fertile seed behind him."

Isabella did not answer. She swayed a little and Ferdinand put his arm about her.

"You should rest for a while," he said. "This shock has been too much for you."

"Rest!" she retorted. "There is little rest left for me. He was my only son and I shall never see him smile again."

She was fighting the impulse to rail against this cruel fate.

Is it not enough that two daughters have gone from me, and even my little Catalina will not long remain? she was demanding. Why should I suffer so? Juan was the one I thought to keep with me for ever.

Perhaps she should send for her confessor. Perhaps she was in need of prayer.

She sought to control herself. This cruel day had to be faced; life had to go on.

She lifted her face to Ferdinand and he saw that the wildness had gone from it.

She said in a clear voice which was as firm as ever: "The Lord hath given, and the Lord hath taken away. Blessed be His Name."

JUANA AND PHILIP

All Spain was in mourning for the Prince of the Asturias. Sable banners were hung up in all the important towns. The streets of Salamanca were silent save for the tolling of bells.

The King and Queen had returned to Madrid. They shut themselves in their private apartments in the Alcazar and gave way to their grief.

Throughout the land the extraordinary qualities of the Prince were talked of in hushed voices.

"Spain," said its people, "has suffered one of the greatest losses she has ever been called upon to bear since she fell into the hands of the barbarians."

But gradually the gloom lifted as the news spread. Before he died his child was conceived, and his widow, the young Archduchess from Flanders, carried this child in her womb.

When the child is born, it was said, Spain will smile again.

* * *

Catalina and Maria sat with their sister-in-law while they worked on their embroidery.

Margaret was more subdued than she had been before the death of Juan; she seemed even more gentle.

Catalina encouraged her to talk, but not of her life with Juan—that would be too painful. To talk of Flanders might also be an uneasy subject, for something was happening in Flanders, between Juana and her husband Philip, which was not pleasing to the Sovereigns. So the best subject was Margaret's life in France, of which neither Catalina nor Maria ever tired of hearing. As for Margaret, recalling it seemed to bring her some peace, for if she could project herself back into a past, in which she had never even heard of Juan, she could escape her anguish for a while and know some comfort.

She made the two young girls see the town of Amboise situated at that spot where the Loire and the Amasse met; they saw the château standing on its rocky plateau, imposing and as formidable as a fortress, and the surrounding country with its fields and undulating vineyards.

"And you thought," said Catalina, "that that would be your home for ever and that you would be Queen of France."

"It shows, does it not," said Margaret, "that we can never be sure of what is in store for us."

She looked a little sad and Maria put in: "Were you unhappy to leave France?"

"Yes, I think I was. I thought it was a great insult, you see, and I knew that my father would be angry. It was not very pleasant to have been chosen to be the bride of the King of France and then find that he preferred someone else."

"But you came to us instead," whispered Catalina, and wished she had not said that because she saw the spasm of pain cross Margaret's face.

"Tell us more about Amboise," she went on quickly.

Margaret was only too happy to do so. She told of Charles and his sister who had been her guardian, and their father Louis XI who delighted to wear the shabbiest clothes.

As she talked to the girls, Margaret felt the child moving within her and began to ask herself why she should wish to talk of the past. Juan was lost to her but she had his child.

She stopped and began to smile.

"What is it?" asked Catalina, and even Maria looked curious.

Margaret laid her hands on her body and said: "I can feel the child . . . mine and Juan's . . . moving within me, and it is as though he kicks me. Perhaps he is angry that I talk of the past when he is about to come into the world, and is telling me that I should speak of the future."

Maria looked a little startled and Catalina was shocked. Margaret's manners were often disconcerting, but they were both glad to see that look in her face. It was as though she had come alive again, as though she had realized that there was happiness waiting for her in this world.

After that she talked to them about Juan; she told them of how she had thought she was going to die when her ship had been almost wrecked. There was no more talk of Amboise. She went over everything that had happened since her arrival in Spain; she could not talk enough of the wedding, of the celebrations, of their triumphal journey across Spain to Salamanca.

Catalina rejoiced and Maria brightened; they looked forward to those times which they spent together.

"Whatever happens," said Catalina to Maria, "however evil our fate may seem, something good will come. Look at Margaret. Juan was taken from her; but she is to have Juan's child."

That was a very comforting philosophy for Catalina; she cherished it.

* * *

Now there was less talk of Juan's death; everyone was awaiting the birth of Juan's son.

"It will be as though he lives again," said the Queen. "I shall feel fresh life within me when I hold my grandchild in my arms."

Ferdinand talked of the child as though it were a boy.

"Please let it be a boy," prayed Catalina. "Then my mother will be happy again."

It was an ordinary enough day. Margaret had sat with Catalina and Maria at their sewing and they had talked of the baby, as they did continually now.

"He will soon be with us," Margaret told them. "How I shall welcome him. I do assure you I do not greatly care to be seen in this condition."

Maria looked shocked. She thought that it was tempting God and the saints to talk in such a way; but Catalina knew that it was only the Flemish manner and not to be taken seriously.

Margaret had put her hands on her bulging body and said: "Oh, he is a sly one. He is very quiet today. Usually he kicks me to warn me that he will not long stay imprisoned in my body."

Then she laughed and, although perhaps it was a shocking subject, Catalina rejoiced to see her so gay.

They chatted about the child and the clothes and the cradle which were being prepared for him; and the fêtes that would take place to celebrate his birth. They grew quite merry. It was an ordinary pleasant day.

Catalina did not know when she first became aware of the tension in the Palace. She, who loved her home perhaps more dearly than any of the others, was always conscious of its moods.

What was it? An unexpected quietness, followed by more activity than usual. Grave faces. Whisperings.

She went to the sewing room. Maria was there but Margaret was not.

"What has happened, Maria?" she asked.

"It is the baby."

"But it is too soon. They said . . ."

"It has come nevertheless."

Catalina's face broke into a smile. "How glad I am. The waiting is over. I wonder when we shall see it, Maria."

Maria said slowly: "It is not good that it should come before its time."

"What do you mean?"

"I don't quite know. But I think they are worried about it."

The girls sat silently sewing, alert for every sound.

Then suddenly they heard a woman sobbing. Catalina ran to

the door, and saw one of the attendants hurrying through the apartments.

"What has happened?" she cried.

But the woman did not answer; she stumbled blindly away. Terrible misgivings came to Catalina then. Was yet another tragedy to befall her family?

* * *

Catalina stood at the door of her mother's private apartment.

"The Queen is not to be disturbed," said one of the two attendants who guarded the door.

Catalina stood desolate.

"I must see my mother," she said firmly.

The attendants shook their heads.

"Is she alone?" asked Catalina.

"That is so."

"She is mourning the dead baby, is she not? She will want me with her."

The attendants looked at each other and, taking advantage of their momentary inattention, Catalina calmly opened the door and walked into her mother's apartment. The attendants were so astonished that the little Princess, who was usually so decorous in her behaviour, should do such a thing, that the door was closing on her before they realized what had happened.

Catalina sped across the room to that small antechamber where she knew her mother would be kneeling before her altar.

She went in and quietly knelt beside her.

The Queen looked at her small daughter, and the tears which before had remained unshed began to flow.

For a few minutes they wept in silence and prayed for strength to control their grief.

Then the Queen rose to her feet and held out her hand to Catalina.

"I had to come to you," cried Catalina. "It was not the fault of the attendants. They tried to stop me. But I was so frightened."

"I am glad you came," said the Queen. "We should always be together in sorrow and in happiness, my darling."

She led Catalina into the main apartment and sat on her bed, drawing her daughter down beside her. She smoothed the child's hair and said: "You know that there is no baby."

"Yes, Mother."

"It never lived. It never suffered. It was born dead."

"Oh, Mother, why . . . why when it meant so much to us all?"

"Perhaps because the shock of its father's death was too much for its mother to bear. In any case—because it was the will of God."

"It was cruel . . . cruel."

"Hush, my dearest. You must never question God's will. You must learn to accept with meekness and fortitude the trials He gives you to bear."

"I will try to be as good and strong as you are, Mother."

"My child, I fear I am not always strong. We must cease to grieve. We must think of comforting poor Margaret."

"She will not die?"

"No, we think she will live. So you see it is not all tragedy. As for me, I have lost my son and my grandchild. But I have my daughters, have I not? I have my Isabella who may well give me a grandchild before long. I have my Juana who I am sure will have children. Then there is my Maria and my little Catalina. You see I am well blessed with many cherished possessions. They will bring me such happiness as will make up for this great tragedy I have suffered."

"Oh, Mother, I hope they will." Catalina thought of her sisters: Isabella who had dreamed she heard the voices cursing in her dreams, Juana whose wildness had always caused the greatest anxiety. Maria? Herself? What would happen to them?

* * *

In the Brussels Palace Juana heard the news from Spain. It came in an affectionate letter from her mother. A terrible tragedy had befallen their House. The heir had died only a few months after his marriage, and all their hopes had been centred on a child of this union who was stillborn.

"Write me some good news of yourself," Isabella begged her daughter. "That will do more than anything to cheer me."

The letter fluttered from Juana's hand. The troubles in Madrid seemed far away, and she had almost forgotten that she had ever lived there, so completely absorbed was she by the gay life of Brussels.

This was the way to live. Here balls, banquets, dancing, festivities were what mattered. Philip implied this and Philip was always right.

Juana could not think of her handsome husband without being overcome by many mingling emotions. Chief of these was her desire for him; she could scarcely bear to be absent from him and, when she was in his presence, she could not keep her eyes from watching him or hands from reaching out to touch him.

This had amused him in the beginning. He had quickly initiated her into the erotic experiences which made up the greater part of his life, and she had followed eagerly, for everything that he did seemed wonderful and she was eager to share in it.

Some of her retinue who had come with her into Flanders warned her. "Be a little more discreet, Highness. Do not be over eager for his embraces."

But there was no restraint in Juana. There never had been; she could not begin learning, now that she was face to face with the greatest emotional experience of her life.

She wanted Philip with her every hour of the day and night. She could not hide the burning desire which was like a frenzy. Philip laughed at it. It had been very amusing at first.

Later she feared he was less amused and had begun to avoid her.

There were the mistresses. She could never be sure who was his mistress of the moment. It might be some little lace-maker whom he had seen on his journeyings through the dominions, fancied and set up near the Palace that he might visit her. It might be—and so often was—one of the ladies of the Court.

When she saw these women Juana felt near to murder. She wanted to mutilate them in some way so that they would be hideous instead of desirable in his eyes.

There were nights when he did not visit her; when she knew that he was with some mistress. Then she would lie, biting her pillow, weeping passionate tears, giving vent to uncontrolled laughter, forgetting everything but her desire for Philip, the most handsome man in the world.

One of the Flemish women had whispered slyly: "He takes his mistress. There are some who would say, if Your Highness took a lover, that you were provoked to it. Perhaps he would."

"Take a lover!" cried Juana. "You do not know Philip. What other man could ever satisfy or please me in the smallest way since I have known him!"

They were beginning to say in the Brussels Palace that Juana's wildness was alarming because it was not merely the fury of a jealous wife. It went deeper than that.

They avoided her eyes whenever possible.

Juana was now finding it difficult to think of her mother far away in Madrid, and this tragedy which had befallen her family. She stared into space trying to remember them all, those wearying days of sitting in the nursery stitching at some tiresome piece of needlework. She remembered being beaten because she had run away when it was time to go to confession.

She laughed aloud at the vague memory. All that was past. Philip would never beat her because she had failed to go to confession. Philip had not a great deal of respect for priests, and life in Brussels was very different from that in Madrid. There was not the same solemnity, the wearying religious services. The rule in Brussels was: Enjoy yourself. The Flemish people, lacking the dignity of the Spaniards, believed they had been put on this Earth to enjoy themselves. It was a doctrine which appealed to Juana.

Everything about Flanders appealed to Juana. It must be so, because Philip was in Flanders.

She was not sure now whether Philip would regard this news from Spain as a tragedy; and if he did not, how would she?

There was another side to Philip's nature besides his sensuality and his love of gaiety. He was not the son of Maximilian for nothing. He was proud of the possessions which were now his and those greater ones which he would inherit. He had wanted Juana for his bride, before he had seen her, because she was the daughter of Isabella and Ferdinand and great good could come to him through union with such an heiress.

Philip was ambitious.

He had been rather pleased, she knew, when he had heard of Juan's death, and not so pleased when he had heard that there was to be a child.

"By God, Juana," he had cried, "now that your brother is dead, who will be the Spanish heir? Tell me that. That sickly sister of yours? The Aragonese are a fierce people. They do not believe women should be their rulers. And quite right too, my love. Quite right too. Do you not agree with me?"

"Oh yes, Philip."

He slapped her buttocks jauntily, because it amused him on occasions to treat the daughter of Ferdinand and Isabella as though she were a tavern girl.

"That's a good girl, Juana. Always agree with your husband. That makes him pleased with you."

She held her face up to his and murmured his name.

"By God, woman," said Philip, "you are insatiable. Later perhaps . . . if you are a good girl. Listen carefully to what I have to say. If it had not been for this child your brother's wife is to have, you and I would be Prince and Princess of Castile."

"Philip, you would be very pleased then?"

"I should be very pleased with my little Juana. But now I am not so pleased. If this child is a son . . . well, then, my little Juana does not bring the same gifts to her doting husband, does she?"

He had caressed her mildly and then had pushed her from him in order to go to one of his mistresses, she felt sure, because he was not pleased with her. A child had been conceived and therefore Philip was not pleased with his wife.

She had cursed Margaret for her fruitfulness. Such a short time married, and already to have conceived a child which Philip did not want! How tiresome of her.

But now there was this news and Philip would be delighted. She must go to him at once.

Before she could leave her apartment there was a knock on her door and a priest entered.

Juana frowned, but this man was Fray Matienzo, a confidential priest whom her mother had sent to Flanders to watch over her daughter; and although Juana was far from Isabella she still remembered the awe in which even she had held her mother.

So she stood impatiently waiting for what the priest had to say to her.

"Your Highness," he began, "I have received a letter from the Queen in which she tells me this tragic news which she also imparts to you. The Queen will be very sad."

Juana said nothing; she was not even thinking of the priest nor of her mother. She was seeing Philip's fair flushed face, listening to her while she told him the news. She would throw herself into his arms, and he would be so pleased with her that he would forget all those big flaxen-haired women who seemed to give him so much pleasure. He would give all his attention to her.

"I thought," said Fray Matienzo, "that you might wish to pray with me for comfort."

Juana looked bewildered. "I do not wish to pray," she said. "I must go at once. I have something important to do."

The priest laid a hand on her arm.

"The Queen, your mother, asks me questions about you."

"Then pray answer them," she retorted.

"I fear they might cause her pain if I told her the truth."

"What's this?" said Juana half-heartedly.

"If I told her that you did not worship as frequently as you did in Spain, if I told her that you did not go to confession . . ."

"I do these things as frequently as my husband does."

"That will not serve you as an excuse before God or your mother."

Juana snapped her fingers; frenzied lights were beginning to show in her eyes. He was detaining her against her will; he was denying her her pleasure. What if Philip heard this news from others before she herself could impart it?

She threw off the priest's detaining hand.

"Go your way," she said angrily, "and let me go mine."

"Highness, I implore you to dismiss the French priests who surround you now. Their ways are not ours."

"I prefer them," she answered.

"Unless you listen to me, unless you mind your ways, I shall have no alternative but to write to your mother and tell her that you have no true piety."

Juana snarled at him between her teeth: "Then do so. Do what you will, you interfering old fool. I am no longer of Spain. I belong to Flanders and Philip!"

She laughed wildly and ran from the room.

Those attendants who saw her looked at each other and shrugged their shoulders. There was little ceremony at the Flemish Court, but no one behaved in quite the same manner as the Infanta Juana. She was more than wild, she was strange, they said.

She found Philip in his apartments. He was sprawled on a sofa, his handsome face flushed. One golden-haired woman sat on a stool at his feet; she was lying back against him, embracing his leg. Another woman, also with brilliant flaxen hair, was fanning him. Someone was strumming on a lute, and men and women were dancing.

It was what Juana had seen many times before. If she could have had her way she would have taken one of those women by her flaxen hair, and have her bound and beaten. Then she would turn her attention to the other.

But she must calm herself. They might flaunt their long flaxen locks which fell over their big bare bosoms, but this was an occasion when she had something more to offer, and she was going to calm herself so thoroughly that she would not act foolishly this time.

She stood on the threshold of the room. No one took any notice of her. The dancers went on dancing and the women went on caressing Philip.

Juana screeched at the top of her voice: "Silence!"

This had the desired effect. There was complete stillness in the room and, before Philip could command them all to go on as they were, Juana cried: "I have important news from Spain."

Philip rose to his feet without warning. The woman at his feet toppled off her stool and fell to the floor. Juana wanted to laugh exultantly as she watched her, but she controlled herself.

She waved the letter from her mother and, seeing it, Philip's eyes gleamed with interest.

"Leave me with my wife," he ordered.

Juana stood aside, watching them file out. She did not look at the two women. She was determined not to lose control of her emotions. She was about to have him to herself and she was happy.

"What news?" he demanded. "What news?"

She smiled at him with all the love she felt for him in her eyes. She knew that she was about to give him something which he greatly desired.

"The child is stillborn," she said.

For a few seconds he did not speak. She watched the slow smile cross his face. Then he brought his clenched fist down on to his thigh. He took her cheek between his thumb and forefinger and pressed it so tightly that she wanted to scream with the joy of it. Whether it was pain or caresses he gave her she did not care. It was enough that his hands were upon her.

"Show me the letter," he said gruffly, and snatched it from her.

She watched him reading it. It was all there, just as he wished it to be.

Then his hands fell to his sides and he began to laugh.

"You are pleased, Philip?" she said, as though to remind him that he owed this to her.

"Oh yes, my love, I am pleased. Are you?"

"I am always pleased when you are."

"That's true, I know. Why Juana, do you see what this means?"

"That my sister Isabella is now the heir of Spain."

"Your sister Isabella! They will not have a woman to rule them, I tell you."

"But my parents have no more sons. And Isabella is the eldest."

"I ought to beat you for not being born first, Juana." She laughed wildly. The thought did not displease her. She only asked that she should have his undivided attention. Instead he went on: "I will show you what an indulgent husband I am. You and I shall be Prince and Princess of Castile, and when your mother is no more Castile will be ours."

"Philip, it should be as you say. But they will remind me that I am not the eldest."

"Do you think they will want the King of Portugal to rule Spain? Not they."

"Not they!" she cried. And she wondered whether they would have the heir of Maximilian either. But this was not for her to say. Philip was pleased with her.

He took her in his arms and danced her round the room. She clung to him madly.

"You will stay with me for a while?" she pleaded.

He put his head on one side and considered her.

"Please, Philip, Please, Philip!" she pleaded. "The two of us . . . alone . . ."

He nodded slowly and drew her to the couch.

Her passion still had the power to amuse him.

He would not stay long with her though, and was soon calling back his friends.

He made Juana stand on the couch beside him.

"My friends," he said, "you have strangers among you, strangers of great importance. You must each come forward and pay homage to the Prince and Princess of Castile."

It was a game similar to those they often played. Each person came to the couch and bowed low, kissing first the hand of Philip and then Juana's.

Juana was so happy. She suddenly remembered with unusual vividness her mother's apartment at Madrid, and she wondered what her parents and her sisters would say if they could see her and Philip now—clever Philip and his wife who had, without their consent, made themselves the heir and heiress of Castile.

She was so amused that she burst into laughter. The restraint of the last hour had been too much for her, and she could not stop laughing.

Philip looked at her coldly. He remembered her frenzied passion, her great desire for him—and he shuddered.

For the first time the thought occurred to him: I know why she is so strange. She is *mad.*

THE QUEEN OF PORTUGAL

FERDINAND and Isabella were studying with dismay the letter they had received from Fray Matienzo. This was indeed disquieting news. Not only was Juana conducting herself in Flanders with the utmost impiety, but she had dared, with her husband, to assume the title of heir to Castile.

Isabella said bitterly: "I wish I had never allowed her to leave me. She should never have been sent away from me. She is unstable."

Ferdinand looked gloomy. He was wondering now whether it would not have been better to have sent Maria into Flanders. Maria had little spirit, it was true, but at least she would not have behaved with such abandon as Juana apparently did.

"There are times," went on Isabella, "when I say to myself, What blow will fall next? My son . . ."

Ferdinand laid his arm about her shoulders. "My dear," he murmured, "you must not give way to your sorrow. It is true that our alliances with the Hapsburgs are proving to be a mixed blessing. We have Margaret here on our hands . . . our daughter-in-law, who has failed to give us an heir. And now it seems that Philip is more our enemy than our friend."

"You have written to Maximilian protesting against this wicked action of his son and our daughter?"

"I have."

"But," went on Isabella quickly, "I do not blame Juana. She has been forced to do this. Oh, my poor child, I would to God I had never let her go."

"Philip is a wild and ambitious young man. We must not take him too seriously. Have no fear. This is not as important as you think. You are upset because one of your daughters has so far forgotten her duty to us as to act in a manner certain to cause us pain. Juana was always half crazy. We should not take too much notice of what she does. There is only one answer to all this."

"And that is?"

"Send for Isabella and Emanuel. Have them proclaimed as our heirs throughout Spain. Then it will avail Maximilian's son and our daughter very little what they *call* themselves. Isabella is our eldest daughter and she is the true heir to Castile. Her sons shall inherit our crowns."

"How wise you are, Ferdinand. You are right. It is the only course. In my grief I could only mourn for the conduct of one of my children. It was foolish of me."

Ferdinand smiled broadly. It was pleasant to have Isabella recognizing his superiority.

"Leave these matters to me, Isabella. You will see that I know how to manage these erring children of ours."

"Promise me not to feel too angry towards our Juana."

"I'd like to lay my hands on her . . ." began Ferdinand.

"No, Ferdinand, no. Remember how unstable she is."

Ferdinand looked at her shrewdly. "There are times," he said slowly, "when she reminds me of your mother."

At last those words had been spoken aloud, and Isabella felt as though she had received a blow. It was folly to be so cowardly. That idea was not new to her. But to hear it spoken aloud gave weight to it, brought her terrors into the daylight. They were no longer fancies, those fears; they had their roots in reality.

Ferdinand looked at her bowed head and, patting her shoulder reassuringly, he left her.

She was glad to be alone.

She whispered under her breath: "What will become of her, what will become of my tragic child?"

And she knew at that moment that this was the greatest tragedy of her life; even now, with the poignant sorrow of loss upon her, she knew that the blow struck at her through the death of their beloved son was light compared with what she would suffer through the madness of her daughter.

Ferdinand on his way to his apartments met a messenger who brought him despatches. He saw that these came from Maximilian, and it gave him pleasure to read them first, before taking them to Isabella.

She is distraught, he told himself. It is better for me to shield her from unpleasantness until she has recovered from these shocks; and as he read Maximilian's reply he told himself that he was glad he had done so. Maximilian made it quite clear that he was firmly behind his son's claim to the crown of Castile. He felt that the daughter-in-law of Maximilian had the right to come before the wife of the King of Portugal, even though she happened to be the younger.

This was a monstrous suggestion, even for such an arrogant man to make. Maximilian also suggested that he had a right to the crown of Portugal through his mother, Doña Leoñor of Portugal; and that his claim was greater than that of Emanuel who was merely a nephew of the last King. There were sly hints that the King of France, Ferdinand's enemy and rival in the

Italian project, was ready to stand beside Maximilian in this claim.

Ferdinand's fury was boundless. Was this what the Hapsburg alliance had brought him?

He sat at his table and wrote furiously. Then he called his messengers.

"Leave at once," he said, "for Lisbon. Let there be no delay. This is a matter of the utmost importance."

* * *

Queen Isabella of Portugal had become reconciled to life. She was no longer tormented by nightmares. For this new peace which had come to her she was grateful to her husband. None could have been kinder than Emanuel. It was strange that here in Lisbon, where she had been so happy with her first husband Alonso, she was learning to forget him.

From her apartments in the Castelo she could look down on Lisbon, a city which she found entrancing to watch from this distance. She could see the Ashbouna where the Arabs lived, shut up in those walls which had long ago been erected by the Visigoths; she looked down past olive and fig trees to the Alcaçova which she and Emanuel sometimes inhabited. Along the narrow streets, which had been made hundreds of years before, the people congregated; there they bought and sold; gossiped, sang and danced. Sometimes in the evenings the sound of a slave song would be heard, plaintive and infinitely sad with longing for a distant land.

The industrious Moors in the Mouraria turned clay on their wheels; they sat cross-legged making their pottery. Some sat weaving. They were adepts at both arts and they grew rich.

It was a city of a hundred sights and beauties. Yet the Queen of Portugal did not care to mingle with her husband's people. She wished to remain in the castle looking on at them, as she wished to look on life, aloof, an onlooker rather than a participant.

In due course many of her and her husband's most industrious subjects would be driven from their country. Isabella could not forget the condition which had brought her into Portugal. The thought came back to torment her: One day they will curse me, those men and women.

But the time was not yet, and something had happened to bring her resignation.

Isabella was pregnant.

She prayed for a son. If she could give Emanuel and Portugal a son she felt she would in some small way have compensated them for the unhappiness their King's marriage was going to bring to numbers of his subjects.

When she had heard the news of her brother's death it had not been merely sorrow which had so stricken her that she had been kept to her bed for some days. That fear, which had been haunting her for so long, seemed to take a material shape, to become a tangible thing, something which would whisper in her ear: There is a curse on your House.

She had told Emanuel this and he had shaken his head. She was subject to strange fancies, he told her. Why, even though Juan was dead, Margaret was to have a child, and if that child were a son there would be an heir for Spain as surely as if Juan had lived.

She had begun to believe him.

And then came further news from Spain.

She had seen the messengers riding to the Castelo and she knew from their livery that they came from her parents. She put her hand to her heart which had begun to flutter uncomfortably.

Where was Emanuel? She would like him to be with her when she read what her parents had to say.

She called to one of her women. "Go and see if the King is in his apartments. If he is, please tell him that I should be pleased if he would come to me here, or if he prefers it I will go to his apartment."

There was only a short time to wait before Emanuel came hurrying to her.

She smiled and held out her hand. He was continually giving her proof of how she could rely on him.

When they were alone, she said: "Emanuel, I have seen messengers riding up to the Castelo, and I know they come from my parents. I was afraid, so I asked you to come to me. Whenever I see my parents' seal I tremble and ask myself: What bad news now?"

"You must not, Isabella." He kissed her cheek gently. She was looking a little better since her pregnancy and that delighted him; he had been alarmed by the thinness of her body when he remembered the young girl who had first come into Portugal to marry his cousin. Then she had not been strikingly healthy, but when he had seen her after the long absence he had noticed at once that she seemed more ethereal, her skin more transparent, her eyes larger because the fullness had disappeared from her cheeks. She was no less beautiful, but that look of not entirely belonging to this world faintly alarmed him.

It had been a great joy to discover that their marriage was to be fruitful. He was sure she had improved in health; and the effect on her spirits had been good.

"It seemed so strange to me that Juan should die. We had never thought of Juan's dying."

"You are too fanciful, Isabella. Juan died because he caught a fever."

"Why should a young and healthy man catch a fever on his honeymoon?"

"Men are not immune from fever merely because they are on their honeymoons, my dearest. It may well be that he was weakened by all the ceremonies. It is unwise to think of his death as an omen." Emanuel laughed. "Why, there was a time when you thought our union was to be ill-fated. Admit it. You thought, We want children, we *need* children, but we shall never have them. And you see, you are going to be proved wrong."

"If it is a boy I carry," cried Isabella with shining eyes, "I shall say I have been foolish and I shall not talk of omens again."

She looked over her shoulder almost furtively, as though she were speaking not to Emanuel but to some unseen presence, as though she were pleading: Show me I was foolish to fear, by giving me a healthy son.

Emanuel smiled tenderly at her and at that moment the messengers arrived.

The letters were delivered to Isabella, who called attendants to take the messengers to where they could be refreshed after their journey.

When she was once more alone with Emanuel she held out the letters to him. Her face was white, her hands trembling.

"I pray you, Emanuel, read them for me."

"They are meant for your eyes, my dear."

"I know, but my hands shake so, and my eyes will not take in the words."

As Emanuel broke the seal and read the letters, Isabella, watching him intently, saw his face whiten.

She said quickly: "What is it, Emanuel? You must tell me quickly."

"The child was stillborn," he said.

Isabella gave a gasp and sank down on to a stool. The room appeared to swim round her, and she seemed to hear those malicious voices—the voices of a thousand tormented and persecuted people—whispering to her.

"But Margaret is well," went on Emanuel.

There was silence and Isabella lifted her face to her husband's. "There is something else?" she asked. "I pray you keep nothing back."

"Yes," he said slowly, "there is something else. Juana and Philip have proclaimed themselves heirs to Castile."

"Juana! But that is impossible. She is younger than I."

"That is what your parents say."

"How could Juana do such a thing?"

"Because she has a very ambitious husband."

"But this is terrible. This will break my mother's heart. This is like quarrelling within the family itself."

"You need have no fear," soothed Emanuel. "Your parents will know how best to deal with such pretensions. They want us to prepare to leave Lisbon at once for Spain. They are going to have you publicly proclaimed heir of Castile."

A weariness assailed Isabella. She put her hand to her aching head. In that moment she thought: I want none of these quarrels. I want to be left in peace to have my child.

Then she felt the child within her, and her mood changed. A Queen must not think of her own personal desires.

It occurred to her that the child in her womb might well be heir to the whole of Spain and all those dependencies of Spain, those lands of the New World.

There was no time in her busy life for lassitude. She had to fight for the rights of this child, even against her own sister.

Her voice was firm as she said: "When could we be ready to leave for Spain?"

TORQUEMADA AND THE KING OF ENGLAND

TOMÁS DE TORQUEMADA lay on his pallet breathing heavily. His gout was a torture and he was finding it increasingly difficult to move about.

"So many things to do," he murmured. "So little time in which to do them." Then because his words might have seemed like a reproach to the Almighty, he murmured: "But Thy will be done."

He thought often of Ximenes, Archbishop of Toledo, who, he told himself, might one day wear the mantle of Torquemada. *There* was a man who he believed would one day overcome carnality to such an extent that he would, before his end, do as great a work as that which had been done by himself.

Torquemada could look back on the last thirty years with complacence. He could marvel now that it was not until he was fifty-eight years of age that he had emerged from the narrow life of the cloister and had begun to write his name in bold letters in the history of his country. His great achievements were the introduction of the Inquisition and the expulsion of the Jews.

He exulted when he remembered this. Alas, that his body was failing him. Alas, that he had his enemies. He wished that he had seen more of this man Ximenes. He believed that such a man could be trusted to guide the Sovereigns in the way they should go, that in his hands could safely be placed the destiny of Spain.

"I could have moulded him," he murmured. "I could have taught him much. Alas, so little time."

He was weary because he had just taken his leave of the chief Inquisitors whom he had summoned to Avila that he might give them the new instructions, in the form of sixteen articles, which he had compiled for the use of the Inquisition. He was continually thinking of reforms, of strengthening the organization, making it more difficult for sinners to elude the *alguazils.*

He believed some eight thousand sinners against the Church had been burned at the stake since that glorious year of 1483, when he had established his Inquisition, until this day when he now lay on his painful pallet wondering how much longer was left to him.

"Eight thousand fires," he mused. "But there were many more brought to judgment. Somewhere in the region of one hundred thousand people found guilty and suffered the minor penalties. A good record."

He was astonished that a man such as himself should have enemies within the Church, and that perhaps the greatest of these should be the Pope himself.

How different it had been when the easy-going Innocent VIII had worn the Papal crown! Torquemada did not trust the Borgia Pope. There were hideous rumours in circulation regarding the life led by Roderigo Borgia, Pope Alexander VI. He had his mistresses, it was said, and had a family of children of whom he was very proud and on whom he showered the highest honours.

To Torquemada, devotee of the hard pallet and the hair shirt, this was shocking; but more so was the fact that the sly and shrewd Borgia seemed to take an almost mischievous delight in frustrating Torquemada in every way possible.

"Perhaps it is inevitable that a whoremonger and evil liver should wish to bring down one who has always followed the holy life," mused Torquemada. "But pity of pities that such a one should be the Holy Father himself!"

Torquemada's eyes gleamed in his pale face. What pleasure it would give him to jostle for power against that man. Even at this moment he was expecting his messengers to return from England, whither he had sent them with a special message for King Henry VII, who might have cause to be grateful to Torquemada.

The wily King of England knew what power the Inquisitor wielded over the Sovereigns. His spies would let him know that Isabella and Ferdinand often visited him at Avila when he was too crippled by the gout to go to them. He would know that the body of Juan had been brought to him at Avila for burial—a mark of the respect the Sovereigns felt for him. It was comforting—particularly in view of the irritations he received from Rome—to know that England knew him for the influential man he was.

It was while he was lying on his pallet brooding on these matters that his messengers arrived from England, and as soon as he learned that they were in the monastery, he had them brought to him with all speed.

The messengers trembled in his presence; there was that in this man to set others trembling. His cold accusing eyes might see some heresy of which a victim had been unaware; those thin lips might rap out a question, the answer to which might cost the one who made it the loss of his possessions, torture, or death.

To stand in the presence of Torquemada was to bring to the

mind the gloomy dungeons of pain, the dismal ceremonies of the *auto de fé*; the smell of scorching human flesh.

"What news of the King of England?" demanded Torquemada.

"Your Excellency, the King of England sends his respects to you and wishes you to know that he desires to be your friend."

"And you told him of my request?"

"Your Excellency, we told him and we had his answer from his own lips. The King of England will not allow in his kingdom any man, woman or child who asks refuge from the Holy Office."

"Did he say this lightly or did he swear it as an oath?"

"Excellency, he put his hands on his breast and swore it. He swore too that he would persecute any Jew or heretic who sought refuge in his Kingdom, should the Inquisition call attention to such a person."

"And was there aught else?"

"The King of England said that, as he was your friend, he knew that you would be his."

Torquemada smiled well satisfied, and the relieved messengers were allowed to escape from his presence.

The King of England at least was his friend. He had given what Torquemada had asked, and he should be rewarded. This marriage between his eldest son and the Sovereigns' youngest daughter must not much longer be delayed. It was absurd sentimentality to talk of the child's being too young.

It was a matter which needed his attention and it should have it.

If only he were not so tired. But he must rouse himself. He had his duty to perform and, although the Queen was going to plead for her youngest daughter, Her Highness, as he had, must learn to subdue her desires; she must not let them stand in the way of her duty.

ISABELLA RECEIVES CHRISTOBAL COLON

Margaret went about the Palace like a sad, pale ghost. She had lost her Flemish gaiety; she seemed always to be looking back into the past.

Often Catalina would walk beside her in the gardens; neither would talk very much, but they had a certain comfort to give each other.

Catalina had a feeling that these walks were precious because they could not go on for long. Something was going to happen to her . . . or to Margaret. Margaret would not be allowed to stay here indefinitely, any more than she would. Maximilian would soon be wondering what new marriage could be arranged for his daughter; as for Catalina, her time of departure must be near.

Catalina said, one day as they walked together: "Soon my sister Isabella will be coming home. Then there will be festivities to welcome her. Perhaps then the time of mourning will be over."

"Festivities will not end my mourning," Margaret answered.

Catalina slipped her arm through that of her sister-in-law. "Will you stay here?" she asked.

"I do not know. My father may recall me. My attendants would be glad to return to Flanders. They say they can never learn your Spanish manners."

"I should miss you sadly if you went."

"Perhaps . . ." began Margaret and stopped short.

Catalina winced. "You are thinking that I may be gone first." She was silent for a moment, then she burst out: "Margaret, I am so frightened when I think of it. I can tell you, because you are different from everyone else. You say what you think. I have a terror of England."

"One country is not so very different from another," Margaret comforted.

"I do not like what I hear of the King of England."

"But it is his son with whom you will be concerned. There are other children, and perhaps they will not be like their father. Look how friendly I have become with you all."

"Yes," said Catalina slowly, "perhaps I shall like Arthur and his brother and sisters."

"Perhaps you will not go after all. Plans are often changed."

"I used to think and hope that," Catalina admitted. "But since the ceremony has been performed by proxy, I feel there is little chance of escape for me."

Catalina's brow was wrinkled; she was picturing that ceremony of which she had heard. It had had to be performed in secret because the King of England feared what the King of Scotland's reaction would be if he knew that England was making a marriage with Spain.

"In the Chapel of the Royal Manor of Bewdley . . ." she whispered. "What strange names these English have. Perhaps in time they will not be strange to me. Oh, Margaret, when I think of that ceremony I feel I am already married. I feel there is no longer hope of escape."

* * *

Isabella watched her daughter from a window of her apartments. She was glad to see Margaret and Catalina together. Poor children, they could help each other.

Although she could not see the expression on her young daughter's face it seemed to her that there was desperation displayed in the droop of her head and the manner in which her hands hung at her sides.

She was probably talking of that marriage by proxy. The poor child would break her heart if she had to go to England. She was thirteen. Another year and the time would be ripe.

The Queen turned away from the window because she could no longer bear to look.

She went to her table and wrote to Torquemada.

"As yet my daughter is too young for marriage. There has been this proxy ceremony; that must suffice for a little longer. Catalina shall not go to England . . . yet."

* * *

Queen Isabella of Spain was often thankful that there was so much to demand her attention. If there had not been, she believed that she would not have been able to bear her grief for what had befallen her family. She had borne the terrible blow of Juan's death, and she had thought at that time that she had come as near to despair as any woman could come; and yet, when she thought of Juana in Flanders, something like terror would assail her.

The truth was that she dared not think too often of Juana.

Therefore she was glad of these continual matters of state to which it was her duty to attend. She would never forget that she was the Queen and that her duty to her country came before everything—yes, even the love which she, as an affectionate mother, bore her children.

Now she was concerned about her Admiral, Christobal Colon, who was on his way to see her. She had a great admiration for this man and never ceased to defend him when his enemies—and he had many—brought charges against him.

Now he wished to sail once more for the New World, and she knew that he would beg for the means to do so. This would mean money for equipment, men and women who would make good colonists.

She would always remember that occasion when he had come home, having discovered the New World and bringing proof of its riches with him. She remembered singing the Te Deum in the royal chapel, praising God for this great gift. Perhaps to some it had not fulfilled its promise. They had expected more riches, greater profit. But Isabella was a woman of vision and she could see that the new colony might have something more important to offer than gold and trinkets.

Men grew impatient. They did not wish to work for their riches. They wanted to grow rich effortlessly. As for Ferdinand, when he saw the spoils which were being brought from the New World, he regretted that they had promised Christobal Colon a share in them, and was continually seeking a way out of his bargain with the adventurer.

Many had desired to follow him on his return to the New World, but to found a colony one needed men of ideals. Isabella understood this as Ferdinand and so many others could not.

It had been a troublous tale of ambition and jealousies which had been brought to Spain from the new colony.

"Who is this Colon?" was a question on the lips of many. "He is a foreigner. Why should he be put above us?"

Isabella understood that many of the would-be colonists had been adventurers, *hidalgos* who had no intention of submitting to any sort of discipline. Poor Colon! His difficulties were not over when he discovered the new land.

And now he was coming to see her again, and she wondered what comfort she would have to offer him.

When he arrived at the Palace she received him at once, and as he knelt before her she gave him a glance of affection. It grieved her that others did not share her faith in him.

She bade him rise and he stood before her, a broad man, long-legged, with deep blue eyes that held the dreams of an idealist in them; his thick hair, which had once been a reddish gold, was now touched with white. He was a man for whom a great dream had come true; but, energetic idealist that he was, one dream fulfilled was immediately superseded by another which seemed as elusive.

Perhaps, thought Isabella, it is easier to discover a New World than to found a peaceable colony.

"My dear Admiral," she said, "tell me your news."

"Highness, the delay in leaving Spain for the colony alarms me. I fear what may be happening there."

Isabella nodded. "I would I could give you all you need. There has, as you realize, been a heavy drain on our purses during these sad months."

Colon understood. The cost of the Prince's wedding must have been enormous. He could have fitted out his expedition on a quarter of it. He remembered how angry he had been during the celebration, and how he had said to his dear Beatriz de Arana and their son, Ferdinand: What folly this is! To squander so much on a wedding when it could go towards enriching the colony and therefore Spain!

Beatriz and young Ferdinand agreed with him. They cared as passionately about his endeavours as he did himself, and he was a lucky man in his family. But what sad frustration he suffered everywhere else.

"The Marchioness of Moya has been telling me of your plight," said the Queen.

"The Marchioness has ever been a good friend to me," answered Colon.

It was true. Isabella's dearest friend, Beatriz de Bobadilla who was now the Marchioness of Moya, believed in Christobal Colon as few did. It was she who, in the days before he had made his discovery, had brought him to the notice of Isabella and given him her active support.

"I am deeply distressed for you and have been wondering how I can provide you with the colonists you need. I think it might be possible to find the money more easily than the men."

"Highness," said Christobal, "an idea has come to me. It is imperative that I have men for the colony. I need them for mining, building and agricultural work. Previously I took with me men who were not primarily colonists. They did not wish to build the New World; they only wished to take from it and return to Spain with their spoils."

Isabella smiled.

"They were disappointed," she said. "The climate did not agree with them, and it was said that they came back so sick and sallow that they had more gold in their faces than in their pockets."

"It is true, Highness. And this is why I find it so difficult to find men who will sail with me. But there are some men who could be made to go. I refer to convicts. If they were offered freedom, in the colony, they would eagerly take it in preference to imprisonment here."

"And," said Isabella, "it would not be a matter of choice. That should be their punishment."

Christobal's sunburned weather-scored face was alight with excitement. "Out there," he said, "they will become new men. They will discover the delights of building a new world. How could they fail to do this?"

"All men are not as you are, Admiral," Isabella reminded him.

But Christobal was certain that all men must prefer the adventure of the new world to incarceration in the old.

"Have I Your Highness's permission to go forward with this plan?"

"Yes," said Isabella. "Select your convicts, Admiral; and may good luck go with you."

After he had gone she sent for the Marchioness of Moya. It was rarely that she had time to be with this dear friend; each had their duties, and it was not often enough that their paths crossed. Yet each remembered the friendship of their youth, and when they could be together they never lost the opportunity.

When Beatriz arrived Isabella told her of Christobal's plan to take convicts to the colony. Beatriz listened gravely and shook her head.

"That is going to mean trouble," she said. "Our dear Colon will find himself keeping the peace among a set of ruffians. How I wish we could send good colonists with him."

"He must needs take what he can get," Isabella answered.

"As we all must," added Beatriz. "What news of the Queen of Portugal?"

"They are setting out at once. They must. I would not have Isabella travel later, when she is far advanced in pregnancy."

"Oh, how I hope . . ." began the impetuous Beatriz.

"Pray go on," Isabella told her. "You were going to say you hoped that this time I shall not be disappointed. This time I shall hold my grandchild in my arms."

Beatriz went to Isabella and stooping over her kissed her. It was the familiar gesture of two friends who had been close to each other. Indeed, the forthright Beatriz, rather domineering as she was, was one of the few who treated the Queen at times as though she were a child. Isabella found it endearing. In the company of Beatriz she felt she could let down her defences and speak of her hopes and fears.

"Yes," said Beatriz, "you are anxious."

"Isabella's health was never good. That cough of hers has persisted for years."

"It is often the frail plants that live the longest," Beatriz assured her. "Isabella will have every care."

"That is one reason why I can feel glad that it has been necessary to call her home. I shall be at the birth. I shall see that she has every possible care."

"Then it is a good thing . . ."

"No," answered Isabella sternly, "it can never be a good thing when there is internal strife in families."

"Strife! You call the strutting of this coxcomb, Philip, strife!"

"Remember who he is, Beatriz. He could make a great deal of trouble for us. And my poor Juana. . . ."

"One day," Beatriz said, "you will find some reason to call *her* home. Then you will explain her duty to her."

Isabella shook her head. It had never been easy to explain to Juana anything which she did not want to understand. She had a feeling that life in Flanders was changing Juana . . . and not for the better. Was it possible for such as Juana to grow more stable? Or would her mind, like her grandmother's, gradually grow more and more wayward?

"So many troubles," mused Isabella. "Our poor sad Margaret is like a ghost wandering about the Palace, looking for her happy past. And Juana . . . But do not let us talk of her. Then there is my frustrated Admiral with his convicts. I fear too there will be great trouble in Naples. Is there no end to our afflictions?"

"No end to our afflictions, and no end to our joys," said Beatriz promptly. "You will soon be holding your grandchild in your arms, my Queen. And when you do so you will forget all that has gone before. Isabella's son will mean as much to you as Juan's would have done."

"You are my comforter, Beatriz, as you ever were. I trust we can spend more time together before we must part."

THE BIRTH OF MIGUEL

TOLEDO LAY before them. Neither Isabella nor Ferdinand, riding at the head of the cavalcade, could help feeling pride in this city. There it stood perched on a lofty granite plateau which from this distance looked as though it had been moulded to the shape of a horseshoe among the mountains above the Tagus. A perfect fortress city, for it could only be reached on the north side by way of the plain of Castile. At every other point the steep rock would prevent entry.

There was little that was Spanish in its architecture, for the Moors seemed to have left their mark on every tower, on every street.

But Isabella was not concerned with her city of Toledo; her thoughts were of the meeting which would shortly take place.

I shall be happy, she told herself, when I see Isabella and assure myself that this pregnancy has not weakened her.

"You grow impatient," Ferdinand whispered, a smile on his lips.

"And you too?"

He nodded. He was impatient for the birth of the child. If it were a son, the unhappy deaths of Juan and his offspring would be of little significance. The people would be glad to accept the son of Isabella and Emanuel as the heir.

"If it is a boy," he said, "he must stay with us in Spain."

"Perhaps," ventured Isabella, "our daughter should stay with us also."

"What! You would separate husband and wife!"

"I see," said Isabella, "that you are thinking there should be more children; and how could Isabella and Emanuel beget children if they were not together!"

"That is true," replied Ferdinand. His eyes strayed to those three girls in the party—Margaret, Maria and Catalina. If his daughters had but been boys. . . . But never mind, if Isabella had a male heir, this would be some solution of their troubles.

They were entering the town. How could she ever do so, Isabella asked herself, without remembering that it was the birthplace of Juana? That memorable event had occurred on a November day when the city looked different from the way it did this day in springtime. When she had first heard the cry of her little daughter she had not guessed what anxieties were to come because of her. Perhaps it would have been better if the child, to which she had given birth here in Toledo in the year 1479, had been stillborn as poor Margaret's child had been. She felt an impulse to call Margaret to her and tell her of this. How foolish of her! Her grief was nowadays often weakening her sense of propriety.

They were at the gates of the city and the Toledans were coming out of their homes to welcome them. Here were the goldsmiths and silversmiths, the blacksmiths, the weavers and embroiderers, the armourers and the curriers, all members of the guilds of this city which was one of the most prosperous in Spain.

Thus it had been at that time when she and Ferdinand had come here to inspect the work on San Juan de los Reyes which they had given to the city. She remembered well the day they had seen the chains of the captives whom they had liberated when they conquered Malaga. These chains had been hung outside the walls of the church for significant decoration; they rested there today and they should remain there for ever—a reminder to the people that their Sovereigns had freed Spain from Moorish domination.

They would go to the church, or perhaps that of Santa Maria la Blanca, and give thanks for the safe arrival of the King and Queen of Portugal.

She would be happy among those horseshoe arches, among those graceful arabesques; there she would ask to be purged of all resentment against the sorrows of the last year. She would be cleansed of self-pity, and ready for the miracle of birth, the recompense which was to be the son her dearest Isabella would give to her and Spain.

It was meet that the Archbishop of Toledo should be in the city to greet them—gaunt emaciated Ximenes de Cisneros, his robes of state hanging uneasily on his spare figure.

Isabella felt a lifting of her spirits as she greeted him. She would tell her old confessor of her weakness; she would listen to his astringent comments; he would scorn her mother-love as unworthy of the Queen; he would deplore her weakness in questioning the will of God.

Ferdinand's greeting of the Archbishop was cool. He could never look at him without remembering that the office with all its pomp and grandeur might have gone to his son.

"It does me good to see my Archbishop," murmured Isabella graciously.

Ximenes bowed before her, but even his bow had an arrogance. He set the Church above the State.

Ximenes rode beside the Queen through the streets of Toledo.

* * *

With what great joy the Queen embraced her daughter Isabella.

This was when they were alone after the ceremonial greeting which had been watched by thousands. Then they had done all that was required of them, this mother and daughter, bowing graciously, kissing hands, as though they were not yearning to embrace and ask a thousand questions.

The Queen would not allow herself to look too closely at her daughter; she was afraid that she might see that which had made her anxious and betray her anxiety.

But now they were alone and the Queen had dismissed all her attendants and those of her daughter, for she told herself they must have this short time together.

"My dearest," cried the Queen, "let me look at you. Why, you are a little pale. And how is your health? Tell me exactly when the little one is expected."

"In August, Mother."

"Well, that is not long to wait. You have not told me how you are."

"I feel a little tired, and rather listless."

"It is natural."

"I wonder."

"What do you mean? You wonder! A pregnant woman has a child to carry. Naturally she does not feel as other women do."

"I have seen some women seem perfectly healthy in pregnancy."

"Nonsense. It differs from woman to woman and from birth to birth. I know. Remember I have had five children of my own."

"Then perhaps this tiredness is nothing."

"And your cough?"

"It is no worse, Mother."

"You think I am foolish with all my questions?"

"Mother, it is good to hear those questions." Isabella suddenly flung herself into her mother's arms and, to the Queen's dismay, she saw tears on her daughter's cheeks.

"Emanuel is good to you?"

"No husband could be better."

"I noticed his tenderness towards you. It pleased me."

"He does everything to please me."

"Then why these tears?"

"Perhaps . . . I am frightened."

"Frightened of childbirth! It is natural. The first time can be alarming. But it is the task of all women, you know. A queen's task as well as a peasant's. Nay, more so. It is more important for a Queen to bear children than for a peasant to do so."

"Mother, there are times when I wish I were a peasant."

"What nonsense you talk."

Isabella realized then that there were matters she could not discuss even with her mother. She could not depress her by telling her that she had a strange foreboding of evil.

She wanted to cry out: Our House is cursed. The persecuted Jews have cursed us. I feel their curses all about me.

Her mother would be shocked at such childishness.

But is it childishness? Isabella asked herself. In the night I feel certain that this evil is all about me. And Emanuel feels it too.

How could that be? Such thoughts were foolish superstition.

She fervently wished that she had not to face the ordeal of childbirth.

* * *

How tiring it was to stand before the Cortes, to hear them proclaim her the heiress of Castile.

These worthy citizens were pleased with her, because none who looked at her could be in any doubt of her pregnancy. They were all hoping for a boy. But if she did not give birth to a boy still the child she carried would, in the eyes of the Toledans, be the heir of Spain.

She listened to their loyal shouts and smiled her thanks. How glad she was that she had been brought up to hide her feelings.

After the ceremony with the Cortes, she must be carried through the streets to show herself to the people. Then she was received in the Cathedral and blessed by the Archbishop.

The atmosphere inside the massive Gothic building seemed overpowering. She stared at the treasures which hung on the walls and thought of the rich citizens of Toledo who had reason to be grateful to her mother for restoring order throughout Spain where once there had been anarchy. In this town lived the finest goldsmiths and silversmiths in the world; and the results of their labours were here in the cathedral for all to see.

She looked at the stern face of Ximenes and, as she studied the rich robes of his office, the brocade and damask studded with precious jewels, she thought of the hair shirt which she knew would be worn beneath those fine garments, and shivered.

She tried to pray then to the Virgin, the patron saint of Toledo, and she found that she could only repeat: "Help me, Holy Mother. Help me."

When they had returned to the Palace Emanuel said she must rest; the ceremony had tired her.

"There are too many ceremonies," he said.

"I do not believe it is the ceremony which tires me, Emanuel," she said. "I think I should be equally tired if I lay on my bed all the day. Perhaps I am not really tired."

"What then, my dearest?"

She looked at him frankly and answered: "I am afraid."

"Afraid! But, my love, you shall have the very best attention in Spain."

"Do you think that will avail me anything?"

"But indeed I do. How I long for September! Then you will be delighting in your child. You will laugh at these fears . . . if you remember them."

"Emanuel, I do not think I shall be here in September."

"But, my darling, what is it you are saying. . .?"

"Dear Emanuel, I know you love me. I know you will be unhappy if I die. But it is better for you to be prepared."

"Prepared! I am prepared for birth, not for death."

"But if death should come . . ."

"You are overwrought."

"I am fatigued, but I think at such times I see the future more clearly. I have a very strong feeling that I shall not get well after the child is born. It is our punishment, Emanuel. For me death, for you bereavement. Why do you look so shocked? It is a small payment for the misery we shall bring to thousands."

Emanuel threw himself down by the bed. "Isabella, you must not talk so. You must not."

She stroked his hair with her thin white hand.

"No," she said, "I must not. But I had to warn you of this feeling I have. It is so strong. Well, I have done so. Now let us forget it. I shall pray that my child will be a boy. That I think will make you very happy."

"And you will be happy too."

She only smiled at him. Then she said quickly: "Toledo is a beautiful town, is it not? I think my father loves it. It is so prosperous. It is so Moorish. There is everything here to remind my parents of the reconquest; there are more than the chains from Malaga on the walls of San Juan de los Reyes. But my mother, while she exults in the prosperity and beauty of Toledo, feels a certain sadness."

"There must be no sadness," said Emanuel.

"But there must always be sadness, it seems, sadness to mingle with pride, with laughter, with joy. Is it not beautiful here? I love to watch the Tagus dashing against the stones far below. Where in Spain is there such a fertile *vega* as that around Toledo? The fruit is so luscious here, the corn so plentiful. But did you notice how the flies pestered us as we came in? I saw the Rock too. The Rock of Toledo from which criminals are hurled down . . . down into the ravine. So much beauty and so much sorrow. That is what my mother feels when she rides into Toledo. In this rich and lovely city my sister Juana was born."

"That should make your mother love it all the more."

Isabella took her husband's hand in hers and cried out: "Emanuel, let there be complete trust between us. Let us not pretend to one another. Can you not see it? It is like the writing on the wall. I see it clearly. As I come nearer and nearer to my confinement I seem to acquire a new sensitivity. I feel I am not entirely of this world but have not yet reached the next. Therefore I sometimes see what is hidden from most human eyes."

"Isabella, you must be calm, my dearest."

"I am calm, Emanuel. But I distress you. I do not want my passing to be the shock to you that my brother's death was to my mother. Emanuel, my dear husband, it is always better to be prepared. Shall I tell you what is in my mind, or shall I pretend that I am a woman who looks into the future and sees her child playing beside her? Shall I lie to you, Emanuel?"

He kissed her hands. "There must be truth between us."

"That is what I thought. So I would tell you. Emanuel, my House has brought greatness to Spain, great prosperity and great sorrow. Is it never possible to have one without the other? On our journey to Toledo we passed through a town where, in the Plaza Mayor, I saw the ashes and I smelt the fires which had recently burned there. It was human flesh which burned, Emanuel."

"Those who died were condemned by the Holy Office."

"I know. They were heretics. They had denied their faith. But they have hearts in which to harbour hatred, lips with which to curse. They would curse our House, Emanuel, even as those who were driven from Spain would curse us. And their curses have not gone unheeded."

"Should we suffer for pleasing God and all the saints?"

"I do not understand, Emanuel; and I am too tired to try to. We are told that this is a Christian country. It is our great desire to bring our people to the Christian faith. We do it by persuasion. We do it by force. It is God's work. But what of the devil?"

"These are strange thoughts, Isabella."

"They come unbidden. See what has happened to us. My parents had five children—four daughters and one son. Their son and heir died suddenly, and his heir was stillborn. My sister Juana is strange, so wild that I have heard it whispered that she is half-way to madness. Already she has caused trouble to our parents by allowing herself to be proclaimed Princess of Castile. You see, Emanuel, it is like a pattern, an evil pattern built up by curses."

"You are distraught, Isabella."

"No. I think I see clearly . . . more clearly than the rest of you. I am to have a child. Child-bearing can be dangerous. I am the daughter of a cursed House. I wonder what will happen next."

"This is a morbid fancy due to your condition."

"Is it, Emanuel? Oh, tell me it is. Tell me that I can be happy. Juan caught a fever, did he not? It might have happened to anybody. And the child was stillborn because of Margaret's grief. Juana is not mad, is she? She is merely high-spirited, and she has fallen completely under the spell of that handsome rogue who is her husband. Is that not natural? And I . . . I was never very strong, so I have morbid fancies. . . . It is merely because of my condition."

"That is so, Isabella. Of course that is so. Now there will be no more morbidity. Now you will rest."

"I will sleep if you will sit beside me and hold my hand, Emanuel. Then I shall feel at peace."

"I shall remain with you, but you must rest. You have forgotten that we have to start on our travels tomorrow."

"Now we must go to Saragossa. The Cortes there must proclaim me the Heiress as the Cortes here at Toledo have done."

"That is right. Now rest."

She closed her eyes, and Emanuel stroked back the hair from her hot forehead.

He was worried. He did not like this talk of premonitions. He had an idea that the ceremony in Saragossa would not be such a pleasant one as that of Toledo. Castile was ready to accept a woman as heir to the crown. But Saragossa, the capital of Aragon, did not recognize the right of women to rule.

He did not mention this. Let her rest. They would overcome their troubles the better by taking them singly.

* * *

Into Saragossa came Isabella, Princess of Castile, with Emanuel her husband.

The people watched them with calm calculating gaze. This was the eldest daughter and heiress of their own Ferdinand, but she was a woman, and the Aragonese did not recognize the right of women to reign in Aragon. Let the Castilians make their own laws; they would never be accepted as the laws of Aragon. The Aragonese were a determined people; they were ready to fight for what they considered to be their rights.

So as Isabella rode into their city they were silent.

How different, thought Isabella, from the welcome they had received in Toledo. She did not like this city of bell turrets and sullen people. She had felt the vague resentment as soon as she passed into Aragon; she had been nervous as she rode along the banks of the Ebro past those caves which seemed to have been formed in this part of the country among the sierras as well as along the banks of the river. The yellow water of the Ebro was turbulent; and the very houses seemed too much like fortresses, reminding her that here was a people who would be determined to demand and fight for its dues.

On her arrival in this faintly hostile city she went to pray to the statue of the Virgin which, it was said, had been carved by the angels fourteen hundred years before. Precious jewels glittered in her cloak and crown which seemed to smother her; and it occurred to Isabella that she must have looked very different when, as the legend had it, she appeared to St. James all those years ago.

From the Virgin she went to the Cathedral close by, and there she prayed anew for strength to bear whatever lay before her.

The people watched her and whispered together.

"The crown of Aragon was promised to the *male* heirs of Ferdinand."

"And this is but a woman."

"She is our Ferdinand's daughter nevertheless, and he has no legitimate sons."

"But the crown should go to the next male heir."

"Castile and Aragon are as one now that Ferdinand and Isabella rule them."

There was going to be resistance in Aragon to the female succession. Isabella of Castile had remained Queen in her own right, but it was well known that she had greater power than Ferdinand. In the eyes of the Aragonese, it was their Ferdinand who should have ruled Spain with Isabella merely as his consort.

"Nay," they said, "we'll not have women on the throne of Spain. Aragon will support the male heir."

"But wait a moment . . . the Princess is pregnant, is she not? If she were to have a son . . ."

"Ah, that would be a different matter. That would offend

none. The Aragonese crown goes to the male descendants of Ferdinand, and his grandson would be the rightful heir."

"Then, we must wait until the birth. That's the simple answer."

It *was* the simple answer, and the Cortes confirmed it. They would not give their allegiance to Isabella of Portugal because she was a woman; but if she bore a son, then they would accept that son as the heir to the crown of Aragon and all Spain.

It was a wearying occasion for Isabella.

She had been alarmed by the hostile looks of the members of the Cortes. She had disliked their arrogant manner of implying that unless she produced a son they would have none of her.

She lay on her bed while her women soothed her; and when Emanuel came to her they hurried away and left them together.

"I feel a great responsibility rests upon me," she said. "I almost wish I were a humble woman waiting the birth of her child."

* * *

The Queen faced Ferdinand in anger.

"How dare they!" she demanded. "In every town of Castile our daughter has been received with honours. But in Saragossa, the capital of Aragon, she is submitted to insult."

Ferdinand could scarcely suppress a wry smile. There had been so many occasions when he had been forced to take second place, when he had been reminded that Aragon was of secondary importance to Castile and that the Queen of Castile was therefore senior to the King of Aragon.

"They but state their rights," he answered.

"Their rights—to reject our daughter!"

"We know well that Aragon accepts only the male line as heirs to the crown."

A faint smile played about his lips. He was reminding her that in Aragon the King was looked upon as the ruler and the Queen as his consort.

Isabella was not concerned with his private feelings. She thought only of the humiliation to her daughter.

"I picture them," she said, "quizzing her as though she were some fishwife. How far advanced in pregnancy is she? She will give birth in August. Then we will wait until August and, if she gives birth to a male child, we will accept that child as heir to the throne. I tell you, our daughter Isabella, being our eldest, is our heir."

"They will not accept her, because they will not accept a woman."

"They have accepted me."

"As my wife," Ferdinand reminded her.

"Rather than endure this insolence of the Saragossa Cortes I would subdue them by sending an armed force to deal with them. I would force them to accept our Isabella as the heir of Spain."

"You cannot mean that."

"But I do," insisted Isabella.

Ferdinand left her and returned shortly with a statesman whose integrity he knew Isabella trusted. This was Antonio de Fonesca, a brother of the Bishop who bore the same name; this man Ferdinand had once sent as envoy to Charles VIII of France, and the bold conduct of Fonesca had so impressed both the Sovereigns that they often consulted him with confidence and respect.

"The Queen's Highness is incensed by the behaviour of the Cortes at Saragossa," said Ferdinand. "She is thinking of sending soldiers to subdue them over this matter of accepting our daughter as heir to the throne."

"Would Your Highness care to hear my opinion?" asked Fonesca of the Queen.

Isabella told him that she would.

"Then, Highness, I would say that the Aragonese have only acted as good and loyal subjects. You must excuse them if they move with caution in an affair which they find difficult to justify by precedent in their history."

Ferdinand was watching his wife closely. He knew that her love of justice would always overcome every other emotion.

She was silent, considering the statesman's remarks.

Then she said: "I see that you are right. There is nothing to be done but hope—and pray—that my grandchild will be a boy."

* * *

Isabella, Queen of Portugal, lay on her bed. Her pains had started and she knew that her time had come.

There was a cold sweat on her brow and she was unconscious of all the people who stood about her bed. She was praying: "A son. Let it be a son."

If she produced a healthy son she would begin to forget this legend of a curse which had grown up in her mind. A son could make so much difference to her family and her country.

The little boy would be heir not only to the crown of Spain but to that of Portugal. The countries would be united; the hostile people of Saragossa would be satisfied; and she and Emanuel would be the proudest parents in the world.

Why should it not be so? Could her family go on receiving blow after blow? They had had their share of tragedy. Let this be different.

"A boy," she murmured, "a healthy boy to make the sullen people of Saragossa cheer, to unite Spain and Portugal." What an important little person this was who was now so impatient to be born!

The pains were coming regularly now. If she did not feel so weak she could have borne them more easily. She lay moaning while the women crowded about her. She drifted from consciousness into unconsciousness and back again.

The pain still persisted; it was more violent now.

She tried not to think of it; she tried to pray, to ask forgiveness of her sins, but her lips continued to form the words: "A boy. Let it be a boy."

* * *

There were voices in the bedchamber.

"A boy! A bonny boy!"

"Is it indeed so?"

"No mistake!"

"Ah, this is a happy day."

Isabella, lying on her bed, heard the cry of a child. She lay listening to the voices, too exhausted to move.

Someone was standing by her bed. Someone else knelt and was taking her hand and kissing it. Emanuel was standing, and it was her mother who knelt.

"Emanuel," she whispered. "Mother . . ."

"My dearest . . ." began Emanuel.

But her mother cried out in a voice loud with triumph: "It is over, my darling. The best possible news for you. You have given birth to a fine baby boy."

Isabella smiled. "Then everyone is happy."

Emanuel was bending over her, his eyes anxious. "Including you?" he said.

"But yes."

His eyes were faintly teasing: No more talk of curses, they were telling her. You see, all your premonitions were wrong. The ordeal is over and you have a beautiful son. "Can you hear the bells ringing?" her mother asked the young Queen.

"I . . . I am not sure."

"All over Spain the bells shall ring. Everyone will be rejoicing. They shall all know that their Sovereigns have a grandson, a male heir, at last."

"Then I am happy."

"We will leave her to rest," said the Queen.

Emanuel nodded. "She is exhausted—no wonder."

"But first . . ." whispered Isabella.

"I understand," laughed her mother. She stood up and called to the nurse.

She took the baby from her and placed it in its mother's arms.

* * *

Ferdinand said: "He shall be called Miguel, after the saint on whose day he was born."

"God bless our little Miguel," answered the Queen. "He's a lively little fellow, but I wish his mother did not look so exhausted."

Ferdinand bent over the cradle, exulting in the infant; he found it hard to take his hands from the child who meant so much to him.

"We must have a triumphant pilgrimage as soon as Isabella is well enough to leave her bed," went on Ferdinand. "The people will want to see their heir. We should do this without delay."

Isabella agreed as to the desirability of this, but it should not be, she assured herself, until Miguel's mother had recovered from her ordeal.

One of the women of the bedchamber was coming quickly towards them.

"Your Highnesses, Her Highness of Portugal . . ."

"Yes?" said Isabella sharply.

"She seems to find breathing difficult. Her condition is changing . . ."

Isabella did not wait for more. With Ferdinand following she hurried to her daughter's bedside.

Emanuel was already there.

The sight of her daughter's wan face, her blue-encircled eyes, her fight for her breath, made Isabella's heart turn over with fear.

"My darling child," she cried, and there was a note of anguish in her voice which was a piteous appeal.

"Mother . . ."

"It is I, my darling. Mother is with you."

"I feel so strange."

"You are tired, my love. You have given birth to a beautiful boy. No wonder you are exhausted."

Isabella tried to smile.

"I . . . cannot . . . breathe," she gasped.

"Where are the physicians?" demanded Ferdinand.

Emanuel shook his head as though to imply they had admitted their ignorance. There was nothing they could do.

Ferdinand walked to a corner of the room, and the doctors followed him.

"What is wrong with her?"

"It is a malaise which sometimes follows childbirth."

"Then what is to be done?"

"Highness, it must take its course."

"But this is . . ."

The doctors did not answer. They dared not tell the King that in their opinion the Queen of Portugal was on her death-bed.

Ferdinand stood wretchedly looking at the group round the bed. He was afraid to join them. It can't happen, he told himself. Isabella, his wife, could never endure this in addition to all she had suffered. This would be too much.

Isabella's eyes seemed to rest on her mother.

"Do we disturb you here, my darling?" asked the elder Isabella.

"No, Mother. You . . . never disturb me. I am too tired to talk, but . . . I want you here. You too, Emanuel."

"You are going to stay with us for months . . . you and Emanuel and little Miguel. We are going to show the baby to the people. They will love their little heir. This is a happy day, my daughter."

"Yes . . . a happy day."

Emanuel was looking appealingly at his mother-in-law as though imploring her to tell him that his wife would recover.

"Mother," said the sick woman, "and Emanuel . . . come near to me."

They sat on the bed and each held a hand.

"Now," she said, "I am happy. I am . . . going, I think."

"No!" cried Emanuel.

But the younger Isabella saw the anguish in the eyes of the elder and she knew; they both knew.

Neither spoke, but they looked at each other and the great love they bore for one another was in their eyes.

"I . . . I gave you the boy," whispered Isabella.

"And you are going to get well," insisted Emanuel.

But the two Isabellas did not answer him, because they knew that a lie could give them no comfort.

"I am so tired," murmured the Queen of Portugal. "I . . . will go now. Goodbye."

The Queen of Spain signed for the priests to come to her daughter's bedside. She knew that the moment had come for the last rites.

She listened to their words; she saw her daughter's attempts to repeat the necessary prayers; and she thought: This is not true. I am dreaming. It cannot be true. Not Juan *and* Isabella. Not both. That would be too cruel.

But she knew it was true.

Isabella was growing weaker with every moment; and only an hour after she had given them little Miguel, she was dead.

THE COURT AT GRANADA

THE BELLS were tolling for the death of the Queen of Portugal. Throughout Spain the people were beginning to ask themselves: "What blight is this on our royal House?"

The Queen lay sick with grief in her darkened bedchamber. It was the first time any of her people had known her to succumb to misery.

About the Palace people moved in their garments of sackcloth, which had taken the place of white serge for mourning at the time of Juan's death. What next? they asked themselves. The little Miguel was not the healthy baby they had hoped he might be. He was fretful; perhaps he was crying for his mother who had died that he might come into the world.

Catalina sat with Maria and Margaret; they were sewing shirts for the poor; and, thought Margaret, it was almost as if they hoped that by this good deed they might avert further disaster, as though they might placate that Providence which seemed determined to chastise them.

The rough material hurt Margaret's hands. She recalled the gaiety of Flanders and she knew that there would never be any happiness for her in Spain.

She looked at little Catalina, her head bent over her work. Catalina suffered more deeply than Maria would ever suffer. The poor child was now thinking of her mother's grief; she was longing to be with her and comfort her.

"It will pass," said Margaret. "People cannot go on grieving for ever."

"Do you believe that?" asked Catalina.

"I know it; I have proved it."

"You mean you no longer mourn Juan and your baby?"

"I shall mourn them for the rest of my life, but at first I mourned every waking hour. Now there are times when I forget them for a while. It is inevitable. Life is like that. So it will be with your mother. She will smile again."

"There are so many disasters," murmured Catalina.

Maria lifted her head from her work. "You will find that we have many good things happening all together later on. That is how life goes on."

"She is right," said Margaret.

Catalina turned to her sewing but she did not see the coarse material; she was thinking of herself as a wife and mother. The joys of motherhood might after all be worth all that she had to suffer to achieve it. Perhaps she would have a child—a daughter who would love her as she loved her mother.

They sat sewing in silence, and at length Margaret rose and left them.

In her apartments she found two of her Flemish attendants staring gloomily out of the window.

They started up as Margaret came in, but she noticed that the expressions on their faces did not change.

"I know," said Margaret. "You are weary of Spain."

"Ugh!" cried the younger of the women. "All these dreary sierras, these dismal plains . . . and worst of all these dismal people!"

"Much has happened to make them dismal."

"They were born dismal, Your Highness. They seem afraid to laugh or dance as people were meant to. They cling too firmly to their dignity."

"If we went home . . ." began Margaret.

The two women's faces were alight with pleasure suddenly. Margaret caught at that pleasure. She told herself then: There will never be happiness for me here. Only if I leave Spain can I begin to forget.

"If we went home," she repeated, "that might be the best thing we could do."

* * *

Ferdinand stood by his wife's bedside looking down at her.

"You must rouse yourself, Isabella," he said. "The people are getting restive."

Isabella looked at him, her eyes blank with misery.

"A ridiculous legend is being spread throughout the land. I hear it is said that we are cursed, and that God has turned His face away from us."

"I was beginning to ask myself if that were so," whispered the Queen.

She raised herself, and Ferdinand was shocked to see the change in her. Isabella had aged by at least ten years. Ferdinand asked himself in that moment whether the next blow his family would have to suffer would be the death of the Queen herself.

"My son," she went on, "and now my daughter. Oh, God in Heaven, how can You so forget me?"

"Hush! You are not yourself. I have never before seen you thus."

"You have never before seen me smitten by such sorrow."

Ferdinand beat this right fist into the palm of his left hand.

"We must not allow these foolish stories to persist. We are inviting disaster if we do. Isabella, we must not sit and mourn; we must not brood on our losses. I do not trust the new French King. I think I preferred Charles VIII to this Louis XII. He is a wily fellow and he is already making treaties with the Italians—we know well to what purpose. The Pope is sly. I do not trust the Borgia. Alexander VI is more statesman than Pope, and who can guess what tricks he will be up to? Isabella, we are Sovereigns first, parents second."

"You speak truth," answered Isabella sadly. "But I must have a little time in which to bury my dead."

Ferdinand made an impatient gesture. "Maximilian, who might have helped to halt these French ambitions, is now engaged in war against the Swiss, and Louis has secured our neutrality by means of the new treaty of Marcoussis. But I don't trust Louis. We must be watchful."

"You are right, of course."

"We must keep a watchful eye on Louis, on Alexander, on Maximilian, as well as on our own son-in-law Philip and our daughter Juana, who seem to have ranged themselves against us. Yes, we must be watchful. But most important is it that all should be well in our own dominions. We cannot have our subjects telling each other that our House is cursed. I have heard it whispered that Miguel is a weakling, that he will not live more than a few months, that it is a miracle that he was not born as our other grandchild, poor Juan's child. These rumours must be stopped."

"We must stop them with all speed."

"Ah then, my Queen, we are in agreement. As soon as you are ready to leave your bed, Miguel must be presented to the Cortes of Saragossa as the heir of Spain. And this ceremony must not be long delayed."

"It shall not be long delayed," Isabella assured him, and he was delighted to see the old determination in her face. He knew he could trust his Isabella. No matter what joy was hers, or what sorrow, she would never forget that she was the Queen.

* * *

The news of the Queen of Portugal's death was brought to Tomás de Torquemada in the monastery of Avila.

He lay on his pallet, unable to move, so crippled was he by the gout.

"Such trials are sent for our own good," he murmured to his sub-prior. "I trust the Sovereigns did not forget this."

"The news is, Excellency, that the Queen is mightily stricken and has had to take to her bed."

"I deplore her weakness and it surprises me," said Torquemada. "Her great sin lies in her vulnerability where her family is concerned. It is high time the youngest was sent to England. And so would she be, but for the Queen's constant excuses. Learn from her faults, my friend. See how even a good woman can fail in her duty when she allows her emotions regarding her children to come between her and God."

"It is so, Excellency. But all have not your strength."

Torquemada dismissed the man.

It was true. Few men on Earth possessed the strength of will to discipline themselves as he had done. But he had great hopes of Ximenes de Cisneros. There was one who, it would seem, might be worthy to tread in his, Torquemada's footsteps.

"If I were but a younger man," sighed Torquemada. "If I might throw off this accursed sickness, this feebleness of my body! My mind is as clear as it ever was. Then I would still rule Spain."

But when the body failed a man, however great he was, his end was near. Even Torquemada could not subdue his flesh so completely that he could ignore it.

He lay back complacently. It was possible that his death would probably be the next one which would be talked of in the towns and villages of Spain. There was death in the air.

But people were constantly dying. He himself had fed thousands of them to the flames. He had done right, he assured himself. It was only in his helplessness that he was afraid.

"Not," he said aloud, "of the pain I might suffer, not of death—for what fear should I have of facing my Maker?—but of the loss to the world which my passing must mean.

"Oh, Holy Mother of God," he prayed, "give this man Ximenes the power to take my place. Give Ximenes strength to guide the Sovereigns as I have done. Then I shall die happy."

The faggots in the *quemaderos* all over the country were well alight. In the dungeons of the Inquisition men, women and children awaited trial through ordeal. In the gloomy chambers of the damned the torturers were busy.

"I trust, O Lord," murmured Torquemada, "that I have done my work well and shall find favour in Your sight. I trust You have noted the number of souls I have brought to You, the numbers I have saved, as well as those I have sent from this world to hell by means of the fiery death. Remember, oh Lord, the zeal of Your servant, Tomás de Torquemada. Remember his love of the Faith."

When he thought over his past life he had no qualms about

death. He was certain that he would be received into Heaven with great glory.

His sub-prior came to him, as he lay there, with news from Rome.

He read the despatch, and his anger burned so fiercely that it set his swollen limbs throbbing.

He and Alexander were two men who were born to be enemies. The Borgia had schemed to become Pope not through love of the Faith but because it was the highest office in the Church. His greatest desire was to shower honours on his sons and daughter, whom, as a man of the Church, he had no right to have begotten. This Borgia, it seemed, could be a merry man, a flouter of conventions. There were evil rumours about his incestuous relationship with his own daughter, Lucrezia, and it was well known that he exercised nepotism and that his sons, Cesare and Giovanni, swaggered through the towns of Italy boasting of their relationship to the Holy Father.

What could a man such as Torquemada—whose life had been spent in subduing the flesh—have in common with such as Roderigo Borgia, Pope Alexander VI? Very little.

Alexander knew this and, because he was a mischievous man, he had continually obstructed Torquemada in his endeavours.

Torquemada remembered early conflicts.

As far back as four years ago he had received a letter from the Pope; he could remember the words clearly now.

Alexander cherished him in "the very bowels of affection for his great labours in raising the glory of the Faith". But Alexander was concerned because from the Vatican he considered the many tasks which Torquemada had taken upon himself, and he remembered the great age of Torquemada and he was not going to allow him to put too great a strain upon himself. Therefore he, Alexander, out of love for Torquemada, was going to appoint four assistants to be at his side in this mighty work of establishing and maintaining the Inquisition throughout Spain.

There could not have been a greater blow to his power. The new Inquisitors, appointed by the Pope, shared the power of Torquemada and the title Inquisitor General lost its significance.

There was no doubt that Alexander in the Vatican was the enemy of Torquemada in the monastery of Avila. It may have been that the Pope considered the Inquisitor General wielded too much power; but Torquemada suspected that the enmity between them grew from their differences—the desire of a man of great carnal appetites, which he made no effort to subdue, to denigrate one who had lived his life in the utmost abstention from all worldly pursuits.

And now, when Torquemada was near to death, Alexander had yet another snub to offer.

The Pope had held an *auto de fé* in the square before St. Peter's, and at this had appeared many of those Jews who had been expelled from Spain. If the Pope had wished to do the smallest honour to Torquemada he would have sent those Jews to the flames or inflicted some other severe punishment.

But Alexander was laughing down his nose at the monk of Avila. Sometimes Torquemada wondered whether he was laughing at the Church itself which he used so shamefully to his advantage.

Alexander had ordered that a service should be read in the square, and the one hundred and eighty Judaizers, and fugitives from Torquemada's wrath were dismissed. No penalties. No wearing of the *sanbenito*. No imprisonment. No confiscation of property.

Alexander dismissed them all to go about their business like good citizens of Rome.

Torquemada clenched his fists tightly together as he thought of it. It was a direct insult, not only to himself but to the Spanish Inquisition; and he believed that the Pope was fully aware of this and it was his main reason for acting as he had.

"And here I lie," he mused, "in this my seventy-eighth year of life, my body crippled, unable to protest."

His heart began to beat violently, shaking his spare frame. The walls of the cell seemed to close in upon him.

"My life's work is done," he whispered and sent for his sub-prior.

"I feel my end is near," he told the man. "Nay, do not look concerned. I have had a long life and in it I think I have served God well. I would not have you bury me with pomp. Put me to rest in the common burial ground among the friars of my monastery. There I would lie happiest."

The sub-prior said quickly: "You are old in years, Excellency, but your spirit is strong. There are years ahead of you."

"Leave me," Torquemada commanded; "I would make my peace with God."

He waved the man away, but he did not believe it was necessary to make his peace with God. He believed that there would be a place in Heaven for him as there had been on Earth.

He lay quietly on his pallet while the strength slowly ebbed from him.

He thought continually of his past life, and as the days went on his condition grew weaker.

It was known throughout the monastery that Torquemada was dying.

On the 16th of September, one month after the death of the Queen of Portugal, Torquemada opened his eyes and was not sure where he lay.

He dreamed he was ascending into Heaven to the sound of music—music which was composed of the cries of heretics as the flames licked their limbs, the murmurs of a band of exiles who trudged wearily, from the land which had been their home for centuries, to what grim horrors they could not know but only fear.

"All this in Thy name . . ." murmured Torquemada and, because he was too weak to control his feelings, a smile of assurance and satisfaction touched his lips.

The sub-prior came to him a little later and he knew that it was time for the last rites to be administered.

* * *

Isabella roused herself from her bed of sickness and grief. She had her duty to perform.

The little Prince Miguel must be shown to the citizens and accepted by the Cortes as heir to the throne. So the processions began.

The people of Saragossa, who had declined to accept his mother, assembled to greet little Miguel as their future King.

Ferdinand and Isabella swore that they would be his faithful guardians, and that before he was allowed to assume any rights as sovereign he should be made to swear to respect those liberties to which the proud people of Aragon were determined to cling.

"Long live the lawful heir and successor to the crown of Aragon!" cried the Saragossa Cortes.

This ceremony was repeated not only throughout Aragon and Castile but in Portugal, for this frail child would, if he came to the throne, unite those countries.

Isabella took her leave of the sorrowing Emanuel.

"Leave the child with me," she said. "You know how deeply affected I have been by the loss of my daughter. I have brought up many children. Give me this little one who will be our heir, that he may help to assuage my grief."

Emanuel was stricken with pity for his stoical mother-in-law. He knew that she was thinking it could not be long before her remaining daughters were taken from her. Moreover, his Spanish inheritance would be of greater importance to little Miguel than that which would come from his father.

"Take the child," he said. "Bring him up as you will. I trust he will never give you cause for anxiety."

Isabella held the child against her and, as she did so, she felt a stirring of that pleasure which only her own beloved family could give her.

It was true that the Lord took away, but He also gave.

She said: "I will take him to my city of Granada. There he shall have the greatest care that it is possible for any child to have. Thank you, Emanuel."

So Emanuel left the child with her, and Ferdinand was delighted that they would be in a position to supervise his up-bringing.

Isabella gently kissed the baby's face, and Ferdinand came to stand beside her.

If I could only be as he is, thought Isabella, and feel as he does that the death of our daughter Isabella was not such a great tragedy, since their child lives.

"Emanuel will need a new wife," Ferdinand mused.

"It will be a long time yet. He dearly loved our Isabella."

"Kings have little time for mourning," answered Ferdinand. "He said nothing of this matter to you?"

"Taking a new wife! Indeed he did not. I am sure the thought has not occurred to him."

"Nevertheless it has occurred to me," retorted Ferdinand. "A King in need of a wife. Have you forgotten that we have a daughter as yet not spoken for?"

Isabella gave him a startled look.

"Why should not our Maria be Queen of Portugal?" demanded Ferdinand. "Thus we should regain that which we have lost by the death of Isabella."

* * *

"Farewell," said Margaret. "It grieves me to leave you, but I know that I must go."

Catalina embraced her sister-in-law. "How I wish that you would stay with us."

"For how long?" asked Margaret. "My father will be making plans for a new marriage for me. It is better that I go."

"You have not been very happy here," said Maria quietly.

"It was not the fault of the King and Queen, nor of any of you. You have done everything possible to make me happy. Farewell, my sisters. I shall think of you often."

Catalina shivered. "How life changes!" she said. "How can we know where any of us will be this time next year . . . or even this time next month?"

Catalina was terrified every time envoys came from England. She knew that her mother was putting off the day when her youngest daughter would leave her home; but it could not be long delayed. Catalina was too fatalistic to believe that was possible.

"Farewell, farewell," said Margaret.

And that day she was on her way to the coast, to board the ship which would take her back to Flanders.

* * *

Isabella's great delight was her little grandson. He was too young as yet to accompany her on all her journeys throughout the country, so after his acceptance by the Cortes of Castile and Aragon, he was left with his nurses in the Alhambra at Granada. Isabella often discussed his future with Ferdinand, and it was her desire that as soon as he was old enough he should always be with them.

"He cannot learn his state duties too early," she said; but what she really meant was that she was not going to be separated from the child more than she could possibly help.

Ferdinand smiled indulgently. He was ready to pass over Isabella's little weaknesses as long as they did not interfere with his plans.

The Court was on its way to Seville, and naturally Isabella would call first at Granada to see her little Miguel.

Catalina, who was with the party, was delighted to note her mother's recovery from despair, and she herself thought as tenderly of Miguel as Isabella did. Miguel was the means of making the Queen happy again; therefore Catalina loved him dearly.

Leisurely the Court moved southwards, and with them travelled the Archbishop of Toledo.

Ximenes had been deeply affected by the death of Tomás de Torquemada. There was a man who had written his name large across a page of Spanish history. He had clearly in his heyday been the most important man in his country, for he had guided the King and Queen and in the days of his strength had had his will.

It was due to him that the Inquisition was now a power in the land and that there was not a man, woman or child who did not dread the knock on the door in the dead of night, the entry of the *alguazils* and the dungeons of torture.

That was well, thought Ximenes, for only through torture could man come to God. And for those who had denied God the greatest torture man could devise was not bad enough. If these people burned at the stake, it was but a foretaste of the punishment which God would give them. What were twenty minutes at the stake compared with an eternity in hell?

Riding south towards Granada, Ximenes was conscious of a great desire: To do, for Spain and the Faith, work which could be compared with that of Torquemada.

He thought of those who were in this retinue, and it seemed to him that the conduct of so many left much to be desired.

Ferdinand was ever reaching for material gain; Isabella's weakness was her children. Even now she had Catalina beside her. The girl was nearly fifteen years old and still she remained in Spain. She was marriageable, and the King of England grew impatient. But for her own gratification—and perhaps because the girl pleaded with her—Isabella kept her in Spain.

Ximenes thought grimly that her affection for the new heir, young Miguel, must approach almost idolatry. The Queen should keep a sharp curb on her affections. They overshadowed her devotion to God and duty.

Catalina had withdrawn herself as far as possible from the stern-faced Archbishop. She read his thoughts and they terrified her. She hoped he would not accompany them to Seville; she was sure that, if he did, he would do his utmost to persuade her mother to send her with all speed to England.

Granada, which some had called the most beautiful city in Spain, was before them. There it lay, a fairy-tale city against the background of the snow-tipped peaks of the Sierra Nevada. High above the town was the Alhambra, that Moorish palace, touched by a rosy glow, a miracle of architecture, strong as a fortress, yet so daintily and so delicately fashioned and carved, as Catalina knew.

There was a saying that God gives His chosen people the means to live in Granada; and Catalina could believe that was so.

She hoped that Granada would bring happiness to them all, that the Queen would be so delighted with her little grandson that she would forget to mourn, that there would be no news from England; and that, for the sunny days ahead, her life and that of her family would be as peacefully serene as this scene of snowy mountains, of rippling streams, the water of which sparkled like diamonds and was as clear as crystals.

She caught the eye of the Archbishop fixed upon her and felt a tremor of alarm.

She need not have worried. He was not thinking of her.

He was saying to himself: It is indeed our most beautiful city. It is not surprising that the Moors clung to it until the last.

But what a tragedy that so many of its inhabitants should be those who deny the true faith. What sin that we should allow these Moors to practise their pagan rites under that blue sky, in the most beautiful city in Spain.

It seemed to Ximenes that the ghost of Torquemada rode beside him. Torquemada could not rest while such blatant sin existed in this fair city of Spain.

Ximenes was certain, as he rode with the Court into Granada, that the mantle of Torquemada was being placed about his shoulders.

* * *

While Isabella was happy in the nursery of her grandson, Ximenes lost no time in examining the conditions which existed in Granada.

The two most influential men in the city were Iñigo Lopez de Mendoza, the Count of Tendilla, and Fray Fernando de Talavera, Archbishop of Granada; and one of Ximenes' first acts was to summon these men to his presence.

He surveyed them with a little impatience. They were, he believed, inclined to be complacent. They were delighted at the peaceful conditions prevailing in this city, which, they congratulated themselves, was in itself near the miraculous. This was a conquered city; a great part of its population consisted of Moors who followed their own faith; yet these Moors lived side by side with Christians and there was no strife between them.

Who would have thought, Ximenes demanded of himself, that this could possibly be a conquered city!

"I confess," he told his visitors, "that the conditions here in Granada give me some concern."

Tendilla showed his surprise. "I am sure, my lord Archbishop," he said, "that when you have seen more of the affairs in this city you will change your mind."

Tendilla, one of the illustrious Mendoza family, could not help but be conscious of the comparatively humble origins of the Archbishop of Toledo. Tendilla lived graciously and it disturbed him to have about him those who did not. Talavera, who had been a Hieronymite monk and whose piety was indisputable, was yet a man of impeccable manners. Tendilla considered Talavera something of a bigot but it seemed to him that such an attitude was essential in a man of the Church; and in his tolerance Tendilla had not found it difficult to overlook that in Talavera which did not fit in with his own views. They had worked well together since the conquest of Granada, and the city of Granada was a prosperous and happy city under their rule.

Both resented the tone of Ximenes, but they had to remember that as Archbishop of Toledo he held the highest post in Spain under the Sovereigns.

"I could not change my mind," went on Ximenes coldly, "while I see this city dominated by that which is heathen."

Tendilla put in: "We obey the rules of their Highnesses' agreement with Boabdil at the time of the reconquest. As Alcayde and Captain-General of the Kingdom of Granada it is my duty to see that this agreement is adhered to."

Ximenes shook his head. "I know well the terms of that agreement, and pity it is that it was ever made."

"Yet," said Talavera, "these conditions *were* made and the Sovereigns could not so dishonour themselves and Spain by not observing them."

"What conditions!" cried Ximenes scornfully. "The Moors to retain possession of their mosques with freedom to practise their heathen rites! What sort of a city is this over which to fly the flag of the Sovereigns?"

"Nevertheless these were the terms of surrender," Tendilla reminded him.

"Unmolested in their style of dress, in their manners and ancient usages; to speak their own language, to have the right to dispose of their own property! A fine treaty."

"Yet, my lord Archbishop, these were the terms Boabdil asked for surrender. Had we not accepted them there would have been months—perhaps years—of slaughter, and no doubt the destruction of much that is beautiful in Granada."

Ximenes turned accusingly to these two men. "You, Tendilla, are the Alcayde; you, Talavera, are the Archbishop. And you content yourselves with looking on at these practices which cannot but anger our God and are enough to make the saints weep. Are you surprised that we suffer the ill fortune we do? Our heir dead. His child stillborn. The Sovereigns' eldest daughter dead in childbirth. What next, I ask you? What next?"

"My lord Archbishop cannot suggest that these tragedies are the results of what happens here in Granada!" murmured Tendilla.

"I say," thundered Ximenes, "that we have witnessed the disfavour of God, and that it behoves us to look about and ask ourselves in what manner we are displeasing Him."

Talavera spoke then. "My lord, you do not realize what efforts we have made to convert these people to Christianity."

Ximenes turned to the Archbishop. It was from a man of the

Church that he might expect good sense, rather than from a soldier. Talavera had at one time been Prior of the Monastery of Santa Maria del Prado, not far from Valladolid; he had also been confessor to the Queen. He was a man of courage. Ximenes had heard that when Isabella's confessor had listened to the Queen's confession he had insisted on her kneeling while he sat, and when Isabella had protested Talavera had remarked that the confessional was God's tribunal and that, as he acted as God's minister, it was fitting that he should remain seated while the Queen knelt. Isabella had approved of such courage; so did Ximenes.

It was known also that this man, who had previously been the Bishop of Avila, refused to accept a larger income when he became Archbishop of Granada; he lived simply and spent a great deal of his income on charity.

This was all very well, thought Ximenes; but what good was it to appease the hunger of the poor, to give them sensuous warmth, when their souls were in peril? What had this dreamer done to bring the heathen Moor into the Christian fold?

"Tell me of these efforts," said Ximenes curtly.

"I have learned Arabic," said Talavera, "in order that I may understand these people and speak with them in their own tongue. I have commanded my clergy to do the same. Once we speak their language we can show them the great advantages of holding to the true Faith. I have had selections from the Gospels translated into Arabic."

"And what conversions have you to report?" demanded Ximenes.

"Ah," put in Tendilla, "this is an ancient people. They have their own literature, their own professions. My lord Archbishop, look at our Alhambra itself. Is it not a marvel of architecture? This is a symbol of the culture of these people."

"Culture!" cried Ximenes, his eyes suddenly blazing. "What culture could there be without Christianity? I see that in this Kingdom of Granada the Christian Faith is considered of little importance. That shall not continue, I tell you. That shall not continue."

Talavera looked distressed. Tendilla raised his eyebrows. He was annoyed, but only slightly so. He understood the ardour of people such as Ximenes. Here was another Torquemada. Torquemada had set up the Inquisition, and men such as Ximenes would keep the fires burning. Tendilla was irritated. He hated unpleasantness. His beloved Granada delighted him with its beauty and prosperity. His Moors were the most industrious people in Spain now that they had rid themselves of the Jews.

He wanted nothing to break the peaceful prosperity of his city.

He smiled. Let this fanatical monk rave. It was true he was Primate of Spain—what a pity that the office had not been given to a civilized nobleman—but Tendilla was very well aware of the agreement which Isabella and Ferdinand had made with Boabdil, and he believed that Isabella at least would honour her agreement.

Therefore he smiled without much concern while Ximenes ranted.

Granada was safe from the fury of the fanatic.

* * *

Isabella held the baby in her arms. The lightness of the little bundle worried her.

Some children are small, she comforted herself. I have had so much trouble that I look for it where it does not exist.

She questioned his nurses.

His little Highness was a good child, a contented child. He took his food and scarcely cried at all.

Isabella thought, Would it not be better if he kicked and cried lustily? Then she remembered her daughter Juana who had done these things.

I must not build up fears where they do not exist, she admonished herself.

There was his wet nurse—a lusty girl, her plump breasts bursting out of her bodice, smelling faintly of *olla podrida* in a manner which slightly offended the Queen's nostrils. But the girl was healthy and she had the affection which such girls did have for their foster children.

It was useless to question the girl. How does he suck? Greedily? Is he eager for his feed?

She would give the answers which she thought would best please the Queen, rather than what might be the truth.

Catalina begged to be allowed to hold the baby, and Isabella laid the child in her daughter's arms.

"Here, sit beside me. Hold our precious little Miguel tightly."

Isabella watched her daughter with the baby. Perhaps it would not be long before she held a child of her own in such a manner.

The thought made her uneasy. How could she bear to part with Catalina? And she would have to part with her soon. The King of England was indicating that he was growing impatient. He was asking for more concessions. Since the death of Juan and his child the bargaining position had not been so favourable for Spain. It was very likely that Margaret would be married soon, and her share of the Hapsburg inheritance was lost.

Ferdinand had said to her during their journey to Granada: "The English alliance is more important to us now than ever."

So it would not be long.

Ferdinand came into the nursery. He too took a delight in the child. Isabella, watching him peering into the small face, realized that he suffered from none of those fears which beset her.

"How like his father Miguel begins to grow," he said, beaming. "Ah, my daughter, I trust it will not be long before you hold a child of your own in your arms. A Prince of England, eh, a Prince who will one day be a King."

He had shattered the peace of the nursery for Catalina. It was no use being annoyed with him. He could never understand Catalina's fears as her mother could.

Ferdinand turned to Isabella: "Your Archbishop is in a fine mood," he said with an ironical smile. "He begs audience. I did not think you would wish to receive him in the nursery."

Isabella felt rather relieved to leave Catalina and Miguel, for poor Catalina's face was creased in her pitiable anxiety.

"I will receive the Archbishop now," she said. "Does he ask to see us both?"

"Both," echoed Ferdinand.

He held out his hand to Isabella and led her from the room.

In a small ante-chamber Ximenes was pacing up and down; he turned as the Sovereigns entered. He did not greet them with the homage etiquette demanded. Ferdinand noticed this and raised his eyebrows slightly in an expression which clearly said to Isabella: *Your* Archbishop—what manners he has!

"You have bad news, Archbishop?" asked Isabella.

"Your Highness, bad news indeed. Since I entered this city I have received shock after shock. Who could believe, as one walks these streets, that one was in a Christian land!"

"It is a prosperous and happy city," Isabella reminded him.

"If it is prosperous, it is the prosperity of the devil!" cried Ximenes. "Happy! You can call people happy—you a Christian—when they wallow in darkness!"

"They are an industrious people," Ferdinand put in, and he spoke coldly as he always did to Ximenes. "They bring great wealth to the place."

"They bring great wealth!" repeated Ximenes. "They worship in a heathen way. They pollute our country. How can we call Spain all-Christian when it harbours such people?"

"They have their own faith," said Isabella gently, "and we are doing our best to bring them to the true faith. My Archbishop of Granada has been telling me that he has learned Arabic and has had the catechism and part of the Gospels translated into Arabic. What more could we do?"

"I could think of much that we could do."

"What?" demanded Ferdinand.

"We could force them to baptism."

"You forget," Isabella put in quickly "that in the agreement we made with Boabdil these people were to continue in their own way of life."

"It was a monstrous agreement."

"I think," Ferdinand interrupted, "that it would be well if the men of the Church confined their attention to Church matters and left the governing of the country to its rulers."

"When an Archbishop is also Primate of Spain, matters of State are his concern," retorted Ximenes.

Ferdinand was astonished at the arrogance of this man, but he could see that Isabella immediately forgave him his insolence on the grounds that all he said was either for the good of the Church or State. She had often defended him to Ferdinand, by reminding him that Ximenes was one of the few men about them who did not seek personal advantage, and that he seemed brusque in his manners because he said what he meant, without thought of any damage this might do to himself.

But she was adamant on this matter of the Moors. She had given her word to Boabdil, and she intended to keep it.

She said in that cool, somewhat curt voice of hers which she reserved for such occasions: "The treaty we made with the Moors must stand. Let us hope that in time, under the guidance of our good Talavera, they will see the light. Now you will retire, my lord, for there are matters which the King and I must discuss, since shortly we must continue our journey."

Ximenes, his mind simmering with plans, which he had no intention of laying before the Sovereigns, retired.

"The monk over-reaches even his rank," said Ferdinand lightly. "Do you know, it would not surprise me if Master Ximenes became so arrogant that in time even you would be unable to endure him."

"Oh, he is a good man; he is the best to fill the position. We must perforce put up with his manners."

"I do not relish the thought of his company in Seville. The man irritates me with his hair shirt and his ostentatious saintliness."

Isabella sighed. "In time you will appreciate him . . . even as I do."

"Never," said Ferdinand, and his tone was harsh because he was thinking of young Alfonso and how grand he would have looked in the fine vestments of the Archbishop of Toledo.

Ferdinand was glad when they left for Seville and Ximenes did not accompany them.

THE FATE OF THE MOORS

XIMENES WAS excited. He looked almost human as he waited to receive his guests. He had planned this meeting so carefully and it was to be the first step in a mighty campaign. He had not asked the Sovereigns' permission to act as he did; he was very glad that they were on their way to Seville. They would be delighted when they saw the results of his work; they would also know that, well as he served them, he served God and the Faith better.

He had had some difficulty with those two old fools, Tendilla and Talavera. They had assured him that his proposed methods would not work. The Moors were courteous by nature; they would listen to what he had to say; they would not contradict his word that the most fortunate people in the world were those who called themselves Christians; but they would remain Mohammedans.

He must understand that these were not savages; they were not as little children to be taught a catechism which they could repeat parrot fashion.

"Not savages!" Ximenes had cried. "All those who are not Christians are savages."

He was not going to diverge from his plan in any way. He was the Primate of Spain and as such was in complete authority under the Sovereigns; as for the Sovereigns, they were on their way to Seville and none could appeal to them.

He ordered that bales of silk and a quantity of scarlet hats should be brought to him. He now studied these with a wry smile on his lips. They were the bait and he believed the expenditure on the articles would be well worth while.

When his guests arrived he received them graciously. They were *alfaquis* of Granada, the learned Moorish priests whose word was law to the Mussulmans of Granada. Once he had seduced these men from their faith, the simple people would be ready to follow their leaders.

The *alfaquis* bowed low. They knew that they were in the presence of the greatest Archbishop in Spain, and their eyes lighted when they saw the bales of rich silk and the scarlet hats which they greatly admired, for they guessed these were gifts.

"I am delighted that you should have accepted my invitation," said Ximenes, and his face showed none of the contempt that he felt for these people. "I wish to talk to you. I think it would be of great interest to us all if we compared our respective religions."

The *alfaquis* smiled and bowed again. And eventually they sat cross-legged around the chair of Ximenes while he talked to them of the Christian Faith and the joys of heaven which awaited those who embraced it; also of the torments of hell which were reserved for those who refused it. He spoke of baptism, a simple ceremony which enabled all those who partook of it to enter the Kingdom of Heaven.

He then took one of the bales and unfurled the crimson silk.

There was a murmur of admiration among his guests.

He wished to make presents, he told them, to all those who would undergo baptism.

Black eyes sparkled as they rested on the bales of coloured silks, and those delightful red hats were irresistible.

Several of the *alfaquis* agreed to be baptized, a ceremony which Ximenes was prepared to perform on the spot; and they went away with their silks and scarlet hats.

There was talk in the streets of Granada.

A great man had come among them. He gave rich presents, and to receive these presents all that was required was to take part in a strange little ceremony.

Each day little companies of Moors would present themselves before Ximenes, to receive baptism, a bale of silk and a scarlet hat.

Ximenes felt such delight that he had to curb it. It seemed sinful to be so happy. He was anxious that Talavera and Tendilla should not know what was happening, for he was sure they would endeavour to let the innocent Moors know what they were undertaking when they submitted to baptism.

What did it matter how they were brought into the Church, Ximenes asked himself, as long as they came?

So he continued with his baptisms and his presents. The costliness of the silk and hats was disturbing, but Ximenes had always been ready to dig deep into the coffers of Toledo for the sake of the Faith.

* * *

News of what was happening came to the ears of one of the most learned of the *alfaquis* in Granada; this was Zegri, who, quietly studious, had not known what was taking place in the city.

One of his fellows called on him wearing a magnificent red hat, and he said: "But you are extravagant. You have become rich, my friend."

"This is not all," he was told. "I have a silk robe, and both were presents from the great Archbishop who is now in Granada."

"Costly presents are often given that costlier presents may be received."

"Ah, but all I did to earn these was to take part in some little Christian game called baptism."

"Baptism! But that is the ceremony which is performed when one accepts the Christian Faith."

"Oh, I was a Christian for a day . . . and for this I received my silk and hat."

"What is this you say?" cried Zegri. "You cannot be a Christian for a day!"

"It is what the Archbishop told us. 'Be baptized,' he said, 'and these gifts are yours.' Our fellows are crowding to his palace each day. We play this little game and come away with our gifts."

"Allah preserve us!" cried Zegri. "Do you not know that once you have been baptized you are a Christian, and do you not know what these Christians do to those whom they call heretics?"

"What do they do?"

Zegri seized his robe as though he would rend it apart. He said: "Here in Granada we live in peace. In other parts of Spain, there is that which is called the Inquisition. Those who do not practise Christianity—and Christianity in a particular manner—are called heretics. They are tortured and burned at the stake."

His visitor had turned pale.

"It would seem," said Zegri impatiently, "that our countrymen have been lulled into stupidity by the beauty of the flowers that grow about our city, by the prosperity of our merchants, by the continued brilliance of our sunshine."

"But . . . they are going in their hundreds!"

"We must call a meeting at once without delay. Send out messages to all. Tell them that I have a stern warning to give. Bring here to me as many of the *alfaquis* as you can muster. I must stop this at once."

* * *

Ximenes waited for more visitors. They did not come. There were his bales of silk, his scarlet hats, but it seemed that now nobody wanted them.

Ximenes enraged sent for Talavera and Tendilla.

They came immediately. Tendilla had discovered what had been happening and was very angry. Talavera also knew, but he was less disturbed; as a Churchman he admired the zeal of Ximenes; never had he seen such rapid proselytism.

"Perhaps," said Ximenes, "you can tell me what is happening in this city."

"It would seem," replied Tendilla lightly, "that certain simple men have become Christians without understanding what this means."

"You sound regretful," accused Ximenes.

"Because," Tendilla answered, "these men have accepted baptism without understanding. They have accepted your gifts and in return they wished to give you what you asked—baptism into the Christian Faith for a bale of silk and a red hat. I should be glad to hear they had accepted our Faith without the bribe."

"Yet there are more conversions in this City since the Archbishop of Toledo came here," Talavera reminded him.

"I do not call this true conversion to Christianity," retorted Tendilla. "These simple souls have no knowledge of what they are undertaking."

"We need not discuss your views on this matter," Ximenes put in coldly. "For the last two days there have been no conversions. There must be a reason. These savages cannot have taken a dislike to bales of silk and scarlet hats."

"They have become wary of baptism," said Tendilla.

"You two go among them as though you were of the same race. You doubtless know the reason for this sudden absence. I command you to tell me."

Tendilla was silent, but Talavera, as an Archbishop himself, although of junior rank, answered his superior's command: "It is due to the warnings of Zegri."

"Zegri? Who is this man Zegri?"

Tendilla spoke then. "He is the leading *alfaquis*, and not such a simple fellow as some. He understands a little of what baptism into the Christian Faith means. He has heard what has been going on and has warned his fellow Moors that baptism demands more of men and women than the acceptance of gifts."

"I see," said Ximenes. "So it is this man Zegri. Thank you for your information."

When they had left him he sent for one of his servants, a man named Leon, and he said to him: "I wish you to take a message from me to the house of the *alfaquis*, Zegri."

* * *

Zegri stood before Ximenes, while Ximenes showed him two bales of silk. "You may take as many of the hats as you wish," he told his guest.

"No," said Zegri. "I know of this baptism. I know what it means. Here in Granada we have not known the Inquisition, but I have heard what it does to Jews who have accepted baptism and go back to their own Faith."

"Once you were a Christian you would not wish to go back to your own Faith. Each day you would become more and more aware of the advantages which Christianity has to offer."

"I am a Mohammedan. I do not look for advantages."

"You are a man stumbling in darkness."

"I live very well, I am a happy man . . . with the love of Allah."

"There is only one true Faith," said Ximenes. "That is the Christian Faith."

"Allah forgive you. You know not what you say."

"You will go to eternal torment when you die."

"Allah will be good to me and mine."

"If you become a Christian you will go to Heaven when you die. Allow me to give you baptism and eternal joy shall be yours."

Zegri smiled and said simply: "I am a Mohammedan. I do not change my religion for a bale of silk and a red hat." His eyes flashed defiance as he stood there, and Ximenes realized that argument would never convince such a man. Yet it was necessary that he should be convinced. This was a powerful man, a man who would sway a multitude. One word from him and the conversions had ceased.

It was not to be tolerated, and in Ximenes' eyes all that was done in the service of the Faith was well done.

"I see," he said, "that I cannot make you a good Christian."

"I do not believe that I could make you a good Mussulman," retorted Zegri, smiling widely.

Ximenes crossed himself in horror.

"Here in Granada we shall continue in our own Faith," said Zegri quietly.

But you shall not! thought Ximenes. I have sworn to convert this place to Christianity, and I will do it.

"I will take my leave of you," said Zegri, "and I will thank you for receiving me in your palace, oh mighty Archbishop."

Ximenes bowed his head and called to his servant Leon.

"Leon," he said, "show my guest the way out. He will come and talk with me again, for I have yet to persuade him."

Leon, a tall man with broad shoulders answered: "So shall it be, Your Excellency." He led the way, and Zegri followed. They went through chambers which he did not remember seeing before, down some stairs to more apartments.

This was not the way he had come in, Zegri was thinking as Leon opened a door and stood aside for him to enter.

Unthinking, Zegri stepped forward. Then he stopped. But he

was too late. Leon gave him a little push from behind and he stumbled down a few dark steps. He heard the door shut behind him and a key turned in the lock.

He was not outside the Archbishop's palace. He was in a dark dungeon.

* * *

Zegri lay on the floor of his dungeon. He was weak, for it must have been long since food had passed his lips. When the door had been locked on him he had beaten on it until his hands had bled; he had shouted to be let out, but no one answered him.

The floor was damp and cold and his limbs were numb.

"They have tricked me," he said aloud, "as they have tricked my friends."

He thought that they would leave him here until he died, but this was not their intention.

Exhausted, he was lying on the floor, when he was aware of a blinding light flashed into his face. It was only a man with a lantern, but Zegri had been so long in the dark that it seemed as brilliant as the sun at noon.

This man was Leon, and with him was another. He pulled Zegri to his feet and slipped an iron ring about his neck; to this was attached a chain which he fixed to a staple in the wall.

"What do you plan to do with me?" demanded Zegri. "What right have you to make me your prisoner? I have done no wrong. I must have a fair trial. In Granada all men must have fair trials."

But Leon only laughed. And after a while the Archbishop of Toledo came into the dungeon.

Zegri cried out: "What is this you would do to me?"

"Make a good Christian of you," Ximenes told him.

"You cannot make me a Christian by torturing me."

A gleam came into Ximenes' eyes, but he said: "You have nothing to fear if you accept baptism."

"And if I will not?"

"I do not despair easily. You will stay here in the darkness until you see the light of truth. You shall be without food for the body until you are prepared to accept food for the soul. Will you accept baptism?"

"Baptism is for Christians," answered Zegri. "I am a Mussulman."

Ximenes inclined his head and walked from the dungeon. Leon followed him, and Zegri was in the cold darkness again.

He waited for these visits. There were several of them. Always he hoped that they would bring him food and drink. It was long since he had eaten and his body was growing weak. There were gnawing pains in his stomach and it cried out for nourishment. Always the words were the same. He would stay here in cold and hunger until he accepted baptism.

At the end of a few days and nights Zegri's discomfort was intense. He knew that if he continued thus he could not live very long. Zegri had spent all his life in the prosperous city of Granada. He had never known hardship before.

What good can I do by remaining here? he asked himself. I should only die.

He thought of his fellow Moors who had been deceived by the bales of silk and the red hats. They had been lured to baptism by bribes; he was being forced to it by this torture.

He knew there was only one way out of his dungeon.

* * *

The blinding light was flashed into his face. There was the big man with the cruel eyes—Leon, the servant of the even more terrifying one with the face of a dead man and the eyes of a fiend.

"Bring him a chair, Leon," said Ximenes. "He is too weak to stand."

The chair was brought and Zegri sat in it.

"Have you anything to say to me?" asked Ximenes.

"Yes, my lord Archbishop, I have something to say. Last night Allah came to my prison."

Ximenes' face in the light from the lantern looked very stern.

"And he told me," went on Zegri, "that I must accept Christian baptism without delay."

"Ah!" It was a long drawn out cry of triumph from the Archbishop of Toledo. For a second his lips were drawn back from his teeth in what was meant to be a smile. "I see your stay with us has been fruitful, very fruitful. Leon, release him from his fetters. We will feed him and clothe him in silk. We will put a red hat on his head and we will baptize him in the name of Our Lord Jesus Christ. I thank God this victory is won."

It was a great relief to have the heavy iron removed from his neck, but even so Zegri was too weak to walk.

Ximenes signed to the big man, Leon, who slung Zegri over his shoulder and carried him out of the damp dark dungeon.

He was put on a couch; his limbs were rubbed; savoury broth was put into his mouth. Ximenes was impatient for the baptism. He had rarely been as excited as when he scattered the consecrated drops from a hyssop over the head of this difficult convert.

So Zegri had now received Christian baptism.

"You should give thanks for your good fortune," Ximenes told him. "Now I trust many of your countrymen will follow your example."

"If you and your servant do to my countrymen as you have done to me," said Zegri, "you will make so many Christians that there will not be a Mussulman left within the walls of Granada."

Ximenes kept Zegri in his palace until he had recovered from the effects of his incarceration, but he let the news be carried through the city: "Zegri has become a Christian."

The result satisfied even Ximenes. Hundreds of Moors were now arriving at the Archbishop's palace to receive baptism and what went with it—bales of silk and scarlet hats.

* * *

Ximenes was not satisfied for long. The more learned of the Moorish population held back and exhorted their friends to do the same. They stressed what had happened to Jews who had received baptism and had been accused of returning to the faith of their fathers; they talked of the dreary *autos-de-fé* which were becoming regular spectacles in many of the towns of Spain. This must not be so in Granada. And those foolish people whose desire for silk and red hats had overcome their good sense were making trouble for themselves.

The people of Granada could not believe in any such trouble. This was Granada, where living had been easy for years; and even after their defeat at the hands of the Christians and the end of the reign of Boabdil, they had gone on as before. They would always go on in that way. Many of them remembered the day when the great Sovereigns, Ferdinand and Isabella, had come to take possession of the Alhambra. Then they had been promised freedom of thought, freedom of action, freedom to follow their own faith.

Ximenes knew that those who were preventing his work from succeeding as he wished it to, were the scholars, and he decided to strike a blow at them. They had declared that they had no need of this Christian culture because they had a greater culture of their own.

"Culture!" cried Ximenes. "What is this culture? Their books, is it?"

It was true that they produced manuscripts of such beauty that they were spoken of throughout the world. Their binding and illuminations were exquisite and unequalled.

"I will have an *auto-de-fé* in Granada," he told Talavera. "It shall be the first. They shall see the flames rising to their beautiful blue sky."

"But the agreement with the Sovereigns . . ." began Talavera.

"This *auto-de-fe* shall be one in which not bodies burn but manuscripts. This shall be a foretaste of what shall come if they forget their baptismal oaths. Let them see the flames rising to the sky. Let them see their evil words writhing in the heat. It would be wise to say nothing of this to Tendilla as yet. There is a man who doubtless would wish to preserve these manuscripts because the bindings are good. I fear our friend Tendilla is a man given to outward show."

"My lord," said Talavera, "if you destroy these people's literature they may seek revenge on us. They are quiet people only among their friends."

"They will find they never had a better friend than myself," said Ximenes. "Look how many of them I have brought to baptism!"

He was determined to continue with his project and would have no interference. Only when he saw those works reduced to ashes would he feel he was making some headway. He would make sure that none of the children should suffer from contamination with those heathen words.

The decree went out. Every manuscript in every Moorish house was to be brought out. They were to be put in heaps in the squares of the town. Severest penalties would be inflicted on those who sought to hide any work in Arabic.

Stunned, the Moors watched their literature passing from their hands into that of the man whom they now knew to be their enemy. Zegri had returned from his visit to the Archbishop's palace a changed man. He was thin and ill; and he seemed deeply humiliated; it was as though all his spirit had gone from him.

Ximenes had ordered that works dealing with religion were to be piled in the squares; but those dealing with medicine were to be brought to him. The Moors were noted for their medical knowledge and it occurred to Ximenes that there could be no profanity in profiting from it. He therefore selected some two or three hundred medical works, examined them and had them sent to Alcalá to be placed in the University he was building there. Then he gave himself up to the task of what he called service to the Faith.

In all the open places of the town the fires were burning.

The Moors sullenly watched their beautiful works of art turned to ashes. Over the city there hung a pall of smoke, dark and lowering.

In the Albaycin, that part of the city which was inhabited

entirely by the Moors, people were getting together behind shutters and even in the streets.

* * *

Tendilla came to see Ximenes. He was not alone; he brought with him several leading Castilians who had lived for years in Granada.

"This is dangerous," Tendilla blurted out.

"I do not understand you," retorted Ximenes haughtily.

"We have lived in Granada for a long time," pointed out Tendilla. "We know these people. Am I not right?" He turned to his companions, who assured Ximenes that they were in complete agreement with Tendilla.

"You should rejoice with me," cried Ximenes contemptuously, "that there is no longer an Arabic literature. If these people have no books, their foolish ideas cannot be passed on to their young. Our next plan shall be to educate their children in the true Faith. In a generation we shall have everyone, man, woman and child, a Christian."

Tendilla interrupted boldly. "I must remind you of the conditions of the treaty."

"Treaty indeed!" snapped Ximenes. "It is time that was forgotten."

"It will never be forgotten. The Moors remember it. They have respected the Sovereigns because ever since '92 that treaty has been observed . . . and now you would disregard it."

"I ask the forgiveness of God because I have not attempted to do so before."

"My lord Archbishop, may I implore you to show more forbearance. If you do not there will be bloodshed in our fair city of Granada."

"I am not concerned with the shedding of blood. I am only concerned with the shedding of sin."

"To follow their own religion is not to sin."

"My lord, have a care. You come close to heresy."

Tendilla flushed an angry red. "Take the advice of a man who knows these people, my lord Archbishop. If you must make Christians of them, I implore you, if you value your life . . ."

"Which I do not," Ximenes interjected.

"Then the lives of others. If you value them, I pray you take a tamer policy towards these people."

"A tamer policy might suit temporal matters, but not those in which the soul is at stake. If the unbeliever cannot be drawn to salvation, he must be driven there. This is not the time to stay our hands, when Mahometanism is tottering."

Tendilla looked helplessly at those citizens whom he had brought with him to argue with Ximenes.

"I can see," he said curtly, "that it is useless to attempt to influence you."

"Quite useless."

"Then we can only hope that we shall be ready to defend ourselves when the time comes."

Tendilla and his friends took their leave of Ximenes, who laughed aloud when he was alone.

Tendilla! A soldier! The Queen had been mistaken to appoint such a man as Alcayde. He had no true spirit. He was a lover of comfort. The souls of Infidels meant nothing to him as long as these people worked and grew rich and so made the town rich.

They thought he did not understand these Moors. They were mistaken. He was fully aware of the growing surliness of the Infidels. He would not be in the least surprised if they were making some plot to attack him. They might attempt to assassinate him. What a glorious death that would be—to die in the service of the Faith. But he had no wish to die yet, for unlike Torquemada he knew no one who would be worthy to wear *his* mantle.

This very day he had sent three of his servants into the Albaycin. Their task was to pause at the stalls and buy some of the goods displayed there, and to listen, of course. To spy on the Infidel. To discover what was being said about the new conditions which Ximenes had brought into their city.

He began to pray, asking for success for his project, promising more converts in exchange for Divine help. He was working out new plans for further forays against the Moors. Their literature was destroyed. What next? He was going to forbid them to follow their ridiculous customs. They were constantly taking baths or staining themselves with henna. He was going to stamp out these barbarous practices.

He noticed that the day was drawing to its close. It was time his servants returned. He went to the window and looked out. Only a little daylight left, he mused.

He went back to his table and his work, but he was wondering what had detained his servants.

When he heard the sound of cries below, he went swiftly down to the hall and there he saw one of those servants whom he had sent into the Albaycin; he was staggering into the hall surrounded by others who cried out in horror at the sight of him. His clothes were torn and he was bleeding from a wound in his side.

"My lord . . ." he was moaning. "Take me to my lord."

Ximenes hurried forward. "My good man, what is this?

What has happened to you? Where are your companions?"

"They are dead. Murdered, my lord. In the Albaycin. We were set upon . . . known as your servants. They are coming here. They have long knives. They have sworn to murder you. My lord . . . they are coming. There is little time left . . ."

The man fell swooning at the feet of the Archbishop.

Ximenes ordered: "Make fast all doors. See that they are guarded. Take this man and call my physician to attend to him. The Infidel comes against us. The Lord is with us. But the Devil is a formidable enemy. Do not stand there. Obey my orders. We must prepare."

* * *

There followed hours of terror for all those in the palace with the exception of Ximenes. From an upper chamber he watched those glowering faces in the light of their torches. He heard their shouts of anger.

He thought: Only these frail walls between myself and the Infidel. "Lord," he prayed, "if it be Thy will to take me into Heaven, then so be it."

They were throwing stones. They had tried to storm the gates but the palace had stood many a siege and would doubtless stand many more.

They shouted curses on this man who had come among them and destroyed their peace; but Ximenes smiled blandly, for the cursings of the Infidel, he told himself, could be counted as blessings.

How long could the palace hold out against the mob? And what would happen when those dark-skinned men broke through?

There was a lull outside, but Ximenes guessed that soon the tumult would break out again. They would storm the walls; they would find some way in, and then . . .

"Let them come, if it be Thy will," he cried aloud.

He stood erect, waiting. He would be the one they sought. He wondered if they would inflict torture on him before they killed him. He was not afraid. His body had been schooled to suffer.

He heard a shout from without and in the light of the torches he saw a man on horseback riding up to the leader of the Moors.

It was Tendilla.

Ximenes could not hear what was said, but Tendilla was clearly arguing with the Moors. There he stood among them all, and Ximenes felt a momentary admiration for the soldier who could be as careless of his safety as Ximenes was of his.

He was now addressing the Moors, waving his hands and shouting, placating them no doubt, perhaps making promises which Ximenes had no intention of keeping.

But the Moors were listening. They had ceased to shout and it was quiet out there. Then Ximenes saw them turn and move away.

Tendilla was alone outside the palace walls.

* * *

Tendilla was let into the palace. His eyes were flashing with anger and that anger was directed not against the Moors but against Ximenes.

"So my lord," he said, "perhaps now you begin to understand."

"I understand that your docile Moors are docile no longer."

"They believe they have suffered great provocation. They are a very angry people. Do you realize that in a very short time they would have forced an entry into this place? Then it would have gone hard with you."

"You are telling me that I owe you my life."

Tendilla made an impatient gesture. "I would not have you imagine that the danger is past. I persuaded them to return to their homes, and they agreed to do this . . . tonight. But this will not be an end to this matter. A proud people does not see its literature burned to ashes and murmur, Thank you, my lord. You are unsafe in this place. Your life is not worth much while you stay here. Make ready at once and accompany me back to the Alhambra. There I can give you adequate protection."

Ximenes stood still as a statue.

"I shall not cower behind the walls of the Alhambra, my good Tendilla. I shall stay here, and if these barbarians come against me, I shall trust in God. If it be His will that I become a martyr to their barbarism, then I say, Thy will be done."

"They believe that they have been victims of your barbarism," retorted Tendilla. "They seek revenge. They will go back to the Albaycin and prepare for a real attack on your palace. They will come again . . . this time in cold blood, fully armed. Do you realize, my lord Archbishop, that a major revolt is about to break out?"

For the first time Ximenes felt a twinge of uneasiness. He had believed he could successfully proselytize without trouble of this nature. If he were setting in motion warfare between Moors and Christians the Sovereigns would not be pleased. Their great aim had been to preserve peace within their own country so that they might conserve their strength for enemies beyond their borders.

But he held his head high and told himself that what he ha done had been for the glory of God; and what was the will the Sovereigns compared with that!

Tendilla said: "I will ask one thing of you. If you will not com to the Alhambra, then stay here, as well guarded as possibl and leave me to deal with this insurrection."

He bowed briefly and left the Archbishop.

* * *

Tendilla rode back to the Alhambra. His wife, who was wai ing for him, betrayed her relief when she saw him.

"I was afraid, Iñigo," she said.

He smiled tenderly. "You need have no fear. The Moors ar my friends. They know that I have always been fair to them. The are a people who respect justice. It is not I who am in dange but that fool of an Archbishop of ours."

"How I wish he had never come to Granada."

"There are many who would echo those words, my dear."

"Iñigo, what are you going to do now?"

"I am going into the Albaycin. I'm going to talk to them an ask them not to arm themselves for a revolt. Ximenes is respon sible for this trouble, but if they kill the Archbishop of Toled they will find the might of Spain raised against them. I mus make them understand this."

"But they are in a dangerous mood."

"It is for this reason that I must not delay."

"But, Iñigo, think. They are rising against the Christians and you are a Christian."

He smiled at her. "Have no fear. This is something whic must be done and I am the one to do it. If things should no go as I believe they will, be ready to leave Granada with th children and lose no time."

"Iñigo! Do not go. This is the Archbishop's affair. Let then storm his palace. Let them torture him . . . kill him if they will He has brought this trouble to Granada. Let him take the consequences."

Tendilla smiled gently. "You have not understood," he said "I am the Alcayde. I am responsible for this zealous reformer o ours. I have to protect him against the results of his own folly."

"So you are determined?"

"I am."

"Go well armed, Iñigo."

Tendilla did not answer.

* * *

Meanwhile Talavera had heard what was happening in the Albaycin. Something must be done quickly to calm the Moors.

They had always respected him. They had listened gravely when he had preached to them of the virtues of Christianity. They knew him for a good man.

Talavera was certain that he, more than any man in Granada, could help to restore order to the Albaycin.

He called for his chaplain and said: "We are going into the Albaycin."

"Yes, my lord," was the answer.

"You and I alone," went on Talavera, watching the expression on the face of the chaplain.

He saw the man's alarm. The whole of Granada must know, thought Talavera, of the trouble which was brewing in the Moorish quarter.

"There is trouble there," went on the Archbishop of Granada. "The Moors are in an ugly mood. They may well set upon us and murder us in their anger. I do not think they will. I think they will listen to me as they have always done. They are a fierce people but only when their anger is aroused, and I do not think we—you and I, my dear chaplain—have done anything to arouse their anger."

"My lord, if we took soldiers with us to protect us . . ."

"I have never gone among them with a bodyguard. To do so now would make it appear that I do not trust them."

"Do you trust them, my lord?"

"I trust in my Lord," was the answer. "And I would not ask you to accompany me if you would not do so of your own free will."

The chaplain hesitated for a few moments, then he said: "Where you go, my lord, there will I go."

"Then prepare, for there is little time."

So with only his chaplain to accompany him the Archbishop of Granada rode into the Albaycin. The chaplain rode before him carrying the crucifix, and the Moors stared at these men in sullen silence for a few moments.

The Archbishop rode right into their midst and said to them: "My friends, I hear that you are arming yourselves, and I come among you unarmed. If you desire to kill me, then you must do so. If you will listen to me, I will give you my advice."

A faint murmuring broke out. The chaplain trembled; many of the Moors carried long knives. He thought of death which might not come quickly; then he looked into the calm face of his Archbishop and felt comforted.

"Will you do me the honour of listening to me?" asked the Archbishop.

There was a short silence. Then one of the *alfaquis* cried out: "Speak, oh Christian lord."

"You are an angry people, and you seek vengeance which, my friends, is not good for those who plan it nor for those who bear the brunt of it. It is a two-edged weapon, to harm those whom it strikes and those who strike. Do nothing rash. Pause and consider the inevitable result of your actions. Pray for guidance. Do not resort to violence."

"We have seen our beautiful manuscripts destroyed before our eyes, oh Talavera," cried one voice. "We have seen the flames rising in the squares of Granada. What next will be burned? Our mosques? Our bodies?"

"Be calm. Pray for guidance."

"Death to the Christian dogs!" cried a wild voice in the crowd.

There was a move forward and the *alfaquis* who had first spoken cried: "Wait! This is our friend. This is not that other. This man is not guilty. In all the years he has been with us he has been just and although he has tried to persuade us he has never sought to force us to that which we did not want."

"It is true," someone called out.

"Yes," cried several voices then. "It is true. We have no quarrel with this man."

"Allah preserve him."

"He is not our enemy."

Many remembered instances of his goodness. He had always helped the poor, Moor or Christian. They had no quarrel with this man.

One woman came forward and knelt at the side of Talavera's horse and said: "You have been good to me and mine. I pray you, oh lord, give me your benediction."

And Talavera placed his hands on this woman's head and said: "Go in peace."

Others came forward to ask his blessing, and when Tendilla rode into the Albaycin this was the scene he witnessed.

Tendilla came with half a dozen soldiers, and when the Moors saw his guards many hands tightened about their knives. But Tendilla's first action was to take his bonnet from his head and throw into their midst.

"I give you my sign," he cried, "that I come in peace. Many of you are armed. Look at us. We have come among you unarmed."

The Moors then saw that it was so, and they remembered too that from this man they had received nothing but justice and tolerance. He had come among them unarmed. They could have slain him and his few men together with the Archbishop and his chaplain without any loss to themselves.

This was certainly a sign of friendship.

"Long life to the Alcayde!" cried one, and the others took up this cry.

Tendilla lifted a hand.

"My friends," he said, "I pray you listen to me. You are armed and plan violence. If you carry out this plan you might have some initial success here in Granada. And what then? Beyond Granada the whole might of Spain would be assembled and come against you. If you gave way to your feelings now you would bring certain disaster and death upon yourselves and your families."

The leading *alfaquis* came to Tendilla and said: "We thank you, oh lord Alcayde, for coming to us this night. We have in your coming proof of the friendship of yourself and the Archbishop of Granada towards us. But we have suffered great wrongs. The burning of our works of art has caused us great distress."

"You have your grievances," Tendilla replied. "If you will go back to your homes and put all thoughts of rebellion from your minds I will bring your case before the Sovereigns."

"You yourself will do this?"

"I will," said Tendilla. "Their Highnesses are now in Seville. As soon as I can put my affairs in order I will ride there and explain to them."

Zegri, who had learned at first hand of what he had come to think of as Christian perfidy, elbowed his way to the side of their leader.

"How can we know," he said, "that the Alcayde does not speak thus to gain time? How do we know that he will not become our enemy and bring the Christians against us?"

"I give you my word," said Tendilla.

"Oh lord Alcayde, I was invited to the house of the Archbishop of Toledo as a guest, and I found myself his prisoner. He changed towards me in the space of an hour. What if you should so change?"

There was a murmuring in the crowd. They were all remembering the experiences of Zegri.

Tendilla saw that the angry mood was returning, the fury which the conduct of Ximenes had aroused was bursting out again.

Tendilla made a decision. "I shall go to Seville," he said. "You well know the love I bear my wife and two children. I will leave them here with you as hostages. That will be a token of my good intentions."

There was silence in the crowd.

Then the leading *alfaquis* said: "You have spoken, oh lord Alcayde."

The crowd began to cheer. They did not love violence. They trusted Tendilla and Talavera to rid them of the trouble-making Ximenes that all might be peace once more in their beautiful city of Granada.

* * *

News of what had happened in the Albaycin was brought to Ximenes. He was now alarmed. He had hoped to continue with his proselytizing unimpeded; he realized now that he must be wary.

Tendilla had come storming into his palace and had not hesitated to say what he meant. He blamed Ximenes for the first trouble that had occurred in the city since the reconquest, adding that within the next few days he was leaving for Seville, and there he would lay the matter before the Sovereigns.

Ximenes coldly retorted that he would do all that he had done, over again, should the need arise, and the need was sore in Granada.

"You will do nothing," retorted Tendilla, "until this matter has been laid before their Highnesses."

And Ximenes had of course agreed to the wisdom of that.

As soon as Tendilla had left, Ximenes fell on his knees in prayer. This was a very important moment in his life. He knew that the version of this affair which Tendilla would carry to the Sovereigns would differ from the tale he had to tell; and it was all-important that Ferdinand and Isabella should hear Ximenes' account first.

It might well be that on the following day Tendilla would set out for Seville. Ximenes must therefore forestall him.

He rose from his knees and sent for one of his Negro servants, a tall long-limbed athlete who could run faster than any other known in the district.

"I shall want you to leave for Seville within half an hour," he said. "Prepare yourself."

The slave bowed, and when he was alone Ximenes sat down to write his account of what had happened in Granada. The need to save souls was imperative. He wanted more power and, when he had it, he would guarantee to bring the Moors of Granada into the Christian fold. He had been unable to stand calmly aside and watch the heathenish habits which were practised in that community. He had acted under guidance from God, and he was now praying that his Sovereigns would not shut their eyes to God's will.

He sent for the slave.

"With all speed to Seville," he commanded.

And he smiled, well satisfied, believing that Isabella and Ferdinand would receive the news from him hours before they could possibly see Tendilla. By that time they would have read his version of the revolt, and all Tendilla's eloquence would not be able to persuade them that Ximenes had been wrong in what he had done.

* * *

The Negro slave ran the first few miles. As he sped onwards there passed him on the road a Moor who was riding on a grey horse; and the Negro wished that he had a horse on which to ride, but he quickly forgot it and gave himself up to the pleasure of exercise.

He was noted for his fleetness of foot and proud of it. Anyone could ride a horse. None could match him for running speed.

But the way was long and even the fleetest of foot grew tired; the throat became parched, and there on the road between Granada and Seville the slave saw a tavern. Tied to a post was the horse which had passed him on the way, and standing close to the horse was the rider.

The man called to the Negro. "Good day to you. I saw you running on the road."

"I envied you your horse," said the Negro, pausing.

" 'Tis thirsty work, running as you run."

"You speak truth there."

"Well, here is an inn and the wine is good. Why do you not fortify yourself with some of this good wine?"

"Oh . . . I am on a mission. I have to reach Seville with all speed."

"You'll go the quicker for the wine."

The Negro considered this. It might be true.

"Come," said the Moor. "Drink with me. Let me be your host."

"You are generous," said the Negro, smiling.

"Come inside and wine shall be brought for us."

They sat together drinking the wine. The Moor encouraged the Negro to talk of his triumphs: How he had won many a race and had not in recent years met the man who could outrun him.

The Moor replenished his glass, and the Negro did not notice how much he was drinking, and forgot that he was unused to such wine.

His speech became slower; he had forgotten where he was; he slumped forward and, smiling, the Moor rose and taking him by the hair jerked his face upwards. The Negro was too intoxicated to protest; he did not even know who the man was.

The Moor called to the innkeeper.

"Let your servants take this man to a bed," he said. "He has drunk much wine and he will not be sober until morning. Give him food then and more wine . . . a great deal of it. It is necessary that he should stay here for another day and night."

The innkeeper took the money which was given him, and assured his honoured customer that his wishes should be carried out.

The Moor smiled pleasantly, went out to his horse and began the journey back to Granada.

Later that night the Count of Tendilla set out for Seville with his retinue. There was rejoicing in the Albaycin. The cunning of Ximenes would be foiled. Isabella and Ferdinand would first hear the story of the Moorish revolt from their friend, not from their enemy.

* * *

When Ferdinand heard from Tendilla what had happened in Granada his first feeling was of anger, then dismay, but these were later tinged with a faint satisfaction.

He lost no time in confronting Isabella.

"Here is a fine state of affairs," he cried. "Revolt in Granada. All brought about through this man Ximenes. So we are to pay dear for the conduct of *your* Archbishop. That for which we fought for years has been endangered in a few hours by the rashness of this man whom you took from his humble station to make Archbishop of Toledo and Primate of Spain."

Isabella was astounded by the news. She had taken great pride in maintaining the treaty. She had always been delighted to hear of the prosperity of her city of Granada, of the industry of the Moorish population and the manner in which they lived peaceably side by side with the Christians. She was overjoyed when she heard of the few conversions to Christianity which Talavera had brought about. But revolt in Granada! And Ximenes, *her* Archbishop—as Ferdinand always called him—was apparently at the very root of it.

"We have not heard his side of the story . . ." she began.

"And why not?" demanded Ferdinand. "Does your Archbishop think he may act without our sanction? He has not thought fit to inform us. Who are we? Merely the Sovereigns. It is Ximenes who rules Spain."

"I confess I am both alarmed and astonished," admitted Isabella.

"I should think so, Madam. This is what comes of giving high office to those who are unable to fill it with dignity and responsibility."

"I shall write to him at once," said the Queen, "informing him of my displeasure and summoning him to our presence without delay."

"It would certainly be wise to recall him from Granada before we have a war on our hands."

Isabella went to her table and began to write in the most severe terms, expressing her deep concern and anger that the Archbishop of Toledo should have so far forgotten his duty to his Sovereigns and his office as to have acted against the treaty of Granada and, having brought about such dire results, had not thought fit to tell his Sovereigns.

Ferdinand watched her, a slow smile curving his mouth. He was anxious as to the state of Granada, but he could not help feeling this pleasure. It was very gratifying to see his prophecies, concerning that upstart, coming true. How different it would have been if his own dear son Alfonso had graced the highest office in Spain.

* * *

Ximenes stood before the Sovereigns. His face was pale but he was as arrogant as ever.

There was no contrition at all, Ferdinand noticed in amazement. What sort of man was this? He had no fear whatsoever. He could be stripped of office and possessions and he would still flaunt his self-righteousness. He could be beaten, tortured, taken to the stake—still he would preserve that air of arrogance.

Even Ferdinand was slightly shaken as he looked at this man. As for Isabella, from the moment he had stood before her she was ready to listen sympathetically and to believe that what she had heard before had not been an accurate account.

"I do not understand," began Isabella, "on what authority you have acted as you did in Granada."

"On that of God," was the answer.

Ferdinand made an impatient gesture but Isabella went on gently: "My lord Archbishop, did you not know that the Treaty of Granada lays down that the Moorish population should continue to worship as it wished?"

"I did know this, Highness, but I thought it an evil treaty."

"Was that your concern?" demanded Ferdinand with sarcasm.

"It is always my concern to fight evil, Highness."

Isabella asked: "If you wished to take these measures would

it not have been wiser to have consulted us, to ask our permission to do so?"

"It would have been most unwise," retorted Ximenes. "Your Highnesses would never have given that permission."

"This is monstrous!" cried Ferdinand.

"Wait, I beg of you," pleaded Isabella. "Let the Archbishop tell us his side of the story."

"It was necessary," continued Ximenes, "that action should be taken against these Infidels. Your Highness did not see fit to do so. In the name of the Faith I was forced to do it for you."

"And," fumed Ferdinand, "having done it, you did not even take the trouble to inform us."

"There you wrong me. I despatched a messenger to you in all haste. He should have reached you before you received the news from any other. Unhappily my enemies waylaid him and intoxicated him so that he did not reach you . . . and then, having failed in his duty, was afraid to present himself either to you or to me."

Isabella looked relieved. "I knew I could trust you to keep us informed, and the failure of your messenger to arrive was certainly no fault of yours."

"There is still this astonishing conduct, which led to revolt in Granada, to be explained," Ferdinand reminded them.

Then Ximenes turned to him and delivered one of those sermons of invective for which he was famous. He reminded them of the manner in which he had served God, the state, and themselves. He told them how much of the revenues of Toledo had gone into the work of proselytizing. He hinted that both had been guilty of indifference to the Faith—Ferdinand in his desire for aggrandizement, Isabella in her affection for her family. Here he touched them both where they were most vulnerable. He made them feel guilty; slowly, with infinite cunning he turned the argument in his favour so that it was as though they were under an obligation to explain themselves to him, not he to them.

Ferdinand was saying to himself: I have found the need always to fight, to protect what is mine and to seek to make it safe; I have seen that only by adding to my possessions can I make Aragon safe.

And Isabella: Perhaps it is sin for a mother to love her children as I have done, to evade her duty in the desire to keep them with her.

Ximenes then came to the point up to which he was leading them.

"It is true," he said, "that there was this Treaty of Granada.

But the Moors in Granada have been in revolt against Your Highnesses. By so doing they have broken the treaty, the core of which was that both sides were to live in amity. It was they who rose against us. Therefore, since they have broken their word, there is no need for us to have any compunction in changing our attitude towards them."

Subtly Ximenes reminded the Sovereigns of the expulsion of the Jews. Much of the property of these unfortunate Jews had enriched the state. The thought of that made Ferdinand's eyes gleam. For Isabella's sake he spoke of the great work that could be done in bringing these Infidels into the Christian fold.

Then he cried: "They have broken the treaty. You are under no obligation. Any means should be used to bring these poor lost souls to Christianity."

Ximenes had won his battle. The Treaty of Granada was no more.

An almost benevolent expression was on Ximenes' face. He was already making plans to bring the Moors of Granada to baptism. In a short time there should be what he called a truly Christian Granada.

THE DEPARTURES OF MIGUEL AND CATALINA

MARIA AND her sister Catalina were at the window watching the comings and goings to and from the Madrid Alcazar. The expression of each was intent; and in both cases their thoughts were on marriage.

Catalina could immediately recognize the English messengers, and on those occasions when she saw these men with their letters from their King to her parents she felt sick with anxiety. The Queen had told her that in each despatch the King of England grew more and more impatient.

Then Catalina would cling to her mother wildly for a few seconds, holding back her tears; and although the Queen reproved her, there was, Catalina knew, a rough note in her voice which betrayed her own nearness to tears.

It cannot be long now, Catalina said to herself every morning. And each day which could be lived through without word from England was something for which she thanked the saints in her prayers at night.

Maria was different. She was as nearly excited as Catalina had ever seen her.

Now she chattered: "Catalina, can you see the Naples livery? Tell me if you do."

Doesn't she care that she will have to leave her home? wondered Catalina. But perhaps Naples did not seem so far away as England.

There was gossip throughout the Alcazar that the next marriage would either be that of Maria to the Duke of Calabria who was the heir of the King of Naples, or that of Catalina to the Prince of Wales.

Maria actually enjoyed talking of her prospective marriage.

"I was afraid I was going to be forgotten," she explained. "There were husbands for everybody else and none for me. It seemed unfair."

"I should rejoice if they had found no husband for me," Catalina reminded her.

"That is because you are so young. You cannot imagine anything but staying at home here with Mother all your life. That is quite impossible."

"I fear you are right."

"When you are as old as I am you will feel differently," Maria comforted her sister.

"In three years' time I shall be as old as you are now. I wonder what I shall be doing by then? Three years from now. That will be the year 1503. It's a long way ahead. Look. There is a messenger. He comes from Flanders, I am sure."

"Then it will be news from our sister."

"Oh," said Catalina and fell silent. That which she feared next to news from England was news from Flanders, because news which came from that country had the power to make her mother so unhappy.

* * *

The girls were summoned to their parents' presence. This was a ceremonial occasion. They were not the only ones in the big apartment. Their parents stood side by side, and Catalina knew immediately that some important announcement was about to be made.

In the Queen's hand were the despatches from Flanders.

It must concern Juana, thought Catalina; but there was no need to worry. Something had happened which made her mother very happy. As for her father, there was an air of jubilance about him.

Into the apartment came all the officers of state who were at that time resident in the Alcazar, and when they were all assembled a trumpeter who stood close to the King and Queen sounded a few notes.

There was silence throughout the room. Then Isabella spoke.

"My friends, this day I have great news for you. My daughter Juana has given birth to a son."

These words were followed by fanfares of triumph.

And then everyone in the room cried: "Long life to the Prince!"

* * *

Isabella and Ferdinand were alone at last.

Ferdinand's face was flushed with pleasure. Isabella's eyes were shining.

"This, I trust," she said, "will have a sobering effect on our daughter."

"A son!" cried Ferdinand. "What joy! The firstborn and a son."

"It will be good for her to be a mother," mused Isabella. "She will discover new responsibilities. It will steady her."

Then she thought of her own mother and those uncanny

scenes in the Castle of Arevalo when she had raved about the rights of her children. Isabella remembered that she had been at her most strange when she had feared that her children might not gain what she considered to be their rights.

But she would not think such thoughts. Juana was fertile. She had her son. That was a matter for the utmost rejoicing.

"They are calling him Charles," murmured Isabella.

Ferdinand frowned. "A foreign name. There has never been a Charles in Spain."

"If this child became Emperor of the Austrians he would be their Charles the Fifth," said Isabella. "There have been other Charleses in Austria."

"I like not the name," insisted Ferdinand. "It would have been a pleasant gesture if they had named their first, Ferdinand."

"It would indeed. But I expect we shall become accustomed to the name."

"Charles the Fifth of Austria," mused Ferdinand, "and Charles the First of Spain."

"He cannot be Charles the First of Spain while Miguel lives," Isabella reminded him.

"Not . . . while Miguel lives," repeated Ferdinand.

He looked at Isabella with that blank expression which, during the early years of their marriage, she had begun to understand. He believed Miguel would not live, and that this which had caused him great anxiety before the letter from Juana had arrived, no longer did so. For if Miguel died now there was still a male heir to please the people of Aragon: There was Juana's son Charles.

"From all reports," said Ferdinand, "our grandson with this odd name appears to be a lusty young person."

"They tell us so."

"I have had it from several sources," answered Ferdinand. "Sources which are warned not to feed me with lies."

"So Charles is big for his age and strong and lusty. Charles will live."

Isabella's lips trembled slightly; she was thinking of that wan child in his nursery in the troubled town of Granada, where the Moorish population had now been called upon to choose between baptism and exile.

Miguel was such a good child. He scarcely ever cried. He coughed a little though, in the same way as his mother had done just before she died.

"Ferdinand," Isabella had turned to her husband, "this child which has been born to our Juana will one day inherit all the riches of Spain."

Ferdinand did not answer. But he agreed with her.

It was the first time that Isabella had given voice to the great anxiety which Miguel had brought to her since his birth.

But all was well now, thought Ferdinand. One heir might be taken from them, but there was another to fill his place.

Isabella once again read Ferdinand's thoughts. She must try to emulate her husband's calm practical common sense. She must not grieve too long for Juan, for Isabella. They had little Miguel. And if little Miguel should follow his mother to the grave, they had lusty little Hapsburg Charles to call their heir.

* * *

Ferdinand at this time was deeply concerned over Naples. When Charles VIII of France had been succeeded by Louis XII it had become clear that Louis had his eyes on Europe, for he immediately laid claim to Naples and Milan. Ferdinand himself had for long cast covetous eyes on Naples which was occupied by his cousin, Frederick. Frederick belonged to an illegitimate line of the House of Aragon, and it was for this reason that Ferdinand itched to take the crown for himself.

Frederick, who might have expected help from his cousin against the King of France, had received a blow when his effort to marry his son, the Duke of Calabria, to Ferdinand's daughter Maria, was thwarted.

Frederick's great hope had been to bind himself closer to his cousin Ferdinand by this marriage; and Ferdinand might have considered the alliance, but for the fact that the King of Portugal was a widower.

Of all his potential enemies Ferdinand most feared the King of France who, by the conquest of Milan, was now a power in Italy. The situation was further aggravated by the conduct of the Borgia Pope, who quite clearly was determined to win wealth, honours and power for himself and his family. The Pope was no friend to Ferdinand. Isabella had been profoundly shocked by the conduct of the Holy Father, whose latest scandalous behaviour had concerned transferring his son Cesare, whom he had previously made a Cardinal, from the Church to the army, simply because that ambitious young man, whose reputation was as evil as that of his father, felt that he could gain more power outside the Church. Ferdinand, believing that nothing could be gained by ranging himself on the side of the Borgias, joined Isabella in accusing the Pope of his crimes.

Alexander had been furious, had torn up the letter in which these complaints were made and had retaliated by referring to the Sovereigns of Spain with some indecency.

Therefore an alliance between the Vatican and Spain was out of the question. Maximilian was heavily engaged, and in any case had not the means of helping Ferdinand. Meanwhile the French, triumphant in Milan, were now preparing to annex Naples.

Frederick of Naples, a gentle peace-loving person, awaited with trepidation the storm, which was about to break over his little Kingdom. He feared the French and he knew that he could not expect help from his cousin Ferdinand who wanted Naples for himself. There seemed no way out of his dilemma except by calling in the help of the Turkish Sultan, Bajazet.

When Ferdinand heard this he was gleeful.

"This is monstrous," he declared to Isabella. "My foolish cousin—I must say my wicked cousin—has asked for help from the greatest enemy of Christianity. Now we need have no qualms about stepping in and taking Naples from him."

Isabella, who previously had been less eager for the Neapolitan campaign, was quickly won over by Ferdinand's arguments when she heard that Frederick had called for help from Bajazet.

But Ferdinand was in as great a dilemma as his cousin Frederick. If he allied himself with the powerful Louis, and victory was theirs, it was certain that Louis would eventually oust Ferdinand from Naples. To help Frederick against Louis was not to be thought of, because he would be fighting for Frederick and that would bring him no gain.

Ferdinand was a wily strategist where his own advancement was concerned. His sharp acquisitive eyes took in every salient point.

When Bajazet ignored Frederick's cry for help, Ferdinand set in motion negotiations between France and Spain, and the result was a new treaty of Granada.

This document was a somewhat sanctimonious one. In it was stated that war was evil and it was the duty of all Christians to preserve peace. Only the Kings of France and Aragon could pretend to the throne of Naples, and as the present King had called in the help of the enemy of all Christians, Bajazet, the Turkish Sultan, there was no alternative left to the Kings of France and Aragon, but that they should take possession of the Kingdom of Naples and divide it between them. The north would be French, the south Spanish.

This was a secret treaty; and so it should remain while the Spaniards and the French prepared to take what the treaty made theirs.

"This should not be difficult," Ferdinand explained to Isabella. "Pope Alexander will support us against Frederick.

Frederick was a fool to refuse his daughter Carlotta to Cesare Borgia. Alexander will never forgive this slight to a son on whom he dotes; and the hatred of the Borgias is implacable."

Isabella was delighted by the cunning strategy of her husband. She said to him on the signing of the treaty: "I do not know what would have become of us but for you."

These words gave Ferdinand pleasure. He often thought what an ideal wife Isabella would have been if she had not been also Queen of Castile, so determined to do her duty that she subdued everything else to that; yet it was precisely because she was Queen of Castile that he had wanted her to be his wife.

His busy mind was looking ahead. There would have to be a campaign against Naples. It was important that the friendship with England should not be broken. He would be glad when he could marry Maria into Portugal.

It would be wise to discuss the matter of England with Isabella while she was in this humble mood.

He laid his hand on Isabella's shoulder and looked serenely into her eyes.

"Isabella, my dear," he said, "I have been patient with you because I know of the love you bear our youngest. The time is passing. She should now begin to prepare for her journey to England."

He saw the fear leap into Isabella's eyes.

"I dread to tell her this," she said.

"Oh come, come, what is this folly? Our Catalina is going to be Queen of England."

"She is so close to me, Ferdinand, more close than any of the others. There are going to be many sad tears when we are parted. She is so alarmed by the thought of this journey that sometimes I fear she has a premonition of evil."

"Is this my wise Isabella talking?"

"Yes, Ferdinand, it is. Our eldest daughter believed she was going to die in childbed, and she did. In the same way our youngest has this horror of England."

"It is time I was firm with you all," said Ferdinand. "There is one way to stop our Catalina's fancies. Let her go to England, let her see for herself what a fine thing it is to be the wife of the heir to the English throne. I'll swear that in a few months' time we shall be having glowing letters about England. She will have forgotten Spain and us."

"I have a feeling that Catalina will never forget us."

"Break the news to her then."

"Oh, Ferdinand, so soon?"

"It has been years. I marvel at the patience of the King of

England. We dare not lose this match, Isabella. It is important to my schemes."

Isabella sighed. "I shall give her a few more days of pleasure," she said. "Let her enjoy another week in Spain. There will not be many weeks left to her in which to enjoy her home."

Isabella knew now that she could no longer put off the date of departure.

* * *

There was an urgent call to Granada, where little Miguel was suffering from a fever. The Queen rode into the city with Ferdinand and her two daughters. The news of Miguel's illness had had one good result, for because of it Isabella had put off giving Catalina instructions to prepare to leave Spain.

How different the city looked on this day. There were the towers of the Alhambra, rosy in the sunlight; there were the sparkling streams; but Granada had lost its gaiety. It was a sad city since Ximenes had ridden into it and had decided that only Christians should enjoy it.

Everywhere there was evidence of those days when it had been the Moorish capital, so that it was impossible to ride through those streets without thinking of the work which was steadily going forward under the instructions of the Archbishop of Toledo.

Isabella's heart was heavy. She was wondering now what she would find when she reached the Palace. How bad was the little boy? She read between the lines of the messages she had received and she guessed that he was very bad indeed.

She felt numbed by this news. Was it, she asked herself, that when blow followed blow, one was prepared for the next?

Ferdinand would not mourn. He would tell her that she must be grateful because they had Charles.

But she would not think of Miguel's dying. She herself would nurse him. She would keep him with her; she would not allow even her state duties to separate her from the child. He was the son of her darling daughter Isabella who had left him to her mother when she died. No matter how many grandsons her children should give her, she would always cherish Miguel, as the first grandson, the heir, the best loved.

She reached that part of this magnificent building which had been erected about the Court of Myrtles and made her way to the apartments which opened on to the Courtyard of Lions.

Her little Miguel could not have lived his short life in more beautiful surroundings. What did he think of the gilded domes and exquisite loveliness of the stucco work? He would be too young as yet to understand the praises which were set out on the walls, praises to the Prophet.

When she went to the apartment which was his nursery, she noticed at once that his nurses wore that grave look which she had become accustomed to see on the faces of those who waited at the sick-beds of the members of her family.

"How fares the Prince?" she asked.

"Highness, he is quiet today."

Quiet today! She was filled with anguish as she leaned over his bed. There he lay, her grandson who was so like his mother, with the same patient resignation in his gentle little face.

"Not Miguel," prayed Isabella. "Have I not suffered enough? Take Charles . . . if you must take from me, but leave me my little Miguel. Leave me Isabella's son."

What arrogance was this? Was she presuming to instruct Providence?

She crossed herself hastily: "Not my will but Thine."

She sat by the bed through the day and night; she knew that Miguel was dying, that only by a miracle could he throw off this fever and grow up to inherit his grandparents' kingdom.

He will die, she thought wearily; and on the day he dies, our heir is Juana. And the people of Aragon will not accept a woman. But they will accept that woman's son. They will accept Charles. Charles is strong and lusty, though his mother grows wilder every day. Juana inherits her wildness from my mother. Is it possible that Charles might inherit wildness from his?

What trouble lay in store for Spain? Was there no end to the ills which could befall them? Was there some truth in the rumours that theirs was an accursed House?

She was aware of the short gurgling breaths for which the child was struggling.

She sent for the doctors, but there was nothing they could do.

This frail little life was slowly slipping away.

"Oh God, what next? What next?" murmured Isabella.

Then the child lay still, and silent, and the doctors nodded one to another.

"So he has gone, my grandson?" asked the Queen.

"That we fear is so, Your Highness."

"Then leave me with him awhile," said Isabella. "I will pray for him. We will all pray for him. But first leave me with him awhile."

When she was alone she lifted the child from his bed and sat holding him in her arms while the tears slowly ran down her cheeks.

* * *

There was little time to grieve. There was the invasion of Naples to be planned; there was the affair of Christobal Colon to demand Isabella's attention.

Her feelings towards the adventurer were now mixed. He had incurred her wrath by using the Indians as slaves, a practice which she deplored. She did not follow the reasoning of most Catholics that, as these savages were doomed to perdition in any case, it mattered little what happened to their bodies on Earth. Isabella's great desire for colonization had been not so much to add to the wealth of Spain as to bring those souls to Christianity which had never been in a position to receive it before. Colon needed workmen for his new colony and he was not over-scrupulous as to how he obtained them. But Isabella at home in Spain asked: "By what authority does Christobal Colon venture to dispose of my subjects?" She ordered that all those men and women who had been taken into slavery should immediately be returned to their own country.

This was the first time she had felt angered by the behaviour of Christobal Colon.

As for Ferdinand he had always regarded the adventurer with some irritation. Since the discovery of the pearl fisheries of Paria he had thought with growing irritation of the agreement he had made—that Colon should have a share of the treasures he discovered. Ferdinand itched to divert more and more of that treasure into his coffers.

There were complaints from the colony, and Isabella had at last been persuaded to send out a kinsman of her friend Beatriz de Bobadilla, a certain Don Francisco de Bobadilla, to discover what was really happening.

Bobadilla had been given great powers. He was to take possession of all fortresses, vessels and property, and to have the right to send back to Spain any man who he thought was not working for the good of the community, that such person should then be made to answer to the Sovereigns for his conduct.

Isabella had at first been pleased to give Bobadilla this important post because he was a distant kinsman of her beloved friend; now she deeply regretted her action, as the only resemblance that Don Francisco bore to his kinswoman Beatriz was in his name.

It was while they were at Granada, mourning the death of little Miguel, that Ferdinand brought Isabella the news that Colon had arrived in Spain.

"Colon!" cried Isabella.

"Sent home for trial by Bobadilla," Ferdinand explained.

"But this is incredible," declared Isabella. "When we gave

Bobadilla such powers we did not think he would use them against the Admiral!"

Ferdinand shrugged his shoulders. "It was for Bobadilla to use his power where he thought it would do the most good."

"But to send Colon home!"

"Why not, if he thinks he is incompetent?"

Isabella forgot the disagreement she had had with the Admiral over the sale of slaves. She was immediately ready to spring to his defence because she remembered that day in 1493 when he had come home triumphant, the discoverer of the new land, when he had laid the riches of the New World at the feet of the Sovereigns.

And now to be sent home by Francisco de Bobadilla! It was too humiliating.

"Ferdinand," she cried, "do you realize that this man is the greatest explorer the world has known? You think it is right that he should be sent home in disgrace?"

Ferdinand interrupted. "In more than disgrace. He has come in fetters. He is now being kept in fetters at Cadiz."

"This is intolerable," cried Isabella. She did not wait to discuss the matter further with Ferdinand. She immediately wrote an order. Christobal Colon was to be released at once from his fetters and was to come with all speed to Granada.

"I am sending a thousand ducats to cover his expenses," she told Ferdinand; "and he shall come in the style befitting a great man who has been wronged."

* * *

So, the people cheering as he came, Christobal Colon rode into Granada. He was thin, even gaunt, and they remembered that this great man had come across the ocean in fetters.

When she heard that he was in Granada, Isabella immediately sent for him and, when he arrived before her and Ferdinand, she would not let him kneel. She embraced him warmly, and Ferdinand did the same.

"My dear friend," cried the Queen, "how can I tell you of my distress that you have been so treated?"

Colon held his head high, and said: "I have crossed the ocean in fetters as a criminal. I understand I am to answer charges which have been brought against me, the charges of having discovered a New World and given it to your Highnesses."

"This is unforgivable," the Queen declared.

But Ferdinand was thinking: You did not give it entirely to your Sovereigns, Christobal Colon. You kept something for yourself.

He was calculating how much richer he would be if Christobal

Colon did not have his share of the riches of the New World.

"I have suffered great humiliation," Colon told them; and Isabella knew that to him humiliation would be the sharpest pain. He was a proud man, a man who for many years of his life had worked to make a dream come true. He had been a man with a vision of a new world and, by his skill in navigation and his extreme patience and refusal to be diverted from his project, he had made that New World a reality.

"Your wrongs shall be put right," Isabella promised. "Bobadilla shall be brought home. He shall be made to answer for his treatment of you. We must ask you to try to forget all that you have suffered. You need have no fear; your honours will be restored to you."

When the proud Colon fell on his knees before the Queen and began to sob like a child, Isabella was shaken out of her serenity.

What he has suffered! she thought. And I, who have suffered in my own way, can understand his feelings.

She laid a hand on his shoulder.

"Weep, my dear friend," she said, "weep, for there is great healing in tears."

So there, at the feet of the Queen, Christobal Colon continued to weep and Isabella thought of her own sorrows as she remembered suddenly the handsome boys she had seen with Colon . . . his son Ferdinand by Beatriz de Arana, and his son Diego by his first marriage. He had two sons, yet he had suffered deeply. His great love was the New World which he had discovered.

She wanted to say to him: I have no sons. Take comfort, my friend, that you have two.

But how could she, the Queen, talk of her sorrows with this adventurer?

She could only lay her hand on his heaving shoulders and seek to offer some comfort.

Ferdinand also was ready to comfort this man. He was thinking that the people would not be pleased to know that the hero of the New World had been sent home like a common criminal in fetters. He was also wondering how he could avoid allowing Christobal Colon such a large share of the riches of the New World and direct them into his own coffers.

* * *

It was a brilliant May day in that year 1501 when Catalina said goodbye to the Alhambra.

She would carry the memory of that most beautiful of buildings in her mind for ever. She told herself that in the misty, sunless land to which she was going she would, when she closed her eyes, see it often standing high on the red rock with the sparkling Darro below. She would remember always the sweet-smelling flowers, the views from the Hall of the Ambassadors, the twelve stone lions supporting the basin of the fountain in the Courtyard of the Lions. And there would be a pain in her heart whenever she thought of this beautiful Palace which had been her home.

There was no longer hope of delay. The day had come. She was to begin the journey to Corunna and there embark for England.

She would embrace her mother for the last time, for although the Queen talked continually of their reunion Catalina felt that there was something final about this parting.

The Queen was pale; she looked as though she had slept little.

Is life to be all such bitter partings for those of us who wear the badge of royalty? Isabella asked herself.

One last look back at the red towers, the rosy walls.

"Farewell, my beloved home," whispered Catalina. "Farewell for ever." Then she turned her face resolutely away, and the journey had begun . . . to Corunna . . . to England.

THE WISE WOMAN OF GRANADA

MIGUEL WAS dead and Catalina had gone to England. The Queen roused herself from her sorrow. There was a duty to perform and it was a duty which should be a pleasure.

"Now that Miguel is dead," she said to Ferdinand, "we should lose no time in calling Juana and Philip to Spain. Juana is now our heir. She must come here to be accepted as such."

"I have already sent to her telling her she must come," Ferdinand answered. "I had thought to hear news by now that they would have set out on their journey."

"Philip is ambitious. He will come soon."

"He is also pleasure-loving."

Isabella was clearly anxious, and Ferdinand, mindful of her sufferings over her recent losses, remembered to be tender towards her.

My poor Isabella, he thought, she is growing frail. She would seem to be more than a year older than myself. She has brooded too much on the deaths in our family; they have aged her.

He said gently: "I'll swear you are longing to see your grandson."

"Little Charles," she mused; but somehow his very name seemed foreign to her. The child of wild Juana and selfish Philip. What manner of man would he grow up to be?

"When I see him," she replied, "I know I shall love him."

"It might be," said Ferdinand, "that we could persuade them to leave Charles here with us to be brought up. After all he will be the heir to our dominions."

Isabella allowed herself to be comforted, but she bore in mind that Philip and Juana were not like Isabella and Emanuel; and she did not believe that Charles could ever mean as much to her as Miguel had.

Still she looked forward to the visit of her daughter and son-in-law; yet there was no news of their coming, and the months were passing.

* * *

In his apartments in the Alhambra Ximenes, while working zealously for the Christianization of Granada, was suddenly smitten with a fever. With his usual stoicism he ignored his weakness and sought to cast it aside, but it persisted.

The Queen sent her doctors to Granada that they might attend her Archbishop. She had now persuaded herself that what Ximenes was doing in Granada should have been started at the time when the city had been taken from the Moors. She told Ferdinand that they should never have agreed to that arrangement with Boabdil for the sake of peaceful surrender. Now she was firmly behind Ximenes in all that he was doing.

She was disturbed to hear that Ximenes was not recovering, that his fever was accompanied by a languor which confined him to his bed; she ordered that he should take up his residence in that summer palace, the Generalife, where he would only be a stone's throw from the Alhambra but in quieter surroundings.

Ximenes availed himself of this offer, but his health did not improve and the fever and the languor continued.

He lay in his apartment in that most delicately beautiful of summer palaces. From his window he looked out on the terraced gardens in which the myrtles and cypresses grew; he longed to leave his bed that he might wander through the tiny courtyards and meditate beside the sparkling fountains.

But even the peace of the Generalife did not bring a return to good health; and he thought often of Tomás de Torquemada who had lain thus in the Monastery of Avila and waited for the end.

Torquemada had lived his life; Ximenes had the feeling that he had only just begun. He had not completed his work in Granada, and that he believed to be only a beginning. He admitted now that he had seen himself as the power behind the throne, as head of this great country, with Ferdinand and Isabella in leading strings.

The Queen's health was failing. He had been aware of that when he had last seen her. If she were to die and Ferdinand were left, he would need a strong guiding hand. The fact that Ferdinand did not like him and would always be resentful of him, did not disturb him. He knew Ferdinand well—an ambitious man, an avaricious man—one who needed the guiding hand of a man of God.

I must not die, Ximenes told himself. My work is not yet completed.

Yet each day he felt weaker.

One day as he lay in his bed, a Moorish servant of the Generalife came to his bedside and stood watching him.

For a moment he thought she had come to do him some injury, and he remembered that day when his brother Bernardín had tried to suffocate him by holding a pillow over his face. He had not seen Bernardín since that day.

These Moors might feel the need for vengeance on one who had disrupted the peace of their lives. He knew many of them had accepted baptism because they preferred it to the exile which was to be imposed on those who did not come into the Christian Faith. They were not such an emotional people as the Jews. He believed many of them had said to each other: "Be a Mussulman in private and a Christian in public. Why not, if that is the only way to live in Granada?"

There would be the Inquisition, of course, to deal with those who were guilty of such perfidy. The Inquisitors would have to watch these people with the utmost care. They would have to be taught what would happen to them if they thought to mock baptism and the Christian Faith.

All these thoughts passed through Ximenes' mind as the woman stood by his bedside.

"What is it, woman?" he asked.

"Oh, lord Archbishop, you are sick unto death. I have seen this fever and the languor often. It has a meaning. With the passing of each day and night the fever burns more hot, the languor grows."

"Then," said Ximenes, "if that is so, it is the will of God and I shall rejoice in it."

"Oh lord Archbishop, a voice has whispered to me to come to you; to tell you that I know of one who could cure your sickness."

"One of your people?"

The woman nodded. "A woman, oh lord. She is a very old woman. Eighty years she has lived in Granada. Often I have seen her cure those of whom the learned doctors despaired. She has herbs and medicines known only to our people."

"Why do you wish to save me? There are many of your people who would rejoice to see me die."

"I have served you, oh lord. I know you for a good man, a man who believes that all he does is in the service of God."

"You are a Christian?"

A glazed look came into the woman's eyes. "I have received baptism, oh lord."

Ximenes thought: Ay, and practise Mohammedanism in private doubtless. But he did not voice these thoughts. He was a little excited. He wanted to live. He knew now that he wanted it desperately. A little while before he had prayed for a miracle. Was this God's answer? God often worked in a mysterious way. Was he going to cure Ximenes through the Moors whom he had worked so hard to bring to God?

The Moors were skilled in medicine. Ximenes himself had

preserved their medical books when he had committed the rest of their literature to the flames.

"Do you propose bringing this wise woman to me?" asked Ximenes.

"I do, oh lord. But she could only come at midnight and in secret."

"Why so?"

"Because, my lord, there are some of my people who would wish you dead for all that has happened since you came to Granada, and they would not be pleased with this wise woman who will cure you."

"I understand," said Ximenes. "And what does this woman want for her reward should she cure me?"

"She cures for the love of the cure, oh lord. You are sick unto death, she says, and the Queen's own doctors cannot cure you. She would like to show you that we Moors have a medicine which excels yours. That is all."

Ximenes was silent for a few seconds. It might be that this woman would attempt to avenge her people. It might be that she had some poison to offer him.

He thought again of Bernardín, his own brother, who had hated him so much that he had attempted to murder him.

There were many people in the world who hated a righteous man.

He made a quick decision. His condition was growing daily weaker. He would die in any case unless some miracle were performed. He would trust in God, and if it were God's will that he should live to govern Spain—by means of the Sovereigns—he would rejoice. If he must die he would accept death with resignation.

He believed that this was an answer to his prayers.

"I will see your woman," he said.

* * *

She came to him at midnight, smuggled into the apartment, an old Moorish woman whose black eyes were scarcely visible through the folds of flesh which encircled them.

She laid her hands on him and felt his fever; she examined his tongue and his eyes and his starved body.

"I can cure you in eight days," she told him. "Do you believe me?"

"Yes," answered Ximenes, "I do."

"Then you will live. But you must tell none that I am treating you, and you must take only the medicines I shall give you. None must know that I come to you. I shall come in stealth at midnight eight times. At the end of that time your fever will have left you. You will begin to be well. You must then abandon your rigorous diet until you are recovered. You must eat rich meat and broths. If you will do this I can cure you."

"It shall be done. What reward do you ask if you cure me?"

She came close to the bed and the folds of flesh divided a little so that he saw the black eyes. There was a look in them which matched his own. She believed in the work she did, even as he believed in his. To her he was not the man who had brought misery to Granada; he was a malignant fever which the doctors of his own race could not cure

"You seek to save souls," she said. "I seek to save bodies. If my people knew that I had saved yours they would not understand."

"It is a pity that you do not burn with the same zeal to save souls as you do to save bodies."

"Then, my lord Archbishop, it might well be that eight days from now you would be dead."

She gave him a potion to drink and she left more with the woman who had brought her. Then she was stealthily taken away.

When she had gone Ximenes lay still thinking about her. He wondered whether the herbs she had given him had been poisoned, but he did not wonder for long. Had he not seen that look in her eyes?

Why had she, a Moorish woman, risked perhaps her life in coming to him—for he knew he had many enemies in the Albaycin and any friend of his would be their enemy. Did she hope that if she saved his life he would relent towards the people of Granada, would restore the old order in payment for his life? If she thought that, she would be mistaken.

He lay between sleeping and waking, wondering about that woman, and in the morning he knew, before his doctors told him, that his fever had abated a little.

He refused their medicines and lay contemplating this strange situation until midnight, when the old woman came to him again. She had brought oils with her and these she rubbed into his body. She gave him more herbal drinks and she left him, promising to come again the next night.

Before the fourth night he knew that the cure was working. And sure enough, as she had said, on the eighth day after he had first seen her his fever had completely disappeared; and the good news was sent to Isabella that her Archbishop was on the way to recovery.

Ximenes was able to wander through the enchanting little courtyards of the Generalife. The sun warmed his bones and he remembered the wise woman's instructions that he should take nourishing food.

Often he expected to be confronted by her, demanding some payment for her services. But she did not come.

It was God's miracle, he told himself eventually. Perhaps she was a heavenly visitor who came in Moorish guise. Should I soften my attitude towards these Infidels because one of them has cured me? What a way of repaying God for His miracle!

Ximenes told himself that this was a test. His life had been saved, but he must show God that his life meant little to him compared with the great work of making an all-Christian Spain.

So when he was well he continued as harsh as ever towards the fellow countrymen of that woman who had saved his life; and as soon as he felt the full return of his vigour he resumed the hair shirt, the starvation diet and the wooden pillow.

THE RETURN OF JUANA

AT LAST Philip and Juana were on their way to Spain.

When Ferdinand received a letter from Philip he came raging into Isabella's apartments.

"They have begun the journey," he said.

"Then that should be cause for rejoicing," she answered him.

"They are travelling through France."

"But they cannot do that."

"They can and they are doing it. Has this young coxcomb no notion of the delicate relationship between ourselves and France? At this present time this might give rise to . . . I know not what."

"And Charles?"

"Charles! They are not bringing him. He is too young." Ferdinand laughed sharply. "You see what this means? They are not going to have him brought up as a Spaniard. They are going to make a Fleming of him. But to go through France! And the suggestion is that there might be a betrothal of Charles and Louis' infant daughter, the Princess Claude."

"They would not make such a match without our consent."

Ferdinand clenched his fists in anger. "I see trouble ahead. I fear these Hapsburg alliances are not what I hoped for."

Isabella answered: "Still, we shall see our daughter. I long for that. I feel sure that when we talk together I shall know that all the anxiety she has caused us has been because she has obeyed her husband."

"I shall make it my task to put this young Philip in his place," growled Ferdinand.

After that Isabella eagerly awaited news of her daughter's progress. There were letters and despatches describing the fêtes and banquets with which the King of France was entertaining them.

At Blois there had been a very special celebration. Here Philip had confirmed the Treaty of Trent between his father, the Emperor Maximilian, and the King of France; one of the clauses of this treaty was to the effect that the King's eldest daughter, Claude, should be affianced to young Charles.

It was a direct insult to Spain, Ferdinand grumbled. Had Philip forgotten that Charles was the heir of Spain. How dared he make a match for the heir of Spain without even consulting the Spanish Sovereigns!

The journey through France was evidently so enjoyable that Philip and Juana seemed in no hurry to curtail it.

Ferdinand suspected that sly Louis was detaining them purposely to slight him and Isabella. Trouble was brewing between France and Spain over the partition of Naples, and both monarchs were expecting conflict to break out in the near future. So Louis amused himself by detaining Ferdinand's daughter and his son-in-law in France, and binding them to him by this Treaty of Trent and the proposed marriage of Charles and Claude.

But by the end of March news came that Philip and Juana with their train were approaching the Spanish border.

Soon I shall see my Juana, Isabella assured herself. Soon she would be able to test for herself how far advanced was this wildness of her daughter.

* * *

As Isabella was preparing to go to Toledo, where she would meet Juana, there was news from England, disquieting news.

Catalina had written often to her mother and, although there had been no complaints, Isabella knew her daughter well enough to understand her deep longing for home. Etiquette would forbid her to compare her new country with that of her birth, or to mention her unhappiness, but Isabella knew how Catalina felt.

Arthur, Catalina's young husband, it seemed, was kind and gentle. So all would be well in time. In one year, Isabella assured herself, or perhaps in two, Spain will seem remote to her and she will begin to think of England as her home.

Then came this news which so disturbed her that she forgot even the perpetual anxiety of wondering what Juana would be like.

Catalina had travelled with her young husband to Ludlow, from which town they were to govern the Principality of Wales. They were to set up a Court there which was to be modelled on that of Westminster. Isabella had been pleased to picture her sixteen-year-old daughter and the fifteen-year-old husband ruling over such a Court. It would be good practice for them, she had said to Ferdinand, against that day when they would rule over England.

Catalina had written an account of the journey from London to Ludlow; how she had ridden pillion behind her Master of Horse, and when she was tired of this mode of travelling had been carried in a litter. She had been delighted by the town of

Ludlow; and the people, she wrote, seemed to have taken her to their hearts, for they cheered her and Arthur whenever she and he appeared among them.

"My little Catalina," Isabella murmured, "a bride of six months only!"

She wondered whether the marriage had yet been consummated or whether the King of England considered his son as yet too young. It would have been more suitable if Arthur had been a year older than Catalina instead of a year younger.

Ferdinand was with her when the news arrived. She read the despatch, and the words danced before her eyes.

"Prince Arthur became stricken by a plague before he had been long in Ludlow. He fell into a rapid decline and, alas, the Infanta of Spain is now a widow."

A widow! Catalina! Why, she was scarcely a wife.

Ferdinand's face had grown pale. "But this is the devil's own luck!" he cried. "God in Heaven, are all our marriage plans for our children to come to nothing!"

Isabella tried to dismiss a certain exultation which had come to her. Catalina a widow! That meant that she could come home. She could be returned to her mother as her eldest sister, Isabella of Portugal, had been.

* * *

Into Toledo rode Isabella and Ferdinand, there to await the arrival of Juana and Philip. The bells of the city were chiming; the people were crowding into the streets; they were ready to welcome not only their Sovereigns but their Sovereigns' heir.

Toledo cared nothing that Juana was a woman. She was the rightful successor to Isabella and they would accept her as their Queen when the time came.

The Queen's nervousness increased as the hour of the meeting with her daughter drew near.

I shall know, she told herself, as soon as I look at her. If there has been any change it will immediately be visible to me. Oh, Juana, my dear daughter, be calm, my love. I pray you be calm.

Then she reminded herself that soon she would have Catalina home. What purpose could be served by her staying in England as the widow of the dead Prince? She must come home to her mother, so that she might more quickly recover from the shock her husband's death must have caused her.

It was on a beautiful May day when Philip and Juana rode into Toledo. At the doors of the great Alcazar Ferdinand and Isabella stood waiting to receive them.

Isabella's eyes immediately went to her daughter. At first glance there appeared to be only that change which would seem inevitable after the ordeals of child-bearing. Juana had given birth to a daughter, yet another Isabella, before she left Flanders. She had aged a little; and she had never been the most beautiful of their children.

And this was her husband. Isabella felt a tremor of fear as she looked at this fair young man who came forward with such arrogance. He was indeed handsome and fully aware of it. My poor Juana, thought Isabella. I hope it is not true that you love this man as distractedly as rumour tells me you do.

They were kneeling before the Sovereigns, but the Queen took her daughter and drew her into her arms. This was one of the rare occasions when Isabella disregarded etiquette. Love and anxiety were everything. She must hold this daughter in her arms, this one who had caused her more anxiety than any of the others, for she had discovered that she did not love her the less because of this.

Juana smiled and clung to her mother for a few seconds.

She is glad to be home! thought the Queen.

The brief ceremony was over, and Isabella said: "I am going to have my daughter to myself for a little while. Give me this pleasure. Philip, your father-in-law will wish to talk with you."

* * *

Isabella took her daughter to that chamber in which, just over twenty years ago, she had been born.

"Juana," Isabella held her daughter against her, "I cannot tell you how glad I am to see you. We have had so much sorrow since you left us."

Juana was silent.

"My dearest," went on the Queen, "you are happy, are you not? You are the happiest of my daughters. Your marriage has been fruitful, and you love your husband."

Juana nodded.

"You are too overcome with happiness at being home to speak of it. That is so, is it not, my love? My happiness equals yours. How I have thought of you since you went away. Your husband . . . he is kind to you?"

Juana's face darkened, and the expression there set the Queen's heart leaping in terror.

"There are women . . . always women. There were women in Flanders. There have been women on the way. There will be women in Spain. I hate them all."

"While he is in Spain," said Isabella sternly, "there must be no scandal."

Juana laughed that wild laughter which was reminiscent of her grandmother.

"You would not be able to keep them away. They pursue him everywhere. Are you surprised? Is there a more handsome man in the world than my Philip?"

"He has good looks, but he should remember his dignity."

"They won't let him. It is no fault of his. They are always there." Juana clenched her hands together. "Oh, how I hate women!"

"My dear, your father shall speak to him."

Juana let out another peal of loud laughter. "He would not listen." She snapped her fingers. "He cares not that for anyone . . . not for my father, nor the King of France. Oh, you should have seen him in France. The women of Blois, and indeed all the towns and villages through which we passed . . . they could not resist him . . . they followed him, imploring him to take them to his bed. . . ."

"And he did not resist?"

Juana turned angrily on her mother. "He is but human. He has the virility of ten ordinary men. It is no fault of his. It is the women . . . the cursed women."

"Juana, my dear, you must be calm. You must not think too much of these matters. Men, who perforce must leave their wives now and then, often find consolation with others. That is but nature."

"It is not only when he has to leave me," said Juana slowly.

"There, my dear, you must not take these matters to heart. He has done his duty by you. There are children."

"Do you think I care for that? Duty! Do I want duty as a bed-fellow? I want only Philip, I tell you. Philip . . . Philip . . . Philip . . ."

Isabella looked furtively about her. She was terrified that Juana's wild shouts might be heard. She must prevent rumour spreading through the Alcazar.

One thing was certain: Marriage had done nothing to calm Juana.

* * *

They must prepare now to take the oath as heirs to Castile. This ceremony would take place in the great Gothic Cathedral, and Isabella was afraid that Juana's wildness would show itself during the ceremony.

She sent for her son-in-law and she thought that, as he entered her apartment, his manner was insolent, but she quickly reminded herself that Flemish ways were not those of Spain; and she remembered how at times she had been faintly shocked by the manners of his sister, Margaret, who had been a good creature.

She dismissed all her attendants so that she might be quite alone with her son-in-law.

"Philip," she said, "I have heard rumours which disturb me."

Philip raised his insolent and well-arched eyebrows. How handsome he is! she thought. Isabella had never seen a man so perfectly proportioned, of such clear skin, such arrogance, such an air of masculinity, such suggestion of power and knowledge that he could do everything better than anyone else.

If Juana had gone to Portugal, to gentle Emanuel, how much better that would have been.

"My daughter is devoted to you, but I understand you are less so to her. There have been unfortunate *affaires*."

"I can assure Your Highness that they have been far from unfortunate."

"Philip, I must ask you not to be flippant on a matter which to me is so serious. My daughter is . . . is not of a serene nature."

"Ha!" laughed Philip. "That is one way of describing it."

"How would you describe it?" asked Isabella fearfully.

"Unbalanced, Madam, dangerous, tottering on the edge of madness."

"Oh, no, no . . . that is not so. You are cruel."

"If you wish me to make pretty speeches, I will do so. I thought you asked me for the truth."

"So . . . that is how you have found her?"

"That is so."

"She is so affectionate towards you."

"Too affectionate by far."

"Can you say that of your wife?"

"Her affection borders on madness, Madam."

Isabella longed to dismiss this young man; she found herself loathing him. She was longing to go back in time and, if she could do that, she would never have allowed this marriage to take place.

"If you treated her with gentle kindness," she began, "as I always tried to do . . ."

"I am not her mother. I am her husband. She asks for more than gentle kindness from me."

"More than you are prepared to give?"

He smiled at her sardonically. "I have given her children. What more can you ask than that?"

It was no use pleading with him. He would continue with his *amours*. Juana was nothing to him but the heiress of Spain. If only he were nothing to her but Maximilian's heir it would be better for her. To her he was the very meaning of her existence.

She said: "I am anxious about the ceremony. This wildness of hers must not be visible. I do not know how the people would react. It is not only here in Castile that she must be calm. There will be the ceremony in Saragossa to follow. You will know that the people of Aragon were none too kind to her sister Isabella."

"But they accepted her son Miguel as their heir. We have Charles to offer them."

"I know. But Charles is a baby. I want them to accept you and Juana as our heirs. If she will be dignified before them, I believe they will. If not, I cannot answer for the consequences."

Philip's eyes narrowed. Then he said: "Your Highness need have no fear. Juana will behave with the utmost decorum before the Cortes."

"How can you be sure of this?"

"I can be sure," he answered arrogantly. "*I* can command her."

When he had left her Isabella thought: There is so much he could do for her. But he does not. He is cruel to her, my poor bewildered Juana.

Isabella found that she hated this son-in-law; she blamed his cruel treatment for the sad change in her daughter.

* * *

Philip came into his wife's apartments in the Toledo Alcazar. Juana, who had been lying down, leapt to her feet, her eyes shining with delight.

"Leave us! Leave us!" she cried, fluttering her hands; and Philip stood aside to let her women pass, smiling lasciviously at the prettiest one, calculatingly. He would remember her.

Juana ran to him and took his arm. "Do not look at her. Do not look at her," she cried.

He threw her off. "Why not? She is a pleasant sight."

"Pleasanter than I am?"

Her archness sickened him. He almost told her that he found her looks becoming more and more repulsive.

"Let me look at you," he said; "that will help me to decide."

She lifted her face to his—all eagerness, all desire—pressing her body against him, her lips parted, her eyes pleading.

Philip held her off. "I have had talk with your mother. You have been telling her tales about me."

Terror showed in her face. "Oh no, Philip. Oh no . . . no, no! Someone has been carrying tales. I have said nothing but good of you."

"In the eyes of your sainted mother I am a philanderer."

"Oh . . . she is so prim, she does not understand."

Philip gripped her wrist so tightly that she cried out, not in pain but in pleasure. She was happy for him to touch her, even though it might be in anger.

"But you understand, do you not, my dear wife. You do not blame me."

"I don't blame you, Philip, but I hope . . ."

"You don't want another child yet, do you?"

"Yes, I do. We must have children . . . many, many children."

He laughed. "Listen," he said, "we have to undergo this ceremony with the Cortes. You know that?"

"Yes, to declare us heirs. That will please you, Philip. It is what you want. No one else could give you so much as that. I am the heiress of Castile and, as my husband, you share in my inheritance."

"That is so. That is why I find you so attractive. Now listen to me. I want you to behave perfectly at the ceremony. Be quiet. Do not laugh, do not smile. Be serious. All the time. If you do not I shall never touch you again."

"Oh, Philip. I will do everything you say. And if I do . . ."

"If you give satisfaction I will stay with you all through the night."

"Philip, I will do anything . . . everything . . ."

He touched her cheek lightly. "Do as I say, and I shall be with you."

She threw herself against him, laughing, touching his face. "Philip, my handsome Philip . . ." she moaned.

He put her from him.

"Not yet. You have not shown me that you'll give me what I want. After the ceremony we shall see. But one smile from you, one word out of place, and that is the end between us."

"Oh, Philip!"

He shook himself free of her. Then he left her and went to find the pretty attendant.

* * *

The ceremonies both at Toledo and Saragossa had passed without a hitch. The people of Saragossa had accepted Juana without protest. She already had her son Charles, and it was unlikely that he would not be of an age to govern by the time Ferdinand was ready to pass on the Crown to him.

Isabella was delighted that the ceremonies had passed so smoothly. She had been terrified of an outburst from Juana.

On the other hand she knew that Philip had ordered his wife to behave with decorum. Perhaps no one else had noticed the glance of triumph that Juana had given her husband once during the ceremony, but Isabella had seen it. It touched her deeply; it was almost like a child's saying: See how good I am.

So much she would do for him. What he could do for her if he would! She loved him with such abandon; if he were only good and kind he could save her from disaster.

Perhaps if Juana remained in Spain it might be possible to nurse her back to health. Isabella had been untiring in her watchfulness over her own mother. She had paid frequent visits to Arevalo to make sure that all that could be done was being done for that poor woman. If she had Juana with her she would watch over her even as she had watched over her mother.

She would suggest this at an appropriate time, but she did not believe for one moment that Philip would remain in Spain; and how could she persuade Juana to stay if he did not?

She tried to think of more pleasant matters. Soon she would have her little Catalina home. Negotiations were now going on with England. Half of Catalina's dowry had been paid, but Ferdinand had refused to pay the other half. Why should he when Catalina was now a widow and was coming home to her family?

Oh, to have her back! What joy that would be! It would compensate a little for all this trouble with Juana.

Perhaps good fortune is coming to me at last, thought the Queen. If I can keep Juana with me, if Catalina comes home, I shall have regained two of my daughters.

* * *

There was news from England. Isabella and Ferdinand received it together.

As Isabella read the letter a great depression came over her, but Ferdinand's expression was shrewd and calculating. The news in the letter, which filled Isabella with sadness, was to him good news.

"Why not?" cried Ferdinand. "Why not? What could be better?"

"I had hoped to have her home with me," sighed Isabella.

"That would be most unsettling for her. It is great good fortune that Henry has a second son. We must agree at once to this marriage with young Henry."

"He is years younger than Catalina. Arthur was her junior by one year."

"What matters that? Catalina can give Henry many children. This is excellent."

"Let her come back home for a while. It seems to me somewhat indecent to talk of marrying her to her husband's brother almost before he is cold in his grave."

"Henry is eager for this marriage. He hints here that, if we do not agree to Catalina's union with young Henry, it will be a French Princess for the boy. That is something we could not endure. Imagine! At this time. War over the partition of Naples pending, and who can know what that wily old Louis has up his sleeve! The English must be with us, not against us . . . and they would surely be against us if we refused this offer and young Henry married a French girl."

"Agree to the marriage, but let there be an interval."

"Indeed yes, there must be an interval. It will be necessary to get a dispensation from the Pope. He'll give it readily enough, but it will take a little time."

"I wonder what our Catalina thinks of this?"

Ferdinand looked at his wife slyly. Then he took another letter from his pocket.

"She has written to me," he said.

Eagerly Isabella seized the letter. She felt a little hurt because, on this important matter, Catalina had written to her father, but immediately she realized that it was the seemly thing to do. In this matter of disposing of his daughter it was Ferdinand, the father, who had the right to make the final decision.

"I have no inclination for a further marriage in England," wrote Catalina, "but I pray you do not take my tastes or desires into your consideration. I pray you act in all things as suits you best. . . ."

Isabella's hand shook. She read between the lines. My little daughter is homesick . . . homesick for me and for Spain.

It was no use thinking of her return. Isabella knew that Catalina would not leave England.

She had a premonition then that when she had said goodbye to her daughter at Corunna that was the last she would see of her on Earth.

Almost immediately she had shaken off her morbid thoughts.

I am growing old, she told herself, and the events of the last years have dealt me great blows. But there is much work for me to do; and I shall have her letters for comfort.

"There should be no delay," Ferdinand was saying. "I shall write to England immediately."

* * *

These journeys through Spain with the Court, that they might be acclaimed Heir and Heiress of Castile, quickly became irksome to Philip; and because he made no ecret of his boredom this affected Juana also.

"How sickened I am by these ceremonies," he exclaimed petulantly. "You Spanish do not know how to enjoy life."

Juana wept with frustration because her country did not please him. She too declared her desire to go back to Flanders.

"I will tell you this," Philip said; "as soon as all the necessary formalities are over, back we shall go."

"Yes, Philip," she answered.

Her attendants, some of whom were her faithful friends, shook their heads sadly over her. If only, they said to each other, she would not betray the depth of her need for him. He cared nothing for her and did not mind who knew it. It was shameful.

None felt this more deeply than the Queen. Often she shut herself in her apartments, declaring that matters of state occupied her. But when she was alone she often lay on her bed because she felt too exhausted to do anything else. The slightest exertion rendered her breathless, and her body was tortured by pain. She did not speak to her doctors about this, telling herself that she was merely tired and needed a little rest.

She prayed a great deal in the quietness of her apartments; and her prayers were for her children, for little Catalina who, with the serenity which she had learnt must be the aim of an Infanta of Spain, was accepting her betrothal to a boy who was not only five years her junior but also her brother-in-law. Isabella was glad that young Henry would not be ready for marriage for a few years.

She felt that Catalina would look after herself. The discipline of her childhood, the manner in which she had learned to accept what life brought her, would stand her in good stead. It was Juana who frightened her.

One day Juana burst in upon her when she was at prayer. She rose stiffly from her knees and looked at her daughter, who was wild-eyed and excited.

"My dear," she said, "I pray you sit down. Has something happened?"

"Yes, Mother. It has happened again. I'm going to have another child."

"But this is excellent news, my darling."

"Is it not! Philip will be pleased."

"We shall all be pleased. You must rest more than you have been doing."

Juana's lips trembled. "If I rest he will be with other women."

Isabella shrugged aside the remark as though she believed it was foolish.

"We must be more together," she said. "I feel the need to rest myself and, as you must do the same, we will rest together."

"I do not feel the need of rest, Mother. I'm not afraid of childbirth. I've grown used to it, and my babies come easily."

Yes, thought Isabella. You who are unsound of mind are sound enough of body. It is your children who are born strong, and those of darling Juan and my dearest Isabella who die.

She went to her daughter and put her arm about her. Juana's body was quivering with excitement; and Isabella knew that she was not thinking of the child she would have, but of the women who would be Philip's companions while she was incapacitated.

* * *

By December of that year Juana, six months pregnant, was growing large. Philip shuddered with distaste when he looked at her, and made no secret of his boredom.

He told her casually one day: "I am leaving for Flanders next week."

"For Flanders!" Juana tried to imagine herself in her condition making that long winter journey. "But . . . how could I travel?"

"I did not say you. I said *I* was going."

"Philip! You would leave me!"

"Oh come, you are in good hands. Your sainted mother wishes to watch over you when your child is born. She does not trust us in Flanders, you know."

"Philip, wait until the child is born, then we will go together."

"It's due in March. By God, do you expect me to stay in this place three more months? Then it will be another month or more before you are ready to leave. Four months in Spain! You couldn't condemn me to that. I thought you loved me."

"With all my heart and soul I do."

"Then do not make trouble."

"I would give you everything I had to give."

"No need to part with that, my dear. All you have to do is say a pleasant goodbye to me next week. That is what I want from you."

"Oh Philip . . . Philip . . ." She sank to her knees and embraced his legs. He threw her off, and she lay sprawling on the floor, grotesque in her condition.

He closed his eyes so that he need not look at her, and hurried away.

* * *

Nothing could make him change his mind. Isabella had begged him to stay with a humility which was rare with her, but he was adamant. His duty lay in Flanders, he declared.

He turned to Ferdinand. "I shall return by way of France," he said.

"Would that be wise?" Ferdinand asked.

"Most wise. The King of France is a friend of *mine*."

While Isabella deplored his insolence, Ferdinand did not, because he could not stop wondering what advantage might accrue through this journey of his son-in-law's into French territory.

"It might be possible," said Ferdinand, "for you to negotiate with the King of France on my behalf."

"Nothing would please me better," answered Philip, secretly deciding that any negotiations he concluded with Louis were going to be to his own advantage rather than Ferdinand's.

"We could ask for certain concessions," said Ferdinand, "since Charles is affianced to Claude; and why should these two not be given the titles of King and Queen of Naples?"

"It is an excellent idea," answered Philip. "In the meantime let the King of France appoint his own governor for his portion, and I will govern on behalf of yourself. As Charles' father, how could you make a better choice?"

"This needs a little consideration," said Ferdinand.

Philip smiled and answered: "You have a week in which to make up your mind."

Juana had sunk into deepest melancholy. All the wildness had gone out of her. This was a mood which Isabella had not seen before. Her daughter scarcely ate; Isabella did not believe she slept very much. She thought of nothing but the fact that Philip was returning to Flanders and leaving her in Spain.

* * *

January and February had passed, and Juana did not rouse herself from her dejection. She would sit for hours at her window, looking out as though she were hoping for the return of Philip.

She appeared to loathe all things Spanish, and when she did speak, which was rarely, it was to complain of her room, her surroundings, her attendants.

Isabella visited her often, but Juana had nothing to say, even to her mother. Oddly enough, in spite of her refusal to eat what was brought to her and the fact that she took scarcely any exercise, she remained healthy.

It was a cold March day when her pains began, and Isabella,

who had demanded to be told as soon as this happened, was close at hand when the child was born.

Another boy, a healthy lusty boy.

How strange life was. Here was another healthy child for this poor deluded girl.

Juana quickly recovered from the ordeal, and now that her body was light again she seemed a little happier.

When her parents came to her she held the child in her arms and declared that he was very like his father. "But I see my own father in him," she added. "We shall call him Ferdinand."

Ferdinand was delighted with the boy. He seemed to be quite unaware of the strangeness of his daughter. She was capable of bearing sturdy sons—that was enough for him.

JUANA THE MAD

Isabella had hoped that when the child was born Juana would cease to fret for Philip and turn her interest to the baby. This was not so. Juana did not change. She scarcely looked at the child. Her one desire was to rejoin Philip.

"You are not strong enough," said her mother. "We could never allow you to make the long journey in your present condition."

"What is he doing while I am not there?" demanded Juana.

"Much the same as he would do if you were there, I doubt not," replied Isabella grimly.

"I *must* go," cried Juana.

"Your father and I will not allow it until you are stronger."

So Juana sank once more into melancholy. Sometimes for whole days she said nothing. At other times she could be heard shouting her resentment in her apartments.

Isabella gave instructions that she must be watched.

"She so longs to rejoin her husband," she explained, "that she may attempt to leave. The King and I are determined that she must be fully recovered before she does so."

A month after the birth of little Ferdinand, Philip in Lyons had made the treaty between the Kings of Spain and France; but it was clear that it meant very little and, as the armies moved in to take possession of their portions of the divided Kingdom of Naples, it became obvious that conflict was close.

It broke out later that year; and the minds of the Sovereigns were concentrated on the new war.

Isabella however contrived to spend as much time as possible with Juana. She was growing increasingly afraid of leaving her, for since the departure of Philip Juana's affliction was becoming more and more apparent. Now it was no use pretending that she was normal. The Court was aware of her mental instability; in a very short time the rumours would be spreading throughout the country.

Juana had written many pleading letters to her husband. "They will not let me come to you," she told him. "It is for you to bid me come. Then they cannot stand in my way."

It was on a November day when she received the letter from Philip. It was ungracious, but it was nevertheless an invitation to return to Flanders. If she thought it worth while making a sea journey at this time; or if she was ready to come through France, a country which was hostile to Spain, why should she not do so?

Juana read the letter and kissed it. Philip's hand had touched the paper. That made it sacred in her mind.

She threw off her melancholy.

"I am leaving," she cried. "I am leaving at once for Flanders."

Her attendants, terrified of what she would do, sent word to the Queen of her new mood.

The Court was then in residence at Medina del Campo, and Isabella had insisted that Juana follow the Court that she herself might be near her daughter whenever possible. Shortly she must leave for Segovia, and when she heard this news she was thankful that she had not already left.

She went at once to Juana's apartments and found her daughter with her hair loose about her shoulders and her eyes wild.

"What has happened, my child?" asked the Queen gently.

"Philip has sent for me. He commands me to go."

Holy Mother, prayed the Queen, does he then wish to rid himself of her? To suggest she should go at this time of the year, with the weather at sea as it is! And how could she travel through France at such a time?

"My dearest," she said, "he does not mean now. He means that when the spring comes you must go to him."

"He says *now*."

"But you could not go in this inclement weather. You would probably be shipwrecked."

"I could go across France."

"Who knows what would happen to you? We are at war with France."

"The King is Philip's friend. He would not harm Philip's wife."

"He would not forget that you are your father's daughter."

Juana twisted a strand of her long hair and pulled it hard in her vehemence. "I will go. I will go."

"No, my darling. Be calm. Let your mother decide."

"You are against me," cried Juana. "You are all against me. It is because you are jealous, it is because I am married to the handsomest man in the world."

"My dearest, I pray you be silent. Do not say such things. You do not mean them. Oh, my Juana, I know you do not mean them. You are overwrought. Let me help you to your bed."

"Not to bed. To Flanders!"

"In the spring, my dear, you shall go."

"Now!" screamed Juana, her eyes dilating. "Now!"

"Then wait here awhile."

"You will help me?"

"I would always help you. You know that."

Juana suddenly flung herself into her mother's arms. "Oh Mother, Mother, I love him so much. I want him so much. You, who are so cold . . . so correct . . . how can you understand what he is to me?"

"I understand," said the Queen. She led her daughter to her bed. "You must rest tonight. You could not set off on a journey tonight, could you?"

"Tomorrow."

"We will see. But tonight you must rest."

Juana allowed herself to be led to her bed. She was murmuring to herself: "Tomorrow I will go to him. Tomorrow . . ."

Isabella laid the coverlet over her daughter.

"Where are you going?" demanded Juana.

"To order a soothing drink for you."

"Tomorrow," whispered Juana.

Isabella went to the door of the apartment and commanded that her physician be brought to her.

When he came she said: "A sleeping draught for my daughter."

The physician brought it and Juana drank it eagerly.

She longed for sleep. She was exhausted with her longing, and sleep would bring tomorrow nearer.

Isabella sat by the bed until she slept.

It has come at last, she told herself. I can no longer hide the truth. Everyone will know. I must have a guard set over her. This is the first step to Arevalo.

Her face was pale, almost expressionless. The greatest blow of all had fallen. She was surprised that she could accept it with such resignation.

* * *

It was past midday when Juana awoke from her drugged sleep.

She immediately remembered the letter which she had received from Philip.

"I am going home to Flanders," she said aloud. "It is today that I go."

She made to rise, but a feeling of great lassitude came over her and she lay back on her pillows contemplating, not the journey to Flanders, but the end of it, the reunion with Philip.

The thought was so intoxicating that she threw off her lassitude and leaped out of bed.

She shouted to her attendants: "Come! Help me to dress. Dress me for a journey. I am leaving today."

The women came in. They looked different, a little furtive perhaps. She noticed this and wondered why.

"Come along," she ordered. "Be quick. We are leaving today. You have much to do."

"Highness, the Queen's orders were that you were to rest in your apartment today."

"How can I do that when I have a journey to make?"

"The Queen's instructions were . . ."

"I do not obey the Queen's instructions when my husband bids me go to him."

"Highness, the weather is bad."

"It will take more than weather to keep me from him. Where is the Queen?"

"She left for Segovia, and she has given all here these instructions: We are to look after you until her return, and then she will talk with you about your journey."

"When does she return?"

"She said that we were to tell you that as soon as her state duties were done at Segovia she would be with you."

"And she expects me to wait until she returns?"

Juana was pulling at the stuff of the robe which she had wrapped about her when she rose from her bed.

"We fear, Highness, that there is no alternative. Instructions have been given to all."

Juana was silent. A cunning look came into her eyes, but she composed herself and she noticed that the attendants showed an immense relief.

"I will speak with the Queen on her return," she said. "Come, help me to dress and do my hair."

She was quiet while they did this; she ate a little food; then she took her seat at the window, and for hours she looked out on the scene below.

By that time the melancholy mood had returned to her.

* * *

It was night. Juana woke suddenly and there were tears on her cheeks.

Why was she crying? For Philip. They were keeping her from Philip when he had asked her to return. They made excuses to keep her here. Her mother was still in Segovia. She did not hurry to Medina del Campo because she knew that when she did come she must make arrangements for her daughter's departure.

It was a plot, a wicked, cruel plot to keep her from Philip.

They were all jealous because she had married the most handsome man in the world.

She sat up in bed. There was a pale moonlight in the room. She got out of bed. She could hear the even breathing of her attendants in the adjoining room.

"I must not wake them," she whispered. "If I do they will stop me."

Stop her? From doing what?

She laughed inwardly. She was not going to wait any longer. She was going . . . now.

There was no time to waste. There was no time to dress. She put a robe about her naked body and, her feet still bare, she crept from the room.

No one heard her. Down the great staircase . . . out to the hall.

One of the guards at the door gasped as though he saw a ghost, and indeed she looked strange enough to be one, with her hair flowing wildly about her shoulders and the robe flapping about her naked body.

"Holy Mother . . ." gasped the guard.

She ran past him.

"Who is it?" he demanded.

"It is I," she answered. "Your Sovereigns' daughter."

"It is indeed. It is the Lady Juana herself. Your Highness, my lady, what do you here? And garbed thus! You will die of the cold. It is a bitter night."

She laughed at him. "Back to your post," she commanded. "Leave me to my duty. I am on my way to Flanders."

The frightened guard shouted to his sleeping companions, and in a few seconds he was joined by half a dozen of them.

They saw the flying figure of their heiress to the throne running across the grounds towards the gates.

"They're locked," said one of the men. "She'll not get any farther."

"Raise the alarm," said one. "My God, she's as mad as her grandmother."

* * *

Juana stood facing them, her back against the buttress, her head held high in defiance.

"Open the gates," she screamed at the Bishop of Burgos who had been brought hurrying from his apartments in the Palace to deal with this situation.

"Highness," he told her, "it is impossible. The Queen's orders are that they shall not be opened."

"I give you orders," shouted Juana.

"Highness, I must obey the orders of my Sovereign. Allow me to call your attendants that they may help you back to your bed."

"I am not going back to my bed. I am going to Flanders."

"Later, Your Highness. For tonight . . ."

"No, no," she screamed. "I'll not go back. Open the gates and let me be on my way."

The Bishop turned to one of the men and said: "Go to Her Highness's apartments and get her women to bring warm clothes."

The man went away.

"What are you whispering?" cried Juana. "You are jealous of me . . . all of you. That is why you keep me here. Open those gates or I will have you flogged."

One of her women now approached.

"Highness," she wailed, "you will die of the cold if you stay here. I pray you come back to bed."

"You want to stop me, do you not? You want to keep me away from him. Do not think I cannot understand. I saw your lascivious eyes upon him."

"Highness, please, Highness," begged the woman.

Another woman arrived with some warm clothing. She tried to slip a heavy cloak about Juana's shoulders. Juana seized it and with a wild cry threw it at them.

"I'll have you all flogged," she cried. "All of you. You have tried to keep me from him."

"Come inside the Palace, Highness," implored the Bishop. "We will send immediately for the Queen, and you can discuss your departure with her."

But Juana's mood had again changed. She sat down and stared ahead of her as though she did not see them. To all their entreaties she made no reply.

The Bishop was uncertain what to do. He could not *command* Juana to return to her apartments, yet feared for her health and even her life, if she remained out of doors during this bitter night.

He went into the Palace and sent for one of his servants.

"Leave at once for Segovia. You cannot go by the main gates. You will be quietly conducted through a secret door. Then with all haste go to the Queen. Tell her what has happened . . . everything you have seen. Ask her for instructions as to how I shall proceed. Go quickly. There is not a moment to lose."

* * *

All through that night Juana remained at the gates of the Palace. The Bishop pleaded with her, even so far forgot her rank as to storm at her. She took no notice of him and at times seemed unaware of him.

The distance between Medina del Campo and Segovia was some forty miles. He could not expect the Queen to arrive that day, nor perhaps the next. He believed that if Juana spent another night in the open, inadequately clothed, she would freeze to death.

All through the next day she refused to move but, as night fell again, he persuaded her to go into a small dwelling on the estate, a hut-like place in which it would be impossible for them to imprison her. There she might have some shelter against the bitter cold.

This Juana eventually agreed to do, and the second night she stayed there; but as soon as it was light she took her place at the gates once more.

When the news of what was happening was brought to Isabella she was overcome with grief. Since her arrival at Segovia she had been feeling very ill; the war, her many duties, the disappointment about Catalina and the persistently nagging fear for Juana were taking their toll of her.

She would return to Medina at once, but she feared that feeble as she was she would be unable to make enough speed.

She called Ximenes to her and, because she feared his sternness towards her daughter, she sent also for Ferdinand's cousin Henriquez.

"I want you to ride with all speed to Medina del Campo," she said. "I shall follow, but necessarily more slowly. My daughter is behaving . . . strangely."

She explained what was happening, and within an hour of leaving her the two set off, while Isabella herself made preparations to depart.

When Ximenes and Henriquez arrived at Medina, the Bishop received them with the utmost relief. He was frantic with anxiety, for Juana still remained, immobile, her features set in grim purpose, her feet and hands blue with cold, seated on the ground with her back against the buttress by the gate of the palace.

When the gates were opened to admit Ximenes and Henriquez she tried to rise, but she was numb with the cold and the gates had been shut again before she could reach them.

Ximenes thundered at her; she must go to her apartments at once. It was most unseemly, most immodest for a Princess of the royal House to be seen wandering about half clad.

"Go back to your University," she cried. "Go and get on with your polyglot bible. Go and torture the poor people of Granada. But leave me alone."

"Your Highness, it would seem that all sense of decency has deserted you."

"Save your words for those who need them," she spat at him. "You have no right to torture me, Ximenes de Cisneros."

Henriquez tried with softer words.

"Dearest cousin, you are causing us distress. We are anxious on your account. You will become ill if you stay here thus."

"If you are so anxious about me, why do you stop my joining my husband?"

"You are not stopped, Highness. You are only asked to wait until the weather is more suited to the long journey you must make."

"Leave me alone," she snarled.

Then she hung her head and stared at the ground, and would not answer them.

Ximenes was pondering whether he would not have her taken in by force, but it was not easy to find those who would be ready to carry out such instructions. This was the future Queen of Spain.

He shuddered when he thought of her. She was inflicting suffering on her body as he himself had so many times. But for what different purpose! He had mortified his flesh that he might grow to greater saintliness; she mortified hers out of defiance because she was denied the gratification of her lust.

Juana spent the next night in the hut, and again at daybreak she was at her post at the gates. And that morning Isabella arrived.

As soon as the Queen entered she went straight to her daughter. She did not scold her, or speak of her duty; she merely took Juana into her arms, and for the first time Isabella broke down. The tears ran down her cheeks as she embraced her daughter. Then, still weeping, she took off her heavy cloak and wrapped it about Juana's cold form.

Then Juana seemed to forget her purpose. She gave a little cry and whispered: "Mother, oh my dear Mother."

"I am here now," said Isabella. "All is well. Mother is here."

It was as though she were a child again. The years seemed to drop from her. She was the wild Juana who had been guilty of some mischief, who had been punished, and who was frightened and uncertain and wanted only the comfort and reassurance her mother could give.

"We are going inside now," said the Queen. "Then you and I will talk. We will make plans and discuss all that you wish to discuss. But, my darling, you are so cold and you are so weak. You must do what your mother says. Then you will be strong and well enough to join your husband in Flanders. If you are sick you could not, could you? Nor would he want a sick wife."

Isabella, with those few words, had been able to do what the fire of Ximenes, the persuasion of Henriquez and the entreaties of Burgos had failed to do.

Her arm about her daughter, the Queen led Juana into the Palace.

* * *

Now that the final blow had fallen on Isabella—that which she had dreaded for so long and which could now not be denied—her health gave way.

She was so ill that for days she could do nothing but keep to her bed. She was unable to make her journeys with Ferdinand, and this was indeed an anxious time for Spain, for the French were threatening invasion.

With the coming of the spring Juana left for Flanders. Isabella said a fond farewell to her daughter, certain that she would never see her again. She did not attempt to advise her, because any advice she gave would not be heeded.

Isabella was aware that her grip on life was no longer very strong.

Even as she embraced Juana she was telling herself that she must put her affairs in order.

* * *

Juana rode joyfully to the coast. The people cheered as she went. There were many in the country villages who did not know of her madness, and who believed that she had been cruelly kept a prisoner, separated from her husband.

As she went, smiling graciously, there was nothing of the mad woman about her. When she was peacefully happy, Juana appeared to be completely sane; and she was happy now because she was going to be with Philip.

There was a delay at Laredo before the sea journey could be attempted, and during that time Juana began to show signs of stress, but before her madness could take a grip of her she was at sea.

What joy it was to be in Brussels again. She was a little worried when Philip did not come to the coast to meet her. Those of her attendants who knew the signs of wildness watched her intently and waited.

In the Palace Philip greeted her casually as though they had not been separated for months. But if she were disappointed she was so delighted to be near him again that she did not show this.

He spent the first night of her arrival with her and she was ecstatically happy; but it was not long before she discovered that his attention was very much occupied elsewhere.

He had a new mistress, one on whom he doted, and it did not take Juana very long to discover who this was. There were many malicious tongues eagerly waiting for the opportunity to point the woman out to her.

When Juana saw her, waves of anger rose within her. This woman had the physique of a Juno. She was a typical Flemish beauty, big-hipped, big-breasted, with a fresh complexion, but the most startling thing about her was her wonderful golden hair; abundant, it fell curling about her shoulders to beyond her waist, and it was clear that she was so proud of it that she invariably wore it loose and was actually setting a new fashion at the Court.

For days Juana watched that woman, hatred growing within her. For nights when she lay alone hoping that Philip would come to her she thought of that woman and what she would do to her if she could lay her hands upon her.

Philip neglected her completely now and the frustration of being so near him and yet denied his company was as great as that of being a prisoner in Medina del Campo.

* * *

Philip had to leave Court for a few days, and to Juana's great joy he did not take his golden-haired mistress with him.

With Philip away Juana could give her orders. She was his wife, the Princess of Spain, the Archduchess of Flanders. He could not take that away from her and give it to the long-haired wanton.

Juana was wild with excitement. She summoned her women to her, and demanded that her husband's mistress be brought before her.

There she stood, insolent, knowing her power, fully realizing Juana's love and need of Philip; in her eyes was a look of pitying insolence as though she were remembering all that she enjoyed with Philip, which favours were denied to his wife.

Juana cried: "Have you brought the cords I asked for?" And one of the women answered that she had.

"Then send for the men," ordered Juana. And several of the men servants, who had been waiting for this summons, having been warned that it would come, entered the apartment.

Juana pointed to Philip's mistress. "Bind her. Bind her, hand and foot."

"Do no such thing," cried the woman. "It will be the worse for you if you do."

Juana in her frenzy assumed all the dignity which her mother had always been at great pains to teach her. "You will obey *me*!" she said quietly. "I am the mistress here."

The men looked at each other and, as the flaxen-haired beauty was about to run from the apartment, one of them caught her and held her fast. The others, following his lead, did as Juana had commanded, and in a few minutes the struggling woman was pinioned, and the stout cords wound about her body. Trussed she lay at the feet of Juana, her great blue eyes wide with horror.

"Now," said Juana, "send for the barber."

"What are you going to do?" cried the woman.

"You will see," Juana told her; and she felt the wild laughter shake her body; but she controlled it. If she were going to take her revenge she must be calm.

The barber entered, carrying the tools of his trade.

"Place this woman on a chair," said Juana.

Again that wild laughter surged up within her. Often she had imagined what she would do with one of Philip's women if she ever had one at her mercy. She had imagined torture, mutilation, even death for one of those who had caused her so much suffering.

But now she had a brilliant idea. This was going to be the best sort of revenge.

"Cut off her hair," said Juana. "Shave her head."

The woman screamed, while the barber stood aghast, staring at that rippling golden glory.

"You heard what I said," screeched Juana. "Do as I say, or I will have you taken to prison. I will have you tortured. I will have you executed. Obey me at once."

The barber muttered: "Yes, yes . . . Your Grace . . . yes, yes, my lady."

"She is mad, mad," screamed the frightened woman, who could imagine few greater tragedies than the loss of her beautiful hair.

But the barber was at work and there was little she could do about it. Juana commanded two of the other men to hold her still, and soon the beautiful locks lay scattered on the floor.

"Now shave her head," cried Juana. "Let me see her completely bald."

The barber obeyed.

Juana was choking with laughter. "How different she looks! I do not recognize her. Do you? She's no beauty now. She looks like a chicken."

The woman who had shrieked her protests in a manner almost as demented as Juana's now lay gasping in her chair. She was clearly suffering from shock.

"You may release her," said Juana. "You may take her away. Bring a mirror. Let her see how much she owed to those beautiful golden curls of which I have robbed her."

As the woman was carried out, Juana gave way to paroxysms of laughter.

* * *

Philip strode into his wife's apartments.

"Philip!" she cried and her eyes shone with delight.

He was looking at her coldly and she thought: So he went to her first; he has seen her.

Then a terrible fear came to her. He was angry, and not with his mistress for the loss of the beautiful hair which he had found so attractive, but with the one who had been responsible for cutting it off.

She stammered: "You have seen her?" And in spite of herself, gurgling, choking laughter rose in her throat. "She . . . she looks like . . . a chicken."

Philip took her by the shoulders and shook her. Yes, he had seen her. He had been thinking of her during the journey to Brussels, thinking with pleasure of the moment of reunion; and then to find her . . . hideous. That shaved head instead of those soft flaxen curls! He had found her repulsive and had not been able to hide it. He had seen the deep humiliation in her face and had but one desire—to get away from her.

She had said to him: "I was tied up, made helpless, and my hair was cut off, my head shaved. Your wife did it . . . your mad wife."

Philip said: "It will grow." And he was thinking: My wife . . . my mad wife.

He had come straight to her and there was loathing within him.

She was mad. She was more repulsive to him than any woman he had ever known. She dared to do this while he was away. She believed she had some power in his Court. This was because her arrogant parents had reminded her that she was the heiress of Spain.

"Philip," she cried, "I did it because she maddened me."

"You did not need her to madden you," he answered sharply. "You were mad already."

"Mad? No, Philip, no. Mad only with love for you. If you will be kind to me I will be calm always. It was only because I was jealous of her that I did this. Say you are not angry with me. Say you will not be cruel. Oh, Philip, she looked so queer . . . that head . . ." The laughter bubbled up again.

"Be silent!" Philip said coldly.

"Philip, do not look at me like that. I did it only because . . ."

"I know why you did it. Take your hands off me. Never come near me again."

"You have forgotten. I am your wife. We must get children . . ."

He said: "We have children enough. Go away from me. I never want you near me again. You are mad. Have a care or I will put you away where you belong."

She was pulling at his doublet, her face turned up to his, the tears beginning to run down her cheeks.

He threw her off and she fell to the floor as he walked quickly from the room.

Juana remained on the floor, sobbing; then suddenly she began to laugh again, remembering that grotesque shaven head.

None came near her. Outside the apartment her attendants whispered together.

"Leave her. It is best when the madness is upon her. What will become of her? She grows more mad every day."

And after a while Juana rose and went to her bed. She lay down and when her women came to her she said: "Prepare me for my bed. My husband will be coming to me soon."

All through the night she waited; but he did not come. She waited through the days and nights that followed, but she did not see him.

She would sit waiting, a melancholy expression on her face; but occasionally she would burst into loud laughter; and each day someone in the Brussels Palace said: "She grows a little more insane each day."

ISABELLA'S END

Isabella lay ill at Medina del Campo. She was suffering from the tertian fever, it was said, and there were signs of dropsy in her legs.

It was June when news was brought to her of that disgraceful episode at the Brussels Court.

"Oh, my daughter," she murmured, "what will become of you?"

What could she do? she asked herself. What could she do for any of her daughters? Catalina was in England; she was afraid for Catalina. It was true that she had been formally betrothed to Henry, now Prince of Wales and heir of Henry VII, but she was anxious concerning the bull of dispensation which she had heard had come from Rome and which alone could make legal a marriage between Catalina and Prince Henry. She had not seen the dispensation. Could she trust the wily King of England? Might it not be that he wished to get his greedy hands on Catalina's dowry, and not care whether the marriage to her late husband's brother was legal or not?

"I must see the bull," she told herself. "I must see it before I die."

Maria as Queen of Portugal would be happy enough. Emanuel could be trusted. Maria the calm one, unexciting and unexcitable, had never given her parents any anxiety. Her future seemed more secure than that of any other of Isabella's daughters.

But Isabella could cease to fret about Catalina when she contemplated Juana. What terrible tragedy did the future hold in store for Juana?

But, sick as she was, she was still the Queen. She must not forget her duties. There were always visitors from abroad to be received; the rights of her own people to protect. Ferdinand was unable to be with her. The French had attempted an invasion of Spain itself, but this Ferdinand had quickly frustrated.

Now that she was ill, Ferdinand himself was ill and unable to come to her; her anxiety for him increased her melancholy.

What will happen when I and Ferdinand have gone? Charles is a baby, Juana is mad. Philip will rule Spain. That must not be. Ferdinand must not die.

She prayed for her husband, prayed that he might be given

strength to recover, to live until that time when Charles was grown into a strong man; and she prayed that her grandson might not have inherited his mother's taint.

Then she remembered Ximenes, her Archbishop; and a great joy came to her. He must stand beside Ferdinand; together they would rule Spain.

She thanked God for the Archbishop.

News came that Ferdinand had recovered from his sickness and, as soon as he was well enough to travel, he would be with her. With a lightened heart she made her will.

She wished to lie, she said, in Granada, in the Franciscan monastery of Santa Isabella in the Alhambra, with no memorial, only a plain inscription.

But I must lie beside Ferdinand, she thought, and it may be that he will wish to lie in a different place. So often during their lives she had felt herself forced to disagree with him. In death she would do as he wished.

She wrote somewhat unsteadily: "Should the King, my lord, prefer a sepulchre in another place, then my will is that my body be transported thither and laid at his side."

She went on to write that the crown was to be settled on Juana, as Queen Proprietor, and the Archduke Philip, her husband; but she appointed Ferdinand, her husband, sole regent of Castile until the majority of her grandson Charles, for she must make arrangements respecting the government in the absence or incapacity of her daughter Juana.

Then she wept a little thinking of Ferdinand. She could remember clearly how he had looked when he had first come to her. In those days she had thought him perfect, the materialization of an ideal. Had she not determined to be the wife of Ferdinand many years before she had seen him? Young, handsome, virile—how many women had been fortunate enough to have such a husband?

"If we had been humble people," she murmured, "if we had always been together, life would have been different for us. The children he begot on other women would have been my children. What a fine, big family I should have then!"

She wrote: "I beseech the King, my lord, that he will accept all my jewels or such as he shall select so that, seeing them, he may be reminded of the singular love I always bore him while living, and that I am now waiting for him in a better world; by which remembrance he may be encouraged to live the more justly and holily in this."

She made the two principal executors of this will the King and Ximenes.

And when it was in order she prepared herself for death, for she knew there was very little time left to her on Earth.

* * *

On that dark November day in the year 1504, a deep sadness settled on the land. Throughout Spain it was known that the Queen was dying.

Isabella lay back on her bed; she was ready now to go. She had made her peace with God; she had lived her life. She could do no more for her beloved daughters, but in these last minutes she prayed for them.

She was conscious of Ferdinand, and she did not see him as the man he had become, but the young husband. She thought of the early days of their marriage when the country was divided and bands of robbers roamed the mountains and the plains. She could catch at that happiness now, that glorious feeling of certainty.

In those days she had said: "We will make a great Spain, Ferdinand, you and I together."

And had they? To them was the honour of the reconquest. To them was the glory of an all-Christian Spain. They had rid the country of Jews and Moors. In every town the fires of the Inquisition were blazing. A great New World across the sea was theirs.

"And yet . . . and yet . . ." she murmured.

She was clinging to life, because there were so many tasks yet to be completed.

"Catalina . . ." her lips formed the name of her youngest daughter. "Catalina, what will become of you in England?"

And then: "Juana . . . oh, my poor mad Juana, what lies ahead for you?"

These things she would never know; and now she was slipping away.

"Ximenes," she whispered; "you must stand with Ferdinand. You must forget your dislike of each other and stand together."

Then she seemed to hear Ferdinand's voice close, filled with contempt: "*Your* Archbishop!"

But she was too tired, too weak; and these problems were no longer for her to solve. She was fifty-four and she had reigned for thirty years. It had been a good, long life.

Those about her bed were weeping, and she said: "Do not weep for me, nor waste your time in prayers for my recovery. I am going. Pray then for the salvation of my soul."

They gave her Extreme Unction then; and shortly before noon on that November day Isabella, the Queen, slipped quietly away.

JEAN PLAIDY HAS ALSO WRITTEN

The Norman Trilogy

THE BASTARD KING
THE LION OF JUSTICE
THE PASSIONATE ENEMIES

The Plantagenet Saga

PLANTAGENET PRELUDE
THE REVOLT OF THE EAGLETS
THE HEART OF THE LION
THE PRINCE OF DARKNESS
THE BATTLE OF THE QUEENS
THE QUEEN FROM PROVENCE
EDWARD LONGSHANKS
THE FOLLIES OF THE KING
THE VOW ON THE HERON
PASSAGE TO PONTEFRACT

The Tudor Novels

KATHARINE, THE VIRGIN WIDOW
THE SHADOW OF THE POMEGRANATE
THE KING'S SECRET MATTER
} Also available in one volume: KATHARINE OF ARAGON

MURDER MOST ROYAL (Anne Boleyn and Catherine Howard)
ST THOMAS'S EVE (Sir Thomas More)
THE SIXTH WIFE (Katharine Parr)
THE THISTLE AND THE ROSE (Margaret Tudor and James IV)
MARY, QUEEN OF FRANCE (Queen of Louis XII)
THE SPANISH BRIDEGROOM (Philip II and his first three wives)
GAY LORD ROBERT (Elizabeth and Leicester)

The Mary Queen of Scots Series

ROYAL ROAD TO FOTHERINGAY
THE CAPTIVE QUEEN OF SCOTS

The Stuart Saga

THE MURDER IN THE TOWER (Robert Carr and the Countess of Essex)

THE WANDERING PRINCE
A HEALTH UNTO HIS MAJESTY
HERE LIES OUR SOVEREIGN LORD
} Also available in one volume: CHARLES II

THE THREE CROWNS (William of Orange)
THE HAUNTED SISTERS (Mary and Anne)
THE QUEEN'S FAVOURITES (Sarah Churchill and Abigail Hill)
} Also available in one volume: THE LAST OF THE STUARTS

The Georgian Saga	THE PRINCESS OF CELLE (Sophia Dorothea and George I)
	QUEEN IN WAITING CAROLINE THE QUEEN } (Caroline of Ansbach)
	THE PRINCE AND THE QUAKERESS (George III & Hannah Lightfoot)
	THE THIRD GEORGE
	PERDITA'S PRINCE (Perdita Robinson)
	SWEET LASS OF RICHMOND HILL (Mrs Fitzherbert)
	INDISCRETIONS OF THE QUEEN (Caroline of Brunswick)
	THE REGENT'S DAUGHTER (Princess Charlotte)
	GODDESS OF THE GREEN ROOM (Dorothy Jordan and William IV)
	VICTORIA IN THE WINGS (End of the Georgian Era)
The Queen Victoria Series	THE CAPTIVE OF KENSINGTON PALACE (Early days of Victoria)
	THE QUEEN AND LORD M (Victoria and Lord Melbourne)
	THE QUEEN'S HUSBAND (Victoria and Albert)
	THE WIDOW OF WINDSOR (Last years of Victoria's reign)
The Ferdinand and Isabella Trilogy	CASTILE FOR ISABELLA SPAIN FOR THE SOVEREIGNS DAUGHTERS OF SPAIN } Also available in one volume: ISABELLA AND FERDINAND
The Lucrezia Borgia Series	MADONNA OF THE SEVEN HILLS LIGHT ON LUCREZIA } Also available in one volume: LUCREZIA BORGIA
The Medici Trilogy	MADAME SERPENT THE ITALIAN WOMAN QUEEN JEZEBEL } Also available in one volume: CATHERINE DE'MEDICI
Henri of Navarre	EVERGREEN GALLANT
The French Revolution Series	LOUIS THE WELL-BELOVED
	THE ROAD TO COMPIÈGNE
	FLAUNTING, EXTRAVAGANT QUEEN
General historical novels	BEYOND THE BLUE MOUNTAINS
	THE GOLDSMITH'S WIFE
	THE SCARLET CLOAK
	DEFENDERS OF THE FAITH
	DAUGHTER OF SATAN
Stories of Victorian England	IT BEGAN IN VAUXHALL GARDENS
	LILITH
Non-Fiction	MARY QUEEN OF SCOTS: *The Fair Devil of Scotland*
	A TRIPTYCH OF POISONERS (Cesare Borgia, Madame de Brinvilliers and Dr Pritchard)
	THE RISE OF THE SPANISH INQUISITION
	THE GROWTH OF THE SPANISH INQUISITION
	THE END OF THE SPANISH INQUISITION

BIBLIOGRAPHY

History of the Reign of Ferdinand and Isabella the Catholic. William H. Prescott. Edited by John Foster Kirk. Two Volumes.
The Heritage of Spain. An Introduction to Spanish Civilization. Nicholson B. Adams.
A History of Spain from Earliest Times to the Death of Ferdinand the Catholic. Ulick Ralph Burke, M.A. Two Volumes.
The Soul of Spain. Havelock Ellis.
Spain and Portugal. Edited by Doré Ogrizek. Translated by Paddy O'Hanlon and H. Iredale. Nelson.
Spain A Companion to Spanish Studies. Edited by E. Allison Peers.
A History of Spanish Civilization. Rafael Altamira. Translated by P. Volkov.
Spain. Henry Dwight Sedgwick.
Christianity in European History. Herbert Butterfield.
Persecution and Tolerance. M. Creighton, D.D.
The Story of the Faith. A survey of Christian History for the Undogmatic. William Alva Gifford.
Queens of Old Spain. Martin A. S. Hume.
Spain. Sacheverell Sitwell.
Spain: It's Greatness and Decay, 1479–1788. Martin A. S. Hume.
The History of Spain. Louis Bertrand and Sir Charles Petrie, M.A., F.R.,Hist.S.
Torquemada Scourge of the Jews. Thomas Hope.
Torquemada and the Spanish Inquisition. Rafael Sabatini.
A History of the Inquisition of Spain. Four Volumes, Henry Charles Lea, LL.D.
Cardinal Ximenes and the Making of Spain. Reginald Merton.

The superb historical novels of

JEAN PLAIDY

A notable trilogy on the life of

CATHERINE DE' MEDICI

Now available in one volume

MADAME SERPENT

The story of the girl growing through bitterness and humiliation into an unholy woman; the story of Catherine de' Medici in love.

THE SPECTATOR—"*Madame Serpent* is the best kind of historical novel —one into which we sink with pleasure and a feeling of undeserved education."

TRUTH—"This is at once an exciting and an intelligent novel."

NORTHERN DAILY TELEGRAPH—"The author skilfully portrays the transition of the innocent girl to the sinister consort of the King of France. A colourful story colourfully told."

THE ITALIAN WOMAN

Catherine de' Medici seen in the middle period of her life as the scheming, conscienceless mother of kings.

THE TIMES LITERARY SUPPLEMENT—"An exciting tale and the author tells it with accurate knowledge of public events."

IRISH PRESS—"An excellent story. The author shows a good understanding of the intricate state policies of the period, and a sure ability to make re-live such people as Jeanne de Navarre, Coligny and the Guises."

NORTHERN DAILY TELEGRAPH—"A penetrating and thoughtful study of Catherine de' Medici with insight and knowledge."

QUEEN JEZEBEL

Catherine de' Medici, the poisoner, the schemer; unloved, ageing, the Queen Jezebel whom all France feared and detested.

THE TIMES LITERARY SUPPLEMENT—". . . the author knows her period and manages with skill a crowded cast."

MANCHESTER EVENING NEWS—"A fascinating historical romance. The protagonists of Catherine's court are vividly drawn. History on the inside."

THE SPHERE—"The author shows the meticulous nature of her research and her ability to tell a good story without fuss or pretension."

Four excellent novels of Tudor times

MURDER MOST ROYAL

The inter-related stories of the two Queens Henry VIII beheaded—Anne Boleyn and Catharine Howard.

SUNDAY TIMES—"In *Murder Most Royal* Jean Plaidy presents Henry VIII's private life, as it concerns his second and fifth wives. Catharine Howard intrudes into fiction less than does Anne Boleyn, and Miss Plaidy has skilfully entwined their two stories."

OBSERVER—"Full-blooded, dramatic, exciting."

BIRMINGHAM POST—"This spirited novel is in the best tradition of historical fiction. Action is swift, conversation natural, background authentic. Miss Plaidy paints the truth as she sees it. It is difficult to present the case of his wives and still be fair to Henry; that this is accomplished makes the book a conspicuous success."

ST. THOMAS'S EVE

The story of Sir Thomas More, his friends Holbein and Erasmus and his family, caught up in the intrigues of a lustful king.

THE TIMES LITERARY SUPPLEMENT—"Miss Plaidy brings home the tyranny of Tudor government. . . . There emerges a charming picture of Thomas More, the wit and man of letters. In manners and customs Miss Plaidy is thoroughly at home."

THE SCOTSMAN—"Jean Plaidy's graceful study of Sir Thomas More and his family makes a novel that the reader can sink into and enjoy. Her portrait of More remains essentially domestic, with the bond between him and his daughter and the whole life of the devoted household at Chelsea sketched vividly and sympathetically. A rewarding book."

THE SIXTH WIFE

Henry VIII's last wife, Katharine Parr, who later married Thomas Seymour for love, only to die mysteriously.

DAILY TELEGRAPH—"Henry is so well drawn that, as in real life, he always holds the stage. But the story, with its alternating lights and shadows, conveys a vivid impression of life at the Tudor Court."

THE TIMES LITERARY SUPPLEMENT—"Miss Plaidy, who knows the sixteenth century very well indeed, brings out the terror that haunted Henry's Court, and the perpetual insecurity that made great men run stupendous risks. She treats her characters with impartial fairness. . . . This is interesting and accurate and makes an absorbing novel."

ROYAL ROAD TO FOTHERINGAY

The whole, fascinating story of Mary Stuart, Queen of France, Scotland and the Isles.

THE OBSERVER—"To tell again the story of Mary, Queen of Scots, and make it *freshly* alive and pitiable (and the politics of the situation *freshly* ferocious) is what Miss Plaidy in *Royal Road to Fotheringay* so admirably succeeds in doing."

BIRMINGHAM MAIL—"Jean Plaidy has already established herself among the foremost of current historical novelists. Her *Royal Road to Fotheringay* tells the tragic story of Mary, Queen of Scots—and tells it freshly. This must surely rank best, or near it, of the many novels about this sadly fascinating woman."

Another outstanding trilogy, on the life of

CHARLES II

THE WANDERING PRINCE

The young Prince, forced to wander Europe as an exile, seen through the eyes of his mistress, Lucy Walter, and his sister, "Minette".

GLASGOW EVENING NEWS—"Miss Plaidy is an accomplished novelist who conveys the gay charm of her hero, Charles II, in difficult days in France."

THE SPHERE—"A romantic reconstruction of the life of Charles II when he was an exile on the Continent. Well done, easy to read and attractive."

THE ILLUSTRATED LONDON NEWS—"Coming from such a reliable and familiar hand, scarcely requires comment. . . . There can be no doubt of the author's gift for storytelling."

EVERYWOMAN—"Jean Plaidy has once again brought characters and background vividly to life."

A HEALTH UNTO HIS MAJESTY

The King in Restoration London, his wife, Catherine of Braganza, and his mistress in chief, Barbara Palmer.

GLASGOW EVENING NEWS—"A lusty, readable novel of the loves of Charles II and intrigues at the Restoration Court."

THE SCOTSMAN—"The narrative moves at a rattling pace against the background of the Restoration. The stage is crowded with personalities in lively comings and goings around the central figure of Charles."

YORKSHIRE EVENING PRESS—"Colourful characters parade on every page in an absorbing plot."

THE TIMES LITERARY SUPPLEMENT—"Miss Plaidy . . . shows most of the reign as a struggle for ascendancy waged between Lady Castlemaine and Queen Catherine of Braganza . . . she has brought the past to life."

VANITY FAIR—"One of the outstanding historical novels of the year."

HERE LIES OUR SOVEREIGN LORD

Charles's intrigues with Louis XIV; his gay court; and the women who influenced him —Louise de Keroualle, Hortense Mancini, Nell Gwyn.

EVERYWOMAN—"Has all the vigour and colour of this author's previous novels . . . history in vivid fictional form."

MANCHESTER EVENING NEWS—"Well up to standard. A fascinating novel."

LAURENCE MEYNELL—"Jean Plaidy writes these historical novels well. A vivid picture of the crude and vigorous London of those days."

GLASGOW EVENING CITIZEN—"Adds yet another successful reconstruction of old history to this writer's commendable account."

Two memorable novels about LUCREZIA BORGIA

MADONNA OF THE SEVEN HILLS

The infamous Borgia story, from Roderigo's rise to the mysterious birth of the Infante Romano *and Lucrezia's marriage to Alfonso of Bisceglie.*

MANCHESTER EVENING NEWS—"A well-written and fascinating historical novel. All the Borgias are here; Pope Alexander, Cesare, Giovanni, Goffredo and Lucrezia—especially the latter. The author has certainly aroused sympathy for her in this first-class novel."

LIGHT ON LUCREZIA

Lucrezia's story from her marriage, through the foundering of her hopes of happiness, to her death.

TIME AND TIDE—"The Borgia story has seldom been told in a manner so conscientious and yet so beguiling."

THE STAR, SHEFFIELD—"Once again Miss Plaidy uses her great power of story telling to cast new lights on a historical figure."

Two fine novels concerning LOUIS XV

LOUIS THE WELL-BELOVED

More than a picture of the early life of Louis XV, this memorable novel presents France at the turning point of her history. Louis was only five when he succeeded *le Roi Soleil*. Ambitious men jostled each other for power, and subsequently Louis soon discovered his overwhelming need of women: the Nesle sisters—Madame de Mailly, Madame de Vintimille, Madame de Châteauroux—and then Madame de Pompadour. These were the years of crisis that led to the Revolution.

THE ROAD TO COMPIÈGNE

In this second novel Louis is no longer the Well-Beloved. His lechery had already earned the contempt of his people. But while they groaned under taxation and poverty, he indulged in fantastic extravagances first with la Pompadour, then with the inmates of the notorious Parc aux Cerfs. These were the years when the monarchy might still have been preserved, but under the pressure of the Seven Years War the King was too indolent and pleasure-loving to do more than murmur, "Après moi le deluge."

And the tragic story of MARIE ANTOINETTE

FLAUNTING EXTRAVAGANT QUEEN

The frivolous, warm-hearted, generous young woman who only wanted to enjoy life.

NEWS CHRONICLE—"One of our best historical novelists brings to life wayward, capricious Marie Antoinette."

SCOTSMAN—"*Flaunting Extravagant Queen* has the colour, liveliness, and sensitivity with which one has come to associate this author's historical novels."